*Dear Be
Potato Queen
xo*

DISCREET DARKMOURN UNIVERSE BIND-UP

BOOKS 1-3

BEN ALDERSON

*Love you more
than Penis!*

Dear Beth, aka Potato Queen
xx

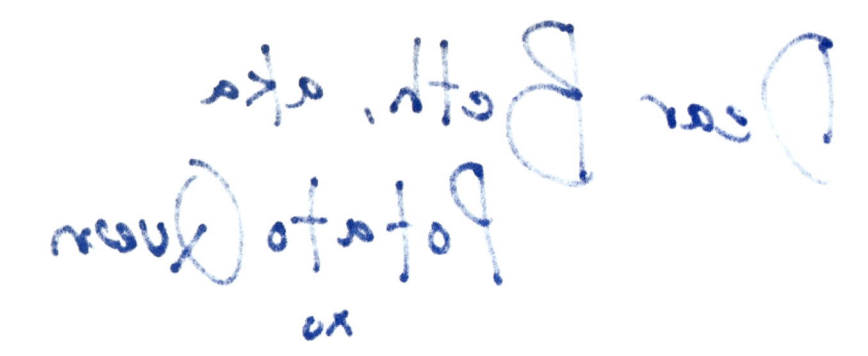

Love ya - name
Other Penis!

Copyright © 2023 by Ben Alderson

The right of Ben Alderson to be identified as the author of this work has been asserted by him in accordance with the Copyright, Designs and Patents Act 1988.

All rights reserved. No part of this publication may be reproduced, transmitted, or stored in a retrieval system, in any form or by any means, without permission in writing from the publisher, nor be otherwise circulated in any form of binding or cover other than that in which it is published and without a similar condition being imposed on the subsequent purchaser.

All characters in this publication are fictitious and any resemblance to real people, alive or dead, is purely coincidental.

Cover Art by - CheshireCath

Character Art by - CheshireCath

Harry, for being my beauty and my **beast**

PART ONE
LORD OF ETERNAL NIGHT

Jak & Marius

LORD of ETERNAL NIGHT

BEN ALDERSON

Please be aware this novel contains scenes or themes of toxic relationships, murder, loss of family members, death, abuse, manipulation, anger, grief/grieving, depression, profanity, adult scenes, adult themes and blood/gore.

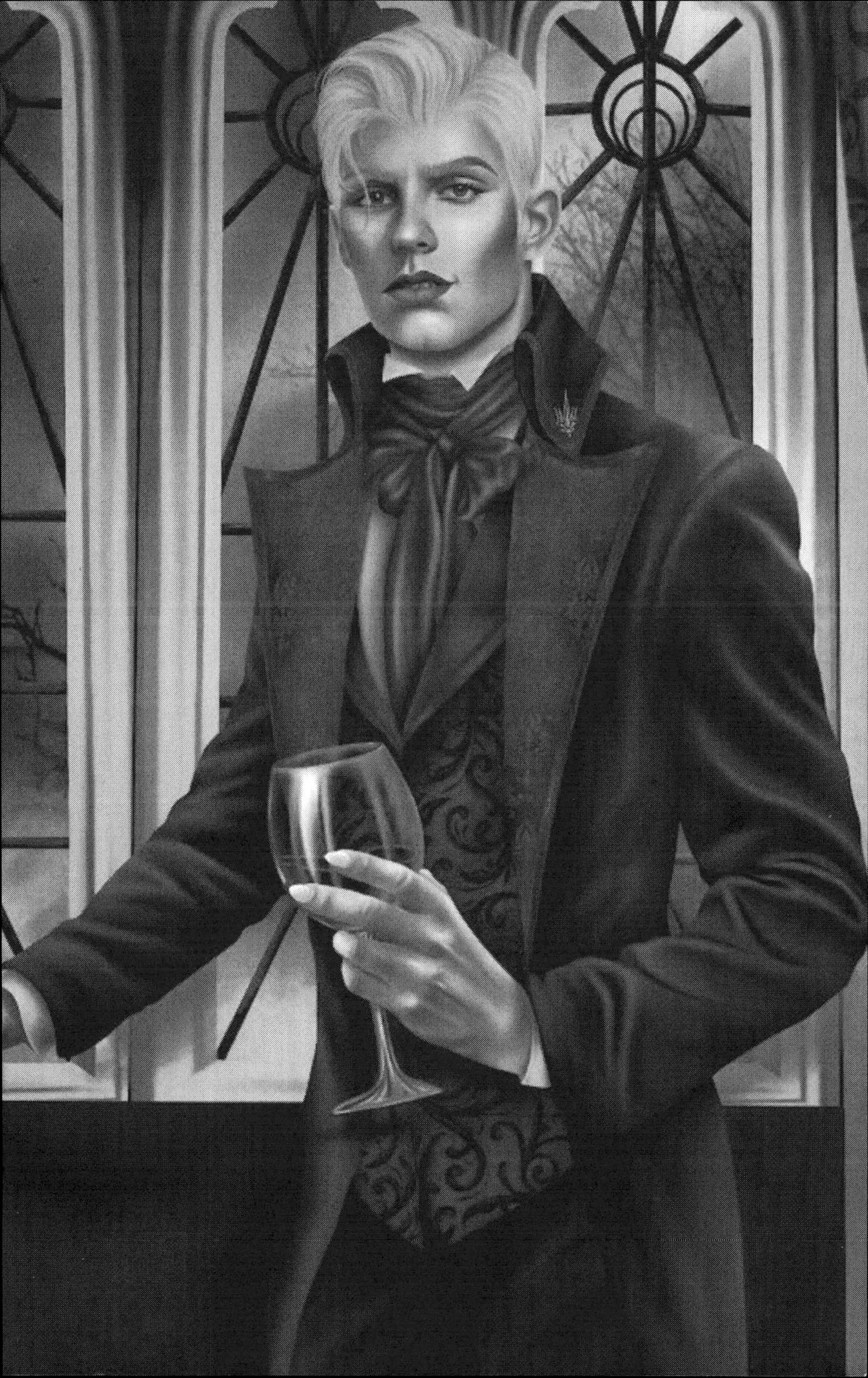

1

FIRE CURLED around my fingers as I watched the pregnant moon rise above the castle. Since dusk had arrived it was impossible not to take my eyes off the monstrosity of stone and mortar that seemed like a toy building so far in the distance. Not even the friendly warmth of the conjured fire could keep at bay the cold dread that had settled, unwelcomely, into my bones.

There was a flurry of snow that drifted across the world beyond the window. The first bout that came as a warning to the harsher conditions that would follow in the coming days and weeks. It did little to help the shivering that passed over my skin.

From my perch on the windowsill, I could see Castle Dread perfectly. It would seem my mother had purchased this humble dwelling for the view alone. A way of reminding me of my life's duty. Not that the view before me was the reminder I needed, not when every day for as long as I could remember I was reminded of it.

Every day was in preparation for this one.

I pulled my gaze from the sleeping castle, giving up on waiting for the countless windows to glow with light. It only happened during the final month.

A signal of warning for the guest it would soon welcome within its empty rooms.

Me.

"Jak, they are waiting for you."

I fisted my hand and the flames winked out. Fire was my most obedient element, the one that came more naturally to me. Tearing my gaze from the castle, I regarded Lamiere who had poked her head around the bedroom door.

"And they can wait a moment longer," I replied.

Lamiere lowered her stare to the floor. It was custom to respect your elders, but that was a wasted tradition for the mundane. A witch never bowed to those with more age. For with age came a lack of power. And I was the last of our kind with ties to magic. It was why they held respect for me.

"Margery has asked for you to join the coven for our last circle. She worries that you will be late before the Claiming."

I sucked my tongue across my teeth and peered at the faint glow of candlelight far down the dark corridor behind Lamiere. "I cannot help but feel that I am being rushed out the door. If they believe me to be late on such a special day, then they do not know me well enough at all."

"You know that your mother holds you to a high esteem... she means well. I can sense her anxiety for your pending separation."

I hated the term Lamiere used. *Mother*. I scoffed at it, knowing that it was likely the very woman before me that deserved the title more.

"She has an awfully odd way of showing it." I moved across the room, sparing it a final glance. I had never slept anywhere but here. For as long as I remembered, these four walls had become my den. A place of safety. Of peace. I was more worried about sleeping away from this place than I was the deed that would soon follow.

"Will you miss me, Lamiere?" I asked, studying her expression closely as I passed her.

"So much that it already hurts." Lamiere pressed an aged spotted hand to her heart and held it there. Her wide, amber eyes glistened with tears of honesty.

I sighed, reaching for her cheek. "I will return. Do not be sad."

"You are a kind boy, Jak."

"Kind boys are not brought up as killers."

Lamiere winced. "Perhaps not..."

"And anyway, I am not a boy. I'm a witch. Has Mother not drummed that into you enough since morning?"

Lamiere laughed through a hiccup, her smile returning to her creased face. "I fear that it is your humour which will finally destroy *it*."

"There are worst ways to go," I said, taking her arm and folding it in the crook of mine. "Do not worry for me, Lamiere. You know as well as I that I am ready for this. I do not believe anyone in this life or the next has ever been more prepared to complete a task as I am."

"This is no simple task, Jak."

"Really?" I tugged her away from the room, leaving it for the final time in a while. "And here I was thinking that it was an easy feat, ending the life of the Eternal Prince."

It was a silly name given to the creature that dwelled within the castle. Even the name of the castle was conjured by youths of past and present. *Castle Dread*. I was certain it would have had a real name lost to the forgotten memory of history. Much like that of the creature that was trapped within the castle's boundaries.

"It is not a laughing matter," she scolded, feet shuffling across the worn, carpeted floor of our home.

"If you do not laugh, dear Lamiere, you cry."

She stopped me halfway down the corridor. The sounds of the coven had picked up. They spoke in rushed whispers, reflecting the inner anxiety I had for the evening ahead of me.

We both were similar heights which made it easier to hold her gaze. Mother would say that the resurgence of my power stunted my growth, that and the insolent human she sired me from.

But I did not mind. It was an inside joke I shared with Lamiere, as I was the same height as the old woman. Lamiere revelled in it.

"Promise me you will be careful."

I averted my eyes, unable to see the worry in her stare. "I will be fine."

"Do not be foolish. He is dangerous and unforgiving. Never has someone returned from the Claiming. You may have the upper hand in training and preparation. But out there..." she pointed to the window far back in the bedroom. "Is different from in here. Be smart. Be cautious."

"There is one great difference between me and the ninety-nine that precede me." I raised my spare hand and wiggled my fingers slightly. Sparks of fire tickled across my skin as a phantom wind blew down the corridor, tousling my loose, brown hair. "I have power."

"And so will he. You are cut from the same cloth, Jak, just be wary."

I could not fight the curl of my lip at her comparison. "We are nothing alike."

Lamiere's brow furrowed as she regarded me. "Come, Jak, before your mother believes you have fled for the night. It is time to say your goodbyes and receive your final blessings."

"I have not wasted a childhood to simply flee at the final hour."

Lamiere's face pinched into a scowl. "You are doing what is required to restore our power. Your life and duty to our kind is the most valuable. That, Jak Bishop, is not a waste."

∽

Whereas I could call upon the elements with a single thought, the only ability my fellow coven members had was the art of staying silent. It was a pathetic ability — passive, unlike those I wielded. The last of my kind to possess the true power which had long since dwindled out.

It was why they all came to give me their final blessing before the Claiming. A moment in our history — the tipping of the scales of fate.

If I would succeed in my task, they would soon share the power they had since long lost.

The room we entered was full of them. Witches. Still and silent they filled the space, heads turning slowly to watch me walk amongst them. I kept my chin raised as the weight of countless stares settled on me.

Lamiere held onto me with firm, stiff fingers, but I did not need her touch to calm me. These men and women would tumble beneath a single gust of conjured wind. I could shake the very room and layer them in broken wood and stone.

They did not unnerve me.

But the woman in the midst of them did.

Her raven black hair draped like rivers of molten shadow over her narrow shoulders. Everything about her face was soft. From the light blue of her gaze to the button shape of her nose. She was a painting of beauty. She was of an age that would expect deep lines to set across her porcelain skin. But she clung to youth more so than me.

"You look divine, my son. Handsome. Likes of which the creature has never seen." *Creature.* The only name she dared speak of him. "The perfect ruse."

I released Lamiere's hand, leaving her at the edge of the circle. "Mother." I bowed to the matriarch of the coven, and my family. The only blood relative I had left.

"Let me take you in for this final time."

The crowd murmured in agreement.

"Do you hold little faith in my return ... Mother?"

She barely flinched at my bite. Her finger snaked beneath my chin and raised it, her nail nipping into skin. "Now, my son, you know there is no room for failure. You have the tools. You have the confidence in your abilities. You... you know what is to be done and when."

I snap my head from her touch, leaving her painted nail to hover awkwardly in the air. "It will be done."

She opened her arms wide, smiling to the crowd that listened in. "To restore our greatness. To break the curse that was laid upon us when the creature was punished for his... greed."

I knew the story well. Everyone in this room and the town beyond had been brought up on it. Even those who came before us. I did not need reminding now.

"Should we not tie this up?" I said. "Unlike you all, I have somewhere important to be."

The sharp crack of Mother's laugh sounded painfully. "With wit like that, Jak, you will fail long before entering the door."

"Do not let it worry you. I can assure you I will play the part well." With that I smiled, relaxing the tension from my face. My lips softened and my forehead smoothed. It was an act — but a simple one. A face I had mastered from years before a mirror. "I have had years of practice... Mother."

Her dress swept across the wooden floor, catching dust among the swirling black fabric as she walked away from me. I kept still, holding my blissful expression as though it were a test to myself.

"You are permitted to take two items during the Claiming. Items in which we have prepared."

There was a clink of metal as she fussed with a clothed table in the middle of the room. Her altar, although organised, was a shamble of relics, candles and jarred herbs.

It was a risk taking anything that would give me away as a witch to the creature. It would ruin the entire plan in a heartbeat if a candle etched with Mother's runes, or a pack of tarot cards would be found in my possession by him.

"I felt these were necessary. You will not be allowed to leave the grounds of the castle. Not for the entire duration of the Claiming, not even if you desire to. The cycle of the moon will be your guide. From tonight you will have until the next full moon. Only when the moon bleeds on the final night will you do what is needed of you. This bowl..." From the plain brown sack, she pulled a brass item. Shallow enough for stew or soup, there was nothing out of the ordinary about its design. "You can use to scry. I have its sister component with me. Simply reach for it if you need our aid. Or ... encouragement."

"I do not imagine encouragement is what I will be craving."

"Jak, do not be fooled. The creature is a trickster. A devil. This cycle of his has gone on many years and he has perfected his own agenda, I am certain. The bowl is there when you need it. Not if."

She put the tool back into the sack. I waited for her to retrieve the final item but her hand came back out empty.

"What of the other?"

"That is for you to decide," she replied, her bright stare trailing me from head to foot. "Perhaps a home comfort would be ideal to take with you."

My brows tugged inward. There was nothing that I could think of that would be of such nature. No comforts but my grimoires and tools that I had to leave behind.

"The bowl will be enough," I said plainly.

Mother tugged at the thin rope that bound the sack closed and handed it to me. I was surprised with how light it felt.

"Then you must take your leave, my son."

Suddenly my legs did not work. I heard her speak but my body seemed to ignore her. Twenty-one years had led up to this night. This moment. Now looking forward at the front door of our home, I lost all ability to move.

Mother was inches from me. A waft of sage and cedar wood filled my nose. "You are ready for this, Jak. I know you are. Go, do what is needed to be done. And when you return, your name will be remembered for an eternity."

She pressed her lips to my cheek and held them there. Beneath her hands that gripped at either of my shoulders I felt her warmth. Human, living warmth.

The last I would feel in weeks. For it would be death that I dwelled alongside. Until I gave him his release from his entrapment. *And my own.* Or I failed and his bindings to the castle would break. Allowing him to be free to spread his disease across the world.

His curse was the flipside of our own. With one that succeeded, the other would not.

As I was guided to the front door I only hoped that I had learned enough. Retained what I needed to know.

The front door opened and with it the cold was invited into the home. Snow dusted by my feet and every dark hair on my arm stood on end.

"After you... Jak. He waits."

This is it.

2

MUCH LIKE THOSE who watched from cracks in doors and behind shuttered windows, I too had been a criminal of the same intrigue. Studying as the yearly Claims walked through the streets of Darkmourn towards the boundaries of the castle that crowned it. But my interest was always educational. Seeing how the Claims held themselves as they walked, or were dragged, towards their doom. I often wondered what my day would be like. I suppose, as I now walked calmly surrounded by the coven, I did not imagine it to be far different from this.

The only difference between those that watched my procession, was they would have revelled in knowing that it was my turn. The son of the very woman who picked those that were sent before me. It was the duty of our family since the first Claiming – to choose whose child would be sent. Knowing that it would one day end with me.

They likely believed this would be a just punishment. My Claiming arrived as they watched on with bellies full of revenge or pleasure. Feelings returned in tenfold to my family from those who already lost loved ones to the yearly sacrifice.

Except I would be the first to return, setting an end to the curse.

A woollen shawl had been draped over my shoulders and with it a welcomed warmth. "This will fight the chill."

I thanked Lamiere with a gentle smile and hugged the itchy fabric close.

It was Mother's idea to go dressed in very little. Exposing the glow of my skin beneath the full moon. To distract the creature upon my arrival. The trousers I wore were made from leather which made them ripple with each footfall up the levelled path towards the castle. The tunic did little to cover me. The sleeves were dramatic – a loose design that hid the nimble curve of my arms. The collar barely touched my neck as it was sizes bigger for me than it should have been. Exposing my neck purposefully. Mother's choice.

If I needed to warm myself a simple call of flame would cease the cold that racked my bones. But I could not use my power. Not yet. Not with fear that the creature watched from the countless windows that speckled across the face of the castle. Each now alight with orange flames. Waiting for my arrival. *It cannot know.* Not until the final day, the final hour when I would break the curse. Only then would I reveal myself.

Darkmourn connected itself to the castle by a bridge of aged stone. Far below the chasms of jagged rock waited potential threats for those who drunkenly stumbled over the unprotected edge. Wind ripped across the bridge, whistling its deadly song as it did so. The brown locks of my hair danced beneath its force — not once did I lift a hand to stop it.

We walked in silence, bathed only in the screaming of wind and the chorus of nightly creatures that dared prowl this close to the castle's boundary line. The place in which the curse began. Or ended, depending on where one stood. The tickle of gazes from Darkmourn faded the further we travelled towards the castle, giving way to another. The feeling was strange. A cold, burning of awareness that someone else watched on. An unseen witness.

I raised my stare towards the towering walls of the castle, looking out for his outline in the many windows. For any sign that he watched my arrival. It made distracting myself from the cold that much *harder*.

Too focused on the feeling and silence, I hardly noticed the shuffle of footsteps slow to a stop.

"This is where we leave you," Mother said, leaning in and pressing a kiss to each cheek, lips close to my ear. "Remember to conceal yourself. Be smart. Be cautious. And return our saviour."

"I know what is required of me," I said, teeth threatening to chatter as the cold spread throughout me. "Mother." She stiffened as I held my voice firm, not whispering back as she did to me.

"Then you may go." Her face remained frozen, lips pulled into a thin, white line. "Take up your position as this year's Claiming."

"I shall."

Whereas the group that followed me here kept back, Lamiere hovered between both parties.

"I will send my thoughts as positive castings, Jak." Lamiere's silver locks billowed in the wind, her own cloak held around her. "When you return I promise to cook you your favourite soup."

I moved towards her, feeling a sudden softening of my heart, and put a hand on the short woman's shoulder. "With such promises you will make the following weeks painfully long."

Lamiere snorted, wiping the bubble of snot that burst from her nose across the sleeve of her muddied shawl. "May *She* guide you."

We both glanced to the moon as if it watched from above. "Do not miss me too terribly, Lamiere. I will return."

There was something about the way she glanced away that told me that she did not believe me. That single moment sunk my heart into the pit of my belly.

"You should take your leave, Jak." Mother distracted me from my moment of self-doubt. "Do not keep the creature waiting."

∽

The wall of shadow was visible only up close. I tilted my head, left and right, admiring the strange power that raced far up into the sky and far below the ground where the bridge met the castle's boundary. Many had tried to break through, but never with success. It was a magic even Mother could not explain. Only the Claim could enter.

I raised a hand and pressed it against the membrane of dark magic. To the touch it was cold. But with a push, my fingers began to slip through it as though it was no more than the dark waters of a lake. My hand reached through first, followed by a foot.

Holding my breath, I proceeded through the strange barrier. Only when the sensation of nightly winter cut across me did I dare open my eyes. I made it.

I allowed myself a moment to catch my breath before walking ahead, not once looking back at Mother, Lamiere and the coven as they witnessed from the other side.

As I passed beneath the crumbling pillared archway, it seemed that the shadows beyond it thickened.

All my focus was on the haunting building before me. The years had not been kind on it. Although it was near impossible to ignore that this castle would have been a spectacle of beauty and architectural prowess long before the curse settled upon it.

A place of grandeur and wealth. Where the vines would have been more than brown corpses clinging to the weathered bricks of the building. The pillars that lined the elaborate walkway would have stood tall and proud. Even the walkway beneath my boots was sodden with weeds and cracks, overgrown to a point that the slabs beneath were close to impossible to see.

Noise in the thick shadows that devoured the overgrown gardens I walked within made me pick up speed. I dared look long enough to see what lurked within.

Was it the creature? Stalking me as I walked towards his front door?

I longed to call on that fire now — to shed light across the hungry darkness around me. A guiding light would come in handy as I stumbled my way up the ruined perron towards the closed door of the castle. But I resisted, hands fumbling across the vine-covered stone banister to keep myself upright.

I waited before the door, unsure to knock or wait. He would know I was here. From the stories I had heard, I knew he likely sensed my presence the moment I stepped foot on his land. Yet the door did not open, but I grew colder and impatient.

Giving up, I raised a fist but before my knuckles could rap upon the dark oak door, it swung inward. I cringed at the sound of old hinges as they screeched.

If he did not know I was here before, he would now.

"Hello?" My voice echoed into the barren entrance before me. I hesitated, foot poised to take my first step into the castle, as I waited for a response.

Silence greeted me in return.

Whereas the world beyond the castle was shadowed in darkness, the inside was not. Although worn, I was greeted by colour. The wooden flooring glowed orange beneath the lit candelabra. White candles dripped furiously among the intricate twisting of metal. Wax melted in frozen drips that puddled across the polished, yet ancient floor. As I stepped inside a wall of stale air slammed into me. I cupped a hand over my nose, trying not to inhale the scent. But it was too late. It lathered the back of my throat and clung to my tongue. This air that had festered without the benefit of an open window or door.

"Hello?" I questioned again, body tense as I reached for the door to see who had opened it. I readied myself for a scare, only to find the space empty behind it.

Years I had readied for this moment, but the fear that stiffened my body was never expected. Its presence shocked me. Mother taught me about fight and flight, always urging me to clench fists and throw power. But now, standing here, I wanted nothing but to turn and run.

The door slammed suddenly. I jumped back, spluttering a shout as I got out of the way of its aggressive swing. The phantom movement shook dust from the walls and rafters until it settled down upon me like snow.

"You rush to leave so soon?" The voice was everywhere and nowhere at once. My fists clenched at my sides as the velvet tone slithered down my spine.

"Forgive me." I kept my gaze down as I turned around, unable to bring myself to look up at the stairway that took up the majority of the entrance. He was there. I knew it.

"It is that time already..." the voice purred. "Another year has passed without much thought. And here I find a Claim standing in my presence. How can it be a year already when I still can taste the last Claim so... clearly?"

I looked up for a moment, long enough to see the towering figure standing at the top of the stairs. Only to snap my gaze back down to my feet in a blink.

Adrenaline flooded through me, setting every vein on fire. I felt the elements stir at my reaction. A readiness that made my bones shake. This is it. My target. That fear that had not long raced through me was blown out with a single exhale.

Should I cower? Force my hands to shake so he thought me weak?

I opted to keep my gaze low as I fought the urge to smile.

Play the part.

"They normally scream, you know." The voice was closer now, yet no more than a whisper. "It has been many a year since one stood without words before me."

"I fear words fail me... in your presence."

There was a shift in the air. He had moved from his perch at the top of the stairs to a place inches before me in a blink. Where the floor was empty before me, now stood boots; black polished leather that caught the light of the candles that hung far above.

"Let me see you," he purred; a sweet brush of breath tingled over me. I breathed it in, images of orchards in spring flooding my mind. But there was something else beneath it. Copper. A sharp tang that hid almost perfectly beneath the illusion of apples. "Do not fear me."

I should have not looked up so quickly for fear that he sensed that I was not scared of him. But my reaction that followed would have covered up any distrust in my forced demeanour.

His eyes were obsidian. No. I squinted closer. Red. Deep red that it seemed they were nothing but pits of darkness.

He was pure light. From the white marble of his manicured hair, to the glow of his skin that seemed to shine from within. His entire body had been crafted from strands of moonlight. My neck ached as I had to look up at him. He towered over me by a foot, or two.

"I do not fear you," I said, eyes darting across his face. A face I had imagined a million times. *Such a waste.* He was handsome, so much so it should have inspired songs and stories. Perhaps it would have been harder knowing the outcome of this visit if I had grown up looking upon his face. Somehow it was easier creating images of it from my imagination all these years.

They were always different. Sometimes human, like the man before me, other times I would play on his title of creature and imagine a beast with horns and a twisted face.

His lips were flushed with colour, as if he had taken a bite from a pomegranate a moment before he smiled. "How... unexpected."

I wanted to agree with him, but I swallowed my words as he exposed two points of his canines. *How unexpected indeed.*

He fiddled with the golden buttons of his dark navy velvet jacket. His nails pointed and sharp. One tug and he would likely slice through the threading with ease.

A shiver ran down my arms as I studied him. Not from fear or disgust. But of anticipation.

"I suppose you wonder what happens next?" he asked. "But I feel as though I should at least know your name before indulging you in such...things."

I nodded, trying to steady my breathing. I felt my desire to lash out with my power now. And it would likely hurt him, maim him perhaps. But the curse was clear, Mother had drilled it into me. Only on the final night when the moon bled would his immortality waver. That was when I had to strike.

Focus. I hissed to myself. *Wait.*

"I asked you a question." His tone dropped suddenly that my stomach flipped with it. He pressed a nail into the bottom of my chin. It pricked my skin until there was a kiss of wetness beneath his touch.

"Jak," I said through gritted teeth. "My name is Jak."

The creature snapped back as though my words burned him. In doing so a sting of cold was left at the mark where his nail touched me.

He stood back for a moment, studying me with his wide, ruby eyes as though he looked for something. Then he lashed forward again, gripping the tops of both my arms and pinching with an urgent hold.

Fire boiled within me.

"Do not fucking touch me," I spat, losing all control. His touch riled disgust throughout me. My hand moved in a blur, knocking against his cheek. The pain that followed had me screaming out. The force sent a shiver of agony up the bones in my arm until it spread across my back. It felt as though my palm had connected with stone.

I stumbled back, hand cradled to my chest as a sob of anguish racked my lungs. I landed on the floor as I tripped over my own feet, landing awkwardly on the sack that was tied around my belt. The bowl jolted into my hip beneath the fall.

"You dare raise a hand to me?" The creature spoke, his voice growing louder with each word. "In my own home?"

His mouth split in a growl that shook the very shadows of the castle. The air vibrated as spit lined his straight bottom teeth to the two canines that grew in size before my eyes. He loomed above me, features distorted. The darks of his eyes seemed to devour all of the white that had been there.

I cowered on the floor, unable to muster the strength to protect myself as pain radiated through me. Fear. Honest, boiling fear.

"Get up," he hissed, raining spittle down over me. "Get up, now!"

Even if I wanted to, I couldn't. With my arm cradled to my chest I could not fight as his hands found me and yanked me from my sitting position.

I winced as he struck out, expecting his own forceful slap to reach me. Instead, a vice grip wrapped around my good arm and lifted me from the slabbed floor. His strength was unimaginable. I was a doll beneath his grasp.

"Stop!" I cried out as he dragged me across the floor, legs dragging pathetically beneath me.

Only moments into my arrival and I had shattered my chances of getting close to him.

As he dragged me across the entrance room, he hissed and seethed. His shoulders rose and fell dramatically. Anger shivered in the air around him, intensifying the strange glow from his skin.

"Please..." I pleaded, shoulder now splitting in pain as it took the brunt of my weight. "You are hurting me."

"You know little of pain..." he hissed, nails biting into my skin as his grip tightened. "But you will. I see now what you want from me. You want the beast. The creature you have heard much about. You will soon come to know that I am what you make me. Fool me once, *beauty*, and you will not have the chance to do it again."

With a heave he threw me to the ground before him. I scrambled across it, trying to put distance between us. The corridor we were in was dark, untouched by the candles that burned in the distance. The darkness played tricks on my mind as it pulled and twisted at his face.

I stopped, not by choice. My back pressed against a door, I felt the rigid wood as it stopped me in my tracks.

"In." He flashed his pointed teeth in warning. "Now."

I barely had a moment to stand. I fumbled with the brass knob of the door, hands coming away covered in dust. I even noticed the mounds of it that now clung to my trousers and dirtied tunic.

I threw the door open, slamming it against the wall behind it. I did not register what lay within before the creature was there, hand gripped around the door, wood creaking beneath his grip.

I stood frozen. Body a mess of aches and pains, and I seethed, "Do... do not touch me again."

He barked a laugh. "You are in my home now. You are my Claim. Did they not warn you of what that meant?"

My lips curled over my own teeth. Through my lashes I looked at him and snarled, "You know nothing of the knowledge I possess of you, demon."

He faltered for a moment, head tilting slightly. "Demon. Hm."

Then the door was slammed in my face. Enough that I flinched, closing my eyes as the wood barrelled towards me.

There was a click. A turning of a key. Then footsteps, sounding off into the corridor beyond the room.

Alone. I was alone.

Countless times I had dreamed about this night. Yet I had not once imagined that this would have ever been the outcome of my first moments within the castle.

I sagged to the floor and unleashed the tears of anger. Far off in the distance of the castle I heard a roar. A feral scream that clawed down my spine.

And deep down I felt Mother's presence and the disappointment towards me.

Day one and I had already failed.

3

I WOKE TO NOISE. A shuffling of feet mixed with the hushed murmurs of low talking. My entire body ached having slept on the floor beyond the door — where he had left me. But I was rid of all grogginess in a single moment.

Sunlight streamed through the large window in the room, slicing spears of light that exposed bouts of dust that danced once unveiled. After being left last night I had not moved from my squat behind the door. How long had it been? Enough for night to pass into day.

The room had been in the cloaks of night and I feared to explore it. Mother always said that what was hidden in the dark was best left there. So I stayed still, listening for the return of the creature, until I had fallen asleep whilst on guard.

In daylight I saw that there was nothing amiss in this chamber room. All but the impossible noise that sounded beyond the locked door. There were others here, in this castle. It should have been empty as all my teachings had informed me. I was not alone. Which went against everything I was led to believe.

The hairs on my neck stood on end as I listened intently, calming my breathing in hopes to catch some word or string of a sentence.

I pressed a hand against the polished wood of the door, covering the multitude of scratch marks beneath. Vibrations tickled across my skin. Their movement was close and their murmured chattering told me that they too were aware of my presence.

On my knees I reached my hand up for the brass knob, knowing that it would still be locked even before my fingers fully grasped around its cold, rusted handle. I had not woken to the click of the key.

"Shit," I hissed, pushing myself to standing and dusting the dirt from my trousers. I had hoped the old lock had grown weak over the years.

It had not.

I breathed heavily, examining the marks across the door. Scars of a battle between another Claiming and a locked door. I had not been the only one locked away in this room. The thought sent a stabbing discomfort through my already aching body.

"Hello?" I called out, not caring for subtly. I waited for a response only to find the noise had quietened. "I can hear you! Please let me out…" I forced my voice to sound meek and pathetic. A plea that would tug at the guilt of someone listening. But it fell on *dead* ears.

I slammed my palm on the door, shaking dust from the frame above. Bang. Bang. Bang. I hit upon it until my wrist ached more than it had when the creature had dragged me into this room.

Fire willed within me, urging to be released. I could burn this door down if I wanted. Devour this entire room until the ancient stones that constructed it broke beneath my heat.

But I couldn't. I mustn't. Not yet.

Whomever filled the rooms with candlelight beyond did not want to help. Perhaps they worked for the creature? I thought that seemed both possible and impossible. I called out for them until my throat itched and I worried my annoyance would break through my pleas. If they had heard me, they did not want to reveal themselves.

Giving up, I moved to examine the chamber.

Dust layered every surface of the dark furniture that filled the modest room. The four-poster bed was far greater than anything I had slept in before. Sheer curtains draped between the four posts, held back by thin ties that revealed deep burgundy bedding.

Had he done this? The question echoed within me. Did he prepare this chamber for every Claiming?

I sat myself down on the end of the bed, a cloud of dust exploding around me. From my seat I could look out of the bay window before me and almost feel the fresh air this room so desperately required.

I wasted no time in unlatching the rusted, black handle of the window and pushing hard to throw it open. The glass almost shattered as the force swung the window wide, slamming it into the wall beyond.

Morning air, fresh and cool, trickled violently into the room.

It swirled around me, encasing me in its familiar touch, finally clearing my nose of the stale scent of the room. The air was brisk. It spurred a shiver to course across my arms and neck.

Then I smelt myself. An odour strong enough to turn my stomach. No amount of fresh air would help that. As soon as I could leave, I needed to wash.

There was a brass tub that took up space across a tiled corner of the chamber. I could only imagine how it would have been filled with warm water for the patron of this castle long before the curse. Now it sat, wasted space, with cobwebs taking home among the curved body of metal.

Like the dusty bed and dull furniture, the tub was only more proof that this room had been untouched.

So who was beyond the room now?

I leaned out of the window, taking in the view. Perhaps I would spot someone outside? Mist clung to the overgrown garden I looked over. Being on the ground level made me see little of Darkmourn that sat nestled in the valley. Would my family be thinking of me? Biting nails in hopes that I succeeded?

I could have reached for the scrying bowl and revealed my first failure to them. Instead I busied my mind, looking at the line of broken white stone statues. Limbs and heads littered the ground beneath those that were left standing. The carpet of mist clung to the ground, dancing and twisting along the blades of overgrown grasses and wild hedges. I reached a hand for the ghostly smoke which licked up the cold slabs of the castle's walls, clambering towards me as if it had a mind of its own. *Perhaps it did.*

Entranced in the moving mist, I was locked in position. Unable to pull my hand away as it grabbed for me. A hand split from the mist, fingers closing around mine.

Panic gripped at my heart. Nails of anxiety stabbed into my flesh as the hand materialised and hardened into skin made of smoke.

Its hold on me was as strong and real as the creature's had been.

Instinct warmed my blood. Just as I had the night before, I called upon my magic. At the tips of my fingers I commanded the air that lingered around them. My most familiar, wilful element. The blast of it exploded from my skin, dissipating the hand of mist in a moment until I was free once again.

I stumbled back, flicking my hand and sending a bout of wind to close the window as I put distance between it.

The glass vibrated within the frame, threatening to shatter from the impact as it closed.

"What in the Goddess's name..." My breathing was uncontrollable as I pressed myself against a bedpost. Watching, unblinking, half expecting a ghostly face to appear behind the glass with a taunting smile.

But nothing happened.

I pressed a hand to my forehead and chuckled, the other held over my frantic heart. "Focus, you fool."

There was a small, quiet knock at the door. It spurred a small scream as my body and soul was already on edge of panicking from the phantom I had just seen. I snapped my head towards the sound, expecting ghostly fingers to slip beneath the crack in the door.

"Are you okay?" a quiet voice called out from the corridor. My heart slammed in my ears, each beat deafening. Slowly I took a step towards the door, trying not to make a sound. "If you have hurt yourself you should tell me. I can help."

There was something songful about the voice. It was light and gentle. Full of youth.

"I am ... fine."

I tiptoed towards the locked door, leaving footprints in the dust covered floor.

"Others have tried escaping through the window. But your fate within the mist is far worse than what you may experience here."

I lowered myself to the floor, my cheek so close to the ground that I felt the coldness of it. Looking beneath the crack in the door, I expected to see feet.

But the floor beyond was empty.

My breath hitched. Closing an eye, I looked again, straining to see who it was that spoke. "I was not trying to escape."

I expected no response knowing that the space beyond was empty.

But the small voice replied, chilling my blood to ice. "Good. Are you hungry?"

"Starved," I said, pushing myself to standing. My stomach ached at the thought of food. Perhaps that was what caused the vision beyond the window. And this strange interaction.

"Then you should be pleased to know that we have prepared you a feast. Eat as much as you want. You can take it back to your chamber if you wish. But heed my warning: you must return to your room before the sun goes down. For that is when he will wake again. Marius will not be pleased to know we have let you out."

Marius. The name rolled off her tongue. And with it brought a vision of the lord of moonlight.

"He... he locked the door. I can't leave."

Something knocked against my foot. I looked down to the key that rested beside it.

"Promise me you will return before nightfall?"

The key was in my hand in seconds, turning in the sister lock on my side of the room. I held my breath as I threw my door open to expose the speaker.

But the corridor was empty.

∼

The castle was a maze. Each turn, each flight of stairs, I found myself lost. No corner was the same. Walls peeled with paper — exposing broken boards beneath. Carpets were worn. Stained sheets covered up hulking shapes that I could only imagine to be unwanted furniture.

And I found no one. No matter how frantically I searched.

As I lost myself in my exploration, I conjured an image of the person I'd spoken to. A young girl, it must have been. She would have to be here somewhere. Her and the rest of the people that made the noise I woke to.

Yet there was no sign of any life among the sunlit rooms. I clung onto the key as if it was the physical reminder I needed to prove I was not going mad. Leaving an imprint of it in my palm as my fist tensed with each undiscovered moment.

It was not long before I caught the scent of the promised feast. Yet another reminder that I was, in fact, not going mad. I picked up my pace, sniffing the air as I followed the scent to its origin. Perhaps the others waited within?

The room in which my nose guided me towards had its door half open. Whereas the other doors I passed were all closed, this one was a clear invitation for me to enter.

Pushing the door, the creak made me cringe as the door's weight struggled against the old hinges. I found myself swearing beneath my breath. My profanities soon dwindled into a breathless sigh as I beheld the vision before me.

Laid out across a long, set table were plates full of food. Delights of all varieties. Steam still curled from sliced meats surrounded by a bed of vegetables. What looked to be buns glazed with sticky honey, and other sweets, broke up the savoury options laid out across it. For such a large table, there were only two seats. One at the side closest to me, the other at the far end.

I found myself hesitating with my hand above the empty, waiting plate before me. Mother's scorning voice filled my head, urging me to wait for the others to pick food first, followed by the sting of a slap on the back of my hand.

But I was alone, and she was far beyond the curse boundaries of the castle. With a smirk I snatched the plate and wasted no time in piling heaps of food onto it, and impatient fistfuls into my mouth. I did not care for the mess I made, nor the questions of how this food came to be, as I lost myself to the lust of hunger.

My mouth exploded in flavour, which was soon washed down by a glass of red liquid that I swept up without much of a thought.

The entire gulp burned as it laced down my throat. Wine. I had drunk it before during rituals and sabbats with the coven. But this taste was… different. As though I drank wealth rather than the scraps of wine Mother could obtain from the town's small market.

I drained the glass until I stared at its crystal bottom. Then I found another and finished that too.

My mind spun but on I ate until my belly ached, pleading me to rest.

Candles burned in holders all along the length of the table. But their purpose was wasted as daylight lit the room from the four, elaborate windows across the far wall. The glass was stained with blue, red and yellow. Its reflection created a rainbow of colour across the room.

Unlike everywhere else I had been thus far, this room was well kept. Sideboards and shelving were kept clean from dust and the table still shone as though it had not long been polished.

I could not imagine the creature doing this. Which only added to my belief that others did in fact dwell within the castle.

Did they too hide from the creature? Coming out during the day when they knew they would be safe from the night dweller?

So many questions — answers of which I would get when I next came into contact with someone.

I stayed in the room, warmed by the food in my belly, until the light began to dim beyond the windows. It may have been time itself that was impossible to grasp, or the aid of the wine that let it slip away from me. But what the wine did not dull was the warning the girl had given me. As the colour changed from bright blues to dark navy I knew it was time to return.

Before I left to find my way back to my room, I grabbed a handful of cheese and bread. It may be a long night.

I should have left sooner as I did not take getting lost on my way back to the chamber into consideration. The longer I took, the more the cold fear returned at the base of my skull, which only intensified by the slicing feeling of eyes following me through the darkening castle.

The sensation of that gaze prickled the hairs down the back of my neck and made me walk faster. But the wine made my legs clumsy and my feet awkward.

The castle was darkening quickly. Quicker than I thought possible. I threw myself down the stairs and back towards the main doors of the castle, turning left down the corridor that led to my chamber. The very same hallway I had been dragged down upon my arrival. Returning to this room was easier than expected, but studying ones surroundings was one of mothers many lessons. And it was now being put to good use.

By the time I entered the room and turned to close the door behind me, I was certain I saw a figure standing at the other end of the corridor.

I did not wait long to be sure of it.

My hands shook as I pulled the key from my pocket, locking the door with awkward fingers. I left the key in the lock to ensure no one could undo it from the other side.

Knowing the power was in my hands, I calmed, pressing a hand against my heart in hopes it would still.

"Get it together…" I hissed, almost laughing at the fear that had found comfort in me. "If he saw me now he would think me pathetic."

Good. The thought passed through my mind. *That is how you want him to see you.*

The room was dark. Void of light which made the room seem endless as the corners were lost to the shadows. It was a long while since I was fearful of the dark — a luxury I was not blessed to have. Sitting on the edge of the bed, I remembered the scorning Mother gave me as a child who struggled to sleep without candlelight.

Do not fear the shadows, for they do not fear you. But what Mother seemed to forget was it was not the dark that frightened me as a child. It was the creature that was warned to command the shadows.

And now I was in his domain.

4

THE CREATURE DID NOT SHOW himself for two nights. And with the time that passed, my anxiety blossomed into a wildflower. Silence bathed the castle both day and night. I hardly slept, constantly waiting for some sign of life. During the daylight the girl did not return, and nor did the beast during the night.

I was alone and it did not fill me with comfort.

Although the castle was seemingly silent and empty, the dining hall was refilled every day when I visited.

So I kept myself busy with eating and drinking. Hardly bothering to investigate the castle beside my chamber and the room that was filled with delicious food.

By the arrival of the third night, I was desperate. Enough to take the scrying bowl from the sack that had been left untouched since I had arrived. It was time to consult with the coven. For guidance, not sympathy at my predicament. Mother was not capable of the latter.

I made sure the door was locked, twice, before calling upon the element of water to open the window required for communication. With one hand gripped on the handle and the other pressed against the door, I pushed and twisted. But the door stayed shut.

It was the only privacy I could ensure. And using my magic was a risk I was willing to take.

Set upon the unmade bed, with the bowl between my crossed legs, I reached out to the water. I closed my eyes to connect with it better. Removing such a mundane sense always helped me connect with my magic. And water was the trickster of the elements. I needed to focus as much as I could for this to work.

Water hung in the air around me. Hidden from sight, but there nonetheless. With my palm held above the bowl, I urged the element to heed my call.

The cold trickle of moisture pooled above my hand in a sphere. It spun, an orb of azure that sloshed in a larger ball the more I pulled from the air around me. Once it swelled, the air dry to the taste, I urged the water into the scrying bowl where it settled. Not a droplet misplaced.

To scry was simple. Look upon the waters cast by a witch and that or who you most desire will be shown. I had done it a few times before. It was easier to visualise my goal in my mind's eye before coaxing it into the water.

I stared at my face among the rippling blue. At my dark brown hair and piercing blue eyes glaring back at me. The same as my mother's. "Show yourself," I commanded, to the water, to Mother, to my reflection.

The command was simple. A snap of will that soon shattered the surface of the water until a face, not much different than my own, looked up at me.

"You should be preoccupied making the creature fall in love with you. I did not think it possible for you to have such time to waste this early on in your task. Why do you call on me so soon?"

I kept my face straight as I replied, "For council."

"I do not like the sound of that, Jak."

"Then you really will not like what I have to tell you."

She knew instantly. I could see it from the slant of her mouth and the pinch of her stare. "Need I remind you that there is no room for failing your task, Jak."

"I know the outcome well, Mother. This is not the reminder I have called you upon for. I need advice."

Her laugh sent ripples through the water. "Entertain me, my son, please."

"The creature, he has not shown himself since my arrival. I have searched this castle for him and have not found him. I am losing precious time."

It was a lie. I had not searched for him, not thoroughly of course. For it was impossible to open most of the locked doors in this wretched place. Not without using magic. So I kept myself busy with eating and drinking. Hardly bothering to investigate the castle beside my chamber and the room which was always refilled with delicious food.

"You still do not know his name?" she asked.

I fisted my hands around the sheets and bit down on my lip. "I hardly remember what he looks like, but yes... I know his name."

Marius. The strange girl had said it, at least this many days into my stay I hoped she had. For I was beginning to believe our interaction was no more than a dream. Only made real by the key that still sat in the door to my side. A reminder I was not going crazy. Not yet at least.

"Then you are on the road to failure. My son, bringing the end to our kind once and for all. Poetic I suppose, but I will not forgive you. Not in this life or the next."

"Quiet the dramatics, Mother. Even from our distance it pains me to listen."

She closed her mouth, silencing whatever comment she was about to snap at me.

"Tell me what I need to do..." I forced a plea into my voice. "What is to say he never returns, not until the final night?"

"Is the beauty I have given you not enough to capture his attention? He is a creature of lust, you should already have him in the palm of your hand."

"Perhaps he is not what you first thought, Mother."

The water in the scrying bowl began to boil at my comment.

"Do not dare think me a fool, Jak. I know what that beast is and soon, if you fail, so will every innocent soul beyond the boundaries of that prison. If you think his unbound hunger will not end this world, you are wrong. I know what he is, for it was my own ancestor that cursed him. And she was also your own. Do what you need to get an audience with him. That is up to you. Burn the castle down if you must. But do what is needed to end this. Or your life will have been a waste."

I leaned back, away from the hot steam of the water as it sizzled from the bowl, muttering to myself. "I am sorry."

Did I apologise to her, or myself for bothering to begin this conversation?

"Do not be sorry, for apologies will not help end this curse. Only action. Next time I see your face I want to hear positive news. Do not ruin my day again."

The last I saw was her hand as it collided into the sister scrying bowl in her possession.

Our connection winked out as the remaining hot water splashed from the bowl and lathered over my legs.

Well that went well. I wasted no time in moving for the window and tipping the remaining water out of it. *You should have known better to call on her. Next time, ask to speak with Lamiere. She would give you sympathy.*

The pressure of my task weighed down on me, more so than before. I was desperate for attention. Just the thought of it alone nearly made a bubble of a laugh burst aloud.

A flicker of flamelight caught my attention. The candlelight danced proudly as if calling my name.

Burn the castle down. Mother's words flooded through me.

I shrugged, reaching for the candle and dislodging it from the iron holder on the wall. With a single thought I could have commanded the flame to jump into the palm of my hand. But if this was to work, I could not have magic be to blame.

"Perhaps you *can* give good guidance, Mother..." I said, smiling to myself as I cradled the candle to the bed.

I had to make it look deliberate but mundane. I clambered back into the bed and held the candle beneath the sheer, lace curtain that framed each side of it.

It caught in a single breath. And the hungry flame turned into a wildfire that circled the bed. I dropped the candle on the mattress, not before blowing the flame out. I was stupid, not irrational. Clambering into the middle of the sheets, I waited as the fire grew around me. The wonderful heat only fuelled the madness that dwindled within me.

Desperate times call for equally desperate measures.

5

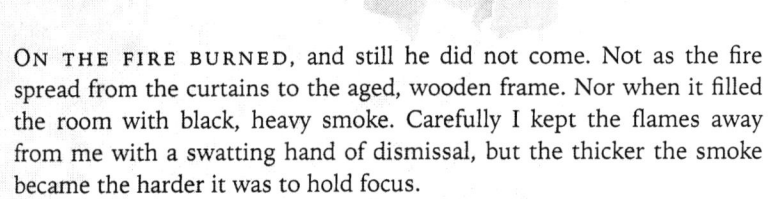

ON THE FIRE BURNED, and still he did not come. Not as the fire spread from the curtains to the aged, wooden frame. Nor when it filled the room with black, heavy smoke. Carefully I kept the flames away from me with a swatting hand of dismissal, but the thicker the smoke became the harder it was to hold focus.

He will come. I hoped.

Although the fire stayed far from my skin, the smoke didn't. With each passing moment it thickened, making each breath as painful as the next.

I coughed into the crook of my arm, trying to keep my lungs clear.

I should stop this. The thought rang true. All around me was the raging red of fire. It burned as though it had been starved for centuries, devouring the area around me in only moments.

My gaze flicked to the door constantly. *Come on.* He had to come. *Come on.* Dread strangled my lungs. *Come on.* Then my heart skipped a beat. The key. I had left it in the lock on my side.

Horror cut its claws down my spine.

I moved, swinging my legs from the bed. But the fire crackled across the bedframe, spitting red fingers out to reach me.

It kept me in place.

The smoke was becoming unbearable. Each breath weaker than the next.

I was surrounded in flames.

Heat seared at my skin, threatening to melt it clean off my bones. I pulled my legs to my chest as the fire found its way onto the sheets.

I was losing my mind. Unable to hold a grip onto reality. Each blink was longer than the last. Each time I fought to open my eyes, the fire was closer than it was before. The open window did little to rid the room of the engulfing smoke.

Mother's voice rang clear across my foggy mind. *You have doomed us all.*

Wooden beams snapped, raining debris over me in sprinklings of burning ash. I raised a hand to batter it away from catching across my hair, my face. In that moment I felt the world slow as the amber glows flew around me. My breathing hitched and my eyes grew heavy, each blink dragging on into an eternity.

My connection to the fire dissolved with my lack of clarity. And in that moment my eyes refused to open again.

Then I felt a touch.

The cold kiss of ice that wrapped around my body, lifting me from the bed. My neck lolled back and I was unable to lift it up. It was as if I watched from a deep cave in the darkness of my mind, unable to act or speak.

The world was upside-down now.

The room moved away from me.

"Be still."

I wanted to breathe but my lungs hurt too much. The pain was terrible, yet in the same moment I couldn't register it.

"You foolish boy."

My chest heaved as I tasted my first gulp of fresh air. Air unspoiled by smoke or fire. It slid down my throat and stretched my lungs. I breathed, in and out, eyes still closed as though if I dared open them, I'd see my skin melting from my body. I feared this was a trick, my mind's way of lulling me into a false sense of comfort whilst my mistake burned away at my skin.

"Wake." I barely registered the growl, even though it was inches from my ear. "You come into my home, raise a hand against me. Now you will for it to burn."

I cracked an eye open, only enough to see a face of woven moonlight hovering above me, nose close to the tip of my own.

Then I forced the other open only to see the points of sharp, white teeth before me.

~

I bolted up to sitting, aware of the way I melted into the bed I was in. The chill of air brushed against my bare chest, kept from my knowingly naked body by a thin sheet tucked around me. I half expected to see nothing but red. But there was no fire here. Nothing but the few candles that barely light the room I was now within.

That and the broad figure that blocks their light from reaching me.

He stood before me. The creature. Shadow cast across his cheekbones which hollowed out the features of his devilish face.

I looked down, unable to hold his blood-red stare and muttered, "You saved me."

Even in my state I knew how to act. Humble and... submissive.

"I merely prolonged your stay. It has been many a year since a Claim attempted to end their visit early... prematurely. I vowed I would not do it again."

I spoke to the sheets that protect my modesty. "It was an accident. A slip of a candle."

"Then you are a nuisance and clumsy. What two... inseparable traits."

"Thank you," I forced out, glancing up into his never-ending stare for a quick moment.

He raised a hand, his eyes closed. "Stop."

I stilled, swallowing my next words. The sheets were stiff in my hands and I gripped on tighter, pulling them up to cover my exposed skin.

His eyes tracked my movements.

"I could not stand the smell of your clothing. It had to be removed."

"Next time ask... please."

I tried hard to keep my face soft. Just like Mother had taught me. I could not mess this up. *Be beautiful, get close to him.*

"I have not needed to ask in years. I will not start with you."

My knuckles paled as I gripped the sheets tighter. "Have I..."

"Burned the chamber to cinders? Likely. Now we must think of a new place for you to stay." His nails were pale and sharp. He tapped one on his chin as he lost his stare to contemplation.

"There are plenty of spare rooms," I said.

"You have explored." His gaze narrowed on me. "Of course you have. Did you find anything of interest on your travels of my home?"

"Perhaps."

"Perhaps?" He tilted his head. "You have little words for an arson criminal."

"It was an accident."

"So you have said."

Before I could shift to move from the bed, he was on it, hands pressed on either side of me. He was like a shadow, no more than a whisper of smoke as his outline settled into physical form again.

"Is my bed not good enough for you, Jak?" he snarled, face inches from mine. "Would you prefer to lay in cinders than comfort? For if that is what you so desire, I can ensure that happens."

I felt my cheeks blush with warmth, no matter how I tried to fight it. I risked a moment to break his entrapping stare to scan the room I woke in. Everything about it was dark. From the patterned wallpaper to the stained furniture. This place was a cavern of gloom and elegance.

"I do not mean to offend," I said.

"We are far past that." He glowered. "You will stay here until a new room is prepared."

Lines creased the sides of his eyes, the only imperfection I could see.

"I—"

His fingers pressed against my lips. Cold, so cold. I almost swallowed my tongue at the shock of his touch.

"It is early so I must retire." The curtains were drawn across the stained-glass window to my left. Although the crack in the middle allowed me to see the lightening of the sky. "Please refrain from setting this room ablaze. I have grown rather fond of these four walls."

His eyes took me all in. Trailing up my bare-chest, my shoulders, and stopping only at my own stare. I spluttered a breath as he released his finger from my mouth, moving it to the strand of loose hair that fell across my forehead.

"Thank you, Marius."

He tilted his head, not once inquiring how I had come to learn his name. In a blink he was off me, seemingly floating across the slabbed floor to the door that my eyes soon found at the far end of the room.

"Where will you stay tonight?" I asked, keeping my voice as gentle as I could muster without dropping his piercing stare.

He paused, face turning slightly, only to show his side profile. "Is that an offer?"

Mother would want me to say yes. I could almost hear her answering for me.

"Am I in a position to make offers in your own home?" I questioned.

He grinned slowly. "No, no you are not."

I blinked and he was gone, his final words hardly finished before he vanished. Only the phantom sensation of his touch was left.

Not even the air seemed to quiver as he simply disappeared. No door was opened or closed, no pattering of footsteps. Just... gone.

I relaxed my hold on the sheets at last, letting them slip over my chest once again.

You have done it. My attempt had got me into the heart of his own personal domain. This was more than a step in the right direction. Even if it meant nearly risking my life to get here. If I failed, I died either way.

I leaned back in his bed and sighed, hands resting behind my head.

Rather die by my hands than his.

6

I WOKE to the itch of sunlight across my eyes, groggy yet comfortable in the creature's bed. I smiled through the sluggish feeling that soddened my limbs as I put my back to the light, face squished against the down-feathered pillows.

Peaking an eye open, I got a view of the room I was in. The night before I had slept straight after my head hit the pillow.

I could not deny, his room was... grand. The bed far larger than the one I had been provided with. Even as I stretched out, I was miles away from feeling the edge.

It was surprisingly easy to feel at ease in this room. I suppose the glaring sunlight helped, knowing the creature, Marius, would not return.

"Marius." I spoke his name aloud. It was strange not only having a face to the creature I had grown hearing about daily, but now having his name felt odd. As though I had obtained some divine secret that I could not share.

The strange girl beyond my own chamber door had called him by that name. But hearing it from his own lips made it seem real. As though I had not connected the dots before he told me himself.

All my life I had envisioned the beast I would soon kill. Never did he have a face or name. Now, only a handful of days into my stay in his cursed castle, I had obtained them both.

I allowed myself to lay back in his bed until my stomach grumbled for attention. It was the cue I needed to finally roll out from the welcoming embrace of the sheets. Just as it had been every day thus far, I knew food would be waiting for me.

Out from the warmth of the sheets, the room was deathly cold. The hearth was empty of cinders or wood. It was clear from the uncharred bricks around it that it had not been lit in a long time.

Which left me, naked, in the middle of the creature's room. With no sign of my clothes around me.

My cheeks warmed at the thought of him seeing me like this, his cold hands removing the clothes from my body.

I could not deny the turn of my stomach, from sickness or something else entirely I was not certain.

Dragging the sheet from the bed, I wrapped it back around myself as I searched the room for something more suitable to wear.

Almost every cabinet, dresser and wardrobe that filled the chamber was empty. Only home to the small creatures that had taken up residence among the dark spaces.

But there, in the top drawer of a grand, wooden carved cabinet did I find clothing.

A nightshirt.

"That will do," I said, shrugging.

I pulled the stiff white fabric over my head until it draped loosely around my ankles. The sleeves were long and baggy, so much so that I had to roll them up to prevent them from getting in the way.

Before a golden mirror I stood and inspected myself. The glass was scratched and worn; the surface almost impossible to see a reflection.

"Jak, you need a wash," I told myself. My feet were still stained black with soot from the fire. My face pale and blue eyes ringed with tiredness. I pressed a hand to my stomach as it rumbled again. "But first it is time to eat."

∼

The door to my chamber had been destroyed. Except not by the fire. No. It lay in parts across the charred room, even the brick of the wall that held it up by the frame had come away. It had been caved in. From the outside.

I inched cautiously into the room, careful not to step on an iron nail or splinter of wood. It was early evening and I had been without shoes all day. After waiting in the great hall for someone, anyone, to come in, I had finally given up and went to retrieve my boots.

Luckily they were where I left them. Neatly lined up beneath the window that overlooked the garden. Now, as the sky was painted a dark purple, it was hard to see the world beyond.

I pulled my boots on, thankful for the break from the ever-cold floor of the castle.

The chamber was close to destroyed. Yet the fire had been put out

— by what or how I did not know. Nor did it matter. My potentially dramatic action resulted in what I required.

Attention.

The scorched scars reached as far as the outer walls but it had been stopped before spreading beyond. The bed was in ruins. Sheets no more than crispy ashes. The posts of the frame now leaned against one another amongst the mound of burned wood and material.

"What a clumsy boy I am."

There was a glint of metal nestled within the pile of ashes. I reached for it, pushing the dusting of destruction out of the way until I got a grasp on the item and pulled it out.

The scrying bowl. It had warped slightly. Not completely broken, but enough to feel as though I would not be able to use it again.

It was the perfect excuse not to call upon Mother or the coven. For a moment, a wink of orange flickered across the dull metal of the bowl. It happened so quickly I almost passed it off as something in my eye. But then it happened again. A reflection of an amber glow. I turned behind me, facing the window to catch what I had seen.

Beyond the window, in the darkening view, I could see it.

What if it was Marius? No. The moon had not reached its apex yet. That was all I knew of the creature before he appeared. It was only in the dead of night that he roamed.

Then it must be the people that live here. The very ones that had done their best to keep out of my way, no matter how I longed to see them.

My heart slammed in my chest as I raced out the room, discarding the scrying bowl back on the floor without a thought. A short run down the corridor and I was there, at the front door ready to find out who lurked beyond it.

But it was locked. *Fuck.* No matter how I tugged and pulled at the large, circular hand, it did not open. Giving up with a breath of frustration, I ran back to the room, hoping to catch the direction the bobbing glow moved in.

I was left with one choice.

It was easy, pulling myself onto the thin ledge of the window and slipping through the gap that it allowed as I pushed it open. I was thankful for the overgrown grass that I landed upon. It not only cushioned my short jump, but kept my footfalls quiet.

The nightshirt did little to keep out the chill of the evening. Mist swirled around my ankles and for a moment I remembered my first night and the hand that reached for me.

I did not stay in one place to find out if that same apparition returned.

Through the darkening gardens I moved, looking for another glare of light to signal where the intruder was heading. My heart thumped in my chest, palms damp with sweat. But on I pushed, desperate to find someone — anyone that was not the beast.

Blindly, I waded through the gardens. Lost among the towering hedges, pathless walkways and monstrous roots and weeds that seemed to have overtaken what must have been a glorious garden once upon a time.

Then I caught it again. Through the gaps of the hedge I almost walked face-first into, amber light that moved beyond it.

I quickened my movements, frantically looking for a way around the hedge wall before me. The twigs scratched at my hands as I searched for a way through.

"Wait!" I shouted, the glow of light disappearing once again. "I see you, just wait!"

I sliced out a hand, reaching for the grounding element of earth. The hedge split in two, parting enough for me to slip through.

It was a risk, using my power. But the blanket of darkness grew heavier. I could hardly see a hand before my face, let alone someone else see me use my power.

I ran. And so did the person I chased after. I was on the stone path now, evident from the loud patter of my footfalls as I took up chase. There was a faint stinging from the cuts I had gifted myself on the soles of my feet. Yet I pushed on. "Please... just wait!"

As if the blossoming night responded, a noise filled the darkening gardens. It seemed to echo from all around me.

I slowed for a moment, searching for the origin of the sound. In the shadows around me my eyes played tricks. I was certain I saw shapes speeding through the dark.

Then the noise occurred again, this time louder, clearer.

A howl.

I picked up my pace, this time urged on by a sudden, piercing fear that tried so desperately to overcome me. Burned wilder by yet another howl that sounded in response to the first.

The nightshirt blew up around my bare legs. I almost tripped on a cracked slab on the path beneath me, but steadied myself as yet another howl pierced through the settling night.

My prey turned a corner, signalled by the sudden change in course the bobbing flame took.

I followed, boots slapping on the ground.

Closing in, I started to see the person. The girl.

Long black hair flowed behind her, caught in the wind she left in her wake. She wore a dress made from dark materials that seemed to blend into the very shadows we ran through.

And her head, like mine, snapped across the darkness surrounding the path as other noises joined in on our chase.

All I heard, above my own heavy breathing, was the snapping of teeth. The shifting of a shape which ran beside me flickered in my peripheral. I risked a look and saw two pools of red glaring back at me.

It happened too fast.

I slammed into something hard, tumbling in an entanglement of limbs, across the ground.

It was not my cry of sudden surprise that rattled across my skull, it came from the girl I had run straight into.

I felt the wet grass around me. Not the hard stone path.

"I am so sorr—"

"Shut up, you fool!" she snapped, pushing herself from the ground with wide, unblinking eyes. Her focus was not on me, but something in the dark before us. I followed her panicked stare to see what captured her attention.

From the shadows stepped a large hound. No, a wolf. Fur made from melted shadows, so dark I could not see where it started and the night around it began. The beast prowled, large paws padding across the ground slowly as it moved for her.

I shifted my arms, trying to get myself from the floor before the creature attacked, its intentions clear as its maw dripped and its lip curled. But it stopped me from moving with a warning snap of its jaws. I could almost feel the stabbing of its red glare as it stared right through me.

"You took us off the path," she muttered, voice laced with fear. "You've doomed us both."

7

THE WOLF THREW itself towards the girl, body melting in wisps of shadows made solid as it blurred through the air. In the brief moment I had fully glanced at her, she must have been no more than thirteen. A small, wiry frame but a face of determined fire.

There was no time for her to scream. That or she did not fear the unbelievable creature that attacked her.

In moments she was devoured in shadows as the wolf landed above her. Only then did she make a noise as her body hit the ground with a hefty crack. The wolf hardly flinched as her shriek split the sky.

Help her. The words were so clear in my mind. An urgent plea. I was frozen to the spot, watching as the wolf lowered its bared teeth, huffing its deathly stench across her face.

The creature slammed a paw upon her chest. The guttural breathless sound that followed sickened me as the beast slammed all air from her lungs. Her hands slapped at the dark paw, both no match for its size. Then she simply stopped as the shattering of bones sang into the night.

Now!

The thought was no longer a plea, but a command.

And my magic answered without further reluctance.

The wind went from still to screaming. A storm of powerful gusts that brewed around the gardens, whistling through trees and broken statues. My air was fearful of the stalking creatures — I sensed it as I willed for it to attack. The mighty force of conjured wind nearly ripped me from the ground as it barrelled into the wolf's sides. I gritted my teeth, jaw clenched as I forced my energy into the element. My heart jolted with relief as the yelp of the whimpering beast sang a song to my very soul. Ripped from its prey, the cloud of shadow and fur was thrown into the night. A useless doll in the grasps of my power.

I wasted no time in moving for where the girl lay across the ground, the wind dwindling to the natural breeze it had been as I relaxed the leash on my power.

"Are you alright?" I said, breathless. I leaned over her, head snapping back towards the dark where the beast still cried and whimpered. My neck threatened to break as I looked from the shadows back to the girl. She was unresponsive, eyes closed and lips parted. I held a finger beneath her nose and felt the tickle of breath against it. She was breathing, but weakly. Her youthful skin as white as snow. I could not deny the small pulse that sounded beneath my touch of her wrist. Even in the dark my eyes adjusted enough to see the small rise and fall of her chest.

A string of profanities spilled across my mind as the whimpering turned into a growl and grew closer once again.

I faced the dark and the hidden creature that lurked within it. A scowl pinched across my face.

Hands readied at my side, I willed the wolf to strike.

"Come on!" I shouted, body tensed, a wall of flesh and bone between the beast and the girl. "Give it another try. I dare you."

Deep, guttural growls responded and more wolves of shadow stepped into view. Each lowered their bodies close to the ground. Ready to strike.

Wind raced around me. Fire warmed beneath my skin. "At last, a fight."

One of the larger beasts shook its mane of shadow and snapped its jaws. It seemed to be a signal as the pack of wolves split and raced for where I kept crouched above the young girl.

My skin burned as the fire beneath my skin itched for release. But as my scream tore out of my throat, yet another shadow joined the chaos. It landed between me and the racing beasts. Pure white hair glowed among the night, body broad and arms wide as though he would simply catch them as they pounced.

Marius.

I could not see his face, not as he screamed towards the pack of wolves. He was bent low, hands curved in a claw-like motion as he gave a single, never-ending screech. I let go of the elements, clapping my hands over my ears to block out the horrific sound.

The very night seemed to shake around us.

I watched in... awe as the wolves dispersed into the night. Each whimpering as they ran, tails between their legs.

Their fear mixed with my own as Marius snapped around to us. His eyes glowed the same red as the beasts he had frightened away. His mouth was split, unnaturally, exposing the lines of spittle connected to his white, pointed teeth.

I could not catch a breath as I looked up at him.

"What have you done?" he growled from the pits of his stomach.

"I didn't — I was..."

"She knows not to leave the path!" he snapped, gaze flaring with anger. "What have you done!?"

Refusing to look away, no matter how I wished to, I seethed my response, "I was not to know."

In a blink he was before me, teeth mere inches from my eyes. "Get out of my way. Now."

I could not move fast enough, flinching as Marius lifted a tensed arm to push me himself.

As he hovered over the girl, his entire demeanour shifted. His body softened and his shoulders lowered. With a long sigh, he scooped her small frame into his arms without much of a thought.

"If she dies..." Marius did not face me as he spoke. But I heard as his voice hitched. "You will soon follow her."

Helplessly I watched as Marius carried the young girl back towards the castle, her pale face resting against his chest. I could hear him whisper to her, but only a muttered sound. I made out not a single word he said.

Did he see my magic? The thought sickened me, but soon melted away as I caught sight of the limp arm of the girl he carried. Guilt fuelled me to get off the floor and follow after him. *Slow, sloppy.* Mother's voice filled the darkness of my mind. My pace only urged to quicken from the fear that the strange creatures would return for me.

Marius did not complain that I trailed after him. He knew I was behind him from the subtle glances over his shoulder. I half expected him to scream at me to leave. But he didn't.

I stayed on the stone path through the gardens, not deviating from it, heeding the warning the young girl had said to me before the creature had hurt her.

I was soon thankful to be back in the castle with the door shut behind me, leaving the reaching mists and moving shadows behind lock and key.

Marius took her to his room. The one I had woken in this morning. I kept my distance as he entered, laying her across the freshly made bed.

A bed I did not make upon leaving the room earlier.

"Will she be okay?" I asked from the corner of the room as Marius ran his hands across her. He did not reply. He carefully pulled at the cords of the dark corset she wore, revealing the top of her chest.

Even from my distance, I could see the dark bruise that had already bloomed across her skin.

He released a breath, one that whistled through gritted teeth. "Broken ribs. She will survive and you… you may live to see tomorrow, Jak."

"Can I help?" I stepped forward cautiously. "It is my fault."

I said it because it was true, and it would have been what he wanted to hear. In truth I did not care for his reaction, but it was clear she meant something to him. And such things become weapons in the right hands.

"Pray tell, what can you do to relieve the pressure her broken ribs are currently causing as they press on her lungs? Do you harbour such power to heal her?"

I harboured power, just not the kind that could heal. Bowing my head, I kept quiet, watching from the corner of the room as Marius moved into action.

He rolled the loose sleeve of his shirt up to his elbow, brought his own wrist to his mouth and bit into his pale skin. My stomach twisted as I watched on. Beneath his lips blood spread, dripping down his chin as he lowered his hand towards the girl's parted mouth, not caring about the drips of ruby that splashed across the white sheets.

He cupped a gentle hand beneath the head of the young girl, lifted her up ever so slightly and held his bleeding wrist over her mouth. My stomach coiled in revulsion. To watch on as his life force fell like fat drops of rain across her paling lips. As if she registered it, her mouth parted, and her tongue slowly unfurled outward to catch the blood.

It was an innocent action, one a child would make during the first rains of spring. Catching the fresh drops of water and drinking from the clouds themselves. But this, this was wrong.

"I smell your disgust," Marius muttered, lowering the girl back onto the pillow. He pulled a laced cloth from his breast pocket and wiped at the blood across his wrist. "Remember it would not have been required if you had not caused this. Be thankful I have the means to help her heal. For your sake."

I closed my gaping mouth shut and tried to clear the revulsion from my expression. "How was I to know that those… things would attack us? It would not seem a handbook is provided upon arrival to this haunting place."

"Blood hounds," Marius said, ignoring my jibe. "Creatures of shadow that hunger for the same thing as I. Now you know, so keep away."

"Noted," I snapped, glancing at his now clean wrist to see not a single mark upon his skin.

He followed my gaze and lifted his wrist up. "Miraculous, isn't it?

How a curse can hold such... beauty. My blood has healing properties and keeps me sustained for years but can also heal others if ingested."

I could not answer. It was far from miraculous, but also far from anything Mother or the coven had warned me about.

"Who is she?" I asked, happy to change the topic.

Marius took his time rolling down his sleeve and buttoning the cuff.

"And you believe you deserve an answer... as if she concerns you?"

My face warmed. "It is a simple question. I know you have people living in this castle. I spoke with one. Is she your... servant?"

"She is no servant of mine."

"Then what?"

The corner of Marius's ashen lips curved into a smile, one of intrigue. "I have never been fond of questions." His sudden laugh bounced across the stone walls of the chamber. "And I have never known a Claim to be so... intrusive. Let me assure you, Jak, there is no living soul inside this castle. She —" he waved to the girl on the bed behind him "—simply visits as did her mother and her mother before that. How else am I supposed to keep in touch with the ever-changing world?"

A shiver spread down my arms. He had an informant from Darkmourn. I looked back to the girl, the traitor, unsure why I did not recognise her.

"And what is it you care to know?" My question escaped me before I could think. "Why do you care what happens beyond this place when you know you can never leave?"

Unless I fail.

Marius silver brow lifted, arched above one eye. "Do not mistake my want for knowledge as caring, Jak. I simply need to know what changes. Because one day, long after you have been drained upon your final night, I will find a way out of this forsaken cage. And when I do, I will be ready for what waits beyond."

"You are confident I will let you feed on me?" The hairs on my arms rose. That part of his curse I knew well. How he would fall into a bloodlust rage — not satisfied until every drop had been devoured from his Claim. Mother told me a story of the first year the curse was laid upon him. It was the one and only time he ever left the body on the boundary of the estate.

Hollow and empty.

He never again gave back the bodies of those he had drank from after that.

"I do not need confidence, Jak. It is inevitable." He traced a finger down my cheek, the nail a hairbreadth away from scratching my skin. "You are the Claim. It is your duty."

Before I could speak, the girl on the bed spluttered a cough. With his unnatural speed he left me, hovering over the girl as her fit of hacking coughs dissolved the heavy tension.

"Steady, Katharine, slowly," Marius cooed. "I have got you."

She pressed a hand to her chest and her coughing soon settled. And I noticed the lack of bruising that had not long covered her skin beneath her fingers.

"What happened... what? I did not leave the path." She spoke fast, her panicked words broken and rushed.

"I know... you did not." Marius cupped a hand to her check. "That was the fault of another."

Her head snapped to me. I expected a growl, but her chestnut eyes only widened. There was a part of me that recognised her, now that I saw her beneath the firelight of the burning candles in the room. And that unnerved me.

I readied myself for her to tell Marius that I was a witch. That I had magic and that was how I helped her. An ancestor to the very woman that laid the curse upon him. *Upon us.*

But Katharine's words shocked me. "Do not be angry with him." Her voice was small, but full of strength for someone of her young age. "Since I am still breathing, he must have saved me. The last thing I remember is the blood hound atop me."

Marius stared at me, eyes squinting. "He did?"

I looked to my feet, clenching my shaking hands into fists. "It was nothing."

"Do not be shy now, it does not become of you."

"I pushed it off her," I forced out the lie.

"You pushed a blood hound?"

I nodded, fearful that another lie would only make it obvious. "It was crushing her so I did what I could." I caught the gaze of Katharine who, unblinkingly, stared back at me. I did not drop her stare as I spoke on. "It was my fault she left the path after all."

"Then I must apologise for my reaction," Marius drawled. "Katharine is very dear to me. I merely acted in a manner I saw fit. Please give me and Katharine a moment. I fear we have much to discuss and would prefer you not to be involved." He smiled, slyly.

I bowed my head, stepping backwards towards the door.

"Jak," the small voice called out. Raising my chin, I regarded the young girl. Katharine. "Do not stray from the path. If you enter their domain again the blood hounds will have a vendetta against you."

"Why?" I questioned, hand hovering over the door handle.

"Because you prevented them from a meal," Marius answered. "One never forgets that."

8

I JOLTED awake to the slam of something on the table before me. Surprised, I kicked out, knocking myself backwards.

"Careful." A hand gripped the back of the chair, stopping it from falling to the floor with me in it. "We would not want yet another accident. Would we?"

I came to quickly, gripping the seat as Marius rocked me back to safety. How long had I been sleeping? Long enough for dribble to have dried on my chin.

"You have had an eventful evening. I am far from surprised that you are tired."

"I'm fine…" I regarded the large sack that now took up space on the empty table before me. But before I had slipped into sleep the table had been completely covered. "The food is gone."

"Were you that famished?"

I shook my head. "No, the food is gone. This table was full and now it is not."

I had fallen asleep with a belly full of more delicious food. Yet there was not a scrap left. "You said no one else lives here. But I hardly imagine you stoop low enough to serve and clean in your own dwelling."

Marius kicked a chair out for himself and sat upon it. He leant his elbows on his knees and rested his chiselled jaw in his palms. "You are wrong. I said that there is not anyone *living* inside this castle."

"But I—"

"Smell terrible. Truly." He leaned back, nose scrunching. "I have drawn a bath in my chamber for you. In that sack is a spare set of clothes. Ones that are not so... revealing. Clean yourself up." His voice was soft yet demanding.

I stiffened in the chair, gripping onto the sides to keep my hands busy. "What about Katharine?"

"She has returned home. The room is yours."

"What about..." I silenced myself.

"Speak, Jak. Do not be shy."

I was far from it.

"Where do you sleep?"

He tilted his head to the side. "I do not sleep."

"Then where do you go? I have seen enough of this castle to know there are other empty rooms for me to stay in."

"Those rooms are not mine." His neck straightened, his deep voice hardened.

"Is that supposed to make me feel a type of way?"

He was still. Burgundy eyes flicked across my face. Searching. I held my breath. But then he smiled. "If I wanted to make you feel a certain way, Jak, I would not need it solely to be in my room."

The chair squeaked across the floor as I stood abruptly.

"Have I said something to offend you?" he said through a sly grin.

My hands shook wildly at my side. "I do not know what you have grown used to, Marius. But I can tell you I am not like the others you have ... played with. Watch what you say to me. And how you say it."

Marius stood now, towering inches over me. "That sounds awfully similar to a threat."

I stepped forward. "What if it is?"

We held each other's stare. Neither one wanting to break it before the other.

"You are right, Jak," Marius whispered, being the first to step back. "You are nothing like the others that have been before you. Nothing."

༄

The water was still warm when I slipped into its embrace. I released a groan until my head went under, mouth filling up with water. I kept my eyes open, watching bubbles escape from my mouth and rise to the surface.

Bliss. And much needed.

Only when my lungs burned for breath did I burst from its warm belly. I hardly cared as it splashed over the edge of the brass tub and splattered over the slabbed ground of Marius's room.

The man... creature, infuriated me. Disgusted me. At least that was what I told myself over and over as I washed the days of dirt from my skin until it was red raw.

I was becoming accustomed to the late nights and early mornings. My normal routine had completely altered since arriving. Before the drawn curtain the sky was lightening and with it brought my tiredness. The short nap I had at the dining table was not sufficient. I longed to swaddle myself in the comforting sheets of Marius's bed. Which had, yet again, been prepared. No sign that Katharine had ever lied upon it nor the dried droplets of blood.

I did not climb into the bed until the water had grown cold and I struggled to keep my eyes open. My arms shook from tiredness as I lifted myself from the tub and trailed a line of water to the bed. I gave little care in letting my bare skin dry. Barely rubbing at it, nor allowing myself time to dry amongst the air before clambering within the sheets.

I turned over in the bed, stretching my exposed body as far as I could. Something stiff scratched against my arm. I fought the tiredness enough to lift my head and look through one eye as to what it was that I felt.

There, on the pillow beside me was a note. A folded piece of parchment that was sealed with black wax.

I ran my thumb over the seal, feeling the ridges of the design that I could not fully make out. It was what I thought to be a cross. But it seemed a rose was etched in the middle of the crosses interlinking lines.

It was a shame to pull the folded parchment apart, breaking the seal too.

Join me for supper.

M.

The note was short. Precise.

"Dinner." I laughed, discarding the note back on the pillow. Turning my back on it, I rolled over, my heart beating calmly in my chest.

Who knew it only took chasing a girl through the gardens to get his full attention?

I almost longed for the scrying bowl to be fixed, so Mother could see how I had changed the tides in my favour.

I suppose she would have to wait and see when I walked back home with his head in my hands.

9

I STUDIED myself before the mirror, this time wearing more than just the loose nightshirt I had found yesterday.

Someone had been in my room as I'd slept. For the pile of clothing had been laid out ready for me at the end of the bed. The thought unnerved me, knowing someone had watched as I slept. Being vulnerable was a new feeling, yet I woke without harm. That was enough to prevent the feeling from becoming overwhelming.

The clothes were grand. Each thread screamed wealth and privilege. The perfect outfit for the supper I had been invited to. One that I clearly had no choice but to accept — not that I would have declined.

The jacket was made from velvet. Each touch left marks in the dark navy material. In the candlelight it looked as though I wore the very ocean captured at midnight. I turned my body, from left to right, taking in the beauty of the material.

The breeches were fitting, hugging my slender legs to the cuff which was held together by a button made from the iridescent belly of a shell.

Everything was tailored to my body. All besides the shirt that was countless sizes too big. If it was not for the jacket holding the shirt in place, it would have slipped over my shoulders each time I moved.

I could have tied it up at the neck with the cream cords that were strung loosely. But I didn't. I kept my neck on show purposefully.

I took my time preparing my brown hair, smoothing it down with the cool water that had been left in the tub. I ran my hand through my fringe, tucking it backwards to expose as much of my face as I could.

My weapon. More powerful than my magic could be against a creature of notable hunger.

He wants a feast. So I shall give him one.

∼

"At last, he arrives." Marius stood at the head of the table. He wore a dark cloak of shadow that swallowed the chair he had only moments before sat upon. "I was beginning to believe you would simply ignore my invitation."

"I did not realise I had a choice," I answered, walking towards the chair that Marius gestured towards.

"One always has a choice."

"They do?"

Marius teeth chattered as he smiled. "You interest me, Jak. I cannot deny that."

I forced my own smile and bowed my head. "I am no more than a boring, simple Claim. I am certain you have had far more interesting company than what I can offer."

"Perhaps," he mused, "there is time left for that to be determined."

I held his stare, and he kept mine, as I pulled my chair out and sat.

"I trust you slept well," he said, still standing long after I took a seat.

"I did."

He lifted his chin, nostrils flaring. "And you took up the not-so-subtle offer to wash?"

As his gaze traced me, I lifted a gentle finger and ran it across my collarbone, slowly until I was certain his eyes followed my every move.

"It was glorious."

Marius sighed as I dropped my touch and picked up the silverware beside the empty plate. Without looking back at him, I began to fill my plate with the delectable foods that waited around me.

Our conversation was a string of short sentences. I found conversation hard to start as I busied myself with the food, whereas I felt Marius was silent for other reasons.

"Not that you need me to offer, but please help yourself." Marius finally sat, which settled the nerves that itched beneath my skin. "You must be hungry."

"Famished," I said, picking a charred leg of cooked meat that must have been chicken.

Marius whispered, enough for me to hear, "You have no idea."

He sat watching me, his stare burrowing into my soul. But not once did I look up, focused on piling my plate even more just to keep myself busy.

I usually preferred the quiet of silence, but as time went on I could not bear it. "Are you not hungry?" I questioned, flicking a forkful of meat at him. Marius had not touched anything, his hands remaining in his lap as he watched me.

"Starving."

My blood chilled, the skin across my exposed neck tickling beneath his stare. "Then eat."

Marius groaned, rocking back in his chair. "There is not a single item on this table that would satisfy me, Jak."

I shrugged, keeping my gaze low. "Suit yourself. I trust you did not prepare all of this for me? Or all the food presented to me since my arrival?"

Marius raised his hands, both of them in surrender. "Do these hands looked overworked?"

I scoffed, taking my time to chew on the chicken that dangled from my fork.

"It seems that little has changed in the way of conversation, Jak. Still your kind discuss small matters such as weather, or in your case, food. Let us have more of a deeper, more interesting conversation."

His comment was an insult buried beneath his posh accent. As though I had been slapped with a feather.

"Then please, ask away," I told him, swallowing the lump of food that struggled down my dry throat.

"There is something about your participation in the previous evening's events that do not sit right to me."

I almost choked.

"Would you be so kind as to explain what happened again. Truly, it is extremely... interesting to me."

I held Marius's stare. He wanted me to trip up, I could sense his distrust. "Is it hard to believe I do not have the bravery to take on one of your hellish beasts?"

Marius huffed, rocking back with his arms behind his head. Muscles flexed, threatening to rip his jacket. "I do not doubt your bravery. You raised a hand to me only moments after I welcomed you into my home."

"You make it seem that my visit here is something worthy of welcome."

"Then we should toast." Marius nails tapped on the glass he raised. "To my hundredth Claim."

"You do not eat, but you drink?" I asked, studying the red wine that sloshed within his glass. He kept looking at me as he raised the rim to his lips and took a swig. The wine stained his already dark lips. The vision of him biting his own wrist flooded my memory.

"I drink because I am thirsty. Wine has been the only substance to curb the deeper appetite the curse bestowed on me."

Intrigue spurred me to question further. "And what is it you crave?"

I knew. I did not need to ask, but I could see the glint in his dark gaze when the subject was brought up. The lust he had for it made his lips part and his tongue traced his lower lip.

"Blood."

I lowered my glass back to the table, shrugging off his comment and digging back into my food even though my appetite had dissipated in that moment. I left the meat on the plate, opting for the boiled and seasoned potato.

"Where do you go during the days?" I asked, changing the subject to one that did not threaten the contents of my stomach to reappear.

"Why do you care to know?"

"You asked for conversation and I am giving it to you. Questions breed answers, is that not what you want?"

Marius released a bated breath. "Tell me about yourself instead, Jak. I find myself wanting to know more of your life before you were so unfortunate to be delivered to me."

"Has Katharine not told you about me? I thought that was the point of her visits."

"I do not care to know about my Claims. It is part of the mystery, waiting to learn of their stories myself."

"Stories," I huffed. "So you are a keen reader?"

"More of a writer. But enough about me. I asked about you, yet I am coming to understand you are skilled at diverting the topic from yourself. It is as if you have something to hide."

As do you, I thought, forcing a smile.

Part of my training was for this moment exactly. Weaving a lie to tell him of myself. To paint a picture I want for Marius to see of me.

"Then ask away." I waved a steady hand, whereas my leg beneath the table was bouncing uncontrollably.

"Tell me of your home."

I focused on the food and let my false story loose.

"My father is a baker. My mother a seamstress. I spend my time flitting between both and helping. Our home is used as the bakery and Mother works from the back rooms."

"You are good with your hands?"

I swallowed the lump of boiled potato. "Awful. Mother will do anything in her power to stop me from ruining her projects. And the most Father lets me do is split the flour, that is it."

"Shame." Marius shrugged. "And do you enjoy helping your parents?"

"I— no."

"No? Then what is it you would have wanted to do in your life?"

I couldn't answer aloud. *To end you.*

"It does not matter what I want now. Does it?"

He knew what I meant. For any other Claim, a visit to this place never resulted in a return home.

Marius's grin melted away, his stare lost to a spot on the table. "Because you are to die." His voice was as cold as his touch. It lasted only a moment before he shook himself out of the strange trance I had watched him slip into.

Opting to steer away from this conversation, I presented Marius with a question.

"What do you do during the rest of the year when you are not... entertaining your Claim?"

It was a question I truly wanted an answer to. I had longed stared up at this castle from my bedroom window. Studying the dark, lifeless windows and seemingly empty place. It was only during the month of the Claiming when the castle came to life.

"I wait."

"That sounds awfully dull," I joked, trying to lighten the suddenly heavy atmosphere that laid upon the room.

"Time is an odd concept in this place. It has taken me years to not dwell on it. For the more I did in the beginning, the more I let myself slip into madness."

A just punishment.

As I thought it, his inquisitive stare settled on mine and held it. His furrowed brow made me believe for a second that he could infiltrate my thoughts.

"It is my turn again." He groaned, lifting the rim of the glass to his lips and holding it there.

"For what?" I said, licking the dregs of wine from my lower lip. Appetite was failing me as the beast bored into me. Instead, I opted for a chug of fruitful, red wine to dull my anxiety at the questions to follow.

"It is my turn to ask you a question." Marius leaned forward on the table, finger tapping his defined jaw. "What did you know of me before you were chosen as my Claim?"

"You want to know?"

He waved a hand, urging me on. "Entertain me... please."

Little is more. Lamiere's words echoed in my mind and my chest warmed at the memory of the old maiden.

"I know you were cursed for killing the betrothed of Morgane De'Fray." My own great-grandmother.

He scoffed, draining his own glass of wine in one fell swoop. "Go on," he said, teeth stained red.

"That you have lived out your days in an eternal cycle. One that can never be broken."

Lie. I will break it.

"I know that those who are sent to your castle never return home."

"Why?"

I kept my face straight, no matter how the wine I had devoured made me want to act. "You kill them."

"Why?" he asked again, a low hiss sounding from the back of his throat.

"To drink from them, to keep yourself—"

"Without pain!" Marius shouted, standing abruptly and slamming his palms on the table. It shook beneath the force, glass and china hitting into each other in a chorus of high-pitched clinks. "I drink because I must. Every year I have asked these same questions hoping that I may hear something else in response. To share in my own confusion as to what the *bitch* turned me into. And every year the same, empty, answers are provided. Believe it or not, Claim, I know little more than you."

I stood, swaying slightly. "My name is Jak."

The flames of the many candles across the table sang to me, willing for me to reach out for them. But I resisted, only just.

"And I do not care."

I pushed from the table, not caring about the chair that fell across the floor in a bang.

"Where are you going?" Marius hissed, demand dripping from his tone.

"To bed." I kept my voice steady, fighting the urge to use magic as a means to shut the creature up.

"Dinner is not over," Marius said, face twitching as it began to relax.

"Believe it or not, I have lost my appetite."

Turning around, I took large steps away from the table, until Marius called out, "Wait... wait." His deep voice cracked. "Please. My... my anger gets the best of me. It is that or I simply forget myself."

I paused, his apology hanging in the air between us. I felt the need for magic slip away like butter over an open flame.

Get close to the beast. Lure him.

"I need more wine," I said, turning back to face him and ignoring his apology. "And something sweet — that is my price."

"Price to stay?"

I grinned, lowering my chin. "Precisely."

"Then forgive my disappearance. I will return shortly." With that he left through the door at the end of the dining hall. From his pocket he pulled a brass key and fit it into the door. One sharp turn and it unlocked, and he disappeared into the shadows beyond.

Marius left swiftly, just as I drank yet another glass of red wine in the same manner. Down to the bottom of the glass I drained it. Then another, and another, until my mind was fuzzy and eyes heavy and slow. It became apparent quickly that Marius was not returning. I must have sat like this for a while, waiting, with the hope that I was finally getting somewhere with him. Getting close to him as I had planned. But clearly, I was wrong.

The sky beyond the room lightened, signalling the arrival of dawn. And the disappearance of Marius for yet another day.

Frustrated, I wobbled from the chair, not caring as it tumbled to the floor. It was time for sleep, I knew that much. But as I walked towards the door I had entered in, I stopped.

Marius had not left for his promise of sweet treats through here. He had gone through the unexplored door at the back of the dining hall. The one that was still left ajar.

On awkward legs I stumbled towards it, ready to explore yet another part of this maze of brick and mortar.

Where do you hide, Marius?

10

I HEARD the murmurings of soft voices as I rounded the dark winding corridors beyond the dining hall. Everything was dark here. I felt the floor beneath my feet slope downwards. The further I walked, the deeper I found myself in the belly of the castle.

There were no windows. No available light to help guide my way. I had to use my hands against the cold stone wall to know I would not collide into something face-first.

I could have called up a flame, but the wine had dulled my senses. That and the clear presence of Marius that was up ahead.

Perhaps hardly any time had passed at all during Marius's absence. I had given in to my own impatience when he would have likely returned to the dining hall soon enough?

But I stilled as the voices rose ahead. Keeping my breathing as shallow as I could muster so I would not miss out on a single word.

"You are slipping," a familiar, youthful voice said. "I would not be the one to remind you, but it was your own request that I keep you in line."

"Your worry is misplaced," Marius replied, his voice a low growl.

"Is it? We all sense your change in mood. We have witnessed it enough; some even have experienced it to know where this path will lead."

A shuffle of footsteps in the dark and the shadows seemed to vibrate. I rubbed a palm over my eyes. Was it the wine?

"It has been years since I have allowed myself more than a word with the Claim. Can this year not be any different?"

"I am merely reminding you as you have requested. Or have you forgotten the oath you made me take?" The voice sharpened. The speaker sounded so young yet held much power beneath her tone.

Marius paused in his response. In my place hidden around the corner of the dark corridor I could imagine him running circles with his forefinger over his chin.

"It all ends the same, Marius. It always will. And you will spend the year to follow in the dark place you made me swear to keep you out of."

"There is something different about him."

Me.

"If this has anything to do with Katharine…"

Marius emitted a low growl from the back of his throat. "Tread carefully."

"Put your teeth away," she said, dismissively. "They cannot harm me. But they can hurt him."

I slowly peered around the corner, hoping to catch a glimpse of the speaker as it hit me where I had heard her before. Beyond the bedroom door during my first morning.

"It is inevitable. For years we have tried to break this curse, yet it always ends the same way. Can I not allow myself one year off from behaving?"

"You make it sound like you are a dog on a leash, Marius."

"Am I not?"

"You are a beast in a locked cage. And there is nothing you can do to break out of it. I will not stand in your way again if this is the path you are going to choose with him. You asked this of me, and I knew a time would come when you would resist. Just know that we will not appear for you when the deed is done, and the blood warms your belly. You can deal with the consequences alone this time."

I jumped at the sound of bone slamming into brick. If it was not for the crack that followed I was certain they would have heard my gasp. Then Marius spoke quietly, so soft I nearly missed it.

"It is his name."

"I knew it had a part to play," she replied softly.

"I feel as if he was sent here as punishment. This is the hundredth year without him yet the pain still cuts deep." A strange chill fell over me. As Marius spoke, I felt the effects of the wine slip away. *Who are you speaking about?* "His name is not the only similarity, which is making it harder for me to distinguish the difference. Perhaps I am simply weary."

"We are all tired, Marius."

"And I am sorry for that, truly."

The girl chirped a laugh. "Do not apologise again. I have heard it enough. You should retire for the day, perhaps some time to clear your head will help you make a decision on which actions to take."

"Have I ever told you how truly blessed I am to have your council, Victorya?"

She laughed again, echoed by the deep, hearty chuckle of Marius. "Who knew the Lord of Eternal Night would be taking guidance from a child."

"Wise, but a child nonetheless."

"You forget yourself. If I was still alive my wisdom would be reflected by my appearance. I have you to thank for my own everlasting youth."

Still alive. Her words thundered through me. The urge to interrupt them and reveal myself was strong, all to get a simple glance at the speaker. But I couldn't. I had to stay unseen so Marius would not know of the upper hand I had just obtained from listening.

He was falling for me and I had barely begun. That was enough to satisfy me. I left them, calling upon the dank air in the corridor to muffle my footfalls as I left for the dining hall again. My magic thrummed through my body as I willed the air to thicken beneath my feet and the slabbed floor. Before I knew it I was back through the dining hall, leaving the door how I had found it.

I would sleep well with the knowledge I had obtained. The weapon in which Marius had unknowingly handed to me.

With a smile plastered across my face, I clambered back to his room and into his bed, revelling in the warmth of the sheets. My chest felt light and free of worry, making it easier to slip into sleep. But as I fell into the darkness I could not rid myself of the face that haunted me.

One that seemed to glow as if moonlight was woven through his alabaster skin.

Marius.

His fingers were tendrils of ice, leaving imprints of frozen burns beneath his touch. Marius held my gaze as his hand trailed up my thigh, effortlessly moving the sheets out of his way. My breath hitched. His mouth parted, exposing the points of his canines.

"Tell me to stop."

I stared deeper into him, shaking my head slightly. "No."

With one hand Marius explored me, and with the other he gripped onto himself. I risked a glance for a moment as his hand ran circles on the protrusion that waited beneath the material of his trousers. The outline of his cock sent a shiver across my arms, until every hair stood on end.

"I am on your mind," Marius breathed.

I arched my back as his hand found what it searched for.

"This is the first time you have called for me."

I could not reply, not as I gripped onto his caressing hand to slow him. His touch intoxicated me.

"Do I fill your thoughts?"

His other hand now gripped my throat, nails biting into my skin as he held me down, stopping me from squirming as he worked away at me.

I was sensitive beneath his touch. It thrilled me. Enthralled me. Marius did not once take his deep, maroon eyes off me.

"Why do you dream of me?"

His words were the crashing wave of water that woke me. I bolted up in his bed, finding the room still lit from the daylight beyond the castle window. Marius was nowhere to be seen. The room was empty.

Breathlessly I waited for my heartbeat to calm for it thundered in my ears. My forehead was damp, as well as my arms and legs. My entire body stuck to the sheets.

It took a moment for the dreamscape to leave me. I lowered my head back onto the pillow and stared up at the ceiling, shocked at myself. My subconsciousness ruled my mind during sleep, and I had conjured that sensual thought. It sickened me.

Or did it?

I rolled over, pressing my face into the pillow in hopes to suffocate the image of Marius from my mind.

"It is the wine," I told myself, promising that I would not touch a drop the next day. But as I closed my eyes again, I half expected to fall back into the scene with him. It had been so clear. Every detail so vivid and real.

The sleep that followed was empty and uninterrupted — but as I fell into its embrace, I was certain I still felt his phantom touch linger across the skin of my thigh.

11

It was a struggle to hold Marius's stare as he made himself known at the threshold of his room.

"May I come in?" he asked, voice dripping with velvet.

I fussed with the sheets, making the bed and puffing the pillows. Doing anything to busy my mind from the dream that had occupied it. But it did not work. "You left me last night," I said through a slight pout.

"I did." I had to admire his bluntness. "And I come with an apology."

I glanced up at him as he clearly held something concealed behind his back with both hands. The jacket Marius adorned today was midnight black and had a cloak attached to the collar which swept proudly behind him. His white locks had been combed over to the side, not a single hair out of place.

I realised all too late that my pause in response was noted as Marius smiled, following my gaze as I searched him up and down.

"Is something wrong?" A single brow lifted in question.

I turned my back on him and sighed. "I am trapped in this castle knowing that my end is weeks away. Of course something is wrong."

It sounded funny, even to me, as I spoke the complaint aloud.

"Well put." Marius voice was right behind me now, forcing a small yelp to escape my lips, silenced by his hand as it rested upon my tensed shoulder. "I did not mean to frighten you."

Beneath his touch, my stomach jolted. Yesterday I was confident that I had him in the palm of my hand. But the dream had left me feeling a way I could not explain.

I turned to him, keeping my face void of expression. Shrugging his touch off my shoulder, I stepped back until the frame of the bed pressed into my lower calves. "To what do I owe the pleasure of your company this evening, Marius?"

Marius pulled a face, fingers flexing where they hovered in the air. "If my disappearance last night has truly angered you, perhaps this will help." He held in his hand a small china plate. Atop it was a single bun, glazed with white icing and drizzled with an amber, sticky substance. "A sweet treat as promised."

"You are far too late," I lied, stomach grumbling in disagreement with what I said. His lips curled upwards as I snatched the plate from his hands. "But I will take it."

My body clock had changed dramatically since arriving. Only a few days of sleeping during the day and staying awake during the night had settled over me with ease. It felt as though I should be eating breakfast now, even though the crescent moon hung in the darkened sky beyond the window.

I used the sweet bun as an excuse not to speak to Marius who stood, longingly, before me as I ate it. Each swallow became harder as my throat dried in response to his stare. He did not look at my eyes as I ate. No. His gaze flicked down to my lips, transfixed by them. I found myself raising my hand to block his view out of discomfort.

As if shaking himself from the trance he spoke. "I was hoping you would join me for a stroll this evening?"

"Where?" I said through a mouthful. The glazing was thick and stuck to my teeth. It seemed to amuse Marius who hid his smile with his slender fingers. "I fear I have searched every corner of this castle and you will not see me stepping foot beyond it because the threat of those creatures are enough to keep me comfortably inside."

"Need I remind you that the blood hounds will not hurt you if I am with you. And I do not mean to disappoint but you are wrong about this place. My home has many rooms in which you have not yet *stumbled* across."

I scrunched my face, lips covered in powdered sugar. Marius leaned forward and, with his thumb, cleared my lower lip. Ice. His touch was so cold my lip faltered beneath it. I could not move, not as he lifted his hand to his own mouth and sucked the remnants of white powder from his thumb.

It became hard to swallow as I watched him take his time making sure not a single speck of sugar was left.

"I forgot the delights of food," he moaned through a grimace.

"You do not eat?" I asked, remembering how he had not touched anything during our supper the evening before.

"There is no need to eat, unlike humans who must feed themselves to survive. For me food is something to busy myself with, but if I did not eat it would not make much difference to me."

I knew so little of him. All my life I had studied this creature yet it was becoming more apparent daily that Mother and the coven's teachings had barely scraped the surface of this enigma.

"Care to join me then?" He turned on his heel, extending a bent arm to me in offering.

I stared at the waiting, crook of his arm as though it was the answer to the universe's deepest secrets. Marius must have sensed my hesitation in taking up his offer. The remnant memory of the dream was still so real. *Too real*. Marius put his arm down to his side and waved dramatically with the other for the door. "Please, follow me."

∽

Marius was right. There was much of this castle I had not explored. As I followed him swiftly through seemingly endless corridors and up curving stairwells, I was left muddled as to where I was. The further we climbed up through the castle, the more the darkness seemed to shift to reveal unseen rooms and unexplored pathways. I almost questioned him on what lay in the deep pits of the castle, the same area I had drunkenly followed him into. Was that where his servants stayed, preparing all the food and drink that had been presented to me? I gathered from their conversation last night the mysterious servants of this dwelling had to keep out of the way. Once again I buried my interest, for now was not the time.

"I was certain I had been everywhere," I said, breathless from yet another climb up a grand staircase to another upper floor of the castle.

Marius carried an iron chamberstick with a single white pillar candle burning. The flame did little to cut through the darkness of the castle, but it did not deter Marius from walking forward with confidence. "The dark can play tricks on one's mind. I did not want you to simply stumble here so the dark acts as a shroud to keep unwanted visitors out. If I will it so."

I skipped up a step, his strides long and powerful. "You make it seem that the darkness is a thing that can do your own bidding."

Marius slowed to a stop, so abruptly that I nearly bumped into the back of him. I caught the shift of his movement as he raised a hand over the flame, fingers outstretched. "It does." He curled his fingers into a fist and the flame in the candle dimmed. Not because it shrunk in size, or was blown out by a gust of unseen wind. I watched as the darkness that hovered beyond the halo of light fought for control.

Shadows of darkness spun around the flame hungrily, blanketing it in gloom. If I squinted, I still could see the glow of orange, but it was faint, like looking through a curtain of liquid obsidian.

"Incredible," I spoke without truly thinking.

"You are not frightened?" Marius questioned.

"More intrigued than fearful," I replied, as the flame sprung back to life with the removal of Marius's hand. "That power should not be possible."

"There is nothing about me that should be possible, Jak."

It was the curse. There was no other explanation for what Marius had just revealed to me. I knew he was not a witch, not when my own ancestor gifted him with this life. He was a greedy, selfish man. One that was mundane and lacking any natural ability. Not like me.

"Your silence unnerves me."

I laid my hand upon his arm, revelling in the slice of surprise that widened his handsome features. "Says the beast that will soon kill me. If anyone deserve the right to be unnerved, it is I."

He winced, even in the minimal light from the candle I saw it. "If I had the choice…"

"What exactly are you going to show me?" I interrupted. "Because I fear my legs will soon give out if you have me walk up any more stairs."

"We are close." Marius faced the corridor. "It has been many years since I last invited a Claim up here."

"You still have not explained where *here* is exactly."

Marius continued his walk forward, leaving me in his wake. "You will soon see."

The destination waited beyond the door at the far end of the darkened corridor. It was closed, like all the others we passed. Marius handed the chamberstick to me as he fussed with a key he had fished from the breast pocket of his jacket. For such dramatic mystery, Marius took his sweet time unlocking it.

He pushed the door open and I was bathed in light. I raised a hand to block out the sudden flare of orange and gold, almost catching my hair alight from the candle I still gripped onto.

Then a warmth washed over me. Its welcoming embrace relaxing both my limbs and mind.

Marius kept the door open as he invited me to enter. "After you."

I did not hesitate to enter a moment longer. Before me was a vision of excellence. Towering shelves of dark mahogany, each filled completely with books of different sizes and bindings. Twin roaring fires sat at either end of the long, yet narrow room. Before the largest fire sat a plump chair. Gold clawed feet held up the velvet upholstery. I could only imagine sitting upon its plush cushioning would have felt like dwelling on a warm cloud.

"What is this place?"

I inhaled, breathing in the scent of sandalwood and ink. On a large desk sat open glass bottles of black liquid that I could only guess was the origin of the smell.

Writing ink. And a desk covered in loose, empty pages.

"A kitchen."

I paused, turning to Marius who chuckled into the crook of his arm. "This is my study. A haven for me of sorts. This room was my sanctuary long before I was cursed to never leave it. I thought you would like to see it. Take it as yet another apology for my... rude disappearance last night."

Walking towards the shelves, I noticed the thick layering of dust across them. Looking back to the desk, I could see where the papers had not been moved for a time as they too were framed with dust. This room had not been used in a long while. All but the newly lit fires had changed. Even they still had the remnants of cobwebs across the piles of untouched brickwork.

"Could you not have dusted before you brought me here?" I held a finger to my nose to fight the sneeze.

Marius looked away for a brief moment. "It was a spur of the moment decision."

"Yet you had the time to light two fires?" I pushed.

"I did not light them," Marius said coldly, closing us in the room. "Besides the obvious need for a—" he ran his finger across the untouched desk "—clean, what do you think?"

"Well I'm not much of a reader, but I must say I'm impressed," I replied, neck aching as I swung my gaze around the room.

"That is the first thing you have said that truly makes me ready to end you."

Silence thickened between us.

"I am only joking," Marius said, rubbing the back of his neck.

I forced a laugh. "Messy and inappropriate. What two charming qualities you have."

Marius flashed a grin, one that did not reach his ruby eyes. He pulled a plain, oak carved chair from beneath the desk and sat down upon it. From his seat he studied me, as I continued to examine the room.

"It has been so long that it seems the chair has forgotten my shape." Marius wiggled in the seat.

"Is there a reason?" I scanned the tomes before me, drifting a careful finger across the leathered spines. Some had ridges, others were smooth. What I had told him was true, I was not much of a reader. Besides studying the coven's many grimoires, Mother did not let me read works of fiction. *Stories distract the mind, and I need yours to be as sharp as a knife. As clear as glass.*

"There are memories in this room that I had long wanted to keep behind a locked door."

"What has changed now?"

I kept my back to him so he could not see me grin when he responded. "I am alone most of the year. Forgive me for wanting company when I can get it."

"Except you are not alone," I said, pulling a book from the shelf. Holding it in both hands, I opened it carefully, worried the ancient pages would simply crumble beneath my touch. "You do not light fires. Nor do you prepare the food that is presented so wonderfully every day. You say no one else lives inside this castle but..." I turned to him, looking up from the book to where he sat. "I do not believe you."

"Kristia," Marius said.

"What?" Confusion furrowed my brow.

"The book you are holding. It is about Kristia."

I flipped the page, revealing the swirling writing of beautiful calligraphy. A single word, just as Marius had said it. *Kristia.*

"She was the fourth Claim that was sent to me. A shy girl, but the further I got to know her the more I sensed the fire within her. I have not met another like her."

"And you just so happen to have a novel about her."

"Wrong... I just so happened to write a novel about her."

I flipped the page yet again. Once, twice, until the pages were filled with handwritten words. The pages so full and sentences so close together that it seemed there was no space left.

"I do not understand."

"I brought you here so you could learn something about me. You think me a beast. Katharine and those before her have told me the stories people believe about me. And most of them are true. But I do not want to... kill anyone. I never have. Unfortunately you will soon see that I am not in control when it happens. I simply cease to exist for that final night. I understand this is strange to you, and you did not choose this. And I apologise for discussing the matter of your demise so frankly. But I too did not choose you. Just like I did not choose those who came before you. In truth, this room fills me with nothing but guilt. It is my reminder of what I have done, and what I will do again."

I could not breathe as Marius spoke. Nor could I take my eyes off his. Not once did he blink as he spoke to me, unravelling his story as I held onto another of his.

"That book, and those around you, are my way of dealing with the guilt. I write stories for those whose lives I take. Create worlds and futures on pages in which I know they will never get to live. It is my way of honouring them."

"Sounds like a lot of effort to me." I couldn't fathom it. Even holding the proof in my hands it did not seem real.

By the time I took my eyes off the page Marius was before me. His movements soundless and light. He took the weight of the book from my hands, closed it and turned it so the spine was facing upwards.

"Kristia is one of many of those stories I have conjured. You are welcome to read them… in your own time though. Just the thought of someone going through my work in front of me unnerves me."

I crossed my arms, unsure what to do with them. What Marius had divulged did not sit well within me. It caused a strange, unwelcome tugging in my chest.

"Will you write one for me?" I asked, sharply.

There I went again, pushing the boundaries of the topic knowing full well Marius would not live long enough to write my name on the inside of a book.

"I will."

I stepped towards him, closing the small gap until the book he held was the only thing separating us.

"And what will it say?"

Marius breathed deeply, eyes flicking across every inch of my face.

"That is yet to be determined."

Being this close to Marius after the dream I had made my stomach jolt. I fought to hold his stare and keep up this illusion of confidence. But being so close made my knees shake.

"I fear I have lied to you about something," Marius muttered, his face inches from mine.

Me too.

"Tell me." I peered deep into his blood-red eyes, wondering how far I could see into his soul.

"There is someone I would gladly kill, without thought or hesitation."

My arms prickled as his voice softened to a whisper.

"Who?" I said, watching his stare follow the movement of my lips.

"The *witch* that did this to me. I know she has since died, but I also know that her family live on. And one day, when I find a way out of this place, I will be certain to rain hell on them all. Out of the memory of those I have been made to kill, I will do it. For them." He gestured to the bookshelves. "And for you, Jak."

His cold touch found my chin and held it.

I parted my mouth to respond, but there was nothing I could say. His warning made the air around me so thick that it was almost impossible to breathe. And I was certain he felt my body tremble in the aftershock of his threat.

There, in that moment, deep in the stormy pits of his gaze, I felt the presence of the beast I had been brought up to hate. I sensed his hatred as though it was a scent in the air. It was palpable, honest and true.

Yet the worst part was the bud of fear that twisted far down in my gut. What Marius said was not a warning.

It was a promise.

12

I awoke the next night from a dreamless sleep. And I could not disregard the disappointment I felt. Rolling over in *his* bed, I surveyed the dark sky beyond the forever drawn curtains and sighed. I was beginning to forget what the sun looked like. Even in my head I recognised the dramatic flare of my thought, but it was true.

Marius's study had only conjured more questions I had for him. And looking at the star-filled sky beyond the dusty windows yet another question sprang to mind.

Why did he hide during the day?

Oh, and another.

Where?

I waited in bed for him to reveal himself. But his absence was obvious. The night before he had not long left after we arrived at his study. It was a change in mood that happened in a blink of an eye. Marius had offered his apologies and left abruptly, leaving me alone with the many stories of his. Stories in which I had started to read through, only giving up when the calls of hunger spasmed in my stomach. It did not feel right to take a book from the room. So I left them, promising silently to return again.

I dressed myself without a thought, pulling freshly folded clothes from the dark, chestnut wardrobe. Much like the outfit I had arrived in I opted for a familiar loose tunic and fitted trousers that buttoned up at my waist tightly.

I had almost expected to bump into him as I found my way into the prepared dining hall. But he was not there.

After I'd finished eating, only one thought passed through my foggy mind. *I have to speak with Mother.*

As soundless as I could, I moved through the castle, taking the route back to the charred room I had stayed in before I set it alight. There was no sign of Marius or the mystery servants that clearly hid among the dark rooms of this place.

Perhaps Marius's strange power of darkness kept them hidden just as he had created the illusion over the wing of the castle that contained his study.

Still the scent of scorched wood clung to the air of the burned room. It was not as pungent as before, but strong enough to smell it before I entered its boundaries.

There the scrying bowl lay, where I had dropped it as I'd ran after Katharine beyond the now closed window of the room. I scooped it from the floor, feeling the warped body of the bowl. It was cold to the touch. Almost lifeless.

Marius could be anywhere, and I had to keep my magic hidden. But the urge to speak with Mother was intense. It was likely a better idea to wait for morning since I knew there would be no risk of him listening.

But that involved waiting. And I did not like the thought of that.

I raced back to his room, scrying bowl held protectively to my chest. The door shut behind me the moment I entered through it. There were many ways I could have kept it closed without a lock and key. I could have melted the ancient bolt. Raised the slabbed flooring inches from the ground until it blocked the door if it was opened from the outside. But this magic would leave such an obvious mark — and Marius would kill me the moment he knew what I was.

Just as he had warned.

As he had promised.

Be quick. I warned myself, nestling into bed with the bowl in my crossed legs. The door was to my back, giving me a moment to act if Marius decided to show himself.

I closed my eyes, inhaling slowly, as I called for the elements. *Water.* I imagined its cool kiss, forceful strength and guiding movement. Above my open palm I felt its trickling presence as I pulled the moisture from the air. By the time I opened my eyes the sphere of azure spun wildly, waiting for its command to enter the scrying bowl.

"Stop before he sees what you are."

The water splashed across my lap and chest in an explosion. My entire body stilled, but the fire within me rose to the surface in response to the intruder that stood behind me.

I turned to face them, ready to rain my magic upon them. To turn them into cinders to prevent them from telling Marius what they had seen.

The figure was no more than a wisp of grey smoke, twisting tendrils of cloud that hung inches above the ground. A body so faint that I could see through it, to the wall behind. It was a small girl, no more than the age of eight, features captured in youth that rippled like the water of a lake.

My mind could not comprehend what I was seeing as the body materialised before me, not completely though as the edges of the colourless girl shivered.

I blinked, unsure what I was witnessing. Flames danced around my fingers, ready and waiting for my release.

"Your magic will not harm me." She kept deathly still. "Calm yourself."

I fisted my hand, closing off my connection to the fire. Everything was silent as I stared dumfounded at the girl.

"What..."

"A soul. A ghost. A spirit. Your guess is as good as mine, believe me. But I am already dead. Your magic will not harm me, so do not waste your time using it."

I studied her shimmering figure, rubbing at my eyes in hopes that it would help make sense of what I saw when I opened them again. My mind could not fathom what I witnessed. Not as the child hovered from the ground in a billow of unseen wind.

Then it hit me. "It was you. The first day, it was you who gave me the key."

"It was." There was something aged about her tone. Her voice was light as a child's, but the hidden undercurrent was anything but young.

"And with Marius." The vision of the night I had followed him into the lower floors of the castle filled my mind.

"He was careless to let you follow," she scorned. "But that is Marius. Careless and foolish. And it would seem you are not different, using your power in this castle, let alone at night when he roams freely."

"I cannot let you tell him." I stood, readying all the elements to wait for my word. All my training and I had never been told how to destroy a spirit. Souls of the dead did not linger on this plane. That's what Mother told me. But here one stood.

"And what are you going to do?" she said, arms folding across her colourless body. "Set me ablaze like you did your room? Blow me away with some gust of stale air?" She almost laughed as she taunted me. "If you stop accusing me and actually listen you would know that I would not tell Marius what I have seen. If I wanted to ruin your plans I could have done so days ago."

It was a strange feeling, being told off by a girl, let alone one that was not alive. "Why? Why not tell him?"

"We have watched you since your first day. If we wanted to inform Marius of your secrets we would have done so. I trusted you would be smart about concealing your power, but you risk exposure when using it during the night. It was a foolish risk you were about to take."

It felt as though I was being scorned by Lamiere. Not a child.

I stepped forward, hands ready at my sides. I would try everything to end this... thing. "And why do you care if I succeed?"

There was no reason to hide the snarl of the beast that lived within me. The one poised and ready to kill when and if required.

"Because we want this curse to end. And I know why you are here and what you plan to do. I heard your last council with the woman in the water. I know you are here to take Marius's life. It is time this ends."

My brows furrowed as I closed in on the spirit. "We?"

"The rest of us agitated souls. We are trapped in this god forsaken castle as part of the dammed curse your bloodline put upon him. For years I have wandered these rooms, seeing others come and die. Only to join me in this haunting existence. It must end. And we will do anything to see it through."

"I heard you speak with him. You are his closest... friend. Yet you would let me go on knowing that I will kill him?"

The spirit closed her pale eyes for a moment. "You will try to kill him and I do hope you succeed. There are countless souls in this castle that know what happens on that fateful night. How he changes into a..."

"Beast." The elements slipped away from me as the realisation hit. Marius had killed her. Her name likely sat waiting upon the shelf in his study.

"His kind is nameless. The first of whatever he is. A twisted creature made by the same magic that runs through your blood and soul. Believe me, I do not wish death upon Marius in the manner you may think. I simply wish him freedom. As I want it for myself."

My body grew heavy as I listened to the phantom. How her face was pinched in sorrow, all but her eyes that seemed to scream with a plea. Pleading for me to do what needed to be done.

"I feel as if I should know your name," I said. "You know much about me, it is only fair."

"Victorya," she replied, blinking her wide, round eyes. It was impossible to imagine the colour they would have been. What shade her hair had glowed beneath the sun. Now she was only shades of grey and white.

"You told him not to get close to me," I said. "I heard you, Victorya."

"Because it is worse for us all. If you fail and your soul does not pass on as it should, Marius will be left with yet another painful reminder of what he did. You will wander the shadows. Unseen unless he requires your presence."

"Where are the others?"

"Hidden. Marius keeps them that way. It has been years since he last let another soul manifest in the way I have. They keep to the shadows, doing what is needed, to set the scene of normalcy in this place."

I felt my breath shudder as it all made sense to me. "It is you who prepare the food. Who fill the tub with water and provide me with clothes to wear. Why have you not shown yourself before?"

"Because Marius has forbidden it." Victorya surged forward, a dusting of shadow left in her wake. "You must not tell him I revealed myself to you."

It was not just her that pleaded to have her secret kept from Marius. And I sensed her fear as if it tugged on my own, overwhelming me.

"Just as you cannot tell him about me."

"It seems we both hold leverage over one another," she murmured. "As long as you follow your plans through." There was something about the way she said it that screamed disbelief.

"You think I will not."

"I have seen others fall into lust with Marius. You are following a similar path as they did. I fear that you may be our only chance to finally… move on. To wherever it is that waits for us beyond the boundaries of this place. Please…" Victorya's light voice took a dive into something deeper, more feral and desperate. "You must finish this."

I swallowed, audibly. "This is an act. A way to get close to him."

"Is it?" Victorya floated back from me, inching towards the far wall of the room. "You will need to convince yourself first before you can convince me to believe that."

I frowned, shaking my head in disagreement. But it seemed she was not ready to hear my counter for her comments. For she moved further away from me, as though she was a leaf caught in a gust of wind. Victorya drifted into the stone wall, her body passing through it in a single, shuddering breath. Leaving me alone, in silence, with nothing but the storm of anxiety blustering through my very soul.

13

"You have been avoiding me," I accused, gripping the doorway as I studied the hunched figure of Marius in the plush, ornate chair behind his desk.

He hardly looked up from the quill that danced across the parchment before him as I entered his study. "No. You have simply not looked hard enough for me."

I scoffed a laugh. "I did not realise we were entrapped in a game of hide and seek."

Marius flicked his ruby stare my way, the corners of his eyes creased by a faint smile. "Oh, had I not made that clear? Why don't you come in and close the door, you are letting out the precious heat."

I did as he said, closing the door gently, feeling the welcoming warm kiss of the twin fires that burned. And I now knew who lit them. It had been short hours since Victorya had disappeared through the wall of the bed chamber, leaving me with that uncovered truth.

"Last night you left and did not return. Now you expect me to hunt for you?" I scoffed. "How entitled you are."

"Yet you came looking for me?" Marius studied me as he dipped the quill into the ink pot. A single drop of black spilled onto the polished oak desk. "It would seem your hunt has been fruitful, for you have found me."

I swallowed my reply, unsure why irritation roiled through me. "It was easier to navigate my way back this time." It was. After Marius had explained his ability over the shadows and darkness I wondered if I would have made it back. But today, it seemed that the walkway was entirely lit by the candles in iron-wrought holders across the walls.

"I willed it so. I told you this study can be used for your... enjoyment. I felt no need to keep it hidden from you."

I had mentally mapped out my walk back to my rooms the evening prior, keeping the direction lodged in my mind. Part of me expected to find the way lost to Marius's shadows, but it was simple to find. How I had missed it before was beyond understanding. But so was his strange power.

I padded across the room, keeping my focus on the bookshelves before me, and not on the devilish creature that sat, muttering quietly, in his chair.

"Have you eaten, Jak?" Marius asked, face alight with concern.

"I am not hungry." My appetite had not clawed its way back to me since seeing the walking spirit.

"Is something bothering you?" I turned from the shelf to Marius who no longer sat behind the desk. Now he stood inches behind me.

I inhaled sharply at his sudden closeness. "You need to stop doing that."

"What?" he breathed; his white hair perfectly arranged. Not a single strand out of place.

I dropped my gaze to my feet, placing my hand on his still chest. "Please, Marius, give me space."

Marius stepped back without the need for me to ask again. "I have had enough company to understand that something bothers you, Jak."

Something had bothered me, but I was not prepared to tell Marius of the company I had shared in his room. Victorya. Now, with Marius before me, I realised just how affected I had been from the interaction. Mother was usually the one to remind me of the heavy pressure of my fate. Now, with her far away, I had a phantom of a young girl to do it in her place.

"And what do you want for me to do? Spill my heart to you?"

"Jak, you do not need to do anything you are not comfortable with. Not with me." His voice was as soft as the expression he made. He took another step back, reluctantly. "I was simply asking."

I thrashed out with my tone, rather than fists as I wished. "Stop that."

One brow raised in confusion above his concerned gaze. "I fear to ask what I must stop doing."

"You speak in such a way that I do not want to hear. Just stop."

Marius's expression melted slightly, his jaw clenching as he regarded my outburst. "If you do not want to hear what I have to say, you are welcome to leave."

Leave. And where would I go? Back to the room, or to another empty place filled with the ghosts of his past? I could not return home, and he knew it. It was strange how quickly the anger took hold within me. Just in time for Marius to close the gap between us, only stopped by the thump of my fist against his chest.

"Get away from me," I warned.

Before I could pound upon him a second time, he caught my fists in his hands. The length of his fingers and width of his palms encased my fists as if they were small apples. His strength was unwavering. His touch cold.

"My kindness offends you?" Marius asked, his grip tightening as I tried to pull free from him. "If you want me to be a beast, then ask me."

"I want you to be…" I couldn't say it. Not aloud. *I want you to be easy to hate.*

There it was. The truth that spilled out in my mind, a fact that spurred fear in me far greater than the *beast* Marius warned of. Marius was nothing like he was supposed to be. Nothing how I was lead, taught, to believe.

"Do not plead shyness now, Jak, go on. Say it." His voice deepened as he hoisted me towards him, my chest crashing into his. He released my hands, wrapped his arm around the curve of my back and held me close. He leaned down until his face was a breath away from mine. "Tell me what you want from me."

"Release me." I forced as much command into my tone, but failed as my voice cracked.

"Make me believe what you ask of me." A snarl erupted from the pits of his stomach as his lip curled over his teeth. Two points flashed in warning.

"Release… me, Marius." Even I could hear how my own tone conspired against me.

I could hardly breathe as I lost myself in his ruby gaze. Deep down I fell through the darkness that curled inside of him. Somewhere in the distance I felt the four elements sing to me. But there was no siren call that would distract me from him.

Marius leaned down, and as he moved I could not take my focus from his mouth. The dream I had filled my mind, and twisted my stomach in knots, sending thrilling warmth through my chest, my stomach, my entire being.

Perhaps this was all it was. A dream. One of him, and his awfully cold touch, pressed against my body. But I knew that was simply wishful thinking.

Thoughts were almost impossible to hold onto as Marius's lips tightened as he spoke again. "If you want me to release you, perhaps you should release me first."

My entire body chilled as I realised what he spoke of. My arms were wrapped far around the lower half of his broad back, grasping onto him. My knuckles tensed as I fisted his jacket and kept him pressed to me.

But even as his words sunk in, I did not release him.

"I—" There were no words to speak, only the muffled spluttering of a sound as I pushed myself onto my toes. Marius's stare was intense, but so was the thrashing river of my heart that I'd lost my control upon.

Then, without thinking further, I crashed my lips into his. Marius's entire body stiffened in response. Enough to make me regret my actions immediately. But before I could pull away, his demeanour relaxed and he melted into me like butter over an open flame.

Only our lips danced together at first. Until his tongue slowly eased itself into my mouth, parting my lips and coaxing my own to join in. A waltz we both partook in.

I finally relaxed my hold on him, busying my free hands by running them up his torso. His shirt rumpled upwards to expose the cold, hard touch of his midriff. Marius's hands held me close, one even reaching for the back of my neck to hold me in place.

I sensed his want to keep me trapped.

But I was not going anywhere.

As we kissed I lost all ability of reason and memory. Gone was the task set at hand for me. All I could think about was his taste. How I inhaled and smelled the incense of sandalwood. His kiss was clean, as though he chewed on clumps of freshly picked mint even now. It also forced any reasoning to a dark cage in the furthest parts of my mind. Locking them away, where I could not reach them.

It was intoxicating.

One moment I was standing, then next he had scooped me up. Instinct had me wrapping my legs around him. I did not fear to fall as his hands now held me up from my behind.

Momentum had us crashing into the shelving. The shock of the crash had me gasping, breaking away from the kiss.

"Did I hurt you?" Marius growled, voice full of allure.

"Not enough." My words were no more than a gasp, a whisper.

His gaze narrowed and he tilted his head as he grinned at me. Marius trailed a pink tongue across his wet lips as he studied me intently. "May I continue?"

I tightened my legs around him, signalling my response.

In anticipation I closed my eyes, ready to give into his kiss again. But his lips did not find mine. Marius nuzzled into my neck, causing my head to tilt backwards.

A moan escaped my mouth as I exhaled in pleasure. Marius kissed and nipped at the skin of my neck, only breaking the intense sensation as he ran a tongue slowly across my jugular onto the other, untouched, side.

I rolled my neck, doing everything I could to make his access easy. My hands found the back of his head. I trailed them through his hair, ruining the perfect style as I held him close.

Marius growled, but not from anger. From something far more sinister. Hunger. It was similar to the sound that the blood hounds made.

"Don't stop," I pleaded as he raised his mouth from my neck. I tried to pull him back but he held firm beneath my grip.

"I need you to tell me you are certain you want this." There was hesitation in his voice. I looked at him, deep in his eyes, noticing his inability to hold my gaze as though he readied himself for disappointment. "If you tell me to stop now then I assure you this will not happen again."

"Marius." His grip on my behind firmed as I said his name. "Continue."

"Have you ever..."

I put my finger to his mouth, almost catching on the points of his canines. "I am grown. I have lived a life before coming as your Claim. And I can assure you I made the most of it."

"There is something dangerous about you."

A grin kicked up the corners of my wet mouth. "Do I frighten you?"

Marius's laugh set my skin afire. "A little. But you also thrill me. In ways I fear I could not explain."

His mouth found mine again, stopping me from responding. Books fell, scattering across the floor as he dragged my body across the shelving. Marius stepped over them effortlessly, lifting me from one shelf to the other.

My body tingled, the feeling spreading through every length of me.

I knew Marius felt the same for something hard pressed into me every time he hoisted me in his hands to get a better grip.

I held firm on the back of his neck, tongues dancing among each other.

Lost in the moment, Marius took a misstep and fell. Down to the wooden panelled flooring we tumbled, Marius pulling me close into him. As his body took the impact he hardly made a sound.

I rolled off him, laying on my back next to him as I lost myself to a fit of giggles. It was impossible to keep my eyes open as the laugh intensified and turned into a chuckle that shook my stomach. I had to press a hand down in worry it would jump out and run away. And I was not the only one who laughed, for Marius's deep chuckle joined in with my own.

"I fear I've ruined the moment," he said, barely catching a breath.

"I can honestly say I've never been dropped before." I rolled onto my side to face him. "Do you have a habit of being so reckless?"

Laying upon the ground his face was more defined. Gravity pulled down upon his skin, carving out his jaw and cheekbones. And his skin, it glowed. At the same level as the burning fires it caught the light and glittered.

It was... beautiful.

"It has been many years since I have been in such a ... predicament. Forgive my clumsiness for lack of practice."

My chest pranged at the thought of Marius with another. I pushed the feeling down to the pits of my belly where I uncovered another I had buried.

He was my enemy. At least that was what I had come to know. Yet here I lay beside him with the phantom touch of his lips across my own.

I rolled onto my back, a rush of anxiety coursing through me as the realisation flooded back through the barrier of reality.

My breath caught as I looked up at the vaulted ceiling. It was painted entirely with dark navy all besides the lines of gold and black that sliced in precise and deliberate shaping's. Peppered across the ceiling were gold markings of connected lines through star-like figures.

It was a celestial chart. A map of the sky similar to those I had seen in Mother's many tomes. Except this, this was far more skilled than anything she could have shown me. Albeit, more beautiful than the night itself.

As though the ceiling was made of glass and I looked up at the constellation of night through it.

Noticing my awe, Marius spoke softly. "It is the very same design that has lasted all these years without the need for repair. It is breathtaking, is it not?"

I leaned back on my elbows, still focusing on the chart of stars and constellations. Although they were not labelled, they did not need to be. I recognized many of the shapes from my short lessons with Lamiere.

"What do you see?"

"Aquila, the eagle." I lifted a finger to point to the shape that had been joined with a line between ten different markings of stars.

Marius too lifted a finger and picked out the very same shape I had seen. "Crowned with the star Altair. You see the one *we* made bigger than the rest?"

I could. Only by a small margin, the shape was slightly bigger than the rest it was linked up with.

"Who is we?" I asked him, latching onto something he had just said. Marius kept his stare on the ceiling.

"A long lost... friend."

The air thickened with sadness as his lashes thickened with moisture. Although I lay mere inches from Marius's side, I felt his body stiffen. Then, in a blink, he was standing. His movements a blur.

I sat up with a sinking feeling in my gut. "I apologise if I have pried too far."

Marius had his back to me, arms folded over his chest as he contemplated in silence. "Tonight I have overstepped, Jak, forgive me."

"What are you talking about?"

Marius faced me with an expression of cold stone. "I should..."

"If you think for a moment that you can just disappear on me again, stop. You cannot keep flouncing in and out, leaving me to ponder my thoughts." The words came tumbling out of me as a result of my pure desperation for him to stay. Deep down this feeling sickened me, but I kept it buried. For now. "There is something you are not telling me. You have said it, I am going to die anyway. Why not spill your secrets to me? Let me listen to your story for you count yourself to be a storyteller."

Marius looked back to the floor. Before he could utter a word, I closed the space between us and pressed a hand to his chest. There was no flutter of a heartbeat within it.

"The mural was completed during a time in my life when I was free. Free of this curse. When I was trapped by another, one who held my love." A single tear slipped down his cheek. "It was that love that resulted in... in this."

The curse. He did not need to say it aloud for me to understand what he suggested.

"When you lose everything you have loved, sometimes the grief can return to ruin the small moments of good that are left. Grief is a silent assassin, lurking in the dark of one's soul, ready to cloak any light in shadow."

I reached up, instinctively, and brushed the cold tear from his equally cold face. It soaked the tip of my thumb where it continued its descent to my wrist. Unlike Marius, I had never lost anything so dear before.

"Thank you for sharing that with me," I said quietly.

Marius took my forearm in his monstrous hand and lifted my wrist to his mouth. He placed a kiss upon my skin where his tear had left a wet trail. "I should be thanking you. It has been simple to grow such habits of running away from these feelings. In all these years that have passed I have run from room to room, shadow to shadow. There is something about you that makes it easier to... cope."

I blushed, guilt stabbing its talon-like grip into my stomach. The need to change the course of the subject was intense.

"Care for a drink?"

Marius grinned through his glistening eyes. "Do you read minds, Jak?"

I stiffened. That was a power that my kind had long lost. "Impossible. It was simply a wild guess."

"Then yes, Jak, I would love a drink. You stay here and I will be back shortly."

"Last time you promised that you did not return at all."

Marius leaned in close, casting a shadow over me. "The difference is that this time it seems we have some unfinished business to attend."

A tickling sensation spread from my feet until it roared through my entire body. Beneath his intense stare I felt my knees buckle ever so slightly. And the promise of his return moistened my mouth with anticipation.

"Do not disappear on me, Jak," Marius said at the doorway to his study.

"Couldn't even if I wanted to," I replied, unable to hide the raw truth in my words.

14

THERE WAS A MISSING BOOK. Someone had removed it from the shelving recently for the outline was still clear from the layering of dust around it. I also knew that this was the first book Marius had written for he had explained they were organised in order from first to most recent. The space between the missing tome and the next was large.

It was not the only thing I noticed as I studied the shelving in Marius's absence. The older the books he wrote, the longer they were. Bindings of pages so thick that two hands were required to hold them open.

But the further I went along the never-ending shelves, the more it was clear that the recent books were shorter. Dramatically so. Small novella's that were no more than a handful of pages long.

What had resulted in Marius writing so little in the more recent years? Was it his lack of want, or the distance he put between himself and the other Claims?

He likely planned my story now. Plotting what my life could have been like if I survived whatever hell waited for me on the final day.

But I knew he would never finish the story.

As I studied the empty shelving, I felt the sudden urge to vomit. Knowing what I had to do no longer warmed me from the inside. It conjured the freezing chill of dread to sit, waiting, in my soul. It was clear to me now that Marius was not the beast at all. *I was.*

"Here you are…"

I jumped at the sudden appearance of Marius. Forcing a smile, I turned to see him standing with a dusty bottle of undisclosed liquid in one hand and two crystal glasses in the other.

"Did I scare you again?" He bit down on his lower lip, likely remembering my previous warning and how that ended up.

"Sorry." I ran a hand through my brown curls, the other resting on my hip. "I was lost to my own thoughts."

The glasses clinked as Marius rested them upon his oaken desk. "No bother. I thought you might like this wine for its vintage. Has been in the undercroft long before my own father was born within these walls."

It was hard to imagine it as Marius spoke of his family. "He must have been a King to be born in such a place."

"He was a man who was no more than lucky to be raised in such a place. From memory his mother was a servant to the ruling house that dwelled here. He simply grew up in the shadow of the great family that lived in this place."

"So how is it you came to claim it as your own?"

Marius slowly popped the cork from the dark-green glass bottle. He lifted it to his nose and took a deep inhale before pouring the red wine in the two waiting glasses. "I inherited it when my father passed. During his childhood he grew close with the daughter of the Lord who owned this castle. They fell in love, married and had me. Their sole heir."

"Which makes you a Lord."

"*Made* me a Lord," Marius interjected. "Now drink with me. All this talk of the past is making me feel like I am sinking internally."

He handed over a glass which I took without question. Our fingers grazed for a moment as I did so.

As I lifted the rim to my lips, Marius spoke up. "Are we not going to toast?"

"Toast?" I questioned, breath fogging the crystallised glass. "To what?"

Marius lifted his glass before him, urging me to copy him. "To discovering new friends. May the exploration only continue."

My mouth dried as our glasses clinked into each-other. Quickly I took a sip, the wine washing away my emotions as it spilled down my throat. "Marius, may I ask you something?"

His pale brows arched above his inquisitive stare. "I fear I do not have a choice."

"There is a missing book." I turned to the bookcase in question. "I was certain that something was in its place yesterday. But now it is gone."

"I felt the need to take it for my own reading pleasure. There are plenty of others for you to borrow if you require."

Marius did not lie about removing it. But I believed there was more of a reason for it.

"It was about the first Claim, wasn't it?"

Stories of the mangled body that had been left on the boundaries of the castle sprung to mind. The one and only time that a Claim had ever been returned. The first of Marius's victims. I knew little of the person for it seemed that the time that had past diluted the knowledge Mother had known of the victim.

"He was not a Claim." Marius's voice grew sharp. "Not in the same manner you are."

Marius revealed more in the first five words than he had meant to. I witnessed his face pinch in frustration as he too realised.

The first person to fall victim to Marius was a boy and he was not a Claim.

I pieced the puzzle together in my mind. "If he was the first, and not a Claim, he must have been…"

Glass smashed into the ground, sending a splash of red wine across the floor. I jumped out of the way of the littering shards, almost spilling my own wine down my front in the process.

Marius stood, hands clenched at his sides, breathing shallow. His face was tilted to the ground, but his eyes glowed like hot coals in a fire. Through his loose white hair, he glared at me.

"Stop pressing for answers. You may not like what you find."

I stumbled back, watching the man before me change into the beast I had grown to know him as. Shadows quivered in the corners of the study as he flexed his sharpened nails and exposed his pointed teeth.

"You… you have only just toasted to continuing our exploration of one another." I tried to keep my voice as steady as I could as his face morphed before my eyes.

"Do not use my words against me," Marius seethed.

"Or what!?" I shouted, my own anger rising to the surface once again. All those buried feelings of guilt at what I had done came barging to the surface. "What are you going to do?"

Marius shook violently. "Go."

"I will not…"

"GO."

His shout shook the very foundations of the castle. Urged on by his sudden, shocking anger. *How dare you.* I longed to throw the glass of wine at him. To hurtle the flames from the hearth and burn away the shadows he threatened to send after me. I watched as they thrummed with his control.

I did not fear him. Not entirely. But the tension that riddled between us was close to unbearable.

Before he could shout again I moved for the door which he partially blocked. I made sure to slam my shoulder into him as I passed.

I do not fear you, for I am the beast. The thought kept me going until the study was far behind me.

I almost expected the spectral figure of the young girl to meet me back in the chamber. To hear her scorn me for acting out.

But I would not let anyone speak to me that way. Not Marius. Not anyone.

There was no risk of Marius following me here. I knew it in my soul. So I sat back upon the four-poster bed and reached for the discarded scrying bowl.

Now it was time to consult with the coven.

15

"Something is wrong. I can tell." Mother's voice cleared through the shimmering water before her face even had time to materialise. "It is still night which means the beast is awake. Yet you call upon me, as though it is the smart decision to make in your situation. Did I not warn you of using your powers during the night?"

"Marius will not come here." Already I longed to pick up the bowl and throw it across the room. But I held firm, biting down into my lower lip to keep my tone free of annoyance. "We are safe to speak."

Her sharp brow furrowed, creating lines across her almost perfect forehead. "You refer to him by name."

"A name I feel that you knew long before sending me here," I snapped.

Mother paused before responding, looking to someone who sat before her out of view of the scrying bowl. "It was not a piece of information I deemed important enough for you to know. His name changes nothing towards the end result. Everything else you have learned from me does."

What else had she kept from me? I narrowed my gaze, holding back the fire from boiling the water in the bowl. "Tell me about the first person he killed. The body he left on the boundary."

"Why does it matter to you?"

I leaned in, hissing through gritted teeth, "So you do not deny knowing more about him? Pray tell what other information have you decided I did not need to know!"

"Whatever has gotten into you can cease immediately, Jak. I am your mother, you do not speak to me in such a manner."

"I do not like being lied to," I said, gripping the sheets beneath me until my knuckles mimicked their whiteness.

"No one has lied to you," Mother replied, voice as cold as Marius's touch. "Perhaps you have never thought to ask the question."

"Then tell me. I ask now, do I not?"

I could not make sense of the quiet murmurings that came from the person sitting out of view. Mother did not hide as she glanced towards them again, listening intently before nodding in agreement. "He was merely a victim. There, now you know as much as I do. His body was drained entirely of blood. Drunk dry by the very creature you should currently be getting close to rather than pressing me for questions. Have you thought to ask him?"

She was keeping the truth from me. I knew it.

"Tell me who he was," I pressed again, not giving up until I was satisfied.

"Jak."

"Tell me."

"What has transpired to get you in such a state?" she asked calmly for the first time, leaning over the bowl until her curtain of dark, straight, hair fell on either side. It gave the illusion that it was only the two of us having the conversation. Although I knew that others listened on from her side. Perhaps Victorya listened on to me, hidden in her astral form. Perhaps she too knew the boiling anger I kept buried, trusting that this was *not* the time to tell me what to do.

"It is not long until the fateful day, Jak. Do not let such insignificant topics cloud your mind and the task at hand. I will do you a favour and tell you everything you seek to know when you return home with his head. Think of it as yet another pending praise for your successful return."

"Why not now?" I rocked back on the bed, burying my face in my hands in defeat. "What if I do not make it back?"

I almost felt the shift in temperature in the room. How the mundane storm that brewed within Mother was moments from bursting out. If she had true power like me, she would have been unstoppable.

"Then you will deserve nothing. If you fail, you deserve what is coming to you."

Shocked, I could hardly hold a breath long enough to string a response together. "Mother..."

"You are different since the last time you called for me. Softer. Not the hard-edged dagger that I have moulded with my bare hands and own sacrifice." Mother took a shuddering breath, battering down the anger she fought so hard to keep in. "I sense a change in you, one that fills me with great concern."

As I kept my eyes closed, the flashes of wasted hours of preparation burst through my mind. Days of magic and physical training, where the other children of town were allowed to go to school and learn mundane matters. They, unlike me, did not have the worries of the survival of their own kind to think of.

"I will not fail," I said quietly. *Will I not?* That mocking voice returned in the back of my mind.

"Say it enough and I may start to believe you."

Her distrust in me caused my heart to harden. It tugged down on my stomach and made me feel sick. Dread. It made me feel worthless beneath her judging, watchful stare.

"Mother, I will not fail."

I came to regret calling upon her. Again.

"I have a piece of advice for you, Jak. Forget the small details and focus on why you are there. I can see that the creature has wormed his way into your mind. Making you ask questions that you would never have uttered before you entered his domain. Keep focused. Not just for our sake, but for your own."

Mother must have knocked the bowl from the table, for the vision of her vanished after one sudden movement. I hardly caught what had caused it. One moment she looked at me, the next the water in the bowl was still and... empty.

In a rage of emotion, I kicked out at the sheets, sending the bowl across the floor in a crash.

Frustration not only caused by her, but what she said. Perhaps she was right about Marius worming his way into my mind. Just thinking of him caused my lips to tingle as though his kiss had lingered. I did have to focus. This was my fault, allowing Marius to soften me with his words. Work me down with his intense presence and reaching hands. *Strong hands.* Yet I had to get close to him, enough to get him at his most vulnerable. Whatever that meant in the end.

Mother's lingering presence made the room feel unbearably cold. I pulled the sheets over my legs, fending off the shakes that caused me to tremble like a leaf in a billowing storm.

Who was the first person to die by his hands? Where was the book? Why did my mother and Marius want to hide it from me?

I sat like that for a while, skimming through the questions only to add more as I went. Sleep was impossible, and the usual hunger I felt non-existent.

Over and over I went through the events of the day, trying to find a reason for the need for secrecy. Marius would be hidden in whatever dark hole he retreated to during the day. Even if I wanted to find him, he would be in...

The undercroft.

The word sang true as it rattled across my storming mind. It was a place, deep in the pits of the castle, far below the very chamber I sulked in. A place vacant of daylight. Perfect for Marius to dwell in until night fell again.

I bolted up in bed, knowing exactly where I had to go for answers. And I had an inkling where I would find the entrance.

16

THE DOOR at the back of the dining hall was still left unlocked. It took all my will power to walk past the deliciously presented food that was waiting upon the long, oak table. Instead, I kept my focus on the task at hand.

To find the book.

As I entered the dark halls beyond the door, I felt a presence around me. In my haste I had not brought a source of light with me. Although it was early morning I didn't have a clue what Marius did during his time away. Did he sleep like I did? Or wait the day out until he made his way back up to the surface of the castle?

The deeper I walked, the more the walls around me closed in. The ceiling seemed to shrink down upon me, and the smell of damp rock and moss only grew more intense with each step. Without light to guide me I had to use my hands to trail along the slick walls. Using my touch and slow, careful footing to make sure I did not fall on some unseen object.

It was not long until the strange foreboding of presence was justified. A kiss of a gaze furrowed into the back of my neck. I slowed, hands falling to my side, as a chill caused my skin to erupt in goosebumps.

"I know you are here," I spoke quietly, although it did nothing to stop the echoing of my voice across the enclosed corridor of stone.

"You should not be down here," Victorya said from before me. Not caring if she witnessed my magic, I lifted a hand in front of me and called upon my favourite element. Fire.

It sprung to life across my open palm. A curling of orange and gold that haloed the strange corridor in warmth and light. Victorya floated in the air, face pinched and arms folded over her see-through body.

"Because Marius is lurking somewhere far down here? Or because it is out of bounds for some other undisclosed reason? I will let you pick your answer."

Victorya hunched her small shoulders. "It would seem that you *also* are in a foul mood."

"You've seen him then?"

The conjured flame illuminated her pale form. I looked to the ground to see that only my shadow lay upon it.

"I have. And if he sees you down here then your chance of... you will not get far."

"If he did not want me to come here he would have locked the door behind him. Shutting me out. He is rather good at that."

"It is habit," Victorya said. "It has been many a year since a Claim dared venture to find Marius during the hours of the living. This would usually be a time that they longed to be uninterrupted. Free of his company... when he was willing to share it."

I hesitated before taking a step to walk past her. Victorya made no move or indication that she would get out of my way.

"You will let me pass," I said. I could walk through her, just waltz between her spectral form as she had with the wall of my bedroom.

"And why are you so certain?"

I took a breath, gaze cutting holes through the already dead girl. "I am tired of being kept from the truth. Let me go so I can..."

"Can wake him? Impossible to do so during the day. Question him? If Marius has ignored your requests for answers he would have done so with a reason. Do not think your presence in his personal chambers is going to sway him to suddenly give up whatever he is keeping from you."

I smiled, having obtained yet more information I needed. This was, as guessed, the way to wherever Marius kept himself hidden.

"Good," I hissed, "because nothing you have said relates to what I am doing here. So... move."

Throwing out the flame, I controlled its hurtling trajectory to land upon the girl. But instead it passed through her. Victorya did not flinch. Instead she zoomed forward until her haunting gaze was uncomfortably close to my own. "Beware how you act around me. For you will find that you go hungry before your stay comes to an end. You will be without fresh clothes. No bath will be drawn. I will... not... aid you."

"Help me!" I laughed. "If you wanted to help you would let me proceed. If he will not wake during my visit then what is the harm of proceeding?"

"What do you hope to find?" she asked, bluntly. "If it is to kill him during his sleep, then you will be wasting your time."

"I would not do tha—" The thought had not even occupied my mind. Killing Marius now, whilst he was at his most vulnerable. "That is not what I hope to achieve."

"Good, because you would be a fool to think that Marius has not tried to end his life before. It never works."

The flame in my palm died down to a simple glow. My connection to it severing as her words settled over me. "He has?"

"Not for a long time. It was terrible. Watching him being so broken. So tired. I will not explain his attempts further but know that you cannot do it."

I spluttered out my response, "I do not wish to."

What made the final night any different? I knew that my powers were linked to his demise, but why?

"As much as that relieves me... for now, we both know that we need you to do it. In the end."

"I need a book," I said, changing the course of the conversation as quickly as I could. I forced more energy into the flame so it burned brighter once more. "Marius has it. I know he is keeping it from me and I want to know why."

"Stealing what you seek will do you no favours," Victorya said. "Have you asked him for it?"

"Yes..." I stilled, shaking my head. "No. No I didn't. The topic got heated and... there is no chance that Marius will give it to me. Not after the way he reacted when I asked a simple question."

"You will ask him next time," Victorya commanded in her small, but powerful voice. "If he does not comply then I will retrieve the book for you myself. But know that I do not like going behind his back."

"You don't?" I scoffed, ready to point out her double standard. "Because you certainly are encouraging me to kill him."

"Trust me, Jak. He would encourage you to do the same if he believed it was a possibility. Now go. Leave him to rest. You do not understand how earned his moments of peace are. From the shadows beneath your eyes it seems that you too need to sleep. Try again with him when you wake."

I looked to the waiting darkness ahead of her, imagining the space in which Marius kept to. Then I nodded, forcing my leaden body to turn back towards the direction of the dining hall. "For someone so young, you surely behave in the manner of an adult."

"I am far older than you, Jak. Do not be fooled by my frozen appearance. Even in this form I have witnessed more of life and death than you could imagine."

I shot a glance over my shoulder to say something in return, but she had vanished. Gone in a single moment. Yet her presence still lingered on the back of my neck until I finally closed the door to the chamber I now called my own.

Until next time, I guess.

~

Katharine returned the next evening. I heard her soft voice which floated up from the lower levels of the castle. Marius was with her, speaking in his usual low tone whilst she did not try and hide what she spoke of. I stayed out of view, hiding behind the splitting banister. On soft feet I had edged closer to try and see the scene as they conversed but the creak of the banister stopped me from leaning over any further for fear it would snap beneath my weight.

"How is your mother?" Marius asked.

"Not well. Every day her breathing shallows. I fear she does not have long left." Katharine's sadness was palpable.

"Let me give you something else to trade in for coin. I have other items you can…"

"Marius, stop. You have done enough."

"Until she heals, I will not feel such a way."

Katharine paced into view. I could see the top of her hair and the colourless, ripped dress she wore. But her expression was hidden from view as I watched from my perch.

"If I turn up with yet more unbelievable goods then they will sure catch wind of my visits. You do not know what they will do to me, to Mother, if they find out. And before you fret about not letting them harm us, you forget you are the princess kept trapped in a tower."

"Waiting for my prince charming to turn up and save me," Marius droned, spurring a weak laugh from Katharine. "If only it were that simple, little one."

"I do not hear any crying or screaming from your Claim. Has he settled into his final days?"

My breath hitched as she looked up. I rocked backwards, just in time for her gaze to miss me.

"Do not speak like that, Katharine." I could not see Marius, but I could imagine the pinching of his expression as he spoke. How he likely brushed the loose strand of white hair from his forehead, lips turned down.

"Have I touched a nerve?"

"Perhaps you have. He has settled well… considering. Did you want me to call upon him so you can thank him for saving your life from the blood hounds?"

Katharine folded her arms across her narrow chest. "It was not his blood that healed me—"

"Ahh," Marius interrupted. "I finally see what you came for."

"It worked on me, it might help my mother. I promise I will not ask for another thing again."

She wanted Marius's blood. A vision of him biting into his own wrist with his monstrous fangs before letting his dark gore drip into Katharine's waiting mouth filled my mind. How her broken body had reformed and healed before my eyes.

Yet another example of the power he held.

"You would take that risk but will not pawn some useless item I can give you for coin?"

"There is no medicine left for her, Marius. I, we, have tried everything to better her state. You should see her coughing. How it racks her body and leaves her exhausted for hours. This is no state for anyone to be in. She told me of your kindness when it was her who visited you. Can you not do it for her?"

I expected him to refuse further. To tell her of what a dangerous risk this would be. Marius did not know what would happen to her. But if my mother or the coven caught wind that Katharine visited, they *would* punish her. If they saw the truth of what she requested from him this evening…

The thought alone turned my stomach.

Katharine was a desperate girl, looking for an equally desperate solution. Come to think of it, I had heard of a woman who was sickly in the town. She lived in a ramshackle house on the outskirts. It was likely why I had never seen Katharine before if that was where she lived. There was never a need for me to leave town that far.

"I will do it. For you. For Paloma. But you must be careful. It is at your own risk as to what happens when you give her it." The warning in his voice caused my fists to tense into balls. "For you both, I hope this works as you wish it will."

"Marius, thank you."

Marius stepped into view, enough that I could see his crown of white hair. Katharine wrapped her arms around him, burying her face into his chest. "Do not thank me yet, little one. Return and tell me of its results, will you? I suppose it is a nice thought that I can help someone beyond this entrapment. For all it is worth, I hope it works."

"So do I." Her voice was muffled as she kept a hold of him.

I rocked back, unable to witness anymore. Guilt riddled through me. It felt wrong watching such a personal moment. So I left them, padding back to my room on bare feet, as quietly as I could muster across the panelled flooring.

Marius is not a beast.

I found myself losing tears as I picked up my walk into a run.
He is not the beast.

How could someone care so much about life, when those beyond this castle cared little about him?

In that moment I saw the truth, I understood it all. The realisation clear to me as I burst into his chamber. A room he never slept in. My vision blurred so much that I almost tripped. I threw myself onto the bed, unable to calm my breathing. My chest ached. I pressed a hand into it, trying to still the feeling of it cracking clean open.

Crying, I was crying. Something I had long left to the past. It was a strange feeling. A breathless, painful ache that spread across my chest as the unfamiliar wetness sliced down my cheeks.

I raised a hand to clear them, only for the moisture to return as more tears were unleashed.

"You want to kill him," I spluttered through chesty sobs. Trying to convince myself of my fate. My only purpose. "You want to kill him."

Want to or *have* to?

17

"If you are cold, I can offer you my jacket?" Marius said, keeping in step with me as we walked to the castle's exit. He must have noticed the shiver of my skin, or how I had wrapped my arms across my chest to keep in the warmth. It seemed colder each night that passed. I suppose, with winter pressing on beyond the castle, it was inevitable for the pathetic fires to hardly keep out the chill. Yet Marius never seemed bothered.

"Will you not be cold?" I asked, staring mostly at my feet as we moved through the castle foyer.

"I do not fear nor feel the cold. So please, it is a clear night tonight and I would feel more comfortable knowing you are not shivering beside me. That and it is… distracting. I would not care for you to catch a sickness and pass before your stay here concludes." Marius shrugged the maroon jacket from his broad shoulders without needing to offer again, carefully straightening out the material before holding it out for me to slip into.

I smiled, not one that was forced or fake. I felt it tug up at my lips as his arms flexed beneath the material of his white shirt.

One hand at a time, I weaved myself into the jacket. There was no warmth left over from his body, but it was far better than the crisp nightly air that scratched at my skin.

"You are certain the hounds will not attack?" I asked, trying not to be overwhelmed by his closeness. Or what happened last time this little space between us was beheld.

"They would not dare if I am with you. They may stalk us, but that is as far as they will go. As long as we stay on the path and do not deviate, we will be safe."

Marius had not mentioned Katharine's visit and I felt that I could not simply add it into the, currently, stiff conversation. It had been a few, long, hours since I had listened in on them and I still felt guilty. Even more so to find out how personal the conversation had been. By the time his heavy knocks sounded on the chamber room's door my eyes had dried, but the sadness had still taken root in my chest.

I had briefly looked to Marius's wrist to see if any marks were left from his bloodletting. But his skin was untouched by scars or marks. As if noticing my stare, he tugged down at the ruffled sleeve of his shirt to hide his perfect skin.

"I thought we would spend yet another day in the study?" I questioned, hugging the jacket around my chest. It was so big the sleeves kept covering my hands.

"Another evening surrounded by books... ugh." He poked his tongue beyond his lip. A tongue I had not long been so familiar with. "There is something I want to share with you that is far greater than that study."

"How mysterious." I laughed, hoping it covered my nerves. There was tension between us. An unspoken conversation left after yesterday's abrupt ending. He had not apologised, nor did I expect him to. Marius was a perfect blend of cautious and polite. Offering a steady arm as we walked down the stairs yet keeping painfully tense beneath my touch.

We hardly exchanged another word until we reached the double, front doors to the castle. The very same that had been locked the last time I had checked.

Of course they now were left open. *How convenient.* As Marius pulled them open the evening breeze rushed into the castle's entrance. The curtains across the windows flapped wildly, sending bouts of dust into the air. The flames across the grand chandelier that hung above us flickered, some even going out beneath the force of the natural, winter winds.

"Quickly," Marius whispered. "Before it blows every candle out. This castle is far more... acceptable beneath the glow of fire."

I moved with haste, tightening the jacket around me as I bowed into the gust and left beyond the doors.

My cheeks nipped beneath the chill, my nose running almost instantly as I stepped outside. The great doors creaked as Marius closed us off from the firelight.

Then we were bathed in night. Only the moon and stars a source of light above us.

"And you expect me to fumble my way around the grounds! I will walk straight off the path and into the jaws of your little pets," I said in jest. However, even I could not hide the true fear I felt knowing they lurked in the shadows. Waiting. My power would be kept within, and that felt as though I was without my most important limb. My weapon.

I was... vulnerable.

Marius's hand found mine and I gasped out of my mindless worry. It was not the warm, lifeful touch that fought away the cold. But it was comforting nonetheless. "I shall guide you. Do not worry yourself."

It took a moment to relax into his control as he guided me through the dark gardens. I could make out some shapes, but without the light of a flame it was impossible for me to figure out where each step would end up. Soon enough my eyes adjusted to the eternal dark and my tight grip on his hand eased. But I did not let go.

"I hope you can swim." His comment caught me off guard. Up until this point he had kept silent during our walk.

"Swim?" I questioned, just the thought alone sent a violent shiver across my skin. From my knowledge the nearest coastal line was days' travel by horse, if you were lucky enough to have the coin to own one.

"One of the beauties of this castle is the hot springs located among the land. Back when I was younger the townsfolk would visit during the winter months to bask in the glory of the warmed waters. It was magnificent. A place in which I enjoyed to frolic. I thought it would be the best way to negate the colder nights."

"And keep away from the books?" I said, looking up at him side-on through thick lashes.

He sighed, eyes unblinking, lips pursed. "Precisely."

"I admit, I have never heard of such a place before." No one ever spoke of the castle before the curse. It was almost hard to believe it did not just conjure into existence the moment it was laid upon Marius. His life before had never seemed to matter to Mother or the coven.

"I thought that would be the case," Marius muttered, keeping his pace slow beside me. His longer legs always kept him a foot ahead, but I could sense his controlled restraint to not pull me along. "We will add the mystery of the hot springs to the ever-growing list of others that I fear has been lost with time."

There it was again, the tugging sadness that seemed to drawl beneath his deep voice. A pause of conversation followed, broken by me clearing my throat and squeezing his hand without thought.

"To answer your question, I cannot swim. There hasn't exactly been any opportunities for practice back home." It was not a lie. My control of the water as an extension of my power meant I did not fear it. Although I had not been submerged in a vast body of water before, I trusted in my ability and instinct to keep me afloat. "You surely do not expect us to go in now? It is dark and cold."

"They are hot springs... Jak." Even as he spoke, I could hear the smile that had returned to his mouth. As though he laughed through each, prolonged word. "I will not solve the darkness issue, but you will be warmer within the spring than outside on the bank."

I shivered on cue. "Then can we get to the springs with haste? This walk is not as relaxing as I thought it would be."

"Patience, Jak, it will be worth the wait."

∼

The body of water sat nestled among the grounds of the castle just as Marius had explained. The crescent moon was painted across its surface as if it were the aquatic twin to the one which ruled the night above us. Tendrils of mist rose from the lake like ghostly fingers. Even from my distance on the grass-bed beside it I felt its enticing warmth.

Everything was still here. Beautiful.

"It is best you do not wet your clothes," Marius explained, no longer holding my hand. "By the time you come out you will be thankful for something dry to wear."

I turned to question him, only to swallow my words. Marius had stripped the shirt from his back, lifting it slowly over his head. His muscle flexed as he tugged his arms from the sleeves last. I watched as he scrunched the material into a ball and threw it to the ground without care. Marius was sculpted with more definition and precision than I could have imagined. His chest was broad, but his hips were narrow. The image of pure strength. Muscles flexed in his chest and stomach, tightening in mounds that protruded from his skin.

"Everything okay?" he asked, hands reaching for the brass buckle of his belt. His smile was sly, his eyes narrowed as if he could read the thoughts that filled my mind.

I shook my head and turned back to the calm surface of water. Hand to my chin, I tried everything to not look back... no matter how loud the siren call to do so was. "You truly want me to get in?"

"That is completely up to you," Marius said. "You are welcome to stand here and watch."

Before I had a chance to act, Marius had thrown himself into the water, disturbing the once glass-like surface. I tumbled back away from the incoming splash of water that had risen up in response. Water soaked the bottom of my trousers and dampened the bank which now squelched beneath my boots.

"What happened to keeping dry?" I shouted, looking back at Marius who kept afloat in the water. My voice echoed across the surface as though it was a skipping stone.

"There is nothing wrong with getting wet," he called out, as his arms moved to keep him afloat.

My mouth dried as I studied him. The water did little to conceal his naked body. Naked. Completely. I quickly looked away, cheeks warming as his alabaster skin glowed proudly beneath the water. The pile of his clothes confirmed all I already thought.

He had removed every article. Even his undergarments.

"You are…" I muttered, covering my eyes with my hand.

"Yes."

"Well, could you not have… I don't know. Kept something on?"

"And why would I do that?" I could hear that gentle swoosh of water as Marius sliced his arms through the spring. "If it makes you uncomfortable you do not need to do the same."

It was not discomfort I felt. No, the feeling was far from it. It was not only my cheeks that warmed but my stomach and chest. My skin prickled with… anticipation. A flashback to the study filled my mind for a moment.

"Turn away," I said, quietly.

"Speak up."

I lifted my stare and looked him dead in the eye. "I said turn away."

Marius's grin widened whereas his eyes narrowed as he nodded. "As you wish."

I only reached for my shirt when the back of Marius's head was all I could see. A giggle threatened to escape me as I caught a glimpse of his behind that rippled beneath the water's surface. I tugged at my clothing and left it in a heap on the bed of the lake. Like Marius, I did not leave a single item of clothing on.

It was easy to forget when my mind was full of thrill and wonder. Deep in the corners of my mind I could remember what I was here to do. But now, out here with Marius, the cold, the water, I gave myself the moment to just… live. Without rule, or fate, or anything really.

The breeze across my bare body sent a shiver through me until it turned into violently shaking. My teeth chattered and my toes curled. I stepped closer to the warm mist of the lake, thankful for the source of heat.

"Can I turn around yet?" Marius called, turning his head far enough for me to pick up my pace.

My heart skipped at the thought of Marius seeing me like this. Exposed. Feet first I stepped into the water and sighed. As soon as I entered it the warm fought away at the cold that seemed to have embedded itself into my bones.

Soon enough I was completely submerged, with the water up to my chin. "You can look now."

Marius turned instantly to face me, the water rippling around him. "Wonderful, is it not?"

I felt completely relaxed as the water hugged me. "Could you not have mentioned this place any sooner? I have an awful feeling that getting out of this is going to be the worst part."

"For you." Marius swam towards me, his large arms treading water.

"Are you just so terribly brave that the cold does not affect you?"

"I am always cold, Jak, even now. It has been a long time since I last felt the warmth of this water. Even now it feels no different to me."

"I do not understand."

"May I?" Marius asked, offering a hand for me to take.

I took it without hesitation. His soft palm pressed against mine as his fingers held onto me and all I felt was his usual chill.

"How?" I asked, squeezing onto his hand as if I would lend his cold skin some of my warmth.

"That is an extremely good question. One that can only be answered by my assumptions. The curse altered me in many ways and this is just one of them. I am cold. Always."

Just the thought made my teeth want to chatter. I tugged Marius closer, enjoying the sudden shock that splashed across his face. His strong chest pressed against mine and he let go of my hand, holding both of his around the bottom of my back. Even as the warm water kept me comfortable it did not stop the shiver of delight that ran across my arms and neck.

"You are dangerous," Marius said, ruby glare piercing right through me. "So dangerous that I fear you know just how to use it as a weapon."

"Coming from the creature that is doomed to kill me."

"You say that as if it does not bother you." Marius's brow peaked.

"Well, perhaps you will not kill me," I whispered, face close to his. Lips only inches apart.

Marius eyes flicked from my parted mouth to my narrowed stare. I sensed his want to kiss me as his hands tightened on my back, pressing my naked body upon his. He parted his lips to match mine and a low growl emitted from his throat, catching me off guard.

I pulled away slightly until Marius let go of me completely. His face pinched in what I could only see as… shame. Then he turned away, running a wet hand through his white hair with his back to me once again.

"What is wrong?" I questioned. "If I said something wrong…"

"It is not you, Jak, but me. I fear I was getting away from myself for a moment."

Marius did not look at me as he spoke, instead he stared off into the dark distance of the lake. I paddled towards him until I was close enough to reach out for his shoulder. As my touch gripped him he shrugged me off.

"Don't..." He turned his head to the side, enough for me to see his forehead creased and lips curled over his teeth. "Please."

I snapped my hand back from him as I took in the profile of his contorted face.

"You do not scare me, Marius."

I felt the need to say it. To tell him. I could raise the water of this lake around him now and encase him in an entrapment if he dared strike for me. But it was what caused his sudden change in attitude that encouraged me to wait out his temperament.

"The hunger never rears its presence so soon," Marius said, stretching his neck from the left then to the right. "Give me a moment and it should subside."

I waited in silence as Marius concentrated on whatever internal battle he was having.

"What do you hunger for?" I finally asked, breaking the painful silence between us.

Marius said one word that had me frozen within the body of warmed water. "Blood."

18

Mother had told me time and time again that the body that was first left for the villagers to discover was completely drained of blood. Empty. A vessel of flesh and bone. The local healer had studied the remains only to find every vein and vessel dried, like a petal beneath the sun. Yet the body had not been sliced, cut or stabbed by a blade. Only the multiple puncture marks that peppered the victim's body gave evidence of what could have caused it.

Two, small puckered marks, the perfect distance of one's clamped jaw.

Blood. Marius's word echoed through me.

"I am not scared of you," I said, unsure where the comment had come from; also unsure if it was truth or not.

"You should be." Marius glared at me, his ruby eyes creased with angst. "Please give me a moment. I will be able to… control this. The feeling will pass."

I paddled in the water, body tense, as I waited for Marius to regain whatever control he desired over his hunger. Hunger for blood.

In those silent moments it began to make sense what occurred on the final night during the blood moon. Did he gradually lose his reality the closer time gave way to the fatal day?

I flinched when Marius turned back around. Gone were the lines across his forehead and thinned lips. His face was once again relaxed, but his eyes glowed with embarrassment.

"It would seem that I have grown well accustomed to ruining the mood." Marius splashed a handful of water across his face, washing away the tense emotion. His hands were so large, fingers incredibly long, that they perfectly cupped his face as he sighed into them for a moment.

I swam towards him, closing the space between us that I so desperately did not desire. "Tell me what it feels like."

Marius lowered his hands and looked up slowly, droplets of water falling off his pale eyelashes. "You truly desire to know?"

The mist from the lake created a wall between us that only my breath could penetrate. Marius stayed completely still until I was before him, my hands reaching for his hard stomach under the water. He tensed beneath my touch. It spurred me on as I trailed my fingers down from the mounds of his stomach muscles to the smooth lines that crowned his hips. I did not look beneath the layer of blue but could sense that his cock was close to where my hands rested.

"I would not have asked if I did not want to know."

"It can only be described as pure, agonising hunger. Although my time before the curse has grown hazy over the years, I suppose it is most likened to the feeling of being withheld from sustenance for a period of time. I was fortunate enough for that not to happen during my youth, but can only imagine how similar the feeling must be."

"But you can control it." My hands slowly moved around his lower abdomen, tracing the lines of his chiselled stomach.

"I would not describe it as control. It is more the sensation of burying a feeling until it is far too great to be kept hidden."

A chill raced across my exposed shoulders and neck. I felt all too exposed as his eyes found that glistening part of my skin which entrapped his attention completely. "You still feel it?"

Marius nodded slowly, his eyes narrowing in on my lips. "Is your plan for me to lose control? You are playing with dark waters, Jak."

I gave up tracing my fingertips and made a point of running my nails across his skin. "I told you that I am not scared, Marius. You will not hurt me."

Now, in this moment, or on the final day. It was a promise to him, as much as it was a promise to myself. Yet for this night I, like Marius, buried the thoughts of the future. Until that fate would become far too great to be kept hidden.

"Won't I?" His hand snaked out of the water and reached for my neck. It was so large his fingers splayed over my entire lower jaw.

As his frozen touch caressed my skin, I felt my stomach jolt. My hands slipped from his stomach, stopping at the definitive V-shaped lines that had burrowed into his hips.

"Are you fearless, Jak?" Marius growled, eyes fixated to my neck. The danger sent a thrill through me. He trailed a nail across my jawline, his other hand now holding me from behind until both our chests pressed together. I craned my neck, thrusting my chin skyward to allow his touch to completely trail my jaw from one side to the other.

"I want you," I breathed. It was both an answer to his question, and my ability to blatantly ignore it. But my words harboured no lie. I did, in fact, want him.

"I will take that as a yes," Marius whispered before diving into my neck. His lips kissed across my skin, teeth brushing close enough to ignite a fire within me. I held tightly onto him as he devoured me. As his kiss intensified I enjoyed the small moments when he sucked hard at my skin. The perfect mix of pleasure and pain. I melted into him, wrapping my legs around his waist to keep myself attached to his touch.

My hands scratched up his back, stopping only when I lost my fingers in his silver hair. Once I had a grip on him I knew he would not stop.

Marius was mostly silent, all but the subtle growls he emitted as he devoured me. But for the both of us, I made all the sound required as he worked away at me.

"Kiss me," I demanded, tugging at his hair to pull him from my neck.

He came away with a sly grin painted across his handsome face. "In due time."

Marius dove back into my neck as my plea echoed as a moan across the still water's surface. "Kiss... me."

I relaxed my hold on his hair as Marius dipped his face close to mine. Closing my eyes in anticipation, I readied myself for his mouth. But it did not meet mine. "Do not rush this. We have time."

His voice was low and silky. The type that would have made my mouth water and legs quiver.

I had been with men before. A handful of times. It was usually quick meetings beneath my home during the dead of night when I was certain Mother was heavily senseless. The moments never meant anything. Not after they had finished in a record time. It was simply a release that I required. But this. This was different.

In the heart of the lake I let the creature explore me. It was what I wanted after all. And I did not realise just how much I needed for this to happen until his hands were already grabbing a hold of my arse. His grip was the perfect blend of firm and gentle. Whereas his nails had tickled across my jaw, I now did not feel them as he squeezed at my exposed behind.

My entire body was on fire. I was bathed in it. Marius still kissed and nipped away at my neck and shoulders whereas his hands now explored other areas of my body.

So, I repaid the favour.

Relying on his hold on my arse and my legs wrapped around his waist, I let my own hands explore beneath the water. In that moment, as the tip of my hand grazed his hard length, he pulled away from me and hissed, "Patience."

"I have none." My voice was firm. I tightened my grip around him with my legs and captured his chin with my free hand, lifting his face until his eyes were on me. "I want you."

"And I want you."

"Then take me. All of me."

There was a pause. "Are you certain? Because once you give yourself to me, I will... take you... all."

Beneath the water, I suddenly grabbed a hold of his cock. *At last.* It was thick in my hand, so much that I could not touch my thumb to my finger. I knew little of its length, but that did not deter me. I wanted him, no matter what he had to offer.

"To my room," Marius said, his deep voice vibrating through me. "Now."

A bubble of a laugh escaped my mouth as I studied his gaze. It was hungry, but not for blood. Not this time.

He wanted me.

Marius kept me wrapped around him as he paddled with one, strong arm towards the bank of the lake. For not a single moment did he remove his stare from mine. Even as he hauled me out of the water. I hardly registered the cold chill of night across my naked body as I lost myself in his eyes. I suppose I was so accustomed to his own cold touch that the nightly air did nothing to distract me from the moment.

He stepped away from the lake, still holding me in his arms. I felt so small in his embrace.

"What about our clothes?" I asked as he began to walk away.

"They will not be required for what is to come."

My entire body twisted and danced as his words settled over me.

Marius leaned his face towards mine and whispered, "Do you trust me?"

"I do."

"Then I ask that you close your eyes, as I cannot simply walk at this pace to our destination."

As he finished speaking, his lips caught me by surprise. The kiss was short, but lingered long after he pulled away. "Now do it, Jak. Do as I tell you."

I nodded, swallowing the lump of desire in my throat. Not waiting a moment longer I did as I was told and closed my eyes.

The world seemed to shift beneath us. As though the ground was turned upside-down and I was falling. I gasped at the sudden jolt, throwing my eyes open a second later to see if the ground had disappeared completely from underneath us.

But we no longer stood outside. The four walls of the bed chamber surrounded us, the hearth alight with a warm welcome of twisting flames, the curtains drawn open across the grand windows for the first time since I had been here.

"How?" I questioned, my head spinning from the sudden movement.

"There are many things you still have yet to learn about me, Jak." Marius kicked the door closed behind him and stalked towards the made bed. "Allow me to show you just some of those things now."

Slowly, Marius lowered me onto the cloud-like bedding. The tickle of the material was welcomed as I sank into it. From my perch amid the white sheets, I finally saw Marius entirely, his body no longer hidden beneath azure lake water, or obscured by clothing.

He stood before me with pride. Chin raised high, arms loose beside him. I let my gaze trail down from his face to his feet. And he stayed still, allowing me to take it all in uninterrupted.

I sat upright, mouth agape, at the length of his cock that hung between his separated legs.

So he does have length.

My cheeks warmed at the thought. It was the largest I had seen before, far greater than the baker's son or my childhood best-friend's brother.

They had been mere men.

Marius was a god. A god of night. A *man.*

"I want to worship you," I said, gripping the sheets. It was all I could do to stop my hands from reaching out for him.

Marius lifted a hand in dismissal. "Allow me to be the one to worship you first, Jak. I assure you that I will give you all the time you desire. But for now, it is all about you."

He stalked towards the bed, and I stayed deathly still. Marius leaned on the mattress, both arms flexing. My eyes did not know where to settle — at his devilish grin or on his cock that seemed to harden with each passing moment.

I leaned back onto the bed as Marius crawled over me, his presence flattening me down upon the bed. His strong arms entrapped me from either side, but he kept himself hovering inches above me. "Well, well, well. Where do I start?"

The question hung between us. I parted my mouth to answer but was soon silenced as Marius dove in and kissed me. For someone so cold, all I felt was warmth. My toes curled and my fingers dug deeper into the bedding as his tongue explored my own. I craned my neck up to him, only for his hand to press me back down to the bed.

He wanted control. I felt it. I bit down on his lower lip, spurring him to splutter in enjoyment as he pulled away from me. His grin sent a wild thrill through me. Then Marius slipped his hands beneath my back and flipped me over until my face was pressed cheek first into the sheets.

"That will stop you from biting," he growled, hands rubbing down my back and onto my arse. I gasped as he spread each cheek with his large hands. I closed my eyes as his thumb brushed against the sensitive spot at the heart of me. My own cock throbbed as it was pressed against the bed. I wanted nothing more than to grab it, grab him and urge him to move faster. Deep down I had wanted this moment to happen for days. Now it was here, I could not wait to begin.

Yet Marius was taking his time.

One moment it was his thumb, and the next it was his tongue. Caressing. Licking. Tracing. Each exhale came out as a sound which only seemed to spur him to deepen his exploration.

I reached back for him, only to be batted away.

"No hands," Marius said quickly, coming up for a breather which I soon regretted. I did not want it to stop.

I had never felt such a way before. In the dark of my closed eyes, I envisioned explosions of colour and imagery. It was pure bliss.

It came to an abrupt stop, followed by a grunt from Marius. I leaned up on my elbows, this time not being pushed back down by his mighty hand. Over my shoulder I looked to Marius who stood, eyes wide and chin wet. He made no move to clean his own spittle from his face. His tongue simply escaped his deep red lips and traced them.

Marius's other hand worked slowly across his hard, length. Up and down, his wrist twisting slightly with each movement. "I want to fuck you."

"Are you waiting for an invitation?" I threw back at him, lifting myself up onto my knees and arching my back.

He did not reply. But I heard the scratch of wood as he pulled open the drawer in the side cabinet beside the bed. I looked back as he retrieved a glass vial of liquid.

"What is that?" I questioned as he uncorked the small vial and tripped the liquid into his hand.

"A way to ensure I cause you no pain."

"And you have had the lubricant sitting in that drawer, waiting for this very moment?" I asked.

"One can never be caught unprepared, Jak."

I flipped myself onto my back, putting my arms behind my head to keep it propped up. "Have you thought about me... Marius?"

His lip lifted, exposing his teeth. "There has not been a moment you have not been on my mind."

I lifted my feet up and spread my knees. "Then fuck me, Marius. Do as *you* wish."

Marius discarded the glass vial. It shattered on the floor beneath his feet, completely empty. All the lubricant now glistened across his cock.

"Jak, I am going to fuck you. Then I am going to fuck you again. I will stop when you tell me, but I have years' worth of energy ready to expel. Are you certain you want me?"

"I do not want you, Marius," I said, staring him dead in the eye. "I need you."

He smiled, a hiss of excitement passing his gritted teeth.

Marius, besides his heated energy, was gentle. His touch was soft as he guided my legs over his sturdy shoulders. His hands not once rushing me, or grabbing me. I could see his want to devour me entirely as it glowed within his dark gaze.

But he was careful.

His calm attitude benefited us both, for it relaxed me entirely as he navigated his length and pressed it up against me. From my past experiences I remembered that breathing was the best way to get through the initial entry. Yet as Marius slipped his considerably sized cock into me I felt nothing but pleasure. It was an explosion as he pushed it all the way within. Not an inch spared. Not an ounce of expected discomfort greeted me.

Marius's exhale was never-ending as he held himself within me. Then, hands gripping my thigh, he pulled out. It was hard to keep still as he thrust himself deep inside of me once again, this time quicker than the first. Marius released a pleasured exhale, cocking his head back as he lost himself in the feeling. Instinctively I reached up to him, wrapping my hands behind his neck and pulled him down above me. Our eyes locked and our breathing synchronised as he began to move. Each time he pulled himself out until it felt as though he would completely leave me. But then he would push back in until his hips pressed against my arse. Momentum built up the more I relaxed into him. Each thrust sent a shiver up my spine. The feeling was pure magic.

My own magic had come close to the surface. As if this connection between us both reduced my sense of my power to a dull cinder. I hardly cared if I lost control in this moment.

I pulled Marius to my neck where he nuzzled into it. He kissed and nipped at my skin whilst picking up his pace.

All I could do was release an endless string of satisfied moans.

I did not question him as his teeth grazed my neck more frequently. I just ran my nails down his back in response. Soon enough he pulled away, lips glistening wet, and flipped me over onto my belly.

"You are… delicious, my Jak."

I let him guide my body until I was on my knees. His hand pushed down at the space between my shoulders until I was, once again, pressed face-down on the bed.

All without the need to remove himself from me.

Unable to reach for him as I wished, I busied my hands by reaching beneath myself and grabbed a hold of my own cock. Everything felt sensitive. The feeling was incredibly new although it was not my first time.

Our bodies conversed with each other. It was a soundless exchange, but one that traversed the need for words.

We were one.

Time was unimportant as he filled me. I let it simply slip away.

"I want to look at you," I demanded, yanking on the sheets. Marius slowed his movements at my request. We had been in this position for a while, and although the feeling was tremendous I wanted to share the climax with him. For I knew it was close. I could feel its arrival racing towards me as though my very spirit threatened to leave my body. And Marius, his breathing was quickening. His grip hardening and deep groans intensifying.

"Here you are," he said, twisting me onto my back once again. Effortlessly he lifted me from the bed, all the while still staying deep within me. I thanked his length for that. The baker's son was hardly able to move without his cock slipping out of me on countless occasions.

Marius held my weight, all without breaking a sweat. I wrapped my legs around him, letting him hold the brunt of me from beneath my arse. Now standing, he moved towards the wall of the chamber, pressing me up against it for extra security.

"You feel unbelievable," he whispered to me as he began working away at me once again. I wrapped my arms around his neck and brought his forehead to mine. We stayed like that, foreheads pressed together, and eyes locked for an eternity.

"Tell me how it feels?" I was breathless, although not from over exerting myself. It was hard to catch a breath as he fucked me.

"Divine," Marius replied slowly. "It is pure divinity."

His eyes were rolling into the back of his head. His muscles tensed beneath my touch.

I knew the ending was coming and I was ready for it. For him. Just knowing I made him feel like that was enough to fill me with pleasure.

Then he surprised me. Grabbing a hold of my cock, Marius moved his hands in ways I never had experienced.

My hold on him slackened as he picked up speed in both his hand movements and thrusts.

I felt my own climax arrive. My breathing quickened as Marius's low grunts built in intensity. Trapped in pure extasy, I gave into the feeling that built within me.

And I released.

Marius did not stop his magic, although did slow it down as I finished. And the prolonged exhales he produced told me he had also reached the same ending.

He leaned his head onto me, eyes closed. "That was..."

"Incredible," I answered for him, breathing shallow.

He carried me back over to the bed where he put me down, gently removing himself from me. I laid back, not caring how I looked as Marius prowled above me.

"I wish it were longer," Marius said, sweat causing strands of hair to stick to his forehead.

"You know I could have managed it," I told him, eyes hard to keep open.

"I have no doubt in that, Jak." Marius leaned down and placed a soft kiss upon my dampened forehead. "It is I who could not last. Not with what you do to me."

As he spoke, his voice silky, I could have pulled him back down upon me. But my eyes grew heavier and it was hard to keep them open.

Marius did not leave me. His body clambered into the bed at my side, his weight shifting the sheets in a way I was not used to. But his presence was welcomed beside me.

We both looked up to the ceiling, breaths still coming out in quickened pants, as his hand slipped into mine.

I wanted to say something, but there were no words. Not as my tiredness rushed over me in a thick, heavy wave.

Marius's thumb moved in circles across the back of my hand as he whispered, "Rest up, my Jak, for I will need you at full energy soon."

I grinned, eyes closed as I spluttered a laugh. "Already thinking ahead of yourself?"

"Oh..." His voice sent shivers across my naked body. "Absolutely."

19

TIME PASSED in a blur of delight. An endless tide of pleasure that I could not break away from. Nor did I want to. Time did not matter, we simply seemed to lose track of it entirely. There was no concept of day and night, which was only enhanced by the heavy, velvet curtains that stayed drawn.

We only slept when we were exhausted, not when our body clocks demanded. When we woke there were plates of food waiting for us, likely dropped off by his host of phantom staff.

I hardly had a moment to contemplate anything before his mouth was on me, and mine... well mine explored without limitation.

I felt... completed. Gone were the thoughts of what I was. What he was. All that occupied my mind was his taste and touch. How gentle he could be, but equally rough if the moment required.

We fucked more times than I could count. It seemed Marius had an endless stream of energy that spurred him to reach for me whenever he required. And when his hands were not touching my body, I only longed for time to speed up until he found me once again.

But Marius listened to me as well. He listened when I told him I needed a break. Not that it happened often. He was frantic, excited, but respected my wishes, my body, my patience.

We did not leave this room. Not for a short walk or a break away from our fucking to explore another part of the castle. There was nothing beyond the closed chamber that I desired more than the naked body that was lying beside me.

I had been awake for a while, Marius still sleeping soundlessly as I nibbled at the sliced apple I had chosen from the plate. It was equally light and fresh, the perfect palette cleanser I needed from the intense entanglement we had not long finished.

His back was to me, muscles moving slowly in sync with his shallow breathing. It was the first time I had not been asleep with him, his large arms cocooned around me as my arse nestled into his crotch. There was something different now. Like I was finally breaking the surface of the entrancing dream I had been locked within. As I stared at the back of his white-haired head, I could think of only one thing.

Our fate.

I bit down on a slice of apple only to cringe at the sudden sickness that flooded through me. Without care I dropped the piece, my appetite running away from me.

I have to kill you.

It was a sobering thought. One that made my hands shake violently. I had crossed a line with Marius but did not regret it. Not even as the weight of my fate fell back upon my shoulders, making it harder to catch a breath.

If I fail... I die.

I was dancing with danger, tiptoeing on the edge of a sharpened blade. The fall was daunting and impossible on either side. Kill the creature I lust for, or die alongside my kind.

Lust. Was that all it was? Just contemplating the word felt wrong. This was more. More than a simple sexual hunger for a stranger.

Strangers didn't share what we had shared. They did not open themselves the way I had, the way Marius had.

Nervous energy buzzed through my bones. I could no longer sit still and watch as he slept and I knew deeply that sleep would not befriend me. Not as a wild storm built within me.

Air. I needed some air, and time alone.

I kept as quiet as I could, opening the chest of ornate drawers to pull out some clothes. I hardly cared what I reached for. Every now and then I would glance back to the man who slept in the bed. But I could not look for long. Not as the guilt only intensified as I laid my gaze upon his calm, emotionless face.

My feet hardly made a sound as I padded across the cold chamber floor for the door. Even after I slipped out of it and closed it behind me, I half expected to hear him call for me. But he didn't.

I let myself wander the hallways and corridors mindlessly. Not caring where I went to. Passing the large windows, I was surprised to see the light sky beyond. How much time really had passed?

I paused to look out, taking in the blanket of fresh snow that had settled over the gardens far below. The heavy mist still clung proudly to the castle's grounds, but the daylight bounced off the snow, making it impossibly bright to stare at.

It then became painfully clear just how cold it truly was as I leaned on the castle's rough wall. Had I grown used to Marius's cold body over the past few days that it took me this long for my body to acclimatize away from him?

Just thinking about him again made me push off from the wall and carry on my walk.

Before I realised as much, I had taken myself back to his study. Numb, I stood before the closed door and loosed a ragged sigh.

Like it had always been, the door was unlocked and the hearths roared inside. I felt my body relax instantly as I entered, but my mind still whirled.

I was unsure what answers I searched for within this room, but anything was better than staring at Marius. My body itched at the thought of his touch. Not because I loathed it, but I did not deserve it.

"This is your fault," I told myself, pacing the carpet without fear of wearing holes in it. "You allowed yourself to forget your task. This feeling inside is deserved. A punishment for losing yourself and stepping off the path."

I answered internally. *If I fail, and miraculously survive whatever awaits me on the final day, Mother will ensure I do not live.*

It was a morbid thought, but I knew it was fact even if Mother had never spoken it aloud. I knew her character as well as I thought I knew my own. She would not let me live.

A new thought sprang to mind, swinging through the mess of worry like a drunkard with a blunt sword.

How long did I have left?

I would have to wait for nightfall to see the moon's phase. It was hard to know what I hoped to see when night did arrive. Part of me longed for more time. Yet another felt the need to rip the thorn from the wound and get this over with. Before I fell any deeper. Because that was what I was doing. Falling. For him, the beast, the creature. Marius. Falling so hard that my bones would likely shatter upon impact on the final day.

Tumbling through this intense oblivion of contrasting emotions.

I tried everything to take my mind off my turmoil. Attempting to lose myself in the painted celestial chart only to bring my mind back to Marius. I attempted to focus my breathing and meditate, only for his face to step out of the shadows in my mind as if he commanded those as well.

Then I studied the bookshelves, running my fingers along the multitude of novels in hopes one would stand out and distract me from how my own story was panning out.

I came to the end of the shelf, but noticed something was different. A space that was now full.

My breathing faltered as I recognised it as the missing book. The one Marius had taken.

I knew the space it left was huge, however it was hard to comprehend just the size of the tome that sat before me. Its spine was so large that it took both hands to pull it from its burrow. The weight of the novel was dramatic, straining my wrists as I wrestled it free.

I leaned back as I carried the tome to Marius's desk, trying to balance out the heaviness in my posture. It was near impossible not to dump it on the oak desk just from the relief of not having to carry it.

Taking a seat, I ran my hands down the gold, embossed cover and readied myself.

"What were you hiding, Marius?" I asked aloud, lifting the front cover back to reveal the aged, yellowed paper within.

Where the answer to my question looked back at me.

A single word. A name. Written in beautiful twisting letters that did not negate the word.

Jak.

My brow furrowed and my forehead creased. Narrowing my gaze, I ran my finger over my name as if it would rub away the illusion and reveal what word truly lay beneath it.

But it stayed the same. Unchanged and proud.

My name.

20

THE CHAIR CREAKED PAINFULLY as I leaned back in it, hands folding behind the back of my head. The tome discarded before me. And my stare did not falter from the page with that one, unbelievable word scrawled across it. I winced at the heavy pounding of my heart as my mind raced for an explanation.

It made no sense. He told me he wrote the stories long after the Claim's final day. Yet here sat a story with my name scripted across the first page.

"It is not what you think." Marius's voice sounded just out of sight. I turned slowly, mouth agape, as he stood in the doorway. He was shirtless, his hair ruffled from his long sleep. Had evening arrived already? Time was truly slipping away from me. My eyes dusted over the unbuttoned waist of his trousers and how it revealed the hairs that crowned his cock. He spoke again, bringing my attention back to his placid face. "Would you prefer for me to explain, or to leave you to read and uncover the truth?"

I would have hauled the book from the table and waved it at him if I had the strength. "I will get clarity far sooner if it comes from you."

He bowed his head, trying to hide the sad glint in his eyes. "When you first arrived and revealed your name to me it was as if that single word had torn down the walls I had built within myself. Your name, his name, had not been spoken in this place for many years. It took me by utter surprise."

"Which explains your reaction…" I added, watching him walk to the other side of the desk.

"I am well accustomed to ghosts. Yet with your reveal I felt the worst of them being dragged to the surface."

I looked back to the book for a moment. "He was your first Claim." The body that was left at the border of his castle. The one both Mother and Victorya had kept so quiet about.

"He was not my Claim. It was those after him that arrived with that label. Jak was..." Marius paused, putting a closed fist to his mouth and clearing the lump from his throat. "Jak was the very reason for why you and I are standing in this room. If it was not for him I would likely be bones beneath the ground. The remains of a withered, old man, who'd died from old age. Instead I fell for him, as he fell for me. And we were punished for it."

I could not speak. All I could do was stay silent and listen as Marius unveiled his truth. A story I had not heard of before. But one that tugged on the familiar strings that seemed to twang within my chest.

"I thought it was some twisted punishment when you arrived, Jak. Beautiful Jak, come to remind me of my undoing. Come — just when I was beginning to forget — to ensure I would not."

"Who was he, Marius?" I asked. "Who was he to you?"

"The love of my life." He looked up slowly, his eyes narrowed and wet. A tear sliced down his cheek, falling carelessly to the ground at his bare feet. "We were young and naïve. Jak was betrothed to another yet we did not care. I was selfish to think he would ever be mine, and he was stupid to believe the same. When we were discovered, we were..."

Marius turned quickly, putting his back to me.

"Were what?" I said, standing from the desk with a scratch of wood against stone. I needed to hear it from him, but I had pieced the story he told to the one I had been taught to believe. "Tell me, Marius."

I paused my plea and waited for prolonged moments. When he finally turned around he no longer held onto sadness. His eyes had narrowed and darkened in colour, as if the ruby of his irises had expanded across the entirety of his stare. His lips had turned white with tension as they snarled above his exposed fangs.

"We were cursed. There were always rumours his betrothed was a witch, but it was never believed. Idle gossip and warnings that we looked over. That was the first and only time I ever underestimated their kind. She discovered our secret and punished us. At first we simply could not leave the grounds. But I grew colder whilst Jak stayed warm. My hunger changed. His did not. I became the beast and he..." Marius choked once again on his words before clearing his throat with an expression of distressed irritation. "Then I killed him. On the day when the moon was full and bled red, I lost myself to the creature that the witch had moulded me into. And I killed him."

Slowly I moved around the desk, unsure if the creature buried within Marius was about to finally show itself. With caution I closed the space between us and pressed my hands against his cool, bare chest. "You fell in love and were punished," I said aloud, more for myself to understand. It was not the version of events I had been taught. Similar in the sense of my ancestor cursing him for stealing someone that belonged to her. Yet I was seeing it from a different light.

"She never cared for Jak," Marius said, looking down his nose at me. "If she did she would have punished me, and not him. Yet she trapped him with me and knew what would become of him."

"I am sorry." My apology meant more than he would know.

Marius gripped a hold of my forearms. "Do not be."

I felt sick, as though my stomach was ready to empty its contents whilst the one revelation raced through me.

Mother had named me after the catalyst for the curse. Knowing I would one day be the Claim. The last Claim, come to end Marius and in doing so be a painful reminder. What did she want to achieve from that? To throw him off guard during my stay? To make it easier for him to fall for me to achieve our end goal?

Or was it more personal? More twisted? A name used as a weapon to slice at Marius whilst he was already down?

"I did not know," I muttered.

"How could you know?" Marius put his finger beneath my chin and lifted my face to his. "From my knowledge the witch died years ago and with it the chance of this nightmare ending. You were not to know."

"But..." I swallowed my words, biting down on my lip so hard the pain was what was required to silence me.

"You have served me a great deal of armistice, Jak. I cannot fully explain how your presence has given me more peace in my mind than I have felt in a long time. Do not apologise. This is not your doing."

He was wrong. It was mine. My Mother's, my covens.

There was not a justified reason for the curse to be cast and I understood that now. I almost took some pleasure in knowing the curse had taken the witch's power and all those who came after her. Until me.

Magic is not taken, without something given in return.

"What did she turn you into?" I reached for his cheek, clearing the stain of a tear from his skin.

"A nameless beast." Marius stared unwaveringly into my soul.

"Nothing is ever nameless," I said meekly.

"Is there anything else like me out there? Tell me, Jak, for you have experienced more of the outside world than I. Have you heard tales of others that hunger for one's life source?"

I knew the answer. Whatever twisted curse had been laid upon Marius was unique. The witch herself had grown mad trying to find a cure for her lack of power. And so did the many that followed after her.

She died with the mad want for her power. Mother told me that it was only on her deathbed when she finally grasped a single slither of magic to prophesise my birth and what the child would mean for our kind.

I used to think it was some cruel play of fate, giving my ancestor her power back just before she passed. As though it dangled itself before her in reminder for what she lost.

But now, standing before Marius who was the product of her jealously, it made me feel satisfied somewhat. Knowing she died, punished in a different manner to Marius. But still punished.

By taking away from him what he desired the most, she gave up her own most treasured love.

Her magic.

"You are unique," I told him.

"I am a demon."

"We all are demons. Some have just learned to hide it better than others."

Marius took my hand in his and guided me to the rugged floor. We left the book open upon the desk and laid upon the ground and looked up at the painted ceiling.

"It was Jak that helped you paint it." It was more a statement than a question.

"He always had the steadier hand."

His reply was short, an obvious sign that he did not want to discuss it further. But I could not cope with the silence. Every break in conversation had my mind full of guilt. Guilt for having the same name. Guilt for the role I had to play in this.

I drowned in the feeling and the silence was the ball and chain strapped to my ankle, keeping me down.

"Just tell me if you do not want to discuss it further," I said, feeling the need to provide him with the option to escape such discomfort.

He rolled his head and faced me, a smile tugging at his lips but not quite reaching his eyes. "You must think me a sappy fool."

I forced a smile in response, my lips quivering slightly. "I have no words as to how I would describe my thoughts for you, Marius."

"Say it again," he breathed, blinking and holding his eyes closed for a beat longer than normal.

"What?"

"My name." When he opened his eyes again they found mine. As though a cord connected us both, that moment sent a thrilling explosion of feeling through my body. "Please, say it again. It... it reminds me of one great difference between you and... please."

I wanted to press him further, but could not muster seeing the wince of his eyes or the paling of his taut lips when the storm of memories coursed behind his gaze.

So I obliged, running the back of my finger down the side of his face. "Marius. Brave Marius. Terrifying Marius. My Marius."

"Thank you." His voice was a bare whisper.

A stabbing sensation in my gut snatched my breath away, but I forced the feeling down.

We lay like that for a while, the book discarded and the room silent. Marius wrapped his fingers between mine and held on tight as though his life depended on it. At one point I thought he had fallen asleep. A place of peace for him, at least I hoped. But as I began to tug my hand from his, he spoke, breaking the quiet.

"Katharine has not returned as she promised she would."

"But she was only here..." I trailed off. Marius showed no sign of caring that I clearly had overheard their last encounter.

"It has been five days. The moon is reaching its third quarter and Katharine should have returned."

I leaned up on my elbows, echoing what Marius had said. "Five days?"

Impossible. I was aware we had lost time to each other, but five days? I shook my head. That couldn't be right.

"Perhaps we missed her?" I asked, having flashes to our entwined limbs.

"I would have felt her presence at the boundary. It is how she can come and go as she pleases."

I faced him, brows furrowed. "You are telling me you could simply let me leave if I chose?"

He shook his head, eyes blank. "It does not work like that. Not for the Claim. Many have tried and you are welcome to if you so desire. But for Katharine and her family, they have remained outside the twisted rules of the curse."

Why? The thought echoed through me.

"So you let her in?"

"In a manner of speaking, yes. I sense her presence and provide her with the invitation to enter."

Intrigue breezed through me, blowing away the cobwebs of guilt for a moment. "Have others tried to enter?"

"Not for many years, but yes. I did not let them in. For fear of what I may have done to them."

"But why Katharine? Why her family?"

Marius paused. "I do not know, Jak."

"I am sure she is okay," I said, but I could not ignore the tugging in my gut. It was becoming hard to distinguish my worries from one another.

"Yes, she must be." Marius did not sound so convinced. He made a move to lie back down on the floor beside me, but instead he ushered my legs apart and leaned forward above me. "My mind is a storm right now. Care to help me calm it?"

His voice grew silky with each word. His invitation to me clear and enticing. This is what I needed, to take my mind off my own storm. Him. His touch that had ways of taking me to different worlds. With him, on me, in me, nothing else mattered.

"How may I help provide your mind reprieve?" I asked, running my tongue across my lower lip. It was not only Marius who was in need for a distraction.

I longed for it. For him.

He lowered himself further atop me, his arms tensing as they carried his entire weight. His face came close to mine until he stopped a mere hairbreadth from my mouth. "Let me have you."

I nipped at his lip, urging a low growl to bubble from his throat and replied, "You already do."

21

With the days that passed, and the lack of Katharine's presence, Marius fell into a dark cave of worry. His mood changed entirely. For a man so still, he did not stop moving. He would disappear for hours, sometimes even entire evenings, and return to climb into bed with me before morning arose.

The curtains in the bed chamber had been kept drawn for so long that I could not remember a time that they were ever open. The thick material kept all daylight from breaking into the room, making time harder to grasp a hold of.

I was thankful when Marius pressed his cold body against mine and finally gave into sleep, I was at peace when he was.

As Marius struggled with the internal storm of his worry for Katharine, I dealt with my own raging emotions. Knowing the final day was growing closer and with it the pending doom of what was to come.

One evening I woke in bed alone. Although I could not recall my dreams, I was certain they had been bad for I woke with a heavy chest and full mind. It caused my body to ache, as though I had been through a fight. Or worse.

Rolling over, I half expected Marius to have shifted to the furthest spot away from me. But the sheets had been left rumpled as Marius had slunk out of the room. Only his lingering scent was left behind.

I swung my legs over the bed and pressed my feet into the cold floor. For a moment I sat like that, fighting a yawn as I also fought at the iron webs of anxiety that had settled within me.

Perhaps he had gone to welcome Katharine? At last. Yet deep down I knew that was not the case. Her absence worried him terribly, and there must have been a reason for it. Not that he dared say it aloud.

Like I did most evenings when I woke alone, I sauntered over to the drawn window and slipped between the heavy sheets of material. The window frame had been upholstered with a faded, blue cushion. A place, I could imagine, reading from and admiring the once beautiful grounds below.

Now I just knelt upon the built-in seat and peered out the foggy windows to see Marius pacing the dark paths. His bloodhounds sulked behind him, their whining only adding to the atmosphere that seemed to spread through the castle.

He did this. Every night. Scouting the grounds as if Katharine had simply got lost among them.

"Victorya," I called, letting my breath fog on the windowpane.

From the reflection I noticed the wisp of grey shadow form into view behind me. "Things are no better."

I had called upon Victorya a lot during the past few days when Marius had left me for stretched periods of time. She ensured I had food and drink, although I had noticed the supplies dwindling as the days went by. Explained from the lack of Katharine's visit. Without her bringing food from the town, there was nothing edible to eat inside the castle.

But hunger was the least of my concerns.

"You are certain I cannot leave for answers?" I asked her again, merely echoing what I had already found out from Marius days ago. "If I can get into town I can find out what has kept her from visiting."

"You cannot leave," she said, floating across the ground to where I knelt. "I can keep telling you, but the answer will remain the same each time."

"I know," I said, pressing my head into my hands. "I just... I cannot keep seeing him in such a way."

"This is nothing compared to what he has been through before, Jak. This mood is a mere wave to the tidal storms we have endured. It will pass, and if Katharine does not return, another will in her place. It has been that way since the beginning."

Victorya had been an open book, answering the questions I had for her. At least in some poetic, twisted way. Sometimes her riddles would stay with me throughout the long evenings, as haunting as my ignorance before she provided me with answers.

But the more I had come to learn, the deeper the seed of anxiety felt within me. Threatening to blossom into an uncomfortable, devouring sapling at any moment.

"It is not in my nature to simply wait. I want to help," I told her, leaving Marius to his pacing as I faced the ghostly girl.

"Can you not speak with your... those who wait on the other side of the water? Ask them to locate her?"

"And give away my concern?" I snapped, realising immediately that I had done so. I peered down to my feet, teeth chewing at my lower lip. "I am sorry, but I cannot do that. Believe me, the thought has crossed my mind. But I cannot let Mother know that I hold some concern for Marius."

The scrying bowl had stayed hidden ever since Marius had been occupying the room with me. Not by myself, as Victorya had explained. She had been the one to store it away to prevent him from finding it.

"Some concern?" Victorya tilted her head and narrowed her opaque eyes. "Even the dead can see you have simply more than just *some* concern. You care deeply for him and do not want to voice that you are dying inside at the thought of what you have to do."

"I know you want the same as my mother does..."

"If Marius knew the release you could give him, he too would be more than thrilled at the thought. I have seen him beg for his suffering to end. Believe me, you do not want to experience it."

"That is not the point!" I said, louder this time. "Have you ever had to kill someone you—"

I silenced myself, releasing to whom I spoke to.

"You forget that I was not blessed with the years of living as you have been, Jak. No, is your answer. I have not had to do the unspeakable because I was never given the chance. You must do it," she seethed.

I bowed my head, unable to apologise to her again. "I feel helpless."

"And pathetic seeking advice from a child, I suspect?"

"I will take the advice where I can these days. Even if it is from you."

It was almost wasted that Victorya did not stick her tongue out and pull a face. But as she had explained before, she may have been stuck in that form, but she was far from a child now. Not after what she had seen.

"I know little of your kind, only that it was believed you should not have access to magic. But here you are. Is there not some spell you can do to find out what is happening with Katharine?"

"My magic does not work like that..." I said. "It is control over the elements. Mother never taught me spells for it was not required. The point of my power is to kill Marius. Not hexes and potions."

"To me it sounds like you have simply been leashed. Taught what they wanted you to know, not what you *needed* to know."

I sighed. "I worked that out years ago."

"Yet you did not demand more knowledge?"

There was no demanding when it came to Mother. Or her coven.

Only Lamiere dared whisper about the other possibilities her ancestors had access to before my ancestor took it away from them all.

"Making me admit aloud how terrible I had it with my family is not going to help us find answers to Katharine's disappearance. If I cannot leave and seek answers myself we will just have to wait for her to turn up when she is ready."

A roar pierced the night, shaking the very foundations of the castle. I first thought it was an illusion brought on by my tiredness, but Victorya's reaction was painfully real. She looked, eyes wide, to me as I felt as though my entire body vibrated.

"Marius," we echoed, already moving for the door of the room.

∽

I found him at edge of the castle where the overgrown paths rolled over to the bridge which connected us to Darkmourn. He stood with his back to me, yet sensed my presence from the slight turn of his face.

"Stay away, Jak," he warned, voice a rumble of thunder that shook the very shadows around us. "Please..."

"Tell me what is wrong." I ignored him, testing another footstep closer to where he stood. Peering over his shoulder, I could see the faint glow of the few buildings that had not yet closed down for the evening. Even from my distance I could imagine the local tavern and the bustling crowd whom would be singing and dancing whilst spilling tankards at such a late hour.

"Tell me, Marius, I am here to help."

"Katharine..." he growled.

I stopped dead in my tracks, my legs going numb. "What do you..." Before I could finish, Marius stepped aside, revealing a mound that lay untouched on the ground before him. The closer I got to it, the clearer it became. A bundle of hair lay by Marius's feet, gathered by a black ribbon that held the loose strands together. It was not just a cutting of hair. It was every strand possible that would have been attached to her head. The blood-stained ends told a story of struggle.

Marius was stiff beside me. Tension rolled off him in waves. But it did not last long. One moment he was still, the next he was slamming his fists against a wall of air before him.

I stumbled back in shock as he battered the unseen barrier that kept him from leaving. Kept us from leaving.

"Let me out!" he screamed. Roared. His voice blended in with the night, causing his hounds to howl.

I clapped my hands over my ears, shying away from his anger.

"Katharine!"

He punched at the barrier, over and over, kicking and throwing his entire body weight against it. All the while screaming her name. "Katharine!" Over and over, he did not stop. Not until his voice scratched along his throat, cracking with each shout.

"Marius, you need to calm down." I reached for him, slowly, only to snap my hands back as he turned on me. His entire face was pinched with lines. They covered his head, clawed at the sides of his eyes and tugged at his lips. In the faded light he look... monstrous. His eyes were as dark as the night around us. His lips almost non-existent as he hissed and snapped fangs at me. Marius was hunched, breathing heavily as he studied me. I saw the disregard in his gaze. How he studied me as if he did not know me.

This was the monster of the curse.

Wind picked up around my body, rushing in familiar and guarding torrents. I fisted my hands, trying to calm the fear that had stunted my ability to take a full breath. *Not now.*

"Marius, it is me." I kept my voice as quiet as I could muster whilst the fear raged wildly through me. "It is me."

He snapped his head to the side, dark veins bulging in his neck.

"Jak, it is your Jak."

My name seemed to anchor him back to reality for a moment. His expression softened, only enough for the whites of his eyes to return. Then his raspy voice broke out of his snapping jaws. "I... want... I want to hurt."

I almost heard the threads of his jacket burst as he slammed his fists into his chest. Pounding one after the other.

I buried the fear and moved for him, throwing myself at his body to stop him from hurting himself anymore. It did not matter to me if he did not feel his actions, if that was the entire reason for doing what he did. I could not watch it.

I wrapped my arms around his waist and buried my head into his chest with my eyes pinched closed. It happened so fast that I readied myself for the slams of his fists into my back. Wincing in anticipation for the pain.

But it did not come. I waited, holding my breath, only to have his hands run softly down my back.

"It...I...Jak, it is me."

His words almost shattered me entirely. I could not speak, instead only tightening my hold on him as if I could never let go again.

I melted beneath his touch as he traced his fingers down my spine and held onto me.

"I am sorry if I frightened you."

I spoke into his body, voice muffled. "I am not scared of you. Only what you wished to achieve by hitting yourself."

His hand stroked the back of my head, as I gripped onto him for dear life.

"That was not even a slither of what I will become, Jak. You need to know that."

"I do not care." Tears slipped from my eyes, wetting the material of his jacket beneath my face.

He took my shoulders and pried me from him. "That was me losing control. But when the final moon rises, I do not simply lose control. That suggests I can find it again. You... I cannot explain."

"Then don't." I stared at him, thankful to see his face soften, erasing the harsh lines that had creased across it.

"You are cold," Marius announced, rubbing his hands up and down my arms.

It was not the cold that made me shake, but the subtle detail of the ribbon that held Katharine's sheared hairs in a bundle.

I had seen it the moment I had laid eyes upon it. Marius showed no sign of noticing what I had, nor did I point it out.

Marius wrapped his arm around my shoulder and guided me back towards the castle, leaving the horror far behind us. I was thankful for the quiet as we walked. Not even the blood hounds that hid among the shadows of the grounds dared make a sound.

I needed the silence to make sense of what was revealed.

Embossed at the end of the black ribbon was a faint marking of a symbol. One I had seen many times throughout my life.

A pentagram etched like a puckered scar across the ribbon's material.

It was a sign. For me.

A message from my mother. A wordless warning.

She had Katharine.

22

I RAISED A HAND, wincing as I blocked the sunlight from my gaze. It had been weeks since I had been outside during the day. It took a moment for the white glare to settle and my vision to focus on the frost covered grounds beyond the castle.

It was pure luck that the front door was left unlocked. Perhaps Marius felt no need to keep me locked within anymore. Not with my knowing that I could never leave. Not until the fateful finale that we were racing towards.

I stumbled blindly down the steps and onto the overgrown path. My boots trod heavily across the bundles of weeds that had split through the cracked slabs beneath me.

The chill of winter had proudly settled over the castle, however the sky was cloudless. As I trudged through the gardens, leaving the castle behind me, I melted beneath the slight kiss of the sun across the back of my neck.

It had taken me two attempts to wake during the hours when Marius was comatose. He hardly left my side since we discovered the offering of Katharine's hair. And I could not scry for answers with him near. So I waited for the safety of daylight to do so.

I settled on the ground, the frozen blades of grass melting beneath me and wetting my trousers. Far away from any window that overlooked this place, I rested the scrying bowl before my crossed legs. I called for the element required until the bowl filled and the surface of water shivered to reveal whom I called for.

"Jak." Mother's voice drifted through the water. I had to bite down on my tongue to stop the unravelling of anger I held towards her. Instead I swallowed the lump in my throat and questioned her calmly.

"What have you done with Katharine?"

Mother grinned, her eyes glowing wickedly. "She has been punished for her actions. I trust I do not need to indulge in what for as I am certain you are already aware."

"Enough of the games, tell me what you have done!" It was not a question but a demand.

"I admit this was not the reaction I expected, although in hindsight I should have seen the signs. All our faith has been put in the hands of a pathetic boy. It should have been me, I have said it all along. If I had your power the task would have had no risk of failing. Yet here you are, worried about what I have done with the creature's little pet."

"Her name is Katharine," I seethed, ignoring her taunt. "I will not ask again."

Mother liked to gloat, it was one of her many flaws. I knew she would share the information and I was right.

"That girl is a blood whore. She was caught feeding her mother the creature's gore and *that* could not go unpunished. The mother was easier to deal with for she was already on her death bed, the poor dear. But the girl, she is still alive. For now."

My stomach hardened and my heart dropped at the thought of murder. Katharine had been caught. If Marius knew...

"Why not kill them both?" I kept my face as straight as I could muster, not wanting to give away the internal turmoil that galloped through me. "Why stop at one when you could have taken them both? Pray tell, Mother, how you held yourself back from committing yet more monstrous acts."

"Because I am smart enough to see that you are a failure. And when you die, and he breaks free of his containment, I will need something, or someone, to use as leverage against his impending rampage."

"I will not..." I could not finish what I had to say as the words came out with no thought. I would fail. Mother was right. I could not kill Marius. No longer caring for this illusion I had upheld, I asked the question that I had longed to know for days. "Was it your idea to name me after the boy he once loved?"

"That creature did not love anything but his own desires. And to answer your question, it was. Poetic, don't you think?"

"You disgust me." I leaned over the bowl, snarling at the woman through the water. "I die happy knowing you will never experience the power that I have. If he kills me, he takes your chance of a legacy with it. And from what he has warned, your kind will be the first to be slaughtered."

"You already have detached yourself from what you are," Mother said, stare glazed over as she regarded me. "And do tell what you believe will occur when he discovers what you are."

My blood ran cold as Mother spoke aloud the one anxiety that I had buried deep. For Marius to know the truth about what I was. I hated myself for the part I had to play, I could only imagine what it would do to him.

"We are doomed in your name. When he drains the life out of your pathetic body I want you to know that it was your doing." I expected her words to sting, but they did not. My body and soul became entirely numb as she spat her hate at me.

"Worthless boy. And if, by any stretch of one's imagination, you make it out, I want you to understand you will have no home to return to." Mother's entire face relaxed for a moment, a soft smile lifting her thinned lips. "Unless you bring us his head, that is."

I had nothing else to say to her but felt the need to stab at her one last time with my words sharpened by knives. "If I cannot stop him, you have no chance, no matter the collateral you hold above him. See you in the underworld… Mother."

I closed my eyes and tensed as all four elements flooded me at once. The power was under my command. I exhaled and the bowl exploded before me, fragments flying far off into the castle's grounds beneath the pure force. Euphoria flooded from my body, filling me entirely with its fresh kiss. It had been days without connection to my power. It had built silently within me, accepting the invitation I offered it for escape. A circle of fire exploded from my chest as I released a scream of anger. It rolled across the overgrown garden around me, devouring every plant and weed in its war path.

I longed to unleash my power, my frustration, on Mother herself. She was the beast all along. And me, a beast of her creation.

All I could do was sit still, a charred mark across the ground where the bowl had once been. Smoke curled into the cold air around me. My breathing was heavy and my mind sodden.

I cried, but not out of sadness. There was no such emotion when it came to my mother. Only fury. It burned within me long after the physical flames across the garden died out, no longer fuelled by the ground. I studied the halo of scorched grass around me, as though a star had fallen from the heavens and kissed where I sat.

There was no hiding this from Marius. He would see and question. The perfect, circular sigil of charred grass and dirt had no natural explanation. I held my shaking hands before me to see the small licks of fire still curling around my fingers.

Anger was the passion needed to keep it alight. And I was riddled with it.

It was long into the day when I finally picked myself up from the ground and walked back towards the castle's entrance. Night would soon arrive. Marius would soon wake.

And I would tell him. Reveal everything to him because keeping it hidden would kill me sooner than the arrival of the fateful final day.

I dragged myself back through the castle doors, slowly taking the steps up towards the level of his chamber where he would still be soundlessly asleep.

There was a small part of me who pleaded with my soul to keep quiet. To do as Mother had wished, what I had trained for all these years.

But as I slipped back into the room and saw Marius's placid face resting upon the swan-feathered pillow, I almost broke down entirely.

He would be free, I told myself as I slipped into the sheets beside him with a warm tear running down my cheek, pulling the sheets up to my chin to try and stop the incessant shivering. Free of the curse keeping him bound here. Free from the trauma and memories that the very walls reminded him of daily.

I closed my eyes, not bothering to clear the wet streaks from my face. And I would be free. Free of Mother and the burden that my life presented.

It was easier to fall into sleep when realisation struck. If Marius killed me, I would no longer be required or reminded of the point of my own existence. Weight lifted from my body mere moments before I drifted into a dreamless, empty and peaceful sleep.

23

It was Marius's wandering hands that woke me. His gentle touch coaxed me from the deep sleep I had lost myself within. Tickling fingers trailed shapes around my thigh which sent shivers across my bare skin. I was facing away from him, but his body was pressed firmly into my back. Each of us slightly curved enough to fit into one another's embrace like two pieces of a puzzle. Pieces that did not fit together, but were forced together and ruined in the process. Yes, that was what we were.

Stifling a yawn, I attempted to stretch out but his cool body kept me trapped within his limitations.

"Can we stay in bed all day?" Marius whispered, pressing a prolonged kiss to the back of my head. His voice was hoarse and raspy, but lighter than it had been the nights past. "I do not feel ready to face the night ahead just yet. Let it be me and you, just us. Just like this. And please do not make me beg."

He slipped a hand beneath my side and wrapped the other atop me. One strong tug and I was firmly in his grasp. And I did not want him to let go. Not even with the bubbling sickness that brewed within, or the haunting knowing of what was to come.

I was still fighting back against the want to fall back into sleep. It was peaceful there. A place without the need to think. Waking this evening felt as though I had been thrust out of a body of warm water into a winter storm.

I barely managed to form words together in agreement. All that came out of my mouth was a string of mumbled, long sounds.

"You are dressed," Marius announced, tugging at the shirt on my back. "But when I last left you I am certain your body was exposed."

My eyes sprang open at his comment. I shifted beneath the sheets and felt the material that Marius still played with at my thigh.

"I was cold." The lie slipped out before I had a chance to claw it back. I had to tell him what I knew of Katharine eventually. And with it the reasoning of how I knew. I was suddenly glad to have my back to him as I was certain my pinched and twisted expression would have given my secrets away.

"Are you now?" His voice rumbled.

"No."

As I said it, his wandering hands quickened in pace as he gripped onto the material of the trousers with full fists and begun tugging them down off my legs. I groaned as the chill of his fingers skimmed up my leg, knowing the trousers were now discarded on the chamber's floor.

"And what of the shirt... do you need it to keep warm now?"

I paused, my breathing shuddering. "No," I said again.

Marius snickered, fingers moving as preciously as a spider weaving a web. Button by button he undid the shirt without needing to be standing before me, all whilst he still lay beside me, his heavy breathing prickling the back of my neck.

There was something different about him. How his hands, although gentle, seemed rushed.

Urgent.

"Has the cold made you lose the ability to say more than one word?"

I pushed back at him, nestling my arse into his crotch. Before I felt the hard rock of his length I could sense his arousal for me. My mouth watered as I rubbed back against him, slowly rocking my hips.

"No," I muttered again, eyes held closed as Marius's enthusiastic grip fondled further.

"If you continue using that word I will be forced to manipulate my further questioning to ensure it ends well for me. Tell me, Jak, will you waste yet another evening with me and not leave this bed?"

"There is nothing else of importance that needs to be done," I replied, accepting his proposal without clearly saying so. Part of me felt wrong for doing this. Keeping the stone of destruction within me. Would one more night really matter before I finally threw it, shattering the glass castle within Marius?

Marius turned me around to face him, his strength enough to complete the movement without my need for assisting. We faced each other, noses a breadth apart. His stare did not linger from mine for a single moment. I was his entire focus, and he was mine.

One more night of peace. It was a promise to myself. Over and over

I repeated it in my mind as I took in his face. His handsome, perfect face.

I reached for the strands of loose, white hair that fell over his ruby eyes. He forced his face into my touch as I pushed the hair out of the way.

"You are the most handsome creature I have ever laid my eyes upon." He did not blink as he spoke. Did not look away. His lips hardly moved as he announced his thoughts aloud.

Him saying that played with the barrier of sadness that I was trying to keep erected. It was almost painful looking at him, knowing what was to come.

I smiled, masking the emotions that stormed within me. "As are you. If you are the very last person I see it would not be terrible. You have not seen the others I have endured back home. You are… different."

Marius winced. "Different is good, is it not?"

"Different is beyond good. It is you."

He parted his lips to respond, but I silenced him with a kiss. I feared that if he spoke I would crumble entirely. So, like the selfish offspring my mother had so perfectly crafted, I buried the feeling and lost myself to Marius.

I pushed at his shoulders until he was laid flat on his back. Hoisting my leg over his, I took my place upon his crotch as though it was my throne. The sheets fell off my back, discarded, exposing both of our now naked bodies.

Marius grinned, exposing his teeth, and raised both his hands and put them behind his head.

"Have your way," he groaned, his sly grin causing my stomach to flip. "I am all yours."

My hands explored his chest and stomach, moving over the mounds of muscle as he tensed beneath my touch. I did not stop until they found his throat. I squeezed at his skin, lowering my parted mouth to his neck as he had done to me.

I started off by simply kissing. Each peck small and soft. But then I brought in a nip which erupted a growl of pleasure and surprise from his, always, parted lips. I sucked, introducing my tongue which ran across his skin, leaving a trail of glistening spit in its wake.

Sounds slipped from him, a chorus of pleasured chirps and deep, thundering growls that only spurred me on further.

Once I pulled away, his neck was as red as his wide, hungry eyes.

I lost myself to the feeling. Marius's hands finally gave up hiding behind his head and he gripped onto either side of my hips. The harder I bit and sucked, the further his fingers dug into me. The pain encouraged me. It was not the type of discomfort that snatched one's breath, but told me all I needed to know about Marius.

He was enjoying this, and I was as well.

Down from his neck, I trailed my tongue across his chest. This close I admired the faint hairs that covered his skin, as silver as those atop his head. Around his nipple was a circle of darker hairs, much like the shadow of hairs that crowned his cock. I licked around his nipple until it hardened, moving onto the next as my hands held firm onto his large, tensed upper arms.

He did not speak. Nor did I. This was not a time for conversation or words for they would not add to the act I was about to commit.

I pushed off from my seat and slipped further down the bed. Marius let me do so, his hands flexing as if he was unsure what to do with them now I was out of his grasp.

My kiss found his hip. The V-shaped lines that framed his throbbing cock stood out proudly. As I kissed at the space just north of his penis, I ran a nail down those lines, stopping only when his large cock was gripped in my hand. My fingers did not touch as I held onto it. Not like the others I had seen and held before. He was... monstrous. And I could not deny the throbbing warmth that came off it in waves. Warmth that did not bless the rest of his touch.

Only this, his most sacred and magical appendage.

My entire focus had been on teasing him that when I finally pulled back to look up at him, his hand now gripped the back of my head and held firm onto my hair.

"Ah, ah, ah." His voice was husky and deep as he commanded, "Do not stop now. Carry on."

I was suddenly self-conscious, unsure if my lack of skillset would suddenly ruin the mood. But Marius urged my head back down towards his cock until the tip was pressed against my closed, wet mouth.

I allowed it to part my lips, my self-consciousness melting away to nothingness as Marius released a moan so wild it shook the very room. It was impossible to fit the entire length in my mouth, but I felt the need to try as much as I could. Over and over I moved up and down, my speed intensifying alongside the guiding hand at the back of my head.

Marius suddenly sat up, pulling me away with his grip. I glanced up, eyes wet, as he took his spare hand and brought it to his mouth. Spit covered his fingers, his stare held to mine. It all happened in a breath.

Marius brought his wet fingers to my opened mouth and rubbed it across my lips.

"Keep it wet."

"You are full of demands," I told him, licking my tongue across my lower lip, his spittle mixing with my own. "How about you try and keep quiet next time?"

Marius's low laugh made my stomach jolt. "It is you who deserves to be silenced." With that my head was guided back down to his throbbing cock until the tip of it filled my mouth once again.

This was what I needed. A different type of peace that sleep would never been able to gift me with.

My mind could hardly focus on the moment at hand as Marius's groans of pleasure shook the shadows around the room.

I felt powerful as my touch conjured such a reaction. My mouth worked at his cock, but so did my hand.

It was impossible to fathom time. I knew from the slight ache in my jaw that it had gone on for a while and the changing tones of Marius's pleasured sounds.

Suddenly it came to a stop, Marius pulling my face from his crotch with both hands around my cheeks.

"Wait..." he breathed, eyes closed as he focused. His demeanour almost... panicked. I stopped my hand movements but could feel him throbbing in my hold. He was close. I was also breathless as I looked up at him, watching him trying to clamber for control of his body as pleasure burned through him. When he finally spoke I could feel pure hunger rolling off him in waves. His eyes were dark, so dark that it made the paleness of his skin stand out. "I am not finished with you yet. It is your turn."

He moved with such unnatural speed that I was suddenly on my hands and knees, no longer looking at him, but facing the bedding beneath me.

I heard the familiar scratch of wood as he opened the bedside drawer and withdrew the only liquid that made sex with him possible.

I bit down on the sheets in anticipation, waiting for the moment that he would fill me.

Marius had touched me before as I had touched him. And it felt incredible. But there was no feeling in the world that could be replaced by the euphoria when he entered me.

The thought alone saturated my mouth even more than it was already.

His hands grasped harder, fingers digging into my skin as he traced lines up my legs and onto my arse. I peered back to see his wide, unblinking eyes almost entirely obscure.

My breath hitched. "Is something wrong?"

Marius turned his head to the side, clicking his neck and sighing. "I hunger for you, Jak."

The words sent lightning through my blood. Marius parted his panting mouth and exposed the two gleaming points of his teeth.

Even if I wanted to wriggle away from it, I couldn't. Not as he held me firm in place. But I did not... not want to move away from him. He did not scare me, no. What he wanted from me, it thrilled me beyond words.

"Are you in control?" The question croaked out of me.

Marius grinned, tongue lapping across his lower lip. "I can smell you, Jak. All of you. I can feel your very essence pumping wildly through your veins. It is a song. A symphony that I find hard to ignore."

He then paused, wandering eyes settling on my stare and holding it. "But to answer your question, yes, I am in control. No matter how I desire to taste you."

I did not know if it was my own thirst for recklessness or the acceptance that my decision was made, but I invited him.

"Marius, I want you to enjoy me. All of me."

His lip curled above his teeth. "Be careful what you say to me, Jak."

"If you want to taste me..." I breathed, pulling my stare away from him and planting my face back down on the sheets of the bed. "Then do it. I trust you."

Marius's grip tightened on my arse, sending fire through my skin. "Are you certain, Jak? I fear I will not have the restraint to caution again."

I closed my eyes, my body calm. "Do it."

A low rumbling growl emitted from Marius, but I was too nervous to open my eyes to watch. I expected his mouth to find my neck or wrist, a place in which my veins shone blue from my skin. But his kiss found my arse and I melted beneath it.

He left a trail of his wet mouth from cheek to cheek. I gasped, arching my back more as his tongue would lap up against a sensitive spot. Then, as I groaned in pleasure, the cold touch shocked me. Not enough to break the enjoyment. But I felt the change.

The feeling was familiar. Reminiscent to when I would stick my gloveless hands into piles of fresh snow when I was young. Until the tips of my fingers would numb and my palms tingled.

But this sensation spread across my arse, followed by a gentle sucking.

My hand reached back and met hair. I tangled my fingers into it and held him firm.

The feeling of his bite was not painful.

No. But for a brief moment I understood that it would be if he so desired it.

Time, as it did so famously in this castle, fell away from me. I was lost on a wave of pure bliss, eyes slow to open and close as he had his way with me.

I lost my ability to hold a thought as Marius moved from position to position. Kissing, drinking, fucking.

Every time his breathing deepened and became uneven I willed him to calm, wanting this moment to go on for as long as I could muster. I refused to touch myself, even batting his own hand away as he reached for me.

At one point he had turned me on my back so I faced him. His lips were apple red, his teeth stained slightly from my blood. Not a drop ran down his chin. Not a drop wasted. Beads of sweat glistened like crystals across his temple, his chest and stomach flexing with each thrust as he re-entered me from his new position.

"I do not want this to end," I told him, legs hoisted above his shoulders as he ploughed into me from above.

I meant it in more ways than just this sex session. I did not want this stay to end. For the final day to arrive and bring death with it. If I could will for time to swallow me entirely I would.

I pushed the thoughts into the darkest pits of my soul and dragged Marius down to my neck. As his teeth slipped into my waiting skin, thoughts simply faded.

There was only me and him. Marius lost to the rapture of our sex. Myself lost to the intoxicating kiss as he nipped at my skin and sucked on my blood gently.

The feeling we shared built like the beating of drums. With intensity and speed, it continued until we both cried out in sync as we shared in the climax we had so longingly kept at bay.

When we were done I felt lightheaded. I laid on my back, body tingling, as I stared up at the dark ceiling of the room. Marius lay beside me, fingers grazing my own as we waited in silence.

"It did not hurt," I finally said, registering the slight tingle that spread across my neck, shoulder and arse. *Which makes the thought of what is to come less intimidating.*

It was the first thing I had said after Marius had finished within me. I had my hand pressed to my lower stomach, feeling just how slim I had become since leaving home. During the earlier days I ate my fill. But it had seemed that food had become less important now.

"I hate to ruin the illusion, but it *will* not feel the same. It did not hurt but I hardly took more than a sip from you." *Really?* "No matter how I longed for more. You can thank the scraps of control I was able to keep, because as soon as that slips away from me I cannot promise you a painless experience."

The silent pause between us went on for an eternity, only broken by Marius who rolled on his side to face me. "Have I ruined the mood?"

Not as much as I am about to.

The moment we had stopped, the returning sickness within me

took me prisoner. His touch no longer distracted me from my thoughts. It simply stopped holding the door closed within me, allowing them free rein to overwhelm me.

"How long do we have?" I asked, voice cracking.

"Two more nights."

It was so soon. And he was so certain as he hardly took breath before answering. I had never felt the want to claw back something so ferociously before. Time. With the power I kept imprisoned within, it was the one concept I could not control.

Not that I ever felt the need to. Except now. I would give all my magic up if it meant that this did not have to come to the destined end.

"I suppose all good things have to come to an end."

Although I had not yet moved to face Marius, I could feel his gaze burning holes into the side of my face.

"The word *good* will never come close to describing what you are to me. You are far more than a good time. I have had plenty of those. But you, Jak, are something entirely different."

"I am different," I murmured, repeating what I had not long ago said to him.

"You are." His hand brushed across my stomach which tensed beneath his cold touch.

"No, Marius. I am different. Different to what you think I am, and I cannot keep pretending. There is no point for my lie anymore."

I did not reach for his hand to hold it, no matter how I longed to do it.

Marius chuckled nervously, pushing himself up on his elbows beside me. "What is bothering you, Jak?"

"I know what has happened to Katharine." Even the very air between us seemed to come to a standstill. I slipped from the bed, leaving him in it as I stood. Nervous energy bubbled through me. "And I wish I could tell you that she will be okay. But I know the people keeping a hold of her, and they would hurt their own if required. Trust me."

I turned to him and watched him where he sat, eyes glaring and body stiff. It seemed every muscle on his exposed body had tensed as my words settled over him.

"Help me understand, Jak, for I fear your words are only confusing me."

This was it.

I raised a hand before us. Marius's eyes settled on it. I reached far within me to the coiling of fire that waited for my call. And it answered. Deep red flames tickled across my fingers, dancing and twisting until the room glowed beneath the flamelight.

Marius was still, all but his mouth that parted slowly and the lines that cut across his forehead as his brows furrowed.

"I am a witch, Marius, and I was sent here to kill you. And those who sent me have Katharine now as leverage."

It seemed that I was unable to catch a breath as he watched on.

Then the flame across my hand died out. Winked out of existence in a single moment. Just as the room shook beneath the sudden roar that spilled from Marius's split, teeth-bared mouth.

24

"Stay back." Marius's two words felt like a stabbing pain through my chest. They barely came out whole and understandable through the hissing that split from him. His face was pinched, pulled between two different emotions. Rage and... was it sadness or shock? Either way I felt each moment as his glare cut into me like the dullest of blades.

I had not even taken a step before he growled them out at me. All that stood between us was the bed. It would not stop him from reaching me if he desired.

I shook as well, but in a different manner to Marius. My forehead dampened and the room seemed to cave in on me.

"I—"

"You... you tricked me."

"No, yes, Marius, let me explain." I could not grasp onto a single thread of clarity.

Marius fisted the sheets, blue veins protruding from his arms beneath the tension. "Why... why!"

One word, that was it. It was all he could conjure, but it stabbed into my gut nonetheless.

"Because it was what I was brought up to do. I had no choice."

"Everyone has a choice," Marius seethed, spittle flying from his lipless snarl.

"Did you?" I said, quietly and unable to hold his glare. "Because from what I understand you were thrown into this situation just as I have been."

Marius's stomach muscles tensed as he threw himself forward, slamming his palms onto the bed. I was certain I heard a snap of wood. "Do not compare me to what you are! We are nothing alike!"

My throat thickened. I found it hard to swallow the lump that had nestled in it. "I did not mean it like that."

"Then tell me, Jak, what did you mean?" He spat my name out like it was a weapon of its own. I recoiled from it, pressing a hand to my chest.

"You do not need to believe me, but what I want is far different to what my family needs. I have learned more about you in these past weeks than I have in years of study."

"Study!" Marius screeched, gripping the sheets in his hands and clenching them. "I cannot believe I did not see this coming. You have ensnared me in a hex, just like that wretched bitch had. All of this... you are no different. Tricking me into bed, forcing my affection. All to get close enough to kill me."

Victorya was wrong. Marius did not beg for what I could offer him.

I looked to the floor, hoping my hair would fall over my eyes to hide the tears that slipped from them.

"I do not hold that type of power over you." Every word he said to me felt as though another rock had been thrown at my very soul, each leaving a scar across my skin as a reminder. "You are in your right to trust me or not, but I have not only learned more about you but myself. I do not want what my coven desires. If you kill me now, or during the final evening, it would not matter to me."

Marius paused, but I dared look up to him, only to witness yet more distrust crease his handsome, pained face.

"Tell me why they... you wish for my death?" His voice was calm, so much so that I almost spluttered on my breath in relief.

I could have told him that it was not my wish. Repeated it over and over again, but the look upon his face told me that it was too late for that. He did not trust that I did not want it. Nor did I blame him.

"To prevent you from being free," I said, voice cracking, lowering my gaze to my feet.

There was a shift in the air, brushing the hair from my dampening forehead. I looked up to Marius who stood inches before me. I could not breathe. Even as he stared me down, my magic was firmly hidden away in the pits of my being. I hardly felt its comforting, familiar presence.

It kept away from me out of disgust. Or perhaps it knew there was no point to aid me. Not when my mind was made up about this outcome.

"Free? If this is yet another trick, do not—"

"It was prophesied, upon my ancestor's death bed, that a witch would arrive upon the hundredth year of the curse. I would be the first of my kind with ties to magic, that would bring the salvation for the witches or... damnation. If I were to kill you upon the final night, then the curse would be broken and the power that kept you locked away here would no longer be required. It would be restored to those witches who have lived without it. Yet if I failed, and you were to kill me as you had the many Claims before, then the curse would also break. Not in favour of the witches, but yourself. You would be free from these grounds. Free to roam the world. Free to dwell without control or restraint. Free to be... you."

I had to slow my words down as I felt the need to rush and tell him. As though I had never said this to anyone, that it flowed freely out of me.

There was urgency in my tale. I watched Marius's face with intent, punishing myself in memorising his reaction.

He hardly blinked as I spoke, only curling his lips at the mention of the curse.

"And I would return to my previous state?" His voice seemed almost hopeful. My heart pained knowing that he would not. Change with magic was irreversible. It was the power keeping him from leaving that could be reserved.

I shook my head, dropping my gaze to the floor. "I am sorry."

"Then I will never be free." Marius turned his back on me and padded away. I wanted to reach out, to stop him, but my arms were frozen to my sides.

"Do not leave me, please. Take it out on me, I deserve it. I need you to know that I am not like them." I paused, disgusted at myself. "Not anymore."

"I warned myself not to trust. To keep my distance from a Claim for the pain in what was to come was far too great. Then you walked in. With that name. Which makes sense now as to why you have it—"

"I never knew..."

"It does not matter, does it? The damage is done no matter what name you have. No matter what your intentions may be. How did they know about Katharine? Did you inform them of her meddling and have known all along that she suffers the price?"

Adrenaline burst through me at the mention of her. "Marius, I had nothing to do with Katharine. I would not have done that to her. Mother told me that Katharine was caught feeding her own mother your blood. That was what captured her attention."

"So this is my fault?" He turned, arms lifting beside him. Around the corners of my vision, I caught the shadows growing from the sides of the room, throbbing like a wave of darkness that swelled in size, fuelled by Marius's anger. "This is what you are trying to say? And dare I ask how you conversed with the outside world?"

"I had a scrying bowl."

"Had?"

"It is currently lying across the lawn of your gardens in shards of charred pieces. Mother knows that I have failed before the final day. She has seen my change. I did not feel the need to keep my lines of communication open to her for I told her my stance."

"And what is your stance?"

"That I have fallen in love with you. It was never on my strict agenda, but I have. And all Mother and the coven's hopes of retrieving their power back with your murder has simply slipped away. I have come to terms with my choice and will die happy knowing they too will suffer when you finally break free of these barriers keeping you tethered here."

Marius kept my gaze as I opened myself to him. The moment I had finished, I felt myself recoil. Out of embarrassment or shame, I was not certain.

But I had said it.

I waited for him to say something back. To see if my words melted the hardness that had returned to his face. The tough expression that I had not seen on him for a long while.

"When I change I suggest you hide. Do what you can to keep me away from you, and you away from me."

Marius turned for the door and walked towards it. I wanted to call for him to not leave. To plead, demand, beg for him to stay with me.

But with each step away from me I felt my soul break apart. By the time he left me, alone, with his words of warning echoing between us, I feared that I would never be able to piece my soul back together.

Not that it mattered now, the thought taunted through my darkening mind.

It would end soon enough. All of it would. But most of all, *I* would end.

25

I EXISTED through the following hours as though I was drifting through a river. Some moments were calm, and others rough and tumultuous. It was impossible to see when I would allow myself moments to breathe, not thinking about the final night that was creeping closer by the minute. Then I would remember what was to come and my uncontrollable emotions took a hold of me.

Marius kept away from me. Even Victorya did not show her translucent, all knowing face to me. Food was not prepared in the dining hall, nor were the candles relit. Even during the long, wasteful hours of daylight, the castle seemed darker. Colder.

A chill raced over my skin as I studied myself in the gilded mirror that was propped against the wall of Marius's chambers. I was thinner, that much was obvious. Shadows in the shapes of half-moons hung beneath my dulled, viridian eyes. The cream shirt I wore hung off my frame as though it was sewn for someone twice my size, exposing my neck and the two marks nestled among the dark bruising across my skin. Raising a finger to circle the area, it still felt tender and sore. Not as much as it had once the evening with Marius had long faded. The skin around the puncture wounds was raised so my finger trailed over the twin bumps gently.

And all I could do was think of him. Marius.

I longed for his presence. Had to bite down on my tongue to stop myself from calling out for him during the darkest of moments.

But I feared that seeing his disappointed, distrusting face would only shatter me further. And I had a few pieces left that were barely being held together.

In the quiet, lonely hours I contemplated the many ways I would see the final evening through. I knew I could not kill him. Not as originally planned. So I allowed my mind to flirt with other possibilities — ideas of holding him off, keeping him at bay just long enough to see that bastard, red moon fall back into its resting place. It had always been discussed that he must be killed on the final night. Yet the possibility of holding him off until that night was over had never been brought up.

As though it was not a possibility I was permitted to imagine. Not for the sake of Mother and the coven and any other powerless witch surviving out in the large world beyond this castle.

No one had speculated what happened after the moon lowered, giving way for the day that followed.

Only that I would survive, and he would die. And I would simply return home just in time for breakfast the following morning.

I had gone over it in my mind countless times, enough to convince myself that I had hope. A small, simmering gleam of hope that we would both see it through.

Then I would remember that I knew nothing of what I was to face. Victorya was not available to give me insight, nor did the books that Marius had written give any indication of what happened during that final, fateful night.

I had seen him lose control, only slightly, but even Marius had warned it was nothing like it would be.

Remembering I was out of my depth seemed to smother that cinder of hope. A vicious cycle as I navigated the final hours in silence.

Tiredness caused my very bones to ache. It took little effort to stay awake during the evening, lying still in the broken bed, waiting to hear a sign that Marius was still dwelling within the castle. But it was silent.

No familiar footsteps, or chatter.

It was as though I was the only person in the world left.

And that was how I felt, even inside my dreams.

∼

I had left the curtains open, rolling over to see the pink tinge that dusted across the full moon's shape. Every time I looked I hoped to see a white crescent. But its colouring was a signal that I knew well.

Tomorrow night it would begin. *And end.*

I pushed myself away from my haunting reflection, giving up on the hopes of sleeping when daylight finally sliced through the dust-filled air of the chamber. When I blinked it seemed that the lingering moon had embedded itself into my dark mind. A constant reminder of what the following evening was to bring.

In a trance I tugged a jacket around my shoulders, and pathetically tied the laces on the boots up whilst I lost my stare to a point on the wall ahead of me. There was only one thought that held enough energy to keep moving forward.

Marius. I had to see Marius. To find and speak to him.

I moved through the castle, a husk of a boy, hardly taking note of my surroundings. Through the dining hall, up to the door that would lead me to the pits far beneath where I stood. To him.

I gave little care for the door as I threw a hand up, calling for my magic to aid me. My fire was the only element to respond. I conjured the flame to cradle the iron handle until it charred to a malleable, weak point. Then I willed for the wind to listen to my call. Unlike the fire, it was reluctant. I forced much strength into my call until a single gust of sharp, phantom wind slammed against the door and snapped the lock in two.

There was no point in hiding now.

Through the following corridor I moved, bumping carelessly into the wall as it turned and twisted. There was no light here and I did not conjure a flame to help.

On I ambled until the path ended. I did not need light to know that a door stood before me. Covered entirely in chains. The padlock on my side. Keeping something in, rather than out.

He was here. Locked away.

I pressed my hands against the wood of the door and leaned my forehead against its surface. Tears flowed freely as my urgency to see him increased. The slams of my fists echoed through the dark. Each one so loud that it shook my skull. But I continued my torrent of hits and punches, intensifying them until the skin across my knuckles ripped and my fingers dampened with my own blood.

I gripped a hold of the heavy, thick padlock and squeezed, hissing through my teeth as a shout of desperation spilled from me.

Burn. Fire danced across my hands and wrists, illuminating the space before me in orange light. *Burn.* I watched, unblinking, forcing more heat into the padlock. *Burn.* It softened beneath my touch, turning into mush as my fist tightened. *Burn.* There was an echoing of pain that spread across my palm, diluted by the fire that glowed across it. *Burn.* A guttural scream exploded from me as I yanked hard on the padlock. It came away in my hand, the web of chains spilling like useless hair across the ground at my feet. The links had been nailed to points in the wall around the door, even threaded beneath the gap at my feet onto the other side.

Yet the iron pulled away like butter, the chains tethered by my flame.

The faint ringing of metal across stone vibrated through the air as I willed the fire to die, returning it to the warm pits within me until I required its presence again.

It only took a gentle push for the door to swing open.

I stood at the precipice, looking into the midnight cavern. Candles burned in every corner, melted into a monstrous pile of wax from years of reuse. The glow was enough to see the sight that waited.

Old wooden barrels were piled atop one another, some marked with scratched and faded numbers and letters. Wine. They had contained wine. I had seen the very same beside the bar at our local tavern. But those did not look as forgotten and... empty as these. Beside them bottles of dark green glass sat, some holding thin pillar candles, others only filled with cobwebs.

But it was not that sight that sent the lightning of disdain coursing through the layer between my skin and muscles.

An open coffin lid revealing its contents rested steps before me. From my stance I could see the glow of pale skin nestled in a bed of ruby, silk sheets. I stepped towards him, hand to my chest, feeling the violent slam of my heart within. Marius slept, like a child coddled with dark material. He looked so peaceful. His arms crossed over his broad chest, hardly enough room for movement if he wanted.

But he was still. Deadly still as he was lost to his dreamscape.

I knew there was no waking him for I had tried when he slept by my side. During the day it was as if he was non-existent. A body, a shell of a man with nothing inside. Only at night did he truly come alive.

I knelt beside him, reaching out a hand to touch his own.

"I had to see you," I whispered, picking up his soft, relaxed hand and holding it in mine. I expected for his hand to be stiff, but it wasn't. I studied his smooth, lineless face for a reaction. For some proof he heard me, registered my presence. But Marius did not even flinch as I spoke. "It has played terribly on my mind, knowing that I lied to you. I know I will not get to tell you now, but I promise you that I will fight. Fight to keep us both alive through the night."

I brought his hand to my mouth and pressed my lips to it. Tears soaked my cheeks and chin. He was so terribly cold but I held on firm, his familiar feeling welcome when I longed nothing more than him to hold me too.

"We will make it through this night to come and I will spend an eternity making up for my lies to you. I promise." My cry was building into a chest-wracking sob. My vision blurred and my forehead tensed as I tried to catch my breath. "I have no one but you. A stranger, but one I know more than my own mother. My own self."

I gave into the sadness that held me hostage. It was impossible to grasp how long I sat there, in the pits of this dark room. Only when my eyes had dried and legs went numb did I contemplate leaving him in peace. As I reluctantly placed his hand back upon his chest, I noticed something in the grasp of his other hand.

I pried a folded piece of parchment from his fist, hands undeniably shaking. It made it close to impossible to unravel the parchment. Holding it up to the flame of the closest candle, I spoke aloud the line of scripted writing that sliced across the yellowed paper.

Do not hurt him. Remember. Do not hurt him.

It was a note. Written in the familiar curves that Marius had scripted across the countless books in his study.

I read it again. The words both echoing in the room and across my mind. *Do not hurt him.* He had locked himself in this room. Had that been Victorya's final task? *Remember.* I knew he changed, and this only solidified that he became something different. A creature without thoughts. *Do not hurt him.*

No matter his anger and hateful stare as he countered me from across the room, he did not want to hurt *me*.

The note was a warning from himself, to himself.

No, not to himself, but to the creature he was about to become.

26

I woke to a deep, thudding laugh. It took a moment to register it as I broke through the grogginess of sleep. I had fallen asleep, back resting against the wardrobe I had pushed against the bedroom door. It was one of many pieces of furniture I had moved to block the only entrance and exit to the room by foot.

The little sleep I had did nothing to clear the cobwebs that wove from bone to bone, and vein to vein.

I listened carefully for the noise again, unsure if it was an illusion from some already forgotten nightmare. All I could hear was the beat of my own frantic heart and shallow breathing. But then it happened again. A laugh that seemed to shiver in the very shadows of the room. It came from here, but also from far away. A noise impossible to pinpoint.

Yet I knew the deep chuckle and its owner.

The open curtains gave view to the dark of night beyond the room. From my perch on the floor, I could not see the blood moon. But its deep, blood-red glow washed across the night and everything beneath it. As though the full moon had been cut down and it bled profusely across the world.

It spilled into the room, waves of crimson that touched everything before me. I raised my hands and saw nothing but the red glow across my skin. There was no time to scold myself on how long I had been asleep or when I had fallen unconscious. I vaguely remembered my eyes growing heavy but blamed it on the lack of food and the long day. It did not matter now.

I stiffened as the laugh shivered around me. A slow, devilish chuckle that dragged on for countless, horrific moments.

The urge to clap my hands over my ears and pinch my eyes shut thrummed through me. To tell myself that this was the dream and I was, in fact, still sleeping. But if my plan was to work, I had to stay vigilant. And no dream begun in such a way. Those types of dreams had other names.

Regardless if I had been trained for this moment, it did not deter the utter fear and panic that riddled through me.

"Calm down," I said, focusing on my breathing. Marius was strong, likely powerful enough to smash through the barrier I had created with the furniture. But his laugh, although near, was also far. His laugh was different. Raspy and deep, as though it was a multitude of different voices overlapping one another.

I stood slowly from the ground, my body useless to stop him if he wanted to enter. Raising my hands in their readied position, I stood back from the door and deeper into the room.

The moments that followed seemed to drag into oblivion. I kept as still and quiet as possible, trying to pinpoint if he was close. It was impossible to distinguish the violent beats of my heart to the footsteps beyond the room.

"Jak." The voice was a symphony as he drawled my name. "Jak, I am hungry, Jak. So, deeply famished."

I longed for the ceiling to crash down upon me. Marius was close. His last warning to tell me to hide trickled into my consciousness. Instead I waited for him in the first place he would have looked.

More moments of silence followed that was not broken by his voice. No. It was a scratch of nails against wood. The sound was so uncomfortable it itched at my skin and made it cold with sweat. Marius was beyond the door, his nails like scraping blades against the barricaded door.

"Do you not want me now?" Marius whispered like a hurt child. "Let me in, Jak, please. Open this door so we can... discuss matters."

I could not muster a reply. My throat had dried entirely, and my tongue seemed to have thickened in my mouth from fear.

"Let me in so I can be with you." Marius changed his tone to commanding as he partially shouted.

"What is stopping you?" I said back, unable to hide the shake in my voice. "You could enter if you wanted."

Marius chuckled, his laugh turning manic. "Where would be the fun in that... witch? Come now, do not be spoiled. Do I not deserve some... fun?" I jumped back as he slammed his fist into the door, wood cracking beneath the force. "Let me in."

I paced back towards the window which I had left ajar during my preparation.

"I am not letting you in, Marius. I am doing as you wished."

"Do not mistake me for the man you think you knew. We are nothing alike."

Magic swirled within my, now, awakened soul. I had a plan to keep him away and this was only the first step. Tiptoeing backwards towards the window, I kept a keen eye on the door. I did not want to encourage conversation for the fear he would hear my voice moving away.

"Beautiful night, is it not?" I shouted, hoping that would distract him from my distance.

"Delightful," Marius purred. "Red has always been a colour I admired. There is something… passionate about it."

"It is not how I would describe it." My hands fumbled against the dusty windowsill, then to the iron latch that had rusted shut before I had pried it open. "I am fonder of the morning if I am honest."

"Shame you will not see it," he replied so quickly it hitched my breath.

I clambered up onto the windowsill until I was in a perch. Readying the element of air, I willed for it to listen for when I called. Its cooperation was imperative to my next plan. I buried the anxiety of the possibility of falling to my death before Marius got to me. An image of him drinking from my broken, shattered body at the ground far below the window sliced through my mind.

No. Focus.

The night beyond the room was crisp as the air swaddled me. It impressed me just how well the thin glass of the window kept the cold out of the room. It was the final night of the final month of the year and the chill of winter was intense. My jaw clenched as I braced against the chill, twisting my wrists and willing the air to follow my command. It was a simple gesture, but one that would keep me airborne for as long as it required to reach the castle's towering roof.

Looking up, my stomach tugged downward as I took in the height. During the daylight it did not seem so impossible. Now, looking upwards, it seemed that the spires moved away from me before my very eyes.

Focus, Jak, I warned again, my hands shaking at my sides as the wind began to listen.

The trick was to hold one's breath, not wasting precious air on breathing when it was needed to keep me afloat.

I closed my eyes, ready to throw myself backwards into the night when a brush of breath tickled my ear.

I spun so fast from my perch that I tumbled onto the chamber's floor in a knot of limbs. Panting, I pushed myself back up to see Marius climbing through the window.

His gaze was obsidian, not a single slither of white left. His lips sliced into a smile, cutting through his cheeks, exposing rows of sharp teeth.

I crawled away from him as his black-tipped fingers bent the wiry frame of the windows and cracked the panels of glass. One leg inside, then another until he stood before me.

"I thought it would take longer than this." He seemed taller, but crooked. And his tone was almost... disappointed, his low lip pouting slightly as he regarded me. "It would be crude to admit that I was hoping for more of a chase. You have made this far too easy."

This was the creature I expected during my years of preparation. And he was far from the man I had come to know. To love.

This being before me was twisted and dark. His face was not soft, but sharp and creased with lines. His tongue, the very same that had explored every inch of my skin, now lapped hungrily across his pale, almost non-existent lips.

"I did not invite you in," I said, forcing as much strength into my tone as I could muster.

"You seem to forget that this is my home. One I do not need an invitation to do what I desire."

I scrambled backwards until my back was, once again, pressed against my barricade. He could not be here. Not like this. His presence ruined the next steps in my plan in a single, horrifying moment.

"You are speechless... it is becoming of you."

My lip curled upward. "If this is what you warned me of, you do not frighten me."

"Don't I?" He rested his hand on one hip, flashing his fangs. "Shame..."

I looked between the open window, feeling the remnants of wind that was still waiting for my command, then back to Marius. "I do not want to hurt you... trust me."

Marius opened his mouth to respond but was silenced as my power slammed into him.

He did not see it coming. Or perhaps the slither of the man I knew simply underestimated me.

The build-up of power still lingered in my bones, waiting patiently for its release. As I raised my hands, and held my breath, billows of wind thrashed across the room at him. It conjured from nowhere and everywhere at the same time. The force crashed into his chest, doubling him over like a doll, and ripping him from his feet.

The window shattered into pieces, flying out into the night with

Marius. I closed my eyes, waiting for the nick of pain to spread across my uncovered skin as glass rained down around me.

But the wind I commanded kept a barrier of protection.

Once the element was expelled completely from my being, I sagged to the ground, opening my eyes to see nothing but destruction. The nightly, natural wind caused the ripped curtains to dance in place of where Marius had stood seconds before.

Panicked, I pushed myself up and ran for the gaping hole my power had created. I hardly cared as I gripped a hold of the glass covered windowsill and peered out to the ground far below.

I expected to see a broken body amongst the scattering of shattered glass.

But I did not.

There was nothing but curling mist and shadow across the overgrown grounds.

Marius was not there. So much relief burned through me that a single sob escaped my parted mouth. My breathing came out ragged and uneven as I fought the urge not to tumble to my knees.

As far as my sight could allow, I scanned the dark garden, looking for him among the shadows, searching for answers as to how he survived the fall.

Then, as I squinted into the dark, the echoing laugh began again.

27

IT WAS a game to Marius as he stalked me through the castle. His domain of shadow and stone.

For hours we played, me the role of a mouse and Marius the hungry, prowling cat. He did not attempt to get close to me, although I was confident he could if he wanted. Instead he let me run from hiding place to hiding place, laughing and scratching nails against walls as he followed me.

My initial plan had been ruined and my panicked mind did not have time to conjure another as I looked wildly for the next place to keep hidden. It was best to keep moving, not allowing him to trap me in one place.

The castle was barren. As I ran the halls, it was not the same place I had dwelled within thus far. Only the light of the red moon gave visual to the forgotten castle. No candles burned. There was no smell of freshly prepared food, or the usual warmth from the lit hearths in every room.

On this night, it was as though I had woken in a place that had been left neglected and untouched.

I found myself down an unfamiliar hallway, one not blessed with windows which made it blindingly obscure. My hands fumbled across the walls, hoping to find a nock to hide within, or a door to hide behind. Gone was the hope to conjure firelight, for that would alert him to my presence. If he was not already aware.

The slack shirt I wore was now plastered to the curve of my back from sweat. If the noise of my bare, running feet did not scream my location, I was certain my odour would.

Just as my hands found the familiar shape of a handle, a scuffle of noise echoed at the end of the hallway.

Reluctantly I glanced back. For painful long moments the hallway was empty. Then my breath halted as a figure ran across it. In a blink it was there, then gone. My heart filled my throat, beating loudly in my ears. Marius had found me.

With damp hands I fumbled for the door handle and thrust it open. Into yet another dark room I ran into, not bothering to shut the door behind me.

I stood, bathed in darkness, as I watched the door.

Come on. My body vibrated with nervous energy. *Show yourself.*

It had become clear that Marius was stalking me. There was no hiding place he would not uncover. I quickly learned to play along. Not controlling my fear as I longed for the adrenaline that came with it, hand in hand, to aid me when the time came.

"Why did you stop?" His voice was all around me. I spun in frantic circles, trying to search for him in the dark. "Do not make this easy for me, Jak… just when I was beginning to believe you were trying."

The hairs on my arms stood on end as his rumbling, drawling tone shuddered from each corner of the room. I raised a hand ignited in conjured fire to battle the shadows, uncovering that he was not physically in the room.

Not yet.

But his power of the darkness clearly aided him.

"It seems you missed an important lesson," I shouted back, waving my fire covered hand as though it was swordplay.

"Pray tell, what would that be?"

A cold chill raced down my spine as icy breath brushed against the back of my neck. My nose scrunched against the copper twang laced among sweet notes of wine. I was rigid and still as a clawed finger traced up my neck, stopping at the base of my ear.

If I closed my eyes it would have been no different to the nights prior when I lost myself to his touch. Although I felt as though I could simply melt beneath him, I stood rigid.

He had not walked through the door, only securing the suspicion that his mundane chase through the castle, hunting me, room to room, was no more than a game to him. He could move through the shadows. And now he had me.

My voice was weak as I finally uttered a reply. "It is rude to play with your food."

"That was a lesson I must have skipped." His nail traced down from my neck to my collarbone. I could not help but tilt my head as he traced my skin. "Why do you not fight back?" His voice was velvet steel, gentle yet sharp.

My mind seemed to scream to a body that simply ignored it. "Is that what you want?"

Marius moved his nail down to my chest, tugging at the string cords that kept the material over my shoulders. He did not stop until the point of his nail pressed against my naval.

"You burn bright yet hold your flames at bay. I sense your want for me. Is that why you keep your power contained? If you will not fight me, then let me have what I desire…"

I hardly registered as flames dripped from my slackened hands like water. The aged flooring hissed as the tongues of hungry fire took control of the dead wood. I blinked, slowly, as the room lit from the ever-growing blossoms of fire.

Marius made no move away from me, not as the fire melted the leather of his boots or flirted with the material of his trousers.

I gasped at the wet lap of tongue that tickled my neck. My stomach jolted, urging the power to burn hotter, higher.

Marius moaned, wrapping one arm around my back, the other grasping my jaw. "You are the greatest I have tasted. Like honey and sugar, so sweet."

"Stop." As I listened to my pathetic voice, it was as though I watched on in astral form, hardly lifting my hands to bat him away.

"Say it louder," he growled, voice vibrating against my skin as he pressed his lips into my neck. "Then maybe I will listen."

I fought against my own reasoning. It would be easy to give in. To close my eyes and see the end.

"Stop," I said again, lifting my hands before my face. Fire dripped down to my wrists as its unwelcome light seared into my gaze.

Marius hissed and his hold loosened. With the lack of his voice, I regained my control. I pulled away, throwing myself over the rivers of fire that ate away at the room. As though the amber glow had brought me out of a daze, I scrambled away from Marius.

Except he no longer stood in the room. It was only me and the fire that devoured the shadows until every corner of the room was bathed in its light. Strange shapes had been covered in dusted sheets, revealed by the light of my fire. Furniture forgotten from years of disuse. A room lost to the dark years that'd passed, unveiled by my power. Yet Marius was lost to the light, not hiding in the corners where the shadows fought to hold their positioning.

He had fled.

For now.

I pushed myself to standing, unable to ignore the slow movements of my limbs. Marius and his touch had done something to me. Kept me in a dulled, calm state, effects which still lingered. I took a step back towards the door and stumbled over my footing. Each blink slow, that when I opened my eyes the room had seemed to shift.

I felt... drunk, my mind foggy and limbs equally useless.

I gripped the door frame as I reached it, noticing the lack of fire across my hands. Behind me the heat from the remaining flames intensified as the room burned. I squinted back at it, watching my lingering power devour the room entirely. It spread quickly, walls and floor creaking as though it screamed in agony.

I could put it out — stop the flames with a single thought.

But I chose to ignore the notion and left them to feast across the room until fire chased after me when I finally left my compromised hiding spot.

⁓

The fire spread swiftly, devouring the floor I had left and the many above it. I thought back to Marius's study, imagining how the books would only fuel the flames that had become the master of this place. Guilt stabbed at my gut as I ran down the stairs towards the entrance. I had my arm held to my nose to keep the intoxicating smoke from dragging me into an unwanted sleep. One I would not awake from.

Marius did not intercept me. Not as I took two steps at once, practically throwing myself down the flight of stairs to the ground floor. The grand doors were open, giving view of the night beyond, a domain of shadow and the beasts that lurked within it.

Yet I still ran for the exit as more sounds of shattering glass and the loud snaps of wood shuddered through the burning castle.

The kiss of night engulfed me as I stumbled outside. I took mere steps before falling to my knees as the hacking coughs overwhelmed me. My fingers dug into the gravel path, mud sinking beneath my nails, as I willed for my lungs to welcome the fresh air, to battle out all remnants of smoke that dared linger behind.

My ears rang violently. As the sound finally calmed, it gave way to a deep growling. A feral, guttural noise that resonated all around me. I looked up slowly, rigid with fear. The fire from the castle cast enough of a glow to bat away the immediate shadows around me. But among that darkness, barely an arm's reach away, was a host of glowing red eyes.

Unlike Marius, his bloodhounds lacked the sophistication and patience to stalk me. Even as I stood on the path, they lacked the rules that Katharine had explained. I supposed rules did not apply during an evening of such horrors.

I sensed its rushed move before its shadowy claws left the dirt ground to pounce for me.

Deeper into the damp, dirt ground, I dug my hands in until my fingers became the very roots that dwelled far beneath me. I called for the earth, urging it to be my protector.

The ground rumbled and split. The level of energy required snatched my breath away. I pinched my eyes closed moments before hearing a wheeze as a root speared through the gut of the bloodhound. Opening my eyes, I saw rows of teeth inches before me, frozen in air as yet more feral roots joined the first. They wrapped around the creature's dark fur, containing its thrashing and snapping jaws.

It is yours. I forced the thought through my hands and deep into the ground. The earth did not linger on my gift. The creature thrashed, feeble attempts to break free. But more roots broke through the ground and encased it, a den of wooden vipers, dragging its feast into their lair.

I sensed the reluctance from the other bloodhounds that watched their foolish pack member disappear beneath the earth.

A warning of what would become of them all.

I lowered my gaze and snarled, baring teeth at those who gazed at me, my own growl of warning echoing around me.

Then the laughing began again, breaking the moment like glass shattering in fire. The pack of bloodhounds parted for the creature that walked between them. One step at a time, his white skin illuminated beneath the ruby glow of the moon and orange flare of the fire.

Marius.

He looked up at the castle behind me, lips twitching as he studied its destruction. "Your kind destroyed my love, my life, and now my home. I see now that you do not run from me, but merely beg for me to punish you." A blink and he was before me, strong hands clamped around my jaw as he lifted me from the ground. "And punish you I shall."

28

I GRIPPED a hold of his hands, thrashing my legs out at him in panic. It felt as though my head would implode beneath the pressure, both hands pushing inward as he lifted me from the ground. All I could do was scream, unable to truly hold onto breath as I fought hard to get out of his grasp.

"You are mine." His muffled hiss hardly registered as I kicked out at him. Marius did not flinch beneath each blow. Pain vibrated through my feet, feeling as though my bones would shatter. But I did not stop.

I clawed my nails down his hands and arms, even thrashing out at his face. All of which he hardly batted an eye towards. Not even as deep droplets of ruby blossomed beneath the cuts I left across his face. Only his tongue escaped his firmly, closed mouth to lap up the droplet that dared fall near it. Before my eyes the marks healed, fresh skin knitting together until his face was once again perfect. Untouched.

I began to beg, his large hands muffling my panicked pleading. "Marius, let me go. Please. Please, Marius."

"Your attempts are wasted, and here I was led to believe you were prepared for this very moment."

I could not mutter a word as his hands clamped harder on each side of my face. I felt my cheekbones scream beneath his touch.

My vision doubled. Tripled. Until the corners of darkness began to close in around me. All I could do was look into his obsidian eyes, searching to see a part of his true self. Hoping the Marius I knew would look back at me and registered what he was doing and stop.

I gave up on my fight, losing energy quickly. Just the thought of calling on my power simply slipped between my fingers. "Please..." I managed again, voice a weak croak. "You are hurting me."

The world dropped out from beneath me in a single moment. I felt nothing as I hit the ground, his touch lingering on my cheek. My neck ached, a terrible pain that spread down my spine and up through my skull.

He had dropped me, my knees now leaking blood from the torn skin and ripped trousers.

Looking up at the looming figure above me, I willed for my vision to calm.

"I wish you had more fight left in you," he growled. "It is a true shame that my feast is too pathetic. So... weak. Promised resistance and I am left with you. I do hope your taste is worth this embarrassment you display."

"I... I will not fight you Marius."

He sneered, teeth bared, "Why!"

"Because I love you. I told you I would not hurt you and I... I hold myself to that promise."

Marius, or the creature he had now become, sucked his teeth in disappointment. "Then let us end it now. I have grown tired of waiting, which is spoiling my appetite. If you refuse me entertainment, then I give up encouraging it."

I rocked back on my hands, slumped in a heap on the ground. All around me the prowling bloodhounds reappeared through the darkness as their leader took steps towards me.

"Marius, if you can hear me, please do not do this." The sky above was lightening slightly, suggesting the arrival of dawn. Had it really been that long? I was tired, exhausted, my body a mess of aches and pains — mine not swiftly healing as Marius's did. It still could be hours away, the red stain across the sky still ever-present.

"*He* is not listening. This is my night, the boy you call for is not present." Marius smirked, dark eyes flashing. "You should know this. More than I. For it is your power that created me."

"I rebuke what they did to you," I spat, broken slabs pinching at my palms as I scrambled away from him. "What she did to you... was wrong."

"She, you. Does it truly matter who tightened the bowstring or who created the arrow? For the outcome is the same. And I am hungry. I admit I have never talked so much with my supper. They usually scream and give in to the hunt long before this point." Marius stopped before me, the bloodhounds faltering to his side where they bared yellowed, serrated teeth. "Stand. Meet your fate."

I winced as I followed his command, not from fear, but from the blast of heat as yet another window exploded from the castle. Bricks crackled and charred as the fire burned on. Marius utterly unfazed that his home was destroyed, crumbling before him with each passing moment.

He hardly looked towards it this entire time, unable to take his hungry focus from me.

"I will not give in to you."

"And you believe I need your acceptance?"

I shook my head ever so slightly, not once taking my gaze off his. "You can try but dawn will arrive and you will go without feeding." Iron laced my words, the bitter taste of determination rearing its head for a final time.

Panic widened his stare, only enough for me to notice. His lips thinned, straightening into a pinched line. Spittle lined both lips as they finally broke into a snarl. "I *will* feed."

Fire.

I unravelled my fists either side of me, opening them like a rose in spring, buds of orange flames twisting in warning. "You will try and fail. Then morning will return, and with it my Marius will return. You will return to me."

Marius's snarl intensified into a growl that seemed to vibrate through the very night. The bloodhounds at his sides echoed his anger at my taunt, each bowing their dark-furred bellies to the ground in preparation for a signal.

Air.

The world around the burning castle began to scream as the winds picked up. A gust of conjured pressure that blew through the grounds, forcing dirt and debris to swirl in torrents around my feet. The fire that reached beyond the destroyed windows bent beneath its force, longing and reaching to join in with the whipping wind's race.

Marius shifted his weight to take a step forward but I gathered air in my lungs and released it slowly, encouraging the wind around us to strengthen in a barrier.

"I will not kill you, Marius, but my life's preparation will not go to waste. You will see."

Water.

The tear that escaped my eye was not from sadness. No. It was the invitation for the fat droplets that began to fall from the sky. I did not need to look up to know that pregnant clouds coated the sky as the red tint from the cursed moon dulled, covered by my power. Rain crashed down upon my head, my skin, hissing as the droplets fell into the balls of flame that were cradled in my waiting palms. I risked a blink, enough to loosen yet another tear. Then the rain thundered down upon us. Each droplet that splashed against my body made me feel refreshed.

Revitalised beneath the kiss of the element's calming, all-knowing power. It thrummed within me, and around me.

Earth.

I grinned, looking through the sheets of rain as Marius teetered side to side. Beneath him the ground shook violently. A gasp of surprise broke his façade as his footing was lost to yet another tremble that jerked beneath him.

"Enough with your games!" he shouted above the elements. Marius raised a clawed hand to shield the lashings of rain and wind that battered against him. It blew the stark, white hairs from his head, exposing glowing skin and hateful eyes. I could not hear what he said next over the howls of his creatures that pounced frantically beside him. He seemed to shout as his mouth opened into a circle of dark oblivion.

Then the bloodhounds attacked.

All at once they threw themselves as balls of shadow, teeth and fur. Time seemed to slow as they each left the ground, throwing themselves with split jaws, towards me.

I cried out, fuelling my emotion into the fire in my hands. I sensed each tongue of flame that burned in the castle. Even the licks of candle-light in the town far away, beyond the barrier of this place. As I willed for the element to aid me, I became it. And it became me.

Light exploded before me, a wave of flame that burst from my hands and grew into a monstrous wall between me and the bloodhounds. I poured my very desperation into the element, causing the heat to intensify and the wall of flame to only burn wild and hot. I half expected the creatures to pass straight through. Like darkness through worn, hole-ridden drapes. But I sensed the bodies of shadow hiss and wink out of existence as they met my power. Not a hair passed successfully through my barrier. It devoured them entirely. Light ended the darkness. Heat destroyed the cold touch of death.

I could no longer see Marius beyond the wall of flame, but I sensed him. In the back of my mind I knew that I could let the wall fall upon him and he would, like his creatures, be destroyed. Like pleading song, I almost gave into it. The power had a mind of its own. I sensed its hunger much like that of which Marius spoke about.

It wanted him. To take his life and return the power that thrummed within him to the witches scattered around the world. All it would take was a thought. A will and the fire would end this.

But in the reflection of the hissing light, I saw the soft face of the boy that hid deep within the creature that currently hosted his body.

I thrust my hands inward, urging the fire to retreat and gather back within me. It rushed for me, like a child returning to its father.

The other elements raged around me, each out of my control as I focused solely on the fire. They would wait for my command. But for now I had to fight the siren song to release my magic entirely and kill him.

The world was suddenly dark again. Only the fire that burned within the castle provided light. My hands were empty and mundane as I surveyed the emptiness before me.

No Marius. No bloodhounds.

Just me and the darkness.

At least that was what he wanted me to believe.

Before I could call out into the dark beyond me, panicked that my power had in fact reached him, a force of shadow slammed into my stomach. I dropped to the ground, winded, clawing at my neck and chest in hopes that it would help hold onto breath.

"So it is me and you. You have got what you want, now it is my turn to play my part."

Another slamming of power collided into me, this time knocking me to the sodden ground. My hands fumbled pathetically to soften the fall but failed miserably.

Laid on my back now, I could hardly keep my eyes open against the rain that crashed upon me. One blink followed by another.

Then the force of a body pressed down above me and a face leaned over me, protecting me from the rain. I finally blinked the water from my eyes.

"I will savour every drop and stop only when you are entirely empty."

I could not use my hands and call forth the fire for his weight kept me pinned to the ground, his hands gripping like shackles onto my wrists, preventing me from lashing out with flames.

Sucking in an inhale of air, Marius clamped a hand down over my mouth to prevent me from exhaling. The gust of air that barrelled within my chest burned me from the inside out, an energy in need of escape that stormed through me.

Marius did not speak again, instead leaning his split mouth towards the curve of my neck. There was no fighting, no kicking or punching, no strength I could muster.

So I did what he longed to do and bit down into his skin. The flesh of his hand was tough, but soon broke to my desperation. A wash of cold blood filled my mouth, threatening to choke me. Taste of copper and, something sweet, like honey. It exploded in my mouth, trailing down my tongue and cheek as though I had no choice but to devour it.

Energy flooded back into my being as his blood entered me. Fuelling me.

Marius threw his head back in a roar, releasing his hold enough for me to heave a blow.

The gust of wind that followed threw him from me as though his body was a feather. Forgotten and light. I forced every ounce of breath from my body until my head tightened and my chest spasmed with longing. The cold droplets of his blood spread down my chin, tickling as it covered my neck and chest.

I did not wait to see where Marius was thrown to. I forced myself from the ground once again, wet with his blood, and bolted.

Towards the barrier at the edge of the castle I ran, blindly throwing my free hands behind me, commanding the ground to split, the air to scream, and the rain to become shards of frozen glass, my attempts to keep him from me.

I did not stop until the barrier was before me, the invisible ending of the castle and where the world beyond began. I stopped only when I collided with the rippling surface of the barrier, slamming panicked, urgent fists against it.

Yet it stayed strong, impenetrable. I turned to face the world behind me, pressing my back against the cold layering of shadow that kept me from leaving.

The castle burned. Now a skeleton of brick and stone. Materialising from the shadows, Marius stalked towards me, a grin cut across his pale, deathly face.

"Nowhere to run. Nowhere to hide. Jak, you will not be able to keep this up. Not for long. You have power, enough from the starved witches that had stayed empty since the curse was laid upon me. But even you will have your limits. And I am ready to discover where they begin. And end."

29

I THREW everything I had at him. Every ounce of magic and energy. With each, thin and quick breath, I commanded the elements as my soldiers. My guard. And it listened, willingly. Volleys of wind, fire and water. Time slipped through my fingers as I lost the ability to think of anything but keeping him from me. It was easy at first, manipulating the emotion that roiled inside of me, feeding it to the elements as they raged as my protection. All whilst my back was pressed to the wall of shadows keeping me, and him, from leaving this cursed place.

I watched in horror as the skin melted from Marius's face as a wave of flame raced across him. It was a moment of tiredness. A lax in my judgement as I did not keep the element from harming him. All control slipped from my hands as I watched, a rasped scream echoing between us, as the fire devoured his skin.

My stomach jerked and twisted, bile creeping up my throat as I pulled the flame back. But I was too late.

Marius was caught in a roar, hand raised to do little as the wave of fire cascaded over him. As he lowered his hand, skin had been burned back to reveal bone. The side of his face less fortunate against the brunt of my wild power exposed the skull beneath, gleaming and pristine, dripping with melted flesh.

I wanted to call his name but my voice was a muddle of rasps and croaks. My throat so dry that each inhale and exhale seemed to encourage a symphony of knifes to cut across it.

His cry of pain and shock soon ceased. One moment it filled the night, next not even my power dared make a noise. The world was silenced. Had I gone too far? Even as I blinked I could not rid myself of the image of melting flesh against charred bone. Had I completed what I had been fated to do?

Marius raised his hand before us and we both watched as skin creeped back over bone. His pale flesh was like a small wave of water lapping back across a sand bank, leaving moisture in its wake.

He was healing, fast, before my eyes.

Marius twisted his wrist, displaying the feat with pride. My focus was entirely on the miracle before me. Dead and burned flesh, healing over, new and fresh.

When he lowered his hand, it revealed his fang filled grin, the last of the skin knitting back across his sharpened cheekbone. "You had me for a moment." Marius clicked his head to the side, the sound painfully loud over the thundering of rain that persisted around us. "I admit, even I was frightened."

My arms ached as I raised them back in defence and threat. "Next time it will burn through bone." I did not believe my warning, and from his intensifying smile, neither did Marius.

He released a hearty laugh at the cracking of my voice. "We both know that you would not maim me. You could have done that a long while ago."

If it was not for the constant force of the barrier behind me I would have fallen to the ground with exhaustion. Dwindlings of fire returned to my palms, but not the strength that it had been before. Even the winds died down to a gentle whisper and the rain calmed to a soothing shower.

"Let this end, give up." Marius walked towards me, sidestepping the curling of fire that I had thrown, missing his foot by inches. "You have fought hard but I sense you're willing to give up. Listen to it. Denying it will not help you in the end. And the end will come."

My stare faltered on his walk, catching the faint limp in his leg. It was so subtle I could have missed it. Then I noticed how his lip curled upward with each step.

He was hurt. Not healing completely as he should have. Marius, although seemingly unharmed, was exhausted.

And the clearing of the clouded sky revealed why.

Gone was the dark of night, but the deep blue of dawn's warning.

A rush of hope thrilled through me at the sight, followed by the pop of a laugh that escaped me. "It would seem you are nearly out of time."

The spark soon exploded into a wildfire of hope that filled every inch of my being.

Marius looked upward, eyes squinting towards the brightening sky. A wince pinched across his face. The piercing red that filled the sky was now pink, dulled by the blue of dawn.

"Enough of this!" Marius face creased with feral panic. Desperation turned his face into a mask of hard lines and pointed fangs. He lunged forward with speed that was unstoppable. Before I could will my magic to help, his hand was around my throat, the other gathering both my wrists and squeezing them together. The bones in my arms and hands felt as though they could shatter, his grip intensified by his urgency.

A nail dug into the side of my neck, piercing my skin with ease.

"Ahh," Marius sighed, dark eyes skirting over everywhere but my own. I could do nothing in his grasp. Not as my head throbbed, longing for air. But his hold kept that from being possible. "Enough time has been wasted."

I closed my eyes, the spark of hope extinguished as his mouth closed in towards my neck. His tongue met my skin first, lapping roughly across the cut that his nail had gifted me. I wanted to cringe away as I felt his entire body tremble with excitement.

This was it. I had tried to prolong this moment, hoping for my own selfish reasons that I would see morning and pass the fateful evening. As his fangs pressed into my skin, I felt a trickling of calmness rush over me.

For me it was the end, but for Marius... it was the beginning. I focused my stare on the lightening sky, hands hanging uselessly by my sides. There was no pain. No agony that I expected. It was the sensual pulling that I had experienced with him in his bedchamber. As he drew blood from me, he took my warmth with it. Starting at my toes, my feet numbed with each deep intake.

But still the pain did not arrive.

Only... relief.

"One feels strange watching on." A voice sounded behind us. I thought it was an apparition until the pressure of Marius's fangs relaxed and he growled, lifting his face from the crook of my neck. All of a sudden that seeping, draining feeling ceased and the warmth kept huddled in a ball deep in my chest. "I did not mean to stop you, goodness no. How terribly ill-mannered interrupting one's... dinner party without an invite."

I believed to have felt fear before this moment. But a new stabbing of horror buried into me at the realisation of whom it was that spoke. The feeling was like drinking water after wine —in that moment, my attention and understanding snapped back to reality.

"Mother."

I could not turn around to see the truth behind me, stood beyond the barrier. Not as Marius's grip on my wrists tightened. The rumbling growl deepened as he hissed towards those who stood beyond my sight. With a sharp tug he turned me around, forcing me to stand before him, one arm around my throat, keeping my head upward, and the other around my waist. I felt like a lost lamb, entrapped within the coils of a snake, looking on at a far greater predator.

It was not only Mother who stood beyond the rippling wall of shadow. Hooded figures of the coven stood with her, each holding lit torches and other, gleaming objects with sharp pointed ends.

And there, exposed to the cold chill of morning, stood Katharine. Hair shaved violently close to her scalp, exposing raw cuts and wounds across her head. She trembled, shoulders bent inward as she did her best to cover her thin, frail body with the scrap of dirtied material that wrapped around her.

This was Mother's final attempt. I could see it in the widening of her eyes. An attempt at a distraction to give me time to end him.

"I fear I missed all the fun." She spoke, her voice painfully calm. "Apologies for the extra guest I have—"

"Do it," I snapped, pushing up against Marius as much as I could. "Finish it now."

I spoke to him and only him. Mother's appearance changed everything.

"A waste..." Mother began, folding her arms across the dark cloak that she wore. "Such a handsome man locked away in this castle for all these years. If I had known of your beauty, perhaps I could have visited as a Claim myself." My stomach turned at Mother's comment. Marius's hold on me tightened. "Goddess knows I would have finished off the task at the end of it. Something my dear son seems to have failed at."

"You look just like her," Marius seethed, spittle and blood dripping onto my shoulder. "If you would have visited I would have taken pleasure in draining you long before the final night."

"For a creature that is so feared and spoken about, you sure are able to string sentences together well. Even on the fateful night. I would have expected a more beastly creature, one who did not enjoy conversation when all he wanted to do is feed."

"You want the beast?" His voice deepened, causing the shadows to curl inward around us.

Mother leaned on one hip and spat, "Well, go on then. Show me. For I look upon not only one, but two pathetic beings. Do as you will with my boy, our kind have adjusted to our pending fate. Yet you will not see the next night either way. I sense it now, the curse on this place weakening. Soon enough the barrier will fall and you will let go of this hungry creature. Jak will die and you will follow. You can either take your fill, the outcome for you and Jak will be the same. But hurry." She glanced up to the sky only slightly, both the corners of her painted lips turning upward. "I give it a few minutes until the sun rears its beautiful face for us all to see."

I followed her stare to the brightening sky. It was light enough that I could see the sleepy town materialise in the distance.

There was hesitation in Marius's grip. A moment that I almost missed as his hold on me relaxed slightly, nails no longer digging into my skin. Yet he did not let go completely.

"Do it," I whispered my plea. "You will be free."

Mother winced as I admitted aloud the outcome that was moments away. I was ready for the end as desperately as Marius was ready for the feast.

He leaned in, cold breath tickling my neck once again. Then he spoke. Subtle words that shattered me into a million pieces.

"I will never harm you again."

His voice was soft in nature. It rumbled slightly, as though he fought for a place in this conversation. I feared that Mother would sense my stiffening and know something was amiss.

"Finish him off, but forgive the aftertaste of failure when you are done," Mother cooed from her position beyond the weakening barrier.

Marius kept his mouth hovering above my neck as he spoke again but his hold on me softened, enough for me to feel but not for Mother to see. "It is me."

My body trembled violently, so much so that Marius had to return the strength to his hold to keep me standing. Deep within I felt the power raise its heavy head as I readied it for what was to come.

Marius breathed his next whisper. The words jagged like a blade, edged and commanding. "Unleash hell, Jak."

It happened so fast that my breath was snatched away from me. Marius pushed me towards the barrier with a roar. I raised my hands, expecting to collide with its layering, but passed through to the surprise of Mother. Into her unexpecting arms I fell, knocking her to the floor.

We tumbled across the paved ground, rolling over limbs as she tried to push me from her. But I became dead weight from my own surprise and confusion.

"No!" someone shouted as I came to a stop among reaching hands. Countless hands from the hooded figures of the coven yanked me from the floor. Mother batted those who dared reach for her. She stood, straightening herself as we all now watched on at Marius who towered in front of Katharine.

"Fool," Mother screamed, her shrill voice that of the dreaded banshee. "You dare play games with me?" If her pointed finger was a weapon, Marius would have been dead ten times over. Her arm shook as she kept it raised towards Marius.

But he looked at me with a pleading, sorrowful gaze. "Fight back."

"You are free," I murmured, eyes brimming with tears.

I could not do anything. Not as the glare of Mother turned to me. In seconds she was before me, blocking my view of Marius. A line of coven members formed between both parties, brandishing their weapons in shaky grasps, each aimed at Marius whose stance was bent and ready to move as he watched them.

"I would take your next steps carefully..." Mother spoke to Marius, but her stare did not leave mine. Not even to blink.

"The barrier is down, the curse is broken and he is free." Spit splashed across her face as I pulled as close as I could to her. But I felt the resistance as those who held me stood strong. "I fail with pride knowing you will die by his doing. That, Mother, is the just ending."

Mother hushed those who held me away like she was swatting bees. Her bony fingers reached for my shoulder and squeezed. Although she was powerless, her touch was enough to silence me. She leaned into me, forehead pressed to mine as she replied, "Then you will die with the same pride."

Confusion pinched lines across my forehead, my eyes searching her face for a sign of a lie. But as she looked up again, a single tear slipped from the corner of her eye.

She cried, but not from sadness or grief. It was something else, something more.

I wanted to shout for Marius as the blade concealed in the folds of Mother's cloak came free. Wind blew at her blue-black hair, pushing each strand from her face so it was impossible not to see her expression. Lines creased over her forehead and I was certain she was shouting.

But the sound did not reach me. No noise did.

One moment the blade was cutting through the air between us, the next sharp tip sliced across my throat.

One fell swoop that was painless. For a split moment I could not register that it had happened as my hands fumbled to discover the truth.

Red. The tips of my fingers were red. Confusion spread through me for a moment, but soon melted away. My mouth parted and I took a breath, gurgling as blood popped like bubbles deep in my throat.

A spray of red splashed across Mother's unblinking, wide stare. That one tear no longer the only thing wetting her face.

But before I could feel the warmth of blood spreading down my body, I was overcome with a chilled, soundless darkness. My eyes met Marius's for a moment. I smiled.

Then nothing.

Just the sweet, calm, uncontrollable lullaby of death greeted me.

30
MARIUS

My body was a prison of agony. Hot, stabbing hunger gripped a hold of my gut and twisted. The pain almost knocked the wind from my lungs, buckled my knees, made my world spin, gripping its sharp talons into my stomach with relentless demand. Yet the feeling was no more painful than the itching that began to spread across my skin. A fire, far greater than what Jak had not long wielded, burned away at me, brought on by the skimming of dawn that washed over the world.

I did not run for cover, not as I watched the river of red spread down his neck, bathing his chest until the dirtied, cream shirt was stained beyond repair. How the colour of life drained from his face, his features relaxing as though he fell into sleep with his wide eyes left open.

So this was what it was like. Death. Inconsolable death, something I had wished upon myself more times than I could count. Usually, when my Claim passed by my doing, I was still in the dissociation brought on by the curse. But Jak had done it, kept me from feeding until daybreak. I had come to hold him in my arms, my teeth grazing his soft, welcoming neck. It was a harsh yanking feeling that felt as though I had woken from a nightmare, gasping for breath as a newborn would.

Jak — despite successfully breaking the curse — had gifted me with a new curse. To watch as he died before me. No longer blessed with being unaware. Detached.

I did not blink. Refused to look away for a moment as the light drained from his beautiful eyes. Eyes I had looked deeply into as I held him. How they would gleam from within when he caught glimpses at me, or spoke on topics he adored. Eyes that I had made weep. Now the bright colouring of blue seemed to fade away to a pale grey, a coating of nothingness passing over them as his stare was lost to me.

One moment he was there, eyes pleading with my own through the windows to his soul. Then like a flame on a candle he was gone. Snuffed out.

"Jak." I registered the lyrics of his name. Did I speak it? Did someone else dare say it aloud?

I waited for him to register the call and respond. To lift his beautiful, soft-angled face with that smile, the one which lifted from the left corner of his mouth more than the right. The smile that creased three lines beside each of his eyes. How it peaked his brow in an expression that screamed mischief.

I registered nothing but him. Watching his death stilled the hunger that scratched across my consciousness. It nullified the pang of hunger. Like the inside of a shell, my breathing echoed throughout my ears, silencing anything else around me.

It did not last, this peaceful moment as I watched death take him.

My own pain intensified as the sun finally threatened to break the curve of the earth.

Wait. I willed the morning to listen, my shadows slipping away from me as the light joined the funeral. *Please, wait.*

She spoke, the woman whose greedy grip held onto Jak, the knife still in her hand, dripping blood across the ground. "Come and fetch *him.*" Her arm loosened around him. My Jak. She spoke again, but I did not register, not over the roaring anger that beat through me.

The noise of his blood dripping across the ground was terrible. Alluring and deadly. My eyes flicked to it, mouth parting, as I watched each splash.

"Jak." His name again, this time I felt the tug of my lips as I finished speaking. Shouting. I was shouting.

The woman smiled and released her hold on him. One push and he was no longer held upright. His body collapsed beneath him. He fell. I moved.

In a blink he was in my arms. All I could register was his touch, as cold as mine, as blood raced rivers across my torn, charred jacket. I lowered his stiff body to the ground, my hand carefully cupping the back of his head. Someone was crying. Was it me?

I barely felt the growing discomfort anymore, not as I lay him down. All I could focus on was him. Jak. His blood. How it never seemed to stop from pumping out the jagged slice across his neck. I reached my finger for it, fighting the urge to pop a digit in my mouth.

Then a hand reached for my shoulder. A nailed finger, tapping for my attention.

I turned, eyes narrowing against the sudden glare of light. Then the person's body moved in view of the growing dawn and I saw her smile. Her thin lips parted, revealing the line of perfect white teeth behind them.

"Being locked away all these years... I feel that it is only just I let you watch the sunrise in peace. See it in its glory and know that you will meet my pathetic son in whatever hellscape you visit in the afterlife."

I registered the murmuring of the group of cloaked figures behind her. And Katharine. Sweet, young Katharine whose scent screamed of fear and panic. She was splayed across the ground, expression a jagged slice of anger and sadness. Her round eyes wet, her lips turned in a snarl.

"Kill them..." I read the shapes of her mouth more than I heard her. The command. Perhaps she spoke something else entirely, but all I could do was think it. Kill them. Kill them.

Devour them.

I looked back to the woman who stands above me, a statue of stone carved from hate.

Her grin hardened. And I smiled back.

"You look just like her," I said, voice a rumble of deep, scratchy tones. "And I often dreamt of what it would be like to devour her blood after she cursed me."

The woman, Jak's mother, lifted the dagger and placed the bloodied tip into the skin of her palm. "And what did you think she would taste like? Sweet revenge, or regret?"

My hold on Jak, his terribly cold body, shuddered as I begun to shake. "I don't know. But I suppose I am about to find out."

Her expression faltered and she parted her mouth to spit yet more hate. But this time I did not let her.

In a blink I was before her, my teeth clamped around her neck. She bled freely into my mouth. I sucked. Hard. Harder. Drinking every ounce of her as the warmth of morning intensified.

But her life source filled me with a renewed strength. So I drank on.

No one dared to interrupt.

She could not speak for my bite had ripped into her throat so deeply that only pathetic gurgling could be heard as she struggled.

The batting of her nails against me soon stopped and her arms hung limply at her sides. Her weight fell into me, dead and stiff. Like her son who lay at our feet.

I registered the knife embedded in my gut as I pulled back from her. Looking down, neck straining, I saw the hilt and grabbed it. The slick, wet song made me cringe as I pulled it from me, still gripping onto the dead body in my arm.

There was no pain, not with the thundering of fresh, weak yet powerful blood, joining my own. I cocked my head back, releasing a sigh as her blood began to dry across my chin.

"It tastes like neither," I spoke to the sky as the euphoria of the feed took me captive for a moment of bliss.

When I was done with her, I did not lower her to the ground gently but simply discarded her with a push.

The sound of her skull cracking against the slabbed ground was a blessing. It echoed through my own mind on a pleasing loop. One I never wished to forget.

I did not bother to wipe the blood from my mouth and chin, not as I roared in the wake of the coven which was already fleeing back towards the waking town. Not a single person stayed to fight. Pointed stakes of wood and sharpened kitchen utensils were discarded across the ground, pointless.

"You need to get to cover." Katharine's kind voice registered somewhere within the internal roaring. "Do not die on me too."

Her words were the anchor I needed from the euphoria. As her soft touch laid across my shoulder, I was brought back to reality.

To this living hell.

I turned to face Katharine who threw her arms around me. She was shaking, violently. Yet I could not find the strength to hold her, not as I looked back to where Jak lay across the ground, whose face was turned away from me.

I winced as more light joined the sky; the first rays of morning finally sliced into existence.

"We need to go now," Katharine murmured.

"Jak." I said his name aloud, hoping he would simply roll over and face me as he had so many evenings with me beside him. But he was still.

Katharine tugged at my arm, but I pulled away from her. I would not leave him, not beside the stiffening body of his mother. Stepping over her, I moved for him, Katharine's pleadings becoming frantic. Jak's head lolled backwards as I lifted him from the ground, his limbs hard and his body heavier as death truly took a hold of him.

Katharine was already moving towards the castle, beckoning to follow. And I did, slowly, allowing the discomfort to become true, burning pain as the light bathed over me. If I slowed to a stop, would I die with him? Together. The thought did not scare me. But Katharine, she caught my attention. I could not leave her behind.

The ruins of the castle were now empty of Jak's fire; it had died as the knife was slashed across his throat. Only thick tendrils of smoke remained, walls of grey and silver which seeped up into the sky.

And towards the remains I walked, away from the now destroyed barrier keeping me from the world. I walked towards the charred memory of my life, my death, my eternal. I walked with him in my arms.

Victorya did not greet me as I stepped over the boundary. Nor did the other phantoms of my past as I made my way, from memory, towards the tunnels that would lead to the untouched chamber of darkness.

Katharine led the way, bare feet patting across the ruined floors. I gifted myself small moments to look up as I followed her, quickly snapping my focus back to the boy in my arms.

To Jak.

My Jak.

It had never ended this way. With me aware as I held the remains of a Claim. Not since the first. Not since I carried another boy named Jak. Full circle. That was how it felt.

I felt tired. More so as we finally stepped beneath the shattered doorway into the shadowed pathway which led to the underbelly of the castle. Only the smell of burning stone and wood lingered here.

It did not matter. His fire could have burned this entire place until it was nothing more than ash. I would not have cared. Not if it meant he was alive.

With me.

Seeing through to morning as he had wished.

I believed Katharine was talking. To me or herself, I was not sure.

There were no words I could muster in return, not as I willed to share in the same deathly silence of the boy in my arms. I feared that I would speak and miss a movement from him. A subtle noise or pinch of his expression that would prove that this was all an illusion. A nasty joke he played on me.

Then I stopped, bumping into Katharine who blocked the way ahead. I then looked up and saw that we were in the small chamber. Melted, broken chains lay at our feet. Did I break out? Did the fire burn them? The padlock was a mess of melted iron.

"You should lay him down, Marius."

I wanted to refuse her aloud, but I barely managed to shake my head to disregard her suggestion.

Then her small, dirtied and worn hands reached for Jak cautiously. "I understand you're hurt. Believe me. But you must lay him to rest."

"He is still bleeding," I croaked, voice hoarse and throat sore. "I pushed him towards her, it's my fault. And he still bleeds, long after his mother has stopped bleeding herself."

"Rest him in the coffin, Marius, lay him down."

Did she not hear me?

I stared at the blood, how it now looked deep obsidian in the dark room. A river of black blood now covered my arms, chest and hands.

But not once did I dare reach down and taste. I was not full, far from it. But the feeling, the craving of urgency had left with the arrival of dawn.

Control had returned, but at the price of his life.

At some point Katharine guided me by the elbow deeper into the room. I kicked the base of the wooden framed coffin and came to a stop. With great regret I lowered Jak down into the coffin, mind screaming for me to keep him in my arms. But a single thought would not let up as I stared down at his seemingly sleeping expression.

"I could heal him," I said to Katharine. "How I healed you. Your mother. Bring him back."

I saw the wince in Katharine's face from across the coffin. But with her mundane eyes she would not see my expression, or lack thereof.

"The dead cannot be healed. Only the living. He is gone, Marius. I am sorry."

I felt a bubble of defiance rush to the surface of my soul. I bit down onto my own lip, breaking skin until my mouth filled with my own blood. I recoiled at the taste of my life force. Bitter, aged and stale.

"How can you explain such philosophy when I am dead, yet can withstand all but daylight...?" I broke the silence, mind burning with determination. "He burned me with fire, I survived. I live years without warmth in my skin. I am death, yet I carry on. If I do not try, I will never forgive myself."

One glance into Katharine's eyes and I witnessed her understanding, far before my own caught up to me.

"Will it work?"

My sharp nail was already pressed against my upper arm. I did not register the nick as it broke my skin as I muttered, "For my sake, and the world beyond this place, I hope so."

I learned long ago that the curse was rooted in blood. A defiance of eternal life that had to be refilled from year to year. For my blood was life force, and not mine at all. It was the remnants from each Claim.

Yet this was different. My body should be filled with Jak's essence. I should desire to feed from him, even now. But I did not.

Had the curse truly broken? Or just fractured?

The trickle of blood ran down my forearm, racing around my wrist like a circlet of ruby before dripping towards the slightly parted mouth of my love. My Jak.

With precision, each droplet never missed the darkness that waited for it. *Drip. Drip. Drip.* His lips were terribly white. *Drip. Drip. Drip.* I traced my nail further down my arm in a straight line, urging for more of my blood to spill. *Drip. Drip. Drip.* My will filled each droplet, carrying my pleading deep within Jak's still, stiffened body.

Drip. Drip. Drip.

My strength flooded from me, flowing into him. Each moment I felt myself growing tired. Blinking became heavier, slower. Each time the skin on my arm knitted back together, I tore it wide open. Shaking my head, I growled with frustration, trying to keep my eyes on him. But they were growing heavier as more of my blood spilled.

Drip.

Drip.

Drip.

"Wake, my love. For I do not think I can bear the wait to see you again in death."

31

I WOKE FROM DARKNESS, to darkness. My hand slapped my chest as I gasped for breath, only to feel it empty. Hollow. Without the tender, gentle beat of my heart. It felt no different than touching an empty shell or a forgotten stone.

Beneath my palm my skin felt strange — cold. I parted my mouth to call out into the darkness, but my throat was dry. I could not form words, only the scratching gasp of a noise that sounded strange to my own ears.

Thirst. The feeling was intense. I smacked my dry mouth together, thinking of nothing but the cool dribbles of liquid that would quench the longing need for something to drink.

It felt as though I had broken free from a dream. A nightmare. Yet the events of what I had experienced were hazy and distant. Kept away by the need for … sustenance.

One hand moved from my chest to my neck. I did not know what to expect, but the soft brush of skin seemed to be a surprise. The other hand moved to my stomach which seemed to spasm deep within, the rippling of a hunger I had not felt before. No. It was not only hunger, but thirst as well. As I woke further, it was as though the feelings awoke alongside me, unfurling like a sleeping cat as it stretched its limbs in waking.

A noise sounded from somewhere in the distance. A shuffling of feet. It was loud, and quiet at the same time, so much so that I could not distinguish its distance. Then, as I came to, I could hear other noises. Sounds I had not registered before. The slight scratching of small legs against stone. A snuffling noise that could only be that of a rat or mouse sniffing for food.

All at once the world, beyond the darkness, came alive, and I heard it all.

Pressing a hand into my gut, I pinched my eyes shut, trying to focus on the one sound that I could understand.

Footsteps walked towards my location. With each step their footfalls grew and intensified in sound.

My stomach jolted and jaw ached as though my teeth danced within my mouth. The burning call of fire spread across my jaw as though it stretched inside my skull. The sensation joined the intensifying burn in my gut and dryness in my throat.

Darkness was a discomfort, a void of agony as I truly woke.

My fingers reached for my mouth as the urge of pressing my teeth back into my gums overwhelmed me. As my fingertip passed my dry lips, I felt a poin—

Voices mixed with the patter of feet.

"... come back to finish you. With the barrier down, you should find cover elsewhere. They have waited years to end you, just as you have waited years to leave. Do not think for a moment they will take their time."

A deep voice responded, lush tones vibrating the darkness around me. "I will not run, nor hide from the likes of them. They can come. It would be a grave mistake."

"You took the head of their queen, but that did not destroy the nest of vipers. I have been around them. I know the plans they have for you — please. You must go."

"Katharine." The name was spoken as a warning. And the name was equally a stranger, and familiar. "I will... not be forced out my home. Let them come, let them see what I will do to them all."

"But you are free." The softer voice responded. "You can leave, Marius."

Marius. The name slammed around my skull, nullifying the discomfort and pain. My finger fell from my mouth and dropped to my still chest as I tried to focus on its origin.

My mind was a storm, but in the eye of it I sensed that the name brought me comfort. It warmed my insides. Cooled my throat like the gulp of ice water. The name, it calmed me.

I opened my mouth, lips moving in the shape of the name. Again, I tried to force the word out.

"M... ari... us."

"Not in the sense that I have long des—" The voice spluttered to a stop. It happened quickly that I felt as though I had simply stopped listening. But I sensed the presence, its closeness to me as something joined the dark around me.

One moment I was alone, the next *he* was with me, weight shifting the coffin, forcing my body to shuffle to the side; the wood creaked in warning, threatening to break beneath the sudden presence beside me.

"Jak." Hands reached for my face and could I do nothing to push them away. Then a face materialised through the shadows and my entire being melted into his touch. *Marius*. Looking into his ruby stare brought everything back. I spluttered for breath, crashing through the hazy surface into the world of reality.

Marius. His eyes did not stop searching my face as though he had lost something and still longed to find it. His hands took a hold of mine with such urgency and squeezed, anchoring me to him, as though some strange wind would come and simply blow me away.

"You..." I forced out, swallowing to try and lubricate my throat enough to speak. "Found me."

I closed my eyes and relaxed into his hands as he cupped both my cheeks. When he replied his voice cracked, and I was certain a splash of wetness clashed against my chin. "You were never lost. Only misplaced for a moment."

He was different, his touch no longer cold. He just felt... normal.

"You are different..." I said, my voice no more than a rasped whisper.

"No, Jak." Marius's eyes misted, his thumb brushing my cheek as though it was a petal. "You are the one that has changed. I am sorry for what I have done. It was selfish not to let you go, but I couldn't. I couldn't not try."

He spoke so fast it was close to impossible to truly take in his words. I scrunched my face and sighed. "What happened, Marius?"

He leaned in, closing the space between us and placed a kiss upon my forehead. A shiver raced down my spine at the touch. He pulled away as he retorted, "What do you remember?"

I blinked, looking into the shadows beyond him. The feeling was like unlocking a gate that had been kept closed, his questioning was the key that unlocked it.

And the memories, the pain, the truth... It all returned.

"She killed me. My mother, my own blood, killed me."

I stared deeply into Marius's gaze, remembering how he had violently winced as the blade sliced across my throat. It was the last thing I could remember before the cold, endless nothingness.

"I am sorry, Jak," Marius murmured, looking down at his hands that now threaded my own and held them. "For everything."

"How... I mean... what happened? I died and... no, Marius, this is too much." The pain in my gut, my jaw, my head, all exploded in one large crash. It rocked my core from the inside. If it was not for his hold my hands would have shook where they lay.

"I watched you die. And I acted upon selfish desperation. I took your choice away from you and made you... this. I made you, turned you like..."

"You." My word was as sharp as a blade. "You turned me, to keep me alive?"

"Jak," he sighed, sorrow and guilt rolling off him in battering waves. "You are not alive, and nor am I. You are... eternal."

∼

Marius was wrong. He had not taken my choice away from me. My mother had. He simply had reinstated what she tried to steal from me.

Life.

Not in the sense of how I had it before. Now my life was different. Never-ending like the man whom had provided me with a second chance.

Night swelled around us as we stood at the boundary of the castle, my hand in Marius's as we both looked down over Darkmourn far below. Not a single home was without light. Perhaps they prepared to come for us, or they knew what was coming for them. My stomach jolted at the promise of what waited within those homes, what pumped within their fine, pathetic, disposal veins.

Katharine waited far behind us, but the nightly wind blew her scent my way. The smell of her sweet, delicious blood. I longed for it. But she was off limits. Marius had said so when she finally burst into his chamber in the bellies of the now ruined castle. I had nearly thrown myself from the coffin in desperation to... feed.

That was what Marius had explained, lending me a sip of his blood that only curbed the desperation enough for me not to rip her throat out.

If Marius was not holding me, I feared for her. For what I longed to do. But Marius promised the feeling would pass once I had my first fill.

And I imagined I would soon be full past the point of bursting.

"What are you thinking about?" I asked, my hand squeezing his as we looked out over the view before us. I sensed his halting anticipation as if it was my own. It was strange, for I sensed more of his emotions now after he had brought me back, as though a tether of shadow kept me pinned to him.

I had wondered if he felt it too. But it was not the time for questions. We would have time for that after I fed.

"I had imagined the possibility of leaving on too many occasions, I hadn't dared to keep count. Yet I always believed, if it would happen, I would be leaving this place alone. Not with someone by my side."

"Someone?" I snapped my teeth, feeling my lips tug into a smile over the new points that protruded from my gums. Sharp teeth that kept ripping at my skin, only for it to heal moments later. Similar to Marius's who had pressed his own deep into my skin, sharing in a lustful, dangerous kiss. "Is that all I am? Just a someone?"

Marius pulled my arm, spinning me around to face him. He was stronger, but I felt as though I could match him with this new strength. It was one of the many differences since waking. I was resilient. My hearing and sight as sharp as the two fangs that pressed into the skin behind my lower lip.

"You are Jak, my Jak." There was still sorrow in his eyes for what he had done to me, yet I felt no pain or hate for his actions. Only... relief. Before meeting him I was equally trapped by the curse, prisoner to the fate I had been born into. And now... Now I was free. From my mother whose corpse was rotting in an unknown location, a place I did not care to know. Marius had shattered the bindings on my fate, just as I had for him.

Marius bowed his head as though holding my stare was impossible. With a hand I lifted his defined chin with a thumb and urged him to stop moping. "I am yours, and you are mine. For an eternity."

"I should have given you the choice."

"And if you had I would have agreed without question."

"You do not know what this means. And I cannot explain it either. It was foolish—"

I raised onto my toes and pressed my lips to his, silencing him. Everything about his taste was an explosion, as though my sensations had been set ablaze as I touched him. I wanted more than to just kiss. The action did not feel strong enough, intense enough, for what I felt deep within. Pulling away slowly, Marius kept his eyes closed and mouth parted slightly, wishing for my return.

"We will discover what it means to be... us. It is a big world out there; we cannot be the only ones."

"And what if we are?" he asked.

I smirked. Was it the thirst or excitement that made me so giddy? "You made me, what is stopping you from doing it again?"

Marius peered over his shoulder to where Katharine hovered in the distance, arms wrapped around her thin frame. "She may not want this."

"Then you can respect that wish. But what if she does? She has no one left living. Like you. Like me. I promise you, Marius, what you have done for me is a gift. Katharine... well, she may feel the same."

Marius lowered his head. "Not yet."

"So, what next then?" I asked, urging for him to look at me. "You are the author. Tell me where you see my story going."

It must have been something I said that encouraged the beautiful yet deadly smile to spread across his face; his eyes lit from the inside and lines furrowed his forehead.

"Perhaps we start with a feast." My stomach grumbled in agreement as we looked back to the town and the unsuspecting victims that waited behind their closed doors. "You will need to feed before the urge becomes impossible to ignore. Then, once you are satisfied… and I, we can spend endless nights lost in one another's bodies. I fear that I have many a thing I would like to do with you, to you."

I did not hide an embarrassed grin.

"And what of your own story, Marius…?"

Marius smiled, flashing the points of his teeth. "For the first time in a long time I feel as though my story can be left open-ended. And with you by my side it will make turning the page that much easier."

If I did not have the growing hunger within me I would have dragged Marius to the ground and devoured him in unspeakable ways. But alas, the feeling was becoming harder to hold back, the want to race for the closest living thing to feed off.

I raised a hand, noticing the ashen tones that clung to my skin, and pointed towards Darkmourn. "I know where I want to begin." Pinching an eye closed, I looked down the length of my finger towards the direction my home would be nestled within. "Leave the coven to me. There are many I would enjoy devouring, whereas some that I would prefer to stay untouched."

Lamiere. I did not need to say her name to conjure a clear image of her. Although my memories from the attack were hazy, I felt deep in my core that she was not with Mother and her coven when they came for us. Just the thought gave me reprieve from feeling betrayed by everyone I had known in my life. Lamiere had always been different.

She would be spared.

"Jak, I will follow your lead. That is your world out there, and this has been mine. I feel foolish to admit, but I think that I would never have the courage to take the first step out there without you."

I squeezed his hand, feeling the tingling of fire deep within my soul. "It is your world now too, Marius. Do not fear it. Make it fear you."

Marius leaned down into my ear, his lip brushing gently across my skin as he whispered, "With you I will never fear anything. Not again."

His words sparked the kindling of fire into a blaze that poured from my skin. Magic. Dark, burning flames curled against my free hand as we witnessed the pregnant moon crown over the town far below. My magic had not left me with death, not as I had expected. It was just as easy to call upon it now, as it had been during… life.

"If Mother could see me now... she would not be happy," I said, raising the curling flames before Marius.

"Then let her roll in her grave and seethe with disgust. She cannot do anything about it now." Marius smiled, flinching slightly from my power.

"I will prove that my power, although the cause of the curse that darkened your life, will light your way forward. I vow it."

"Then let us destroy, raze and devour, my Jak," Marius announced, speaking to the night as his own power shuddered the shadows around us. It passed over the moon, blocking out the minimal pearlescent light that kissed down upon us. "Then let us take it and claim the night as our own."

I grinned, forcing my stare from Marius, my handsome Marius, back to Darkmourn. "Let us take it... together."

PART TWO
KING OF IMMORTAL TITHE

Arlo & Faenir

KING of IMMORTAL TITHE
BEN ALDERSON

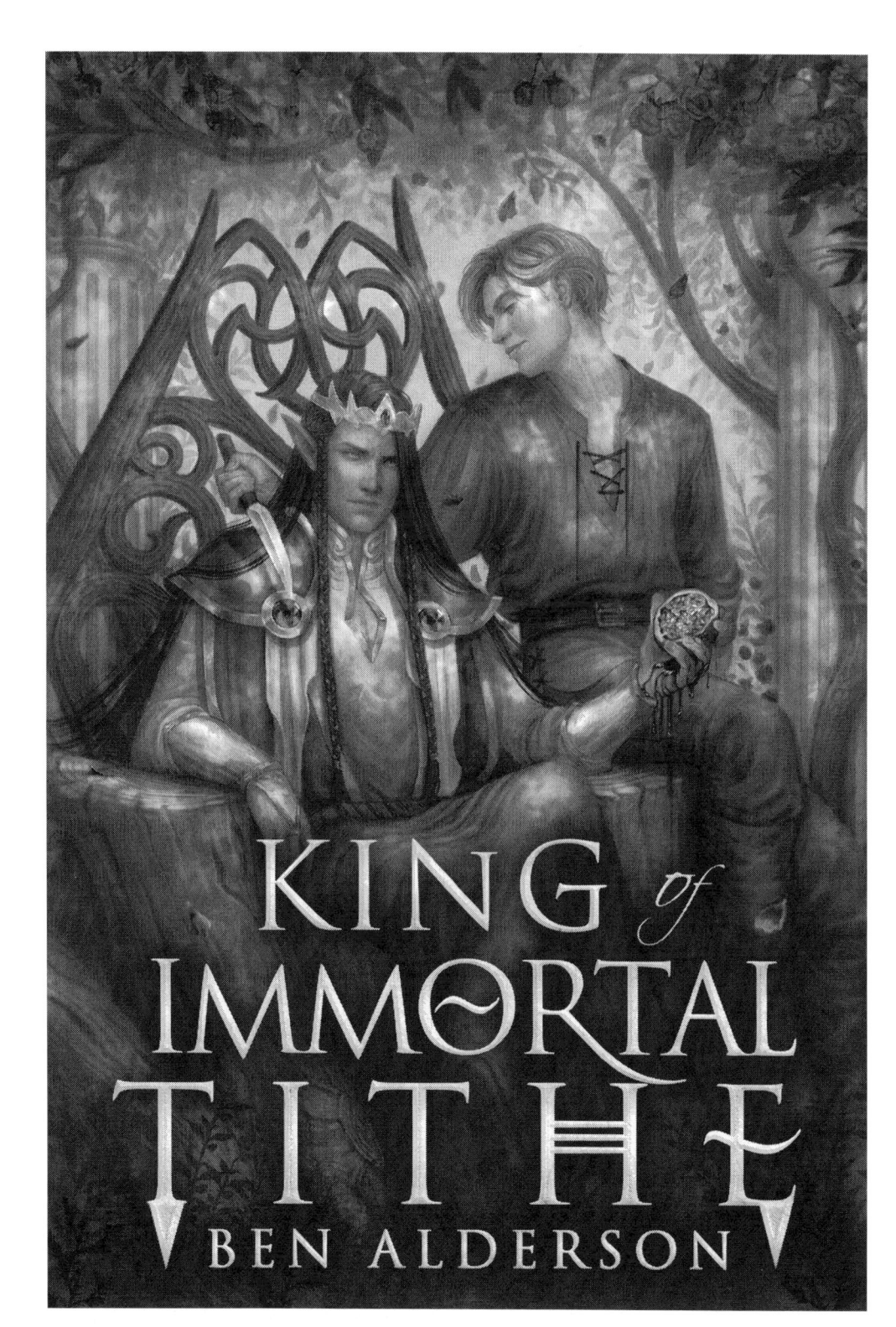

Please be aware this novel contains scenes or themes of toxic relationships, murder, loss of family members, death, abuse, manipulation, anger, grief/grieving, depression and blood/gore/ suicide.

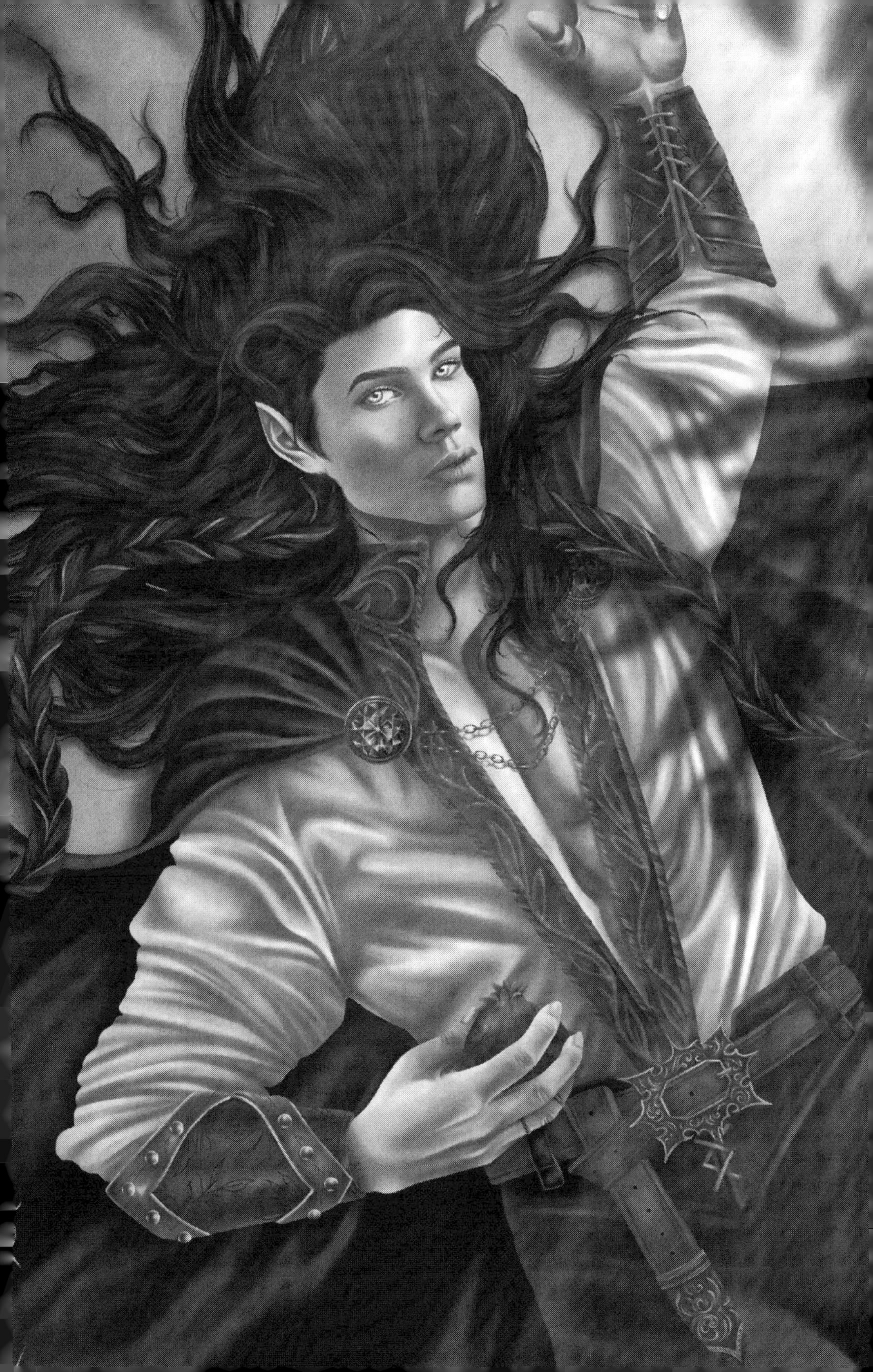

1

I SMILED in the face of death, welcoming it like an old friend.

My reflection was etched into the wide, moon-round eyes of the vampire pinned beneath me. Even in the lightless cavern, my smirk was visible.

But to a vampire, I was no friend. Far from it, because friends rarely plunged stakes into each other's chests and watched the insignificant life they had left drain away into nothingness.

Killing a vampire was easier than one would have imagined. It involved a good deal of stealth, for the fuckers were known for having a keener ear than an owl. There was also a healthy helping of fearlessness required. Vampires were monsters of nightmares, except no longer figments of imagination but real. As real as me and the stake I had gripped hard in my hand.

I no longer feared them. I couldn't. Being scared was not an option. But I could still recognise the danger they possessed. There were hordes of vampires. Thousands. The figure likely higher than I could ever imagine, which made them far more deadly than I. I couldn't pull the true number out of my ass to tell it even if I wished.

The corpse beneath me would have been young when he was turned. Its creaseless skin and innocent eyes revealed as much. His harsh face was crowned by sun-kissed locks of yellow and gold, long enough to fall around his skull like the petals of a picked flower.

I usually followed a rule I'd set for myself, as strict as a religion. Don't kill the young ones. The discomfort which followed once I buried wood in their heart was too much to bear at times.

However, today was an exception.

I had slipped from Tithe later than I would have liked. It was easier to clamber out of the town during the shift of the wall's guards around early dawn. The Watchers, as they were aptly named because it was all they ever seemed to do, were tired by the time they were swapped out, which meant they grew lazy—lazier than normal at least. Not that I complained. For years I had been completing this dance of leaving town before dawn and returning all before the break of the morning fast.

All day I had searched for the undead, seeking desperately through the ruins of long-forgotten buildings overgrown foliage had claimed. Usually they were easier to find, but it seemed today every single vampire had fled the world entirely.

If only.

Darkmourn, a city lost to death and time, nestled in the shadow of Castle Dread, was a major nest for the creatures. Today, the old town was utterly dry of the bounty I required.

When the sun ruled the skies, the creatures would flee to the darkest corners of the world. Light, much like my trusted stake, was deadly to the undead.

The more time slipped by, the harsher my desperation grew. Then I heard the familiar weeping of the creature, which finally led me to my prey.

The vampire was cowering in the cellar of an old bakery in Darkmourn. Years ago, this building would have been filled with the luscious smells of fresh bread and the tickling scents of sweet delights. Now it was a cavernous place, home to rats the size of cats and shadowed corners hiding other unseen horrors.

Fuck, I hate rats.

The vampire was whimpering in the dark belly of the bakery, its light voice enough to slice the skin of anyone without a stomach forged of iron. I knew it had been a child the moment I caught the dulcet tones lifting from the shadows of the cellar.

I had paused for only a moment, looking up at the rising sun and knowing my window of time to return to Tithe was short.

I could have turned my back and continued searching for one of older age. If I had the supply back home, perhaps I would have. But being picky with my prey was not a luxury I possessed, and I refused to return to Tithe without what I needed.

Blood. To be more specific, vampire blood.

I had made sure the vampire's death was as swift as I could gift it. It had hardly had a chance to scream in terror before I had pounced into the shadows of the cellar, straddled it and then drove the stake into its heart.

Even after years of the Hunt, the sound of wood through flesh turned my stomach. It was wet and loud, like the smacking of lips as a greedy Watcher chewed on meat.

I sat there for a moment, watching the pale colouring of the child's skin darken, as though years of rotting caught up to it within seconds. Guilt stabbed through me, but only for a moment. It was all I allowed.

Reaching for my leathered belt, I tore the short dagger from its sheath alongside two glass vials I kept in a pouch as easily accessible as my weapon.

"Sorry," I muttered, taking the dagger and lifting the blade toward the creature's throat. With a keen, swift slice, the flesh tore open and dark, pinkish gore splashed across the vampire's chest.

"At least you have found peace," I told the corpse as its cold, thin blood poured over my hands as I filled the vials to their rim.

There was a time I used to fill more than a couple of glass vials at a time, but then my sister grew older, and her eyes sharpened alongside her mind. She was inquisitive, which I had convinced myself was a bad thing. Sometimes those with watching stares noticed flaws as though it were their gift.

Auriol could not discover my greatest secret.

The pale colour of the blood and its almost transparent texture revealed the vampire had not fed in a while, likely because of the absence of prey. Humans who were lucky enough to survive since the curse of the vampires spread across the world, now lived within walled communities like Tithe. For years, the blood-thirsty creatures had little but vermin and wild beasts to feast from.

This child was certainly a victim to starvation. But regardless, its blood would do. It would serve its required purpose.

Once the vials were filled, the vampire's corpse melted beneath me, staining the ground in a puddle of bones and mush. Two was not as much as I had hoped to get, but it would do. It would keep me from needing to leave Tithe for a month or so. Two vials for two blissful and painless months. Only then I would have to hunt again.

I left the bakery's cellar and the melted stain of death in my wake. Vials tucked carefully into the pouch at my waist, the knife gripped in my hand. Who knew when another vampire would take their opportunity to show themselves to me.

The world beyond was quiet, almost peaceful. I walked the empty, forgotten streets of Darkmourn, cutting down the main cobbled pathways with my bounty bumping against my hip. Only the clink of the full flasks and my padding footsteps gave me company as I began my return to Tithe.

I could hardly imagine what life was like for the occupants of this town before the curse had spread. But one thing I was certain of was they had something I did not: freedom. Must have been nice. I admired the wall-less view around Darkmourn, looking towards the faint outline of rolling hills and the dense forests which filled the horizon for miles.

Even the towering, charred remains of Castle Dread did not displease me. I drank it all in every time I came, hoping the vision would sustain me until my next visit.

Tithe was not like this. It was not a place of freedom like the outside world. It was surrounded by a wall so high it blocked out the view of anything and everything beyond it. Many of Tithe's occupants hardly cared for the world beyond the walls. But I did. Even when I did not need to leave to get blood, I longed to step outside if only for a moment, just to see, to look around and let my eyes stretch for as far as they desired.

Trading freedom for safety was the price to pay for being kept alive. Most felt it was a fair trade. I was still not convinced.

The coughing began as I stood knee-deep in a shallow lake closest to Tithe's boundary, scrubbing the vampire's melted flesh from my leather breeches until the body of water turned grey. The sound was terrible. Wet gargles scratched up through my throat and made my lungs feel as though they would implode if I took a full breath in.

A sudden pain clamped across my chest and squeezed. I stumbled a step, almost falling completely, as the world seemed to shudder beneath my feet. If it was not daylight, I would have sent a message to all the vampires close enough to hear that I was ready for the taking.

I caught the droplets of blood in my cupped hands. It filled my mouth with the taste of copper, staining my teeth red and leaking out the corners of my lips. At least it happened now. The thought was not helpful. These fits were warnings my body was failing. They would start small, tickling spasms in my chest. Soon, becoming heavy rasping breaths which sounded wet and gargled in my chest, as though water filled my lungs and I drowned in it.

It was the warning I needed to know when it was time to devour a vial of my bounty. Vampire's blood was the only thing which gave me relief from the pain and the impending doom the agony revealed. I was dying, and only one form of medicine could keep death from claiming me. Medicine. I had tried to convince myself that was what the blood was. It made drinking it less... sickening.

It took a while for the coughing to finally calm before I had the energy to clean myself again. Only when I scrubbed my blood from my hands and face did I sit myself on the bank of the lake, weak and tired.

Begrudgingly, I accepted my need to drain a vial immediately. I just sat there, trying to catch my breath as I felt the familiar draining sickness dance through my body, as though it rejoiced to be overcoming me again.

A shiver passed across my arms. The weather was growing increasingly colder with the welcoming of autumn, my most hated season of all. I could only face sitting in my stupor for so long before taking one vial from the pouch, uncorking it with my teeth and draining the contents into my mouth.

As I drank the vampire's blood, I allowed myself to think of him. Small and pathetic, crumbling beneath my touch as I held the stake in his chest. I recognised the guilt as I did the sickness within me, trying to justify my murder by reminding myself why I did what I did...

And who I did it for.

Get up.

I repeated this mantra to myself four times before I got the strength and courage to stand again. It would take hours before the vampire's blood finally took effect. Until then, I just had to hope another fit did not return.

One vial left. Fucking pathetic, I should have found more.

Angry at my truth and failure, I discarded the empty, pink-stained vial and smashed it beneath my feet as I trod back towards Tithe's outer wall.

Today had started like shit, and I had a feeling it would not end any better.

2

I SQUEEZED my tired body through the narrow gap beneath Tithe's boundary wall, far later than I would have liked to return. It was still morning, but I'd wasted precious minutes waiting for the Watchers atop the towering stone wall to turn their backs for me to slip inside town.

Any other day, I would scrutinise my narrow frame compared to the built, muscled bodies of the other young men within Tithe. At the fruitful age of twenty-five, I was still slight and painfully short. My body knocked years off my appearance, but without it, I would never have been able to leave and enter Tithe at my leisure. I was thankful for that.

Dirt and crumbled stone scratched across my chest and belly as I dragged myself through the hole which time had worn away. Only when I passed entirely beneath could I surrender a breath of relief.

Tithe was a cramped place. Narrow streets, and old black beamed and white painted buildings which seemed to lean on one another for support. I could see it now, through the thinning of trees I stood within.

My hand went to the pouch at my belt, fingers dusting over the swell of the glass vial within. Then I ran, as fast as my legs allowed, through the small patch of woods, across a field littered with the sheep who grazed upon the little patches of grass they could find this time of year.

With any luck, Auriol would have still been asleep when I reached home. At least I hoped so. It would have saved me the need to lie and if there was one thing I hated more than the Watchers and the immortals who commanded them; it was lying. Even if I was the self-proclaimed master of it.

~

Auriol was awake by the time I pushed open the door to our home. Home was at least one word which could be described for the run-down apartment we dwelled within. Located in the upper floors of Tithe's most infamous apothecary, it was a place where the floorboards screamed and every window rattled, as though the very building expressed its displeasure for us living there.

Two steps inside and she called out for me. "Are you ever going to learn that your bed is likely a better place to stay than lurking in the sweat-drenched sheets of Tom's?"

I winced, still feeling the tickle of the cough lurking at the back of my throat. It took a lot of effort to keep it at bay.

Auriol must not know.

"But his bed is far warmer... and bigger," I called out, dusting the dried mud from the sleeve of my jacket. The gilded mirror which hung drunkenly upon the wall beside me revealed the complete state I was in, as if I had been pulled through a bush over and over. Or through a wall. My straw-blond hair was a mess and heavy bags hung proudly beneath my mismatched eyes.

At least I looked the part of a dishevelled, tired patron of Tom's company. Even if he was not the reason for where I had been.

I could hear the smile in the way my sister responded, distracting me from the way I looked. "Out of all the men in Tithe and still you keep returning to him. When are you going to see Tom for what he is and leave him behind you?"

Ah, time to lie.

"I don't imagine you would appreciate me listing the reasons as to why Tom has me ensnared, sister, unless you want me to go into very long detail..."

She forced a fake gag, which conjured a deep laugh from me in response, and I said, "I shall take that as a no."

The first doorless frame to my left led into the main room of our apartment. I tore my jacket from my back and rested it on the back of the chair tucked under the worn dining table. By the time I looked back towards the slightly wonky corridor, Auriol's head had poked around her bedroom door.

"Arlo," she said, stifling a yawn. "Even Tom's long ego would entice no one else into his bedroom. At least not anyone with a lick of taste. I had believed you would be more interested in meaningful conversation."

"When I'm with Tom, there is no need for conversation... put it that way."

Auriol huffed, rolled her eyes dramatically and grimaced without diluting any of her expression. "Men, you are all the same."

"Hungry?" I said, happy to divert the conversation before she picked up the truth that I had not, in fact, been at Tom's. Well, not the entire time, at least. I had warmed his bed before leaving Tithe at dawn, but she did not need to know that part.

"As if I am going to let you cook." Auriol wrapped her arms around her slender frame and padded barefoot down the corridor towards our kitchenette. "The last thing I need is to catch a sickness before tomorrow. If I miss out on their arrival for another year, I will be pissed. It could be my turn and I'm not missing that for the sake of your cooking. Sit. Eggs?"

My skin crawled at the brief mention of tomorrow's festivities. I hated the elves on any day, but the idea of their visits always made me feel terrifying dread. Especially with the idea that Auriol was seen by them. My sister was beautiful, stealing her looks from our mother, from the flow of her thick, chestnut hair that fell all the way down to her tailbone, to the sharp etchings of her face. High cheekbones, narrow chin and eyes so wide it seemed she held the secrets of the universe within them.

The only thing that signified us as siblings was our eyes; one a deep brown, the other a bright diamond blue. Everyone in Tithe knew us from them, just as they had known our mother before she had passed.

Looking at Auriol was both wonderful and painful, unknowingly dragging memories to the surface, ones I had spent years burying.

"About tomorrow," I started, already sensing Auriol's dramatic roll of her eyes and tongue kissing across her teeth in displeasure. "What if I told you I would prefer that you sit it out?"

I watched her crack an egg into the lip of a bowl, noticeably harder than it needed to be. "Every year you do this. And every year I obey like the good little sister I am. This time, Arlo, I am going."

Inevitably, this conversation was to happen one day. Auriol was twenty years old, younger than me by five years. But she had become an adult years ago. It forced Auriol to grow up far younger than she deserved. As scarless as her skin was, there was no denying the mark the lack of childhood had left upon her.

Upon us both.

Last year was the first time she had pushed against my refusal for us to both sit out the immortal's visit to Tithe. So, I made her breakfast the morning of their arrival, which left us both bedbound with the shits. It was the effect of ensuring she was not placed before them like willing meat to the slaughter. Because I knew, if she was to have been seen by the elves, she would have been taken from me.

For that was what they do. Take. It was payment. At least that was what the Watchers reminded us of. A tithe for our safety. It was the reason our commune was called Tithe. Payment to be protected from the vampires beyond the wall.

But Auriol was worth more than keeping the occupants of this godforsaken hovel safe. I could not see, nor allow her to be chosen. Selfishly, I needed her.

Likely more than she needs me.

"What if I begged?" I said, looking through my lashes as I watched her beat the eggs into a scramble. "Pretty please with a cherry—"

"I am allergic to cherries so you can shove your pleading in the same dark cavern that Tom sticks his long ego…"

"Okay, okay!" I forced a smile, trying to hide the true torment the idea of her going made me feel. "Stop whilst you're ahead before you put me off your wonderful cooking."

She lifted the egg splattered spoon at me as though it was the greatest weapon, one that won wars and defeated ancient demons and witches. Auriol looked down her nose, with narrowed eyes which screamed with threats. "No more then, understand? I am going and that is the end of that."

"Then I am coming with you."

"But you never go." Auriol almost sounded disappointed in the idea of me following.

"Nor do you." I shrugged, trying to keep my expression void of the genuine panic I felt inside. "I suppose it will be a first for us both. Don't you just love the idea of spending some time with your brother? Quality time? We could feast on sweet breads and eat cured meats until our bellies explode. Make the most of it."

Even though I had stayed clear of the immortal's visits, I still watched the festivities that Tithe put on in honour of their return. Stalls overwhelmed with food and the contagious laughter that came from unlimited tankards of ale and stronger spirits. The streets were full of Tithe's blinded occupants dressed in finery which they could hardly afford, and only came out of their closets once a year. It was as if they were peacocks exposing feathers to catch the attention of the fey-kind. For the unlucky few, it worked.

But no one was like my sister. Not a single person in Tithe could come close to comparing. And that fact had me pushing the pile of peppered eggs around the plate as I tried to keep my anxiety from overwhelming me entirely.

"You are welcome…"

I shook myself out of my head, forcing a smile that even I knew Auriol would never believe. "Are you not joining me?"

She had only given me a plate, her chair left neatly tucked beneath the table, forgotten and unwanted.

"I am a wanted woman," she said, brows furrowed as she scanned my face for a hint as to what caused my turmoil. She would never outright ask. Auriol had learned never to pry, which I respected. "I am heading into town to pick up some last-minute supplies for tomorrow. Kaye is helping me put together my outfit for the festival."

It took everything in my power not to kick up from the chair and demand that she did nothing of the sort. Instead, I focused on the plate, stabbing the fork into the pillowy clumps of egg I toyed with.

"Have fun," I lied.

"Could you at least pretend to be excited with me?" Auriol leaned in, wrapping her arms around my shoulders, her fingers interlocking over my chest where she held on.

"I just don't want you getting your hopes up," I replied coldly. It was not a complete lie.

"That I might not get picked?" Auriol's voice was equally cold. She pulled away from me, clearly over my lack of enthusiasm and vibrant displeasure at the idea of her being chosen by the elves. "Do you really think it is such a terrible thing for me to be chosen? How can you sit there and tell me you do not wish for a better life when you spent half our childhood conjuring fantasies of leaving Tithe and living in the world beyond as though those fucking bloodsucking pricks haven't poisoned it all!"

I stared at my plate, arms and legs numb. Auriol stood behind me, breathing heavily and although I knew I should turn and face her, tell her she was right, and I was wrong… I couldn't do it. That was one lie I was not prepared to say.

I kept silent, counting each of her deep breaths as I waited for her to lash out again. I deserved it.

"Sometimes you need to remember…" Auriol trailed off.

"Say it." I knew what was coming. It had been for a long time and part of me desired for her to speak the words aloud.

"It doesn't matter."

I pleaded, "Say it."

Auriol sighed, one filled with years of turmoil and dark emotion. She was always better at letting it out and making sense of how she felt. I admired her for it.

"You are not them, Arlo. I do not blame you for stepping into their shoes and doing what you had too as the oldest of us both. But you are not Dad. You are not Mum. I think it is time you remember that and release the burden. It would be a shame if it ruined what little we had left."

She left swiftly, feet slapping against the floor as she hurried towards her room.

Just like the coward I recognised myself to be, I swallowed what I truly wished to say and kept it buried in the darkest part of my soul, wondering how much room I had left there before those feelings I kept hidden had nowhere else to go but out.

3
FAENIR

CLARIA WAS NOT the Queen of Evelina by choice. The title should have been passed to my mother many years ago. She should have been the one to retire my grandmother from the heavy burden of the crown.

Should have.

Except I had killed my mother and prevented that from ever happening. And Claria had spent the hundred years that followed, making sure I did not forget.

Not that I ever would.

"It has been many a year since you last requested an audience, Faenir." Queen Claria's voice was rugged with age. It cracked and popped as though she needed to clear something from her throat. I hated many things in life, but her existence made everything pale in comparison. "I admit I would have preferred not to have seen your face for an even longer period of time. Looking upon you is a painful reminder of what you took from me. Tell me, child, what has dragged you before me like the unwanted mutt you are?"

Child. Even now she degraded me as though a century was nothing but a blink in time. I supposed to be someone so withered and ancient, one hundred and thirteen years of living was youthful in comparison.

I stood rigid before the curved oak throne her hunched frame sat upon. She looked small within it, like a child sitting on a chair meant for adults. The twisting, intricately woven back of the throne was polished and twisted together like the antlers of the proudest stag. It had been carved from a stump of dark wood, with its roots still rising and falling out of the earth beneath it.

The heart of Evelina.

Where the dense foliage reached above the throne, explosions of blood-red roses crowned the glade as their petals fell like snow around us. If one did not look close enough, they would have been fooled by the trick of life and beauty. I was not privy to such blindness. The glade should have been a place of colour, now it was far from it. Dull and muted, entrapped in the grasp of death. Every year, Evelina seemed to retreat into death a little more than the one before.

I recognised death, for it sang to my soul.

We were one in the same.

"Apologies if my presence disturbs you. My visit will be brief," I replied, hearing the careless tone that had entered my voice as it echoed across the enchanted forest we stood within.

Claria waved a veined hand as though she wished our meeting to end quickly. "Then get on with it so your presence does not encourage Evelina to perish any more than required."

I fought the urge to drop her hateful, judging stare. With great effort, I swallowed the stone of defiance and cleared my throat. "I request to be pardoned from the day's Choosing."

"Denied," she barked quickly.

My breathing quickened, my body growing stiffer where I stood. "It is not required for me to visit Tithe. You know what will happen if I partake in the Choosing. It would not bode well for our relationship with the humans."

As Myrinn had warned me.

Claria leaned forward in the throne, thin arms resting on each armrest as they trembled to hold her weight. "There could have been a time that your Choosing of a human mate would have been celebrated. As heir to this world, it would have secured your succession and ensured your mother, my dearest Eleaen, to step down. You could have been King."

"Could have," I echoed back. "Being the optimal words, grandmother."

"Indeed," she said through a scowl. All at once she rocked back into the throne, bones cracking with even the most subtle of movements. "You, like your dearest siblings, will visit Tithe and take your mate. If we have hopes of preventing the demise of our kind, then we must continue with the Choosing. I understand you may not see the importance and the part you have to play... you have always been such a selfish, twisted child."

I am no child. I wanted to scream it. My shadows coiled within the far corners of the forest, begging for me to call upon their comfort.

The child had died when I was old enough to recognise what I had done, what my being alive had caused and why it had made me so hated by Claria. By my family.

"You are aware of what will happen if you force my hand to do this."

My grandmother smiled. It was the first time I had seen her smile in countless years that I believed it was not something she had the potential for. Bright and gleaming, it smoothed the many wrinkles of her bitter, old face and caused her amber eyes to glow from within. "You will kill the poor soul that you pick. For that is what you do. Your touch is as cursed as you are, Faenir. And it will further prevent you from stealing the crown I have worked tirelessly to keep from you."

"I never desired to be King, Claria," I spat, sensing the dancing shadows as though they waited for my command to devour her where she sat. "I have said it many times, yet still, you do not listen. Or simply choose not to."

"It is all well and good, but until it is proven to the realm that you are barren of possibility to find a mate to rule beside, then I will go to all measures to ensure your failure."

At that, I dropped her gaze just before her light, amused chuckle spilled out.

"Let the humans see you in the same light that we do. Let them come to know the monster that is Faenir."

4

TOM WAS RUSHING, made clear mostly from his frantic thrusts and his not so careful hands. The most telling sign was his lack of focus, chestnut eyes flicking towards the window as if the impending light of dawn would reach Tithe quicker every time he would look away.

It killed the mood for me. He was so distracted by the arrival of morning that he hardly noticed when I stopped gyrating on his hard, long cock.

It took Tom a moment to look back up at me, beads of glistening sweat tracing down the prominent bones of his strong face. His brows furrowed with a mixture of confusion and annoyance.

"What's wrong?" he asked, deep voice enough to clear my frustration and lose myself in the sex again. I was certain his voice alone could remove my clothes from my body.

Among many other things, some not as nice as the others, Tom was handsome. For me, it was his only redeeming feature that kept me returning most evenings. I had slept, tangled within his sheets, far more times than I had my own. He served his purpose, of course, acting as a distraction from my mind and the world around me.

His chestnut eyes, the same colour as wet oak after a downpour of winter rain. Tom was a labourer on a farm north of Tithe towards its outer walls. Close to where I would escape.

Working beneath his father, he would tend to their livestock, mainly sheep, but with the odd milk cow. His physical work had crafted his body in ways that should only be possible for the heroes of ancient stories. Arms as hard as boulders, every muscle defined with proud lines. Tom was strong, not that it was required when dealing with me.

He often reminded me how he just loved to pick me up and throw me around. Unlike me, Tom was obsessed with my body; he worshipped it.

With the turn of the last month of summer, Tom's skin was kissed and golden. Freckles dusted across his broad shoulders, matching those that spread over the bridge of his sharp, straight nose. And now, looking up at me where I sat upon his crotch, sheets a knot around us, I could not deny his heroic beauty.

"At least have the decency to give me your full attention when you are fucking me, Tom," I said finally.

He did not laugh like I expected, instead rolling his eyes as he harshly pushed me off his lap. I was forced to lie beside him, feeling stupid for even speaking. If I had thought the mood was ruined before, it was destroyed now, shattered into too many pieces to possibly put back together.

"Sometimes you are impossible to please... do you know that?"

I gazed up at the beamed ceiling of his room, admiring the intricate spiderwebs that had lived among the shadows for as long as I could remember. No matter how many times I asked Tom to clean them, he never did. And why would he? For someone who was so engrossed in his vanity, Tom was excellent at pushing the not so pretty parts of his life into the dark corners of himself. Like the spiderwebs, they were out of sight and out of mind.

"Harsh," I said, rolling over and placing my palm across his chest. Coarse hairs tickled beneath the tips of my fingers. "Just forget that I said anything."

I could see from the proud, tall cock still raised skyward between his legs that Tom was not satisfied. It glistened in the light of dawn that filtered through his window, covered in the lubricant that he purchased from the apothecary beneath my home.

"How about we go again..." I encouraged, running my fingers from his chest, down the mountainous lumps of muscle across his stomach, following the lines that pointed down to his lower hip. I didn't get close to the manicured hairs that crowned his cock before Tom grabbed my hand and tore it from his skin.

"Perhaps we'll finish later." Tom swung his legs over the edge of his bed, which groaned with every slight move. No wonder his father and mother could never look me in the eyes. They knew what happened when I visited, ratted out by the noise his bed made when I dwelled within it. "Arlo, I think you should leave... or like just go home and get ready or something."

I popped my elbow up, resting my head in my hand as I watched him stand. Tom stretched, the glow of morning outlining his deliciously conjured body with a halo of light.

"But I would prefer to stay here with you all day. Tom, come back to bed. I promise we will have a more enjoyable day within it than out there." There was a forced pleading in my voice. It was not exactly Tom I wished to spend time with. But his body and the power of distraction he held were what I needed to get me through the day and those who came with it.

The elves.

Hanging off the wooden pillar at the end of his bed was my jacket, tunic, trousers, and most importantly, my pouched belt. Tom reached for it, fisted my clothes and threw them upon me before I had a chance to raise my hands to protect myself.

"Get up," Tom scoffed, pulling his own trousers up over the bulges of his thighs before tucking his still hard cock into the band over his waist. "May I remind you, Arlo, that you are the only person in Tithe that does not wish to see the elves. I am going, like your sister. You can either wallow at home all day or join us."

I should never have told him about the conflict between me and my sister the day prior. Tom didn't care for my emotions and turmoil, but he listened like a patient dog, knowing that his treat would come for his good behaviour. My sex. It was always the same. Even if I could practically feel Tom's discomfort when I expressed the worries of my life, I still never refrained from talking. Tom was a shit conversationalist, but it was better than speaking to a brick wall. Similar certainly, but better.

"You are like the rest of them," I said, gladly climbing out of his sticky sheets. I was damp with sweat and my arse glistened with lubricant. I needed a wash as desperately as I wanted this day to be over.

"Always thinking this will be your year to be chosen. Tell me, Tom, are you going to get yourself ready and parade yourself hoping to claim the attention of the elves that visit?" It was not a question, more of a statement fuelled by a speck of jealousy at the idea of the elves taking him from me as well.

Tom was handsome enough for the elegantly pompous creatures to choose him as their boon. The creatures were equally vain and loved pretty and lovely things. Auriol. Tom. If they were taken from me, I truly would be left alone.

"Would it be so bad?" Tom turned on me with wide eyes full of pity. "A new life where you could live like a king whilst knowing your family's lives would be changed. No more work. No more poverty. Unlike you, I actually care what happens to my family and if being picked by the fey will give them a better life, then so be it."

My blood chilled. Arguing with Tom was not how I saw this morning going, but since he was clearly so ready for one, I supposed I could give him what he wanted.

"That is not fair, Tom." My feet smacked onto the floor as I began dressing myself hurriedly.

"Is it not?" His voice peaked, mouth drawn into a fine line. "You are so adamant to keep your poor sister trapped in your depressive life that you can't possibly imagine what it would be like for her to be given a chance."

"Fuck you."

"I already did."

I was almost lost for words. Tom grabbed at my insecurities and brandished them towards me like a weapon, sharp and thirsty for blood, slicing me open.

"Don't speak about matters you could not possibly understand."

"Understand?" He barked a laugh. "How can I not understand when you waffle on about your problems and emotions every time you visit? Arlo, for your own sake, face the day like a man and stop trying to stop others from doing what it is they wish to do."

My fingers were numb as I buttoned up my tunic. There was no doubt the wrong buttons were put into mismatching holes as I focused entirely on not letting Tom see me cry; not from sadness, but from anger and humiliation. Those were the worst tears to shed.

"You can be a real prick, Tom. Do you know that?" I was shouting now, mouth laced with copper from the blood that spilled from my bitten cheeks.

"The truth can hurt," he replied, brushing past me as he paced towards his bedroom door. "I think you should go. Take the day to think how your moods affect others, and maybe if I am still here tonight, which I really do hope I am not, you can come back, and we will finish where we left off."

I could have vomited across my bare feet. Tom truly believed that I would come running back, even after what he had said. And the truth was... I would.

Auriol was right about him—of course she was; my sister was a keen judge of character when it came to everyone but me. The price I paid for Tom and the distraction he provided was this. When things were good with him, they were amazing, but when they were bad... well, he had a way of worming into my feelings and causing more pain than the sickness that the vampire blood kept at bay.

Sometimes I wished to tell him. To see if he would have not had any lick of honest, caring emotion if I told him I was dying. Then someone would know. But he would use it against me... I had no doubt.

The door to his room screeched open, and Tom held it wide, standing beside it like a silent guard.

I was not fully dressed, my boots lost in the mess of his room. There was no time to find them. Defeated, I kept my head down as I walked away from his bed. I could have said so much to Tom as I left, but instead I bit down on my tongue to keep myself silent.

A firm hand reached out and grabbed my shoulder. His touch shattered the spell of silence. "Arlo, I hope I see you among the crowds today."

He didn't. Tom's emotionless tone told me as much. It was as though he forced himself to say it, his own way of apologising for his brash reaction this morning. Tom didn't care. He was simply saying what he thought I wished to hear to feed his own twisted conscience.

I looked up at him, standing half a foot shorter than him. "For your sake, I hope you are chosen by them."

Tom smiled; it reached his eyes, as though the idea of it brightened his very soul. Then he replied, voice alight with hope, "As do I."

5

MANY YEARS HAD DILUTED the story of how Tithe came to be. Although the story was Darkmourn's ugliest scar, those who still clung to the realm of the living chose to forget it. Mother used to tell Auriol and me the tale repeatedly, as though it was her most important lesson for us to remember. Not that I could ever have forgotten.

It started with the witches, as all things do. Selfish beings whose personal vengeance destroyed the world as it was known. Vampires may be creatures of nightmares, but witches were the masters who pulled the strings of that dreamscape.

The beginning of the story was hazy, or unimportant, as I had deemed it. But I remembered it started with heartbreak; most called it that, but I recognised it for its ugly truth. It was revenge and jealousy, or love if you wished to give it a name.

It was the end that mattered most, like all stories. The world changed when a male witch had been sent to Castle Dread to kill the creature that lurked within its walls. He failed and thus doomed Darkmourn and the world around it. Jak, his name still a painful reminder to everyone, was the last Claim of the old world…

Which was why I never understood why Tithe had given a name to the elves' visits and made a festival out of it: the Choosing. It was no different to the old Claiming, reminiscent of the tales of the old world. The Choosing was simply a way of giving a terrible thing a pretty name in hopes to hide the truth of what the day came with: thievery, elves stealing what didn't belong to them, taking loved ones away as payment for keeping us safe from the vampiric curse that spread through the outside world.

I had vowed to never take part. It was my parents' last wish before they both passed. And like the witch boy who could not kill the first vampire, I had failed. Now I raced through Tithe, searching frantically for Auriol.

I pushed through the crowded streets, slipping past people squashed together like fish in a barrel. A trail of disgruntled sounds and comments were left in my wake, likely because of the sharp elbow I provided those who didn't hurry and get out of my way. I didn't care, I just had to find Auriol.

Searching for her among the crowd was like locating a needle in a haystack. A fucking big haystack. The streets of Tithe were full of colour. Every person I passed was dressed in their best clothes; jackets of deep azures and red dresses so lush that it looked as though they soaked the material in their blood, and I wouldn't have put it past them. Desperation could lead one down a strange path, and the occupants of Tithe were certainly desperate to get the attention of the feykind.

In comparison, I looked dull. From my knee-worn trousers, pale cream tunic and the brown leather jacket which had more missing buttons than remaining ones, I stood out in the crowd far more than those around me did. Everything about the way I had dressed screamed my obvious lack of care or interest.

Tithe sang with excitement. It was filled with voices of the town's occupants and had been from the moment I was kicked out of Tom's house until I returned home to find Auriol had already left.

Find her. Mother's voice filled my mind. It wasn't her, of course. The dead stayed dead unless changed by a vampire, and Mother was never given enough time for that to happen. Nor had father when he died weeks later.

I had to shake the thought of them both. If I was to find Auriol among the swollen streets, I would need to focus, not be distracted by the conjured whispers of ghosts.

Living close to the centre of Tithe, there was one window in our home that gave the perfect view to the cobbled-stoned square and lonely ash tree that stabbed through the ground at its heart, and I knew that was where I would find her. No matter the season, the tree never lost a leaf or its colour; a deep emerald green blended seamlessly with the dusting of gold that spread over the thick foliage of the tree.

Leaving home, I ran for the tree and stood beneath its shadow that the endless spread of its foliage cast across the heart of the town. The human that was named Tithe's first Watcher had said he witnessed the tree burst suddenly from the ground, and the elves followed shortly after. It was such an outlandish story that I wished it was nothing but.

I was surrounded by youth. Faces I recognised well were adorned in face paints and hair twisted into ridiculous nests of curls. The boys stood taller, faces unreadable and mysterious, as though they believed their allure would be what the elves would find most asserting.

My eyes flickered across the crowds in search of her.

I had to remind myself to breathe as my chest stabbed with anxious pain. One hand was pressed over my heart, the other gripping onto the vial hidden within the pouch at my waist; its closeness had always comforted me.

"Welcome," boomed a voice so great it made me jump. "I cannot express how warm my heart is to see you all so poised and primed. Tithe has always been overflowing with beauty, and every year I only imagine how hard it must be for our guardians to pick one to take with them. This year may be the hardest choice yet!"

Dameon Slater, head Watcher of Tithe, had ambled his way onto a podium erected to the side of the tree. He was a towering man, white hair always kept from his face which revealed how unkind the years had been to him; lines creased his brow, and deep crow's feet bracketed his eyes. Even when he smiled, like now, the emotion never seemed to reach his eyes.

It was not his appearance that could silence conversations and demand respect, but the knowledge that his family had been one of the first to flee Darkmourn. They'd stumbled across this very place, which years later had come to be what it was today. It was what gave him his title as Watcher. Just as his father had been, or his father's father before that... Dameon Slater was believed to be in direct communication with the elves within their realm.

And as the people of Tithe desired nothing more than to worship those creatures in hopes their lives would change, they treated Dameon as though he was one of them.

Respect was earned, and in my eyes, he didn't deserve a scrap of it.

"Another year has passed, and we are all still here. Safe from the poisoned world beyond without the need for fear or worry. A gift our guardians provide us..."

I forced his baritone waffle to the back of my mind and continued pushing my way through the crowd. It was harder now. Instead of slipping through a moving stream, everyone had stopped and gathered within the courtyard to listen and soon witness the elves' arrival. It was like navigating around immovable rocks.

"Excuse me," I muttered. "Sorry."

"No fucking chance," a woman growled, grey hair pulled across her shoulder in a messy, knotted braid. "If you wanted a better view, you should have got your place earlier. Shift it."

I raised my hands in defeat, forcing a smile before disappearing off into the midst of sticky, sweat-damp bodies.

It was a warm day, not surprising for the turn of summer to autumn. With close to every occupant in Tithe filling the streets, it was as though a furnace of warmth had been lit around me.

"This year is special, for it is the first time in which our visitors are each from the same family. On a good year two, maybe three of you, would have a chance to have your lives changed and your families made for life. This year there will be five. Five luckily souls who will be swept from our dear Tithe and taken on an adventure alongside your mate."

My skin crawled. Just hearing him speak the words aloud had my stomach twisted into knots.

"Let us hear your willingness for the Choosing. Share your excitement with your town and hope our guardians can hear you through our realm into theirs."

The world exploded with cheering. I ducked as dried petals were thrown from balconies of those who watched from the safety of their homes. Arms were thrown skyward, feet stomping on the cobbled streets as the skies filled with cheers and shouts.

That was when I saw Tom. A line had formed, almost in a semicircle around the base of the tree. Not a single person faced away from it. He, like the surrounding people, was garbed in finery. Clothes I could never have imagined a man like him would ever own.

And my initial thought sent lightning through my veins: He will be chosen today.

His jacket was crafted from a dark velvet, threaded with gold and silver. Naturally, he was tall, but the pads that filled his shoulders and the low cut of his tunic made him look as regal as the creatures he was wishing to impress.

Prick. It had taken until today to realise that he truly saw nothing in the future for us. Even after the evenings of his whispers and repeated promises, this was what he wanted.

He never wanted me. Why would he, compared to a life of riches and wealth? A life no one truly knew, for when the elves picked their humans, they left and never returned.

I should not harbour a possessive desire for Tom, but I did. Deep down, seeing him scream among those who stood with him conjured an envy I didn't know I possessed over him. For his sake, I hoped he was chosen. It would save the wrath that would follow if he was not.

"Where is she?" I spat, reaching for his arm and pinching it with a steel grip. Tom was so focused on his ridiculous thrill he had not noticed as I had stepped up behind him.

The surprise on his face was genuine. If I was a painter, it would have been an image I would have desired to immortalise forever.

"You actually came."

"Auriol, I need to find her."

He rolled his eyes, a reaction I was all too familiar with. "Even now you cannot just give it a rest. Leave Auriol and let her enjoy the day."

Tom shrugged free from my hand and turned his back on me with dismissal. I could see the disapproving looks from the two girls who flanked his sides before they too dismissed me.

"Tom," I said through gritted teeth. "If you don't answer me, I swear I'll tell the elf that is stupid enough to choose you that your cock is limp and has the inability to create an orgasm that isn't forced."

I was certain even Dameon heard, for his speech dwindled. Everything had become terribly quiet as the crimson spread of embarrassment crept across Tom's face.

Before he spat out his words, I heard her. My name was called out, soft like the flutter of a bird's wing, except it was not a welcoming sound, more broken and breathless.

Auriol. She had stepped out from the line and faced me. My breath stuck in my throat as I caught sight of her. Even the thunderous swear from Tom faded into nothingness as I stared at her. It was as though Mother had called for me. Auriol looked beautiful, not tacky and forced like those around her, but truly remarkable. Natural. As though her very presence among the crowd was justified.

"Your interruption is not smiled upon, Master and Mistress Grey. Return to your stations and wait as those around you are," Dameon called out, narrow gaze fixed on both of us.

I could see that Auriol was mortified by the outburst. Her shoulders had raised, chin forced down to her chest as though she wished to disappear. But she could never disappear, not looking the way she did. The dress she wore was lace and the purest of white. I had only even seen design work so intricate on the spiderwebs in Tom's bedroom ceiling. Her brunette hair was not backcombed and obnoxious but sleek and tumbling, like waves of rich chestnut rolling down her back. She did not need to paint on her beauty, for she was blessed with it in abundance.

I watched, helpless and pathetic, as she dusted off her embarrassment, faced Dameon and delivered a smile so beautiful that even the lines upon his face seemed to soften. "Apologies, Watcher Dameon. It would seem my brother is as excited as I am for the chance to change his fate. Let us hope our guardians pick one of us."

"Yes," Dameon replied, lips twitching. "Your family could do with some good fortune." His comment felt like a slap.

There was no time to dwell as Auriol's pink-blushed lips pulled into a tight line and she gestured to the space beside her. I could see the words form upon her lips. "Here. Now."

Every eye within Tithe watched as I rushed to my place beside my sister. Dameon did not speak as I did so, allowing the muted whispers of those who watched as they burned at my soul.

"I can't believe you are doing this," Auriol said, body pinned straight at my side. She didn't look at me as she spoke but faced towards the tree as Dameon started up once again. "There will never be enough words to express how upset you have made me."

I was frantic, not caring for the scene I had caused, but only for the burning desire to get my sister as far away from the Choosing as possible. "I can't let you go. Not with them."

"Can't or won't? Do you wish for me to be miserable until the end of my days? Cooped up in a hideous home that's haunted by the memories of everything we have lost?"

"You don't understand..."

"No, Arlo, you are right. I don't."

A few of those near us pressed fingers to lips and sneered to silence us.

"If you go, then I will lose you." Just speaking it aloud made my heart crack inside my chest. If you go, then everything I promised our parents, everything I do to stop the same sickness from taking me, will be for nothing.

My body was frozen as I screamed in my mind at her.

If you go, then there is no reason for me to stop fighting it. Leaving seals my fate, and I am not ready to face death yet.

I had wished to tell Auriol that I had the same sickness that stole our parents from us. For years, I had fought the urge to speak it aloud for fear of what it would do to her. To us. I had kept it buried, swallowing my words even when my will was weak.

But now, standing before the tree, which would soon ripple like water as the elves passed through from their realm, I desired to tell her more than ever.

Maybe she would understand.

Maybe she would stay.

Or perhaps it would only solidify her desire to run from me.

Auriol surprised me by taking my hand. Her fingers slipped within mine, skin warm and fingers trembling slightly. She gripped onto me like she did years ago, holding on as though she wouldn't dare let go.

"Today is promised, but tomorrow is not. We both know far too well what can happen and I cannot just wait around in a life I am not happy in. Not anymore. Let me have this moment. Arlo, please listen to me."

I bit down on the insides of my cheeks and glanced at her, fighting hard to keep the stinging tears at bay. "I am listening, always."

"There is no saying I will be chosen by them, but I just want this moment to dream. If they leave and I am still here, then I promise you I will try to make better with the life we have been given. But please, just today, let me pretend."

Pretend. That was what I had been doing this entire time. Pretending I was fine. Filling my body with the sickening gore of the undead to just pretend.

How could I deny her that?

"Okay," I forced out, knowing it was still very much far from okay. "But I refuse to leave your side. I can't and won't leave you."

As always, I could hear the smile in her voice without having to look at her. Auriol squeezed my hand, and I returned it with a squeeze of my own. "That is all I could have wanted. Oh, and about Tom... I told you he was an idiot."

I almost spluttered a laugh. "That you did."

There was a shift in the air. It thickened, like when a summer storm settled over the world, and the warm air crackled with lightning as the icy winds clashed against it. It laced a strange taste across my tongue, stifling any further words from spilling out from my mouth.

Auriol's grip on my hand tightened, the crowd inhaling a breath at the same time. Expressions melted with wonder as she and every person looked towards the tree.

I had only ever watched the Choosing a handful of times from the perch of the sole window in our apartment, only a brief glance before I shut the heavy curtains and blissfully blocked out the events from my reality.

Being here was different— thrilling, yes, but that coiling of fear I had felt this entire time turned from a spark into an inferno.

Then Dameon spoke, his voice crystal clear over the completely silent town of Tithe. "People of Tithe, here they come."

6

The elves swept out through the tree's surface as though the bark were no more than water. It rippled around their frames, not shifting a single hair upon their heads. Not even the light breeze that coursed through Tithe dared touch these creatures; it left them alone. From fear or respect, I was unsure.

I held my breath the entire time, fearful that I would say something obscene from shock or disbelief at what I witnessed. I counted them to keep myself occupied, one by one, as they strode into Tithe from whatever realm lay beyond the strange, unnatural tree.

Like a row of ducklings, the elves stayed in a perfect line, each one moving with a grace that was not possible for humans. It was as if they floated. Everything about them was effortless and perfect. Four, I counted. Not five, as Dameon had suggested. I repeated my tally as though I had missed something.

The air still crackled with impending tension even after they all had left the confines of the tree. It was the movement of the four elves, each glancing over their shoulders with a shared expression of annoyance, that warned that someone was left to come through. The broad, red-haired man tapped a polished boot upon the cobbles with impatience.

Then he showed himself, much to the excitement of the crowd compared to the clear displeasure of his peers. The Elven man stumbled across the threshold; feet awkward as though they were heavy with ale. His sloppy entrance conjured giggles from the surrounding girls, which did not go unnoticed. I expected that he would have enjoyed their reaction, yet his frown remained.

I couldn't focus on a single elf long enough to truly drink in their appearance. Even to blink would have been a crime for missing out on any details of the otherworldly creatures. At that moment, I forgot why I hated them; their aura of beauty blinded me from my preconceived emotions.

"I can't believe it," Auriol said, echoing my thoughts. Even if I wanted to, I couldn't look at her. "I can't…" Her voice tapered off as she finally succumbed to the same spell I was frozen beneath.

The elves had entrapped us, rooted me to the spot as they lined themselves up before the crowd.

Somewhere behind them I was aware of Dameon who hovered upon the podium, out of place and almost displeased that the fey-kind had not paid him any mind.

"Welcome, all—"

"That is more than enough, Dameon. Please cease your tedious chatter so we can get this started." It was the final elf who spoke. Hearing his deep voice rattle with the thickness of some powerful spirits confirmed that he certainly was drunk—that and the subtle sway of his tall frame and the deep-set shadows beneath his piercing gold eyes.

Beside him stood a woman, a lithe figure draped in a dress of emerald and jade. Her skin was a dark brown which glistened as though painted with the dusting of silver stars. She kept an expression of glee across her face. However, I noticed the subtle shift of her gaze, as though wincing in reaction to the elf that had belittled Dameon.

"Now, brother, that is no way to greet our dear host," she said. Her voice was soft, like the tinkering of bells swaying in a gentle breeze. It sent a welcoming chill down my spine, the feeling not as unpleasant as I would have wished it to be. It pleased Dameon also, whose crimson cheeks dulled in tone. He bowed his head as the woman looked at him with an honest smile.

"It is no bother, my lady," Dameon forced out, his smile the greatest of lies.

"Grand. Then, as Faenir so eloquently put it, shall we proceed?" she asked, removing her touch from the drunk elf and clasping her hands before her.

Faenir. His name settled over me like fresh snow. It melted upon my skin, sinking through, chilling my bones, making my body ache. Somewhere deep in my consciousness, I recognised the reaction as ridiculous, pathetic, as though I was pining for a person I had never met before. But that was soon smothered as my attention returned to the drunk.

"Would you not care for a walk around Tithe?" Dameon asked nervously, gesturing with a swollen hand at the surrounding crowd.

"This being your family's first year here, we thought you may wish to..."

"That would not be necessary," the woman replied. "We are afraid that our visit to your realm must be kept short. Me and my siblings will pick our mate and leave with haste."

I recognised an urgency buried beneath her words, emphasised by the flickering of the elf's eyes and the slight quiver of her taut lips.

Before, I would have been thankful for the idea of them coming and going without their presence leaving much of a mark upon Tithe. Now, seeing them in the flesh only a few broad steps before me, I never wanted them to go.

Faenir ran a ringed hand through the length of his thick, obsidian hair. It was so long it fell in wisps to his waist. He pushed it back from his face, revealing the two elongated points of his ears and the sharp lines of his jaw and cheekbones. Until now it had fallen mostly over his face, concealing his otherworldly beauty, but the taut lines of his mouth and the endless wonder in his eyes had me fearing him more than those he stood alongside.

Regardless, I wanted his attention. I wished for him to look at me, to trail those golden eyes over me just to see if I was deemed worthy enough for his consideration. It was a haunting feeling, one I recognised to be nothing more than deliria conjured by his appearance. Was this how Auriol felt?

It seemed he settled his narrowed stare upon everyone but me. I hated it. When his eyes found that of Auriol's, I almost jumped before her. It lasted only a moment before sweeping over me and continuing down the line.

I followed his trail of interest where it stopped on Tom. From my position, I caught his handsome profile, one I had enjoyed many times. But compared to the creature before me, Tom paled in comparison. But the elf's attention lingered upon Tom longer than I cared to admit. And that coiling of jealousy made itself known within me once again. Then I remembered Auriol. If Tom was chosen, that would be one less chance for her to be taken from me.

I'd rather it be him.

Or me.

"If that is what you wish," Dameon eventually replied.

Returning my attention to the Watcher, I watched as he paraded towards the edge of the podium, then cleared his throat. Taking a gulping, noticeably shaking breath, he called out again, "As thanks for your continued protection against the evils that lurk beyond the wall, please, the people of Tithe would be honoured to be chosen."

It was the red-haired elf who spoke next. "Ensuring the legacy of your kind prolongs the test of time. We gladly offer our powers up to secure your futures."

He cast his hungry gaze across our line, not stopping on a single person long enough to give a hint who it was that caught his interest. There was something calculating about this one. His eyes were a burning red, as though fires twisted around his pupils in an eternal dance.

"May I, Myrinn?" he said to the elven woman, not once removing his eyes from the crowd.

She replied, gesturing elegantly towards the crowd with a sweep of her hand, "Choose wisely, Haldor."

And choose he did.

His choice lasted only a moment.

Auriol groaned as my hand squeezed hers. I had to relax it, not knowing that I had hurt her without realising. I thought he was walking towards us for a moment, which sent a sharp stab of panic through me. Then someone caught his eye.

Haldor stepped towards the line with sure footing and a chin held high with pride that came from growing up around power. His jacket was fitted across his powerful frame, crafted from a golden velvet that gleamed with the dull light of day. It rippled as he walked, much like the tree that the elves had entered through. As he grew closer, I saw how similar his jacket was to that of a flame, shifting between shades of gold to darker, more warming reds and ambers.

"You," he said, standing before a short, blonde-haired girl that I somewhat recognised. "Tell me your name."

"Her..." Auriol scorned quietly, only enough for me to hear. However, I was certain the elf, Haldor, turned his head slightly as though he had picked her murmur out. "He surely can't choose her."

"Samantha," the human girl replied, looking up at the significantly taller elf through pale lashes.

He stood there, contemplating her name as though it were the oddest thing he had heard. Then he turned towards Myrinn and nodded before returning his attention to the girl and raising a hand.

I was the only one to gasp. Unfamiliar, cold eyes fell upon me, but I couldn't care to see who they belonged to. Never having witnessed a Choosing, I was confident that the elf was preparing to strike the girl, but he didn't. He placed a hand on the girl's head and the crowd erupted in cheers.

"It is done," Dameon hollered. "The first tithe has been made."

An older woman and man pushed their way through the crowd in a fit of tears and laughter. Haldor stepped back, allowing the girl to be swept into the arms of the couple. It must have been her parents, mother and father coming to say farewell to their child.

Samantha cried alongside her parents, not from sadness or fear, but from happiness. Anyone close enough to her shared congratulations in the forms of hugs and words of praise. Haldor simply stood and waited, his face stoic and expressionless; only the tapping of his boot upon the ground signified his desire for this display to hurry and end.

"That is enough," he finally said, shattering the excitement as though he took it in his hands and crumpled it. "Come, Sam-an-tha. Join me." He reached out a hand for her to take, not because he wished to, but because he had to. Haldor practically pried the girl from her family, and she happily obliged.

One down.

The thought doused the flames of my anxiety for only a moment before I counted the elves that were left. Four to go.

Next to choose was a shorter elf by the name of Frila. She, like Haldor, had pale skin with a bridge of freckles across her pointed nose. Her hair was a tumbling of white that gathered at her waist in braids. As she walked the line of humans, lips pursed in concentration, the bottom of her azure-toned gown slipped over the cobbles like the billowing of water. She chose a male of Auriol's age. I recognised him well and from the exhale of frustration from Auriol at my side; she was not happy to see him picked.

Like Haldor to Samantha, Frila raised a hand and placed it upon the young man's head. She had to raise up on tiptoes to do it. Even I found the action sweet, perhaps sickly sweet, in fact.

His name was James, and he promptly placed his arm into the crook of Frila's elbow before they swept off to stand beside Haldor and his chosen mate.

"Another down," I recounted aloud to Auriol's displeasure. That relief I felt was growing ever so slightly, but enough to notice, as though a weight was being lifted from my shoulders.

Auriol straightened next to me, brightening her smile as she gazed towards the remaining elves. "I only need one chance and I see three. Odds are in my favour."

Gildir was next to retrieve his claim. His skin was golden, his brown hair trimmed close to his scalp. As he drew closer, I could see that each strand of hair was a tight curl upon his head. A feathering of a beard spread across the lower side of his face, which he brushed a thumb and forefinger over as he surveyed the crowd.

"I promise to leave you the best pick, brother," Gildir called back towards Myrinn and Faenir. Faenir's upper lip curled over his teeth, urged by the giggling of Frila, who held delicate fingers over her red-painted lips. It was an odd encounter.

"Gildir," Myrinn scolded through a tight-lipped smile. "Not now."

He spun around on the spot, hands raised to his sides and shoulders, shrugging in a signal of defeat.

I watched Faenir intently, seeing how he whispered to Myrinn, whose expression waned. The crowd was so focused on Gildir as he pointed his finger over them, they did not notice the interaction with the remaining fey.

Faenir boiled with anger. His forehead was furrowed with countless lines, I was certain each one told a story. Even Myrinn looked flustered as she replied. Then the strangest thing occurred. Faenir raised his hand in gesture, and she flinched, stepping back from it in a hurry.

A chill sliced down my spine. I couldn't fathom what I had witnessed between them, nor could I have time to work it out as the crowd exploded around me. This time, it was not all from cheering. Three of the elves had chosen and those waiting somewhat patiently for their chance were growing impatient. Much like Auriol.

By the time I looked back to Faenir and Myrinn, there was not an ounce of tension between them. Well, not from Myrinn at least. Faenir seethed silently at her side now with a noticeable distance between them.

Gildir had claimed a stunning girl with curls of ginger hair that circled her face in a halo. She reacted calmly to his touch upon her head, however, her eyes brimmed with undeniable thrill. No matter how hard she tried to keep her composure, I could see the truth through the cracks of it.

"Whose up next?" Gildir asked as he passed the remaining two. Frila laughed again, silenced only by Haldor, whose burning stare shot upon her. "May I suggest it be you, sister? Leave the best for last, I think…"

Myrinn shared a look of sympathy with Faenir before sweeping off towards the crowd with a glowing smile. As she did, I caught Gildir whisper into his Chosen's ear. The girl spluttered a cry and practically threw herself away from Faenir, who tried to pretend as though he had not noticed.

But he had. The pain in his golden eyes told as much.

I knew Auriol was safe from being chosen by Myrinn. Never, in Tithe's history, had an elf picked a claim of the same sex. It was a strange concept, to only limit yourself to those opposite to you. Tithe was a place where sexuality wasn't restricted, and it was always a concept of the Choosing I never understood.

When Myrinn passed Auriol, she gifted her a brilliant smile. Auriol, who had only even come home with a boy's name on the tip of her lips, shuddered at the Elven woman's presence as though she would happily have thrown herself before her.

But alas, Myrinn moved on and ended up claiming a strapping

young man who towered beside an extremely disappointed Tom. For a moment, I had believed it was him and felt almost disappointed that it wasn't. For my sake, more so than his.

"It will not happen to me, will it?"

I tried to hide my grin as I looked at my sister. Her mismatched eyes scanned my face as though looking for a reason to hate me for my happiness that she was right. I couldn't do it to her. Even though I prayed to anything or anyone that would listen for her not to be taken, I still wished she would have another moment of wishing. Because when this was over, as she promised me, her want for this chance would be left behind.

"One chance you said. There is one more left to claim," I murmured in support.

Faenir.

"Your turn, brother," Gildir called out again before Myrinn even had the chance to join her siblings. "Don't keep us waiting."

Faenir did not move. His hands balled into fists at his sides, his chest heaving, as though he shared the same anxiety as I. Then he said a word I did not expect. "No."

Gildir laughed to the horror of his Chosen. "Go on, Faenir. Place your hand upon the one you find most alluring and see if she still stands long enough to return home."

"I will not indulge in this fantasy."

"Faenir." It was Myrinn who spoke up. "Please, just try."

"You know what will happen."

"Grandmother will not be pleased if you do not follow custom."

We all watched in complete silence at the interaction. Dameon leaned down from the podium, speaking out of the corner of his mouth. "There seems to be a problem. Accept our apologies if we have disrespected you in any—"

"Silence yourself," Faenir snapped, whipping his temper towards the Watcher, who practically fell back on his arse. The shadows of the tree which the sun cast upon the street seemed to shiver. I blinked, and they were still once again.

"Perhaps it should be left," Myrinn added quickly, unable to keep up her façade that everything was fine by smiling.

"This is your chance," Gildir said, as if reminding Faenir of something. "To prove her wrong."

Faenir stepped forward, looking from the elf to the line of confused, silent humans.

Myrinn considered her thoughts. "If you do not want to do this, then I will petition Grandmother for…"

Faenir raised a hand into the air, his fingers twitching as he did so.

"As always, cousin, my hand is forced. This is what she wants, then I will do as she wishes."

"We should leave," I said without realising. Auriol pulled her hand out of reach as I tried to take it. "Something is not right with that one."

She ignored me, instead muttering the same words under her breath, "Me, please choose me. Please. Please."

Faenir's eyes fell upon my sister and stayed there. He did not smile. His face did not warm at the sight of her. Instead, he looked sorrowful. It was an expression we both knew well. After the death of our parents, anyone we passed, anyone who visited us, looked at us the very same way. I didn't have a chance to understand why as the shift of his cloak hushed across the ground as he walked towards us.

Toward me.

Toward her.

Auriol's breath hitched. My heart stopped. Three words lingered across Faenir's lips as he closed in on us. "I am sorry."

Somewhere behind him, the elves buzzed with a dangerous excitement, Gildir and Frila's voices reaching over the rest of them.

Faenir stood before us, inches from Auriol, as he faced her down.

I tried to move, but I couldn't. My mind screamed for me to say something, do something, to stop him as he raised his hand.

Faenir closed his eyes, handsome face wincing as he lowered his palm towards my sister's willing and waiting head. The world seemed to stop for a moment. All the sound drained from existence until it was only the haunting whisper of my parents which remained.

Do not lose sight of her. Do not leave her as we have. Stay together, promise us.

I broke free from my prison of horror and reached out my hand. Snapping my fingers across the man's wrist, I clamped down with a vice-like grip. His skin was soft like downy feathers, yet it was cold, as if I'd buried my fingers in snow. My hand was not big enough to wrap entirely around the width of his wrist, but my strength was unwavering, fuelled by my desperation to keep him from the only person I had left.

"You. Cannot. Have. Her," I spat, wrist aching beneath the weight of his arm.

"Arlo, stop it!" Auriol pleaded.

Faenir looked at me with widening eyes. I saw my reflection in his stare, stern face twisting among the gold flecks.

No longer did his siblings laugh and coax him on. Instead, they were as silent as the crowd who watched on as I had interrupted the Choosing.

Then he spoke to me, eyes furrowed, and mouth parted in a mixture of disbelief and something else. Something I should have recognised sooner. Terror. "This should not be possible."

Heart thundering like the cantering of a hundred wild mares, I tossed his wrist away and stepped between my sister and him. Like many men, Faenir was taller than me, but I did not let that deter my territorial stance. "Pick someone else. She is not for you."

Faenir cocked his head, looking at me as though he was a hound, and I was something new to him. As he spoke again, I discerned his words were for me and me alone. "What are you, *Arlo?*"

The way he said my name felt as rancid as it clawed up my spine. Not only that, but it was a strange question, one I never imagined being asked by anyone, let alone an otherworldly creature such as him. I replied the only way I felt like I could, "Not of any interest to you, elf."

He smirked, surveying me with those burning, honey eyes. "You could not understand how very wrong you are."

7

THE CHILL which slithered up my spine was not caused by the gale of cold winds that brushed through Tithe. It was the silence, sickening and endless. That was what conjured the reaction. Even with the streets of Tithe full to bursting, I could have heard a pin drop. Every set of eyes were focused on me.

Whereas my attention was frozen upon the elven man.

Faenir stumbled back as though moved by an unseen force. His hands were raised before him, fingers splayed. Without so much as a blink, he studied them as if it was the first moment he had realised he even had hands, turning them over, inspecting every inch of skin with such intensity it seemed he searched for the true meaning of life upon them.

Myrinn was behind him in moments, her movements rushed but still dripping with grace. "Faenir, we should leave."

"Did you see?" he murmured in response, still not taking his eyes from his hands.

Myrinn looked at me, only for a short moment, eyes tracing me from head to toe. "I saw enough. We all have."

Faenir finally broke his concentration and focused on me with the same wide-eyed expression. And he was not the only one who did. Myrinn, Haldor, and the other two fey whose smug expressions had been scraped clean from their pleasant faces. Not a single one tore their gaze from me, not even as Gildir and Frila shared whispers behind their hands.

The human occupants of Tithe also observed in horror at what I had done; some gazes were gentler than others.

Above the lot of them, it was Faenir's I cared for.

His shock was so palpable that it encouraged the hairs upon my arms to stand on end.

"Impossible," he muttered, eyes flicking back and forth from his hands then back to me.

My breathing was heavy, my heart thundering painfully in my chest. The ability to form words failed me as I felt buried beneath the weight of the elves attention. Names were powerful, not something I wished to give out so easily. Father had taught me that.

A tingling spread across my palm. No matter how many times I flexed it at my side the feeling would not stop. Faenir had left his impression upon me, and I was unable to decide how I felt about it.

"Faenir," Myrinn said, turning her back on me as though I was not worthy to listen to. "Now."

Faenir waited for me to answer him. I held my breath, urging him to leave as he was being asked to do.

When he finally turned away, I could have fallen to my knees.

"Wait," Auriol called out, breaking the line as she begged for the elf's attention. "Please, he didn't mean to do that. Take me with you. Let me be your Chosen!"

My skin crawled as I listened to her pleading. Watching her race forward, the skirt of her dress held in two tense fists, I saw the reality of what I had done. The severity of it.

The elves sauntered towards the tree, five with their Chosen mates and Faenir without. *She should be with him. She will hate you for this.*

Dameon didn't have the chance to speak as they brushed past him and disappeared into the rippling body of the tree.

It happened so quickly.

Only when the last slip of Myrinn's straight back passed from view did Auriol turn to me. Her eyes burned, wide and red. A single tear escaped, slicing down her cheek where it traced the curves of her jaw and stained her dress once it fell. It seemed that the ground trembled where she stood rooted to it, but it was her body. She shook violently, physically trying to stop poisonous hate from bursting beyond her pale lips.

The peace lasted a second.

"You ruined everything," she growled. When her mouth moved again nothing more than a slip of exhausted air came out.

"Auriol, I'm..." *Sorry?* No. I wasn't sorry. I did what I had been tasked by our parents to do. I kept her safe. She could hate me for the rest of her life and it would be the *tithe* I would pay for knowing she was safe. Safe from the unknown. Safe from them.

Safe... from Faenir.

Dameon pounced upon the scene, face flushed, scarlet staining his neck and cheeks. He took my upper arm in his hand, pinching my skin between careless fingers. "One of you needs to explain what has just happened. Right. Now. Do you understand the severity? The disrespect would be the downfall of Tithe!"

"Get off me!" The pain Dameon inflicted on me was the anchor I needed to focus. I tore my arm free just as the wave of the crowd flooded over us. Auriol was lost to it, but I had nowhere to go, not with the furious form of the Watcher in my way and the occupants of Tithe at my back.

I was trapped in the net of furious chaos.

"You are not going anywhere, Arlo Grey." Dameon attempted to reach out for me but missed as I began slipping away. "Something needs to be done in hopes to plead forgiveness for your disregard to our customs."

I didn't care for what he said next. Dancing around the crush of bodies, I ran, head down and mind focused as I tried everything to find Auriol.

People tried to stop me, but their effort was in vain. Nothing would prevent me from finding my sister. I had stopped her from being taken from me, I would not lose her now without a fight.

~

I could hear the song of destruction before I even reached the front door to our home. The shattering of glass. The splintering of wood. My legs burned as I bounded up the stairs, two at a time. I was greeted by our door left ajar. Shards of broken plates and cups littered the floor beyond like blades of deadly grass. My boots betrayed me, announcing my arrival with loud crunching, as did the screeching door hinges that screamed as I pushed it wide.

Auriol waited for me with a chair held above her head. She grimaced, a cat-like shriek spitting out of her as she hoisted the chair forward and threw it towards me. It shattered across the wall at my side. Splinters exploded across the side of my face, cutting and scratching.

"I hate you!"

I lowered my arm, recognising the wet warmth of a cut across my cheek. "I know."

She stood there, breathing laboured and eyes wild with fury. Her hair was unkempt, her dress ruined by the smudging of dirt along its seam. "Do you? Do you know how selfish you are? How completely consumed by your own wants and needs that you cannot see that your actions will be the ruin of us!"

I shouldn't have let her words hurt me, but they did. Because she was right.

"Everything I do is to keep you safe—"

"From what?" She laughed, barking as she interrupted me. "Answer me that, Arlo. Nothing you do is for me. Nothing. It is all for you. Years I have ignored the comments from friends, even from people who I care little for. But I can't pretend they are wrong anymore. They see what you are, and so do I."

I felt heat rise from the ground, through my boots and into every vein and bone within my body. It was a discomforting feeling, knowing that other people spoke about us. I had known the people of Tithe looked at us with sorrow after our parents passed. Was I truly blind to how they saw me?

"Listening to what others say is pointless. Auriol, please consider why I do this. We don't know what happens to those who are Chosen. The risk of the unknown is too great."

She paced forward, arm raised and finger pointed towards me until her nail found my chest and pressed into it. "I know that whatever waits within their realm would be a far better future than what I would have here. Stuck, poor little orphan Auriol whose parents couldn't even stay alive to care for her and whose brother keeps her imprisoned for his own need for control. I want a life without the constraints that have been shackled upon me. And my one chance, the chance I was given and deserved, has been taken by the person I should trust the most."

I lowered my stare to my boots, unworthy of my sister. "I did it because it was what our parents wanted."

Auriol spun from me, moving so fast I was sure she would raise her hand back and slap it across my face. "So you commune with the dead now?"

"Don't be ridiculous," I snapped, stalking after her as she frantically searched for the next item to throw and break. We passed holes in the walls, dents made by the broken objects that lay forgotten at the floor beneath them. "You could never understand the pressure I have been under since they died. Everything I have done is because they asked it of me. It is their wish..."

"They are dead! *Fucking dead*, Arlo. It doesn't matter what they wish or want; if they are not here to say it then it is pointless. When are you going to realise that you act on your own behalf and not that of the dead?"

"That isn't fair."

"Fair? What isn't fair is our dear mother and father gave up on us."

"Auriol!" I couldn't believe the words that came out of her mouth. It was a lie, but as she said it I knew she believed it was truth. "They could not help the sickness that infected them. Do you really think they gave up without a fight?"

I knew the fight, the struggle as my lungs filled up with my own blood, drowning me from the inside out. "You... we cannot even begin to imagine what they went through. You are saying that because you are angry."

"Don't you dare speak on my behalf. You know nothing about me."

I had to keep my anger buried. I wished, nothing more, than to lash out and hurt her with the truth. Auriol didn't understand the very lengths I had gone to ensure our parents final wishes were kept. How I filled my body with the sick gore of the vampires I killed just to ensure she was not left in this world alone.

"What now?" I asked, pacing behind her as she burned marks into our floor which each rushed step. "Are you going to take your anger out on me, on everything we have left? Smash our home into pieces only for us to patch it up together again? You might not understand why I have done what I have, but you will one day. When you are older and realise that you can have a life within Tithe, one you can carve for yourself."

"One where you can continue being my shadow and keep my happiness from reach, is that what you mean?"

This was getting nowhere and if I continued arguing with her I would soon spread my own destruction alongside hers. "I am going to go. Take the time you need to think this over. Perhaps when this entire place is overturned, we can sit down among the mess and chat like adults."

"That's right, Arlo," she sneered, teeth bared. "Run away from the truth. Do what you do best and disappear. You think you do everything to keep this family together when you cannot even stay in this fucking house for long enough to be a part of it. Run to Tom. At least one of us is granted the freedom to live other lives. And do not worry about me. I will be here when you get back like I always am, waiting like the doting sister who is willing to disregard her wants in life to please you."

I stopped myself from telling her then and there. My hand reached for the pouch at my belt and the glass vials within. The urge to tear them free from their leather confines and smash them upon the ground at her feet was almost too strong to ignore. I wished to see the dead, cold blood of the vampire drip through the floorboards and wash away.

It took a will power I did not know I possessed to turn my back on her and walk towards our open door. Each step was forced. My heart thundered in my chest, almost leaping into my throat and stopping me from swallowing or gulping a big enough breath to calm down. I felt a bulging vein in my forehead, throbbing as though it was a worm beneath my skin. And with each step towards the boundary of our broken, split home, I still longed to hear Auriol call my name.

She didn't. And deep down, beneath the anger and embarrassment, I could understand why.

I threw the hood of my jacket up, concealing myself beneath its welcoming shadows, before I reached the last stair beyond the building's outer door. The streets were still crammed with people, no longer alive with excitement for the festivities but horror for what had happened. What I had done.

The worst part of it was that I still felt Faenir's presence across my palm. I needed something to scrub away his touch and the memory of it.

Auriol was right. Only Tom had the power to do that for me.

8
FAENIR

I was all too familiar with the golden hue of life force. How it glowed around a person's body as though they stood before the mighty sun which burned brilliantly behind them.

All until I touched them and stole it away.

My affliction made me a moth to a flame, always drawn to those who brimmed with life. They teased me, urging me to reach out and touch their warmth, all for me to take it from them and leave them dull and cold.

That was what would have happened to the girl. All before *he* had reached a hand, wrapped his slender fingers around my wrist, and stopped me.

I had never felt anything like it. A decade with only feeling the cold and yet I could feel the boy's warmth as though he still held me.

"He touched you," Myrinn repeated for the umpteenth time since returning to our realm. I sensed her own want to try. My sister, kind and glowing like a star, always hoping for the best for everyone.

"Don't." I pulled back before her fingers could move another inch towards me.

The rest of my relatives whispered with caution as guards came and swept their humans from them. I could see the confusion creased across the humans' faces as they overheard the commotion that lasted a moment as they were removed from the room.

"Queen Claria must hear of this immediately," Frila said. Was that panic I heard beneath her tone?

"Hold your tongue," Myrinn snapped, turning her attention upon our youngest sister. "Until we understand what has occurred there will be nothing to report. As much as you do enjoy the chaos, little sister, I demand that you keep silent about this."

I should have told Myrinn that I did not require her help to fight my battles. It had been years since I had even seen her last and I had done fine coping without her.

"For now," Gildir added, seemingly the most unbothered by the display.

"The Choosing is over," I reminded them all. "What has happened can be forgotten. It makes no difference for I have still returned empty-handed."

As I spoke, I could not stop the wheels turning in my mind. The entrance to Tithe waited behind me. I would have until nightfall to visit and return before the veil between our worlds sealed, if only to see him again and inspect his halo of life, to find the answers as to why he could resist the death my touch granted.

How? Why? Only two of the many questions that swam within my pulsing mind.

My relatives, as powerful as they each were, would not notice if I melted into the shadows. They had no domain over the darkness, not like I.

I retreated to the quiet chamber within my soul and waited for the conversation to end. With great effort, I forced a smile at Myrinn, who looked back at me with motherly concern that was almost similar to pity. She then turned with the rest and left me alone.

Perhaps I had decided upon my actions before I truly realised.

Impatient and starved for that warmth once again, I slipped into the shadows, pressed through the base of the Great Tree of Nyssa and entered Tithe with my sights and desires focused on finding the boy again.

Arlo.

9

I WAS BEING FOLLOWED as I weaved through the bustling streets of Tithe like a mouse. No matter if I stopped and looked blatantly around, or briefly glanced over my shoulder, there was no one there to see.

I narrowed my stare, searching through the shadows of shops, homes and alleyways, just to find the owner of the eyes that caused prickles across the back of my neck.

Still, there wasn't anyone noticeable.

Continuing through the narrowed side streets of Tithe was my best option. Tired, old buildings leaned on either side of the crooked passageways. The shadow they cast across the cobbled path was dense. With my hood up and quick feet, I kept pace.

Dameon likely had a price for my head after what I had done. It was best to stay clear from him until things died down. *If they ever did.* Yes, not all of the fey-kind had left with a Chosen, but four of them did. That was better than nothing. Surely, they would see sense and not punish Tithe for what I had done.

The tickling sensation didn't cease. It continued to flirt with me, spreading goosebumps across any exposed skin it could find. At one point, seemingly alone in the back alleys of Tithe's outer reaches, I almost stopped and shouted for the person to reveal themselves. Seeing sense that I was likely crazed, I kept my head down and my feet quick.

I reached Tom's house to find it empty. The dusty windows were dark and there was not a sound of life from within. I sagged, back pressed against the paint-worn door with the perfect balance of relief and disappointment. He would have likely still been thrown into the throngs of what little festivities were left.

It was not the best choice for me to wait for him to return. So I went to the only place I knew I was welcome.

The Wall.

I needed a distraction, and the ancient oaks couldn't provide that, but it was my only option. I couldn't return home to Auriol, not yet. Perhaps things would have cooled down by the rise of tomorrow's dawn. Until then I would have to wait and play out our argument over and over in my head.

Since I had left Tom's house, I had not felt the presence following me. It was easy to push it to the back of my mind when I had far too much to worry about.

I sat beneath the trees at the edges of Tithe's boundary, hidden beneath the foliage from the towering wall and the Watchers who paraded across it. When evening arrived, I would return to Tom and allow him to divert my mind from my reality.

I only hoped he would.

༄

Night had fallen upon Tithe and with it a chill that sank into my bones. I woke beneath the trees freezing and stiff. At some point I had fallen asleep, giving into the peace of that rather than the punishment my waking brain put me under.

Stretching out my aching limbs, I made my way towards Tom's house, sprinting through shadows. By the time I got there, I was relieved to see the glow of orange and red flames dancing within the windows.

He was home.

"Hello?" I called out, pushing the already ajar door to Tom's home open. It screeched painfully; if they had not heard my call then the noise it made would surely alert them to my presence.

After several moments passed with no response, I called out again, stepping carefully through the threshold. "I would have knocked but the door was…"

My mouth clamped shut, silencing the horror from spilling out as I saw what waited before me.

Tom's mother, Kate, was splayed out across the floor. In her hand she gripped the iron prongs that would be used to push wood about in the hearth. Beside her was a perfectly stacked pile of logs still waiting to be placed into the flames.

It looked as though she had fallen asleep before finishing her task. But Kate was not sleeping. No…

She was dead.

I knew that from the grey sheen of her skin, as though it had turned to stone, cracking in places and allowing blood to spread like a lake of scarlet beneath her. Her hair, once full of warmth and colour, was drained to tones of silver; strands like cobwebs, lying within her blood and staining it in wet clumps.

My stomach jolted. I rocked forward, hands on knees, as vomit erupted out of me; the wet splatter only made me sick again, over and over until my stomach cramped and a cold sweat broke out over my forehead.

I called Tom's name, recognising the deafening silence more than I had before I found Kate's dead body. It was close to impossible to wait for his response or hear it over the thundering of my heart. It echoed through my ears, synchronising with the thumping pain that filled my head.

Perhaps I should have left then, run back out the door and screamed Tithe down until someone came to help us. But my feet moved forward. I sidestepped around the outstretched legs of Kate as though I navigated a narrow path on the side of a sheer-face cliff.

My hand went to my belt and to the short knife that offered its comfort. I gripped the hilt, not pulling it free from the sheath just yet, but I was ready if I needed it.

I found Tom's dad in the darkened kitchen. I almost passed him as I moved for the stairs but stopped when I saw the dark outline of his figure sitting upon a chair by the dining table.

"Are you okay, sir?" I asked, rushing in to help him. In the dark it looked as though he was simply sitting at the table waiting patiently for his supper to be put before him. I was wrong.

The stench of decay greeted me as I got closer to him. With the little light that spilled from the living room I finally saw the truth of what waited for me. Like his wife, he too was dead. His wide eyes were black, bulging from his skull as though the skin around them had retreated. His face was sunken and hollow; it was as though he had died weeks before. What was left of the grey skin still clinging to the bones of his face were melting off before my eyes. It dripped alongside his darkened blood, across the table before him where his hands rested. His mouth was open in a silent scream, the little amount of teeth he still had were yellow and brown; most laid among the dripping puddle of gore beneath him.

My mind raced for what had done this. Vampires? No. It couldn't have been. The Watchers would have been alerted if a vampire had broken through the boundary. Or maybe they had. My disrespect at the Choosing had done what the Watchers had threatened for as long as I could remember. The magic that kept us hidden from sight of the undead creatures had been taken back by the elves and we were left, holed together in a pen like sheep, waiting for the wolves to come and pick us apart.

I unsheathed my pathetic knife, the bone handle worn from years of handling and the blade dull. It was better used to cut steak than an enemy, but it served me well against the vampires that I hunted when I needed their blood.

If there was one here, I would kill it. Take its blood for my own use and call upon the Watchers.

I would be a hero. They would see past my actions and acclaim me for...

No, Arlo. Focus.

Swallowing the urge to vomit again, I lifted the blade to Tom's father's neck. Even in the sagging, melting skin I could not discern teeth marks. I then looked at his arms—

There was movement above me, the familiar creak of floorboards beneath heavy feet. I could have died on the spot from the fear which crawled up from my feet and spread across my skull; the feeling was painful.

"Tom," I forced out, trying to put as much confidence into my voice as I could muster. I had chased vampires into the darkest pits, far more frightening than this place. But it was different. I was normally the one hunting, but now it felt like I was being hunted. "Please, Tom... let it be you."

I left the dead body in the kitchen and padded quietly towards the bottom of the stairs. My knuckles were white with tension as I gripped the knife and held it out before me.

If it was a vampire, I had to kill it, not because I was desperate to collect its blood this time, but because if it got out of this house and spread its disease around Tithe until it reached Auriol... The thought alone had me taking the steps up to next floor of the house.

I had to keep Auriol safe.

The creak sounded again. I recognised its location from being in Tom's room. I prepared myself to find him dead, like his mother and father. The stairs replied to the noise that waited for me, squeaking its betrayal of my presence.

There was no point in sneaking. Whoever, or whatever, waited upstairs knew I was coming.

I burst into Tom's room, the cry of battle wetting my lips and filling my chest with a false sense of confidence.

"Arlo..." Tom stood still in the centre of his room; darkness danced around him. Only the light of the silvered moon cutting paths through his window illuminated us.

"You are alive."

"It is your fault."

I lowered my knife. The shock at finding him alive sent a violent tremble through my legs. I hardly registered what he said as a new urgency spread through me.

"We need to get out of here, Tom. Whatever has killed your parents will be back." Getting my words out was hard. I rushed, urgent and frantic, as I raised my hand towards him.

Tom stayed still, chin raised high as though an unseen hand had lifted it. "You brought this. You killed them. You..." Tom began to cry now, spitting with each shaking breath. Snot leaked down his nose, spreading with the dribble and tears until it coated his pale skin.

That was when I felt it, a shift of the shadows as a hand reached out behind Tom and hovered in the air above his shoulder. Tom flinched as though sensing the presence but did not turn to see it. It was not the clawed hand of a vampire. The light of the moon dusted across it, catching the almost diamond glint of its skin, perfect nails, and a deep ruby ring set in a gold band that stood proud upon its middle finger.

"Get back!" I shouted, throat dry and tongue feeling too big for my mouth.

"You never answered my question," a voice spoke from the shadows, deep and rich. It caused the air to vibrate as though it danced in command to it. The hand that belonged to the shrouded figure twitched, fingers rising and falling one by one as if he was playing the ivory keys of an instrument.

Tom snivelled like a pig being led to slaughter, eyes rimmed red with the knowledge of what was to come for him.

I pointed my knife, narrowing my gaze as I tried to navigate the shadows for the speaker. It was as though they had thickened into a cloak, and *he* wore it. However, he did not need to step free from his hiding place for me to know who spoke. I recognised his voice as if it was as familiar as my sister's.

"Faenir..." I said his name aloud, hoping speaking it would shatter this illusion. Perhaps I still slept beneath the trees in the outskirts of Tithe. Surely this had to be a dream. This death. This horror. How else could it be explained that an elf stood within Tom's room? When it went against everything I knew about their visits.

As if hearing my thoughts and wishing to prove me a fool, Faenir freed himself of the shadows. He did not move. They did, shifting away from him as if someone else had pulled his cloak free.

My breath hitched. Tom spluttered a light scream that belonged more to a young girl than him.

"I see I have made an impression on you just as you have on me."

I cringed. My skin felt as though it would melt from my bones just as it had for Tom's parents.

"Do not hurt him," I pleaded. "I disrespected you. I refused your

Choosing, not him. Why come and hurt these people when they had nothing to do with it?"

It felt natural to close the space between us. I wanted him to know that I did not fear him. But should I? If Faenir had caused the death within this house, then I should be frightened.

"I thought you were *all* free from my curse. Now I see that was wrong." Faenir did not smile as he spoke, although his voice was full of excitement. He did not take his golden eyes off me, not as he lowered his lips towards Tom's neck where they waited a hairsbreadth above it. "You interest me, Arlo. I wished to see you again and make sure that it was not I who was crazed and mad. I almost left without trying again."

"Please," I said through gritted teeth. "Let him go."

"Why?" Faenir pouted, lips growing closer to Tom's neck.

"If you hurt him, I swear I will kill you."

Faenir smiled, welcoming my threat. "I am not scared of death. Why should I fear something that belongs to me?"

He kissed Tom before I could do anything to stop it, pressing his lips into Tom's neck gently and for only a brief moment. Tom relaxed, shoulders lowering, and all creases of fear and panic vanished from his face until he was the handsome man I remembered him to be.

The peace lasted only a moment.

Tom's eyes were thrown open as the first warning. He went to scream but a gargle came out instead. Then, like his mother and father, a shadow of grey passed over his skin. Tom died where he stood; life drained from his body with each prolonged second. I had never seen a body decay so quickly apart from the vampires I had staked myself.

I couldn't mutter a word. The knife shook in my hand, my body rooted to the spot, as Faenir released Tom and he tumbled to the floor like a sack of rotten shit.

"You see what happens to those I touch?" Faenir asked, voice peaked with the question. "Then tell me why you still stand. Why did you not die as you should have when your fingers took my wrist and stopped me? What, *Arlo*, makes you so different?"

I did not take my eyes from Tom's rotting corpse as Faenir stepped towards me. It was as though the shadows in the room closed in around us, blocking out the light from the moon and covering every wall until we stood within a hellscape of darkness in another realm.

"Until you can answer me," Faenir said, voice urging the darkness to creep closer as if his presence commanded it. "You will be mine."

10

I WAS LOST to a sea of darkness. Its current was resilient, dragging me from my feet and throwing my world into chaos.

I had a sense I was moving but not because I was walking. It came in the unsettling jolt that filled my stomach as though I was looking down at the world from a great height, except there was nothing for me to see, only the endless darkness as though hands were held over my eyes.

There was no use in crying out, to scream from fear or wail like a broken-hearted creature from the memory of Tom dying before my eyes. No one would hear me. My throat would fill with the shadows the moment my lips opened, blocking my airway and silencing me with its greedy hands.

Was I dying? It was the clearest thought that I could latch onto. Faenir had reached for me, fingers grazing my cheek in what should have been an affectionate touch. But then the darkness took over.

Perhaps his touch, the one that had killed Tom, his father and mother, had taken me too.

An image of Auriol's face flashed through my mind suddenly. It was an explosion of brilliant light fighting away the shadows so I could see her clearly. Life. That was what the halo that surrounded her frame was.

The edges of the vision were blurry, but the life that encompassed her was bright and frightening. I was beside her. My body glowed with the same aura of light as hers. I could see the horrific embarrassment on her face and the determined hatred in mine. How my mismatching eyes glared at the person's viewpoint I was getting a glimpse of. Faenir. I was seeing from his eyes during the Choosing.

It lasted only a moment.

Then everything stopped. The world stilled. The darkness quietened its siren call.

Only four words seemed to whisper in the silence, so faint, it was the only thing for me to cling to.

You will be mine.

It was the cold breeze that dusted across my sodden skin that woke me.

Then I heard the gentle brush of... water, lapping up against a shore of smoothed stone which joined in with a chorus of bird calls. I laid there with my eyes pinched closed, enjoying the calming feeling my senses kept me entrapped in.

But then I remembered that in Tithe there was no body of water large enough to cause such a sound and certainly not one close to home.

I bolted upright, eyes snapping wide, to find that I was laid out across a bed I did not recognise in a room I had never seen before. It was a vast bedroom constructed from walls of white stone with veins of dark grey that spread through them like rivers. Directly before the bed, which was big enough for at least five grown men to fill, was an arched doorway generously giving view to the world beyond.

Sheer curtains moved in the breeze, twisting like ghosts dancing to the chorus of nature.

I focused on the open, cloudless skies and the faint outline of what looked like the peaks of a mountainous range far in the distance. This world was certainly not the one I knew.

I was no longer in Tithe.

Heart pounding, I threw myself from the bed. The sheets that had been draped across me almost caused me to fall flat upon my face as they tangled with my feet. Steadying myself, head thundering in harmony with my heart, my hands went to my belt. One hand clasped the pouch hiding the vials which calmed me somewhat. The other went to the empty sheath that should have held my knife, the one I had last brandished towards Faenir whilst standing above the dead body of Tom.

"I thought it best to keep this from you. It would be foolish to allow a weapon to be kept in your hands when I do not know what you do with it."

I turned on my heel, fists gathered into balls before me, and faced the speaker.

Faenir leaned against a doorframe at the other end of the room. His legs were crossed at his ankles, rivulets of dark hair falling over his chest like waves of shadow. A shiver spread down from my skull as I watched him, stupefied, as he twisted my knife in one hand with the tip of the metal spinning upon his finger. He pulled it away to reveal a droplet of ruby blood before swiftly sticking his finger in his mouth, raising his golden stare to me, and cleaning the blood with his tongue.

"Where have you taken me?" I hissed, nails cutting crescent moons into my palms.

"To my home."

I wished to take my eyes from the elven prince and glance across the room once again. But I knew that would have been foolish.

Never take your eyes off your enemy, for it is what they do when you cannot see which makes them your greatest threat.

"We are not in Tithe." It was not a question, but more a statement to confirm what my mind had already come to terms with.

"Far from it," Faenir confirmed, flashing pink stained teeth. As he pulled his finger from his mouth, I noticed the cut was no longer visible.

You can take him. The thought was sudden. That possibility faltered into nothingness as I registered the fact that Faenir, as well as being over a foot taller than me, had the power to kill at his touch. If I was to get out of this place, I needed to be alive.

"You killed them..." I snarled, lip curling over my teeth as though I was no different to the vampires I hunted. "Tom. His family."

"That bothers you, does it?"

My skin crawled as his gaze traced over me. Faenir studied every inch of me, drinking my details like a dehydrated sailor. I didn't answer his question, aware of my lack of control if I did. Perhaps I would have given into the haunting image of their deaths which lurked at the back of my mind, or even raced across the room and tackled Faenir in a furious hurricane of fists and teeth.

Instead, I inhaled deeply, hoping it would help me stay calm, and presented my demand. "Take me back."

Faenir pushed himself from the doorframe, amusement alight across his devilish face. "I am afraid I am unable to do that."

My eyes frantically searched for signs that he was lying; the twitching of a lip, or the narrowing of an eye that was the usual response when someone was being deceitful.

"Take. Me. Home."

"Are you not going to ask where it is you are before demanding to return to a place which holds no future for you compared to what I can give you?" Faenir was serious as he spoke. Two, perfectly manicured dark brows furrowed above his squinting stare. His angular face was hauntingly handsome. The way he looked at me screamed with confusion as though he could not understand how stupid I could be not to see sense in why I was here.

I stepped closer to him, knuckles white as I still bared my fists. He stared at me and sniggered softly which burned the furnace of anger inside of me to a new level of heat.

"I am not the one to be laughed at, *elf*," I said, muscles trembling with anticipation. "Careful how you regard me."

An urgency was building. I wanted to get home to Auriol and would do anything to make that happen.

"Your threats are meaningless to me, *human*."

"Tell me what you want from me and get this over with."

"You are my Chosen, Arlo." He drew my name out as though enjoying the way the sounds rolled over his tongue. My skin crawled to see his misplaced enjoyment. "What I want is you. Now, are you ready to answer the pressing mystery? I am dying to know."

Nothing else mattered about what he said besides his first four words. "I am nothing to you. Not your Chosen. Not your mystery. Nothing. Now, if you do not take me home, I swear to tear this entire... this... fucking, where the fuck have you taken me!?"

My blustering, wordy anger entertained Faenir who could not hide the twitching corners of his lips. "Haxton."

"What?" I gaped, breathing heavily as though I had run up a steep hill and back down again without stopping.

"You are currently residing in the guest suite of my home, Haxton Manor."

"Well fuck your home," I spat, scowling at the elf who hardly flinched from the droplets of spit that shot towards him. "Smile again and I promise to wipe it clean from your face."

"As you have said," Faenir replied, calmly. Even with me inches from him the elven prince showed no signs of concern. That irked me. "And as I will tell you again, returning home is not possible. I have chosen you, Arlo. Just like my cousins have picked their mates before you, when you so interestingly interrupted. I suppose you simply delayed the inevitable and I admit I am thankful for that. If you had not stopped me from choosing your sister then we would not be here now, together."

Faenir's gilded eyes drifted away from me, lost in thought. "Perhaps she is the same as you... She can resist my—"

"Do not *dare* think of her." I threw my fist forward, which the elf sidestepped effortlessly. Angered, I tried to punch him again, only to miss for a second time.

"I would not concern yourself, Arlo. My interests are entirely upon you."

I stepped back from him, wishing nothing more than distance as my mind stormed with anxiety. Quickly, I put together the pieces of this scene. Faenir had taken me, unwillingly, from Tithe. Wherever this Haxton Manor was, it was far from the doorstep of mine and Auriol's home.

Auriol. My heart panged in my chest, and I did everything I could not to show him the pain.

Faenir seemed to notice anyway for his face lost all remnants of humour. It was hard to focus on him when my panic made breathing hard. It seemed each breath in was weak and the air too light to have real benefit. My heart was pounding harder, my head feeling as though I had drunk an entire bottle of aged wine or at least had been smacked across the skull with the bottle instead.

"What is the matter?" His voice was quiet as he spoke. Faenir was so close to me now that I caught the scent that clung to his silver-toned shirt, rosewood entwined with something sweeter. I found myself pondering what it was and forgetting about my concerns as he drew closer.

"You..." I muttered, having to look up at Faenir as he stood before me. He was far taller than I first believed. My position accentuated the sharp structure of his face. The tips of his cupid's bow were curved perfectly. His nose was straight and proud. Faenir's skin was kissed by sun, golden like his eyes which only stood out as the tumbling of raven-black hair fell over his shoulders. Up close I could see plaits woven into his hair; red string twisted amongst them.

His closeness only entrapped me for a moment. As Faenir slowly lifted a hand towards the strand of stubborn, blond hair that had fallen over my eye, I snapped out of my stupor and attacked.

"Take me fucking home," I cried over the crunch of my fist as it finally slammed into his face. That perfect nose was not perfect anymore; it was bent. Streams of red blood poured freely; some splattered across my knuckles while the rest spread across the lower half of his face.

"I... cannot." Faenir rocked back, bright eyes wide but not from fear, from intrigue. He raised a hand to his broken nose and traced his finger down it.

I struck out again, slamming my fists into his rock-solid chest. Faenir didn't move an inch. He stood tall, hardly moved by the thundering of my fists. Nor did he stop me. Blood ruined his shirt. *His blood*, pouring freely from the damage I had caused.

"I fear I have made a mistake," Faenir said only when I stopped.

I cried furiously, tears of frustration and desperation rolling down my face. My blood covered hands hurt, the bones in my knuckles each screaming with the demand to rest.

"This is not how I imagined this day to be."

"Please..." I dropped to my knees, not caring for the pain as they met the marble floor. Fat, red droplets of his blood splattered like spring rain around his feet. It was both beautiful and frightening. "I just want to go home."

"Arlo."

I winced as he said my name but dared look up.

"If it makes you feel any better, know that your sister will be well rewarded. Just as the families of the other Chosen are."

I bowed my head, chin to chest, from exhaustion. Deep down I did not want him to see me cry. Holding back such emotion was impossible when one felt lost and terrified.

"Why...?" I said, eyes stinging as I looked back up at him. "You left without a Chosen and came back. Why me?"

Faenir knelt before me, still keeping his hands to himself. I hardly blinked as I watched him with intent, not wishing to miss a single movement. I had seen what his touch could do if he wished, and I was not prepared to die. Even if he had kept himself from me this entire time.

Not yet. My mind raced to the vial of vampire blood in my pouch. One. It would only last near a month at most... that was all.

"If what you desired most in the world was suddenly presented to you on a gilded platter, would you not do what you could to take it?"

Faenir's question was given in answer to mine, however I could not make sense as to what it meant.

"Would you?" he asked again, breath coming out softly. Even with his face covered in his own blood and his deathly power a horrific reminder he was dangerous, I was not scared of him.

"I have faced monsters far more frightening than you, elf."

Faenir paused, regarded my comment and then stood. "Then you will be well suited to your new home. Monsters." Faenir laughed dryly, turned his back on me and walked towards the open door. "There are plenty of those lurking this side of *my* realm."

"Wait..." I shouted, pushing myself up with urgency.

Faenir stopped briefly. He did not turn back to face me, but instead rolled his shoulders and straightened his posture as though preparing to walk out of this room and into another filled with a crowd of adoring followers. "I suggest you rest. We will speak further on the matter over dinner."

I watched, helplessly, as my captor left the room, his swishing dark ruby cloak the last thing I saw. Even as the door shut behind him, I expected to hear the turn of a lock.

The door was not secured.

Standing deathly still I waited for as long as I could handle, using the thumping crashes of my heart to make sense of the time between when he had left me. I managed until the twenty-fourth count before I gathered myself and followed him.

If Faenir was not going to take me home, I would find my way back myself.

For Auriol's sake.

And mine.

11
FAENIR

The grace of his touch was the most wondrous feeling in the world, no matter if it conjured shattered bone and blood. I prevented myself from healing, holding back the magic from knitting together my skin and mending the bones that had fractured in my nose. All because I did not desire to forget what *his* touch had felt like for fear I would believe it had never happened.

For years I had felt agony like no other, but not in this way, not as real as this; as physical and undeniable, caused by another's hand. It was always my hands that hurt. Maimed. Killed.

Arlo was the harsh reminder that others, like me, could do just as much damage.

Blood had dried across my bare chest. Some clung within the braids of my hair, making them as stiff as straw. The person who looked back at me in the reflection of the steam-coated mirror was not the same I had grown used to seeing. This one had hope in his eyes, eyes surrounded by purple bruising and swelling from Arlo's attack. I could have looked at myself for hours, spent days even, trying to discern the undeniable truth that Arlo had done this...

With his fists upon my skin, and still lived to do it again.

I reached a cupped hand into the basin of warmed water then splashed it over my face. I did what I could to clean my face and the gore that covered the bottom of it like a mask. Droplets of pink and red splashed across the white stone basin and turned the water a ruddy colour.

Finally, my nose healed, the dark bruising retreated to the glowing hue of my skin. I felt the rush of fresh air as I inhaled deeply, testing the limits of the way my body mended itself.

If I could have put it off anymore, I would have.

Just as I feared, looking back at the pinkish droplets of water that fell from my almost clean face, it was as if it had never happened.

My fingers reached tentatively to the smooth bridge of my nose, expecting to feel some memory of discomfort. But there was nothing. No pain. No bump of bone or cut of skin.

And just like that I forgot. My mind was willing to cling to the feeling of Arlo's touch for long enough to memorise it, just as it had when he had gripped my wrist back in Tithe. It was no more than a dream and I was still the monster whose touch could kill.

12

I REQUIRED A WEAPON. *Preferably something fucking sharp and pointy.*

The thought was one of many as I tore through Haxton Manor. It was certainly one of the louder thoughts, alongside my urgency to return to Tithe and get as far away from here as possible.

Faenir had not shown himself again, nor did I feel as though I was being stalked as I trailed through endless high ceiling rooms and chambers adorned in furniture I would never have dreamed of seeing. Grand, stone and wood creations that seemed only suitable for a god, not an elf like Faenir.

He didn't deserve this luxury.

It became apparent quickly that Haxton was a hollow and empty place. Although beautiful, with its marble floors and white stone pillars that helped hold aloft the towering ceiling, it was… dead. It was deafeningly quiet, so much so that what should have been the tapping of my light feet sounded like the thundering of countless hooves as I ran, trying to find my escape. Everything about this place was cold; it seemed to seep from the floor and walls, covering me with its icy embrace.

The endless open windows did not help with the winter-like freeze, but without them I would have felt trapped in a perfectly pristine box with no hope for escape. It was encouraging to see the stretch of azure lake that seemed to wrap around Haxton Manor entirely every time I looked beyond them.

At one point I had stopped to catch my breath, peering out the stone-arched window and looking down to see how far the drop was. Could I have jumped and made my escape easier? A trellis of red flowers that looked as breath-taking as roses but as full as carnations covered most of the wall beyond. The roots and stems were thick and woven amongst one another like the braids in Faenir's hair. They could likely hold my weight but the intense drop that still lingered beneath the window was not worth the risk of trying.

The fall would kill me.

You are dying anyway, I reminded myself harshly. It was what I needed to push from the ledge and carry on running blindly through the wide and empty corridors.

By the time I reached the ground floor of the manor I had broken out into a barrage of hot flushes. My tunic felt sticky on my skin, material clinging unwantedly to every press of bone and curve of what little muscle I had.

Like the windows, the large doors that signalled the main entrance of the manor were wide open. It was much like when Auriol and I would spring clean our apartment in hopes to frighten away the dust and moths who took up residency with us. We would open every window we had just to allow the aid of fresh, spring air to speed up our clean.

Just the thought of her and the memory caused me discomfort. Gritting my teeth and pushing it to the back of my mind, I continued for the door.

Faenir was a terrible captor. It was as though his lack of presence and unlocked doors was his way of encouraging me to take leave. Not wasting the opportunity, I burst out into the open, squinting slightly as the bright glare of sun danced off the swell of water before me. Freedom.

Keep going.

My boots slapped down sloping steps towards a dark stone gravel path that led to the lake.

It is not over until you are home.

I had no idea where I was running to, but something told me Tithe rested beyond the lake. It was as though a compass within me had spun wildly, waking from years of slumber. The arrow twisted and twisted in circles until settling in the direction of the mountains across the lake. To Auriol. I knew it.

The closer I got to the water the more I could see beyond the haze of clouds in the distance. The mountainous outline grew clearer, allowing me to make out the white tipped peaks and harsh giant bodies of each one.

But then I saw what that compass was trying to tell me. The top of a tree, a tree far taller and monstrous than any dared to be. It towered over the tallest of the four mountains peaks but was fainter to look at.

Set back at a distance I could see the luscious outline of its full branches and shadowed trunk.

It was much like the tree within Tithe, except bigger by a thousandfold.

Tithe. Home. That was my way back to Auriol. I could not explain it, this feeling, but that tugging of the compass within me was too demanding to ignore.

The lake was miles long. Only a fool would swim it. And I was many things, but a fool was not a title I cared to accept.

My boots left prints in the golden sand as I raced alongside the shore. When I turned back to look behind me, the gentle lapping of water would devour the mark I left as though I never had been here.

Perfect. If Faenir came looking, he wouldn't know the way I took.

Maybe he chased after me now? I half expected to hear my name called out in fury but then the elf did not seem the type to voice his feelings so vocally, not that I knew anything about him, nor wished to.

Eventually I found what looked like a dock of some kind. Wooden and rotten, the panels had holes and the stilts that disappeared into the water looked gnawed and weak. A brown rope slithered within the lake as if toyed with by unseen fish... or other creatures.

This was a good sign at least. Evidence of a boat that would glide across the water far quicker than I could swim it. But if swimming the length of the azure depths was my only option, it would have to do.

The sky was darkening quickly, and with it my hopes of finding a way out. From within Haxton it had certainly felt like the lake stretched around it completely; running along its shoreline only confirmed it.

Haxton was nestled on a piece of land completely surrounded by water. There was no boat in sight, nothing I could use to get free from this place. And with night fast approaching, the lake went from a soft blue to a darkened grey that no longer looked inviting.

Now, I felt the need to turn away from it and head back to the manor. I couldn't place my finger on why I felt a creeping chill of fear up the back of my neck. But whatever it was did a fantastic job at putting me off giving into my desperation and swimming.

It was when I was close to giving up, I saw something that had my heart leaping into my throat. A light hovered far out in the distance. The familiar curls of fire, orange and red, danced like a bud captured within a glass lantern which hardly reflected over the water it glided across. It was held upon a pole, gripped by a hand of a figure who stood tall on the prow of a small vessel.

A boat.

It was a *fucking* boat.

I waded into the water, waving my hands like a mad fool above my head. "Here!" I shouted, voice skipping over the still water like a stone

I had thrown. With each bounce the echo grew quieter and quieter. "Please, I have been taken from my home. He stole me. Please. Quick!"

I walked out further into the frigid water, cringing at the noise my desperate cries made. I was knee-deep when I turned back towards Haxton Manor and the soft, bluish glow that emanated from the many windows. They were like dull eyes, watching my escape as though it was the greatest entertainment it had ever witnessed.

Perhaps Faenir watched in glee, smiling with his shattered nose and blood covered face as I tried to leave. Or maybe he wanted me to; after what I had done to him, he would see that I was the wrong choice and wish for me to return home.

"Hurry up!" I shouted, shivering as the cold water soaked into my trousers. I was waist-deep now.

The boat did not seem to pick up its speed, but it was hard to tell when the darkening sky made every small detail impossible to notice. The view of the mountains had retired to sleep, the tree no more than a darkened smudge across the landscape before me.

I was freezing to the bone, I knew that. My teeth chattered violently, catching the skin of my inner cheeks without prejudice. The water was now up to my chest as I fought my way out as if it would get me to the boat, and the person within it, quicker.

"Please!"

My feet fell from the muddied ground until I was forced to swim.

"Pl-please."

Water splashed into my mouth. Salty but fresh, it made the insides of my cheeks clench and my tongue sting with the distaste of it.

I was not making progress. Turning back towards the shore, it looked so far away that I could not believe I had swum such a length so quickly, yet still the boat and that mocking light did not grow closer.

Something brushed up against me. It halted my breathing, my legs and arms turning to stone. I tried to look down into the dark pits of black that surrounded me and saw nothing.

It happened again, this time beneath me. Something pushed up against my feet and I kicked out, slipping beneath the water in a moment of panic. I scrunched my eyes closed, treading the water with my arms as I attempted to keep myself from drowning.

I managed a single breath before the unseen danger wrapped a grip around my ankle and pulled.

"Arlo!"

The cry of my name was the last thing I heard before I was dragged into the cold depths of the lake.

I threw my eyes wide to see bubbles stream before them, disorientating me. My lungs burned as I held onto the pathetic, final breath I had managed before I was taken under.

I kicked out in vain. It did not dissuade what had me. I had often thought of the creatures that lurked in deep waters but never thought I'd ever set foot in such a place.

Oh how life changed so quickly.

I clawed at the lake as though it would save me, eyes stinging as the harsh, bitter water infiltrated them. Then I saw them. *People.* Figures of silver and white so stark against the dark waters that I gasped at the sight of them. I realised suddenly that my gasp had expelled the little air I had left. My weakening hands reached for the bubbles as though I could take them in my fingers and draw them back to my lips.

A fool you are.

The opaque bodies drifted around me. I followed one, the figure of a small child, a girl whose body was not full but wispy and see-through like morning fog. She drifted beneath me until I saw what had a hold of me.

It was another figure of white shadows. Its hand gripped my ankle, anchoring me through the water with terrifying strength. It glowered, judging eyes cutting straight through me with unmeasurable intent.

Suddenly it was not a lake I drowned within, but a swell of ghostly figures. Each of them reached for me with hard, strong grips and helped guide me down into the pits of my death.

My eyes grew heavy as the swelling pain in my chest faded. Suddenly I did not care for air to fill my lungs with breath and life. It was peaceful, surrounded by the dead as they held me and greeted me, taking me home as if I was one of them.

13

I REFUSED to look down at Arlo, to study the way his limp body was curled up in my arms, or how his cheek was squashed against the sodden material of my shirt. I didn't need to look to know he was there because I *felt* him.

Arlo's hard press against me was so entirely intoxicating that I could not focus on anything but keeping one foot before the other.

Myrinn waited at the entrance to Haxton, fingernails chewed between teeth as she waited to hear the verdict of Arlo's stupidity. She likely expected him to be dead, drowned by the ruthless shades who dwelled within Styx.

I had not yet dealt with the fact that Myrinn had arrived at Haxton without invitation as though she was above it. Charon would face my wrath for bringing her upon his boat once Arlo was awake; I would take out this feeling on them both.

Arlo would have been dead if I had got to him any later. The glow of life that haloed around his body was the beacon I needed to find him within the waters. Even now it still shone as bright as any star.

I felt rage as though it was a new emotion, furious at myself for being so distracted and letting him get into this predicament. I had convinced myself that Arlo was indestructible because he could withstand my touch. But he was not, tonight proved that.

"He is breathing," I confirmed as I swept past Myrinn.

Myrinn instantly relaxed, pulling her hands from her pale lips and loosing a breath. "Have you not warned him of the dangers that lurk here?"

I paused before replying, trying to focus on her rather than the fluttering of Arlo's heartbeat as it echoed across my chest. I had felt my own before, strong and proud; others would dwindle beneath my touch.

Not Arlo. *But why?*

"He has not been susceptible to conversation."

Myrinn stepped aside to allow me to pass into the manor without slowing a step. "Can you blame the boy? Stealing a mate is certainly the opposite of what the custom is. If we are to keep our relationship with the humans strong, we should not make ourselves seem anything remotely like a threat."

"I care little for what they think of me. Nor did Claria when she sent me to Tithe with the sole purpose of me killing a human for her own enjoyment."

"And yet you proved her wrong," Myrinn replied, pacing behind me on quick feet. "I understand your years of seclusion has affected your ability to think of anyone but yourself; however, your actions have shattered your perfectly crafted cage and left you open to the same rules as the rest of us. Think, Faenir. Keeping your Chosen alive is the first step of claiming your fate."

"His name," the growl slipped out of me without control, "is Arlo. And you truly believe I care for what others wish to see me do with this life?"

The patter of her feet ceased. I almost stopped and turned around, an apology dusted across my taut lips. Instead, I kept my focus on the hallway before me. "If you have come all this way to Haxton to remind me of the repercussions then perhaps it can wait until I deal with this."

Myrinn replied sharply, "Then I will prepare supper."

"That will not be required. You will not be staying long enough to break bread, cousin."

She ignored my disregard. "When he wakes and you both are ready, I expect to see you in the dining hall."

The conversation was closed before I could refuse her anymore. Myrinn's presence retreated into the belly of Haxton whilst I was left to carry the body of Arlo back towards his room.

He had begun to shiver so I held him closer. Only when I was certain I was out of Myrinn's earshot did I dare speak.

"I am sorry," I said softly, knowing it would be the only time I would say the words aloud to him, or anyone. "You are safe with me."

Arlo stirred against me. I slowed my pace just steps away from the entrance to the room he had run from. For the first time since I had reached for his hand in the depths of the Styx, I looked at him. He winced as though dreaming something horrific. I wished to draw my thumb across the lines of worry that scrunched across his forehead until his skin was smooth once again.

I resisted.

14

I BOLTED UPRIGHT, a scream clawing up my throat. My hands reached up for my neck as though I expected to choke on water. My legs kicked out to rid them of the phantoms' fingers that pulled me down into dark depths.

But there were no dead here...

Only the tangling of sheets around my frantic legs and the darkened sky which gave a view beyond the opened balcony of the bedroom.

It took a moment to calm my laboured breathing and thunderous heart. Every time I blinked, I believed I would see them again, faint whispers of silver bodies who longed for me to join them in death. They did not come for me, yet I still recognised their presence in the haunting glint of the lake that taunted me beyond the balcony.

"Are you so desperate to leave my home you would throw yourself into shades and think you would simply swim free?"

Faenir stepped into the room with hands full of folded clothing. He paced straight towards the bed with a pinched expression and fury filled eyes. The pile of clothing thudded upon the bed as he discarded them, then he stood back and folded his arms across his chest.

"If I had known..." I began but swallowed the rest of my excuse and swapped it with something harder. "They were going to kill me."

"Indeed, shades are bitter spirits who dwell within the Styx and harbour the hate and anger that prevents them from moving to another realm of peace. Even I do not dare bother them... often."

Shades. "You expect me to believe that the lake is filled with ghosts?"

"Ghosts, spirits, phantoms. All different words for the same truth.

And I do not care if you wish to believe me or not. Thanks for saving your life would have sufficed."

"My captor and saviour," I sneered. "Anything else you wish to add to your ever-growing list of titles?"

Faenir's frown deepened as I pushed myself from the bed. My body ached with every slight move. It felt as though I had been pulled and tugged from all angles and my limbs hated me for it.

Where I had laid within the bed, the sheets were no longer white and pristine but muddied and all shades of brown. The evening breeze drifted across the room and revealed the stench of stale, dirty water that clung to me and the mess I had left behind.

Then I noticed a similar patch across Faenir's chest. He caught me looking but said nothing to confirm what had caused it.

"Your face looks better than it had been when I last saw you," I said through a sly grin.

Faenir ignored my jibe. "I suggest you wash and change before you come down for dinner. Those clothes will have to do until more supplies reach us in the coming days. A bath has been drawn in the chamber beyond those doors, filled with water that is not infested with shades might I add. Clean yourself up and we will be waiting for you downstairs."

"We?" He had said so much but I had only cared for that comment.

"Myrinn is persistent; she wants us both to join and I truly would not ignore that request. She can be rather persuasive if required."

Myrinn, the beautiful elf who had seemed so innately protective over Faenir during the Claiming. Her name and splendour were so unique I would have remembered them until my final day.

"She is here?"

"Arrived with the ferryman, the same one you threw yourself into Styx in hopes to board." Faenir peered at me down the length of his sharp nose. I felt the silent judging in his golden eyes and could not gleam why, someone who so clearly detested me, stole me from my home.

If he hated you, you would be dead.

"You cannot keep me here," I said, fists clenching at my sides once again. "I will not stop looking for a way home."

"I can *and* I will."

It was harder for me not to throw a punch and break his nose for a second time.

"Clean yourself up," Faenir added before turning on his heel to leave. "I trust that this time you will not go searching within Haxton's grounds. If you fear the shades, they will seem like kittens in comparison to what else lurks within my home."

I listened beyond the doors which had been left ajar before me. Pressing my back to their cold, wooden presence I devoured the one-sided conversation that happened in the room on the other side.

It had not been hard to find my way here. All it took was to listen to the voices, for sound was such a foreign concept within Haxton Manor. Sound suggested life, and this place was void of it.

"... must you be so infuriating, cousin? There will be no good to come from trying to entice Arlo to stay when Haxton remains a home for ghosts and regret."

I did not need to peer through the gap to know it was Myrinn who spoke. Her light, powerful tones conjured a vivid image of her in Tithe.

"What is done is done," Faenir replied. He spoke as though every word was an effort. Even from my vantage point I could hear his very want to be left alone. Speaking seemed such an effort for the brooding elf.

There was a familiar scratch of metal against plate, a clink of glass then followed by the glugging rush of liquid. "You are lucky he still lives. Faenir, will you look at me and at least show some interest into what I am saying?"

"This conversation, and your presence may I add, is unsolicited. I did not invite you to visit, nor embark in an inquiry as to what I have done and why I took the human from his realm unwillingly."

"Someone must be the harsh reminder that you have made a grave mistake stealing him from his home," Myrinn replied, her voice deepening with an unseen power.

Faenir barked, followed by a screech of chair against the floor. The sound made my skin crawl. I held my breath to stop myself from gasping in response.

"You keep suggesting I have stolen him, *taken* him, that my doing is different to what you have partaken in, Myrinn. Did you not willingly enter their realm and pick a mate without asking if they even wished to return to Evelina with you? No. Do not come to my home and look at me as though I am less than. I am simply following the very tradition Claria and the rest of you believed I would fail in. Keeping him here puts all your hopes of succession at risk... that is why you are so invested, I imagine."

Myrinn stood now, evident by the loud clatter of her chair as it was thrown across the floor. "How dare you even for a moment believe I care more for the crown than your well-being."

"Do you not?" His question was quiet, words dangerous as though opening a wound that he knew would cause pain.

I chose that moment to enter. With a gentle push the door swung wide and revealed me standing, red cheeked, and my narrowed gaze locked on my captor. "It would seem your *kind* are not above the mundane limits of arguing with family. Shall I take this terrible atmosphere as the excuse I require to return to my room?"

"Arlo." Myrinn stood straight, face softening before my eyes from one of unleashed anger to controlled temper. "I apologise that you had to hear that."

Faenir said nothing, but his wide, golden stare screamed many silent thoughts.

He didn't think I would come. The rising of his pristine brows told me that he was happy I did.

"Please," Myrinn said, stepping back from the table and gesturing to the vacant chair that waited patiently, tucked beneath the long table before her. "More than anyone, you have been through a lot today. I would feel better knowing you get some food in you. It will help... I hope."

The table had been dressed beautifully; I could not deny that. It was long and made from thick cuttings of dark wood. Across its length, a black runner of material had been laid. Upon it waited silver plates of food, far more than enough for three people to devour. Goblets of wine, deep red and pale grape-white, had been nestled among the delights of food, all mostly untouched beside the goblet closest to where Faenir had been sitting. That one was already half empty.

As I walked into the room, I tried to keep my chin up and my expression unbothered. However, I could not shake the feeling of eyes following me, golden, intense eyes that belonged to my captor. They were the chains that bound me to this place. Heavy and anchoring, Faenir studied me as though he had never seen me before.

"Do all your captive humans get offered such luxuries?" I asked, reaching for the back of my chair and gripping it in hopes they both did not see how my hands trembled. "Because it will take far more than warmed meats and sweet fruits for me to forget that I am a prisoner within this place."

Myrinn winced at that, forcing a smile and a laugh as she reached down for her chair, righted it and sat back upon it. She was dressed in a gown of silver that complimented her brown skin. Around the narrow bodice was a web of straps and belts that gave structure to her dress before it fell around her waist like clouds of tumbling mist. Myrinn's hair hung across both exposed shoulders, thick braids woven perfectly together with the addition of jewels and golden clasps that completed her regal aura. At the crown of her head, hair had been twisted to give the impression of wearing a tiara.

If I had ever believed in Kings and Queens, I would not have doubted that she was the greatest of them all.

Faenir was the last to move. There was still tension between them both, but it seemed to dissipate with every passing moment.

"If you keep persisting that you are my captive then I will insist on tying chains around your wrists to keep you bound to me. Perhaps that would stop you from being such a... fool."

"Faenir, please."

I ignored Myrinn's pleading as my knuckles turned white upon the top of the chair. "You're insufferable."

"*You* bathed."

I tried to ignore Faenir's strange comment but couldn't. It came out of nowhere and completely derailed the fury that had thickened across my tongue ready to be spat at him.

"It is what you asked of me, was it not? I would not want to displease my captor." I bowed dramatically. When I raised my eyes back to his I held that wide, golden stare in contest.

It took him a moment to reply. Faenir did an incredible job at keeping most emotion from his bored, frowning expression as though he was not able to show anything else. "Just sit yourself down."

"You arrogant—"

"Perhaps we should begin," Myrinn said hurriedly, reaching for a bowl of what could only be described as a cloudy, thin soup. "Would not want the food to get cold before it is even enjoyed."

Faenir reached for his glass of wine instead of the food. Still holding my stare, he lifted it to his lips and exhaled, fogging the inside of his glass before taking a long sip. He won. I tore my attention from him and sat, hating that I did exactly as he commanded.

In truth I was starving, but the idea of eating food was beyond me. All it took was the reminder of where I was and what had happened, and my hunger ran away from me.

Instead, I focused my attention on Myrinn. "I wish to return to Tithe."

She almost choked on her soup. Carefully she placed the spoon down beside the bowl and raised a napkin to her lips. It was all an act to give her time to decide on her answer.

"That," she said before patting her painted lips, "I am afraid is not possible. As much as I understand... and agree, that your being here is wrong, there is nothing I can do to return you home."

I believed her. How could I not when her gaze was so trusting? I studied her expression and did not see a glimmer of a lie across it.

"I have already told him this. He chooses not to listen."

My hand gripped the knife beside my empty plate. Its polished, bone handle in my hand was familiar. All it would take was a sure aim and a strong arm and it would have been thrown across the table and buried between Faenir's eyes. In that moment I decided it would be leaving this room with me.

Just in case.

"What of your human?" I asked, trying to still the frantic thunder of my heart in my chest.

"Yes," Faenir added, leaning forward with the hint of amusement across his stern face. "Where is your mate, cousin? Is it not custom to spend your first night together?"

Myrinn shot Faenir with a glare that made him snigger into his glass. "Haxton Manor does not scream in welcome. After my brief visit, I shall return to him, do not concern yourself. However, for tonight, I feel that there are more pressing matters to deal with."

"Has he attempted to kill himself already? Escape his fate perhaps?"

My palm dampened as I tightened my grip on the knife.

"You are drunk," Myrinn snapped.

"I need to be to get through this meal."

It was comforting to know that Myrinn also shared disdain towards Faenir. Even though I was still captive, I felt as though she would protect me with more than just her words if required.

Myrinn struck out with a hand as though reaching for something unseen across the table. It was a strange action filled with intent and focus. I followed it and watched, in disbelief, as the wine in Faenir's glass leapt out and splashed across his face before he had so much as a chance to hold in a breath.

Magic. Such an open display scared me more than anything else I had seen.

The glass shattered in Faenir's hand. A growl built within his chest before spilling beyond his lips in a string of anger. "Leave!"

Myrinn stood again, chest heaving and hands open, waiting at her sides. "The years of your chosen solitude has ruined you, cousin."

I watched as power radiated from Myrinn's skin. The air grew heavy with moisture. The goblets of wine trembled upon the table as the liquid within sloshed and twisted like a hurricane controlled them.

"Get. Out. Now." The shadows that hung naturally in the corners of the room seemed to shiver, slithering outwards like snakes that coiled and twisted over one another.

"There is no helping you. Years I have fought your corner with our family. Trying to make them see that your bitterness is simply a making of the way you have been treated. Silly Myrinn, always hoping to see the good in everyone."

"I do not need you or your help. Not now. Not before."

I could do nothing but watch as both elves gathered power. The air crackled with it.

Stories of magic had been left in the history of Darkmourn. Humans capable of magic, witches, had been the downfall of humanity and not a single soul left within the vampire-riddled world beyond cared to speak of it.

Except now I stood between two storms of power that were ready to clash into one another at any given moment. I could do nothing but watch, knife resting upon my thigh beneath the table, ready in case I had to use it against them.

"This was your chance to prove yourself," Myrinn shouted across the tables, glass cracking beneath the weight of the liquids she controlled. "To Claria, to them all. To yourself."

There was much unsaid between them, a story that I longed to dig my claws into and uncover but all I cared about was getting free of this place and returning to Auriol.

As if sensing my fear, Myrinn glanced towards me, and her power embedded away like water over rocks. The tension in the room retreated as her expression changed from anger to regret.

I waited for her to say something but instead she stood from her chair, leaving her soup forgotten, most of it now splashed across the table and soaking into the dark wood and sodden material; then she dropped her gaze and walked away.

"Wait." I stood, not caring for the shadows that still gathered around us. It was Faenir's power, the same I had seen in Tom's room as he lay dead between us.

Faenir did not stop me as I followed after Myrinn. Nor did he notice as I slipped the knife into my belt that kept the oversized, leather breeches Faenir had supplied, from falling from my thin waist.

"Please, don't leave me with him," I called out, breathlessly chasing after her.

"I am sorry, Arlo," Myrinn murmured, long legs keeping her a pace ahead of me as she moved through Haxton.

"No. If you are then take me with you," I begged. My urgency filled my throat and threatened to make me gag with desperation.

"There is nowhere for you if I do."

I reached out and gripped her forearm. "You have said that my being here is wrong. There must be a way for me to return home. I have to get back to her."

"Your sister," Myrinn said, lips pulled tight. "It is the girl you had stopped Faenir from touching?"

"Yes," I spluttered, almost melting beneath the sorrow in Myrinn's bright eyes. "I am the only person she has left. She is the only person *I* have left. I need to return to her."

"Even if I wish I could, there is nothing I can do for you, Arlo. The veil between Evelina and Darkmourn is weak. Unpredictable. There is a lot to be said about the powers that Queen Claria has sacrificed keeping your kind safe within the boundary wall. Because of this she only has enough reserves to open the door between our realms at the turning of a season. Only she has the power to grant your return home. Even if she does, it would not be until the next turn of the seasons."

I gripped the pouch at my belt and clung to the vial of blood that waited within. As my mind raced, I tried to calculate how long the blood would keep me alive before winter became spring.

"Then you must take me to her! To your Queen."

Myrinn's gaze fell to her feet. "I cannot."

My legs gave out. I fell to the floor, the crack of my knees against the slabbed floor did not dampen the pain that filled my soul and threatened to rip me apart.

To Myrinn it looked as though her confirmation of my fate in this realm had caused this reaction. The truth of what brought me to my knees was far beyond my ability to admit. *Would I die before I could ever return home?*

She knelt before me, skirt billowing out around her. I did not flinch as her fingers reached for my chin and lifted it up so I could do nothing but look at the screaming sympathy that spilled from her.

"I will do what I can to send word to the Watchers of your home and pass a message on to your sister. It is frowned upon, but I will do it as my apology for my cousin's actions. You are a victim of his selfish choice, and I cannot do anything but express my regret for what has occurred."

Tears filled my eyes. I feared to blink for them to spill and reveal my weakness. "I... I need to speak to her."

Myrinn dropped her hand and stood. She towered above me, her frame casting a shadow over my kneeling frame. "You belong to Faenir. You are his property. There are rules we must uphold and interfering with another's Chosen is forbidden. But..." I looked up at her as her whisper settled over me. "There will be a ball within the coming days. Encourage Faenir to take you and I will be there waiting to share news of your sister. Queen Claria will be hosting, if you wish to speak with her then you can do so... but it must seem like it is on Faenir's terms."

"I don't understand what you want from me... what *he* wants from me," I said.

Myrinn turned her back on me in more ways than one. She moved for the main doors of Haxton Manor as she replied, "Faenir is troubled, but he is not dangerous. Not to you at least."

"He kills. I have seen it," I shouted, my words echoing across the empty, cold manor.

"You are different, even I cannot make sense of it. Faenir is many things, but I leave knowing you are safe in his care."

"Care?" I laughed, finally allowing the tears to fall down my cheeks.

"Make him come to the ball, Arlo, and I will give you the news of your sister. Take it as a peace offering between you and our kind."

Myrinn left swiftly, not allowing room for my pleading to continue.

I could have chased after her. But I didn't. Not because I did not want to, but because I knew, deep down, that Faenir watched from the darkness and waited to spring forth and stop me from leaving.

He would not let me go.

Myrinn's own words had confirmed that. *You are his property*. Perhaps my parent's death when I was so young had made the concept of belonging to anyone incomprehensible to me. *You belong to Faenir*. The thought alone made my skin crawl as though spiders danced upon me.

Faenir had me trapped in his web.

Then cut us free.

15

I WAITED for Faenir to come for me, knife in hand and poised ready to kill.

It had begun with me watching the door with intent, keeping my breathing as featherlight as I could muster to ensure I did not miss a sound. I burned holes into the closed door as my body ached with anticipation for his arrival.

Years of chasing the undead among the forgotten streets and barren landscape of Darkmourn had me in fighting, fit shape. Even with Faenir's unknown powers over darkness and death, if given the chance I would attack before he could do so little as blink in wonder.

After Myrinn had left early that evening and I had returned to the chamber where Faenir had last been, there was only the table of food left untouched. It had been the goblets of wine and water that had seen me though until now. The water dulled the physical pain of my body, the wine calming the wild torment of my mind.

Minutes of waiting for Faenir turned to hours, hours to days. He never came for me. I had done well to keep the sleep away at first but then I would find myself vulnerable, giving into my heavy eyelids and falling into the comforting embrace of darkness.

When I woke, startling as though a pail of water had cascaded over my head, the knife was still gripped in my hand.

Perhaps reading minds was another one of his sickly powers. Could he sense what I wished to do to him? How my next action would create pain and damage far greater than his healing abilities could battle?

My thoughts of destruction wavered with the time that slipped away. My grip loosened on my knife. Myrinn's promise of providing me with news of my sister burrowed its way into my consciousness and infected my mind.

The more Faenir stayed away, the want to cause him pain turned into desperation for his return. I needed him if I was ever going to get free of this place. I needed him if I was to meet Myrinn at the ball and hear if Auriol was well. Not that I could have done anything about it if she was not okay. We had been torn from one another and kept separated by the steel bars between our worlds.

It was on Faenir's third day of vacancy when my inner thoughts betrayed me. I gave in to walking the many halls of Haxton Manor in hopes to distract myself from what my mind tried to convince me of. *She will be happier without you.* Would she have smiled when I had never returned home? Had she released a sigh of relief to know that the chains I had kept upon her had shattered with my own demise?

Our last encounter had not been positive in the slightest. My disappearance would give her the life she desired, one away from me. Auriol had made her feelings for me clear. Her words replayed vividly in my head, over and over, as punishment.

I grew used to being alone. I counted the slabbed flooring I walked across in my attempts to distract myself. It worked for a short while before the festering poison of my thoughts grew louder.

There was no dulling my anxiety, no counting or distracting that would stop me from hearing Auriol's hate-filled voice. It was so clear, I could have convinced myself that she followed in the shadows as I ambled aimlessly through Haxton.

I forgot my purpose in those three days. Even the knife I had so dearly clung to was left discarded on the bed in the prison I now saw as my room.

For a time, I had to stop myself from leaving the front doors and throwing myself back into the pits of the Styx; at least there would have been peace waiting for me in the darkest parts of that lake.

It was growing dark beyond the manor on that third day when the silence cracked. I had reached the outer doors of the dining chamber and smelt rot and mould. The stench was so pungent it tore me from my thoughts, and I was left standing beyond the room as though I had slept walked the entire way here. Not that I felt hunger anymore, but the smell was enough to ensure I would never wish to eat again.

Haxton was empty, a shell of dark thoughts and vacant rooms. The lack of presence had caused the food that Myrinn had made to spoil and turn. It made sense at least; this was a place of death after all.

There was only a single goblet of paled-grape wine left within my own room. I had finished the water the day prior. If my own mind didn't kill me before the sickness claimed my body, the lack of sustenance would.

Careless and lost, I wandered back into my chamber to find Faenir sitting upon the bed as though he belonged there and had never left. I stopped, dead in my tracks, unable to fathom what I was seeing. Blinking did not remove the scene, nor did rubbing my closed eyes.

"I made a mistake," Faenir's monotone voice grumbled across the room. My skin crawled in response.

"You left me," my voice was hoarse from days of neglect. I repeated myself, unsure if he could have made sense of the scratchy words. "You left me... alone."

"Did you miss me?" Faenir did not lower his stare although it seemed that he winced ever so slightly.

"Not in the sense you would hope for." I longed for the soft curve of the knife in my hand.

"My leaving you was a lapse in my judgement."

"Why?" The single worded question snapped out of me.

"I believed you would prefer my absence after everything that has happened."

Day's worth of aggression came flooding out of me at once. My weak, tired legs paced the room until I was inches before him. Faenir did little but move his knees apart, allowing me to get closer. I didn't notice this at first, for my gaze was solely on his, not on the way his body moved gently, or how his hands gripped the sheets for support... or comfort.

"If you wish to leave me then I beg you to take me home. Take me anywhere from here, just do not leave me again." I spoke so quickly that I was not truly in control of the words that came out of my mouth, nor the way I said it.

"Do not be concerned," Faenir muttered quietly, so much in fact that the beating of my heart did well to drown out his words. If I was not watching his lips, I would have missed what he said.

"I have no desire to leave your side again... Arlo."

Faenir shifted forward, moving his placement until he sat upon the very edge of the bed. I looked down at him, breathing laboured and face flushed red, as he regarded me from his seat.

"Where..." I felt stupid for asking but I wished to know. "Where did you *hide*?"

"I have found that the shadows provide the greatest solitude when wishing to escape."

"That doesn't answer my question," I said, catching the glint of the knife I had taken from the dining chamber all those days ago. Faenir had moved it from the place I had left it upon my bed, to the oaken side table beside it. He caught me looking but did not make a move to reach for it.

"I was far enough away for you to have time from me, but close enough that I could stop you from doing anything untoward. I admit... time fell away from me. I would not have wished to stay away for so long, but I had believed you made your thoughts clear on our proximity when you shattered my nose."

Was that a smile I caught? A smirk in jest or teasing? Either way I wished to wipe it clean from his face and demand he never raised his lips to me again. "And if you wish to keep your face unmarred then you best tell me what it is you want from me."

"The same as my family wants from their mates."

I caught the retort from leaving me by gritting my teeth into my tongue. *I am not your mate!* The scream echoed in my mind. "Then what do *your kind* want from the humans?"

Perhaps if I knew why they took us, it would lead to the answer of how we could get home.

Faenir sighed, turning his face away from me, his raven black hair ruffled as though moved by a hidden breeze. "There is so much to say, I fear I do not know where to begin."

"Start with me. You left Tithe without a Chosen, but you came back."

His demeanour changed within a breath, turning back to look at me with eyes brimming full of desire. "All my life I have killed just by touching another. I had grown used to taking the glow of life from another as though it was as natural as taking a breath. Not a single person has ever survived my touch."

His deep voice vibrated through me.

"Until me."

Faenir stood then, forcing me back a step to allow him room. It was so sudden that I almost tripped over my footing. "You are smarter than I gave *your kind* credit for."

He mimicked the insult I had not long shared. His slight grin brightened until teeth shone through parted lips. Faenir's smile lasted only a moment as I reached out for him.

My hand wavered in the air beside his face. I let every part of Faenir stiffen. He looked beyond me as though I did not stand before him at all. However, his entire focus was on me, even if he did not truly look.

"You took me from my home because I am the first person who will not die when you touch them," I repeated, fingers inching closer to the carved structure of his cheekbone. "You came back for me. Ripped me from my life... and for what?"

Faenir exhaled a quivering breath, eyes flicking towards the tips of my fingers as they edged closer to his skin.

"The stench of desperation is ripe on you, *Faenir*."

I was not scared of death. The years of prolonging my own demise caused the thought of dying to mutate. It became as familiar as a friend. I had chased the dead to keep my own death at bay, devouring the blood of vampires without much thought. And before me stood the very embodiment of what I had fled. *Faenir.* I had seen what his touch had done to Tom and his parents... and still I reached for him.

"Do not do this..." He exhaled as the tips of my cold, shaking fingers brushed against his sharp cheekbone.

"Why not?" I carried on, ignoring his desperate plea. My fingers melted onto his warm skin until my palm caressed the side of his face. "Is this not the reason why you took me? Because you desired to feel something you have been deprived of for your entire pathetic existence?"

Faenir's eyes flickered closed, too lost in the feel of my hand to recognise my insult. The lines across his brow softened and the frown that seemed permanently etched into his face thawed away before my very eyes.

I studied him, feeling the heavy beating of his pulse beneath my palm. *Or was it my own?*

"Arlo..." he groaned my name, reaching up to place a hand upon mine to stop it from ever moving.

I took that as my moment. Jolting out with my spare hand, I reached up and wrapped my fingers around his exposed throat. Faenir's golden eyes flew open as I tightened my hold.

"I do not pity you," I sneered. Faenir did not squirm beneath my grip, or wince as my nails dug into his soft skin. "If you think I care for what you have been through, then you could not be further from the truth. I will spend the time you have trapped me here making you wish you never set eyes on me. And if I ever find out that my sister is harmed by your actions then I swear to make you feel pain that you never believed possible."

I was breathless, my knuckles white as I gripped tighter. All the while Faenir just stared at me with a doe-eyed expression that I could not place between fear, surprise or judging.

When Faenir finally broke his silence, all manner of his serenity had vanished. "Have you quite finished?"

I made sure to squeeze into his throat before releasing him, not that it mattered for clearly it did not affect him as I had hoped. I pulled back from him and caught the crescent moon marks my nails had left upon his neck. I grinned, knowing my warning had at least left a mark.

"For now," I replied, turning my back on him and facing the open balcony. I did so, not because I couldn't care to look upon his face another moment, but because my body began to tremble as the adrenaline slowed. I would not let him see the weakness in me. "I think it is best you leave."

"As do I, but first I must know something."

I gritted my teeth. "There is nothing else for me to say."

"I am required to provide confirmation of our acceptance or refusal to my grandmother's pending ball. From your actions this evening I trust you would rather forgo the event than spend it with me."

"No," I spun around, unable to stop the sudden desperation from poisoning my voice, "Wait. I wish to go."

Faenir nodded, his face showing no sign as to him knowing why I wished to visit. "Then I will send word to Myrinn of our decision. Since her departure from Haxton she has been persistent with sending messages. I fear if I ignore her anymore then she will return."

There was nothing for me to say, no words to provide him that would deter my mind from the promise of the ball. I had convinced myself that it had already passed during Faenir's absence. The rush of relief to know I was wrong made my knees tremble.

"Goodnight, Arlo."

"When is it?" I said, failing myself as I tried not to display any more of my desperate nature to him. "The ball... when is it?"

Faenir paused as he reached the door. "Tomorrow evening."

I swallowed my next words. My silence confirmed to Faenir that it was his time to take leave. I could not pretend to care for the ball and what the event entailed; all I could think of was finding out if Myrinn had had word from my sister.

Regardless of the answer, this was my chance to get away from Haxton Manor, from Faenir, and to carve my own way back home.

16

Faenir stood and watched me with such interest I almost believed I was on fire. Why else would he keep his stare trapped upon me? Golden eyes trailed me up and down, so slowly, like a dragon guarding treasure, just as the old stories told. I wished to demand that he averted his attention. Instead, I swallowed that urge as I paraded down the steps beyond Haxton Manor to where he waited for me.

It could not have been what I wore that interested him, that was for certain. Before I had left my room, I had surveyed how unimpressive I looked, dwarfed by the oversized, moss-toned tunic and boring trousers that were sizes too large. If it were not for my belt, it would have looked as though I was a child playing dress up in my father's spare clothes.

That, of course, was impossible on two accounts. One: my father was dead, and two: the tunic belonged to Faenir.

The black laces that should have tied up at my collar were left loose, exposing the skin of my chest. The trousers I wore were crafted from a brown, sun-stained leather that the long boots mostly hid up until below my knees.

I had never been to a ball, for such luxuries did not exist in my world, but I had heard enough tales as a child to know I should have been dressed in finery, like Faenir was now.

It was dark beyond the manor. Night had claimed the skies and brushed its jewelled tones of dark navy so that it appeared black. However, it seemed the moon, proud and glowing white, idolised Faenir for it bathed him in its glow and outlined every possible inch of him.

Faenir's raven hair fell behind him, tousled in the nightly winds. Only the twisted twin braids tumbled across his chest. He was a vision of ruby, white and gold. The tunic he wore was far grander than mine. It was lined with a strand of gold at his neckline which dipped dramatically to expose the shadowed curves of muscle hidden beneath. Across his shoulders were plates of gleaming brass metal which draped into a cloak of similar toning at his back. What kept his outfit in place were the vivid, large stones of ruby pinned at his chest. He dripped in wealth, and I realised quickly that I gawped at him as he did me.

"I was hoping you would have changed your mind and this evening's festivities would be forgotten and thus missed," Faenir said as I reached the gravelled path he stood upon. That was his greeting, not that I expected a polite hello or cared for it.

"You would have liked that, wouldn't you...?" I brushed past him, uncaring, as though I knew where I was walking to. In fact, I did not. What was left before me was the Styx, yet I could not imagine how else we would leave Haxton.

"It would have saved a rather large amount of discomfort, that I cannot deny."

I smiled at the idea of Faenir being uneasy. "What a shame."

The sound of his footfalls, crunching over the pebble-stoned gravel informed me that Faenir followed. Within a few strides he had passed me, strolling towards the stretch of water that spread out around the manor. "Come, it is best the ferryman is not kept waiting."

I didn't get a chance to question him as I was forced to quicken my pace to keep up.

The same wooden dock I had seen days before was now glowing beneath the light of a hovering flame. A boat had moored against it, rocking gently by the lapping of dark waters it rested upon. In it stood a figure draped in heavy folds of material that even the lantern he held could not penetrate to reveal his face.

Although I could not see his features, I felt his hidden gaze follow me, judging and cold. My hand moved for the handle of the knife I had brought with me, buried in the belt of my trousers, one that Faenir did not know about. Or perhaps he did, and he enjoyed the idea of me being armed.

I faltered a step as we reached the haunting figure. Faenir did not share my sudden discomfort as he took to the dock in silence. I allowed myself only a moment of hesitation before I chased after him.

"May I?" Faenir offered a hand as he stood beyond the boat. Not once had he regarded the figure who stood within it or cared to notice that a third person was even among our presence.

I glanced to his outstretched hand and frowned naturally. "That will not be necessary."

I wondered if Faenir could hear the lie in my voice. Standing upon the rickety dock I was more than aware of the shades that waited within the darkness of Styx's water. I could not see them, but their presence was as real as the silent figure within the boat and Faenir's outstretched hand. He did not lower it, not until I forced myself to take a cautious step into the boat which swayed awfully beneath me. It stilled only when Faenir climbed in; his presence was the heavy pressure that kept it from rocking.

"With haste, Charon." It was the first time Faenir spoke to the figure, and I found myself loosing a breath in relief that my mind was not making his appearance up as some cruel vision. "And may I take this moment to remind you that strays are not permitted entry to Haxton without my consent."

The figure turned, hoisting the pole the lantern was draped across. Water sloshed and I soon noticed that the pole extended far beneath the dark waters of the Styx. With a great heave, the boat began to move.

"Myrinn Evelina wished to speak with you, Master," a whispered voice replied from beneath the folds of his cloak. The sound was both awful and pleasant, like the scratching of nails against glass. It rattled the evening winds as though echoing among the dark in which it spoke from. "I cannot deny the bloodline of *life*."

"Bloodline or not," Faenir responded, voice tight as though he held back his true wrath, "You are mine, Charon. Not theirs. If you are so careless to make such mistakes again then you shall find yourself returned to the pits of the Styx where I dragged you up from all those years ago. Do you understand?"

"Indeed," Charon replied softly.

Faenir did not respond, clearly satisfied the hooded figure would listen to the reprimand as a result of escorting Myrinn to Haxton.

Neither spoke again. Instead, their silence gave way to the rushing of water that sang beneath the small vessel as it cut across the lake. We glided across the Styx with ease, aided by the motion of the staff-like pole that Charon pushed in and out of the water.

Faenir simply watched me as Haxton Manor became a dot in the distance. I was glad for the quiet, for I had nothing to say to him. Although the tracing marks his eyes left across my body made me want to itch the feeling from my skin. All I wanted was for this journey to end so I could speak with Myrinn. I cared little for anything else.

"You are cold," Faenir broke the silence suddenly. It was not a question, more a statement, and he was not wrong.

I had not noticed the chill until he spoke. Then I realised the ache in my jaw was from the chattering of teeth and my limbs quivered violently as our boat ripped through the winds.

"Do not concern yourself with—" Before I could finish Faenir had shifted the cloak from his back and threw it over my shoulders. It settled upon me like the falling of a feather, slow and gentle. But I could not deny the warmth his body had left imprinted upon the material. I chose not to refuse him as I hugged it closer to me, giving into a moment of weakness for the reward of comfort.

There was no thanks to share, nor did Faenir expect it.

We fell back into our silence as the boat moved towards the far-off shore and the outline of mountains that crowned it.

Home. Auriol. Run.

My attention fixated on the silhouette of that monstrous tree. The closer we moved towards it, the sharper the edges of its blurred outline became.

Noticing my attention, Faenir spoke up. "The Great Tree signifies the very heart of our realm. Nyssa, it is called by the same name of the Goddess that planted its seed at the beginning of time."

It felt as though I held a coveted book in my hands, ready to open the page and uncover wisdom that no other had the luxury of knowing. No matter how my interest burned I had to show a lack of care to Faenir.

"It looks like the tree back home..." I muttered, breath fogging beyond my lips, fingers tugging the cloak closer around my shoulders to fend off the chill.

"That is because they are linked, intrinsically connected as though they are doors joined by a string that bounds each to one another. Without one, the other cannot survive." Faenir confirmed what that persistent spinning compass within my chest had suggested. It was home, at least my way back to Auriol.

"What makes Tithe so special?" I asked, turning my gaze from the view to Faenir who still looked at me with far more interest.

"Tithe is simply one door among many others. Nyssa is a gateway to all of the world beyond."

"That does not answer my question."

Faenir sighed, blinking for what seemed like the first time since this entire journey. "Your home is one of the few left standing, unmarred and protected from the deathly curse that has spread across your world."

"What happens if it falls to *them*? The vampires," I asked, mind wandering to the glass vial hidden within the pouch at my waist.

Faenir looked at the hooded figure of Charon who, as I expected, did not utter a word nor the hush of a breath. Knowing that the haunting figure was not prepared to come to Faenir's aid, the elven prince looked back at me with a face of forced steel.

"The end. For us all."

A carriage waited for us as we climbed out of the ferryman's boat. At least Faenir climbed, my disembark was more of a clambering on wobbling knees.

The world had not stopped rocking before the ferryman changed course and pushed the boat away from us. I watched as he disappeared, the folds of his obsidian cloak melting with the dark sky in which he moved towards. Within moments Charon, and the ruby flame that burned proudly from the lantern at the crown of his stick, vanished into nothingness.

I had long confirmed, aided by Faenir's prior comment, that Charon was not part of the living world. He was dead, a shade covered in clothing to hide the truth. And the unsaid truth did not concern me.

Faenir hesitated as he waited upon the sandy bank for me. His hand twitched at his side, fingers flexing, as he asked me with forced politeness to follow him into the wooden box on wheels which waited upon a distant path.

There was no hesitation from me to enter. I was the first one inside the darkened carriage, Faenir following shortly behind me. The exchange from the boat into the carriage happened so quickly that I hardly noticed the two bodies who sat upon an elevated seat at the head. They held onto the reins of four, brilliantly white horses. Unlike Charon, these people were very much alive.

As the whip of reins sounded and the carriage jolted gently forward, I decided to break the tension for fear it would devour me completely.

"Is there anything you wish to warn me about?" I asked.

Faenir's attention snapped from fussing over his nails, to me in a heartbeat. "Only that, no matter what impression you receive, we will not be welcome." His reply shocked me.

"Care to elaborate?"

"My *family* has a strained relationship. Not everyone is as pleased to see me as Myrinn has been." There was so much unsaid, evident from Faenir's comment.

"Then I get the impression that I will thoroughly enjoy this evening no matter what it brings."

Faenir grimaced, returning his attention to his nails. "You will not be the only one…"

Within the carriage, we were no longer exposed to the elements of night. Yet still I clung to the cloak Faenir had given to me with no desire to give it back.

Conversation with Faenir was as deathly as his touch. It was clear he did not wish to speak, not that his blatant refusal should have annoyed me.

It did.

He had seemed entirely focused on me within the boat. Now, I could not discern the distance he was putting between us, his lack of care for my presence made clear by his focus on anything but me.

I reached for the velvet blue curtain that blocked the world beyond the carriage and moved it back an inch so I could see. Everything moved past the window in a blur. It was so sudden my stomach jolted, and I fell back into my seat. It took a long moment of frantic blinking to settle my eyes. It was as though the carriage moved at such a speed that it turned the world beyond into smudges of dark shapes.

Faenir did not elaborate. *Of course he didn't.*

There was nothing else to occupy my thoughts but Faenir and his cryptic words. The rest of the journey to our destination went by seemingly quicker than Charon's boat ride. I had busied myself with thoughts of Tom as I felt he was a safer person to fill my mind than Auriol. His memory was less of a punishment until I recalled the dead bodies of him and his parents.

Had they been discarded yet? Stiffened bodies were usually thrown over the wall by the Watchers in order to prevent the dead from rising again as they did in Darkmourn.

Every time I blinked, I could see their bodies falling from great heights, splattering across the grassland and staining it red.

Of course, Tom and his parents would never have risen as vampires. They had not been bitten; anyone with sense knew that the disease spread from teeth devouring skin. I almost vomited at the thought.

"Arlo," Faenir muttered moments before the carriage slowed to a stop. "We have arrived." He sounded less than pleased, but I didn't care.

Urgency and desperation at finding Myrinn blinded me as I reached for the door. Faenir stopped me. He threw out his hand and pressed it upon mine. The sudden touch anchored me back into the moment. "I need you to understand something very important before we do this."

I swallowed a lump in my throat, unable to deny the urgency that lit his golden eyes from within. "Are you worried what your parents will think when they see who you have chosen?" My question hung between us.

Faenir's expression of concern deepened into one that frightened me. It was the first time since seeing him in Tom's room that I truly felt the need to put distance between us.

"Unfortunately, my mother and father will not be joining us this evening."

"Why is that?" I pressed, my bravado faltering with each drawn-out moment.

Whatever he was going to tell me was replaced with something darker. In hindsight I should have kept my smart mouth shut, for I would never have been prepared for what he was going to say.

"Because I killed them." He removed his fingers, leaving the cold press of his touch across the back of my hand. "That is why."

17

WE ARRIVED beneath the shadow of the Great Tree Faenir had named Nyssa. With its monstrous heights, it was not impossible to imagine how the elves believed it to be planted by a Goddess. In a world of vampires and magic, Goddesses were not an impossible fable to believe.

Faenir's words repeated within my head long after we disembarked from the carriage. It was as though he called out into an empty cavern, his deep voice singing back on a loop.

He had not offered me a hand as I clambered out, nor did I believe I would have taken it after he had revealed what he had done to his parents. Although he had not elaborated on the cause of their death, I imagined it was related to his touch more than poison or a dagger.

"Cousin," a shadow spoke as it peeled away from the darkened landscape we had entered. Both of my feet had yet to touch the ground before the speaker was revealed.

Faenir looked into the darkness, positioning his body before mine with a single step and spoke. "Haldor, has Myrinn already come to regret our invite that she sends you to turn us away?"

Haldor. The red-haired elf that had been the first to choose his mate in Tithe. Samantha, I remembered the human girl he had picked and wondered if she lingered within the shadows he had slipped from. That thought was soon banished by an explosion of light. I winced as flames conjured from nothing erupted across the wall of the strange building we had been brought to. Fire danced to life, encouraged by the twisting star of flame that hovered above Haldor's hand. The display of frightening power was so sudden even Faenir rocked back a step but soon stiffened in retaliation.

Besides the light, I was not prepared for the warmth that kissed my cheeks. His flame reached me even from a distance. Bright and all-revealing as it banished the dark and revealed what the tree's shadow had hidden.

"I have no doubt Myrinn would have preferred to have welcomed you this evening; however, she is currently having her precious ear chewed off by our Queen."

Faenir's shoulders lifted at the mention of Claria. It was so clear that even Haldor seemed to notice and shared a smile at his discomfort. "Claria was unaware of our invitation?"

Haldor pouted. The fire within his hand died with a closed fist; only the fire that had sprung along the line of torches across the towering wall remained. Even as the two men's interaction distracted me, I could not help but notice how the wall had the same texture of a tree, rough ripples of oaken flesh that seemed to shiver beneath the flames.

"If Claria had known of your visit, she would have cancelled the ball entirely. And that would have been a mighty killjoy for us all."

Haldor was tall, but still fell inches beneath Faenir's height, made more obvious as Faenir drew closer to him. Now the unease shifted to Haldor for the first time since he stepped from the shadows.

He was handsome, which I could not deny, but even his beauty could not hide his discomfort at Faenir's closeness. Haldor's jaw was cleanly shaven, his ivory skin dusted with freckles. Red curls fell perfectly across his forehead as though twisted by a finger.

"Such a daring choice of mate," Haldor said, narrowing his embered-red eyes on me. For the first time since being taken from Tithe I felt a familiar warmth spread across my groin, a burning encouraged as Haldor's attention devoured me. "I remember this one from the line-up. How could I forget someone with eyes like tha—"

"You would do well to turn your attention," Faenir replied, voice dripping with warning. "He is mine."

I wished to shout at them both and refuse Faenir's comment, but my confidence had seemed to run away from me.

Haldor flashed a wolfish grin towards me which conjured a growl from the man who stood between us. He held it in contest, and I was certain Faenir was going to lash out.

"*She* wishes to speak with you," Haldor said to Faenir whose growl only deepened.

"That was not included on the invite."

"Even you, Prince of Evelina, are not above refusing the Queen for an audience. My suggestion would be that you go and relieve Myrinn before our dearest grandmother unleashes her wrath upon her."

"Myrinn has made her bed. She can deal with the repercussions of orchestrating my visit... we are leaving."

"No," I snapped as Faenir began to turn back towards the carriage.

I dug my heels into the ground, literally, showing Faenir with my firm glare that I was not going back to Haxton.

"You allow your Chosen to speak to you in such a manner?" Haldor enjoyed every moment of this interaction.

"My name is Arlo." I turned my attention to Haldor. "Call me by anything else again and I will cut your tongue from your head."

Haldor laughed. Faenir didn't.

"Trust me, *Haldor*," Faenir said, amusement flirting with his frown. "The human is not lying. If you believe my touch should be feared... well, it pales in comparison to what Arlo is capable of. Take my word for it."

Faenir's strangely placed compliment made my stomach jolt. I had to fight my expression to hide my reaction.

"How well-matched you both are," Haldor muttered. All at once he turned on his heel and faced the carving of a door etched into the strange wall. "Perhaps there is hope for your succession after all."

Nothing else was said as Haldor walked away. I expected Faenir to force me back into the carriage. Once again, he surprised me.

"Shall we?" Faenir said, gesturing a hand before him in a sweep. There was no denying the trepidation lost within his wincing stare nor the tension that furrowed lines across his brow.

Something had set the elven man at unease. And whatever waited for us alongside Queen Claria conjured something strange in Faenir. Something I had not believed possible for him.

Fear.

I expected Queens and Kings to live within a castle, similar to Castle Dread that languished within Darkmourn, buildings with towering walls and turrets draped with fluttering banners. Each room within should have been full of luxurious furniture and plush beds stuffed with the softest feathers. Every possible detail should have been coated in wealth.

My imagination could not have been further from the truth.

As we followed Haldor through the dark passages, he would throw out gestures towards the walls which then blossomed with a rose of fire. His light revealed all. The walls at our sides were much like what I had seen outside, the rough bark of a tree we now moved *within*.

I had been within many buildings and establishments, but never a tree believed to have been planted by a Goddess. However, it was not the most impossible thing to believe since being brought to this realm, not compared to lakes filled with ghosts, or elves with the power of fire and death lingering at their fingertips.

The narrow corridors soon opened up to hallways much like that in Haxton. Stone constructions of white and marble, wood from the tree's inners devoured the rooms we passed through; it was the perfect melody of stone and timber. I could not fathom how a tree could have grown to such mountainous heights, nor how an entire dwelling of rooms had been built within the honeycomb maze of the tree's belly.

My fingers trailed the rough walls as I navigated over knots of roots beneath my feet, and I thought of the tree in Tithe. Somewhere within this maze of rooms would be the answers to getting home, I believed it wholeheartedly.

I was all-consumed with my thoughts that I had not noticed when Faenir stopped walking, not until I crashed into the back of him, tripping over his feet and mine.

He did not react to me, I could *hear* why. Towering before us stood large arched doors; they were closed but that did not stop the raised voice within from spilling beyond.

Haldor leaned up against the wall beside the doors, one leg bent which stretched the midnight black trousers that hugged the strength of muscle beneath; I had to force my eyes away to stop my imagination from running away with me.

"Never did I imagine a day when Claria would raise her voice towards her golden child. The right thing to do would be to enter and save Myrinn from her wrath but I admit it is nice for Claria's rage to be placed on another for once," Haldor said.

Myrinn was on the other side of the door, silently taking the muffled berating from the aged voice. I looked to Faenir, and he showed no urgency to enter and help her. Instead, his eyes were pinched closed, wincing every time the voice raised in pitch as though he was at the other end of the ire.

"Do something," I muttered, naturally reaching for his hand. My fingers slipped within his. Faenir's eyes snapped open, and his frown of discomfort melted into one of tempered determination.

He gritted his jaw, muscles feathering. Then, without dropping my hand, he walked us forward and threw the doors open with a powerful push.

"Good luck, Faenir...." Haldor whispered as we passed.

It was not another room that we entered, but another world. A landscape of forest and glade, vines of branches crowned the skies. Pillars of old stone stood like proud guards throughout the area.

Swollen buds of deep, red fruit hung from vines; each one shifted on an unseen breeze.

I inhaled deeply, my nose filled with the sweet nature of fruit and fresh flowers. Across my tongue, I could taste it; the burst of strawberries in summer, and the bite of crisp apples picked happily from an orchard. This place thrummed with life. The air sang with it. The moss-covered ground shivered with it.

My eyes trailed the wondrous place until I came across something misplaced in the heart of it. Before us sat a throne made of wood and in it cowered a hunched, old woman.

Myrinn stood next to the throne, her head bowed, and hands clasped before her. She barely looked up as we entered.

"So, it is true?" the broken, rasped voice broke free from the vessel of sagging, wrinkled skin.

"I cannot imagine what you must have thought when you first heard the word, grandmother."

"Faenir," Myrinn groaned, eyes flashing with caution. "Don't."

I tensed at the unspoken tension between the three elves.

"Leave us, Myrinn," the crooked Queen said. "Let our conversation be a reminder that your foolish actions *will* aid in Evelina's downfall. And to think I had high expectations for you when all you wished to do was sabotage our survival due to your misplaced, idyllic thoughts."

"It was never my intention," Myrinn curtsied, voice barely a mumble over the swishing of her elaborate skirts, "Grandmother."

I tried to catch Myrinn's eyes as she swept between Faenir and me. All the while she kept her head down. I almost reached out and stopped her, to demand if she had an update from my sister. With great restraint, I resisted my urge. Because I now stood in the presence of a Queen, and I could only imagine that if anyone had the power to return me home... it was her.

No matter how ancient and weak she looked within her chair, she practically glowed with power.

Myrinn's clipped footfall faded, finally silenced by the slamming of the doors behind us, before Claria spoke again. "Show me." The demand came out of the Queen in a rush.

"There is nothing to see."

"That is exactly why I have asked, which I will not do again."

Faenir turned to me, lips twitching and face full of fury. He extended a hand to me and I couldn't help but notice the twitching of his fingers. I looked at his hand with confusion which lasted only a moment. I soon realised what she wished to see: Faenir's touch and the lack of affect it had on me.

Disregarding Faenir's outstretched hand I took a step towards the throne and ensured my chin did not lower. "He stole me from my home."

The Queen leaned forward. "As I have heard."

I swallowed a lump in my throat and continued. "I wish to return. He has refused and I do not want this... I just want to get back."

Claria studied me for a moment then erupted in bellows of laughter. She threw her head back, the nest of grey hair falling around her sagging face. "Even your mate does not wish to be with you. How does it make you feel, dear Faenir, to know that the only being known to survive your touch wishes to be far from your side? Does it sting as I hope it does? All these years and the one thing you have desired cannot fathom desiring you in return."

I looked between the frantic Queen and the stoic prince of death. My plea faltered on my lips as a great unease settled in the pit of my stomach like a stone thrown into a body of water.

"Unfortunately for us all, human, you cannot return home. There was once a time when your world was full of life and it fuelled Evelina, allowing such transactions more frequently. Gone are those days. Now, only at the turn of the next season, will the veil open again."

Anger boiled in my stomach, replacing the unease. At the tip of my tongue, I felt the need to demand my return, to reveal that I would die without it. But the wild look of madness in the Queen's hooded eyes told me that my demise would please her.

I swallowed my plea and returned, like a wounded animal, back to Faenir's side.

"Do you truly believe I will let you do this, Faenir?"

He tilted his head, deliberating her question with a click of his bones.

"If I indulge in this union, it will be the end of Evelina. I have prolonged my reign to prevent your destructive touch from shattering this crown. Not before. Not now. Not tomorrow or the days beyond."

"I do not want your crown."

My mind tried to piece together what was happening but was distracted by the twinge in Faenir's jaw. His entire focus was on the old Queen. It left his profile open for memorising and I soon noted that the muscles across his jawline had a way of revealing the emotion he fought to keep at bay.

"Your lack of want will not stop it from falling into your hands," she shouted, voice echoing across the landscape and drawing back that sweet power of life as though she was the source of it. "Faenir, your actions have put me in a position in which I wished never to be in."

Her gaze snapped back to me. The pressure of it made my limbs feel heavy. Even if I wished to step back I couldn't. This time her eyes were void of humour, instead narrowed and sharpened like a blade.

"Ensuring your union fails before the turn of the season will solidify the court's decision to let the crown surpass you and fall upon one of your cousins."

"Whatever this is about," I started, sensing the presence of the knife beneath the belt of my trousers. If I needed it, it was only a quick swipe from reach. "I do not want anything to do with it."

"A waste..." she sang with fury. It was as though she had not heard me or cared to. "Life is precious, and we need the humans to flourish if Evelina ever has a chance of seeing through these dark times. But if I am forced to sacrifice the life of this one then it would be for our greater cause..."

I gasped as the view of the Queen disappeared. I blinked, wondering if the world had gone dark. But it was Faenir. His body was a shield between us.

"If you even dare to contemplate harming Arlo, I swear to destroy everything your bitter, long life has spent trying to salvage. Do not make me be the monster you so wish me to be."

My throat dried, my lungs constricting as Faenir's words settled over me. There was no denying he meant every word he spoke. It was the first time he had truly retorted with equal power against the Queen. And it nearly took my breath away.

"You dare threaten me?" She pushed forward, long nails pinching into the arms of her throne.

"A promise," Faenir snapped. "I am far too determined to give threats, Claria."

Shadows crept across the luscious landscape like a living wave. The warmth seemed to vanish from the air within moments. It was Faenir. It was all him.

"Leave," Queen Claria shouted, her own glow of power pushing against Faenir's with contest. "Enjoy the festivities of the evening. For the sake of your life, and that of your mate, I do hope you fail by your own accord. Otherwise, I too will provide a promise and I am certain to keep it for far more years than you would believe possible. *Demon.*"

18

FAENIR

THERE IS no cooling the boiling of my blood. My fury is all-consuming. It thundered across my mind, swelled in my veins until they screamed with the desire to explode.

I could not think clearly, thoughts of sense fell violently between my fingers as though no more than sand. All my mind could capture was Claria's threat against Arlo. It replayed over and over, fuelling a violent crash of energy that built and grew.

There's a storm within me and it's all-consuming. It stole my anger and fed it to the dark mass of power. For years that storm had been kept at bay, the cord of control pulled tighter with each encounter with Claria or my family.

There would come a time when I was powerless to control it.

When the cord would snap.

And soon the storm would break free.

19

Demon.

Queen Claria had made her lack of love for Faenir clear. Even now, as we navigated the strange maze of corridors on hastened feet, I could hear the hateful title she bestowed on my captor.

Unbeknownst to me, I had found myself in the middle of a family war. Blood against blood. As Faenir tugged me away from Claria in a cloud of screaming silence, I was able to piece together what I had learned. Faenir had killed his parents; still the *how* was a mystery but one I was determined to uncover. His grandmother, the Queen of Evelina, despised him for it as though the crime had been committed recently, her hate potent and undeniable. She kept the crown from Faenir, expecting he would fail to ever grasp the possibility to succeed from prince to something more.

Until now. Until me.

The thought that this man could ever be a King had my footing fumble and nearly trip as I chased after him.

Somehow my presence in Evelina potentially solidified his right to succession and Claria had threatened my life to ensure that did not happen. It was not Faenir's touch that put my life at risk, but his proximity.

The whisperings of music interrupted our silence. First it was so hushed I could barely recognise it over our footfalls, then it grew, building into a crescendo that filled the barren rooms and echoed from all around us.

"What is that?" I asked, fighting to catch my breath as Faenir continued to stalk ahead. It was evident he wished to put as much distance between Claria and us as possible.

Faenir replied through a tight-lipped grimace. "The ball. You wished to partake in it did you not?"

I swallowed, skin shivering in sync with the dramatic notes of the melody. "I would have thought you wanted to leave after..."

Faenir stopped suddenly, his gilded eyes hardly blinked as he surveyed me. There seemed to be so much he wished to say for his expression spoke volumes of unsaid concerns. "You may hate me for what I have done. It is a feeling I am well accustomed to. But I wish for you to know that I will not let anything happen to you whilst you are in my care."

"This is about Claria's threat?"

He nodded softly. "I vow, as penance and apology for my actions, to see you home safely. I will make your stay within our realm as peaceful as I can. Every day that I have with you will be spent proving that I am not the monster they all see me as." There it was. The harsh truth of his inner mind spilling free as though he lacked the control I had grown used to him claiming.

I was lost for words. Even though I wanted nothing more than to look away from him, I fought myself to hold his stare, no matter how heavy it became. "What if I don't make it to the turn of the season?" I replied, hiding the truth of what I alluded to beneath the real threat of Claria.

Faenir did not need to know that I had only one vial of vampire blood left or why I had it. It would not change how this story reached its finale. Once the blood was gone and my sickness was freed from the prison it was kept in, I... would die.

"That," Faenir said through a harsh breath, "is not an option."

The grey-stoned floor vibrated beneath us as the melody continued to build with tension and beauty. I could not place the instrument that could have conjured such a sound. There was a magic laced within it, something Tithe, Darkmourn and the world away from this one would never have known possible.

I felt as though we were striking up a deal. One that I had, in truth, no choice but to agree to. Since my own parents' demise, I had spent my days convincing myself to prolong the same fate. Every time I left the walls of Tithe in search for my poison, all I did was hold back the ticking hands of my doom's ticking clock. Soon enough it was going to catch up with me.

Now the hands spun quickly. My fate raced towards me, and nothing would slow it down.

We stood there, each of us silently trying to read the other's expressions and failing to grasp the thoughts we hid from one another.

"If your mind has changed about the ball then I am more than willing to take leave." Faenir's arms lifted, his hands reaching out but falling short before they could touch my arms.

Perhaps he expected I would have flinched. I did not.

"No." That was what Claria would have wanted. Our presence here upset her. By leaving Nyssa we would allow her to win whatever game both Faenir and her had been locked within. A game of crowns. A game of family.

I love games.

Before Faenir could lower his hands, I reached out and took one. His mouth parted in a gentle gasp that spread across his face and melted the lines of tension once more. His touch was deadly, mine seemed to be the opposite for him.

"It is clear I do not know your politics, but I can understand that turning our back on this ball only means that the true *monster* has won. I am not one for being a participant and allowing that to happen. So, as you have so perfectly suggested, I wish to make a deal with you too."

Faenir's fingers gripped ever so harder, and it sent a thrilling bolt up my spine. "It would not be wise to poke the bee's nest, for doing so will sting," Faenir whispered.

I wanted to ask how he had heard that saying. It was one Mother had used on me and Auriol many times, a way of warning us that playing with fire always caused hands to burn.

"Faenir," I said, returning the grip on his hand. I was overly aware of the sodden skin and more so the fact he did not hurt me. He could not hurt me. *Why?* That was another mystery I added to the ever-growing list in my mind. "Do not think for a second, I wish to poke the bee's nest. If I am going to be forced to stay here, then I will destroy it instead."

"Arlo, you have a treacherous tongue."

I laughed at that, smiling naturally towards him for the first time. "Oh, you could not begin to imagine."

We entered the ballroom, hand in hand. Of course, I had not known what waited in this strange place for it was a mystery with each turn of a corridor and opening of a door. The closed doors blew open without our need to do anything. Beyond them the air swelled with music. A balcony waited before us with twisting, wooden carvings that formed a barrier between it and the great drop on its other side.

Faenir guided me into the room until I could see the sweeping staircase that fell from each side of the balcony until it reached the black and white patterned floor below. We stopped at the edge of the balcony and looked down at a sea of people, and every single one of them looked at us, not a pair of eyes wasted on anything else. Even the music seemed to quiet. The air thrummed with tense intrigue.

I forced out a shuddering breath and held my head high as I stared down at the crowd. This was a symbol. Faenir displayed me beside him as though I was a jewel, and from the look of everyone beneath us they could not fathom what they saw.

Expressions morphed from shock to horror then to disbelief. Some smiled falsely, flashing teeth as though they were wolves surveying prey. It did not deter me, for I was the wolf in this story. Others gleamed upward with pure happiness. Namely Myrinn whose arm was held in the crook of her human mate.

"Faenir Evelina, and his *mate*, Arlo."

I could not see who it was that announced us, nor did I think it was needed. Everyone knew Faenir because of his reputation and thus they had likely heard of me.

"I have not even asked for your full name," Faenir murmured out the corner of his sharp lips.

"And nor will I tell you."

He paused, swallowing audibly. "May I ask why not?"

"Names have power, Faenir. They are also earned, and you have not yet proven yourself worthy of my last name."

He chuckled softly, the sound vibrated across my skin until the hairs upon my arms stood on end. "Then that is all well and good for those who look upon us now will soon expect you to take my last name. That is all that matters to them."

"How disappointed they will be," I replied, pulling away from his side and shifting towards the steps without his lead.

Faenir moved after me, fingers gripping harder on my hand so I could not pull away. It was Faenir's hand woven with mine that finally broke the crowd. The murmuring of conversation began, and eyes turned away from us, all the while I still felt their interest pinned to our union, even if their eyes suggested otherwise.

By the time we reached the last carpeted step the music picked up in volume and pace once again.

"That was an entrance," I said, finally feeling like I could breathe without the weight of so many eyes upon me.

"Indeed, it was," Faenir replied. "It would seem our message has been received. We should leave before any further damage is done."

"And miss a dance?" My legs felt far from dancing as they trembled with anxiety. "I think not."

Myrinn waited for us at the bottom of the sweeping, red-carpeted stairs. Her human was steps behind her as she navigated the swell of the crowd that seemed to press in around us. I was lost in her embrace as she threw her arms around me. "I am so glad to see you. And I am sorry for anything my grandmother has said…" When she pulled away,

I could not remove the scent of sea-salt that danced across the breeze. It was not an unpleasant smell, but I preferred the one that clung to Faenir, not that I would admit it.

"Have you heard from her?" I whispered, forgetting instantly of everything that had occurred around me.

Myrinn's smile dimmed, and my heart seemed to plummet within me. "The Watchers have confirmed your sister is well. As the families of all the Chosen, she has been moved to her new settlement and is being provided with thanks for her *sacrifice*."

I wished to ask her more, but Myrinn tactically shifted the conversation. "Faenir, your presence at court is for the best. I hope you know that."

"We will not stay for long," Faenir cut her off with his reply. I glanced up at him, seeing how his mask of emptiness had returned to his face. He spoke to his cousin but looked over the crowd as if hunting for something. "Arlo wishes to dance. Then we will return to Haxton Manor."

"Dance?" Myrinn practically choked on the word. "You?"

He scowled down at her, but not without a glint of something softer in his eyes. "That is what I said."

Myrinn closed her mouth and drew her finger across her lips. This made the human boy I could still not name chuckle as though she had just spoken the most humorous tale.

"Then Gale and I will join you." She took the human man back into the crook of her arm and beamed from ear to ear.

"That will not be necessary," Faenir groaned.

"Oh do stop moaning, Faenir, it is unbecoming of the future King..." With that she melted into the crowd, a teasing grin brightening her beautiful face.

We stood looking out at the throng of people, side by side, and silent, both as out of place as the other. There was a noticeable space between the crowd and Faenir. If he took a step, they moved. Their potent fear of his closeness left a sour taste in my mouth, one I could not deny.

"Shall we?" I asked, reaching my hand back out for his.

Our fingers grazed one another. There was a reluctance before he took my hand. His eyes left their warm trail from my hand, up my arm, and to my face.

"You can at least force a smile," he said. "We are about to put on a show, are we not? At least pretend like you are enjoying yourself."

I pulled a face, halfway between a frown and a pout. It felt more natural to stick my tongue out like a child; I chose to keep that imprisoned behind my clamped teeth.

"Don't you dare step on my feet," I warned.

Faenir pulled me in close and inhaled deeply. "It is best that you keep up then, Arlo."

20

It was awkward at first, our bodies pressed close together, our feet fighting with one another as we stepped on toes and tripped over the strange pacing. I had danced before, but never with another. Usually, it was before a mirror as I imagined a man pressed behind me as I moved my hips in soft circles.

This, undoubtedly, was a different type of dancing. And Faenir, I imagined, had done neither type before. Yet there was no denying that he was a fast learner. Soon enough Faenir took control and we twisted and spun, his hand pressed into the small of my back, mine reaching up and gripping his broad arm for support. The music melted within our bodies until we were one in the same.

It was easy to get lost in the moment, to forget the crowd of elven gentry that stood from the edge of the room and watched as we seized the floor as our own. Soon enough I was aware of other couples who braved the floor and joined us.

Myrinn glided across the tiles in the powerful arms of her human, Gale. I then recognised the red curls of Haldor and his human Samantha. Another recognisable face could be seen, the youthful, heart-shaped visage of Frila. Her white hair spilled down across her shoulders like strands of silk which swayed as her human mate danced with her.

Evelina royalty danced around one another as the rest of the court watched. Except, there was one elven prince I could not find. Gildir. Perhaps he watched from the crowd, that was close to impossible to confirm as those watching swelled like a wave.

"Your heart is thundering," Faenir said, demanding my attention once again. His fingers tensed on my back, pressing deeper into the skin beneath my clothing. There was something intense about his hold, it had to be as he controlled our movements and kept us dancing. "It is a beautiful thing."

"And yet you still do not smile," I retorted, finding his powerful gaze almost too hard to keep.

"Is that what you wish of me?" Faenir's lips hardly twitched, but his golden eyes seemed to glow as though smiling from within.

"I wish nothing of you," I replied, finding my tongue thickening in my mouth. "However, if you want us to truly leave an impression in spite of your grandmother then perhaps you can convince those watching us that you are actually enjoying yourself."

"Oh, Arlo," Faenir murmured. "Let it be known that I am *thoroughly* enjoying myself."

We were so close now that I felt his warmth spill from him. My chest was inches from his torso. I gripped onto the material of his jacket as his own fingers tapped across my back as though he stroked the ivory keys of a piano.

The music changed the longer we spun amongst the room. The melody slowed then quickened in pace as the sounds began to tell another story.

"Have you danced with many men before?" His question came out of nowhere and had me faltering over the wrong step. Faenir caught me though. His arms wrapped tighter around my waist and kept me pinned to him.

"Not that it matters." I caught Myrinn smiling out the corner of my eye, whispering something to Gale who, in turn, returned her mischievous grin. "No. At least not dancing in the same sense as this."

Faenir's jaw tightened as strands of raven hair blew across his face to obscure the flash of an expression. It did not hide it well. *Jealousy.* It was the reaction I wanted, to toy with him as I would food on a plate.

"I think it is time to leave." He came to an abrupt stop. The crowd audibly reacted to his suddenness.

"Going so soon?" Haldor swept across to us, detaching from the striking Samantha and breaking us apart from his powerful presence. "Faenir, not that you would know, but it is custom for partners to swap during a dance." He then looked to me, hands held out and asked, "May I?"

"Do not—" Faenir began but I cut him off.

"I would love to."

Haldor smiled from ear to ear. "Samantha, dearest, wait for me. It is best my cousin keeps his hands off you. For your sake..." With that Haldor took me into his arms and pulled me away. The crowd took this as their moment to swell onto the dance floor and I lost Faenir to them.

I felt the burning warmth of his eyes bore into me even when I could not see him.

"He will not like this," I muttered, looking up through my lashes at Haldor. Whereas Faenir did not take his eyes off me, Haldor seemed more interested in the reactions around us.

"Faenir is not one for liking anything," he replied finally, rough hands holding me close to him. His warmth was not as welcoming as I would have imagined. It boiled and crackled, as though a fire filled his veins instead of blood. "But if you are to help him claim the crown from Claria's clawed grasp, then I feel I should do my best to get to know you."

"I get the impression that you all do not like the Queen... which is strange since you are family."

"Family does not constitute love as I am sure you have been led to believe. You cannot choose your family; love is earned not granted just because of shared blood."

My skin crawled at his comment. Auriol had not earned my love, and yet she owned it.

"I imagine you share the same wish that Faenir does not take the crown. Would this not ruin your opportunity to become King?"

Haldor laughed at that. The space beneath his hand grew hotter and I was certain my clothes could combust. "Myrinn is the eldest and thus the next in line."

"You didn't answer my question."

Haldor closed in, his face lowering to mine, and I was certain I felt the ground tremble beneath a far-off growl. "Faenir is many things, and a King is not one of them. Evelina is a place of life. If he succeeds, then he will ruin this realm and everything it stands for."

I tried to pull away but couldn't. My heart picked up in my chest, the music also reached a painful crescendo that vibrated through my bones and skin.

"Is this the part where you warn me?" I scowled at him. "Because anything you are going to say has likely been covered by your most welcoming grandmother."

"I am not going to threaten you," Haldor replied, voice no more than a whisper beneath the music. "Even I know that would be a mistake."

"Then what do you want from me?"

Haldor's hands relaxed. His expression shifted from his narrowed gaze to a softening smile that smoothed out every inch of his handsome face. "The same thing we all want from your kind. A chance."

I could not ask what he meant by that as I slipped from his weakening embrace, and he melted into the crowd. He left me alone. Bodies of strangers pressed in around me. Turning frantically, I searched for a way out, for a face that I recognised.

For *Faenir*.

There was a wave of them, coming in at once and drowning me in rich clothing and judging faces. Although they did not speak to me, I felt their stares trying to drain answers from me. Hands tugged greedily at my arms and tunic, likely testing that I was, in fact, real. For how else could I still be alive?

How I could be touched by the prince of death? Why did I still live when others didn't?

Through the crowd I caught the blur of a body. Gale, long stemmed glass in hand filled with the bubbling of honey-toned wine; in it bobbed seeds of pink. He was moving from the dance floor as though following someone like a lost puppy, likely bringing a drink to Myrinn who he longed to find among the overwhelming crowd.

I followed him. If he searched for Myrinn she was likely a safer person to be with then Haldor or the grasping crowd. Not caring for those I hurt or upset, I pushed my way through the bodies, not discriminating to whom received a harsh jab of my elbow on the way out. The thought of reaching Myrinn had me rushing forward.

I wanted to know more about Auriol, to uncover how I could send word to a Watcher like Myrinn could. If that was all I could do to feel close to my sister again I would take it.

Gale left the room through an arched door within the shadows of the staircase Faenir and I had come down from. His body disappeared behind the door as it closed. I reached it seconds after him, pushing it open and calling out, "Wait for me. Gale, Myrinn?"

It took me a moment for my eyes to adjust to the darkness of the corridor beyond. This place must have been a hallway for those who worked within this strange place. From what details I could see, there was no wealth or luxury on display here; it was more like the burrowing of a rabbit's den, dark and cramped with a stale moisture to the air.

Footsteps sounded up ahead.

"Gale?" I asked the darkness which pressed in around me. "Myrinn?"

Onward I pushed, but with each step a strange feeling took hold of me. It told me to turn around and return to the main ballroom. Nothing good came from those who lurked within shadows, even I knew that.

I lifted the hem of my shirt and pulled free the knife I had smuggled here, all without a second thought. All of a sudden, I was back in Darkmourn, moving through the ruins of a once brilliant town in search of a vampire. My ears focused on the darkness. My breathing quietened.

The footsteps up ahead slowed, and I copied, except I did not stop. I kept pressing forward just on lighter feet. The outline of a figure came into view and the hand on my knife relaxed.

"Lost?" I called out as Gale turned around to look at me. I searched the shadows for Myrinn but I knew she was not here. Deep down my soul was screaming at me to turn away but it was only Gale. He was alone. Yet I still gripped the knife for instinct commanded that of me.

"I think so," Gale replied calmly, hardly caring for the knife I held between us. "I was looking for something... but I can't find it."

"There is nothing good to come from searching the dark," I said, sidestepping to allow room for Gale as he paced close to me. "We should get back to the ball. Myrinn will be looking for you."

"Myrinn," he muttered, repeating her name another three times as though he could not place why he knew it. Then he said something that tugged at the tension between us. "Who?"

Gale threw himself at me, taking advantage of my sudden confusion. The floor fell from my feet. Strong hands wrapped around my throat and slammed me down until my head cracked into the ground. In a blink I was blinded by pain. My mouth filled with blood as my teeth clamped over my tongue. The gushing of copper choked me as much as Gale's large, powerful hands squeezing my neck.

It happened so quickly.

The anchoring body of the knife no longer filled my hand. In the fall I had dropped it, not that it would have helped.

Gale straddled me as he strangled hard. I slammed my fists into his chest, recognising the feeling slipping away. When that did not help, and my vision began to blur, I tried slapping his face. My nails dug into his cheeks as I raked down them. At some point, as my eyes began to close and my pain became muted, I felt the warmth of his blood wetting my hands.

Gale was going to kill me.

I stared deep into his wide, unblinking eyes and felt terrifying dread. My vision grew heavy and each time I blinked it seemed to take longer to pull myself from the darkness. But still I tried to focus, to see my frightened, paling reflection in his eyes as my life finally gave up on me.

Perhaps it was my delusion, brought on to protect my mind from the truth that I was going to die, but I was certain Gale was crying.

My lungs burned for air, but his hands ensured that was kept from me.

I closed my eyes and did not fight it anymore. Auriol was waiting there. So was Mother and Father, standing in a line with arms outstretched for me in greeting. Peace. Wondrous, welcoming peace which lasted only a moment.

My eyes flew open as I inhaled a desperate breath.

Gale's presence was gone, only his phantom touch pinched across the skin of my neck. I swallowed mouthfuls of my own blood which now tried its best to finish the job Gale was unable to complete.

Had he run off? Given up at the last moment?

I blinked. Perhaps I had fallen into sleep for a moment because when I opened my eyes once again, I looked up to see Faenir. He towered above me, sharp-red blood splattered across his pale face. It dripped down his grimace and fell upon me like droplets of fat rain. Then his mouth split open, and he shouted violently until every shadow rushed over and devoured us both.

21

Dark, mottled bruises circled the skin across my neck, a necklace of purples, greens and yellows that I could not remove. I studied them in the reflection of the floor-length mirror, tracing my fingers over the colourful hand marks Gale had left upon me. It hurt to touch, but that didn't stop me from doing so. Each time my fingers even dusted lightly across the tender skin I inhaled through a hiss.

"Looking at it will not make it go away," Faenir said.

I tore my concentration from the bruising to Faenir who sat in a grand, deep green velvet chair. Even in the reflection I could make out his cold expression and his frown that had been on full display since I had woken moments before.

"And prey tell what it is you suggest I do?"

"Rest." His answer came out short and fast.

We were back in Haxton Manor. The last thing I remembered was being laid across the floor in the dark corridor in Evelina, fighting to keep consciousness. My thoughts were a string of disconnected memories that made little sense and only added to the pounding in my head.

"That is easier said than done." I was restless. My limbs ached with extreme exhaustion, but my mind whirled violently as though entrapped by a storm. "How long have I been out for?"

"Not long enough." He leaned forward, clearing sleep from his gilded eyes with a lazy swipe of his hand.

When I had woken back in *my* bed in Haxton, it was to the gentle purring of Faenir as he slept in the very chair he had not yet vacated. Before I had time to even register where I was or remember what had happened his eyes had burst open as my name slipped from his mouth in a gasp. It was a moment of concerned weakness in Faenir that he hid quickly behind a wall of moody temper.

"Please," he said, gesturing back to the mound of twisted sheets upon the four-poster bed. "Sit. Let me look over your wounds."

I shook his offer off, pacing before the mirror instead. "I am fine. I… I just can't make sense of why he would do it."

"Arlo," Faenir said, a hint of warning in his voice.

I ignored him, allowing the pain across my throat and the throbbing at the back of my head to intensify alongside my anxious confusion. "Before you even think to scorn me for following after him, don't waste your breath. I thought Gale was looking for Myrinn, and why else would he have left the room? I only wished to speak with her."

"Arlo," Faenir tried again, his voice deepening.

"Gale was following someone, I am sure of it. But—"

"Arlo, sit!" Faenir snapped, half in a shout and a plea. "You have been through a lot and this incessant movement is not going to help. Do not make me force you back into that bed."

There was something about his warning tone that had my cheeks warming. For an entire moment I lost a grasp on what I was saying. Faenir was standing now, his off-white tunic untied at the collar to reveal lines of hidden muscle. He had rolled his sleeves up to his elbows and left his cloak draped carelessly across the arm of the chair.

"Fine," I forced out, walking back to the bed like a scorned pup. As I clambered back into the sheets Faenir was beside me, moving the full pillows towards the headboard to create a back support.

For a moment we were so close that his breath tickled across my neck. Our eyes locked. I was certain that moment would have lasted a lifetime if I did not force myself to break his gaze.

"I will do my best to answer your questions, but as you can imagine that even I will be falling short on many. Haldor has yet to send word regarding the inquisition that has been raised."

"Inquisition?" I said, allowing the unknown word to fill my mouth and familiarise itself in my mind.

"We must find out what happened and why, the inquisition raised will investigate what happened at the ball."

My throat was equal parts sore and dry. Before I could reach for the glass of water at my bedside it was in Faenir's hand as he brought it to my lips.

"May I?" he asked softly.

I could have refused and taken the glass from him; it was not that I required help to drink after all. But, as if by instinct, I moved my lips closer to him and it was greeted by the cold kiss of glass.

I drank until it was almost finished, muttering my thanks through glistening, moist lips, lips that Faenir seemed to watch intently until I spoke again.

"How difficult is it to question Gale?" I asked as Faenir put down the glass and returned his focus to me. When he did there was dread in his eyes; it shrunk his dark pupils to mere dots that seemed to disappear among the sea of gold that surrounded them.

"Difficult. Impossible, in fact."

I could not remember much of what happened, only that Gale had been atop me and the next he had not. But there was something else, another memory that wished to reveal itself through the haze.

"It was you, wasn't it? You stopped him."

It was Faenir that reminded me. "Yes, and in doing so I have killed him." He flinched as he said it.

My mouth dried once again, but it was not water that would help quench it. "You found me."

"Of course I found you. If I did not get to you when I did then we would not be having this conversation. He was intent on killing you. By the time I found you the glow of life that haloes you was faltering. Another moment and it would have been extinguished."

The truth of knowing that Faenir had killed Gale did not disturb me as I thought it would.

"And Myrinn, is she okay?" She was the first person I thought of as he said it.

Faenir seemed to rock back a step. "Does it not concern you that I killed him?"

"Like you said, we would not be having this conversation if you didn't do it."

I watched as my words physically settled over Faenir and his body seemed to lose some of the tension that had kept him strung tight. As if realising, I noticed he turned his back on me and paced back for the chair.

"Myrinn is coping well considering," he finally answered my question as he took his seat again. "Claria is furious of course but considering the justification of Gale's actions I am free from her open berating for the time being."

"Furious because you killed someone, or furious that I survived?"

Faenir answered plainly. "Both."

"Charming," I muttered. "She can join the line. Haldor is not exactly thrilled that I am here. Gale wanted me dead."

"Excuse me?" Faenir spoke and the shadows quivered. I felt the pressure of his sudden anger as physically as if the air itself pressed in on me.

"When he danced with me..." With each word Faenir's dark mood was intensifying. "It doesn't matter."

"Everything matters. I have put your life in danger, Arlo. By me giving into my selfish desires I have brought you into a realm that does not wish to see you live."

There was so much to unpack from what he said. Too much. However, I could not help but grasp one certain comment.

"This is all because you can touch me and that means you could become King."

"I do not wish for that."

"As you keep saying."

"And yet my family seems to not hear me."

"I hear you," I said softly.

Faenir dropped his gaze, the lines around his eyes smoothing.

"What is it you wish for?" I asked. "You stole me from my home and for what... why?"

"To *feel*," Faenir snapped. "I wish to finally feel the mundane truth of touch without consequence. Such a simple thing for everyone else to experience. So simple that you may not even realise how being deprived of such a thing can drive you to do things you never imagined you were capable of."

"Like stealing innocent people from their homes. From their families."

Faenir looked down, focusing on his hands which were balled in fists upon his lap. "Perhaps I should leave you to rest."

"If you dare leave me. You promised not to leave me again." I didn't expect my sudden panic at the idea of being left alone. Just the thought of Faenir leaving me had visions of Gale flooding back into my mind.

Faenir looked back up at me. Hope swirled within his eyes. "Nothing will happen to you in Haxton. I promise that. Soon the inquisition will find out why Gale wished to harm you and who put him up to that challenge."

I felt numb, defeated and pathetic. Not from what had happened, but how desperate I had been to keep Faenir with me. My captor. The person who had sealed the promise of my death in more ways than one.

"Myrinn is horrified. She thinks you will hate her. Blame her."

"And should I?"

Faenir shook his head, raven hair falling out from its neatly tucked position behind his pointed ears. "Myrinn is not capable of hurting. That is her curse, just like death is mine. And she would not have risked her Claim's life for such a thing."

"Why? Because it takes her out of the running for the crown?"

Faenir pulled a face, but his lack of questioning made it clear that he knew what Haldor and I had spoken about.

"There are many reasons as to why the elfkin take humans from

Darkmourn. It is not always about ensuring succession. In fact, that is the rarest of reasons, one only my family are limited to."

"Then why else? Faenir, help me make sense of the world you have forced me to take a part in."

There was hesitation. He opened his mouth but closed it again. I began to believe he would not speak again until words slipped out of taut lips. "I could risk your life by telling you."

That almost made me laugh out loud. I had to swallow back the bubble of frantic chuckles as though I could not believe he had said such a thing. "I think it is clear my life could not be more at risk because of you."

He paused, contemplated his thoughts silently, then revealed something I never could have thought possible. "Our races are linked. Our survival is reliant on one another. If the humans perish in your world, so will the life of this world. We are nothing without one another."

"If that was the case, where was your kind when the vampires spread their disease across the world?" I had always wondered about it. It was one of the reasons why I had a deep hate for elves long before I had been taken to their world.

Why had the elves chosen the desperate moments before the human's demise to show themselves? Sweeping into our world as our saviours, except all they did was throw up walls and concealed us within them.

"There is much to learn about Evelina and its history. We are a realm which has been around far longer than you could even comprehend. But for the sake of your head and my patience you should understand that we thrive off the humans. Their life force feeds Evelina—it keeps us powerful; it keeps us alive. If you, the humans, perish, we follow afterward."

"It still doesn't explain why you take us. If the elves wish for the humans to live then why not leave us in our homes? The more you take, the less you leave."

"Because the elves believe that the only way of ensuring the humans future is by giving them one."

"How so?" I felt myself teetering over the edge of an abyss, with a great discovery lying just out of reach.

"You called them witches, I believe, strange name."

"Those *creatures* destroyed themselves," I interrupted, mouth filling with disgust at the mention of witches. "Darkmourn history tells us that they even had a second chance with the last witch who fell for the creature he was meant to kill and allowed the disease to spread. On two accounts they ruined my world."

"And Queen Claria believes they will save it anew. It was not the plan the elves had for them. The name the elves had gifted them long ago was one more unique. *Halflings.* If we are to give your kind a fighting chance against the vampires that roam the world beyond the walls my ancestors erected, then we will need to right the tip in balance. Magic must return to your realm."

I couldn't believe what Faenir was suggesting. Pinching my eyes closed, the daylight that spilled into the room suddenly became too much to bear.

"Humans are taken and used to sire halflings, beings with power belonging to the elves, but in vessels of humans. Since the downfall of Darkmourn our kind has been creating you an army."

"…that is why they never return."

"I have not lied to you, Arlo. You and any other Chosen can leave Evelina if you so desire. It just so happens that life in Evelina is better than what it can be for you back in Tithe."

I put my head in my hands, finding it easier to block out the world and the horrifying truth Faenir had revealed. There was no denying the intense relief I felt knowing that Auriol was back in Tithe. *Far away.* If Faenir had picked her, and she had the same unknown resistance to his touch, then her life would have not been as she hoped—not one of luxury without costs. Auriol would have been made to bear children. *Halflings.*

"Do they wish me harm because I ensure your succession, or because you picked a mate who cannot sire your children. Which is it?"

Faenir repeated a single word he had said earlier, this time just as cold and sharp. "Both."

I laid down in the bed, unable to hold myself up anymore; I wished only to close my eyes and block out everything that had happened and had been said.

"They see you as a wasted choice, a way of me scorning their beliefs by spitting at the feet of their rules and customs."

"And what do you see me as?" I asked, rolling onto my side and putting my back to him.

As I buried my head into the feather-stuffed pillow, not even I could drown out Faenir's reply. "The only choice."

22

I WOKE, cheeks slick with tears, my breathing shallow. Auriol's name whispered across my trembling lips. I sat up and found that Faenir was still in the chair. Relief flooded through me, and I fell back onto the pillows.

Faenir slept soundlessly. Simply reminding myself of his presence helped pull me from the dregs of the night terror. He was the reminder I needed to understand I was no longer in that nightmare, for the real world was one far more frightening.

It was hard to focus on what I had dreamt which made me wake with tears. Auriol had been there as she had most nights, waiting for me in the dark. Sometimes she welcomed me, other times she wept as though she could not see me, as though I was already dead.

This time the dream was different.

Her stomach was swollen, her hands cradling it as if she required some assistance with its heavy presence. She sang to it, a beautiful voice full of hope and promise. Then she stopped. Her pregnant belly was gone. She looked down at her hands, now sodden with blood, and she screamed. Auriol's gentle face split into a drawn-out cry that warped her features. She howled and thrashed, begged for her child to be returned to her.

I woke before I saw any more.

I laid like that for a while, looking up at the towering ceiling above whilst listening to the Faenir's soft breathing. Beyond it was the gentle lap of the Styx, one of Haxton's greatest lies. It sounded so peaceful, yet I knew it was far from that. How could both sounds be so calming yet come from such dangerous things?

A chill blew in through the balcony doors, causing the brush of lace curtains to skim over the stone flooring. It cooled the tears across my face and chilled my skin until I shivered from more than just the low temperature.

Despite all the sounds of night it was Faenir's breathing that captured my attention. Soon enough that was all I could focus on. How both his inhale and exhale was feather soft. It was so terribly quiet that I fixated on each breath just to make sure he didn't break his rhythm.

I drove myself mad listening to him.

So, without much thought, I slipped from the bed and padded over to the chair; the floor was cold against my bare feet. Perhaps it was my delusion that drove me to his side. Maybe my exhaustion or the bang to my head when Gale had thrust me to the floor. Deep down I knew it was neither of those things. It was my own selfish need, a want to fill my mind with other thoughts, more delicious and consuming. Tom would have been that distraction for me... but Faenir killed him. Yet that still did not deter me from reaching down and tracing my fingers across the hollow curve of his cheek.

Faenir's breathing faltered; his golden, tired eyes crept open. "Why are you crying?"

Embarrassed, I cleared the stubborn dampness with the back of my hand. "I had a bad dream."

I didn't expect for Faenir to console me, nor did I know why I had come over to him. But his distraction was a powerful thing and I feared if I closed my eyes again, I would see Auriol and I couldn't handle that again.

"Tell me what it is I can offer to help ease your sorrow."

I played with his words, toying with all manner of thoughts that speared through my mind. My legs wove between his, pushing his knees apart with a soft nudge. Soon enough I stood between them, all the while Faenir had hardly moved a muscle; his attitude burned with anticipation and wonder.

"May I?" My eyes flicked to his strong thighs in silent suggestion.

Faenir's hands reached for the arms of the chair and gripped them tightly. He opened his mouth as if to reply but a string of jumbled stutters followed. The chair creaked as I climbed onto it, straddling Faenir's thighs until I sat perfectly upon them. He watched me with wide, unblinking eyes. "It feels as though I am the one dreaming now."

"Isn't this what you wanted?" I asked, leaning into him until my lips brushed across his neck; Faenir still gripped the chair as though his life depended on it. "To be touched. To feel what others do?"

"Arlo," Faenir groaned as my tongue traced the skin at his neck in intricate circles. "You have been through a lot. You are confused."

I pulled away enough that I could look up at him through the stubborn strands of ash blond hair that covered my eyes. That frown that Faenir wore so well had vanished. "I know what I am doing. If you wish for me to stop, then say so."

"...I..."

"What?" I said quietly. "Believe me, Faenir, if I did not want you, I would not be doing this." I did want him. But I wanted Faenir like I did with Tom, a way of filling the nights with more than just bad dreams.

Faenir shifted beneath me. I jolted as his hips moved and his legs widened in stance. Before I could fall two strong hands pressed against the tops of my ass and held firm. "Careful," he said, fingers tensing. "I would not want you getting hurt."

"But that is the point. You *can't* hurt me."

I almost cried out when he removed one of his hands from my ass. My breath shuddered as his fingers surprised me, brushing across the side of my face and pushing the hair out of it. Faenir's gilded eyes followed the movement of his own finger as though it was the most fascinating thing in the world.

"I still cannot fathom that you are real. Sometimes, for a moment, I trick myself into believing you are just a figment of my imagination, conjured from years of longing and wasted wishes... Yet here you are."

I reached up and gripped his hand so it pressed against the side of my face and could not move away. "Well, I am real. So tell me what you wish to do with me."

Perhaps I had said the wrong thing. My words caused Faenir to hesitate. The softness in his face hardened, his frown returning to its rightful place.

"Many things." Faenir tore his hand out from under mine and forced himself from the chair, taking me along with him. He was strong. His grip on me was assured and placed to keep me from falling out of his hold. Instinctively I wrapped my legs around his waist as he stalked over to the bed, all without dropping his gaze from mine. "And all can wait until the morning. What I want from you tonight is for you to sleep. Rest and allow yourself to heal after what has happened to you. If you still feel the same about me, come dawn then I welcome you to pick this up where I regrettably stop it. If not, then we will put this all behind us."

I narrowed my gaze, burning holes through him. "I am not the delicate flower that you believe I am. You could pick from me from the root and still I would bloom. I know what I want..."

Faenir lowered me to the bed, depositing me into the cloud of sheets and then stood back at the bedside. "Not once did I imagine you to be delicate. However, I have waited hundreds of years for the chance to feel. I can wait a few more hours if it means I will not need to add the worry of your regret to my mind."

"I do not regret anything," I replied quickly. Desperately.

Faenir looked back at me, rolling back his shoulders as he exhaled his reply. "You will."

23
FAENIR

I COULD HAVE TAKEN ARLO, torn the clothes from his body and explored him in ways my mind had tortured me with. I wanted it with such boiling, undeniable desire that it set my skin aflame.

But that would have been wrong to do so.

Not even hours before Arlo sat upon my lap, slowly rocking himself upon me, had he wished me harm. He had looked at me with such disgust and hate that I had once believed I was accustomed to. His feelings could not have changed so quickly. I would not let him make a decision that he would spend the rest of his days regretting.

My conscience was already broken; with that regret upon it, I feared it would shatter completely.

I waited for him to fall back to sleep. Then I waited a few more moments to know that the nightmare that had thrown Arlo into my arms did not return. Only once his breathing had slowed and his face melted into placidity did I leave.

Each step away from the room pained me. I was breaking his promise, leaving him alone when he begged for me not to again. Part of me expected him to wake suddenly and call out my name, the idea alone was not enough to keep me though, not when my body and mind needed cleansing.

I could not have sat in that room whilst his touch still teased across my skin. Most indulgent of all was the wetness of his tongue. It took everything in my power not to touch my neck and feel the dampness on my skin. If I allowed myself to truly focus on the closeness of his lips and the way his teeth grazed over my neck, I knew I would not have found the restraint to stop myself from devouring him.

Years without touch had not made me a stranger to it. It made me desperate for it.

I walked through the unkind corridors of Haxton in search for the only place with the power to clear my mind. A place of quietness and death. The Styx.

Keep your distance, Charon, I speared the thought across the great lake towards the loyal spirit that lurked within his boat.

His reply shuddered through the link that tethered us, *As you wish, Master.*

Leaving Haxton behind I kept my focus on the dark expanse before me. At night the Styx looked like glass, cut through with obsidian so dark that it mixed seamlessly with the sky. One began where the other ended.

My clothes littered the ground as I closed in on the water. I tore my tunic free with one hand. My trousers came next, undoing them at the waist before they fell to my ankles. I gripped the hard erection that Arlo had cursed me with, forcing it downward in hopes to banish it; just holding my cock urged it to throb harder. As I reached the shore my toes curled as the freezing water rushed over them in greeting. I did not stop, walking until the water covered my nudity in a cloak of darkness.

Shades drifted towards me, grey slithers of shadow and mist that formed figures. They cut through the water, encouraging me to join them. But they would not take me as they had with Arlo. Even the dead feared my touch.

I let the water slip over my head until I bathed in freezing, endless darkness. Only when the Styx closed over me entirely did the voices start, the shades screaming and pleading for freedom. Begging. Crying. Demanding that I set them free from this place. It was the distraction I needed. At last, my cock softened in my grasp. The water of the Styx did what I required, ridding Arlo's touch from my skin.

When not a whisper was left did I finally forget.

There was no room for thought in the Styx, not as the dead distracted me with desperate pleas for freedom, not when I allowed them to punish me for what I had done to them.

That was what this place was, a prison for the souls I had stolen. A reminder of the monster that Arlo convinced me to forget.

24

I HAD, unwillingly, entered into a tournament of silence. Days passed in a slow and torturous dance of stubborn quiet and close proximity. Faenir, although never straying far from me, hardly spoke a word since that night when I had clambered onto his lap in hopes for more than just a seat. And I, stubborn as Auriol had always told me I was, refused to be the first one to speak either.

It had been three days, although it felt more like an eternity. I counted by scoring marks into the stone flooring beneath my bed using a knife I had stolen. It was becoming a game to store Faenir's silverware like a magpie, hiding it beneath the bed alongside the single vial of vampire blood. I felt carrying the vial around in a pouch at my belt would only raise questions, ones I was not prepared to provide answers to.

When Faenir would leave me alone I felt as though I could breathe properly. It was not that I despised his company, but the silence drove me mad. I longed for him to ask me other questions that did not relate to the rate of my healing or how he fixated on the fading bruises across my neck.

I replied with short, one-word answers yet he still did not seem to understand, or care, that there was a taut string of tension, and it was mere moments from snapping.

It was on the third morning, with the long oak table between us, that the string finally broke.

"I regret it." I slammed my hands down upon the wood, shaking the glass of water Faenir had tentatively poured for me. "Is that what you wish to hear? I regret getting out of bed and throwing myself at you. I should have forced myself back to sleep. If I could go back and change my choices, I fucking would have."

Faenir looked over the parchment of cream paper that he gripped in both hands. It was likely a report from the inquisition into my attack. They had arrived every morning from Evelina's council, every single one lacking real information.

"Is that truly how you feel?" he asked, eyes swirling with interest. Faenir hid the lower part of his face with the parchment, making it harder for me to read him, although I was certain he was grinning behind it.

"Well," I huffed. "That is why you have been practically ignoring me, is it not? Have you finally realised that taking me was a mistake?"

"You," he replied, voice cut with seriousness, "are not a mistake. And we are talking now, are we not? Humans, your kind are strange. If you were so in need of conversation, why did you not start it?"

That stumped me. I swallowed the excuse I was preparing to throw back at him and picked another root. "You ignored me."

"I apologise if that made you feel uncomfortable."

It felt ridiculous to accept his apology, but rude not to acknowledge it. "So you admit it."

"Perhaps my silence has suggested that I do not care for your company, but rest assured you have been on my mind this entire time."

"Well..." I stumbled over my words. "Don't!"

He lowered the parchment so it no longer concealed part of his face. "Care to elaborate?" Faenir's frown deepened, his pruned brows furrowing like daggers above his eyes.

"Think about me. I have not given you that right."

"That is a fine shame. But with or without it, you have burrowed far too deeply that I do not believe I could pry you out."

My throat dried. I almost choked on the pure seriousness of his expression. I plucked the glass of water and downed its contents in hopes it would calm the rising scarlet in my cheeks.

Faenir grinned and raised the parchment back across his smug, knowing face.

"Usually, the letter is thrown into the fire by now," I said again, not wishing for the silence to return so soon. "Has the council provided more clarity into what happened with Gale and why he attacked me?"

"No," Faenir replied. "Their investigation has not uncovered anything substantial since yesterday's mention of the knife they had found in the corridor. It is still to be determined why Gale chose to strangle you when he could have stabbed you instead..."

"Don't act coy with me, Faenir," I added.

"Ah, that is right. The knife was yours, wasn't it? Or mine to be precise, you just took it from me."

The way his eyes gleamed hinted that he had already known that. Perhaps he too noticed the dwindling supply of knives as the days passed. If only he looked beneath the bed and he would find them.

"And do you blame me? In a world where I am destined for death, it would be foolish for me not to be protected."

"I protect you."

I looked back to the now empty glass of water and wished for it to be filled. Those three words had the heat in my cheeks flooding back in abundance. I felt its hungry presence spread down my neck and constrict around my chest.

Nothing else needed to be said about the knife. Faenir knew I had taken it and did not scorn me further.

"This parchment is not an update from the council." Faenir pushed back his chair, letting it squeak terribly across the floor. Then he walked to me, footsteps heavy, his deep burgundy cloak sweeping behind him. "It... is an invitation."

"Not another one."

Faenir lowered the parchment over my shoulder and held it before me. It took a moment for me to focus on the swirling words upon it as I was too distracted by his closeness.

"Read it to me," he whispered, cool breath tickling my ear. "Hearing it aloud might help me make sense of it."

I stiffened at his nearness. Each blink reminded me of his hesitant touch when I had straddled him upon the chair he still used as a bed.

"Go on..." he encouraged. "I am waiting."

I snatched the parchment from his hands and began.

Faenir Evelina & mate are hereby invited to the Joining Ceremony of Princess Frila Evelina & mate.
Proceedings will occur within the capital, Neveserin, by Queen Claria the Light.
Blessed be.

"A Joining?" I questioned, looking back at Faenir after I had read it aloud twice.

"Your kind, from my understanding, used to celebrate such partnerships and name it a wedding. This is Evelina's equivalent."

There was no stopping the barking laugh that exploded from me. "A wedding! They have not known each other more than a number of days."

"It is custom." Faenir took the parchment, crumpled it in his hand and threw it with precise aim into the burning hearth, as he did with all the other letters that arrived each morning. The invite crackled upon impact, singeing as the fire devoured it. "Elves who chose a mate will always sanctify their union and Join with one another. It is the first step towards the... necessary."

"Children," I echoed, remembering back to what Faenir had revealed to me. "You pick your human that fits your taste and desire, then marry them before fucking. Seems an awful lot of hassle to get your dick wet?"

"The production of halflings is far more important than just... sex." I shivered with delight at the discomfort the single word caused the elven prince. "Frila is the youngest of our family, a spritely girl who has always, if I must admit, irritated me with her presence alone. For that we will not be going."

"Hold on," I snapped, twisting in the chair to get a better look at him. "Why?"

"I could list the reasons... The most important is your safety."

I scowled at Faenir down the point of my finger. "Don't you dare use me as an excuse to continue hiding from your family and the responsibilities that come with them."

"May I ask why you show such interest in forcing me to do things I do not wish to do? First it was the ball, now this. It is not safe beyond Haxton, not for you."

I stood from the chair, squaring myself off against Faenir who crossed strong arms over his chest. Standing so close that our toes almost touched, I looked up at him and made sure his gaze was fixated on mine. I wished for him to see the honesty in my soul alongside what I was about to say.

"If we do not go then you allow *them* to win. Claria. Haldor. Anyone who has shunned you for being something you cannot help yourself from being. You may be complacent with letting the bad ones succeed, but I am not. Swallow your pride, Faenir. We're going."

Faenir's fingers twitched, I caught them out of the corner of my eye. "It is not the right decision to make. Believe me, I have spent far more years than you could imagine keeping my distance from family relations. This invite has only reached Haxton because it is a challenge, one I would gladly lose if it means keeping you out of harm's way."

I spun back to the table, snatched the knife from beside the plate and twisted back around all within a blink. Faenir spluttered a gasp, one mixed with surprise and pleasure, as I pressed the blunt blade to his neck. "Don't fear for me. I can handle myself. And this time... I am far more prepared."

Faenir's exhale fogged against the metal of the blade, his chest rising and falling heavily with each breath. "If we accept Frila's invitation we will be openly disrespecting Claria before all of Evelina. I highly imagine she does not have an inkling that the invite has reached us."

"I am relying on that. Which is exactly why I wish for us to go," I replied, reaching up on tiptoes until our faces were inches apart. "Disrespect."

~

Neveserin, the capital of Evelina, was the most ethereal place I had ever laid eyes on. I drank it in, face pressed against the glass window of the carriage, as though I was a child and freshly baked cakes waited for me on the other side. The city was carved into the mountains that Faenir had named Cul Nair.

The Goddess Nyssa fell from the skies and left her dent in the world. Where she touched, life blossomed. Neveserin is believed to be the birthplace of our kind.

Domed roof buildings and arched walkways connected one another through a pathway of bridges that seemed to float over cascading waterfalls of azure and opal blues. Trees broke up the countless constructions, each locked in the autumnal shades of amber, gold and brown.

Neveserin seemed to be constructed in levels. The lower levels, which melted from cobbled streets to wide pool-like glens of water and fields, housed small buildings. Above them towered far larger buildings, spiralling towers and monstrous stone temples.

I could not fathom how many elves must have dwelled within this city.

Far in the distance I could see the outline of Evelina's heart, the Great Tree we had visited during the ball, Nyssa. If Neveserin was the birthplace, Nyssa was the place where the Goddess went to die. The Great Tree seemed to guard the city with its shadowing presence.

Once the carriage finally came to a stop after journeying for countless hours, I almost felt disappointed. I could have ridden around the city over and over and never grown bored. Being here amongst such architectural beauty made it hard to believe that Tithe was even real and made it even easier to believe in the Goddess; only someone of such great power could have created such a place.

"Do you remember our deal?" Faenir asked as he stood beyond the carriage and offered me a hand. This time I did not refuse it. Still distracted by the city's physical attraction, I was not prepared for the soft kiss of the air and how it hummed with magic. Using Faenir's hand to steady myself, I inhaled a lungful of lavender and cherry blossom.

"Yes," I replied meekly, unable to look at him for longer than a second for fear of missing out on the wonder of the city. "I don't leave yours or Myrinn's sight."

"I understand Neveserin is overwhelming for the likes of your kind, but do not let its grace distract you from the danger that lurks behind it."

I tore my hand from his. "Stop worrying."

"Never."

"You made it," the light, blissful voice called out.

I turned, feeling the easy slip of Faenir's hand fall protectively upon my lower back.

"I cannot express how glad I am to see you. Both of you."

Myrinn watched us from the arched doorway of the grand building that stood guard before us. The lowering sunlight cast a golden glow across her dark skin. Her bare shoulders seemed to glisten as though shards of stars had dusted across them.

It seemed normal for Myrinn to wear only the finest of dresses. Each time I had seen her, she was wearing something that belonged in the pages of books instead of real life. The dress she currently wore was the shade of burnt amber. The cowl neckline was held up by thin straps and the dress seemed to skim across her frame, highlighting each curve and perfectly drawn line of her body.

Faenir tipped his head into a subtle bow. "Thank you for hosting our stay."

I dipped my knees and bowed a beat behind Faenir. "It is good to see you, Myrinn."

Her smile warmed at my comment. Faenir had told me at the beginning of the journey that Myrinn still housed a lot of guilt for what Gale had done to me. I looked forward to telling her that not once did I blame her. She had been the only one to show me kindness since Faenir had brought me to Evelina and I would not forget that lightly.

"As they have been before, and will be going forward, my doors are always open to you, cousin." Myrinn stood aside, sweeping a hand towards the elegant, curved doorway of light cedar wood. "Perhaps we should catch up over wine… there truly is much to discuss."

25

Tailors fluttered around me like frantic birds; hands pulled at fabric, fingers pinched my skin carelessly. I gritted my teeth as needles wove in and out, stitching a deep navy material to fit my outstretched limbs. I dared not hiss or show my discomfort for fear that Faenir would explode at the handmaids, for he watched from the shadows of the room, leaning against the wall with a knee angled up for support. Not a movement went unseen by him. Myrinn had already scorned him for snapping at one of her handmaids whose needle grazed the skin of my arm.

Myrinn laid across a grand chair, plucking grapes from the plate beside her and inspecting each one with intense interest. "It is important you look the part, Arlo," she said through a breath.

Faenir had refused Myrinn's request for her to escort me through Neveserin to collect a wardrobe of clothes. I guessed he preferred seeing me in his oversized hand-me-downs which he had provided. Instead, in her passive act of defiance, she had commissioned the tailors to her home hours after breakfast that morning instead.

If I cannot bring you into the city, then I will bring the city to you, she had said as the tailors and handmaids floated into the room with arms full of cases overwhelmed with fabric. Faenir glowered and shrunk into the shadows of the room in defeat, yet still he watched.

"He does not need to be paraded like a prized bull," Faenir grumbled from his shadows.

"*He* can speak for himself," I retorted through a hidden smile as Myrinn rolled her eyes dramatically. "If our presence at the Joining is a test, then it is important we prepare to pass it."

"I was thinking of it more as a message." Myrinn popped a purple grape into her mouth and bit down on it. "It is encouraging to know you hold such interest in Evelina's politics. If that is a result of your change of heart to your circumstance, I cannot express how glad I am."

I caught Faenir's piercing gilded stare as Myrinn spoke. Within the reflection of the standing mirror before me I held it, until another needle poked my side and distracted me from him. "It is not like I have a choice in the matter. If I cannot return home, then I must make the most of my visit. I'm not one for hiding from those who wish me harm."

I was certain I heard Faenir swallow hard at my comment.

"Nothing will happen to you during your visit, I promise that." Myrinn glanced subtly over her shoulder towards Faenir. "You will have us both to protect you. After what... what Gale did." She quietened, as though losing herself to a darkening thought. "I will not let it happen again."

"Do not make promises you cannot keep, Myrinn," Faenir grumbled. "Now the inquisition into Gale's actions have been dropped by the council there is no knowing if it will happen again."

Myrinn had been the one to share that update with us when we had arrived the night prior. Queen Claria had closed the investigation and labelled Gale as volatile. Jealous. There was no pressuring the investigation. In the eyes of the Queen and her council, the matter had been dealt with. Except it hadn't, not in Faenir's eyes.

"Rest assured nothing will happen in my home." Myrinn's fingers pinched the grape, letting juice spread down her wrist and staining her silk dress. "And if your hunch behind Grandmother is correct, no pass will be made for Arlo during the Joining. She would not wish to interfere with such a spectacle and ruin Frila's day."

The tailors shared glances with one another. They did not utter a word, but from the look in their eyes I was cautious not to speak ill of the Queen. *Not yet at least.*

"I'm not frightened," I announced, feeling the need to make them aware that I did not need protecting. It was suffocating. Both Myrinn and Faenir, although speaking from a good place, spoke on my behalf. And I didn't like it. For a moment I felt as though I wore Auriol's shoes. "And perhaps the council were right, and Gale was simply mad? When he spoke to me it was like he did not know who you were, Myrinn. His mind was not in a clear place."

"Arlo could be right, Myrinn. What is to say you simply picked a rotten apple from the orchard?" Faenir enjoyed watching Myrinn squirm under his words.

"What is done is done." Myrinn sat up straight, clapping her hands together in dismissal. As though dispersing from the surprise of the noise, the tailors gathered their belongings and parted from the room with haste and whispered breaths.

"We will make the most of your visit to Neveserin, and when you leave it will be alongside a horde of my staff. Now I no longer have a human to host, my rooms are rather full of wasted bodies. I am certain you could find use for them in Haxton more than I can."

"That will not be required."

"It certainly will be," Myrinn replied quickly, rising from her seat. The conversation was done, for now. "Arlo, let me see you."

She winked at me as though recognising the seething elven prince behind. It made me grin, which seemed to calm him quicker. "It is beautiful, is it not?" Her eyes trailed me from head to toe.

I looked down, admiring the clothes the tailors had pinned, strapped and sewed together whilst I had stood for what felt like a millennium. The jacket was a deep shade of navy. It looked almost wet from the way the velvet material caught the spilling daylight that flooded into the room through the glass-domed ceiling above us. The stitching thread was silver. It matched the formfitting trousers, and the unbuttoned jacket revealed the open necked tunic of cream with buttons made from black shell.

"Don't I look stupid?" I asked, running my hands down the arms of the jacket and feeling the small, seven lined stars that they had stitched upon the material. It was as though I wore the surface of the Styx, dark blue with the reflection of burning stars glinting across it.

"No," Faenir said softly. "Far from it."

Myrinn chuckled into her fingers, one brow raised above pleased eyes. "Faenir seems to like it which is the most important thing." She leaned forward quickly and added in a whisper, "So do I. Do not feel *stupid*, but brilliant. If you are to stir the politics of my family, then you may as well do it in style."

"In doing so it will only anger powerful people."

Myrinn took my hand in hers and squeezed. "We are all powerful people. Some—" her eyes flickered, gesturing towards where Faenir lurked. "—more than others."

"It would be best that you do not fill Arlo's head with such ideas." Faenir paced towards us. His closeness made Myrinn flinch slightly, although I could see the regret in her face the moment she did; the reaction did not go unnoticed by Faenir either. "Arlo has a tendency to steal knives. He doesn't need to concern himself with our family."

"He certainly does." Myrinn spun as fast as a viper. "If you are both to complete your own Joining then Arlo will be thrust deep into the heart of our family and its secrets. Hiding from it will only encourage failure."

"Remind me why you care all of a sudden?" Faenir asked, eyes narrowed. "How many years have you all forgotten to reach out to me? The estranged killer of the family. Poisoned fruit, is that not what Grandmother refers to me as during the many dinners, parties and events I have been left out of?"

Myrinn swallowed hard, eyes widening.

"Please," I said quickly. Last time they had come to blows the room almost crumpled beneath the presence of their magic.

"I wish to hear your answer..." Faenir pressed on, ignoring my plea.

"Faenir, enough." I put myself between them both. "I wish to have some time alone with Myrinn."

"Absolutely not."

"Faenir." I glowered. "It was not a request."

His face softened in outward concern. "*It* is not safe to leave you."

"You can disrespect many things, but not my promise to look after your mate, cousin." Myrinn was not pleased at his blatant disregard of her ability to keep me from harm.

Before he could reply I stepped before him, reached up and cupped his cheek. He practically melted into my touch. "I will be fine. Please."

Faenir bit down on his lip as I removed my touch and let the real world and its worries return to him. Then he nodded, one quick tilt of his head as though he could not utter the words it took to agree.

"Take him beyond the boundaries of your home and I will destroy it," Faenir snapped, frantic and rushed as he took steps towards the door. "And everyone unlucky enough to dwell in it."

Myrinn pouted, wrapping one hand around my waist and waggling her spare hand in a farewell gesture. "He will be returned in one piece. I promise."

∼

My head felt foggy, my arms and legs were heavy and slow. Yet I still drank the wine as though it was water from a never-ending source. At one point I had gone from sober to drunk in what seemed like a blink, most noticeable when I closed my eyes only to reopen them to a room spinning before me. It was not a pleasant feeling, but that did not stop me from knocking back each glass until my teeth felt rough with fermented grape. No matter how many glasses I consumed, I could not get rid of the strangling discomfort that gripped my heart.

"Faenir can hurt with his words, his actions, but you understand now why I cannot begrudge him?" Myrinn did not clear the jewelled tear that rolled down her cheek. "He has been punished... punished from the moment he was born for something he cannot control."

It had been easy manipulating the conversation to get answers that I had longed to uncover. Myrinn was an open book, willing for me to flick through the pages to find out about Faenir and his past.

"How did it happen?"

It felt wrong to ask Myrinn to spill the perfectly crafted chest of secrets without consulting the person it related to, but I had to know. Selfishly, it would help me make sense of him.

"Claria tells it as though it is her greatest story. Repeating it over meals with dignitaries and high esteemed members of Evelina's realm. Anyone who would listen. The part that sickens me the most is that they laugh, chuckle like wild beasts over someone else's misery."

I swallowed a lump in my throat, laying my fingers on the back of Myrinn's hand. "Help me understand."

She gathered herself, inhaling deeply as she regarded me through the low-lit room. "Then I will tell it as Claria has. Forgive me for the lack of sensitivity."

I gripped the glass and watched Myrinn without blinking for fear of missing the truth of Faenir's beginnings.

"Faenir was born to Queen Claria's eldest daughter, my father's sister. Her name was Lilith. During her pregnancy it was prophesied for a child to be born that would finally relieve my grandmother of her duties. Evelina is a place of life. So, when Faenir was born, the perfect vision of our realm was shattered as though captured in a glass ball and thrown from a great height. Lilith died as Faenir passed out of her. Her partner, Faenir's father, Croin, took Faenir into his arms and the moment he did so he joined his beloved in death, all before he had realised what had happened."

I blinked and my mind filled with scenes so horrific I wished never to close my eyes again. A body slick with the grime of birth, skin cold and as stiff as marble. I saw a child, its wailing scratching across my soul like a knife pulled across stone.

The wine was left cold in my hand, my grip on the glass threatening to shatter it at any given moment.

"Claria tells the tale as though she found them. Mother, father and the unknowing maids that rushed to help and calm the crying child. Faenir was discovered, naked and subdued, surrounded by a mound of the dead."

Myrinn was crying hard now. If there was more to the story, she couldn't speak through the sobs that wracked her chest.

I sat there in numbed silence.

Faenir was branded a monster for simply being alive. His curse was unfair and had moulded him into the person who had seen me in Tithe and acted upon desperation.

Just as I do with the vampires.

Just as I do with suffocating my sister and her life.

In a twisted, warped way, I did not blame Faenir for stealing me. Maybe that was the wine that dulled my sense between what was wrong or right. But in the back of my mind I felt as though I would have done the same.

"How did he survive?" I asked. If he could not have been touched, then it made little sense to understand how a child was nursed and brought up all without even being able to pick him up from the floor.

"He was never meant to," Myrinn replied. "Claria misses this part out in her stories, but our family knows the next chapters well. It took twenty royal guards to return Faenir to his family dwelling. Once bundled in cloth they were able to touch him... he was gathered in a sack and taken home."

"To Haxton Manor."

"They swaddled him in cloth, the first guards dying upon impact with his skin. Those who were lucky enough to gather him from the trail of death were safe for longer moments; protected by the material. Claria did not care for the material that covered Faenir's mouth. Sometimes I imagine she must have wished him to suffocate after what happened to Lilith."

There was a storm in my stomach. It jolted like wild seas, threatening to break free and spill the morning's food across my new outfit and the chair I sat upon.

"The orders were simple. Take him to Haxton and discard him into the lake."

"No." The glass slipped from my hand and shattered across the floor in a littering of diamond-like shards. "He was a baby!"

"That did not matter. Faenir was a monster from the moment he was born. Claria had him thrown into the Styx in hopes that he would drown. Condemned as poison. His crime of death punishable by death."

I grieved for that child. My heart twisted into knots in my chest, the feeling reminiscent of when my own parents had succumbed to the sickness that claimed them.

"But he survived."

She nodded as the lit candles cast shadows across her striking beauty. "Faenir's power goes against Claria. Life and death. He, like her, is powerful enough to rule a realm. His magic is unexplainable, and Claria despises that. Whatever happened to Faenir in that water changed it forever. You saw what lurks within the waters... you know that death lingers and so does Faenir. Some stories tell that a servant of the family jumped into the Styx and dragged the child free from the water. Faenir has never been one to reveal what happened. Nor do I think he will ever expose that part of his past to anyone."

I stood suddenly, rocking on my feet. "I need to see him."

Myrinn reached out and gripped my arm. "I am sorry if I upset you."

"Before I said I was not scared," I said, my chest rising and falling wildly. "Now I understand that Faenir is not the monster in this story. He is simply the product of another."

She released me. "Go to him. See him in the same light I have for many years."

I paused at that, turning to face her over the shattering of my glass and the melted candle that spilled a river of wax across the table between us. "Why do you treat him with kindness when the rest of your world shuns him?"

Myrinn took a deep breath, rolled back her shoulders and resolve returned into her strong expression. "Whereas everyone sees Faenir as the end to Evelina, I see him as its revival. I do not wish to perish in a dying world."

"And why do you believe he can save it?"

"Because like calls to like," Myrinn replied quietly. "Faenir was destined for birth for a reason. And he is family. He is my blood. I can never turn my back on the truth of that."

26

FAENIR STOPPED PACING the chamber the moment I burst through the door. By the time I saw him my heart was in my throat and my eyes were blurred with tears. I could hardly hold a full breath for fear of it breaking free in a sob.

"What has happened?" Faenir spluttered, cutting across the room so quickly that I was sure he floated on a violent breeze.

I threw myself into his unexpecting arms. My face crashed into his chest, my hands gripping one another behind his back as I allowed my tears to stain his tunic.

Faenir hesitated to return my embrace. But he gave in, gentle hands reaching for the sides of my face and forcing me to look up at him. "Speak to me, Arlo."

Faenir's thumb brushed a tear from my cheek as I struggled to find the right words to say. The haze behind his gilded stare changed from concern, to anger and back to worry. I could almost see him trying to silently work out what had happened.

"Myrinn," I managed finally, "she told me what they did to you."

He immediately stiffened. I felt his desire to pull away and hide himself from me, but there was no hiding anymore. Even in the darkness of the large room with the amber glow of candles being our only source of light, I saw Faenir clearly.

"Why didn't you tell me?"

Faenir loosed a tired breath and pinched his pained eyes closed. "I had burdened you with enough by bringing you here. It would not have mattered if your time passed without you knowing the truth."

I reached up and brushed my shaking hand down the line of his jaw.

My fingers traced it down to his neck, to his chest where I laid them above his heart. "I'm sorry for what they did to you. What they do. I understand now. All of it. I understand." Forming a sentence was hard through my laboured breathing. I spoke what I could, through broken, rushed words.

Faenir's heart hammered beneath my palm, the pace quickening with every passing moment. "Do not cry for me, Arlo," he whispered, opening his eyes once again as his steel resolve had returned to them.

"You have lost so much," I replied. "Even more has been taken from you."

"In this moment I feel like I have everything."

His comment was so precise it stabbed through my soul and buried itself within my mind. It was as though he repeated it, speaking that sentence over and over in torment. It destroyed me. Unravelled me. Devoured me.

"I could give you so much more," I said.

Faenir's eyes widened in knowing. Before he could say anything further, I gave into the taut tension of our cord, the unseen one that had grown shorter every day during my time in Evelina. Now it was mere inches long; there was no pulling away anymore.

Rising on my tiptoes, cheeks slick with tears, I brought my face up to Faenir's until our lips waited a hairbreadth apart. I felt his breath as he felt mine, a cool and welcoming breeze.

"What are you doing?" he asked.

"What I should have all those nights ago."

Our lips pressed together. At first it could not have been called a kiss. It was feather soft and slow, lips simply touching. Existing as one. Faenir watched through wide eyes as though he feared I would perish at any given moment. It lasted a few heartbeats before I retreated from him. His lack of response made me self-conscious and embarrassed.

Faenir was a frozen statue of disbelief. He did not stop me from pulling away. Instead, he let go of my cheek and raised fingers to his lips and touched them.

The sudden realisation flooded over me. That was Faenir's first kiss. In his long life, that had been the very first.

I turned away before he could see my sadness turn to boiling embarrassment. Then a hand clasped my wrist, tugged me back again, and a body crashed into me.

Faenir kissed me back. This time it was far from gentle and inexperienced. It was heavy and passionate. Our faces melted together; mine held by Faenir's desperate hands as he guided the kiss. It started as lips crushing together. I gripped his tunic in my fists and held him to me. Then my mouth parted, tongue encouraging its way into his mouth to greet his. They coiled. Wet and hungry.

Faenir's hand moved and cupped the back of my head. There was no pulling away, nor did I want to. I gave into the wave of his desperation and happily drowned within it. A spreading of numb tingles filled every finger and toe, all twenty digits until I could no longer feel them. I could have lost myself in him like a maze with no desire to ever escape again.

When we finally pulled away again, I felt disappointment that it was over. Then I recognised the desire in his fiery gaze and I knew that it was far from being done. It had only just begun.

"You taste…" Faenir said, voice a low growl. "Divine."

I smiled, my stomach jolting with anticipated excitement. "For someone who has not kissed before you certainly did well."

"Arlo," he breathed my name as though trying to control himself. "You could not possibly comprehend what the many years of imagination has given me."

"Show me."

Faenir stared at me without blinking. His entire focus was on me, creating a thrilling jolt that awakened every sense in my body. It was as though he was starved, and I was his meal; he contemplated which part of me he wished to devour first.

"Are you certain you want this?"

"I want *you*." And I did, as desperately as he wanted me; I was confident of that. My head was full of him, with no room for any other thought. In that moment it was only us, and the world and the realms beyond this room no longer mattered.

Faenir grinned slowly, his red-stained and swollen lips tugging at the corners. I spluttered a breath as he moved, gathering his raven locks in his fist and twisting it into a knot. I had not seen him so clearly before. With his hair pulled back from his face I could see every perfect curve and line. He was handsome, more so than I had first believed. Everything about him was sharp, from the length of his nose and the protruding of his jawline. His face had been carved from the dagger of the gods.

No. He was a god. In every sense as power curled from his tall, broad body in undulant waves.

"Do *you* want this?" I asked, unable to bear the tense silence as Faenir gathered himself.

"In every possible capacity you could imagine."

"Then have me," I breathed, shrugging off the new jacket the tailors had made for me until it slipped freely from my shoulders and fell to the floor. "Do with me as you wish. I give myself to you, body and all."

"Oh, darling," Faenir groaned. "You cannot imagine how long I have waited to hear that."

Without taking my eyes off him I lifted a finger to pull the dark cords of my tunic.

"No." Faenir put a hand on mine to stop me. "Allow me."

A shiver spread up my spine. I lowered my hand to my side and gave Faenir the control to undress me. He did so with careful hands. Faenir treated me as though I was made of glass. However, all I wished was for him to shatter me.

Patience, his eyes commanded me. The shattering would come.

"Arms up," Faenir demanded.

I listened, raising my arms as he lifted the tunic over my head. His knuckles grazed my stomach; my slight muscles rippled in reaction. I was surprised when he turned his back and walked towards the chest of dark oak drawers. He folded my tunic, placed it carefully upon the chest's sideboard and then turned back to me.

"I do not wish to rush this," he said from a distance.

I stepped forward desperately. "Do you wish to torture me then?"

"Perhaps."

I swallowed hard.

Faenir leaned back upon the chest of drawers. The shadows around him seemed to twist and snake. "Now let me watch you take your trousers off."

My hands fumbled for the belt in haste. The pouch with the glass vials knocked against my hip as I carefully discarded it atop the rumpled jacket that waited on the floor.

"Slower."

I glowered at him. "Give me one good reason to."

"I have waited many years, I can wait a few more seconds."

My tongue spread out and traced my lower lip before sucking it in and nibbling upon it. It was a test for my hands not to shake as I popped the button of my trousers. My fingers were numb as I worked on unbuttoning the final two golden clasps. My trousers fell at my feet and I stepped free of them.

"Oh my, Arlo," Faenir said, pushing from the chest and walking back towards me. "Look at you."

"I do not want you to look. I want you to touch me."

"Is that so?" He closed in on me and brushed both of his hands across my abdomen. Faenir marvelled at the shivering bumps that appeared across my skin in the wake of his touch. For a man who held such power, it was as though he had only just discovered it. His gilded eyes lit from within, impressed that he could cause such a reaction.

"Take my clothes off," Faenir commanded. "Would you do that for me?"

He asked as though I had the choice to refuse. That would never happen.

I did not take my time to remove the clothes from Faenir's body. My hands fumbled pathetically as I tore them free. He was amused by my manner, lips practically glistening with desire as he bit down on them. As his tunic ripped, tearing at the seams from my hard desperation, he lowered his face to mine and kissed me. I was blinded by his mouth and taste, running my hands over the stone-like muscles that had hid beneath his clothes. I wished to pull away and admire his build, but in the same breath, I did not want to stop feeling his mouth upon mine.

I could not understand how long we kissed for. By the time we pulled apart we were both breathless, my lips sensitive to the touch. Even Faenir's mouth blossomed with red as though sore, but it did not bother him.

My focus moved from his handsome, serious expression to the trousers that still hung from his hips, before shifting back to his face. Staring at him deep in his eyes I lowered myself to my knees. I allowed my hands to trail down the hills of his broad chest to his stomach until they passed from skin to material. My fingers curled into the waistband and pulled it down enough to see the lines that pointed towards the shadowing of coarse dark hair.

Faenir's breathing became laboured, shuddering with each exhale as he watched me unbutton the trousers and tug them downward. I was already aware of the hard mound that rested beneath it. My hand moved over it and my chest warmed. I could not wait another moment to see him in his full, exposed glory.

Yanking the trousers down, his cock fell free, mere inches from my face. My own throbbed within the undershorts that Faenir had left on me. He, however, did not wear any.

"What is the matter, my darling?" Faenir spoke as he looked down at me with a knowing smile upon his face. "Is there a problem?"

"No," I said, unable to take my attention from the length of his thick, hard cock. "Far from it."

Faenir had controlled every moment until now. But, as I wrapped my fingers around his cock and felt its warmth pool in my palm, the power was handed over to me. No matter how commanding his aura was, up until this moment he soon melted into my touch in a murmuring of pleased groans.

I leaned in close to the pink curve of his tip, mesmerised by the thickness. Tom had been well endowed. But this... This was beyond anything I had seen, held or taken before. My mouth watered at the fact.

"I am going to make up for all your years of wondering," I said, lips brushing against the wet tip. It glistened with his own excitement, flinching in my hand as though it had a mind of its own. "Let us see just how long you can last."

"My darling..." Faenir's voice dissipated into a long, pleased sigh as I wrapped my lips over him and sucked the head of his cock as though it was a freshly picked cherry.

His taste laced across my tongue as it worked around and around the curves of his tip. My jaw ached within moments but that did not deter me. I started slow, moving up and down his shaft with a quickening pace. There was no fitting it all in, not with this position; the angle was all wrong. I longed to lie him down upon the bed that waited patiently at the other side of the room. There would be more possibilities there... but that would have to wait.

Faenir's groans intensified as my hand joined in. I pulled free from his cock with a pop of my mouth and looked up at him as I licked my palm. He didn't utter a word as he watched my lips retake him, until my wet fingers gripped his cock; he released a swear that made the shadows of the room tremble.

"I forbid you to stop."

"As you wish," I said, words muffled by the mouthful of flesh I held within it. "My lord."

I sucked Faenir until his strong demeanour crumbled; his knees shook, and hands gripped hungrily at the back of my head. Before now I had always done everything I could not to perform for another in such a way. I had found the lack of my own pleasuring dull. This was different. My own cock throbbed with anticipated excitement as I worked away at the elven prince. I knew this was not the end, even as his tip leaked sticky sweetness that coated my tongue, Faenir still held onto control with confidence.

I hardly registered the ache in my knees when Faenir tugged back at my hair and guided me to stand up. Not caring for the spittle that painted my lips and dampened my chin, he dove in for a kiss that burned with passion.

"I was not finished," I said, words smudged across his mouth.

"We." Faenir bent his knees and wrapped his strong hands at the curve beneath my ass. With an effortless jolt he picked me up from the ground; my legs snapped around his waist to keep myself from falling. "Are far from finished."

He paraded across the chamber room with his fingers gripping into the skin of my ass, his hardened, wet cock slapping into me with each measured step the only sound in the room. "Do you wish to know what I am to do next?"

My chest warmed. Heat rose into my cheeks, making my mouth more sodden than I believed possible. I slipped a finger over his red-stained lips to silence him. "Do not spoil the surprise. Show me instead, Your Highness."

He lowered us to the bed until the gentle embrace of silken sheets tickled across my bare skin. "What is with the sudden use of titles? Do you mean to mock me?"

I grinned, turning my head so Faenir could dive into my neck. His lips and teeth tormented me as I spluttered out a reply. "It is a title you deserve."

"How so?" he encouraged, pulling away from my neck as though he came up from the deepest belly of water for air.

"Only a prince is worthy of my body. Take me, Faenir. Show me what you desire. Use me. Destroy me."

"You, Arlo, my darling, are the only person that I wish to be the making of."

The kiss he gave me was softer than the rest. There was no flickering of tongues or clashing lips. It was like a petal falling through a spring breeze which gently landed upon my skin. The brush of a feather. The song of wind.

The calm before the storm.

"I may need your guidance." Faenir's fingers traced down my thighs, digging into my skin but not going so far to cause me discomfort. "The last thing I wish is for you to be hurt."

"You could never hurt me."

"Do not say that."

I reached up, took his face in both hands and pressed my forehead to his. "Enough of this talk. Fuck me until words become meaningless."

He tore my undershorts off me, hoisted my legs up and jolted me forward. I screeched with thrill. "Then fuck you I shall."

Faenir stood at the edge of the bed. My legs were thrown over his shoulders, my ass pressed up against the length of his spit-covered cock that twitched at my entrance. I could not take my eyes off Faenir as he gathered spit in his mouth and, with undeniable precision, allowed a trail of it to fall from his lips and fall upon his cock.

My breathing was heavy, my heartbeat filling my ears as though to block out everything else.

Faenir spat a total of three times. Once he was done his thumb spread out the lubrication as evenly as he could across the curved tip of his cock. Then his hand ran circles up and down his length which drew long, pleasured groans from him.

He had commanded me to touch myself as he prepared for what was to come. Faenir watched with such interest I felt like he was memorising every part of me, searing every single intimate moment we shared into his mind; I could see his enjoyment as he studied me.

There was a second where I had to remove my own hand in a panic, worried that I was going to explode and end this before it had truly begun; the feeling had come over so quickly as Faenir took some of his spit and traced around the sensitive centre of my ass with two, soft-touched fingers.

"Breathe deep for me," Faenir commanded.

This was his first time having sex yet I felt like the one with no experience. The way he looked at me spoke of an abundance of knowledge. There would come a time when I would find out how he could be so confident in the face of a new challenge. Now was not the moment for a history lesson. This moment was for the *now* and *here*.

Faenir Evelina entered me with ease. A cry of pure, devouring pleasure stole my breath away and filled the room. His shadows responded as though singing and muffling my own cries.

I did not catch a breath until his hips pressed into my ass. He was inside of me. All of him.

"You are so deliciously tight," Faenir called out with a dreamy sigh.

I gripped the pillow behind my head and squeezed. What I truly wished to do was rip it from beneath me and place it over my face so I could release the storm of shouts that twisted within me. Instead, I managed a reply, though breathless and broken, "Fuck. Me. I beg you."

I could see Faenir's mask of control shatter with each thrust of his cock. His lips trembled, his hands gripping harder on my thighs as he moved in and out of me. He would not last as long as he wished, as long as I desired.

But there was always time for another try. And another.

I was faintly aware of the darkening room as Faenir's cloak of shadows covered us and left us in the safe haven of their concealment. I did not understand his powers but assumed that the noises we made would not reach past this boundary.

I let go of my inhibitions, giving into the pleasure that stretched me out as he rode within me, and I expelled each overwhelming orgasm in shouts and groans. Faenir soon joined in, unable to hide his growls behind the biting of his lip for another moment. He could not help himself as his grinding quickened. His hands ran across my body, touching every inch. Beads of sweat rolled down his face like diamonds which fell upon me as he leaned over to kiss me. I could tell he concentrated on prolonging this moment.

It was impossible to know how much time passed as he pounded into me over and over. Seeing his thrill had me creeping closer to the edge of bursting and I feared I would fail to stop it.

"Do not stop," I murmured, lips pulling away from his, my fingers interwoven with his knot of raven hair. "I want to feel you."

"I will break into millions of pieces if you dare speak like that," he replied, licking his lips to taste me and the salt of his own sweat.

"Break, Faenir, shatter within me. I wish for it."

My words were the confirmation he needed.

Faenir threw his head back and roared into the shadows. I joined in, my hand moving vigorously in tune with his pounding. We raced towards the edge of the cliff and threw ourselves off as one.

The final orgasm lasted the longest. As Faenir came within me, slowing his grinding to a gentle lull, I finished upon my stomach, uncaring for the splattering of cum that reached my chest.

Faenir crumpled over me, and I embraced him. I closed my eyes to help the sudden throbbing that filled my skull. We laid like that for a long moment, heavy breathing and strong beats of hearts, a chorus of one.

"Words cannot express…" Faenir began sleepily. "I have never felt anything as divine. In a world I had come to believe was full of terror and hate, for the first time I have seen pleasure."

His heart cantered in his chest, echoing across mine as he laid atop me. I held onto him, fingers tracing stars and circles into the damp skin on his back. "You are more than I could have ever imagined."

"You imagined me before this?" He raised his head, a smile creased across his handsome face.

I squinted at him in earnest. "As a monster."

"Entertain me, Arlo, darling. Am I the monster that everyone titles me as such?"

I nipped at his lip, tugging him in so his lips were pressed dutifully against mine once again. "You are my monster. My destroyer. And I count down the moments until you have the energy to terrorise me again."

Wrapped up in his arms I thought of nothing but his warmth. Not of Auriol, of Tithe, nor of the vial of blood that promised me stolen life. There was no past or future to cloud my mind with worry and anxiety.

There was only now, in his arms, and that felt like peace.

"Forgive me, my darling, if my eyes close." Faenir rolled off me and onto his side. I looked down and exhaled at the sight of his large cock resting across the V-shaped muscles of his hip.

"Rest," I told him, closing my eyes and smiling without effort. "We will need it."

"Indeed," Faenir replied, his hand gripping onto mine and holding it tightly. "We shall."

27

THE SKIES of Neveserin were filled with song. From the moment I had woken, encased in Faenir's protective embrace, to now as we followed the parade through the city's main road, my ears rang with it. The sound was similar to tinkling bells, as though they had been strung and draped from building to building. Except there were no bells. Elves sang in harmony, crafting sounds I could not have imagined possible without witnessing it first-hand. It was both beautiful, and *haunting*.

My steps were muffled over the fresh layering of scarlet petals that fell around us. *Magic, it had to be*. For there were no trees to cause such a mess. A light breeze danced among the crowds, whipping hair from shoulders and causing dresses and cloaks to flutter like flags in the wind. The petals drifted among the airstreams as though pulled by a ribbon of unseen power, one clearly conjured by Princess Frila who led the procession, sitting upon a carriage of pure, polished wood.

I knew little of magic and frankly did not care to find out, but I had seen enough to know that Myrinn commanded water, her brother Haldor controlled fire, and Frila claimed the air as though she owned it.

That left the fourth sibling, Gildir. He had not presented himself at the ball days prior. And since knowing of my arrival in the city, he showed a lack of interest. Gildir had ignored me with such ease that he made it seem like I had not stood between Myrinn and Faenir as we prepared for the procession. Now he walked beside his twin's carriage like a silent guard. His element must have been earth from his stubbornness alone.

"It will be over soon," Myrinn said as though reading my mind. She offered me a warm smile and I took it. She held a bouquet of white lilies that dramatically spilled a waterfall of orange-dusted ivory petals. The stems glowed with gold powder that matched what was spread across her eyelids and dusted over the apples of her cheeks. The gold complimented the dress she wore. It was crafted from layers of azure and aqua blues and seemed to float like a body of water with each step she took.

"Even that will not be quick enough," Faenir grumbled from my side. Each time he spoke I could not help but smile. It was pathetic. I was dependent and cursed by what had happened between us the night prior. Even now, dressed in the creased outfit that had been left discarded on the bedroom floor where he'd devoured me, I still felt his touch lingering. On me. *In me.*

Myrinn had not outwardly told me that she knew what had occurred. However, the knowing glance she had given me as she greeted us in the main hall of her home was enough to reveal that she knew. Then the blush of crimson across my cheeks confirmed it.

"What is the rush, cousin? Do you have somewhere else to be with more *pressing* matters to attend?"

Faenir shot Myrinn a terrifying glare. She only giggled in response.

"Be on guard," Faenir said, turning his attention back to the crowd ahead but for no other reason than hiding his embarrassment from view. "The day is far from over."

I stiffened at his comment. No matter how beautiful the day had been thus far, he still believed my life to be at risk while being out in public. In truth he likely wished to lock me away to keep me safe, and the thought of that was not terrible, but hiding away was not an option.

"I will tell you again, and a thousand times after that... I will be fine."

Faenir's jaw clenched, the muscles feathering lightly in his cheeks. "The knife you have hidden in your trousers suggests you are, in fact, as concerned as I am."

I had not realised he had seen me slip it from the silver tray provided at breakfast. My mind went to the vial of vampire blood hidden neatly away in the inner breast pocket of the jacket. Had he seen me move it from the pouch at my belt to the pocket? Having the belt ruining the outfit Myrinn had commissioned for me would have surely drawn unwanted attention.

I resisted the urge to reach for the small lump in the material above my heart. "I am not concerned, simply prepared. If anything happens, I am ready to greet it this time."

"Believe me, darling, no one will get close enough for you to be able to pull it free. You have my word."

Myrinn leaned in and whispered with a voice full of glee. "Perhaps, when you are finished with the knife, you would be so kind as to return it."

I bit down on my lip to stifle a grin. "You have my word, Myrinn."

I walked until my legs ached, winding up through the city as though climbing mountains in zigzagging lines. Faenir nor Myrinn showed any effort or exhaustion, whereas I could have fallen to the floor and given up.

By the time we finally slowed to a stop before the grand construction of timber and stone that overshadowed the parade before us, I finally found out the true meaning of relief.

I glanced over my shoulder and admired the thunderous crowd of elegantly dressed elves who had flooded in behind us as we had passed them; it seemed the entire city was here. As I swept my attention over the crowd, I was suddenly aware of just how many of them looked to me and Faenir. Anticipation for our presence was seemingly the most exciting part of the day instead of the pending Joining Ceremony that would soon begin.

The crowd fell to their knees in a bow. It happened in a wave of movement that took my breath away. I almost believed it was in reaction to me, but that misplaced thought quickly dwindled when I turned back around to see the true reason for the display of respect.

Before the door of the impressive construction stood two figures, standing high above us. My heart skipped a beat at the sight of Haldor whose arm was outstretched, aiding the hunched women at his side. Queen Claria was held up by Haldor as though her own minimal weight was too much for her age to bear. Yet no matter how frail and ancient she looked, her gaze screamed with power and authority as she swept it over the city.

Myrinn cleared her throat, which should have been a subtle sound, except the silence around us made it sound monstrous. I looked to my side to find empty space. She, like the rest of the city, was kneeling. Her eyes were wide in a signal as she watched my own horror bloom.

I realised that Faenir and I were the only ones left standing. It did not go unnoticed.

Claria's wrinkled face pinched into an undeniable scowl before she was blocked by the crowd who stood tall once again and erupted in cheers.

"If today had the chance of going well, then I think we have just spoiled it," I spoke to Faenir softly, whose gaze seemed to be lost to a spot in the distance.

He blinked, snapping out of his trance, then turned his full attention to me; I almost buckled under the weight of it. "Respect should be earned," he replied. "Not granted because of the metal placed upon your head."

There was a storm that passed behind his narrowed eyes. His reaction unsettled me more so than Claria's. "What is wrong?"

"All of this," Faenir answered. "I will be content when we can leave this city and return home." He reached out and plucked a crimson petal which had fallen upon my shoulder. I released a hardened sigh as he touched me even only for a brief moment.

"You always seem to be in a rush," I said, watching him pinch the petal between his fingers. It wilted and died, turning brown and falling to the ground at his feet.

"I wonder why."

"You do not deny it?"

Myrinn cleared her throat again, but it was no more than white noise as I focused on the elven prince. He leaned in, both of us hearing the collective inhale of the crowd who watched us. Faenir hesitated as though remembering how exposed we were. He almost pulled away before I scolded him.

"Don't you dare," I said, eyes narrowing. "Touch me. Let them see... even if the reason is that Claria will hate it. Do it."

His eyes flicked in the direction of the Queen as though concerned what she may do if she saw. Then that emotion dissipated within a breath. Faenir's hand lifted to my chin, took it within his thumb and finger and guided my face to his. The kiss was soft and far different to those he had laid upon me the night prior, yet the symbol was clear enough. The crowd had seen that I, unlike the petal he had taken from my shoulder, was left living and well.

I understood their collective shock. Such a simple, mundane act had made the people of Neveserin see Faenir in a new light, different to the picture Queen Claria had painted him as.

"Is that better?" Faenir asked.

"Much," I replied.

Myrinn's hand found my shoulder and Faenir shot her a look that had my knees quivering. She removed her hand almost immediately, but her voice was still firm and guiding. "Your presence will displease grandmother greatly, let our tardiness not contribute to her mood."

～

For the entire length of the long and painfully drawn-out ceremony, Haldor watched me like a hawk studying a mouse. I tried not to reveal just how much his stare caused me discomfort, or how it reminded me of the underlying threat he gave me during the ball... and what happened after.

My legs became numb from standing as Claria slowly wrapped golden cords around Frila and her human's arms. It was laborious to watch and more so to hear the calling of pleased sighs and comments from those around us.

All the while he watched me. I wished to either escape from Haldor's line of sight or scream threats at him to stop looking.

Haldor had spent more time staring at me instead of paying attention to his human Claim, Samantha. She noticed, grimacing at his lack of interest. I could tell from each perfectly curled strand of sun-bleached hair to the fitting dress of the deepest ruby that Samantha had tried everything to physically capture her elf's attention.

And, for my sake, I wished it had worked.

I had fought myself not to tell Faenir for fear of what he would do. Myrinn also didn't notice as she watched the Joining with tearful eyes.

Did I recognise disappointment from Haldor as it creased the corner of his lips and kept his frown rooted upon his face? Or was I reaching for a reality that did not exist? Allowing my anxiety to clamp its claws into me and conjure stories. Perhaps it was never Haldor's doing in the first place. The inquisition had not listed him as a suspect before Queen Claria had closed it. Regardless, his stabbing interest unnerved me.

Princess Frila and her human Claim, Kai, had not been pronounced Joined mates for a few moments before Faenir stood up and offered me a hand. "Care to take a walk with me?"

"Sit down," Myrinn hissed. "It is not over."

"Unfortunately for you, it is not. Arlo, may we take leave?"

I reached up, not caring for the grumbling of annoyance from the guests who sat nearest to us. Due to their trepidation of Faenir's proximity, the row to his side and those closest to both the front and back had been left empty. It made slipping out of the bustling chamber easier.

"Go then," Myrinn whispered, shooing us away with a flick of her hands. "It is not my wrath you will face." Her soft gaze flickered to Faenir who waited with silent patience. "Do not dare disappear back to *my* home. We have the rest of the evening to survive first. Together."

I smiled apologetically for leaving but felt a great relief to be finally taken out of Haldor's line of sight.

"Save me a glass of something strong," I muttered to her.

Myrinn nodded, pressing a finger to her lips and replied quietly, "You will regret saying that to me."

Faenir pulled me away before I could say anything more.

"Dare I ask where you are taking me?" I focused on not tripping over my footing as we moved through the crowd with haste. It parted as Faenir closed in, elves practically throwing themselves from his path.

"I have sat through that entire service without so much as a moan," Faenir grunted, keeping his gaze focused on the path ahead. "I believe I deserve a treat for my patience and good behaviour."

My cheeks warmed and I suddenly felt aware of every set of eyes and ears that seemed focused on us. Far in the background I could still hear the grumbling chatter from Queen Claria who'd begun untying cords from around Frila and Kai's arms.

Faenir guided us before the grand door of the chamber. On quick feet and pulled by his persistent strength, we made it out into an empty hallway when he stopped just out of the sight of those within the room.

"I cannot wait another moment," Faenir groaned, taking my jaw in his hand. His fingers gripped in desperation and his presence forced me steps backwards until the cold, solid press of a wall met my spine.

I gasped, writhing beneath his touch as my body reacted to our closeness. "Is this all you wanted from me?"

His lack of patience thrilled me. I could see my reflection in his wide, unblinking eyes and the smirk he had conjured; it was sly and all-knowing.

"I despise everything about today. How dare such a self-absorbed event eat into the time in which I could be touching you. The concentration it has taken not to lay you on the pew and take you right there... for all to see." Faenir had to stop to control his breathing. "I want you."

"Why didn't you?" I asked, heart beating heavily in my chest. "Take me, that is? Do not mistake me... I would not care if it was put on display for the entire world to see."

After last night, it was true.

I suddenly felt suffocated by my clothes. I wished to rip them free from my skin until only Faenir's hands could warm me.

"Myrinn wishes for me to make an impression on the people of Evelina. Tearing your clothes off with my teeth and fucking you before them all, I am confident, was not what she had in mind."

I looked around, pouting as his fingers gripped tighter into my jaw. "We are all alone now. No one to see us."

His brows lifted, full lips wetting beneath his tongue. "Tell me you want me."

I leaned in, pulling against his hold until my lips brushed over his. "Faenir, I do not waste time on wants. Only needs. And I *need* you."

As the crowd within the chamber hall erupted in cheers of glee, I exploded in moans of pure gratification. Faenir had twisted me until my cheek was pressed against the stone wall. With the doors still open wide at our side, he called upon his shadows to provide us shelter, especially as the crowd suddenly flooded out in a wave.

Hidden away in our pocket of darkness, none of the guests noticed us as they left the Joining. Not as Faenir, with frantic hands, pulled my trousers down until they laid around my ankles; or as he retrieved his hard cock from the band of his breeches and wet it with the strings of spit from his mouth.

Faenir fucked me before them and not a single one noticed.

"Scream for me," he commanded. "I promise they will not hear a single sound."

Sex with him last night had been beautiful and connective. This made me feel giddy as he ground within me, each thrust hard and enthusiastic as the one before.

I moaned within the blanket of darkness as he pounded me from behind with long, fulfilling strokes. I reached back for him, gripping awkwardly at his jacket, his hair, anything to keep a grasp on reality and not give into the overwhelming wave of pleasure that wished to steal me away.

Bodies of unaware elves flooded around us, outlines blurred as though looking through a murky window. They laughed and spoke highly of the ceremony. Some had Faenir's name lurking upon their lips; I could not hear what they said over my own moaning and Faenir's hefty panting.

I almost broke away when Myrinn moved into the hall, deep in conversation with Haldor who looked utterly displeased. I would have lingered on their hushed words and ruined the mood if Faenir had not pulled himself free of me, turned me to face him, and lifted me from the ground until my back was pressed to the wall and my legs were wrapped around his waist.

"Focus on me," he demanded. "Not them. *Me.*"

"Faen—" His cock found its way into me in this new position and my words turned to an exhaled breath. My head clashed upon the stone wall with a thud as I lost myself to the way his cock stretched and filled me. Gone was my concern for Haldor. Of anything.

There was only us, lost, far away from prying eyes.

"You are so beautiful," Faenir said as his eyes rolled into the back of his head.

I wrapped my arms around him, fingers tangling in waves of dark hair. "I forbid you to stop."

"Oh," he groaned, pounding harder each time he pulled his cock free of me. "Arlo, you feel incredible. Tight and welcoming, I would slay a thousand stars to never forget this."

My skin felt sticky beneath my jacket and tunic. I was aware that my hair was plastered across my forehead as I exerted myself with little effort. I, like Faenir, would have wished for this to continue.

It was when our lips met, and our tongues joined in with the dance we were entrapped in that I felt Faenir rush to his finish. As he slowed, burying his face in my neck in a string of moans as he came, I felt satisfied without the need to pleasure myself. My legs gripped him tighter, my fingers pulling on the strands of his dark hair until he peeled free of my skin.

"Do you feel satisfied now?" I asked, noticing how my voice echoed within the cloaking of his shadows.

Faenir pinched his eyes closed and smiled until every line and crease of his usual mask faded away. Pulling himself free from me, Faenir lowered me back to my feet and placed a feather soft kiss upon my forehead. "For now. But I cannot promise I will not steal you away again from the rest of the Joining. I starve for you in ways I never knew possible."

"You are a demon," I said through narrowed eyes. Faenir surveyed me as I pulled up my trousers and buttoned them back up at the waist. "But I admit that even I wish to stay hidden with you. Give me a good reason not to leave like you wished instead of facing the day again."

As the joy of his sex faded and the sounds of the bustling crowds around us peaked through the shadows, I was reminded of what waited. Claria. Haldor. Everything here and far beyond Neveserin.

Faenir took my face in his hands; they felt damp, but I did not care. His touch alone was soothing from the haunting reality that crept back into the front of my mind.

"Believe me, my darling, I wish nothing more than to take you back to Haxton and keep you all to myself. Do not tempt me for I am a weak man and will do it for you."

Remembering Myrinn's story from last night helped me hold my chin high. "No. We face them all together. Myrinn wishes for the people of this realm to see you through eyes no longer glazed with fear. We do not leave until they see you as I do."

Faenir released my face and stood tall. The shadows around us crept inward like smoke dispersing after a candle had been blown out. Soon enough the crowd beyond audibly gasped at our sudden reappearance. I watched as some stumbled back, while others looked at the way our hands held one another and did not retreat with the fear I would have expected.

I was helping them *see* Faenir compared to what his grandmother had made them believe he was.

"Great ceremony," I said softly, forcing a smile at the huddle of elves closest to us. "We do apologise for our sudden... interruption, don't we, Faenir?" I gripped his arm and held him close.

It took a moment for him to force a response as he worked out what I was doing. "Yes. Splendid Joining indeed." He focused on me, and the world faded away once again. "I believe we should get a drink to celebrate dear Frila's special day. I cannot speak on your behalf, darling, but I have built up a rather desperate thirst..."

He winked and I melted.

Faenir gripped my hand and walked through the crowds with focus and poise. Until now I had seen him as he presented himself, different and unwanted in a crowd. But the way he guided me through the cramped hallways of the grand castle made it seem as though he owned it. He was its King and he practically oozed with confidence that only deserved a crown.

Doors were opened for him without the need to ask. People stepped out of the way, not from fear of his touch, but from respect, respect simply earned from his aura.

"We must find Myrinn before she begins to form stories that we have stolen one another and left the city. I would not want to offend our host and I admit, I am beginning to enjoy Myrinn's company. Just do not tell her."

I smiled at his comment, admiring Faenir from his side as we entered a room overwhelmed with the sweet kiss of roses which bloomed across vines that wrapped around pillars of white, carved stone.

"And by the looks of it she is not pleased. Whatever are we going to tell her?"

I locked eyes with Myrinn as Faenir nodded in her direction. She turned from her conversation and beamed at us both, sweeping her arms in greeting, and Faenir's concern fell away.

Before I could call for her, a figure stepped in our line of sight. Someone familiar shouted her name in a tone filled with condemnation. I locked eyes with the person to see the human, Samantha. At first there was nothing strange about her presence despite Haldor not being by her side. She strangled the stem of a lipstick-stained wine glass which seemed to shake slightly.

"Are you lost?" Faenir asked with amusement lightening his voice.

She did not reply. Samantha looked around with wide eyes and trembling lips. A frown turned her beautiful face into a grimace that looked odd upon such a beautiful face.

I pulled my hand free from Faenir and stepped towards her. Her blue eyes seemed darker than they had before, the pink coating of her lips smudged from the wine glass. "Something is wrong..."

Samantha thrashed out before I had the chance to do anything. I was frozen in shock as the glass she carried was lifted skyward. She smashed it into her skull. Glass shattered and wine splashed, staining her hair red.

Someone shouted her name again; it was Haldor, pushing through the swelling crowd behind her. But before he could reach her, Samantha lunged, face pulled into a silent scream, with the jagged remains of her glass outstretched for me.

28
FAENIR

I was detached from reality. *Distracted*. Still, as Arlo and I glided on a cloud of pure divinity, I recognised the tight welcoming embrace across my cock which lay resting within the confines of my trousers. The memory of his touch was haunting. It invaded my mind from the night prior until now as we walked into the swell of people who had no sense of what we had done in the shadows.

Arlo's sex made me drunk. Focusing on anything but keeping that feral part of me under control was almost impossible. It was why I had become slow, why I did not act with haste as the human attacked. My body was here, but my mind elsewhere.

Everything happened quickly.

Arlo fell with the human girl, whose name I could not recall. His hand was torn from my own as her weight stole him from me. The room burned with the terrified screams of elves. Many ran, others stayed and watched as the two bodies tussled upon the floor like bickering children. But fighting children usually didn't lead to smashed glass or blood, deep scarlet that stained my vision.

I snapped, breaking free of my thoughts and throwing myself towards them.

"Faenir," Myrinn cried out. She was somewhere at my side. I cared little to check. "They are watching."

The very air before me thickened with moisture. My nose crashed into the wall that had not been there moments before, encasing me in a cage. I slammed my fists against Myrinn's damp power. It did not shatter, yet that did not deter me; not for a moment did I give up. My heart thundered within my chest, and I felt as though it would rupture through my bones, my flesh.

Beyond my watery prison Myrinn threw her hands out towards the scene. Liquid from the glasses upon tables and in hands lifted and gathered within the air. Like the wall before me, she crafted something new, a spike of glistening, sharpened ice that hung suspended; within a blink it shot towards Samantha.

Light exploded. Heat flared. I did not flinch as the warmth collided with Myrinn's wall of power. Water hissed as fire kissed across it. Haldor had met his sister's attack with a wave of his own magic. The spear melted upon impact, leaving a puddle of boiling liquid upon the floor.

"Enough!" Called a voice. Grandmother.

I continued pounding my fists, recognising the roar within my ears as my own which erupted from my open mouth.

"Free me!" I shouted. "Myrinn, I swear…"

Haldor ran towards Arlo, his face pinched in honest and terrifying disbelief. Myrinn didn't have the chance to attack again as Haldor tore his Claim from atop Arlo and threw her across the room. Her head cracked into a pillar with a resounding clap.

Beneath my fury, the sound pleased me.

My anger quickly turned to desperation as I was trapped, unable to do anything but watch. All the while I begged to hear Arlo, to know that he was okay. I fixated on the glow of life that haloed his outline and waited for it to dull with death. To my relief, his aura burned strong, brighter than I imagined stars would be if they were plucked from the sky and held carefully on one's palm.

Myrinn withdrew her power, and I could have fallen to my knees as the wall around me dissipated. Never had I felt so weak before. This time, no one stopped me from running towards Arlo as he lay immobilised on the ground amongst the smatterings of glass. And blood.

Blood.

"Darling." My voice cracked as I knelt beside him.

Arlo's eyes were wide with horror, his skin as pale as snow. He shook violently, his hands reaching towards his chest. It took little searching to find what had caused the reaction. Above his heart, clothes glittering with glass, was the spreading puddle of red; it seeped through the dark material of his ruined jacket, staining his white tunic beneath to a wet scarlet.

"Arlo." Myrinn threw herself to his side and reached out for him. Before her fingers could come near enough to touch, I broke into more pieces than the glass upon him.

"Do. Not. Touch. Him." Each word came out harsher than the one before. "GET AWAY FROM HIM."

The room darkened.

I could not think straight as the one thing I had held so dear began slipping through my fingers like sand. Arlo was hurt. How much so I did not yet know. And my mind dared to torture me with the idea of losing him. It was all that occupied my thoughts.

"I wish to help," Myrinn pleaded, trying again to reach out.

"Did you not hear me!?" Shadows curled between us. I cared little for the hurt that pinched at Myrinn's face. She had kept me from him. *I could have... I could...*

Cold, trembling hands reached up and traced softly across the skin of my jaw. "Faenir... calm yourself down."

Myrinn broke into a sob as she looked down at the boy beneath us. I did the same, unable to truly believe that his touch was real.

"I am okay," Arlo forced out. I did not believe him, but those three words gathered the broken parts of my soul and did wonders to stitch them together again.

"Oh, my darling." My head fell upon his stomach, and I allowed myself to melt into him. "I thought I had lost you."

Bloodied hands gathered in my hair and held on tight. I feared if I looked up the entire chamber would see tears forming in my eyes. They could not see. It was a weakness that I did not desire having attached to my name.

"Arlo has lost a lot of blood," Myrinn recounted aloud as though her thoughts had no limit. She looked up from Arlo, cheeks flushed as she cried out to the watching crowd, "Someone, call for a healer, now!"

A shadow passed across us; in my muddled thoughts I believed it was one of my own, until *it* spoke. "I have had one sent for."

I ripped my head from Arlo's stomach and looked up to see Haldor. Sudden, devouring anger had me standing. No matter the death my touch could cause him, Haldor did not step back.

"I did not know," Haldor said quickly, grimacing as his eyes flicked down towards Arlo for a moment. "Faenir, I promise you; this has nothing to do with me."

I did not know what to believe. Thinking of anything but Arlo took strength, and I was void of it. In my eyes every person here was responsible. I should never have agreed to come. It was a mistake. One of my gravest.

"Look at me," said the broken, crackling voice beneath me. Arlo tried to sit himself up. Seeing the steely resolve across his face as he grimaced in pain made my knees week. "I am fine," he lied. "It's just a small scratch."

"A scratch would not cause such a spill of blood," Myrinn replied, her voice soft as she echoed my thoughts.

I could barely stand to look at Arlo, not as my mind began pointing the blame back at myself. Seeing him in such a way felt as though glass had punctured *my* chest over and over. I wished for nothing but to steal him into my arms and return to Haxton.

We would never leave again.

Unable to look at Arlo, I focused my fury upon the human girl instead. Her body was unconscious across the side of the room, the glow of life still prevalent around her. The last one who tried to harm Arlo had died before I could question him. This time would be different.

Arlo's blood covered hand reached for Myrinn and pulled her down towards him. Jealousy flared within me, but their closeness lasted only a moment.

"He wishes for me to take him to the healer." Myrinn was already helping Arlo from the floor. Her expression had altered, hardening into a mask to hide something beneath. It was something I was all too familiar with. *Secrets.*

"Absolutely not," I growled, causing those who watched from the outskirts of the room to step back.

"Faenir, Myrinn." Queen Claria cut through the crowd, the tear-streaked face of Frila racing behind. Gildir followed with a hand upon his sword. *Little too late for weapons now.* "I demand an explanation. Now."

"Samantha." Haldor put himself between us, his body acting as a shield, not that I required it. For the first time I felt no fear looking upon my grandmother; there was no room for such a feeling when only anger dwelled within me. "My human attacked him. I saw it—"

"You've ruined my day!" Frila screamed, stamping her feet like a child. "My Joining has been marked by your presence and now you caused this."

"Swallow your tongue, girl," Myrinn snapped, silencing Frila from making another comment that would encourage me to truly ruin her event.

Claria could not hide her half smile. "*He* still lives I see."

"Dissatisfied?" I asked.

Haldor raised a hand to stop me from saying, or doing, anything else.

"It would seem your presence is a bad omen, cousin." It was Gildir's turn to add in his opinion. All the while their words did not affect me; those weapons dulled years ago.

Claria ignored my comment, instead pinning her attention to Myrinn. "Take the boy to a healer and see that he is fit and well. Haldor, gather your mate and the rest of you will meet us in the council hall. The Joining is over."

With the aid of Gildir's arm for support, Claria turned to face the crowd who still watched. "Thank you," she forced a smile that did little but accentuate the deep wrinkles across her displeasing face, "for coming."

Arlo was draped across Myrinn's shoulder. His gaze was unfocused, pinned to something unimportant on the floor as he was lost and confused.

"He will be fine," Myrinn said softly as though her words were only meant for me.

Arlo looked up at me with those mesmerising eyes, one as blue as the skies, the other richer than the earth itself. His lips trembled as they tugged upward at the corners. He winced but still forced the grin nonetheless; it never met his eyes.

"Deal with this," Arlo commanded me. "Find answers. Then come to me."

I swallowed hard, unable to refuse him. If Arlo had told me to kill every person within Evelina in his honour, I would have done it here and now.

No one uttered a word to me as I watched Myrinn escort Arlo from the room. They were not alone as the silver-garbed guards of the Queen's assembly gathered around them in a cloak of metal and steel.

Only when they had left did I turn back on my family.

"When I find out who is behind these attacks, I will take pleasure in causing you terrible pain. Do not think I will let you die quickly. You will suffer just as you have made me suffer."

I looked to Haldor who tugged his human from the floor. She was waking now, moaning as though waking from a night of heavy drinking. Gildir stood guard, unease of the events keeping his usual, misplaced humour silent. Frila was encased in her human's arms as he wasted his breath trying to console her.

"Hold your threats," Queen Claria said coldly, looking at me with an expression she had not granted me before. "It is unbecoming of a prince."

"Do not mistake me, Claria," I replied, hissing through my teeth to stop myself from screaming. "My words are bond. It is a promise, not a threat. Remember that."

29

I HELD out the broken shards of blood-coated glass, not the shards that littered my jacket, but the smatterings of it that filled the pocket at my chest. There was no need to care about nicking my fingers on glass as I had fished them out of the pocket to show her. Pain was not a luxury I held.

Myrinn had to steady my hand by holding my wrist. It shook so violently that I could have dropped the pieces and let them scatter across the floor. It wouldn't have mattered if I had.

Nothing mattered anymore.

"Help me understand," she pleaded, eyes wide, as though blinking would cause her to miss what I had to say.

It had taken great persuading for me to convince Myrinn to dismiss the healers. She refused at first. Of course she had, as she regarded the blood covering my chest. The pleading in my eyes convinced her to do as I wished.

It was not my blood that coated me. If the healers removed my clothes, they would have found my skin bruised, but not marked. It would have created more questions than answers.

I could have laughed at what happened. Although I had known that the vial of vampire blood shattered upon impact with Samantha's stabbing attack, it still did not feel real. A dream, a bad one, but surely this was not my reality.

Even as I had whispered into Myrinn's ear, pleading that she kept Faenir away, I still did not fully grasp that I was finally being forced to tell my truth. To face it head on.

When Queen Claria requested that Myrinn be the one to take me to the healers, I almost believed she could read my mind. For a moment, I liked her, because she kept Faenir from coming here and finding out my deadly secret.

I was not prepared for him to find out. Not this way, at least.

"The blood is not mine." My voice was firm. Tears dribbled down my cheeks.

Myrinn tried to reach for my jacket as though to prove me wrong herself by revealing a wound beneath it. She would have found nothing. "You are in shock, Arlo," Myrinn fussed, trying to push me back upon the bed. "It was silly for me to send the healers away... Faenir would kill me if he knew."

"He can't find out," I said, fisting the glass in my hands; every fragment bit into my palm, but I did not care.

Myrinn gasped in response.

"Listen to me," I cried. "Please."

"Okay," Myrinn said, holding her hands up in surrender. "I am listening."

It took me a moment to catch my breath.

"The blood belongs to a vampire. I kept it in a glass vial for the single need to drink it when the time was required. That caused this. It... broke."

The world spun for a moment, as though someone had yanked it harshly out from beneath me.

I allowed my words to settle over her. Myrinn's face twisted from emotion to emotion. Disbelief to horror. Shock to disgust. The expression she settled on turned her mouth into a small O-shape and colour drained from her cheeks.

One word escaped above the rest. "Why?"

"It kept me alive. Without the blood, I will die."

Myrinn shook her head, huffing out an exhausted breath as though she had heard enough. "You are not dying, Arlo. This is just..."

"I am dying, and I do not care if you wish to believe me or not because it is true." I waved my fist before her, letting the minor cuts that broken vial had made across my palm deepen and sting. "This was all that was keeping me from falling to the same fucking sickness that killed my parents. Years I have hunted vampires. Drained them of the very thing they desire from us, then using it for my gain. All to stay alive. To ensure I did not leave my sister in our world alone..."

I pinched my eyes closed as my throat constricted. The pressure of my truth was too much to bear. All this time I had held it all in and refused to let anyone know I hid from death.

But death found me and snatched me from my world. He kept me locked away from my family and now I would never return home. I would truly die here. Except it was not only Auriol I felt guilty for leaving behind. Faenir would lose me too.

"Arlo." Myrinn wrapped her arms around me, and I crumbled within them; my face pressed to her shoulder as I opened the floodgates. "I am sorry... I am so sorry."

There were no questions. No prodding and poking to find out more. There was simply Myrinn, and she held me up with caring hands as she embraced my secret as her own.

"You can't tell him, Myrinn," I said through heavy sobs.

"It is not my secret to share. Your truth is safe with me."

She held me as a mother would, swaddling me against her. If I closed my eyes, I could imagine that it was my mum. Years had gone by since I had last felt the support of another in such a way.

"Does your sister know?" Myrinn asked finally.

I retreated from her embrace and tried to sit up on my own. Although my eyes still leaked, my breathing calmed at the mention of Auriol. "No."

Myrinn chewed on her lip as she lost herself in thought. "How long have you sustained yourself with vampire blood? Our kind only know of the creatures from what we have learned by watching... I cannot imagine how something derived from the undead can keep you alive."

"Before my father died, he had told me a story that was brought to Tithe by one of its founders. An old woman brought tales about vampire blood and its benefits. No one believed her. They condemned her as a powerless witch. No one wished to listen to someone crazed enough to suggest such a thing. When my father had told me this tale, I had dismissed it just like the old patrons of Tithe had... but I became desperate after he passed when I showed symptoms of the same disease that took them both. I had promised them to never leave Auriol. She was still so young and when the spots of blood smudged across my hand as I coughed, I knew what it meant. I couldn't leave her..."

Myrinn placed a hand on my knee to remind me she was here with me. Her touch grounded me from the overwhelming pull of my story, one I never imagined telling.

"Desperate people are forced to do desperate things. Father's story lingered with me. My options were die trying to fix myself or die anyway. I fought."

"You went hunting for death, hoping to find life."

Hearing it aloud broke me. I nodded, confirming what Myrinn had to say as truth.

"My first kill was the hardest. I was sloppy and unprepared. I spent most of my energy breaking out beneath the wall your Queen created. The vampire was practically waiting for me on the other side. I was badly injured by the time I had hacked the creature to death. I drank my fill that night. Fresh wounds healed, and the sickness retreated like a scorned mutt. I never stopped going after that."

Myrinn listened in stunned silence, not once interrupting me as I told my story. Only when I finished speaking did she take a hulking breath in and spoke. "The wall should be impassable. Queen Claria erected it around Tithe to protect your kind from being picked off by the very creatures you have hunted. If you have been able to break free without the Watchers or Claria noticing a tear in her power, then there is no saying how truly weakened she is becoming." Myrinn took my hands into hers and squeezed. "Do you think the blood that you have been taking is what prevents Faenir's touch from harming you?"

I had not thought of it but hearing her ask it made sense. "We will soon find out, I suppose. When the dregs of the last vial I took wear off, my body will fall back into death's grip. Perhaps Faenir will kill me before the sickness in my body finally has its chance to catch up."

Concern spilled across Myrinn's bright gaze. It was hard to watch the pain deepen the lines at the corners of her eyes and mouth. "You must tell him."

"No," I snapped, urgency clear in my tone and wide eyes. "He can't know."

"Why?"

"Because he will lose the only thing that he has ever wanted. That would break him... I cannot bear the thought of watching him know he is losing me... selfishly I cannot handle that. I have been there before with my parents, trapped in the grasp of impending doom... there is nothing more destructive."

Myrinn winced as she replied, "So you would rather he found out when the inevitable occurs? At least prepare him, Arlo. For the sake of Evelina."

I could not explain further why I did not wish Faenir to know. Perhaps I couldn't answer because I did not know myself.

"I wish to help him whilst I have the time left."

"What if we can find a solution? I understand you have been driven to extreme measures to stay alive, but our healers are far greater than those in Tithe, with access to magic your realm has been severed from."

A spark of hope curled within me. I feared to recognise it for getting my hopes up would be detrimental. "If I let you try to help, you must promise me that Faenir does not find out."

"Only if you promise to tell him if I fail."

I bit down on the insides of my cheeks until all I could taste was the sharp tang of copper. "If we are going to make a deal, then I have something I will require from you if I die. My sister Auriol... I cannot stand to leave her in this world alone. Promise me you will watch out for her."

Myrinn dropped my gaze, and the hope diminished in a single breath. "If you die before the Joining with Faenir, much like Gale, then your sister will find the grace we have given her will be taken from her. There is nothing I can do to stop it."

Adding this knowledge atop of everything else was too much. I buckled under the weight, falling back into the white-sheeted bed the healers had ushered me into.

"I have failed my parents... Auriol. Myself."

"Arlo, you cannot think like that."

I buried my head in my hands, the light of the room suddenly becoming too much to bear.

"We can fix it," Myrinn added, fingers gripping onto me with urgency. "Together, we will find a solution."

Sighing through my anxiety, I recognised the way my breath trembled. "I have tried to fix it... for once, I understand that is no longer an option for me. I'm broken, Myrinn, with missing parts."

Noise sounded beyond the room; heavy footsteps followed by the thundering of a guttural growl. Faenir. He had found the dismissed healers loitering outside. Even from beyond the door, I could hear his fury; it shook the very walls.

Myrinn stood abruptly. She angled herself before the door, stance wide, as though to stop him herself.

We had run out of time.

I reached forward, bed creaking beneath me. Scooping up a shard of glass, I brought it to my now exposed chest and sliced it downward. Skin split, blood gushed out over my hands. A rush passed over my mind like a cloud. Somewhere in the distance, as the pain registered and unleashed its scream within me, Myrinn had called out my name.

I blinked, seeing through eyes now filled with agony. Myrinn had torn the glass from my hand just as the door kicked open. She held it behind her back.

There was no time for questioning why I had done it to myself. Faenir had to believe the blood he had seen was my own. That Samantha had caused it.

In my haste, I placed faith in the promise that Myrinn's healers could save me, at least from bleeding out on the bed. And if they couldn't... well, I would die soon anyway.

30
FAENIR

I FELT the fibres of the wood beneath my hands. They cracked and splintered, breaking under my grip, yet I could not let go of the chair's armrests for fear of what I would do. I could take my anger out on it instead of the human slumped in the chair in the heart of our circle.

"Speak, human. Exercise your own free will or be forced to answer," Queen Claria croaked from her throne.

I admit Claria forced just enough concern into her voice to make me believe she wished to know the motives of the human. If I had not glowered across the space towards her, I would not have seen her disinterest deepening the wrinkles across her face.

The human's silence persisted; lips sealed shut as though forced by other means. And perhaps they were.

"Samantha," Haldor said, sitting on a grand chair to my side. He leaned forward; amber brows furrowed over his tortured eyes. He did not care for the human, but more for the knowledge of what was to happen next. "Tell me. Be truthful and I promise to keep you from harm."

I would punish Samantha for her crime against Arlo. Haldor knew that, and he grieved the reality even now. If Samantha died, it would remove him from succession, which made one fact clear.

Haldor was not behind the attack.

Part of me wished he was. I longed to unleash myself upon him, an excuse was all it took. But even in the storm that raged within my mind, I understood Haldor would not purposefully forfeit the only grasp he had on the throne.

Someone had ripped it from his hands.

Who? The question filled my head like a parliament of owls.

My eyes fell back upon Claria and the wood beneath my left hand completely caved in. The snap was so sudden that it made the human gasp out of shock. It was the first sound she had made since the attack.

Claria rolled her tired eyes, which enraged me further. Every wasted moment that we waited for this human to tell us why she had done it was another that kept me from Arlo.

I had to keep myself from blinking. The darkness usually provided me peace and relief, but now it only gave room for the vision of his body covered in blood and glass. Urgency forced me to my feet. "I am not partaking in this game. If the human wishes to cower behind her silence, then I will be forced to act accordingly."

Haldor stood abruptly, calling out for me as I paced towards his Claim. "Don't hurt her... Faenir, please. Allow her to tell us."

"Sit down, Haldor," Claria snapped. "Let Faenir be the one to kill her. That is what he wants... it is what he always wants. Death. Destruction. He cannot restrain himself."

Frila chuckled into her fingers, falling silent as I gave her my full attention. "Stop hiding behind your hands and say something, Frila. Does it please you to know that you will be Queen if Haldor's mate is killed?"

"Beast," she hissed through bared teeth. For such a beautiful creature, her eyes were feral. "Grandmother is right. You ruined my Joining. Bringing your mate here... what did you expect was going to happen?"

Unseen winds gathered around Frila and twisted her white locks into a vortex. Her ivory dress fluttered like strong wings, snapping in the stillness.

My vision narrowed as my fury intensified. Every shadow around the room whispered into my consciousness, pleading for me to call upon them and carry out vengeance, echoing the sentiments of the furthest and darkest parts of my mind.

And I would have acted then if the small, strange voice that had buried into my conscience didn't speak up. *Prove them wrong. Calm.* I recognised the lullaby tones as Arlo, a siren, cutting through my anger and calming me from the inside out.

"We would not have visited if you had not insisted on sending an invitation," I replied smoothly, "Except your words have clarified that it was never you who sent it."

"Why would I ever wish for you to celebrate alongside me?" Frila said, withdrawing her conjured winds as Claria placed a motherly hand on her arm to calm her. "If you believed the invitation was genuine, then you confirm yourself a fool. Your presence is wrong, and I hate it. I hate you. We all do."

"Enough," Haldor snapped, turning his fiery stare upon her. "This is not helping."

"The truth can hurt," Gildir said, a wolfish grin plastered across his face.

I did not care for her revelation, nor was it required to hear it aloud to know what they thought of me. Their disdain had been clear in the looks they gave me, in the way they had shunned and ignored me.

Claria had attempted to murder me as a baby; that alone made their hate abundantly clear.

Frila may have expected her words to hurt me, to stab into my chest and twist inside my blackened heart. It did not. I wouldn't let them have that power over me.

I looked around the room, allowing my eyes to settle on each of them. Frila, who wouldn't meet my eyes, done with acknowledging my existence. Claria, who cared more about putting a gentle hand upon Frila's to calm her. Gildir, who, as always, cared more about his fingernails than anything else around him. And Haldor, who nodded subtly as I stared at him.

"Which one of you wished for me to bring him?" I asked. "We are all together now. Do not be shy."

Not a single one of them spoke up.

"After all these years, do you truly believe I care for the crown you so desperately clamber over one another for? I do not want it. I do not care about it."

Claria spoke up, turning her sharp eyes upon me and covering me in slashes and cuts. If her gaze could kill, it would. "You think it is that simple, boy? This crown." She gestured to the twisting of gold metal and the deepest red rubies buried within it that sat atop her nest of grey hairs. "Does not care for wants. The people of this world have followed tradition and rely on it. You are the eldest born. You have chosen your mate. They will expect you to take this crown from me."

"Then I will tell them. Remove myself from the race I never wished to partake in."

Claria exploded in light. I squinted as her old, hunched figure burst into whites and golds. Power radiated from her. She was a star among us. It lasted only a moment before she fell back to her chair, exhausted.

"Grandmother," Gildir cried out, leaving his chair and moving to the throne's side.

Panting with shaking breaths and all without opening her eyes, Claria raised a hand to stifle Gildir's worry. "I am fine, dear boy. Give me a moment."

He did so, reluctantly, not before giving me a look of pure disgust.

"Faenir," Claria finally managed. The display of power was inspiring, but equally showed how weak she had become. Time had finally caught up with her and I couldn't help but admit that it did not hurt me to think that she would one day perish.

I longed for it.

"Tradition shall not be ignored simply because you so wish for it."

My hands clenched into fists at my sides. "So you mean to kill Arlo? To take the one thing I truly want just to make sure that fucking crown is kept from me?"

"I do not care for your mate enough to kill him. Time will catch up with you, and I am confident in my belief that you shall complete that task yourself."

"Then who is it!?" I shouted, feeling Claria's backhanded threat sting across my cheek. "Who—"

The human spluttered a wet gasp behind me. I turned to look at her and saw how she clung to her neck; her face painted red; the whites of her eyes darkened with veins.

"Stop that, Faenir!" Claria commanded.

I stared at my hands as though they were to blame, but it was not my doing.

Haldor was up, racing across the space and reaching out for her. "Samantha, I have got you!"

"It is not me." No one seemed to listen to me as chaos gripped the room.

The ground rumbled beneath my feet; stone slabs cracked as Gildir threw out his power towards me. "Enough, leave her."

An icy chill spread through my body. I raised my hands up to my sides, trying to prove that I was not the cause of the human's sudden pain. "I am not doing this."

Claria was the only one left sitting as Gildir and Frila raced towards Haldor to help him. That was when the convulsions began. Samantha's eyes bulged in her head. Foam began gathering past her pale lips and dribbled down her chin. No matter how hard Haldor had hold of the girl, she did not stop the violent spasms that had her body rocking in the chair.

It was over in moments.

Samantha's mouth split into a scream, which never made it out. Her head lolled backwards, neck at a terrible angle. Her body finally stilled. The glow of life that surrounded her extinguished in a blink, as though it was a candle's flame devoured by the weakest of winds.

Dead.

Haldor pressed his head into her lap and wept like a child. Frila expelled a cry of horror which was muffled by the chest of her twin, who gathered her into his arms and shielded her face. The only noticeable reaction on Gildir's stoic face was the peak of a single, dark brow.

Claria sat quietly, watching me with eyes overwhelmed with hate. It twisted her face into a mask of disdain that I had taught myself to mimic. It was an expression that I was most familiar with when looking at my grandmother.

"Are you happy now?" she asked.

I ignored her, pacing towards the dead body of the human. "Haldor, I promise it was not me."

He replied into her lap, his words muffled; I could not make a single one out.

"You demon," Frila spat, eyes swollen but lacked the tears I had expected.

I ignored her. Looking down upon the face of Samantha, I expected to feel relief. She had attacked Arlo, and she deserved death. But the feeling did not rear its head. Peering down upon her, I registered the greying of her skin. It seemed my proximity sped up her decaying as though my aura demanded it. For a moment, it surprised me. Being with Arlo and his resistance to my power had numbed me to a point of forgetting what I was capable of.

I had not been the one to kill her.

A strange, overwhelming urge to place a hand upon Haldor's shoulder overtook my mind. I wished to console him, that felt natural to do so. Instead, I turned my attention to the girl's tormented face, how her wide-open eyes made it seem that she looked at something horrific before her death. I studied every detail of her, searching for the cause, all the while repeating that it was not me, over and over, as though I willed myself to believe it.

As they fussed over her stiffening body, I noticed something fall from the foam upon her chin. A seed. Haldor looked up, heat radiating from his body, as I reached towards her chin. He said nothing to stop me as he also noticed what had captured my attention. I plucked it from the foam, noticing how cold the human was; where the tip of my finger brushed over her skin, it flaked away as though turning to ashes beneath me.

"What is it?" Haldor whispered; his voice as steady as steel.

As I held the seed, it rotted in my hand. I fisted it, nails digging into my palm as my mind whirled with possibilities. "It would have been easier for you to become King," I said to Haldor, ignoring his question. "Believe me when I tell you I did not wish for death, as you may all think. I am sorry for your loss and more so what it means."

He blinked, grimacing as my words settled over him.

I did not stay to hear what he had to say in reply. As the seed turned to liquid in my hand, decaying quickly beneath my touch, I left the room. No one stopped me. I focused on my breathing, wishing to hear Arlo's calming voice in the back of my mind. But it never spoke up over my inner thoughts that thundered and crashed as violent as a storm.

All I desired was to take him far away from this place. To lock him within Haxton to keep him safe. But how could I do that when my presence still threatened to kill him? Even if my touch would not, just him being mine put him in danger. And the seed that was now nothing but rotten ash in my hand held the answers, I was certain of that.

Each step further from my family was another closer to him. I should never have left his side, even with Myrinn's promise to…

Myrinn. The invitation.

It was her.

Suddenly I was running, dropping the ash from my hand as I raced through the castle towards Arlo.

My shadows gathered behind me until I felt every part of the castle they graced.

Then I found them, slithers of glowing life among the dark.

Two figures. One burning far brighter than the other.

The other dwindling in life.

Arlo.

31

NEVESERIN PASSED in a blur of ivory-domed buildings and white pillars. Faenir sat beside me in the carriage, facing his window, not once uttering a word. Silence hummed between us so taut that no knife would have been able to cut it.

Even as wheels clambered over the cobbled streets and the hooves of the steeds clattered evenly, I still could hear Faenir's thunderous fury as he had entered the healer's chamber. I winced at the memory, trying to focus on the details in the world outside this moving box, anything to clear what he had said to Myrinn. He had burst through the door in a storm of shadow; never had I seen someone so far gone to rage as I had Faenir. His anger did not calm when he found me bleeding on the bed with the fresh wound I had given myself.

In a gaggle of fear, the healers had raced in behind Faenir for aid. Strapped beneath their hands as they held me to the bed, I could do nothing but watch as Faenir unleashed himself upon Myrinn.

The pain in my chest had choked me, even if I'd longed to scream and tell him to leave her alone, I couldn't. The scene haunted me as we rode out of the elven city. Guilt was my fresh wound, and it pained me more than the healed slash across my chest had.

It was you.

Myrinn had not denied him.

The invite, you sent it. Not Frila.

I did. Two words, that was all she'd spoken. As fingers had pinched at my skin and white clothes soaked up blood, I found it hard to truly understand those two words.

He could have died because of you. Or is that what you want? It would seem all this time you wished to protect him, yet it was you who has put Arlo's life at risk time and time again.

The mask of steel Myrinn erected had come crumbling down. I'd seen her longing to grab Faenir and shake sense into him; it'd burned in her eyes as they filled with tears.

Myrinn had persisted in her case, but Faenir had kept the blame heavy upon her. Heated words were shared, some I did not think I would ever forget, and at the end of it, there was no solution.

Regardless of what happened with Faenir before he found us, and what came after… I never would have believed Myrinn was to blame. In time, he would see sense. Faenir had to.

I had not seen Myrinn since she stormed from the healer's chamber room. She left, carrying my most precious secret in her hands as though it were a butterfly waiting to be released. Or crushed.

My mind was filled with the promise of death. No matter where I looked, what I thought, it all came back to it. I had grown used to the glass vial's presence. Even now, as we flew over bumps in the road, I reached up for the breast pocket to find it flat. Empty.

It was a painful reminder. All of it.

"You were too hard on her." I severed the silence before the dark thoughts devoured me completely. "If you truly believe that Myrinn is behind the attacks, then I have mistaken you for something other than a fool."

Faenir turned from his window and focused on me. I hated the way he looked at me, eyes searching for pain. His eyes had dulled to tones of honey, as though a light had perished within, yet the worst part was the heavy fear that clung to them. Faenir looked at me as I imagined a poor man looked at coin, with honest, sickening desperation. Part of me wished to snap at him, demand that he look away. If he saw me in such a way now, what would happen if he knew the truth?

He can't find out.

I dropped my eyes to my hands, which fidgeted in my lap. Faenir sighed knowingly.

"Even if Myrinn did not force the hands of the human that hurt you, by her forging that invitation she signed the warrant of your life. I cannot forgive her for tricking us into coming."

"Stop convincing yourself of her intentions when you know little as to what they are."

Faenir recoiled as I threw my attention back to him. Such hot and sudden anger filled my body. I wished to lash out like a child gripped in a tantrum. The new, puckered scar across my chest pulled awkwardly, sending a sharp spread of discomfort across my torso, restricting my breathing for a moment.

"Please," Faenir said, reaching up but hesitating before he touched me. "I should not have said anything to work you up. You have been through a great deal, I only wish for you to relax now."

I was not giving up the conversation that easily. "Stop placing your guilt upon Myrinn. It is not her presence that threatens my life." I regretted the words the moment they left my mouth. Faenir's handsome face screwed into one of agony. If my words were a knife, it would have cut deep.

"I am sorry..." I began as Faenir turned back away and peered beyond the window.

"But you are right. Nothing you said is incorrect. I am to blame, I know that."

I was, but my deliverance did not need to be so careless. "All Myrinn wants is for the people of your realm to see you as more than what you have been painted out to be. There was no malice behind what she has done."

"And she told you this?" he muttered.

"Myrinn petitions for you to become King. She thinks you are the only one powerful enough to prevent the death of Evelina and I think she is right."

"So, she is setting me up and going against my own wishes?"

I reached out and gripped his hand, which was balled into a fist beside him. As soon as I touched him, Faenir released a breath and his hand relaxed. "Beside the fact that you have been told your entire life that you are not to be King, why are you so adamant about not making your own decision on the matter? Tell me, Faenir, help me understand why you do not want such a thing."

"How can I rule a world in which I cannot touch? A King or Queen should inspire love in their subjects. I embody the very opposite of what love is."

"You do not need to physically touch a heart to make an impact on it. Love is not physical; I only wish you would recognise that."

"*Love*." Faenir practically shuddered as he spoke the word. It seemed to hurt him. "I am a killer. My own parents brought me into this world as a product of their love and yet I killed them. Everything I touch is destroyed. If the crown falls upon me, then I will destroy it as I have with everything else."

Something white flew past the window so fast that I hardly registered what it was.

"Yet here we are, my hand upon yours, and you have not destroyed me. In fact, I would say you have had the opposite effect. There is love in you, Faenir. You just need to trust it."

Another blur of white beyond the window. This time it thudded against the glass and distracted us both.

"What...?"

I leaned over Faenir, hands propped against his thigh as I peered outside. The carriage moved with such speed that it was hard to focus on anything. Again, another thud occurred as something unmistakably white fell beneath the wheels of the carriage and out of view.

"Slow down!" Faenir commanded, slamming a palm to the wall that separated us from the coachman. He did not need to ask again. We both jolted as the carriage slowed suddenly.

As the world calmed beyond the window, it was clear what was waiting. Lining the streets were elves of all kinds, children, adults, huddled together so close that they formed a wall between the city and us. In their hands were bundles of beautiful white flowers; long, pointed petals so white I first believed them to be carrying handfuls of snow. They threw them as we passed, letting the flowers rain down upon the carriage. They littered the road, crushed beneath the wheels as we rode over them.

"Why are they doing that?" I asked, breath fogging on the glass.

Faenir replied as gentle a whisper, "Lilies. In Evelina, the flowers represent forgiveness. It is a message."

"They ask for our forgiveness?"

"No," Faenir replied sharply. I turned to look at him, noticing the lines of his profile and the returning spark in his golden eyes as he studied the faces of every elf we passed. "They are asking for your forgiveness. For what has happened to you."

A shiver coursed up my arms as I added, "To us."

"No," Faenir said. "They owe me nothing."

"This is what Myrinn wished," I said, pleading for Faenir to see what I now saw. "For the people of this world to sympathise with you. Can't you see? Look at them, Faenir. Truly look at them and recognise the truth in their faces."

"I do not require their sympathy."

"No, you don't." I couldn't hide my smile as I looked back beyond the window and watched as the sky rained with lilies. "But you require their support if we are ever going to see you take what is rightfully yours."

The crown.

"We?" Faenir's eyes tickled across my face. His lips were so close to my cheek that I felt his warm breath.

There was so much I wished to say at that moment. Looking at the city of elves, at the symbol of their actions, I made my mind up on a decision that I had not given space to think of yet. I did not wish to die and simply cease to exist. If I was going to go, then I wanted to make a mark on the world. It was what my parents had done with Auriol and I. We were their legacy, but until now I did not have one.

Faenir, he is more than my legacy.

"*We* have much to do, Your Majesty."

Faenir tugged me onto his lap and the crowd beyond the carriage shouted with glee as they watched us. He did not care or notice, but I did. "Careful, Arlo, if you speak in such a way, you will force me to rule you; body and soul."

"Do it." I pressed my face towards his until our noses touched. "Rule me."

And he did, cramped in the back of the carriage upon velvet pillows. As our lips crashed together, Faenir reached for the golden cord that held back the curtain from the window and tore it free. We were bathed in darkness.

"That is much better. It would be untoward for anyone to see what I am about to do with you."

Faenir dove into my neck, spreading his tongue and lips across it. I ran my hands through his length of raven hair and held tight. It was easy to forget the world and its worries when pressed to Faenir in the shadows.

"No more talking..." I said, wishing to give in completely to his touch.

"Mhhmm," Faenir replied, his deep voice vibrating against my skin.

I closed my eyes and was greeted with nothing but desire. No death. No thoughts.

Only him.

Me.

Us.

Opening my eyes and slowly adjusting to the dark, I watched Faenir take the golden cord and tie it blindly until my wrists were bound at my back. He gently forced me with a hand until I was on my knees in the carriage's footwell. His bright eyes sliced through the darkness, glowing proudly once again; it thrilled me to see.

"Suck my cock, Arlo."

There was a click of a belt unbuttoning. The brush of material over skin as Faenir pulled down his slacks.

"Of course, Your Majesty."

Faenir groaned, reaching forward and gripping my chin. His large fingers groped around my skin and pulled me towards his exposed crotch. I giggled in the darkness, silenced by the warm, curved flesh pressed to my lips. My tongue lapped up the pleasant coating of his excitement. Faenir growled, and the shadows danced. All before he could capture a deep breath, I wrapped my mouth around his cock and twisted my tongue in circles across the top.

"Fuck."

With my hands tied behind my back, I could only work my tongue to cause him pleasure. Faenir raised his hands behind his head and leaned back. He enjoyed every long moment. There was no stopping my spit from falling beyond my lips and wetting my cheeks and chin.

My jaw had a dull ache, but that did not hold me back. Guided by the sudden presence of his hand, and my ever-constant enthusiasm, I sucked his hardened cock for an unknown amount of time. At one moment the carriage jolted, moving from the cobbled street to something smoother. Faenir's cock was forced deep into my throat, and I gagged, eyes watering.

He chuckled, pulling my head back to allow me to catch my breath. "You are spectacular, my darling," Faenir whispered, clearing the wet spit from my lips with his thumb.

"Don't," I growled, teeth bared, "stop me again. Understand?"

My heart leapt at my own demand, eased by Faenir's chuckle. "Certainly, my darling. I apologise. I am all yours."

Explosions of sweetness filled my mouth as I worked vigorously at Faenir's cock. I knew Faenir was going climax before he likely knew. I tasted it. A warning. I allowed his sweet juices to fill my cheeks and clog my throat. Powerful, that was how I felt. Even with my hands bound and my head held down by Faenir's hand, I was the most powerful creature in the world.

Faenir finished in a string of explosive groans. The hardening in my own trousers throbbed, spreading a damp patch within as I shared the same climax all without the need to touch myself. It was magic. That was what this was. And, even exhausted, all I could think about was doing it again.

Forever.

At least for the rest of my forever, however short that time may be.

32

THE FERRYMAN'S boat rocked viciously as he moored it across the disturbed surface of the Styx. The weather had noticeably changed in the days since our arrival back at Haxton Manor. Perhaps it echoed the storm that brewed with me? Impenetrable clouds did well to block out the sun. The days were overcast, the nights darker, which made everything seem more sinister.

It was not the best of days to stand outside on the stone balcony connected to my chamber. However, it had become part of my daily routine, watching the ferry of new people to help fill the manor and make it feel... alive. A shiver passed unwantedly across my arms. I tugged the rough blanket tighter around me as I watched the visitors within Charon's boat grip the edges as they traversed the dark blue water towards the manor.

Haxton had quickly filled with serving staff that Myrinn had continued sending. I supposed it was her way of apologising for what had happened in Neveserin, not that I believed she needed to.

Other members of Haxton's staff waited upon the shore for the new arrivals, winds battered them from all angles. Children ran in between their parents' legs, sometimes braving the Styx by sneaking up on it, but never did they get too close. Even those in the boat that moved closer with each moment peered over the edge of the wooden vessel in fear. They must have known what lurked and waited beneath the waters. I gathered the shades waited longingly for someone, one poor soul, to fall overboard.

This visit was the second boat today that had arrived. Still, it surprised me when I saw Charon carting the living across to Faenir's home. The prince had done little to refuse the serving staff, but, from his disappearances when new ones arrived, I only imagined what warnings he gave them. He viewed each and every one as his enemy, a threat. I only hoped he would soften in time.

As of yet, Faenir had not permitted me to visit them alone. I understood why but could not ignore my frustration at being kept in a cage like a bird with broken wings.

A door opened and closed in the chamber room behind me. I heard the familiar gait across the marble floor. It was silly perhaps, but I held my breath in anticipation of Faenir and his touch, which always followed. I longed for it more, which only intensified my anxiety, my guilt for the secret I harboured selfishly.

"You will catch your death standing out in the cold," Faenir said.

How wrong he was.

"I enjoy watching them arrive. It gives me something to do with my mind instead of staring at the same four walls."

Faenir did not miss the lacing of annoyance hidden beneath my tone. "If you wish to go for a walk, simply ask. This is your home for the time being, not your prison," he said.

Finally, I turned to look at him. Faenir carried a silver platter that took both hands to hold up. Piled upon it in a pyramid of scarlet orbs were what I thought to be apples at first. How wrong I was. Pomegranates glistened like fat jewels upon the platter, each one coated with a sheen of mist. My mouth watered in anticipation for the tarty and sweet flavour that waited within the hard, red shell of their outer layer.

"How did you get these?" I asked, rushing to his side.

I had never seen the fruit in person before but had heard of them. Long before the vampire's curse spread across Darkmourn, pomegranates and other unusual fruits came over from far-off lands where the climate was far different to ours.

"Gildir sends his apologies for what occurred in Neveserin. I can assure you; I am equally surprised."

"They," I pointed to the platter, "are from him?"

"Indeed. The first arrivals to Haxton this morning brought the gift with them. If you would prefer I had them disposed of, I would happily do this for you."

"There will be no need," I said, my mouth salivating. "However, I can't stop trying to imagine what exactly he feels the need to apologise for."

Faenir's brow furrowed. "Darling, I believe the saying suggests that great minds think alike."

He placed the platter on the bedside cabinet. As he did so, the pomegranate that balanced precariously upon the top of the pile rolled from its perch and fell. He caught it swiftly, snatching the fruit in one hand before it hit the ground, which likely would have been better for the fruit because the moment it met Faenir's touch, the pomegranate rotted; it decayed with haste, colour draining from its shell, leaking inky-black liquid between his fingers.

"Such a waste," he said, letting go of the rotten fruit which became ash beneath his touch and floated to the ground. "Gildir would see that as a sign of great disrespect, I am sure."

"I am surprised you have even let me receive the gift, considering how much of a threat you have treated every person who has been sent here. You would trust your cousin is not out to poison me with his gift?"

"They are not poisoned," Faenir said matter-of-factly.

My brow peaked as another shiver passed across my skin. "What have you done?"

"I ate one. Poison would not kill me, but I certainly would sense the effects."

I could not explain why his action had angered me, but it did. "You shouldn't have done that. I do not require you to be my taster... when are you going to realise that not everyone is out to kill me?"

"Would this be the wrong moment to admit that I have been tasting every morsel of food prepared since we came back home?"

I forced out a sigh. Mother had always taught me to pick my battles, and this was not one I had the energy for. Despite my want to fall into his arms and let his touch lighten the storm in my mind, I turned my back on him. I moved back towards the balcony, leaving the disagreement behind me.

The winds had grown stronger in the moments I had been inside. It whipped at my hair, tugging at the blanket across my shoulders until it forced me to hold on tighter.

Charon had now reached shore. The four elves practically threw themselves from the vessel in fear, or relief, I was unsure.

Faenir stepped in behind me and I immediately relaxed into his warmth. I did not protest for space, because that was not what I longed for. His arms came around me, each hand gripping the smooth-stone wall of the balcony as we both watched the swell of the crowds below.

"I cannot express my discomfort at knowing they all dwell in my home."

"Because you long for your own space, or because you are frightened of what might happen?" I asked.

"All my life I have kept a distance from the living. Each one of them burn with the glow of life and sometimes it makes looking upon them hard. Uncomfortable. I imagine it is what it would feel like to stare at the sun for a time."

It made sense. When I had seen Faenir pass the huddles of serving staff dusting long-forgotten frames and sideboards, he always kept his gaze on the floor.

"Give it time. It will become easier."

Faenir's arms closed in on me. His breath joined the winds and played with the hair across my ear. "I hope it does. However, time will not stop my touch with doing the very same as it had with that pomegranate. What is to say I touch one servant by mistake? All it would take is a glance of a hand, a brush of skin, and I would kill them without that ever being my intention."

I took that moment to reach a hand and place it upon his. Mine was deathly cold in comparison. "Faenir, you are far too conscious to act in such a way. Do you see them running from you? Hiding when you pass? I may not be able to speak on behalf of them all, but I am confident they are not scared of you. Take that as you will. Find comfort in knowing that the elves you have allowed into your home understand the risk and still continue as though it is normal because it is. It is your normal and there is nothing wrong with that."

Faenir rested his chin on the top of my head. I could hear his smile as he expelled a laboured breath. "There is power in the way you speak. I am grateful for it."

For it. I longed for him to repeat himself and change his last word to *you.*

The light burst of laughter reached us from the grounds that stretched out beneath us. Three children ran and danced, playing games with one another without a single care in the world. Faenir grunted at their presence but held back any comments.

"Those children," I said, choosing my words carefully, "Are they the halflings you told me about?"

"No," he said. "Not in the sense you are thinking."

"What do you mean?"

"Look closer at them. Tell me what you see."

As I narrowed my gaze on their heads, I thought it was a trick question. I did not know what, in fact, I searched for. "If you wish to provide a clue, I would be ever so grateful, Your Highness."

Faenir lowered his mouth to my ear and placed a kiss upon it, soft lips brushing the rounded tip and pulling away as he whispered, "Look again."

It took a moment to distract myself from his kiss to truly understand the hint he had provided. Then I saw it. The children, hidden beneath hair that bounced as they ran from one another, were ears—as there should have been, of course—but they weren't elongated and pointed like Faenir's. No. They were rounded and... mundane, like mine.

"They are humans..." I muttered.

"It is common for the less noble members of Evelina's community to be burdened with the human babies that are swapped out when a halfling is taken and left in your realm. Although the halflings look human, their blood is far from it; that is the only noticeable difference —so slight, in fact, that the humans would never notice when their blood child was swapped out."

"That," I said, looking at the children in a new light, "is cruel."

"I agree," Faenir replied. "My ancestors had abolished the practice for thousands of years, all until the vampire spread his curse across the world. My grandmother plans to aid the humans' survival by reinstating magic in your realm. Doing so would take years… but it was an investment she was willing to make."

"At the cost of families who bring up children that do not belong to them?"

Faenir stiffened, his stomach hardened like a wall behind me. "Only time will determine if that sacrifice will become beneficial."

"Would you have sanctioned such a thing if you were King?" I asked.

Faenir took a moment to ponder my question. "Claria wants an army to defeat the vampires with the very same being that created the first. Although I understand her efforts, mine would have been different, not that it matters."

I wanted to tell him it did, in fact, matter. All of it did. "I am still trying to wrap my head around all this. Is it possible that I have come across a halfling? If Claria has been swapping children out for years, then surely there is enough of them in Darkmourn to fight back?"

"Not every halfling can become what you know to be a witch. It is magic that lays dormant within them all, but it takes something great and unknown to make it bloom into pure power. The witches that caused the damage to your realm are products of hundreds and hundreds of years' worth of practice, religion and focus. Intervention from our kind helped them along. The halflings in Darkmourn are still young, an army who are yet to understand what they are required for, but an army nonetheless."

Queen Claria had focused her energy on creating an army, years wasted allowing the vampires to devour our kind and keeping us in pens, just for the potential of restoring balance. She played the long game. Not the right game.

My head throbbed at the knowledge Faenir had bestowed upon me. I began racing through my mind, picking out names of people I had known and trying to remember anything that might've suggested that they may have been halflings themselves.

I second-guessed my heritage. The jarring thought was short-lived as I reminded myself of the mismatched eyes Auriol and I got from our mother. And, more horrifically, the sickness I had been unluckily graced with.

"You are quiet," Faenir said.

"My mind isn't," I replied.

Faenir turned me to face him, and I didn't put up any resistance. "Would you like me to fill your mind with other matters?"

His lips curved upward, and I could not help but smile back. Something about Faenir was so entirely consuming. And he was right. It was early afternoon and already I would have preferred to climb into bed and hide away from the world.

"What is it you have in mind?"

Faenir's fingers laced through mine, and he began stepping backwards. He guided me back into the chamber, which was just as cold inside as it was out. "I may not be able to touch Gildir's kind offering of apology, but you can."

"I sense you are missing some elaboration as to what you mean exactly."

There was a glow of mischief behind his gaze. "Follow my commands, darling, and you will find out just what I am thinking."

33
FAENIR

"There is something I would like to ask you, but if you wish to refuse me an answer, I will understand."

I knew a question was coming, for Arlo's fingers suddenly stopped tracing circles across my skin. He spoke not a moment after placing his entire palm upon my chest.

"I have nothing to hide from you, Arlo. For you, I am a book to open and rifle through the pages at your leisure," I replied.

My heart leapt as Arlo raised his head from its place upon me and looked up at me. His wide eyes glistened. If he blinked, I was certain he would have cried. I longed to know what thoughts had troubled him, so I added pressure onto his back and pulled him close. "Talk to me, darling. What is it that concerns you?"

He looked away, not quick enough for me to see the single tear betray him as it rolled freely down the peak of his cheekbone.

"Seeing the children running through your grounds cannot help but make me grieve a childhood you never had. It is not fair what they have done to you. There is a part of me who is trying to make sense as to why Claria gave the orders to…" Arlo swallowed his words. They stopped so abruptly it conjured a shiver to race across my skin.

"You can say it. The memory is harsh, but I do not give it power to hurt me."

He looked back up at me at that moment. He pushed himself completely from my chest and shifted his weight on the bed until he was sitting cross-legged, facing me. The dull light of early evening danced across his skin. It revealed every mark, every freckle, which I longed to memorise. To touch. As I did every time I looked at Arlo, I gave into the wonder that sang to me. How my shadows and his life light swirled as one. My shadows never took from him. His light was quiet, not demanding as others were around me. Theirs would sing for me to steal it, whereas Arlo's life light simply existed without a melody.

"How did you survive what she did to you?" he asked.

Without thought, my gaze shifted from Arlo towards the cloud-peppered sky beyond the balcony. A storm brewed as it had for days, growing braver with whistling winds and downpours of rain that lasted hours. It was not the weather my mind drifted to, but the sole figure that I felt, even from a distance: Charon.

"Perhaps your answer will be better suited for another, for the mind of a baby cannot remember the details of such an event... even if the trauma left deep scars. It was Charon who found me."

"But he is..." I watched Arlo silently contemplate what he was to say. "Dead, is he not?"

"Charon was once a man who lived and breathed as we do. During a time when he was not the ghoul that dwells upon the waters of the Styx, he was a man, a member of my family's court. He worked in the gardens and heard me wailing upon the shores. Luckily, he had picked me up with gloved hands. His wife, however, was not so lucky. Nor was my family's head healer. It took three bodies to pile up for Charon to know that he only survived because of the cover he wore on his hands."

It was easy spilling my story to Arlo. The words fell out of me naturally and Arlo listened without interrupting.

"All this time I imagined you had been alone..."

I cringed at the sadness in Arlo's voice, how it passed like a storm cloud behind his eyes. "Do not be sad for me, enough of such emotion has been spent throughout my life. I was not always alone, and with you here, I won't be again."

Hurt pinched Arlo's face. It lasted only a moment as I witnessed him steel his expression. I was certain he bit down on the insides of his cheeks to stop himself from reacting again.

"Charon must have loved you, to look after you even after the unfortunate end his wife met."

Allowing myself only a moment to the dark, I closed my eyes and reached out my shadows to Charon. He, unlike the other shades within the Styx, had been crafted of physical darkness as my grief as a child broke open when he died of natural causes. I could not explain with words as to what I had done to provide Charon such a form when the other souls I stole lingered within the dark waters. Could I release them too? Free them from the eternal prison my presence had locked them within?

"He loved me, I do not doubt that." I said. "When Charon passed, I had not even reached a decade of age. All the other members of my family's household had fled. They did not desire to be near an omen of such peril, they left only Charon and me. He did his best, with what was provided. I owe that man a debt that I fear I will never be able to repay."

When I opened my eyes again, I could see the thoughts churning within Arlo's mind, hows and whys dancing among each other, deciding which was more pressing to ask first.

"My heart hurts at the thought of you being alone, but I am thankful that Charon gave you his time and love. Knowing you have experienced such simple honours of life makes me happy."

He did not look happy. Far from it, in fact.

I swallowed the lump that had invaded my throat. There was a swelling in my chest that grew the more I looked at Arlo. From his determined stare to the way his spine curved as he leaned forward over his now crossed legs. Everything about him made me react physically.

"Charon has not been the only one to show me such things." I leaned up on my elbows, stomach flexing, and reached a hand for Arlo's knee. I gripped it as though winds threatened to blow me away from him. "You, Arlo, have given me so much more in such a short time."

With bated breath, I waited for Arlo to say something. Anything. I could see he longed to from the subtle opening of his mouth. Silence crept between us, pulling taut, like a cord with knots that wished nothing more than to unwind.

Instead, it snapped completely when Arlo finally broke the silence. "Are you hungry?"

The insides of my cheeks pricked as Arlo reached across my body, his chest brushing precariously over the hardening length, as he snatched a pomegranate from the platter alongside the ivory-bone handle knife. He held it before me, in offering with a grin lifting the corners of his lips.

"Dare I ask what you are going to do with that?"

Arlo exhaled, "Feed you."

I forced my brows to furrow. Arlo lifted the hard, crimson shell to his lips and pressed it there. It took tremendous effort not to take myself into my hand.

"What of the sheets? Careful, or they will become sticky and then where will we sleep?"

He shrugged, pink tongue escaping the confines of his glistening lips as it traced circles across the fruit. He knew what he was doing, the glint of allure in his mismatched eyes revealed as much.

Without saying a word more, Arlo clambered upon my lap, each leg resting on either side of my hips. It did not look as though he moved, but I felt him rock on my cock, encouraging it to throb against his bare skin with equal excitement. He leaned over me, lifted the silver knife and traced it across the mounds of my chest. A shock of cold metal had me gasping, as did the feeling of the sharp edge scratching across the coarse, curled hairs while Arlo ran it across me.

"I am beginning to believe you have an interest in sharp, culinary utensils," I said, eyes flicking between Arlo's smirk and the knife he drew across me.

"You trust me, don't you?"

Nodding, I lifted my arm from the bed to reach for his face. Lightning fast, Arlo jabbed the tip of the knife at my throat. "Ah, ah, ah. Keep your hands to yourself. Let me please His Majesty and show him exactly how he should be treated."

"There is danger in your eyes, my darling," I purred. "Trust, yes. Thrill, even more so."

"Good." Arlo sat back up, withdrew the blade from my skin and brought it to the pomegranate that had, until now, become more of an afterthought during the past moments. "Open your mouth."

A warmth spread across my stomach, hardening the muscles upon it. Shivering anticipation made my hands twitch; to still them I brought them up behind my head to ensure I followed Arlo's command. Between the mischievous glow behind his gaze, and the fluid flashing of the knife, I did not want to disappoint.

Arlo was not as gentle with the knife as he drew it across the pomegranate's casing. It split, and juices dripped in streams down his hand, his wrist, where it splattered across my torso.

"Oh dear," Arlo cooed, not stopping until the fruit was cut into pieces. "It would seem I've made a terrible mess."

"Indeed." It was the only word I could muster strength to form aloud. Every other possibility I wished to share involved much darker thoughts. Things I wished to do to Arlo. Many, countless ideas I longed to see come to light.

Like a cat bowing over a bowl of cream, Arlo lowered himself to my chest. His tongue slithered free, teeth flashing.

My hands gripped the back of my head. The feeling of his tongue lapping the sticky residue of the fruit from my skin made me groan. I pinched my eyes closed but still recognised the throbbing of my cock and shadows which seemed to beat in tune with my heart.

He did not stop. Somewhere the knife and the pomegranate had been discarded for both his hands were on me. My greedy fingers reached behind his ass as he gripped my length and stroked it. His other hand scratched across stomach as though he longed to memorise each dip and peak with his touch. Seeds and spit shone across my stomach. Arlo marvelled at his feast, lips stained red and swollen.

There was something feral about his stare, as though he was lost in thought for a moment.

"Have you had enough?" I asked.

Arlo snapped out of his mind, his smile bright, and replied, "Far from it."

I sighed heavily, shivering, as Arlo dipped back down upon me and continued his meal. With Arlo, there was not much room to think of anything but him and the now. Humans should be powerless, but this one defied such concepts.

There was a small concern, eating away at the back of my mind, that attempted to convince me that Arlo filled his mouth with my skin because he did not wish to speak. The conversation had ended abruptly. If I had not been distracted by the kitchen knife and the juices that dried upon my body, perhaps I would have asked what had caused the sudden end.

Such thoughts were impossible.

I closed my eyes as the dripping of fresh juice spilt upon my length. Arlo had slithered downward in the bed, gripping onto the base of my cock to steady himself as he squeezed the fruit in his other fist.

If I watched him, I feared I would race towards the end before I could stop myself, for I felt the urgency building in the pit of my stomach as though a flock of birds prepared to take flight.

Arlo wrapped his warmth around the tip he held carefully in his grasp. I could not comprehend the sound that burst from my very soul as he twisted his tongue in soft, yet frantic circles. His hand moved in tandem. He sucked the juices from my flesh with burning desire.

It became impossible to control myself. I raised my hips, forcing myself deeper into Arlo's throat. He pushed me back down. The sound he made as he struggled on my length had my blood burning me from the inside out.

As much as I desired to give into his pleasure and relieve myself, I would not. This was not like the carriage ride where he had taken me into his mouth and swallowed everything I gave him. This would be longer. More controlled. Arlo had ways of seeing me pleased, but I wanted nothing more than to tear him from me, twist him upon the bed, and bury myself in him until my hips slapped against his ass.

I could not wait another moment.

Gripping Arlo's head by his hair, I pulled him from my cock. His wet mouth made a popping sound as it came free. The look of surprise and thrill painted across his face was an image I never wished to forget.

My mouth crashed into his. Sweetness burst across my tongue. My fingers wove deeper into his hair until they brushed across his scalp with urgency.

"I am going to take you," I growled into his lips, coming away for breath. "Completely."

My shadows did not need to gather to hide us from sight this time. There were no crowds to watch or Joining ceremonies to defile. I left the shadows alone, allowing our moans to join the thundering rumble of a storm that sang within the darkening skies beyond the room. It was Arlo and me. We were all that mattered in my mind. Not the crown. Not Claria or my family.

"Faenir." Arlo spoke my name as though it was the most beautiful thing in the world. "I was wondering how long I could make you last before you would have me bent over so you could ruin me."

"Ruin you?" I chuckled. Arlo shivered. My cock throbbed. "When I am finished, you will feel remade. Unless you wish for me to destroy you instead?"

"Make me, destroy me. Whatever you decide, do it now."

Arlo turned himself around, lowered his belly down on the bed and kept his knees raised until all I could see was his ass. He presented himself to me, smooth curves of flesh gave way to the light pink star of his centre.

My fingers lifted to my lips. I spat. Once. Twice. Arlo peered over his shoulder, stare narrowed with taunting lust, as he watched me lower my hand to his centre. Arlo's eyes rolled back into his head as I slowly entered my finger into him. His groan was my guide, telling me if it was hurting or not. From the way he bit down on his lip and the way his hands pulled the sheets into fists, he enjoyed it. I did not stop until it was completely inside.

"More," he begged, voice muffled by the sheets. "Give me all of you."

"Soon." The sharpness of my tone surprised me. I wanted this to last. For hours, days or more.

My arms ached, but that did not deter the way I slipped my finger in and out. Arlo loved it. His moans revealed as much. I was able to include another finger which I spat down upon for more ease.

It did not take long for the desire to replace my finger with my cock to overwhelm me. Arlo called out with glee as I pressed the head of my cock to his centre and forced it within. Arlo threw himself back onto my length with a need for pleasure. I gripped his thighs to keep myself upright as I was lost in the tight embrace of his ass. When he grew tired, I began thrusting, pulling out almost completely before thrusting myself back into him.

If I finally gave into death that I had staved off, I would have done so happily. This feeling was divinity. Complete, intoxicating lust that fuelled me with more energy than I could have deemed possible.

I leaned over Arlo for support, still pounding into him although my body was tired and my hair damp with sweat. I spared a hand for him, reaching beneath his hips and gripping his own length. It was selfish for me not to. For a moment I could not find the rhythm of my fucking and my wrist, but as soon as I did our breathing entwined and we raced towards the cliff's edge of pleasure.

There was no understanding of how long we did this for. In another time I would have wished to pick him up and explore other positions but sensing his building pleasure in tandem with my own, I knew we would not last.

Pleasure should be enjoyed, not prolonged. It was for the here and now.

"Faenir, keep doing it."

A growl erupted from me. "Are you close?"

"Yes," Arlo spluttered through harsh, heavy breaths, "Yes."

I could not answer that I too was almost at the end.

My pace intensified, both my wrist and my hips worked faster. Light flashed through my mind, fire boiled in my chest, and the entire world cracked open at the moment we both broke through the sex as one combined soul.

There was nothing to spoil the moment of peace that followed, not as Arlo fell onto his side, drawing me down onto the bed with him. I curled my damp limbs around his body. Arlo panted in my embrace, trembling hands holding onto mine as I wrapped them around his chest.

"Would you forgive me if I wished to be bedbound for the entirety of tomorrow?" I admitted, stifling a yawn. A deep, unsettling tiredness had overcome me. It made my bones feel as though they were made from iron, my blood from hardened silver. "I don't imagine my knees will work for a long while."

"Sleep," Arlo replied, voice as meek as my own. We had driven each other to the edge of exhaustion; it was near impossible to keep my eyes open as I nuzzled into his shoulder. "You have earned the rest."

I wished to say more, do more, but I gave into the wave of peace and closed my eyes. "Good night then, darling."

Arlo inhaled deeply, worming his way back into me until we were completely connected. "Night, Your Majesty."

34

I HAD LOST count of the days which passed both painfully quick and torturously slow. Hidden beneath the bed I was splayed across, etched upon the slabbed flooring, were the marks I had made, my countdown which I no longer had a need for.

Death crept up on me, a silent assassin waiting in the shadows of time to strike. To take me. And I waited for it. My fists clenched and jaw gritted, preparing myself for a fight. I would not be taken without one.

Every day since we had returned from Neveserin had been the same. I woke hours before Faenir, as though freezing waters had been dumped upon me. Each time I took my first breath, I expected to feel pain in my lungs. Every time I coughed; I would pull my hand back as though preparing myself to see the splattering of blood upon it.

If the sickness did not come to claim me soon as it had my parents, the sense of impending doom would likely take me first. Or I would be murdered instead. The person behind the attacks had still not been found, nor did it seem that Claria cared to locate them. How hard was it to locate the killer when all she had to do was look in the mirror to see them? Faenir believed it too, which was why he refused for me to leave Haxton's boundaries again. Faenir trusted Claria would never come to Haxton, whereas I didn't count on that.

I dared move from my position, head resting upon Faenir's chest, feeling the rise and fall and every strong beat of his heart. Unlike most days, when I would come to realise that I was alive and the sickness kept at bay, I happily laid upon him, waiting for him to wake. This evening was different. Today I needed to move, to do something that would distract my mind.

"You have a habit of sneaking out of bed," Faenir groaned, tugged unwontedly from sleep as I slipped from his chest. I winced, face crumpled, as I woke him. Sitting myself upon the edge of his bed, I buried my face in my hands. The bed creaked as Faenir reached over and placed a hand on my shoulder, urging me to lie back down.

I shrugged him off. "I thought it would be a gracious gesture if I offered to help Ana in the kitchens this evening."

Ana was one of the many serving staff that Myrinn had sent to Haxton when we had left. Faenir couldn't refuse them entry even if he wished to. Aided by my demand, he allowed them to come.

During the short time in Myrinn's home, I had grown used to the subtle noise of life. Haxton was desperate for such a thing. Witnessing people as they floated up and down hallways, their chatter echoed throughout the many rooms, had made this place more... tolerable. But my thanks for their presence went far beyond what they did to Faenir's home. It was what they would do for him in time. Faenir would never be alone again and if that was the mark I left upon his life, then it would be a scar worthy of pride.

"Not that I care to speak on her behalf, but she has already got the help. Come back to bed. I can give you something to assist with if you so need the distraction," Faenir replied. "And if I told you I enjoyed helping? It makes me feel less... useless."

Faenir chuckled deeply at that. The muscles across his stomach rippled mesmerisingly. For a moment, I almost forgot what my mind had been set on.

"I am beginning to believe you and Ana are having a flippant love affair with your disappearances," Faenir said, grinning wildly. "Is there something you wish to share with me?"

In all honesty, having company besides Faenir was refreshing. Cleaning pots or helping prepare food worked wonders at taking my mind off my looming death. It was another tactic of distraction that didn't end with having my clothes torn from my body, not that I minded the latter.

"Far too old for me," I said.

Faenir did not miss my wink; he flashed teeth. "What a relief. Now, stop teasing me and get back under the sheets. I am growing ever so cold without you. We have an entire platter of pomegranates that should not go to waste. Just imagine how offended Gildir would be if he knew they were left to rot."

"I'm going. There is nothing you can say or suggest that will make me stay," I said shortly. Images of the night prior were still vivid in my head. Even now, hours later, and the taste of the fruit's juices made my teeth sticky. "May I be the one to remind you I couldn't care for Gildir's gift, or feelings. Let them rot and send them back to him with a ribbon, if you so desire."

"Oh, that would truly be a waste when you seemed to thoroughly enjoy his... apology last night."

"And what about you?" I asked, cheeks prickling from my smile. "Did you enjoy yourself?"

"Enough to not allow you to leave my side!" Faenir said in jest. Except he was not entirely joking. I could see in the concern that darkened his eyes that he did not trust me in anyone else's care.

I stood from the bed, keeping my back to him. "Believe it or not, not everyone is out to kill me. If Ana wished to see me harmed, she could have spoiled many meals and finished the job long before this very moment."

He had undoubtedly struggled with the change in Haxton's climate and the proximity of others in his home. Although he moved out of the way of anyone he crossed, ensuring he was far enough not to cause them pain, he also spent most of his time hiding within this very room. Here, with me, limbs entangled or not, Faenir did well at becoming a ghost in his own domain.

"If you will not be cautious about your own life, then I must."

I could have told him he was wasting his time, snapped and shouted at him for thinking in such a way. But I gathered myself as I had the hundreds of other times. My anger was not a result of what Faenir said, but the truth I kept from him.

My lies were poison, eating me away from the inside.

There had been so many times I had wished to tell him, but every time the words nearly left my mouth, I would see a vision of him, the contorting of his beautiful face into the very expression I had made when my parents died. I was resilient, but not strong enough for that.

"Well, I am going." I forced a smile over my shoulder. I could only bear to look at him for a moment before my knees felt weak. His long, naked body was outstretched across the crumpled sheets, only his modesty was covered by a pathetic slip of material that one gust of wind could move. Locks of obsidian hair splayed out across the pillow in a halo. His tired, rich eyes narrowed upon me with hungry intention.

Surely, he was satisfied. It had been hours since I had last sat upon him as though I was a King, and he was my throne. My chest warmed as my eyes flicked over the knife that lay forgotten on the bedside cabinet. I had to fight the urge to climb back into his arms and distract myself with his company instead of breakfast.

"Then we will both assist Ana if you are so adamant," Faenir said, kicking his legs over the bed to stand. As he did so, the little covering of the sheets fell away from his cock as though reminding me what I was missing out on.

"Myrinn will be pleased to hear that Faenir laboured in his kitchens. What would she say, knowing you are finally *mingling* with the people?"

I threw on a newly made black tunic and matching leather trousers which Haxton's seamstress had made for me. Faenir changed also, his outfit overwhelming with grandeur, from his billowing ivory cloak to the formfitting shirt and trousers beneath. All the while, he did not stop looking at me.

Faenir always watched me as though he were searching for something. It was one of many quirks that thrilled me about him.

Once changed into something more suitable for being seen, we moved through the bustling manor hand in hand. Faenir grew quiet as we passed the many serving staff, who each bowed at him. He kept his gait proud and chin raised, as if he did not see anyone at all. I imagined he expected fear from the people, but the way they looked upon Faenir was with nothing of the sort. Admiration. Excitement. He did not seem to notice it.

In time, he would. At least I hoped.

I realised something was amiss before we reached the kitchens located in the lower levels of the manor. Usually, as we reached the main atrium in Haxton, the air would sing with the smells of freshly cooked foods, cured meats, fried potatoes and an array of delicious wonders that Ana prepared daily.

Today the air was empty. My stomach grumbled in response to the lack of scents. Ana had not yet missed a meal, and she prepared many.

By the time we navigated through the dining room, down the curved steps and into the kitchen, we came to find it void of the songs of cooking and warmth. Ana was nowhere to be seen.

Her maid danced around the cold stone room until he saw Faenir and I. He gasped. The pots he carried clattered to the floor, then the spewing of his apologies burst out as he bowed deeply to hide the scarlet staining his youthful cheeks.

"Your Highness, I am sorry for the delay. Terrible! I feel truly embarrassed that you have had to come looking for food. I have failed you. Please, do not trouble yourself down here. If you would..." He hardly stopped for breath.

"We did not intend to surprise you." Faenir stopped him from vomiting any more excuses; his voice was crisp yet edged with honest concern.

"We came to offer to help," I said, eyes scanning the room for Ana as though she would burst beyond the pantry with arms full of dried goods.

"No help required," he spluttered, then stumbled over his words quickly, "But I don't wish to tell you what to do, Your Highness. If you want to help, then you are welcome. I mean, this is your home, you can do what you like—"

"What," Faenir said, interrupting the panicked boy, "is your name?"

He swallowed hard and loud, the lump in his throat bobbing. "Harrison."

"Harrison, where is Ana?" I asked.

The poor boy looked as though he was about to cry. Harrison's lower lip quivered, and his full cheeks flushed a deeper scarlet. It was not from fear that caused such a reaction this time. He exhaled, dropping his raised shoulders and practically folding in on himself.

I looked up to Faenir, who tilted his head inquisitively.

"I am so sorry…"

"You have got nothing to be sorry for, but please answer Arlo's question. About Ana, what has happened?"

"It is her little girl," Harrison finally said, fat goblets of tears leaking down the curves of his face. Strands of snot joined, spilling ferociously, before he swept them away with the back of his sleeve.

"Go on," Faenir implored as the boy had to catch his breath. "If something is the matter, then it is important we know so we can help."

I pulled free of Faenir's hand and edged towards the boy. Taking his shaking shoulders into my hands, I encouraged him to calm down. "Do not be scared. Take your time."

Ana was one of a handful of elves who had brought children to Haxton. The manor had housing for serving staff that was kept separate from the main building itself in the northern grounds; I had passed it on my first day. Forgotten from years of disuse, it had been covered with overgrown greenery. I imagined that was where Ana was now.

Harrison took a moment to steady himself. "Ana's little May is sick. She has been for a while. It's why she had to bring her here. Ana had no family to leave her with in the city."

"What is the matter with her?" Faenir asked, visibly tense from what Harrison said.

"She is dying. Ana didn't come to work because she dreads to leave May's side."

The floor could have fallen away from me at that moment as the reality of what Harrison had said fell upon me. "Take us to them," I demanded as the fingers of dread spread a shiver down my spine. "Now."

35
FAENIR

THE CHILD LOOKED HORRIFICALLY SMALL, nestled within the arms of her weeping mother. Her body did not glow with the halo of life. Instead, shadows danced around her skin like vipers longing for blood; beneath was a slither of light that they worked hard to suffocate.

I felt the shadows tugging at me the moment we had entered their room, a cord pulling me with urgency. I wished to greet it as the death demanded, to reach out and claim the shadows for my own. If it was not for Arlo's hand in mine and the way his presence grounded me, there would have been nothing stopping me.

The woman, Ana, hardly looked up from the child as we entered. It was as if she expected our company. She was singing a lullaby, rocking the child back and forth. The haunting sound made me want to flee the room, flee this place entirely. I wanted to demand that she stopped, yet it felt wrong to stop a mother consoling a child. Unjust. Monstrous.

Tears fell upon little May's grey hued skin as Ana finally choked on the lyrics. I believed the little girl was sleeping until two dulled blue eyes creaked open and looked towards where we stood.

Did she sense the pull between us?

"That is the prince, mummy." May's broken voice scratched at my soul like nails across stone.

Ana nodded, swiping her hand over the small forehead of the little girl to gather the damp, red curls that hung around her hollow face. "A special visit for a special girl."

"I want to see him. He is so far away."

Ana looked up and stared directly into my eyes. Without

outstretching a hand for me, she beckoned me towards her. "Your Highness, please... for a moment. Come and meet my princess."

I could not reply, could not move a muscle as that ominous shadow lingered across the little child's skin. The room was silent to everyone else, yet to me... the shadows cried out with wanting.

"Go to her," Arlo whispered, sadness thickening in his throat. His voice tore me out of my thoughts.

"I do not wish to hurt them." My voice did not sound like my own. It was distant and echoed as though I stood at the end of a long, barren corridor and shouted at myself from the other end.

"You may find," Arlo said softly, "that your words may have the opposite effect."

He urged me forward, fingers slipping out of my hand with ease. Without him holding me back, there was nothing stopping me from following that sinister pull.

Ana said something to me, but I could not focus, not as the child watched me with doe-wide eyes. I knelt down at her side, squeezing my hands upon my thighs to keep them from reaching out.

"Hello," she said, her small voice wheezing with great effort.

"Hello," I replied, unsure of what else to say.

"You are not scary." May's small, bloodshot eyes raced across my face. Her attention left featherlight touches, like little fingers tracing across my features to memorise them. "They said you were a monster, but you don't look like one."

"Perhaps you are just braver than the rest of them?"

Ana sobbed, pressing a wet kiss to the child's forehead. "May is the bravest of them all. She has faced far greater pains than many could ever comprehend."

"I do not doubt it," I replied softly.

"Mummy," May gasped, wincing as she tried to sit up, but couldn't. "Don't be sad." The girl, with great effort, lifted her hand to her mother's cheek and held it there, not concerned for the tears that raced over her small fingers.

"My sweet girl, I do not wish for you to be in pain anymore," Ana said.

"I feel it going away now, mummy, like you promised. It is slipping away like the sand through my fingers... do you remember?"

"Nothing could ever make me forget."

"I don't hurt anymore."

Because you are dying.

I felt it. Unlike Ana and Arlo, whose bodies sang with the light of life, May did not. I wondered if Ana knew that the child's time was ending. May seemed to know and took comfort in the fact. Had her suffering been so terrible that death was the better choice for her?

For someone so slight, so fragile, I could not deny her strength. I admired it—admired her.

"Why are you crying, mummy?" May asked.

"Because I am not ready to let you go…"

Somewhere in the shadows behind us, Arlo exhaled a cry, stifled by a hand. I wished to find him and comfort him, but May needed me now.

"Mummy is scared," May said with such clarity, "I am dying, and that makes her sad."

"Are you frightened of what will come to pass?" I asked. Perhaps the question was meant for someone of far greater age. Children were a strange concept to me.

May seemed to understand. She nodded, her hand falling from Ana's face before reaching out towards me. I flinched backwards, not wishing for her time to come to its end so quickly. She noticed, face pinching into a frown. "Are you scared of my death like my mummy, prince?"

I sighed, closing my eyes and blocking out the scene for a moment whilst I gathered my thoughts. "I cannot fear death, nor should you."

May replied meekly, breathing taking up most of her ability to speak, "He is not scary, is he, mummy?"

"No," Ana replied, voice a mess of grief. "He is kind."

"Death is not something to be feared. Death is peace. It is quiet. It is relief. It is more than sadness and pain. Death…" It was my turn to choke on my words. I had to stop and clear my throat before I carried on; something strange pricked in my eyes as I did so, opening them didn't help. "Death can be unfair. It does not follow anyone's rules but its own. Yet, no matter when it comes, it will never let you be alone."

"Is that true?" May blinked, as though fighting sleep. *But it was not sleep that was coming for her.*

"I believe you are required elsewhere more than you are here. Such a brave and strong soul. Destiny has another place in mind for you."

"Ahh…" the small, broken child groaned as her mother covered her with a smothering of kisses. "Will you miss me, mummy?"

"So much that it hurts."

"One day, soon or far, you will see one another again," I said, wishing to provide them comfort.

May fought to keep her eyes open. Ana brought the child to her breast and held her close. May's voice was muffled as she spoke, but her words rang true. "I will see you again, mummy. Just like the prince said."

Ana could not respond through her sobs.

"Farewell brave, little May." I stood, feeling my frozen, hardened heart shatter one piece at a time. "May you find rest without pain and burden."

I turned my back on her. Before I fully tore my gaze from the mother and child, I noticed the faint glow was gone from the little girl's skin. Like a candle blown out, or the stars blinking out of existence, May died in her mother's arms.

The harrowing scream that tore out of Ana shook the very foundations of Haxton Manor. It confirmed what I had thought, the child was gone. I wished to throw myself into Arlo's arms to hide from the grief, but he was not standing in the shadows.

Arlo was nowhere to be seen.

36

Tears blinded my vision as I ran through the gardens of Haxton Manor. Far behind me I could hear the terrorising scream of grief as it crashed into the darkness. The very stars shuddered beneath it, blinking out of existence as though they too could not bear witness to the death of a child.

The frigid air stung at my face. It ripped the tears from my cheeks greedily, yet more spilled. My throat burned with each inhale, my chest aching as though hands gripped and squeezed. And all I could think about was the way Faenir had softened before the child, his calm and guiding voice as he eased her departure with words of comfort.

Death is not something to be feared.

His resounding voice echoed throughout my mind.

Death is peace.

Since my parents had died, I had never truly felt peace. Chaos ruled my life. I lived on the edge of a knife, kept there only by drinking the blood of the undead. Peace was a concept I had not experienced, until Faenir.

It is quiet.

My mind was roaring as it had since that fateful day, filled with the promise I had made to my mother, my father. *Look after Auriol. Do not fail her as we have.* I had failed them all.

It is a relief.

Was it? Was that what waited for me when death finally caught up? In a way, I believed it, longed for it. No more worry. No more pressure. No more promises.

It is more than sadness and pain.

For whom? For the one who died, or the family they left behind? Because I had lived with shards of grief in my chest, edging closer to my heart every day that passed.

I cut through the night until Ana's screams grew quieter, only stopping as water splashed beneath my boots and the ground seemed to swallow me up slowly. The calm waters of the Styx stretched out before me. Dark waves reached my boots as though encouraging me to give in to it.

Far in the distance I saw the bobbing glow of a light. The ferryman brave enough to journey through the waters patrolled the far edges of the lake. Faenir had commanded it of him, ensuring unwanted visitors were kept away.

I blinked away the tears and attempted to catch a deep enough breath to steady the thundering in my chest.

The waters of the Styx seemed to sing to me, questioning with each lap of a wave against the dark sands of the bank.

Why are you here? What do you come searching for?

Perhaps it was the peace Faenir had spoken about. The quiet. I could have thrown myself into the waters and found peace sooner than the sickness returned. Standing before the Styx, I contemplated ending it. The thought was fleeting and fast, but there undoubtedly.

At least death would be on my own terms. If there was peace, then I longed to find it. It was what I deserved.

"Arlo..." Faenir spoke behind me.

I had not sensed his presence, but as I glanced over my shoulder, face slick with sadness, I saw him there. Wind whipped his obsidian hair around his shoulders as his piercing gaze watched me.

"She is gone, isn't she?" I shouted above the wind. I did not need to ask to know the answer, nor did Faenir need to reply, because the sombre expression etched into his handsome face answered for him. "Death is not fair. It is cruel and wrong."

Faenir stepped cautiously towards me. "My darling, you are not wrong. Death is like a coin, two opposing sides and truths depending on which way it lands and to whom still lives long enough to flip it."

I steeled myself as I turned my back on the Styx. "I couldn't stay and watch. Perhaps that makes me a coward... so be it."

Faenir was close now, hands out, reaching for me. Part of me longed to throw myself into his embrace, yet the other part had me rooted to the spot. As I looked upon him, I could only imagine his reaction when I finally was taken from him. Would he scream as Ana had? Fill the night with his grief until the stars burst and the sky shattered?

"Do you wish to speak about them?" His question caught me off guard. He noticed my trepidation and continued. "Myrinn told me about your parents. She explained your urgency to return to Tithe because of the promise you kept for them."

What else had she said?

I prepared myself for him to drag forth the truth about the sickness and how it, too, claimed me. I, like my parents, was the *tithe* paid to death himself.

I could not speak from fear I would expose myself, or the weakness that longed to burst through the cracks across my soul.

"I understand you will leave me, Arlo, and I do not resent you for it. When the door opens up between our realms, you will return to your sister, and I will not stop you. No matter how hard, I will *not* stop you. I want you to know that."

My knees buckled, and I dropped to the ground. I gripped fistfuls of sand, hoping to feel something real.

Faenir was there before me, hands reaching for my downturned face. "Speak to me, darling. Tell me what is wrong."

"What if I can't leave?" I managed, voice breaking with each word.

Faenir misinterpreted me; I did not correct him. "I long for you to stay with me. Selfishly, I desire nothing more, but I love you enough to know that I must let you go home. It is my punishment for stealing you from it, one I must endure."

I looked up; my eyes once again blinded by grief. "Say it again?"

Faenir's cool fingers dropped from my face, and he rocked backwards on his knees. "What?" He had not realised he said it aloud.

"You love me?"

His stare was lost to a spot on the ground between us, dark brows furrowed as he frowned, trying to make sense of his own words. "I am not worthy of such a thing, but I cannot help it."

Something cold and wet kissed upon my skin. I looked up at the dark clouds that swelled over the night sky like a blanket. Droplets of silver rain fell down over us.

"Who told you such a thing?" I asked. It was my turn to reach for Faenir, who gathered me willingly into his arms. "Let me be the one to tell you how wrong you are, Faenir. Are you truly blind not to see how surrounded you are by love? Do you not see it in Myrinn's admiration for you? Have I not proven to you enough how deserving you are of love?"

Faenir cradled my head to his chest, his hands working in calming circles across my wet hair as the rain fell harder and faster upon us. "I took you from your life because of my selfish and desperate need to feel your touch. Every day, I feel nothing but the burden of guilt for my actions. I do not deserve your love, Arlo."

"Stop it, Faenir," I said, rain and tears blending into one. "I love you. Do you hear me? I love you."

"Say it again," Faenir repeated my previous statement beneath the thundering of a brewing storm. Lightning sparked across the sky. A deep rumbling echoed throughout the blanket of clouds as though encouraging the weather to worsen. Still, we did not move from beneath it.

"I love you," I screamed in chorus with the thunder.

Faenir gathered my face in his hands and crashed his lips upon mine. The kiss was deep and urgent. It was a wave of wordless emotion that gathered me up and covered me. I drowned willingly to it.

"I am not deserving of you, Arlo," Faenir said as he pulled back. "I know it is just to let you leave me, but my soul screams for me to beg you to stay. Our time is limited, I recognise that, but I do not wish for you to go without knowing you will always have a place with me. I will carve out an eternity just for you to be with me."

The lie was the easiest for me to tell, because it was not entirely false, but simply lacking the details that I should have provided him. "I will never leave you, Faenir."

His golden eyes widened. I reached for the strands of wet, dark hair that had plastered across his face and moved them so I could see every inch of his expression. The sharp edges of his jaw, the heart-shaped bow atop his lips. All of him.

"I do not understand, Arlo... help me make sense."

I swallowed the sadness in hopes he believed every word I had to say. "Bond with me."

"Do not say such a thing."

I took his wet face in my hands to ensure he could not look away. "Bond with me. Do so and I will stay by your side willingly. Show me you want me and do it."

He blinked away rain that fell before his eyes. "If we do this, then it will not bode well."

"Because it will solidify your right to take the throne and become King? Do it. Take what is rightfully yours, take me and the crown and you can have me forever."

This was the mark I was to leave on the world. If Myrinn was right, Claria was growing weak. Faenir was the only one strong enough to protect Tithe and keep the wall surrounding my home, my Auriol, strong and secure from the evil beyond it.

Faenir deserved his destiny and if I was to die, then it would be knowing I could ensure Auriol's protection. Deep in the shadowed parts of my mind, I recognised it was my way of keeping my parents' promise.

"I would destroy this world if it meant you would stay by my side."

"Faenir." I cleared a droplet from his sharpened cheek. I could not tell if it was rain or a tear that cooled across my thumb and ran down my wrist. "Do this and I will always be with you. Do it for me, but more so... do it for you." Again, I spoke aloud my half lie. I would always be with Faenir, perhaps not physically, but like the spirits that dwelled within the Styx behind us, I would never be far from him.

Faenir pressed his head to mine and closed his eyes in contemplation. I allowed him the silence as the rumbling storm crashed above us, sky flashing with forks of blue-white shards of jagged light. When he opened his eyes again, they were void of sadness but brimming with confidence. "Arlo, it would be my honour to Bond with you."

I smiled into his kiss, gripping the back of his neck and holding him to me. His wet hair tangled in my fingers as we lost ourselves to one another. Time could have stopped completely as I gave into the relief of his agreement to my request.

"What next?" I asked, my chest full of warmth, as though it would burst with relief.

"If we are to Bond, it must be agreed by Claria."

The bubble popped as soon as he spoke. "She will never agree."

"I know," Faenir replied, lips brushing over mine. "There is, dare I admit, another way."

I looked up through clumped, wet lashes at the determination that oozed from Faenir. "How?"

"We take the throne from her. With the support of Myrinn and my family, it will be enough for the right of succession to fall to *us*."

I exhaled deeply, feeling the hammering of my heart shudder within the confines of my chest. "You mean to kill her?"

Faenir nodded, wincing in discomfort at his confirmation. "If she forces my hand, then so be it. I told you, Arlo, if it means keeping you, I will end them all. After all, it was Claria who had me thrown into the Styx hoping to have me killed. I am only repaying the debt... if it comes down to it, I will do so without guilt. That lack of emotion will be one we both share."

37

I WOKE ABRUPTLY, coughing so terribly that my throat burned as though I had swallowed fire. There was nothing else I could focus on but trying to catch my breath. I was panicking, hands clutching at my throat as though it closed in on itself. Each dry inhale was harsh and felt as though daggers pierced my lungs. It took a moment to finally calm myself, forehead damp with sweat and body covered in icy chills—not from the cold, but dread.

I felt the tickling of warmth across my palm and did not need to look to know that blood covered it. There was already the taste of it across my mouth, covering my inner cheeks, the sharp flavour turning my stomach into knots.

I sat there, hands upturned upon my lap, as the blood dribbled between my fingers and stained the white sheets. All I could do was watch it, a physical confirmation of what was to come. An omen.

The sickness rattled around my lungs with each breath. I waited patiently, trying to calm myself, until my breathing cleared and all that was left to prove that what had happened *had* happened was the red across my palms.

There was a storm brewing in the sky beyond Haxton. Each day it was becoming worse, with no sign of it passing; it mirrored that of the one within me.

I was thankful that Faenir was not in bed beside me, lucky in equal measures. He had taken to waking early since May's death to visit Ana; that, and the preparations for our Joining were well under way and consumed most of his time.

With the sun beyond the balcony devoured by the blanket of

ominous clouds, it was hard to know what time of day it was. Usually, he would come bearing a tray of food late morning.

Which could be any moment.

Pushing away the discomfort that lingered in my chest, I threw myself from the bed. Tearing the sheets free, I bundled them into a ball in my hands and ran frantically around the room for a place to hide them.

The serving staff could not see the blood without alerting Faenir. And with my plan so close to fruition, he could not know of it either. *Or what it meant for me.*

I bundled the bloodied sheets beneath the bed. Hiding them in plain sight seemed to be one of my only options. As I clambered onto all fours and thrust the sheets forward, I caught a glance at the carving marks I had left on the stone floor, forgotten and pointless.

How long did I have? Days? When the first spotting of blood showed, I would have been preparing to leave Tithe to secure more of the vampire's blood. I never let it pass long enough to play with the knowledge of how long I had left.

Soon you will find out.

Shut up, I scorned myself, inner voices fighting as one.

I raced towards the basin of water that had been left in the adjoining bathing chamber. The cloudy water that filled the brass tub was tepid. Memories of the night prior passed through my mind; Faenir and I, sitting in the water, our naked bodies in constant contact.

There was no room for fussing as I stripped myself bare and climbed into the tub, wincing as it passed every sensitive inch of my body. Until I was completely submerged, blood melting from my hands in smoke-like ribbons, did I finally relax.

I laid like that for a while. Testing out my lungs, I held my breath and lowered myself until I was fully submerged. The tickling in my chest began before I reached the count of ten. Over and over, I slipped beneath the water and held my breath, hoping that this was all a trick. It was not.

I did not leave the bath when an unfamiliar clipping of feet announced a visitor.

"May I come in?"

My hands moved to clutch my groin as Myrinn's voice echoed throughout the marbled room.

"You came," I spluttered, water splashing beyond the tub and puddling on the floor.

Invitations for our Joining had been sent to all of Faenir's family, strapped to the claws of proud crows. Myrinn, Haldor and Gildir had responded within a day. Frila and Queen Claria had not yet responded as of the night prior.

"How could I not? I only hoped Faenir would have agreed to a Joining with you, Arlo, but what powers do you possess to have swayed his mind so quickly?" Myrinn beamed the most beautiful of smiles. It curved her eyes and painted her rounded cheeks with a pink blush. "The moment the invite arrived, I had practically thrown myself into a... what is the matter?"

I dipped my face lower into the water, annoyed that my expression had given my inner thoughts away.

Myrinn, regardless of my naked state, sauntered over to the tub's side. As though reading my mind, she snatched a softened towel that hung upon a wooden railing and thrust it towards me.

I reached and took it, knowing there was no hiding from the conversation. "It is happening quicker than I thought it would."

Myrinn's eyes glanced behind her as though searching for anyone that might hear. She turned her back on me as I stepped free of the tub. Satisfied we were alone, she replied, "I brought my most trusted healer with me. Arlo, I should have gotten to you sooner, but with how things were left with Faenir, I would have had no passage to Haxton if he did not permit it."

"You can look," I said, gripping onto the towel I had wrapped around my body as I was overcome with chills. When Myrinn turned around the pity in her eyes was too much to bear.

"I will send for her immediately."

"No," I snapped, taking a moment to calm my racing heart. "I need to see Faenir first, before he comes looking for me. Your healer can wait until later... not that their visit will have much effect."

Myrinn's hands were warm compared to my skin. She took me by the shoulders and stared deep into my eyes as though searching for my soul. "Have faith, Arlo, it is not over yet."

"And it will not be over until the Joining is complete." I pulled away from her hands and paced back into the bedroom.

Myrinn's light feet padded after me. "I admire your determination," she replied. "However, I cannot help but feel it is misplaced."

My body vibrated with nervous energy. "Frila, and your grandmother, have they bothered to provide a reply?" I asked, changing the subject somewhat, and pulled free the clothing Myrinn's tailors had recently made for me. These, much like the clothes I had arrived to Evelina in, were simple and durable, leather trousers and a plain, simple tunic with loose brown ties around the neckline.

"I would be lying if I said that Frila took a little more convincing to come than the others. However, I regret to inform you that Queen Claria has not been contactable since the previous Joining, although I am sure you are not surprised to hear this."

I could not say I was shocked at Queen Claria's lack of interest to come to the Joining. In doing so, it would mean she accepted our union, which she'd made clear that she did not.

Faenir's words came to mind. *If it means keeping you, I will kill them all.* The more time went by, the less they bothered me; a fact that should have disturbed me had the opposite effect.

"How did you do it?" Myrinn asked. "Convince him? He was adamant he wanted no part in the crown, yet I cannot help but notice that this sudden Joining was a silent acceptance of his fate."

"Faenir believes I will not leave him to return to Tithe if we go through with the ceremony. I have tricked and deceived him, manipulating Faenir's... love to get what I want."

Myrinn frowned, shaking her head. "Unfortunately, it will take more than those words to convince me you do not want this."

"It does not matter what I want. I will die either way. But I will not give up on my life until I am certain the lives of those *I* care for are secured."

"Auriol is not the only one you care for," Myrinn said quietly. "I see the way you look at Faenir. Even those who now work for Faenir have sent word of your love for one another. I understand you are dealing with turmoil that I, nor anyone else, can relate to... but even I do not need you to tell me you are doing this for any other reason than love for my cousin."

I raised my arms at my sides. "Oh, Myrinn, you caught me. Am I that predictable?" I despised the way I sounded, how angry I felt at the world, but everything that was being said was just another slash to my soul, reminding me I was dying and leaving more than I dreamed of ever having behind.

"Love is as predictable as it is a surprise. A blessing and a curse. It is love because it hurts as much as it heals and I wish it was not so, but it is."

"I am sorry," I said, lowering my stare to the floor. "My head hurts and I am tired. I should not have taken it out on you."

Myrinn stepped towards me and embraced me with open arms. I inhaled her scent, salt of the ocean and the light buds of fresh flowers. If I closed my eyes, I could almost imagine it being Auriol.

Ever since my parents' death, it was rare for me to lose myself completely to grief. Often, I had felt the urge, but never did the tears come so violently, until now. Myrinn held my head and allowed the shoulders of her navy silk gown to soak up the tears that spilled from me.

We did not speak. She simply let me be. It was the grief of my future which clamped down on my chest this time, not the sickness. It made breathing hard. Myrinn's hand rubbed circles into my back which helped somewhat.

I focused on her touch to draw me back out long enough to calm myself down. "When I die…"

"If," Myrinn corrected, tone ablaze with her belief.

"If, or when… please send a message to my sister. I have so much to say to her. So many things to apologise for. I cannot say goodbye on my terms, and I know I have already asked a lot from you…"

"Arlo," she said, breathless. Myrinn placed a finger beneath my chin and raised it until our gazes were levelled. "With your agreement to Bond with Faenir, it will not only save himself, but our world. The least I can do is to ensure your message reaches your sister, so she understands what has happened. I swear to you I will make sure she knows… everything."

"You know, I will miss you too," I blurted.

Myrinn chewed down on her lower lip as her azure eyes glistened, mist passing over them. "Never did I think I would care for a human as I do for you."

"What about your mate?" I asked, clearing my tears with the back of my hand whilst Myrinn dabbed hers away with the edge of a napkin she drew from her chest.

"Faenir was blessed to have… picked." We both grinned nervously at her choice of words, knowing how my being here was far more than being chosen as a Claim. "Chosen someone whom he truly connected with. Perhaps if Gale had not perished so prematurely, I may have come to love him too."

"Still no more news on whom is behind the attempts on my life?" I asked, being reminded of what she said.

"All fingers point towards Claria."

A clap of thunder echoed beyond the balcony. Myrinn jumped, both of us turning towards the noise as patter of rain fell heavily outside.

"If you are right, then she will stop at nothing to make sure the Joining is not seen through," I said finally, a shiver creeping up my arms and leaving them covered in goosebumps.

The feeling of dread had become a constant in my life. It twisted among my bones, squeezed through my veins and took root in my heart. This time it was not dread for me, but for the Queen herself, for what Faenir would do.

She deserved what was coming, but at what cost?

38

THE STORM BROKE above Haxton Manor, bathing the world beyond in darkness. The building trembled beneath the howling winds. A blanket of clouds coated the sky, split only with beams of jagged lightning; they overlapped one another, some coal grey and others midnight black, each as impenetrable as the next.

Throughout my stay in Faenir's home, I had grown used to the windows always being open. No matter if it was day or night, Faenir had an unspoken lust for fresh air. It was a rarity for them to ever be closed. Now they had each been secured, locked as rain battered across the glass with demanding cracks. Scratching of rain and sleet warred against the glass windows. The noise was terrible.

This weather was far more than any storm I had encountered. This one had brewed for days, only seeming to grow more tempered with time; it crackled with magic. The air was thick and charged. I could not ignore the hairs on my arms as they stood on end. There was no keeping away the cold that had seeped into my marrow until my bones ached. I couldn't discern if it was the weather that caused my discomfort or the growing sickness within me.

Warm hands brushed over my bare chest, drawing me out of my thoughts. I gasped, causing the healer to flick me an apologetic glance before continuing to study my skin, and more importantly, what lurked beneath.

"Is there anything that can be done to help?" Myrinn asked, hardly removing her knuckles from between her teeth.

We both waited for the healer to respond as the golden glow of magic emitting from between her fingers dimmed. The light had been conjured from nothingness, as though the woman clasped a strand of sun beneath her palm. It was not cold, nor warm, but pleasant, nonetheless. "No." Concentration deepened the lines of age across the older elf's face, which only added years onto her age. Her reply was finite and sharp, like a blade driven into one's heart without missing its mark.

Myrinn held her posture straight. However, even I could recognise how hard she focused to keep her honest reaction hidden from me. I watched her, unmoving and straight-backed.

For no other reason but to stop my hands from trembling, I began buttoning my shirt back up, focusing on the task at hand; at least it would stop me from torturing myself with the look of defeat in Myrinn's opal gaze.

"Thank you," I said; each word was as forced as the one before. "For trying, at least."

The healer backed off, her distance truly signifying that there was nothing else to be done.

"Try again," Myrinn said.

"Your Highness, I cannot heal decay—"

"Try again!" Myrinn snapped this time, interrupting the healer who cowered from the lashing of fury. "I refuse to hear your excuses. You have barely tried. Get back and try…"

"Enough." My knees shook as I snapped my attention to the scarlet-flushed princess. "Myrinn, please. It is done."

"It cannot be," she replied. "This is… I do not dare believe it."

I turned my gaze to the healer, whose eyes boiled with sympathy. It made me sick, more so than the extinguishing of hope that her confirmation had just caused. "You tried, which was all I could have asked of you."

"Your lungs…" The healer said, hesitantly looking between Myrinn and I. "Never have I felt such a thing before. They fill with blood, and they feel… wrong. Rotting slowly until…"

"Tarha, that is very much enough." I was thankful for Myrinn's interruption. "I trust I do not need to remind you of the importance of keeping this between the three of us. It would be truly awful if something unwanted was said."

Tarha, even in her advanced age compared to the princess, bowed as though Myrinn was the elder. "Threats are not required, Myrinn, not in my line of care. I simply wish to help ease the pain which," she looked back at me, burning holes into my head, "will come soon enough."

Myrinn blinked, keeping her steely expression. "If Arlo requires your help, then I give him authority to call for you."

"There will be no need," I said, still struggling with my buttons. My fingers were numb. I was more focused on swallowing back the urge to cough. It seemed a tickle had embedded into my throat like a thorn, refusing to clear.

Tarha bowed, dismissing herself without the requirement of another word. As she swept from the room, a worn cream habit clutched in her hand, a shadow passed before the door.

"I have been wondering where you have been."

I fumbled with the remaining buttons as Faenir looked between the escaping healer, Myrinn, and me.

"She came to check on the scarring," Myrinn said quickly, yet still Faenir's gaze studied me as though searching for the unsaid truth. "Being human means his skin will blemish no matter the healing or tonics provided. There is no denying a healer from checking upon their patient."

"Darling," Faenir said, completely ignoring his cousin. "Are you well?"

I smiled brightly, trying not to jump as a violent rumble of thunder echoed beyond the chamber door. "Couldn't be better," I lied.

Faenir did not believe me, that much was clear. Myrinn noticed it too, for she began fussing like a bird as she edged towards the door. She said something about supper and how she would see us there, then she was gone.

Leaving Faenir and me alone.

"Stop looking at me like that," I said, sounding like a demanding child.

"How can I not? I feel as though I have been deprived of your company," Faenir replied, kneeling suddenly beside the chair I had sat myself down on. If I had not, I was certain I would have fallen.

Noticing I struggled with the shirt, Faenir gently swept my hands upon my lap. His fingers, fast and assured, began buttoning up my shirt. I groaned as his knuckles grazed my stomach. "I have wanted to come for you hours ago, but the rest of our guests arrived at the most inconvenient of times. There has been much preparation, and I did not want to concern you with it."

"Well," I said, trying to stop myself from demanding that he began undoing his helpful work and rip my clothes from me. "You are here now." I leaned forward and placed a gentle kiss on the end of his nose.

The soft touch conjured a purring groan from Faenir as he finished dressing me. "I missed you. Is that pathetic to admit aloud when you have been mere hallways and rooms away?"

"I…" My chest tickled. Panic surged through my body and mind as I prepared for the fit to come.

Faenir's grin faded once again, and he leaned forward, fingers brushing over my chin. "Something bothers you."

I shook my head, giving myself time to appease my breathing. Part of me believed I would open my mouth to reply, and the coughing would begin. If it did, there would be no hiding the truth when blood spluttered beyond my lips.

"It is the storm," I replied, thankful that my voice was clear and the tickle in my chest subsided. "I've never liked them. When I was younger, I would steal into Auriol's room, take her from the crib, and hide inside the wardrobe. Mother would find us come morning and no matter how many times she did, every storm always ended the same." It was a relief to speak aloud the truth to Faenir, to share a part of my past.

"Your sister has always been important to you."

I nodded, eyes pricking. "Even before my parents died, I had wished to protect her. Perhaps on more occasions than required."

"There is nothing wrong with wishing to protect the ones you love."

"Even if they did not wish to be protected?"

As the sickness grew within me, greedily clawing at my body in desperation, I could not forget how Auriol and I had left off. Just as the blood suffocated me as it filled my lungs, I had done the same to her. It would be a regret I would carry with me to the grave.

"I have no doubt that your sister loves you. How could she not?" Faenir glanced towards the closed balcony doors and narrowed his gaze as they rattled in their frames. "The storm will pass as they always do. However, between me and you, seeing Frila and Gildir nearly thrown from Charon's boat into the Styx has been a moment I will not forget in a hurry."

"I feel cheated for not having seen such a wonder," I replied, recognising the warmth in my chest as hope. Myrinn had arrived at Haxton alongside Haldor. It had only been a matter of time before their siblings arrived. "Only one more to arrive."

Faenir looked downward. His hand dropped from my chin and gripped my thigh. "Claria has declined."

I expected it, but still the news stung. "When did you find out?"

"Gildir informed me upon his arrival. It was the first thing he said as sick still dribbled out the corner of his mouth after he expelled the contents of his stomach upon my shores."

I gritted my teeth, jaw aching with tension as I bit down on my response. "Do I wish to know what this means?"

"Tomorrow I will leave Haxton to speak with her."

"Kill her," I corrected.

Faenir gripped his hand into my thigh and focused in on my eyes as though I were the only thing of importance to him. "She has decided her fate, as I have decided *ours*."

Ours. I blinked and saw the horror in Tahra's face as she discovered the rot of sickness that was unrepairable. There was no knowing how long I could fight it. Even now, I felt weaker than I cared to admit. My neck ached as I held my head up, my arms tired and numb. Our fate raced towards its end, and Faenir did not know it.

"Tonight, we shall feast together," Faenir announced. "With what is coming, I will still need my family's support. I do not wish to go from living with knives at my back to ruling with newly forged swords at our fronts."

"And what if they do not listen?"

"If they turn their back on what I have to say, then they, much like Claria, will seal their own fates." His response was cold and honest, but it did not scare me.

I cared little for Faenir's family and the lack of kindness they had shown me, apart from Myrinn, who had been nothing but supportive; Haldor, Gildir and Frila had shown no loyalty to Faenir. I hoped that changed... for their sakes.

I pressed my forehead to Faenir's, delighting in his proximity. Inhaling, I took him all in, breathing in his scent of sandalwood and feeling the soft brush of his dark hair which tangled in my fingers.

"I can tell something plays on your mind," he said.

"Only that you will be forced to leave me tomorrow."

Faenir's lip brushed closer. "It will not take me long."

"I do not want you to leave me. Ever."

"Oh, darling." Faenir pressed his lips to mine. The touch was so soft, so gentle that if I did not watch him, I would never have known his lips were upon mine. "I will never leave you."

"What if I die?" I asked, not needing to tell him when or how soon it would happen. "You are an elf. Immortal and powerful. I am still a human, and my demise will come far sooner than yours."

A shadow passed beyond his eyes, darkening the gold until they glowed like embers in a hearth. "I command death. It has been my curse. For as long as I control it, I will never let you leave me."

I smiled. "How lucky I am to have found you."

"I hate to correct you, my darling, but it was I who found you. And I vow to never lose you... not in this eternity or the next."

Grief played with me as though it was a hound, and I was its bone. I drowned in the emotions; each wave was both anger and sadness, denial and clarity, not one moment was the same as before.

I closed my mouth upon Faenir's and felt calm. In contrast, the storm outside of Haxton seemed to grow restless. A bolt of lightning flashed throughout the room, highlighting everything so clearly.

Pulling free from him, against my want or better judgement, I spoke, "Not that I wish tonight's supper away, but the sooner it is over, the sooner I can take you away and feast upon you for dessert."

"With promises like that, I would gladly skip the meal entirely."

I smiled into him, and he into me. "It will be worth the wait."

"Darling," Faenir whispered, fingers gripping tighter into my skin. "I have no doubt. Come, let us not keep our revered guests waiting a moment longer."

39

The food laid across the elegantly dressed table was left untouched. Wasted. I felt guilt for ignoring Ana's hard work, but the thought of eating was displeasing. Not a single person reached for a fork or knife. Instead, the six of us clung to the goblets of sweet wine as though our lives depended on it. I could not decide if the lack of feasting from Faenir's cousins was because of an abundance of mistrust or a display of blatant rudeness. I guessed the latter, as they each had no problem with draining their goblets and refilling them without question. If they would have believed the food to be poisoned or tampered with in any way, then they would have left the wine as well.

"It would seem that even the weather is against your union," Gildir said, smiling into the rim of his glass; he revelled in the tension that sparked through the air in the dining hall, toying with it as though it was his to command.

A clap of thunder sounded beyond the walls as though the storm had called out with its agreement. And Frila giggled softly at her brother's comment, giving him a side-eyed look, wolfish grin contorting her face from one of beauty to beastly.

I could not draw my attention away from the red scratch marks that flexed down the side of his face. No one had made a comment about the scratches, but I sensed everyone had seen them. Shifting my focus elsewhere, I studied the rest of his appearance. His moss-toned cloak was draped across his chair. The tunic that he wore had been rolled up over his elbows which rested—without manners—upon the table. He made me feel overdressed in my obsidian jacket with the threading of embroidered silver stars across it.

"I care little what nature has to say," Faenir replied, his deep voice rich in darkness. "It is not her support I require. It is yours."

"Support?" Gildir replied, focusing more on the swirling of red wine that spun in the glass he whirled. "I was wondering why you requested for us to visit. Did you think some old wine and dull company would gain our seal of approval for your union?"

Only minutes into the meal and I already wanted nothing more than to throw the wine at him. I grinned to myself at the thought. Faenir seemed to sense my wishes as his hand laid across mine where it rested upon the table; his touch spoke a thousand words.

"That is not why we are here," Myrinn replied, scowling at her brother. "You understand our laws. Grandmother is the only one who can bless the Joining. Can family not simply be family?"

Gildir glanced towards the empty chair that sat at the head of the table. "Disfunction is the groundwork for any family, Myrinn, you should know that. So, do you wish to get to the point in why you persist with this Joining so we can get on with our lives?"

"Faenir needs our support," Haldor spoke up, offering me a sympathetic look. "It would seem you have made your mind up, Gildir. Which if that is the case, then care to explain why you are here?"

"Why are we all here?" Frila countered, voice light and sweet, but expression pinched in contrast. "Haxton is a miserable place. I wish nothing more than to leave it and never look back."

"Has anyone ever told you how insufferable you are?" I spat, unable to hold my tongue.

Frila pouted, white hair shifting around her shoulders as an unseen breeze filtered through the room. "Do not dare speak to me... *human.*" She spat the word as though it was the greatest of insults.

This was not going well.

"Enough." Myrinn slapped her hand on the table. I felt the wine within my goblet shiver as though listening to her call. "All these years and we still cannot sit together in peace and discuss matters as families should. How do we expect Evelina to survive if we still treat it with such destructive care?"

"Evelina will thrive once Faenir steps down from succession and allows Queen Claria to pass it on to someone deserving." Gildir's knuckles paled as he gripped his goblet, and muscles feathered in his jaw.

"Unfortunately, to your great disappointment, I cannot let that happen," Faenir replied. He was the calmest of us all, back straight as he sat beside me, a rock of clarity, as though unbothered by the growing tension.

"It should first be clarified that I would have happily abdicated the throne. Not once have I ever desired to take it. Of course, all that changed when Claria forced me into Tithe. You see, my choice has never been my own. Just as she has poisoned you to hate me, she wished for the same with the humans. I am certain you do not need me to repeat just how differently that ended."

Faenir squeezed my hand and continued. "Claria's stubborn hate for me will be what kills this world, not I."

Myrinn's glass clattered against her plate as she placed it down. Haldor did the same, not until after he took a swig that drained his goblet.

"May I add... I believe Faenir is the only one strong enough to save our world," Myrinn said. Her gaze brushed over each of us to ensure she had our full attention. "To some of you, this may seem like a game, but it is far from it. Such a decision is serious, and I will do anything to ensure it happens."

"How disappointing," Gildir said, shaking his head. "Myrinn, the golden child. Turning her back on her family for some idealistic idea that Faenir, who kills whatever he touches, will not do the very same when given the crown to rule over our world. Sadly, you are alone in your views."

"No. She is not." All eyes snapped to Haldor, who sat rigid in his chair.

"You seem to have changed your tune so suddenly," Gildir said, lips tugging into a menacing smirk. "Not long ago, you gloated about being the next King of Evelina. Now you are out of the running with the... terrible... passing of your human, you change your mind?"

"It has nothing to do with her murder," he snapped, blazing eyes wide. The many candles that fought against the ominous gloom of the room spluttered higher, fuelled by his emotion. "If you speak about Samantha's death, then do so correctly. Do you not worry that your mate will be next?"

"My mate is secure with our Queen. Do not waste energy worrying about her, dear brother. Instead help us understand why you suddenly desire to see a monster take the throne." Gildir drew out his plea, only emphasising how unserious he was.

"Safe from you, I gather?" I said, glaring at the marks on his face.

Gildir's oak-brown eyes narrowed as he raised fingers to his cheek. "My mate has been hesitant of late. I am sure some heavy encouragement will soon calm her."

Frila giggled knowingly.

"Death rules the human realm thanks to the vampiric disease the witches spread," I said, ignoring the unease in my gut. "Claria does not have the power to counter the hordes of the undead that ravage our world and push it closer to complete annihilation. Faenir... he is the only one with the power to counter it, and I believe, stop it. Regardless of what you think of my kind, without us, you are nothing. You cease to exist."

Gildir studied me up and down with a look of disgust. "I do not understand how Faenir stomachs one with such unwanted—"

Shadows shook the room. Flooding across the table, they snuffed out each candle flame with ease. Left was the dull silvered light that entered from the few windows across the room. It happened so quickly that Gildir swallowed what he had to say next as fear silenced him. A small gasp escaped Frila's taut lips.

"Watch your tongue, Gildir," Faenir growled, now standing from the table with a cloak of shadows twisting at his back. "Speak to Arlo in such a way again and I will use you as an example of what happens to those who oppose me."

I reached for him, threading my hand into the fist at his side. My touch alone had the effect I needed, and Faenir's power seemed to retreat.

Haldor gestured towards the table, and the candles sprung back to life. I flinched at the sudden light as I willed Faenir to take his gaze from Gildir and look at me.

"I shall take the throne," Faenir confirmed his intentions, speaking through gritted teeth. "I requested your presence in hopes you would see sense. To ask that you stand with me, not against me, as I finish what is required. I see now that my hopes have been misplaced with some of you."

Frila glanced towards Gildir, but he did not notice as he watched Faenir with such burning contempt. I was certain he would have burst into flames if he held Haldor's powers. She then stood from the table, chair kicked out behind her. "I, for one, have heard enough."

Gildir stood too, chest heaving with each breath. "If we are done here..."

"Sit down," Haldor shouted. "Both of you. Stubborn as the woman who has poisoned your minds."

"We are wasting time," I said to Faenir out of the corner of my mouth.

"Gildir, Frila, please," Myrinn pleaded, taking another approach as I watched on at the family drama with a parched mouth and headache that thundered far more powerfully than the storm beyond the manor.

"Let them go," Faenir spoke coldly, waving a hand in dismissal. "I have no patience to entertain the minds of fools. Their decision is not important. What is to be done will be done regardless if they stand for me or against me."

The ground rumbled as Gildir flexed his hand. His power over earth echoed across the room. Glasses clinked against plates. Food toppled from their piles and rolled across the table before disappearing onto the floor. "Careful, Faenir, that sounds an awful lot like a threat."

"A promise," I spat before Faenir could gather his shadows again. "Why did you bother coming if you were never willing to listen to what we had to say in the first place?"

"It was not for the wine," Gildir sneered.

"Then what?" I persisted, noticing how Frila pulled back at Gildir's arm as though to stop him.

Gildir puffed out his chest, smiling down his narrow nose as his eyes trailed me up and down. "What makes you so special? That is what I wish to know."

He did not need to explain further what he meant. Suddenly, I recognised Faenir and his closeness, his touch, how it lingered across my body from the last time he had worshipped me.

"All these years and the bodies Faenir has left in his wake, yet you resist it. Why?" Gildir looked to Myrinn and smiled; it was only for a moment. I followed his gaze to find Myrinn looking defeatedly at her empty plate. There was a glint of amusement that passed across his eyes, one that suggested he asked a question when already knowing the answer; Myrinn seemed to confirm it.

My hand edged towards the knife upon the table. I would slit this man's throat before he said another word.

He knows. He knows.

"Is it fate… Arlo? Or something more tangible?"

A ruckus sounded beyond the closed doors to the dining room. My knees could have given way as the attention was quickly diverted away from me. Raised voices and the thundering of heavy footfalls grew in volume. I looked towards the doors the moment before they burst open. They slammed against the walls, shaking the dust from the rafters.

A huddle of figures raced in. Ana was at the head, tired face hollowed in horror. Something was wrong, that was clear before her rushed voice spoke. "There is a fire!" Ana shouted at the table of royalty, not caring who she disturbed; I loved that about her. "In the apartments for the serving staff. We tried to stop it… they are still in there."

As she explained what was going on, I noticed the smudging of ash across her face. The others behind her, panting and breathless, showed signs that they too had been close to flames, cheeks red and skin marked with soot.

"How did it start?" I asked, unsure if she could hear me over the others shouting.

"Lightning. The storm worsens. A bolt struck the building." Ana looked from me to Faenir, her eyes filling with tears. "Children, there are children stuck inside."

Faenir was moving for the door before Ana had the chance to finish. I raced after him, only to be stopped by his firm hand. "No, Arlo. Leave this to me."

I could not refuse him as Myrinn placed a hand on my shoulder, nodding to Faenir in agreement. "I will look after him. Go."

"The fire, I can stop it. Allow me to help." Haldor was beside Faenir in a blink.

To my surprise, the short frame of Frila joined them too. Her face was void of humour and as serious as the rest of her family. "I will join you both."

Faenir did not waste a moment in accepting or refusing Frila's offer of aid. He was angry, not stupid. Instead, he looked back at me, planted a kiss on my forehead, and whispered a promise, "Stay safe. I will return for you soon."

Myrinn hugged my shoulders as we watched them rush from the room.

"Well, well," Gildir's voice drawled behind us. "It would seem we have some much-required time to discuss some matters."

I could hardly stand how placid he sounded as my mind was filled with the flashing of fire and storm. In the back of my head, I heard the screams of those trapped; they haunted me as I turned my attention back to Gildir. "Why am I not surprised you have not offered to help?"

Gildir smiled, oddly calm, considering what was happening beyond the room. He took his seat, kicking his feet up and resting them on the table, and snatched his glass of wine back. "Because that, human, was never part of the plan."

40
FAENIR

Frozen sheets of rain hammered down upon me; it stung at my skin, tore at my cheeks and face as I ran towards the fire. My clothes drenched through within moments of leaving the confines of the manor. I bit down on the cold ache that made a home in my bones. My discomfort was an afterthought.

Dark flames towered into the storm-cursed sky. There was nothing that could have prepared me for the destruction. It was both terrible and beautiful. Fire devoured the serving staff's quarters, wood and stone no match for the power of the wild element.

Not days before had I been kneeling before a child in one of those rooms. I glanced in the direction of Ana and May's apartment and saw nothing but flames dancing proudly beyond charred, glassless window frames. Haldor and Frila kept pace at my sides as we reached the blaze. I was thankful for their company. My power was great, but I had my limits. There was nothing my shadows could have done to stop this.

"*Nyssa,*" I cursed the Goddess's name above the rain. "Help them."

Haldor stepped up to my left. His amber curls were plastered to his head, ivory skin illuminated as the fire raged before us. His narrowed gaze did not tear free from the fire as he sized it up.

"Can you hold it from spreading?" I asked, voice muffled by the powerful storm.

Determination fortified his expression. Droplets of rain fell from the tip of his nose as he nodded, shouting his reply, "I shall do what I can."

Frila slipped to my other side. Winds ripped around us, howling so viciously it sounded like a chorus of souls crying in pain. Whereas

Haldor watched the fire as though it was his greatest enemy, she watched me.

"The winds are feeding the fire," I said. "Deflect the flow away and starve the fire. It will help Haldor attempt to put it out completely."

I did not wait to see if she listened to my command as I threw myself into the chaos.

Ana was aiding people from the scorched doorway. They came stumbling from it as dark, thick smoke billowed around them. Choking, spluttering. Some hardly kept their eyes open as others helped them run free.

Haldor stood before the burning building; arms held before him in worship. He leashed the flames with his power. Immediately, their frantic movements seemed to calm, dwindling slightly, but not completely.

Glass exploded from one of the higher floors. An outward burst of orange and ruby tongues reached out into the night. Not even the heavy rain could aid in putting the fire out.

I was helpless as I watched.

"This is terrible," Frila's small voice whispered beside me. "So much death. None of them deserved such a fate."

I turned to look down at her. Still, she did not aid Haldor. Frila kept her hands at her sides as she marvelled at the destruction.

"You are wasting precious time, Frila!"

Thunder rumbled in the skies above. Not a moment later, a burst of white-hot lightning forked across the sky. It illuminated the darkness, long enough for me to recognise the humour in Frila's wide, grey eyes.

"How are you to protect our world when you cannot even look after your own home? Death follows you no matter where you step. It always has and it always will."

Haldor roared into the night; my name mixed with his cry of desperate pleading.

I wished to turn and help him, but something stopped me; a whisper of my shadows forewarning that something was wrong.

Seared into Frila's cloud-silver gaze was my reflection. Tired, horrified eyes looked back at me. Frila cackled, and the storm echoed in response.

I reached for my shadows a moment too late. Frila was prepared. She threw her hands skyward, and a fork of lightning reached down as though to touch her. Winds billowed as Frila's power fed the storm.

Her storm.

I gathered my shadows in time, for the burst of bright light crashed towards me. The energy crackled across my arms. Inhaling, I smelt singed hair. I threw the cloak of shadows across me as her power slammed into mine. The ground fell away from me, and I spun wildly through the night. A sudden cry tore out of my throat, silenced only as my body slapped back into the muddied ground.

I clutched at my chest, unable to gather a breath. The pain stabbed through me, slicing up my back as though knives slashed out at me.

"What have you done?" Haldor shouted.

I blinked away the rain and looked up at his tired face. Dark smudging of ash had brushed across his cheek. "It is her..."

Haldor turned back, flames spreading across his hands. They hissed as the storm fell upon them, but still they burned bright. He was haloed by the flames that were still devouring the serving quarters as he faced off the deranged figure whose storm whipped around her.

"Dear Haldor, please do not stand in *our* way," Frila groaned.

I pushed myself from the ground, each small movement boiling agony, but my anger soon dulled the pain as it growled throughout me. Darkness swelled around Haldor and me, preparing to shield us if Frila attacked.

"It did not have to end like this, you know..." Frila called out, long-white hair twisting around her as a vortex of power formed into a cyclone. She stood before us, possessed with her element, eyes glowing with the crackling of lightning that she commanded.

"Never did I expect that you had the capacity to arrange such chaos," I replied, breathless from my fury. "Perhaps I should admit I am impressed, but that will not matter with how this will end."

Bolts of white light crackled across Frila's forehead. Even from a distance, I recognised what it was. A crown.

"Not all of my ideas." Frila laughed and thunder rumbled above. "Actually, it was not my idea at all."

"Then whose?" I asked, taking a cautious step forward. Fearing to blink as if I'd miss her next move, I readied myself to hear the name of our grandmother, to confirm what we had always known.

"Take a wild guess," Frila said, head bowing as her grin sliced across her face.

"Gildir," Haldor said.

The ground swayed beneath my feet, sounds diminishing to a soft whisper as Haldor's accusation settled over me.

"How fabulous, you got it in one!" Frila replied. "And I was hoping to play a little game to draw out this finale. Shame."

I had to get to him.

Fire dripped from Haldor's fingers, melting onto the wet ground at his feet. "It makes sense at least, sending you out to do all the hard work to ensure he benefits from whatever this is all for."

Frila pouted. "Oh, brother, are you finally seeing that you are not grandmother's favourite? Do not be too upset, will you?"

"Fuck you!" Haldor roared.

My head throbbed, skull aching as thoughts slammed within it. I took a step forward but the fizzing of Frila's power popped across my skin in warning.

"Now, now, Faenir. Another step and I will be forced to see if you can survive my lightning. I have always wondered what would become of you in the face of my power."

There was nothing else of importance but Arlo and the girl who stood between us.

"Go to him," Haldor said, his words meant for me only. "I will deal with this one."

Frila's fingers tickled the air, and the winds whipped towards us. "Care for me to kill you the same way I did with your sweet little human? Want to feel what she had when I choked the air from her lungs?"

Haldor faltered.

"I would be careful with such claims," I added, sensing the growing heat that spilled from Haldor's presence.

"Claims?" Frila barked. "You have grown soft, Faenir. Gildir was confident you would kill Haldor's human, but it seems compassion has weakened you. Your lack of action simply forced me to do what you could not."

Haldor attacked without another word. He ran forward before my shadows could stop him. Frila welcomed him, bending her knees like a cat ready to pounce. Whips of pressurised fire grew from his fists. He lashed them out towards the place where she stood. Her laugh resounded through the winds, a warning that this was exactly how she wished for this encounter to go.

Haldor stopped dead in his tracks. His fire diminished as his hands clamped towards his throat. His head was thrown backward, mouth pulled open by unseen hands.

The conjured winds grew stronger. Wilder. I forced my way through them as Frila picked her brother up from the ground and dangled him in a web of her power, as though he were only a child's doll. A burst of lightning cracked across the ground before me. Her shot was meant in warning, to keep me in place so I could do little but watch, all without paying much mind to me.

Frila focused solely on Haldor as she ripped the air from his lungs. The glow of life that encased him flickered. His feet kicked out beneath him, eyes bulging out of his skull as the whites turned blood-red.

I pushed on, trying to reach him. The shadows willed me forward, unable to break through the winds which roared between us. More lightning cracked. The ground burned. Hands raised before me, I pushed at the wall of air, trying to force myself through. My body had become leaden beneath her power. She kept me pinned in place, unable to do anything but watch.

"You. Shall. Not. Stop. Us!" Frila screamed, imprisoned by her deranged mind. "It is ours. OURS!"

Desperation clawed out my throat and fuelled my shadows forward. Dark fingers of my power reached out to Haldor. My attempt was futile. The golden light of Haldor's life force spluttered. Before my eyes, it blinked out of existence and bathed him in the shadows of death.

Haldor's arms dropped to his side, his neck falling at an awkward, sickening angle. Then he tumbled to the ground as Frila's winds threw him carelessly. There was a moment of clarity that followed Haldor's death, his shadows reached out for mine and joined as though we were one.

Frila, breathless, fell to her knees and clutched the ground. Not once did she take her wild eyes from the body laid out before her. Then she did something that sickened me. *She cried*. Eyes red and tears rolling freely down her face, she unleashed a howl that broke the storm apart.

The winds were amicable enough for me to walk freely. Frila did not take her eyes from Haldor's body as I stood above her, my shadow falling across her small, hunched posture.

"Was it worth it?" I asked, kneeling before her. Part of me expected a fight, but the realisation of what she had done caused her to break into pieces upon the ground.

Frila did not look away or answer me. I watched the very understanding pinch her beautiful face into a mask of horror. Slowly, she peered up at me. I could only imagine what she must have seen, as my shadows spread like wings behind me.

"It was inevitable," she hissed, fingers digging into the ground. "The tithe to pay for taking the crown. It always was."

The murder of Haldor had broken Frila. She was not made for the burden of death. Only I was.

"Gildir will see that your human dies just as he has with all the others."

I should have left her at that moment, but the hunger that cramped my soul was too powerful to ignore. There was nothing I had left to say to Frila. Words would not relieve my anger. Only death had that power.

I reached for Frila. Determination filled her eyes as my fingers closed in on the skin of her jaw. My shadows flared against her life-light, serpents thirsting for its energy. Willingly, she reached out her dirt-covered hands and gripped the sodden shirt at my chest. It was as though she longed for the release I could gift her. As soon as my touch graced her face, I devoured her. The rush of her life had me crying out into the night. The feeling was euphoric. I gripped her jaw tighter, leaving bruises across her cold skin as I drained the life from her.

I let go long after Frila died. Her skin rotted, melting from bones as muscles blackened and turned to ash. She crumbled beneath my hand.

Light broke through the thick clouds as they dissipated. At the back of my mind, I was aware of the many servants who watched on. Ana called out my name for aid as the fire still raged on.

My focus no longer belonged to them.

Shadows gathered around me, blocking out the world entirely. The silence I called for was welcome. It did well to drown out the turmoil that warred through my bones and blood. Yet there was only a single name clear enough to cut through the booming in my mind and the agony that clawed through my soul.

One name.

My mate.

Arlo.

41

Dread speared down my spine. It carved its way across my skin and flayed me in two.

Faenir.

Gildir seemed relaxed considering the chaos of the storm and the fire it caused, disinterest smoothing every line of worry that I expected to pinch his face. Everything about his laid-back demeanour made a shiver of alarm spread across my arms.

Myrinn stood by my side, silent as a guard of stone. I glanced sideways at her to see if she too sensed something amiss. She was looking wide-eyed at me, but not from surprise or horror... from sorrow.

"Dare I ask what plan you are referring to?" I glared towards Gildir.

He smiled in return. As he did so the four scratch marks across his jaw flexed as though he was a peacock, and the marks were his feathers.

"Well," he said, voice light and full of amusement. "The one in which we separate you from your oh-so-deadly-mate for a chance to discuss matters."

"The storm..." My tone practically glowed with accusation that I did not need to finish my sentence.

"I am surprised it took you this long to work it out. Was it not obvious that the weather turned alongside our arrival? Frila always loved a show and this one has been spectacular." He raised his glass as though in cheers, then took a long swig with pride.

"Myrinn," I said, unable to take my eyes off the elf as the truth settled upon me. "You need to help Faenir."

"Faenir is not in danger," her reply was cold.

"That is right," Gildir added. "Frila simply needed to remove you from one another long enough for the necessary to occur."

It no longer mattered what Gildir said as I looked upon my friend with horrified confusion. She could hardly hold my gaze, constantly looking down to the hands that she had clasped before her. There was no ignoring the way those hands shook.

"You knew about this?"

Myrinn swallowed hard. "It was never how I wished for this to end."

"To end?" I choked on my words as my mind raced to piece together this puzzle. Myrinn's betrayal stung. A dull ache echoed throughout my chest, and I gripped at it, unsure if the sickness caused it or the revelation.

"I am sorry." Myrinn's reply was short. I stood frozen to the spot as she turned her back on me and paced to the room's edge.

"Would a glass of wine help wash down what we have to discuss or…"

"Fuck your wine," I spat, body trembling with rage.

"What a mouth you have." Gildir chuckled, placing his fingers before his lips. "I must say I can recognise Faenir's interest in you. You are an interesting boy. I only hope Auriol turns out as thrilling as you."

It took a moment for my mind to catch up with the name the elf had spewed. Gildir, who until now enjoyed hearing the sound of his own voice, paused as well, revelling as he witnessed me work out what he had said.

"What did you just say?" The storm became a distant memory as a new roaring screamed within my ears. I paced towards the table, needing to hold myself up for fear my legs would give out.

"Your sister, Auriol," Gildir continued. "Pretty girl I must say. I can speak little of what her mouth can accomplish but I admit her hands, although wild, have great potential."

I watched as he brought his fingers up to his scratched jaw and rubbed it caringly.

"How do you know her name?"

Gildir raised his glass in toast again, this time gesturing towards where Myrinn stood. "My sister shared such interesting information, like your sister's name, not that I needed it to find her. Those eyes… One as blue as cobalt, the other as brown as ancient oak. Such mesmerising eyes and the moment I found her in Tithe I knew her to be your kin. Yet the most interesting news was to learn that you are dying, that all my attempts before have been nothing but wasted effort because you would always have perished in the end anyway."

My legs gave out. I gripped the table, arms suddenly numb, as I tried to hold myself up.

"Arlo." Myrinn was beside me once more, hands reaching out.

"Get away from me," I spat; tears welled in my eyes.

"Steady now," Gildir's calm and steady voice sliced through me like knife through hot butter. "We do not have long before we are to leave, and I need you in one piece."

As my hand fell, my fingers wrapped quickly around the ivory handle of a knife. Neither one of them noticed as I slipped it into my sleeve, slightly nicking the skin on my arm as I did so.

"I don't believe you..." I said finally, breathless as I looked up at Gildir from the floor.

"I do not require you to believe what I have to say. Your trusting of my words will not have an effect on the outcome."

"But you had a Claim..." I spluttered, although my mind kept telling me I had not seen her with him since the day in Tithe. "The door between our realms is sealed..."

"It was. Sadly, the first human I took was rather boring. Auriol, I am confident, will be completely different," Gildir said proudly. "The barrier was closed until I convinced Claria to tear it apart to allow me to retrieve my *new* Claim. Only she has the power to do so, even if it has made her substantially weaker. Grandmother knows her time is coming to an end and with Frila, likely moments from being slaughtered when Faenir discovers the truth, that will leave only myself left to take the crown."

"Why?"

Myrinn winced at my broken, meek voice. "I wanted nothing more than Faenir to take the crown. For years I have petitioned for such a thing. But you are dying..." It pained her to say it, visible from the grimace across her face, and it pained me to hear it. "If Faenir loses you I do not believe he would be strong enough to endure. Evelina has had one unstable monarch; it will not survive another."

"Myrinn saw the light."

"I was given no choice," she snapped. "Do not mistake my decision for anything more than wishing to see this world continue. Gildir, you are the last resort, not the preferred."

"Faenir trusted you." I glowered, ashamed of the tears that ran down my cheeks. "I trusted you."

Myrinn pinched her lips into a tight line. Her dark brows furrowed. She did everything to hide the hurt that desired to flash across her face. She failed at it. "Auriol will be safe," she replied finally. "That is one promise I have not broken."

Safe? The scratch marks upon Gildir's face suggested she felt anything but safe. I almost laughed at the notion before the jolting sickness in my stomach silenced me. The fear I had felt when Faenir had first taken me from Tithe flooded back. Did she feel that same fear now? Scared and lost in a new world filled with danger and betrayal.

Where families sent one another to the slaughter for the one purpose of feeling the weight of gold upon their heads.

"So, what now?" I asked, clammy hands holding onto the knife I had taken. If Gildir thought the scratches my sister gifted him were bad, then the one I would leave would be more... lasting. "What was the purpose of all of this?"

Gildir turned his head to the side, studying me as though he was a dog looking at a bone. "Do you wish to see your sister again?"

The question caught me off guard. The answer fell from my mouth as though it was the easiest thing I had ever had to say. "Yes."

Gildir stood from the chair, casting his shadow across me. "Then we must leave before our opportunity fails us."

He offered me a hand. I stared, stupefied, as though not knowing what to do with such a thing.

"Why not just kill me now?"

"Do not tempt me," Gildir groaned, eyes rolling into the back of his head.

"Gildir, stick to the agreement." Warning laced Myrinn's words.

He sighed, dropped his hand back to his side, then glanced to Myrinn where she loitered behind me.

Do it. This was my chance. *Finish him.*

I gathered myself up onto one knee, slipped the knife free and lunged.

The tip of the dull knife gleamed in the candlelight. It was fast. But Gildir was quicker. One moment I was facing him. The next Gildir stood behind me in a blur, hands gripping my shoulders as he turned my body to face Myrinn...

The momentum of my attack did not stop. Myrinn didn't have a moment to blink. Then the knife stabbed through the bottom of her jaw, jarring through sinew and skin, until the hilt slammed into bone. Blood spilled from her open mouth; the gore-stained blade visible between the gaps of her open lips.

I fell backwards, hand letting go of the knife which stayed buried in her face.

"No," I screamed, gagging for breath as vomit filled my mouth before splattering onto the floor at my feet.

Myrinn gargled in response. Her hands violently shook as she reached up towards her face.

"You have saved me a task," Gildir whispered into my ear. He sounded both close and far away. "Two perhaps, for once Evelina finds out what you have done to one of its beloved princesses, they will never wish for you, or Faenir, to take the throne."

I had no fight left in me as Gildir steered my body from the room. Myrinn gagged and spluttered on the blood that filled her mouth. As we left her, I was certain I recognised the thud of a body falling to the floor.

I had killed her.

As my feet moved through Haxton Manor, the thundering boom of the storm still raging outside, I could not stop looking at my hands, at how red they were. My fingers were sticky and slick with her blood. I smelt it, harsh copper that made my mouth water in warning for more vomit.

Soon enough the blood washed away as Gildir pulled me outside. I cared little for the cold, or the sting of the harsh rain that fell upon me. Even with the blood vanishing from my hands I could not stop seeing red. It was everywhere, cursing my mind with each blink. No matter how I willed for it to go, it did not.

"I didn't mean to."

"Yes, you did," Gildir replied, voice raised above the crashing storm.

From somewhere in the distance, I could see the glow of fire. Even through the heavy winds and devouring rain I could smell the harsh scent of smoke.

"She betrayed your trust. She sold your sister to the enemy and for that you wanted to punish her."

"No…"

"It will be easy to convince them all." He leaned in close, lips brushing my ear. "Thank you for that."

The water of lake Styx thrashed furiously beneath the weight of Frila's conjured storm. Charon waited at the end of the wooden walkway that extended over the lake. His boat knocked against it over and over.

Gildir sat me down within the boat which began to slide away from Haxton Manor. I was helpless to stop it. Charon guided us across choppy waters, his dark cloak billowing behind him.

The further the ferryman took us from Haxton the more I could see. Fire grew from beyond the manor, outlining it with a scarlet halo. Dark clouds of smoke stretched up for as far as I could see, mixing perfectly with the clouds as they willingly joined as one.

Faenir's name was a whisper against my sick-covered lips. I wished to say it but the pain was too much. I couldn't conjure up enough energy to do so. Each breath of mine fogged beyond my lips, my lungs rattled as though my grief encouraged my sickness to take me here and now.

"He will come for you," Gildir confirmed; his words did not bring me relief. "But he will be too late."

The storm broke suddenly. I felt the air still as the winds calmed and the waters beneath the boat settled into its glass-like face once again. Above, the clouds seemed to part to reveal a sky blanketed with stars. All at once the magic that had crackled within the air had vanished.

"Ah," Gildir sighed, his shoulders relaxing as he slumped forward in his seat. "It would seem you are not the only one with blood on your hands this eve. How poetic, the prince of death and his mate cut from the same cloth."

The ferryman skimmed across the Styx like a pebble thrown with force; the speed ripped the tears from my face.

"King or not, Faenir will kill you if anything happens to me."

"I am counting on it," Gildir said through a grin. "He will come and prove himself to be the monster he is. You may have softened him in the eyes of our people but that was doomed not to last."

"Fuck you."

"Careful, Arlo, I would not wish for you to ruin the chance to see your sister before you die. Myrinn told me your wishes… I know you would do anything for her."

I stilled, swallowing hard as the image of Auriol filled my mind. Within my chest, tied in knots around my heart, was a cord. At one side it pulled towards my sister as it always had. The other yanked back towards Haxton, towards the man I had left behind.

"Monsters are for slaying, Arlo," Gildir muttered at my side, facing towards Haxton as though searching the darkness for Faenir as I did, "Never for ruling."

42

For the sake of your sister, play your part convincingly.

Gildir's threat clawed through my mind. *Play your part.* During the carriage journey Gildir had explained how my visit to court would proceed. How I would be presented before Claria and the crowd of gentry as a witness to Faenir's crime. Except that was not all I was here for now. My *part* had altered, from being a witness to a partner in his crime.

Myrinn's death was never meant to happen. Gildir wanted me to know that he enjoyed watching my expression as he drove home just how I had killed her... it was my doing. This deviation from Gildir's perfectly planned story only aided in proving both Faenir's and my crime to the people of Evelina as a way of ensuring they would not wish to see us take the crown.

There was no proof that Faenir had killed Frila, but Gildir was confident nonetheless, only confirming to me that he'd sent his own sister, one who'd stood firmly at his side with equal views, to her death.

What of Haldor? He had left with Faenir. Could he have stopped him from falling into the trap laid out for him?

Hope was a strange concept as Gildir guided me through the ominously lit corridors woven within Nyssa. With each shuddering inhale I smelt the thick scents of damp earth. The further we got into the Great Tree of Life, the more my legs ached. My chest tightened with each breath, rasping in the pits of my throat as though liquid was within it.

I could feel my life bleed away with time. The rotting sickness I had delayed for so long finally caught up with me. It was greedy and rushed, racing to claim me before I could dodge it for another time.

Gildir led the parade ahead, a circle of decorated guards who regarded me with all-consuming hatred behind him. To them I was no longer the man who could withstand the touch of death. I was a killer.

There was nothing I could do but keep my stare ahead, focusing on each step to ensure my legs did not give out. The promise of seeing Auriol once more before it was too late kept me going.

What will she think when she sees me? Tired and weak, would she know the moment her eyes laid upon me? In my mind's eye the cloudy vision of my sister broke through the chaos. I saw her glaring at me with the same look the guards shot my way. Gritting my teeth, I could not dwell on what could be, when I was moments away from finding out.

I recognised the destination from my first visit to Nyssa. Unlike before, the doors leading to the throne room were left open due to the crowd of people that overflowed from them, so large that they could not fit completely within.

A path was made between them. No one needed to move a muscle to allow us to pass through. Once they bowed as Gildir swept before them, chin raised and shoulders rolled back, they glowered at me. The weight of their hateful glares forced more pressure upon me. Although I cared little for what they thought, I knew there was no coming back from this, no changing their minds now. Some elves spat across the floor before my feet. Others cursed my presence. Many wept with Myrinn's name, a whisper across their lips.

"Bring forward the killer." Claria's aged voice was recognisable even at a distance. It rang out across the crowd, silencing them. If I closed my eyes, I would have believed that no one was left around us. "I wish to look into his soul when he tells me why he decided to take the life of my darling Myrinn."

A sharp sword was suddenly at my back; it kept me moving until the twisted throne of wood came into view with the hunched figure of Queen Claria sitting upon it like a child. The Queen's expression was void of any knowledge of this charade, yet I could see the satisfied glimmer in her grey-glazed eyes that she was enjoying every moment of this.

Gildir stopped before his grandmother and bowed. The bend of his back was so dramatic I was surprised he did not extend a hand and wave it before him. The crowd was so focused on me that they did not notice the hungry grin he flashed my way before he took his place at the Claria's side.

That was when I saw her. Stiff and straight-backed, her face covered with a white, lace veil, Auriol stood waiting for Gildir's return. I knew it was her as though I knew my own self. Through the veil I could feel her gaze piercing through me. I longed to see her face, to know the truth of how she saw me, exhausted and covered in someone else's blood. Blood the storm's rain had done more to smudge then wash away completely.

My knees cracked against the ground, the pain no more than a whisper.

"Do you have anything to say for your crime?" Queen Claria bellowed.

Play your part.

As if to remind me Gildir reached out for my sister, longer fingers curling around Auriol's hand. She tried to pull away, but he held firm. As his knuckles paled, I longed to scream out and beg him to stop.

Play your part.

"I have means to make you talk if required," Claria called out, attempting to draw my attention back to her.

"I did it," I spluttered, urgent and rasped. "I killed Myrinn."

She did not ask why because the reasoning did not matter. All that did was the blood staining my clothes and the effect it had on the crowd. "What do you have to say about Prince Faenir?"

My throat closed as though hands gripped tightly around it. As I opened my mouth to reply a spluttered cough came out. It sounded as though stones filled my lungs. It took over my body, cramping and stabbing with agony.

The crowd reacted in a chorused gasp.

My hands slapped atop the strange forest floor as I tried to catch my breath. Wide-eyed, I watched droplets of deep scarlet fall from my lips and splatter across the stone. They blended seamlessly among the red petals around me.

By the time I pushed myself back on my knees I could hardly stay still. My body rocked. My mind groggy and slow.

His shuffling of feet caught my attention. I drew my eyes slowly from Claria back to Auriol who was being restrained by Gildir. His smile had faded and in place was a fearsome expression of annoyance. The fading scratch marks that she had gifted him gleamed across his skin; that made me smile.

"Faenir will answer for his crimes when he comes for you," Claria said, unbothered. "For your sake he will behave or find that you will meet the same end as Myrinn, as Frila."

"Fuck," I exhaled, blood and spit spilling down my chin, "you."

Claria's shoulder relaxed. Her lips twitched upward at the corners as she turned her attention to the crowd. "I trust another life does not need to be taken to prove that Faenir and his Claim are not worthy to rule our beloved Evelina? Nyssa looks down upon our fading world with great sadness at what has happened… she has lost faith in us. It is important that we make amends before it is too late."

I felt a chill race across the back of my neck. I looked over my shoulder to see if death waited behind me, ready to take me, but only the sharp tip of a sword winked back at me. There was no reason to fear the blade; my sickness would take me long before it could.

Knelt before the twisted, bitter queen of Evelina, I clung to life more desperately than I ever had. Each blink was slow. Claria spoke and her voice seemed muted and muddied. I picked out a few words, trying to focus on them as blood hummed through my ears.

Crown. Gildir. King.

More coughing grasped my body and had me bent over, mouth filling with blood. A strange, starving feeling lingered in the back of my head. It dulled the copper tang of my blood and changed it into something sweet.

"My reign as Queen has come to an end. To give Evelina the chance to stop Faenir and save this world from the undead that steal those we require for sustenance, it is time another takes up the mantle. Gildir, once Joined with his Claim, will be granted my blessing for succession. I hand over the crown and its power willingly. I forfeit my…" Claria stopped speaking suddenly, or perhaps my ears gave up.

All at once there was a silence that thrummed around the room. The falling of soft, red petals from the trees that crowned the room seemed to slow… then stop all together.

I blinked.

Gildir had Auriol's hair gripped in his fist, sword drawn before him as he faced off something behind me.

Claria stood, skin glowing with light as though stars beamed beneath her wrinkled skin.

I wished to see what had scared them, but the world was askew. *No.* I laid splayed across the ground; cheek pressed to the mossy floor bed. As the cough came again, in a wave far greater than before, I could do little to sit myself up. Blood pooled within my cheeks, threatening to choke me where I lay. Unmoving, I was far too weak to hold my eyes open long enough to see what caused the room to swell with disorder.

My eyes closed again. The darkness was so welcoming I did not wish to force myself to see, all until hands brushed over my body. Seeing through narrowed eyes, I looked up at the flushed face of my sister. Auriol. Her lips were moving quickly, the veil ripped from her face to reveal the knowing horror that ruined her beauty. I could not hear her. I tried to say her name but gargled on blood as though my lungs no longer had room for air.

That look… I had seen it upon her face before, when it was much younger, many years ago.

Auriol's ivory dress was stained red. Her fingers dripped with my blood. Droplets even graced the skin of her jaw as slick, horrid coughs continued to devour me.

I gasped for air but the blood filling my mouth, throat and lungs prevented it. The world was far too bright. Before I pinched my eyes closed again, I saw Auriol throw her head back, mouth split as her silent scream made her face feral.

This time I did not open my eyes again.

I was surrounded in darkness, freefalling through it as obsidian winds clawed at my body, pathetically trying to catch me. I went willingly, my mind's clarity was as clear as crystal.

Somewhere in the distance I was aware of Auriol's presence as death guided me away from her. Beyond her was Faenir, a presence of shadow and silence that this calming void recognised. They both occupied my mind. Their memories, both new and old, had my soul singing with glee.

I stopped falling. It felt as though my body hit the floor which had come up to greet me. My conscience recognised something was wrong. I should have kept falling forever and ever until I was so immersed in death that there was no return.

Yet something had stopped me. I felt the dark void regard me, judging my presence as though to see if I was worthy of it. Its decision was clear. Death chewed me up and spat me out. And as my eyes snapped open all I could feel was *hunger*.

43
FAENIR

I PULLED the knife free from Myrinn's jaw. As the metal slipped free of flesh, she let out a howl. It sliced through me, itching nails of urgency across my soul which anxiety had grabbed hold of. I was careful not to touch her blood-coated skin and discarded the blade across the floor.

"Where is he?" My question was a growl.

Myrinn's lips trembled, teeth dark with blood. The only sound she made in return was the whimpering of an injured animal.

I looked across the room, studying the knocked over chair. The emptiness of Arlo's presence.

Gildir.

Myrinn was trying to say something. Each time she forced a noise, more blood spilled from the wound beneath her chin. It gushed across her body, spilling free, until her gown looked as though it was crafted from the richest of rubies.

I stood, leaving her reaching for my jacket. Never had one come so close to touch me willingly, other than those seeking death. The shock of it had my attention snapping back down to her.

Myrinn continued to splutter words that made little sense. I wished to clasp her shoulders and shake sense into her.

"You promised to protect him," I shouted down at her, spittle flying. "You owe it to him to tell me what Gildir has done!"

Myrinn's weak fingers dropped from my jacket, staining the hem red. She gagged on her own gore. It splattered across the floor, almost black in the ominously lit room, as though red wine had been spilled carelessly upon the floor.

A waste.

My world was in turmoil. Still, the fire grew in the servants' dwelling, the bodies of children and their families stuck within. Ana had called after me as I left the bodies of Haldor and Frila discarded across the ground; I did not turn back to help her. All I could think of was Arlo. His name thrummed through my mind. I felt his lack of presence as physical agony. My bones ached as though they grew brittle in my arms and legs. Even the blood in my veins seemed to thicken and boil. The worst of it was the tremendous crack that formed deep within my chest.

Gildir had been behind the attempts upon Arlo's life. Gildir had wanted power at any cost. Gildir had taken him from me—my Arlo, snatched from my grasp. In that moment, I felt as though the meaning of my life had slipped through my hands, never to return. Darkness swelled within my soul, an overwhelming ache that clouded my vision and shackled me with a slew of terrible thoughts.

I will kill them all. They took everything.

Arlo, my heart.

It all shattered.

I felt the Styx shiver as my cry broke free. The souls who slumbered within the dark waters came alive. Even from a distance, I felt them crawl free from their imprisonment. They harboured my hate and *welcomed* my anger, begging me to share my burden so it did not consume me.

Powerful, disturbed shadows spun around me like obedient hounds returning to my side. The presence of the dead pounded within me for release, and I gave it to them. I lost myself to the power. To grief. I cared little for Haxton, for Evelina, and the innocents that dwelled among those who wished nothing more than to punish me for being alive. They had finally broken me. After all these years, it took a human boy to drive the fatal weapon into my cracked heart to see it shatter completely.

They wanted the monster. They wished for it. For an age, Claria and my family had forced me onto a path I never wished to journey down. Here I was, at the end, alone and broken. Hollow. Carved from the inside out.

They had taken the one thing that kept my love for humanity and life ablaze.

It was time for them all to feel as I do now.

Myrinn's blood-slick fingers clamped around my ankle. Her touch was steel, fingers gripping my skin as nails dug into it. The touch broke through the darkness within me, like sun peeking between clouds. I looked down as the glow of life drained from her body. Her death came swiftly and instant, my shadows fuelled with hunger for it. Had her pain become too much to bear? She wished for peace she likely did not deserve and found it by pressing her skin to mine.

No. It was not that simple.

Before her, strokes of blood had been painted across the floor. She had wished for me to see, her way of giving a message, one provided only with the sacrifice of her life. Drawn in blood was a single word. Even upside-down I could make sense of it.

Nyssa.

My shadows closed in around me so suddenly, devouring my skin, my body, until we were one and the same.

Myrinn's final message was simple. Gildir had taken Arlo to Nyssa.

∾

I could only imagine what those around me thought as I swept into Nyssa. In their wide, horrified stares, I could see myself, passing through the innards of the Great Tree with shadows billowing from my back like the wings of some dark being come to claim its prey. Hidden within my shadows, the dead withered, twisting and coiling among one another like snakes forced into a basket.

Phantom arms reached out towards the crowd that waited beyond the throne room. Their screams of terror set my soul on fire. Some ran, many stayed standing, frozen to the spot. They all shared the same fear, I could taste it, sweet as honey, making my mouth salivate with yearning.

Did they come to witness Arlo's murder? A crowd of people who had once shown us love now thirsted for revenge, to witness Arlo suffer because of falsities and lies.

No one stopped me from sweeping into the throne room. My dark reflection flickered across the metal breastplates from the soldiers who tried to calm the panic my presence had caused.

I lashed out with my shadows in warning to any who got too close. My touch would not be what killed them. The power they had scorned had now changed. It was poison, leaking into my shadows, as though they hungered for death more viciously than before.

The countless elves parted for me. Bodies moved to each side of the forest.

Then I saw them.

Claria sat forward on her throne, smiling with hysterical glee. Gildir stood before her, sword drawn and raised, towards where I walked. It did not deter me from taking another step. I regarded them both, lips curling above my teeth.

Then I heard a sound that seemed misplaced. Crying. I turned my attention to the sobbing woman to my side. She looked up at me, not with horror, but sadness. One blue and one brown eye blurred red with tears. I recognised her. How could I not with such telling eyes? Arlo's sister. Auriol.

There was no time to make sense of how she was here. Not as I regarded the cause of her grief. Arlo was cradled in her arms. His skin was grey. His arms limp at his sides. And the glow of life that I had memorised so perfectly... was gone. In its place was thick, lingering darkness. The mark of death.

"Careful where you step, cousin." Gildir was before me, his sword still brandished between us. Now there was little distance between the tip of the blade and my chest.

I glanced down at it with no concern. The sword was pressed through my jacket and into my skin. I could not feel it. Did not care. My shadows curled around the blade like armour.

"Arlo is dead," I confirmed aloud.

"It was not I who killed him," Gildir replied. "Did you not know? Did your dearest Arlo not reveal his lie whilst he had the chance?"

I glared down the sharp edge of the blade towards the hand that held it. Unlike the crowds, thin now, as many had run—*clever choice*—Gildir showed no concern at my proximity.

"Lies," I hissed, my shadows echoing the sound as though starved serpents dwelled within them.

He shrugged. "Faenir, for the murder of Frila, Haldor and Myrinn Evelina, it has been established that you are not worthy of succession."

I did not deny it. Their deaths, one way or another, had been caused by me. But their lives did not compare to the one that lay wasted across the lap of a grieving girl.

"You took him from me," I said, shadows crawling up the blade, inching close to Gildir with each passing moment. "All I wished was to be left alone. Never did I care for the crown. For Evelina. For any of this, yet on and on you forced this idea that I wished to rule down my throat... and at what price?"

I spoke to Gildir. To Claria. To anyone left listening as the grinding, painful reality that Arlo lay dead near me slammed through me, and there was nothing I could do; no power over death itself could prepare me for seeing his cold, stiffening body in the hands of his loved one.

"It was never as simple," Gildir whispered, for only me to hear.

"What have I done to deserve this?" I felt oddly calm as I asked.

"Well," Gildir laughed sharply, as though my question was ridiculous, "you were born." His words had no effect on me. He intended to cause me pain, but pain was an ally. I longed for it, desired it in more ways than one.

"As Nyssa's chosen heir," Claria called out, voice hardly heard over the shouting and screaming and pounding of running feet. "I decree Gildir will be King. It has been decided."

"I lay no claim to your throne," I spat, stepping forward as the sword pierced further into my chest. Gildir's steeled expression faltered at this. His eyes widened only slightly, enough for me to notice his confidence waning. "Have it if you are so desperate. But you will rule over a world of waste, I promise that."

Gildir stepped back. I strode forward, skewering myself upon his blade in hopes it would finish me. I wished to die, to give into that peace which had been dangled before me for years.

I glanced over his shoulder to Claria, who sat watching. "Rather, a powerless runt takes the crown and seals the fate of Evelina. The death of a few may stain my hands, but the destruction of us all will scar yours."

"I will save it."

"Just as Claria has? Keeping the humans in pens like cattle, instead of dealing with the threat that our own creations caused? I look forward to seeing you fail."

Gildir dropped his hands from the hilt of the sword. He stumbled back. Onward I stepped.

"Stand down," Claria warned, bones clicking menacingly as she stood. "You have caused enough damage to this family."

Hate boiled within my bones. My shadows gathered and grew, draining what little light that still spewed from the haggard Queen of Evelina. There was not one person I despised more.

"It is done, Faenir," Claria's voice cracked as she spoke. "My last decree is to banish you to your dark dwelling and ban you from ever leaving its shores for the sake of our people and their safety. You, devil, are not welcome here."

"I will see that you pay." I glared at Claria, then to Gildir, who still looked with shock at his sword, which had pierced through me. Where blood should have spilled, shadows danced in its stead. The forest bed beneath my feet withered and rotted.

"Take your death and leave," Claria warned.

She spoke of Arlo. My death. My Arlo. I could not bring myself to look at him. If I did not look, then it was not real. Even if my shattered soul twisted into knots at the knowledge that he was lost to me.

"Do you wish to know why you could touch him?" Gildir said with a smile.

I looked back at him, shadows screaming for the chance to reach out and drain the golden glow of life that encased him. "I care little for your lies."

"Did Myrinn never reveal what she so willingly told to us? How your dearest Arlo had been dying all along. His life was already entwined with yours, Faenir, even if you were too blind to see it."

I hesitated. Gildir took this as his chance to spill more lies. Where his words did not hurt me before, these cut deep.

"He drank the blood of vampires, concealing his death but not stopping it."

"Liar."

I studied his face for proof that he had lied, the shifting of an eye, or the twitch of a lip.

"Even the very thing you command wishes to escape from you," Gildir said, leaning forward slightly as though preparing to share the greatest secret of all. "And the worst part of it all was my attempts to see that Arlo died were in vain. When all that was required was waiting... patiently... as I have for this day all my life."

My shadows flared like wings at my back. A roar filled my chest and exploded outward as another fleeting cry joined in chorus with me.

Gildir looked away from me, brows furrowing over narrowed eyes at the girl, Auriol, who held the unconscious body of my beloved. I followed suit.

She was standing, arms now empty, and her brother's name carved into her cry. "Arlo!" She looked at Gildir, as Gildir looked at her; it was a strange encounter.

"Impossible..." Gildir muttered quietly, drawing my attention back to him.

My heart jolted in my chest, as though starting again after slumbering in the darkness.

Behind Gildir, with eyes glowing the purest of scarlet against pale, ivory skin, stood Arlo. Clawed fingers gripped Gildir's shoulder, pinning him in place. Arlo's mouth was parted, revealing two sharpened points of teeth that seemed to extend before my eyes.

Arlo regarded me like a predator. His pink tongue brushed against his pointed canines one by one. His attention then fell to Gildir's exposed neck. Spit ran from the corners of his parted lips as though he was a starving hound looking upon a carving of raw meat.

"Darling?" I whispered.

Arlo did not reply, his focus locked elsewhere.

Gildir did not move. Could not move, no matter how he fidgeted beneath Arlo's grip.

"This," Arlo hissed, his voice different from before; it sounded harsh and forced, like nails pulled across stone, "is for them *all*."

Claria could not so much as gather breath to shout in warning as Arlo threw back his head, opened his pale lips wide and dove his teeth into Gildir's neck.

44

It was believed the kiss of the undead led to the spread of their disease, teeth sinking into skin, the drawing of blood from a victim until they were left an empty husk of flesh and bone. We were all wrong. I was proof that we were fools ever to believe such a thing. With the nectar-like liquid filling my cheeks and slithering down my throat, I had been brought back not because of a bite… It was the blood that I had drank willingly.

It had poisoned me.

Changed me.

And most of all, it did what Father had suggested, kept me from the grasp of death—now for an unfathomable amount of time.

Before me, Faenir was a creature to be feared. Wings of shadows spilt from his cloak. His golden stare was wide, his head cocked. It took tremendous effort not to close my eyes and give in to the euphoria that filled my body as I drained Gildir, who I had entrapped beneath my grasp. I was stronger than before. Renewed. Famished. *Starving*. I gave little room for Gildir to move, digging my nails through his shirt and into flesh until more sweet, divine blood spilt across his chest; every drop that did not grace my lips was a waste.

The hunger had its own voice, desperate and pleading, like a child locked in a cage in which the key had been long lost. The moment my eyes opened, and I saw Auriol, I almost wrapped my jaw around her arms. Even in my desperation, I knew not to, enough to press away from her and choose my victim. Gildir was the easiest one to pick. Even with the overwhelming thunder of hearts that chorused through my head, or the scent of blood that tickled within my nose, he was the one who called out to me above the rest.

I moaned into his neck; lips smudged with blood. My tongue lapped against his slick skin as though I was a cat drinking cream from a bowl. It was glorious. The more I consumed of him, the more soothed I became.

"Darling," Faenir spoke finally. It could have been seconds or hours since I had first clamped my jaw around Gildir's soft neck. Time was pointless, a silly concept that meant little to me now. "That will be enough."

A strange, unwanted feeling crept into my consciousness. Was it guilt? Disgust... no. It couldn't be when his blood was so holy. So beautiful.

"Arlo," Faenir said again, this time his voice harsher. More commanding. The shadows that spread around him shrunk with each passing moment.

Reluctantly, I withdrew my teeth from Gildir's neck. He groaned, sounding more pleasured than pained. I could only imagine what Faenir saw. My lips were coated with dripping red gore, my chin and chest covered with my ravenous urgency.

"Abomination!" someone cried.

I cared little for the speaker. Words could not hurt me now. Faenir's lip curled above his straight teeth in reaction.

"Your light." Faenir reached out his fingers, toying with something unseen an inch beyond the skin of my arms. "It has gone."

"Because I am dead," I replied, mouth watering as the copper tang of blood teased my nose. My meal still waited, unmoving and spellbound, in my arms.

"That I can see."

I searched his expression for revulsion. There was none to find. Even I was oddly calm with the deep-rooted understanding of what I had become. I did not fear myself or give room to contemplate just what I was doing to Gildir. It simply felt right. Just.

"Why did you not tell me of your sickness?" Faenir asked.

I dropped my gaze downward, suddenly feeling the creeping of emotion flood back into my chest—my empty, still chest. "I cared for you enough to hide the truth. I did not wish to watch you break if you lost me..."

Faenir pondered that, eyes glazed over in deep thought. He was silent for a long moment; I soon believed he would never speak again. "You are far from lost, my darling."

I did not flinch as Faenir reached those gentle, caring fingers and brushed them across my jaw. His touch was featherlight and... real.

Warmth like nothing I could have expected. It shocked me. I gasped, lips parting as the points of my teeth nipped at them.

"Skin as cold as forgotten marble." Faenir's voice trembled. His eyes traced across me as his other hand reached out, marvelling at how he did not kill me with his touch.

I groaned into his touch, hands gripping hard upon my prey so he could not escape me.

"I feel as though I should ask how this is possible?" Faenir's question was no more than a whisper. He did not need to elaborate for me to know what he wished to uncover.

My desire to live *had become my curse.*

"Perhaps," I replied, wishing to melt into his hands and forget the world. "We will discuss this soon."

I sensed the presence of someone familiar join at my side. It was Auriol, I knew it from her scent alone. She smelled like home, dust and old wood with the undertones of freshly picked roses. I closed my eyes and saw a bunch of flowers within a vase on the table of our home in Tithe.

"What have you become?" she asked it aloud as though it would make it seem real. "I watched you die in my arms. Arlo, the one I knew has gone... haven't you?"

Part of me longed to reach out and embrace her, to hold my sister close and never let go again but I feared what I would do. My eyes flickered between hers and then her neck. Her skin fluttered above the plump artery, as though enticing me to greet it with my teeth.

I gripped tighter on Gildir's limp, living body as though to anchor myself.

"Perhaps I am still the same. Maybe not. Either way this is my doing." My words came out in a hiss.

Faenir's attention was drawn elsewhere to the clattering of metal and the shouting of an old woman whose voice was likened to the unimportant buzzing of a fly, one I wished to swat.

"How long have you suffered without me knowing? The way you coughed... that sound has haunted me for years. I would never forget such a noise."

I nodded, tongue tracing my lower lip to savour the sweetness that coated it. Her eyes, those same eyes that had tied us together as siblings, watched my tongue as though it was the most dangerous thing she had ever seen.

"It began not months after Father died. I knew from the first spotting of blood that I could not put you through the suffering that still scarred you. Auriol, the choices I made were to ensure you were never left alone. And now I have become a nightmare of flesh..."

"I don't know what to think," Auriol replied, looking towards the limp elf in my grasp. "But I cannot say I am not relieved either way."

"He hurt you, didn't he?" I asked. I feared if the answer was yes, my hands would twist, and his neck would snap beneath them.

"Given the chance he may have. After he came for me, there has been little time alone enough to know his capabilities, although his intention was clear."

"Auriol, I wanted none of this to happen."

"Me being here, or you becoming..." She could not say it.

"Everything."

Auriol grimaced, reaching out her hands, but not for me. "Give him to me."

The protective growl erupted out of nowhere. Auriol did not step back but pushed her hands forward to show she was not scared of me. "Enough blood has been spilled, Arlo. This is not you."

It was not me before. But it is now.

Faenir's demanding voice distracted me. I turned as Auriol took her chance to pry the elf from my arms. I caught a fresh scent on the wind as I regarded Claria, standing guard beyond the throne as though she protected it. Her attention was on Faenir entirely, who had snaked his way towards her.

"This ends now," Claria croaked.

"Indeed, it does," Faenir retorted, wings of shadow flaring out behind him. "It could have been different, Grandmother, I want you to know that."

"No," she spat, eyes wild. "I saw the destruction of our realm the moment you were born. Evil. Death. Decay. Everything Evelina stands against and yet you stand before me, the very omen of our destruction."

"Your words do not—cannot—hurt me."

Claria tore the crown from her head and cowered. There were no soldiers to protect her. They had run from the room along with the crowd who had been led here. "You will not have it. It is not yours."

"If that's true, then allow Nyssa to be our judge. You are not a Goddess as she is. You are a bitter old crone who led this world down the path it is on. Hand in hand, you have guided us to this moment. You may see me as the demon, as you have declared me, but I am merely a product of your hate."

Claria fell backwards, stumbling over her weak footing. Still, she did not let go of the circlet of gold with the inset of opal and rubies. Her wrinkled fingers held on as though her life depended on it. All this blood and death because of that crown. It had inspired hate, greed and malevolence; it represented nothing of life and the beauties that came with it.

"Give it to me," Faenir commanded, the grass rotting beneath his feet. "Make the end easier for yourself."

She pressed her back against the base of her throne. Her gaze flickered between the crown, to Faenir and then to me where I stood. "As breath fills my lungs, I will never lay my blessing upon you."

"Then you force me into a corner that I did not wish to be kept in. Just as you have done from the moment you had me thrown into the Styx in hopes of my demise." Faenir's voice cracked with sorrow. Whereas I wished to rip into her rumpled, old body and drain blood from her veins, he did not want death.

"You. Shall. Not. Have. It."

"I will. Once I pry it from your cold, dead hands."

I watched understanding glaze across her eyes. Her time was up. Her reign ended. Faenir gathered his shadows and sighed, dispersing them until they melted away and he was left mundane without them.

"Do it," I hissed quietly. Faenir flinched, continuing his stride towards his grandmother.

"They will never accept you," she spat, forcing her face as close to his as he knelt down before her.

"*My* people will not have a choice in the matter. Just as they did not have the choice when you were given the crown. I will be forced to prove myself worthy. Earn it. Whereas you believed respect and admiration was given just because of the chair you sat upon and the gold that weighed down your head."

"I hate YOU!" Claria screamed, clutching the golden circlet to her chest protectively.

Faenir replied, calm and clear, "I, Grandmother, forgive you."

Queen Claria Evelina pinched her eyes closed as the King of Death brushed a careful hand across her cheek and claimed her soul as his own.

45

Days later and I longed for Claria to be alive just for my chance to take my fury out on her withered body. I did not imagine her taste was pleasing, but still I longed for it, now even more so than before.

"Tithe may not be standing by the time we return," Auriol reiterated, looking between Faenir and I.

"What has our captive revealed?" Faenir asked coldly. He sat on his throne, arms resting on each side whilst he twirled a pomegranate around his hand. He always had something in his hand, testing the limits of his renewed power. Days since he'd laid the crown upon his head with the rotting carcass of Claria beneath him, his power had changed.

Even as my sister spoke to him, his focus was never entirely on her. He watched the pomegranate, waiting for its pink skin to melt to black rot. It never happened.

"Claria paid a price of power for Gildir to take me from Tithe. He had no problem gloating about the exchange of magic in which Claria had paid. Taking it from the protection around Tithe to regain energy to open the door between our realms. If the Watchers have failed, our home will be no more than a feeding ground for the…"

Auriol's words trailed off as she looked at me. I held her unwavering stare in contest.

"You can say it," I told her.

"Vampires."

Faenir reached out and placed a hand upon mine. I was perched on the edge of the throne, one hand occupied, toying with the silk of Faenir's dark hair, the other gripping a vial of blood, Gildir's blood. As soon as I felt the singing of hunger, it was safer for me to pop the cork and drink it. It would stave off the famished cry and keep those close to me safe.

"It has been days now and still nothing has been done," Auriol scorned. Her tight-lipped expression proved that she had far more to say but didn't. She had taken it upon herself to become Gildir's keeper, the carrier of the key to his imprisonment. She had yet to tell me what he had, or had not done, when he took her from Tithe. And I learned to keep my questions to myself. Auriol did not need me to protect her, the scratch marks on Gildir's face had proven that.

My sister was determined and clear-headed. Faenir had not asked for her council, yet she provided it brilliantly when it seemed the rest of the elven realm had turned their backs on the new King.

"Something must be done," I said to Faenir, my breath causing the strands of hair to dance.

Faenir nodded softly, contemplating. I wished to reach out my fingers and turn his face to look at me, to help ease the deep-set lines of pressure that had pinched his handsome face the moment the crown and its responsibilities rested upon him. "Auriol, I vowed to ensure the humans survive."

Auriol grimaced, fists clenching at her sides. "Easy words to say sitting comfortably upon a throne."

I winced. Faenir did not react.

"It is clear your grandmother wished for the same. Keeping us penned in walls like sheep hiding from wolves. You should be more concerned with us humans thriving, not surviving. Stop hiding us away. Deal with the issue that your own magic has ultimately caused."

Auriol did not require a sword and armour to make her look like a warrior before us. Straight-backed, chin raised high and eyes burning with fierce determination, she was prepared to take the cause in her own hands and save the world.

I smiled, pride swelling in my chest. "My sister is right, Faenir," I said, catching her quick glance at me. She regarded my smile and her own lips twitched.

Faenir stood from the throne, fingers gripping tighter across the pomegranate until its juices spilled down his wrist. He regarded Auriol. "If all humans share a soul as strong as yours, I do not doubt they will prosper. There are many wounds across your realm and mine that need healing. I only wish you to consider staying with us to provide your strength to aid them."

Auriol had made her wish to return to Tithe abundantly clear, and I had not tried to change her mind. It was her choice to make, not mine. Those lessons had been hard learned. Much had been said between us since Claria's death, and still there were many things left unsaid. I revealed the promise I made to our parents and what I had done to ensure it was kept. I did not do so to encourage her forgiveness for my actions and control, nor had she given it to me.

It took a while for her to look at me for more than a fleeting moment. When she did, she would usually avoid my eyes, now deep red like swirling pits of blood, instead of the once blue and brown that we shared.

Yet it was Auriol who had collected Gildir's blood during her visits to him in his cage in the deep prisons of Nyssa. It was her unspoken acceptance of what I had become, that was all I had needed.

"Auriol, thank you." Faenir bowed to my sister as red petals fell from the trees above her. They landed upon her crown of brown hair as she stood tall. "It is a wonder to have your guidance. I only hope that I do right by you."

If my heart still beat, it would have skipped in that moment.

"What will you do?" Auriol questioned, shifting her stance to prepare to leave us.

Faenir looked over his shoulder to where I sat, lounged across his throne. I still expected him to look at me with loathing at the creature I had become. Never did such an emotion fill his golden stare. In its place was warmth and admiration.

I was no longer living, but beneath his attention Faenir made me feel alive.

"I believe the opportunity is now to infiltrate the hive, to deal with our problems rather than hide them behind walls."

∼

Haxton Manor was deathly silent around us. Peaceful.

I picked up the scents of scorched wood and charred stone. It clung to everything. Faenir had done little to deal with the damage of Frila's lightning. He had revealed that he did not wish to either.

When we had returned to his home, we had found it empty. Ana and those who had survived the fire that Frila's lightning had started had left. Even the Styx was uninhabited; the spirits and souls that had been trapped among the water had found freedom. No longer did they dwell in the dark depths; now they lived within Faenir's shadows. He did not call for them often, but when he did, I saw the silver glow of the phantoms dancing happily among *his* darkness.

Charon had also found freedom. The ferryman's boat was left moored upon the shores of the Styx when we had returned. Faenir did not say a word as he pushed the boat back into the water and helped me inside. Charon, like the dead that left the lake beyond Haxton mundane, had found peace alongside Faenir. I was glad about that.

Faenir's hands gripped my thighs, the pinch of his nails into my skin was thrilling. He refused to let go as he rolled his hips, encouraging his hard length to push in and out of me.

My arms straddled either side of him, keeping me leaning over him with our lips inches from one another. I looked down at him as I bounced upon him. My sudden control over the sex had him groaning as he bit down on his lip.

"*Fuck,*" I breathed as Faenir's pacing intensified. I gripped the sheets as my teeth grew in my mouth, the tips pricking my lips and drawing blood.

"You take me so well," he groaned; his pleased words warmed me just as his hands did.

"I don't want this to end."

"Arlo, darling." Faenir slowed, moved his hand to the back of my neck, and brought me close to his mouth. "You are mine forever. I am yours."

"Forever is a long time," I replied. "You may grow bored with me."

"Never," he said, thrusting into my ass until his hips pressed against me.

I howled with pleasure, throwing my head back as my stomach cramped with hunger.

Faenir noticed. He brought his wet lips to my ear and whispered, "Drink from me."

I could not deny him. His invitation was what I longed for. I studied him beneath me. Dark hair fanned out across the pillows in a halo of raven shadow. His cheeks were flushed red. Lips glistened as though coated in honey.

"Are you certain?" I hissed, finding it hard to restrain myself from sinking my teeth into his flesh.

"I am going to need you at full strength, my darling," Faenir said softly, "For what is to come."

My tongue traced my teeth, running across the points of my canines as they sharpened. This hunger differed from the emptiness of my stomach. It was lust; it spread across my chest and warmed my cold body from the inside out.

"Come." Faenir continued fucking me, guiding my head down towards his neck. I pressed my hands to the muscles of his chest, my nails scratching across his skin with excitement. "Feast, my darling. We leave soon."

Night was upon us. I felt it coming more than I could see it. Faenir had thrown walls of thick, impenetrable shadow around the room to stop the sunlight from bothering me. The night's arrival signalled our departure. Auriol readied herself back in Nyssa. She would expect our return soon.

"Promise me when we come home, to steal me back into this room and keep me captive just as you always wished," I said, lips pressed to the skin at his neck. My teeth grazed across him, drawing a breathy sigh from my King.

"We are eternal," Faenir replied, pounding softer into my ass as his hands clawed down my back. His touch was warm against my cold skin. It left trails upon it, marks that would linger. "You are my forever."

"Oh, Faenir." My voice was muffled as my mouth was filled with skin. One bite and his nectar would fill me; the thought alone wetted the tip of my hard cock. "I love you."

The King of Evelina pinned beneath me groaned as I bit into him. My teeth spilled through his warm skin as painless as I could make it. Sweet, powerful blood filled my cheeks, and I drank.

Faenir fucked me harder. I closed my eyes as my body burned with euphoria. Faenir squeezed my ass with one hand and held the back of my head to his neck with the other. Above the roaring of pleasure, I heard his breathless reply. "And I love you. My eternal. My forever. My darling."

46
WHEN SHADOWS COLLIDE

CASTLE DREAD LOOMED BEFORE US. The shards of dark brick and aged stone was a stain against the landscape of Darkmourn. Its turrets glowed beneath the silver of the full moon. The light did wonders to outline the many details of this haunting place, brick by brick, at least those that still stood. Much of the castle was left in ruins, torn apart by a witch's power countless years ago, yet the great doors at its entrance were left unmarked and closed.

I had never been this close before. It looked empty to the eye, but my keen ears picked up movement from deep within. A shifting of light feet. A murmur of voices.

"They're inside and know we have arrived," I said.

Faenir stood beside me, shadows crawling beneath his hands in readiness. Auriol was at my other side, hand clutching mine tightly.

Even within the shadows of the castle grounds, we were being watched. Stalked. Creatures with glowing red eyes prowled. The warning yip of a wolf sounded from our side. They watched, but never came close enough to be seen beside a flash of red and the sharp snapping of jaws.

We waited beyond the doors of Castle Dread for our host to welcome us.

An elven King. A vampire. And a human.

What a sight.

A shiver passed across my skin as the doors finally opened. The sound of ancient hinges screamed, scratching at my mind with claws of horror. I felt my elongated canines nip at my lower lip as I tried to keep fear from my face, especially when I saw whom we came to visit.

Two figures were outlined by the warming glow of fire within the castle. One was taller than the other. He stood forward as though to reveal himself. Hair of white moonlight crowned his head. His eyes were the richest scarlet. His face was carved and hollow, with strong bones and dark brows that stood in contrast to his ivory skin. Two points of sharpened teeth overlapped his lip which twitched as he regarded us.

"What *do* we have here?" His voice was as deep and rich as the velvet navy jacket that rippled when he moved. He cocked his head skyward, nose flaring as he snatched our scent from the windless night. "I did not realise an invitation had been sent for visitors. Jak, did you call for our guests without my knowing?" There was humour and teasing in his voice. However, there was no denying the sharpness hidden beneath it.

The second figure stepped free from the shadows of the doorway. He was beautiful. Curls of brown hair perfectly laid across his forehead. He wore a loose tunic of white that billowed at his arms and sat low across his shoulders. His skin was deeper in tone than that of the man he stood besides, but it still gleamed with the grey of death. "No, Marius, it would seem they are lost."

I hissed as they laughed in chorus. Auriol squeezed my hand in warning.

Faenir's shadows twisted like snakes as he stepped forward. "I expected more, I admit."

Marius, the vampire of legends, lowered his head and smiled. His tongue escaped the confines of his tight-lipped mouth. He drew it slowly across his teeth, ensuring we each saw the glistening tipped points as though he were a peacock, and they were his feathers. "What do we have here?" Marius said. "Such an unlikely group of visitors, I must say."

"Invite us into your home and we can discuss our presence, among other things," Faenir commanded.

The petite figure, Jak, stiffened. Then flames spread across his closed fists until each hand glowed with curling tongues of orange.

My breath caught in the back of my throat. The last time I had seen such power was in Haldor. The thought alone soured my mouth, especially because Jak was no elf. He was as formidable as the witch-turned-vampire he stood proudly beside. *Witch*.

"This is all your fault," I spat. I did not need to elaborate for them to know what I meant. Vampires. The death. The undead that ruled Darkmourn more than the living.

"Now, now," Faenir sang. "Darling, let us not offend our hosts just yet."

"Your presence alone offends me. Leave before I call for our hounds to chase you out," Jak warned, fire spreading to his elbows. "Or better yet, I could be the one doing the chasing."

Marius chuckled at that. I felt his burning red stare bore into me, studying me from head to foot. Faenir did not like that his attention had turned. "Dare I enquire as to why one of my own creatures," Marius mused, drinking me in, "hangs stakes from his belt as though they were jewels or something of worth? How amusing."

My fingers twitched. I longed to pull out one of the carved stakes to show it off as he had with his teeth.

"Cut the shit. We all know you are not going to turn us away. So, are you going to let us in or not?" Faenir asked, voice raising above the darkness as though to prove he controlled it. "We have come a rather long way."

"Step closer," Marius said, lifting a finger and curling it inward in beckoning. "I do not think I have seen the likes of you before…"

Faenir sensed the danger behind his words but stepped forward anyway, not without snarling in warning at the bloodthirsty creature. Perhaps it was his curled lip that made Marius react, or the fact he finally sensed the elf's power. The strangest thing occurred. Shadows lingered behind Marius like a cloak, a power similar to that of my King. Faenir noticed, flaring his shadows in response. They regarded one another for a moment.

Jak stared, with narrowed and distrusting eyes, between his lover and mine.

"Ah, perhaps you should come in," Marius said finally, breaking the strange competition of power. "You are welcome to join us for a drink. That is as lenient as my hospitality can stretch. However, as our hosting has been forced upon us, I am afraid the wine I offer has long spoiled, yet I see that you have brought your own drink with you."

I wished to stand before Auriol to protect her from Marius and Jak's sharpened stare. Her grip on my hand kept me in place. She snarled, far more deadly than anything Faenir and I could have done in that moment.

"I long to be the one to kill the first vampire," Auriol warned, glancing to Jak. "Perhaps it will be I that finishes the task that you failed at all those years ago."

Jak bucked forward with a snarl. Marius reached out a hand and stopped him, not caring for the fire that burned his skin. Jak recalled his power instantly. Then they both shared a whispered word, before shifting their attention back to Faenir.

"Long have I wondered when your kind would reveal themselves to me," Marius said, releasing his hold on the witch-boy. They both stood aside in offering. "It would seem we have a long night ahead of us."

With that, our hosts turned on their heels and enticed us to follow them inside the belly of Castle Dread.

∽

Jak studied me over the lip of his glass. Eyes like a viper, tongue just as loose, he left a trail of spit across the rim. There was no question that blood filled his glass, and that it was human. I could smell it, pungent, even from a distance. It reminded me of my sister, who sat stiffly beside me.

"Why should I concern myself with the death of your kind?" Marius questioned, bored as he laid back in his chair.

We were surrounded by shelves of books towering on either side of the room. I could have lost myself to the gilded lettering across the spines and the smell of the pages if I was not in such... unpredictable company. Fire glowed in the many hearths within the study; they had been lit before we had entered.

"Have you wondered what would happen to you when the last human is drained of the precious blood that keeps you... reanimated?" Faenir's question was pointed and precise.

"That is not a matter that should concern you, elf." Unseen wind lifted the brown curls from Jak's forehead.

"Oh, but it does. Greatly, in fact."

"Do go on," Marius said, amused. "What holds your interest in whether or not humans survive the might of my kind?"

Faenir had not touched the wine that Marius had poured for him. The cork spun around within the dark liquid; even the bottle was covered in dust, the label unreadable in its age.

"To put it simply, my world will cease to exist."

"And this concerns me?" Marius replied with a disinterested hum.

Shadows twisted from the corner of the room and gathered in a cloak around us. "It should. If pushed, I will do anything to ensure the human race does not perish."

"Ah," Marius breathed, pointing towards where I sat. "Yet if I read your subtle threat correctly, by destroying me you will not only remove the threat of my kind from this world but also your *friend* here... he would turn to ash alongside us all."

Faenir flinched at the term Marius used. *Friend*.

"If that ensures the human race survives..." I said, one brow raised in jest.

"Will you reduce yourself to drinking the blood of rats when you wipe us from existence?" Auriol glowered towards the Lord of Vampires. "And what will you do when you kill the last of those? When all creatures are drained, and you are left to starve? What then?"

"Finally, we reached the heart of this conversation." Marius laughed.

"I'm not one to laugh at," Auriol growled.

Marius studied her for a moment, a grin etched into his demonic yet handsome face. "You remind me of a human girl I once knew."

"What became of her?" Auriol asked. I felt her fingers linger close to my belt and the stakes that waited upon it.

"She willingly gave herself to the death I could gift her. Perhaps I will introduce you to Katherine before you leave... I imagine she would admire your strength a lot. She has such a weak spot for women with spirit of steel."

Jak slapped a hand down on the table, the many glasses chimed in response. "I've been betrayed before by my own blood. What makes you think we will trust you? *Strangers.*"

"What if I could promise you a cure? A way of keeping you satisfied," Faenir murmured, drawing their attention back to him.

"You suggest we are in need of fixing?" Jak spat.

Faenir did not flinch at Marius's shadows that joined our conversation suddenly. "Careful, my love, let us not ruin the evening just yet. I have interest in what this... elf has to say."

"I do not mean to fix your curse," Faenir said, leaning forward on the table. "That power is even beyond me. But what if I could provide you sustenance? Blood. An eternal source to keep you and your kind full and the humans untouched. Auriol is right. I do not imagine such powerful beings as yourselves drinking from the likes of vermin. Even I can see that you are above such desperation as that."

It was a gamble coming to Darkmourn to bargain with demons. To play on a weakness that Auriol had brought to light. To pick out a pending concern of blood for the creatures that required it in order to prevent their own inevitable destruction if humans and animals became extinct.

It would seem Auriol was right. Marius and Jak shared a look that sang with concern. It gleamed through the cracks of their confidence and allure.

"Would you like for me to continue?" Faenir's shoulders relaxed as he recognised the reaction before him.

"You have come all this way, elf. Do not stop on our behalf."

"Good." Faenir lifted a hand to his side and flicked his fingers with dramatic ease. The shadows peeled away, revealing another being we had brought with us. Both vampires reacted as though sunlight had burst through the night. "A gift," Faenir looked towards Gildir, who stood rigid as the shadows melted away from him, "A peace offering between us, if you will."

Jak and Marius hissed, nails scratching into the wood of the table. They had not felt, nor sensed, the extra presence and reacted as such.

"What is this!?" Marius growled.

"A trick!" Jak snapped.

I could not fight the smile as their shock melted into expressions of interest. Noses flared and tongues pressed beyond lips as they glanced at the marks my teeth had left upon Gildir's throat.

"We could offer you beings that live as long lives as you. Whose bodies, if cared for, would continue to thrive and provide you an eternal source of the blood you cherish so dearly," I said, revelling in the reaction of the creatures.

Jak broke free from the trance first. "If you are right, one would not be enough."

"Then I would provide you more," Faenir confirmed.

"What *King* would throw his own people into a pit of snakes?" Jak's question hung between us.

"A desperate one," Auriol confirmed, looking between us all. "It is time our kinds come together instead of tearing one another apart, don't you think?"

"Careful, human. Let us not get away with ourselves." Marius's glowing eyes snapped between Gildir and Auriol as though unsure who deserved his attention more.

"I understand the decision has come upon you quickly, but an answer is required before we depart," I said.

Faenir gripped my thigh beneath the table and squeezed. His touch thrilled me. Even in the presence of such creatures, I could not hide my lust that spilled from my pores in waves.

Marius seemed to notice. Jak too, as they both licked their lips hungrily.

"And if we refuse your offer?"

"You die," Auriol said quickly.

"But we are already dead," Marius replied through a wide grin. "That has brought you all here, has it not?"

"You do not know death as I do, vampire." Faenir stood from the table, his hand leaving a mark of warmth upon my thigh. "I wish for you to have the choice of how this meeting ends. Do not mistake my offer for anything more than a request of allied peace between us."

"Peace," Jak barked. "Humans never wanted peace. If they did, we would not be sitting here discussing such matters."

"Yet here we are, together, with a choice to change the world or destroy it."

Marius pondered Faenir's words in a moment of silence. He looked back to Gildir, whose soul had been broken. He no longer moved or made a sound. *Auriol's doing.*

"Such an interesting offer. I admit you may convince me, but the creatures that dwell within the shadows of Darkmourn do not follow my command. Even if I agree, they still have their own desires."

Faenir nodded to Marius in understanding. "I propose a covenant, one that protects our kinds from one another. There would be rules, ones on which we must each agree upon, rules that we would each be responsible for ensuring that our respective people would follow or be punished."

Marius stood from the table and faced Faenir. Both creatures equalled each other in height. But in power? That was not determined. Faenir did not wear his crown by choice. Our presence in Marius's domain was threatening enough; being recognised as a King would paint a bigger target on his back. Faenir was not the King of vampires, nor humans; he had made that clear to me it was not his desire.

"I am interested," Marius said finally, reaching out for Gildir, who did not flinch as the vampire drew a nail across his skin. A bead of deep blood blossomed beneath his mark. Marius drew a finger to his lips, eyes rolling back into his head, as he savoured the taste of an immortal.

Jak stood, unable to resist the smell of the blood; even I struggled to stay in my seat.

"If your suggestion is to work, it may take time," Marius murmured.

"Then we are blessed to have such a concept in the palms of our hands." Faenir lifted an arm and held out a hand in offering. "Are we not?"

Marius looked again to Jak, searching for agreement. The freckles across Jak's nose wrinkled beneath the scrunch of his nose. I readied myself to hear his refusal, but then he nodded.

"There is much to discuss," Marius said, turning back to Faenir. He glanced towards his extended hand as though it held dangers.

You have no idea, I thought as I watched Marius reach for Faenir.

The King of Death and the Lord of Night clasped hands in agreement.

It was done. It had worked.

Auriol relaxed back in her chair, tension evaporating with a sigh. I looked towards her, feeling a swell in my hollow, still chest. It was such a human feeling I almost forgot my lust for blood.

The covenant had been agreed between two great powers of death to cherish life above all else. Yet, as we raised a glass of blood, or wine, I could not ignore the voice that lingered in the far reaches of my mind.

Just as it was Auriol's suggestion for the evening's meeting, it was Faenir's to refrain from mentioning the halflings in our conversation. They were our failsafe, as he had explained. Only time would tell if this agreement would work. And if it did not, there were means to deal with the traitors even if it meant we would be reduced to ash.

For rules, as each of our presences proved, are destined to be broken.

PART THREE
ALPHA OF MORTAL FLESH

Rhory & Calix

ALPHA of MORTAL FLESH

BEN ALDERSON

Please be aware this novel contains scenes or themes which readers may be triggered by. This book deals with the topic of domestic abuse, gaslighting, physical abuse, mental abuse and control.

Other content warnings are as followed:

Toxic relationships, murder, loss of family members, death, abuse, manipulation, anger, grief/grieving, depression, profanity, adult scenes, adult themes, blood/gore, mentions of suicide.

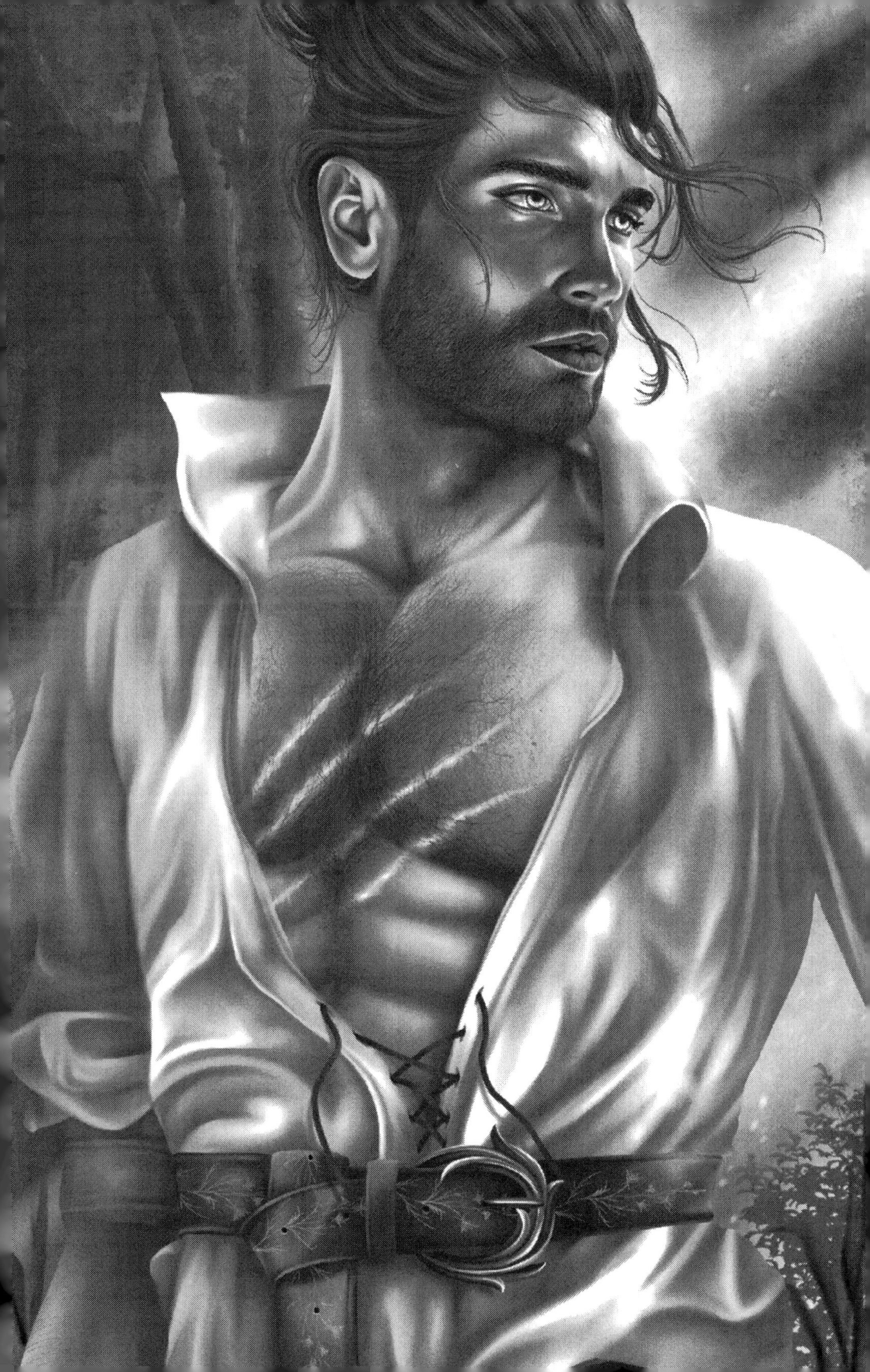

ALPHA OF MORTAL FLESH

Rhory & Calix

1

25 YEARS BEFORE

Drip. Drip. Drip.

Warm droplets of blood fell across my upturned face. If I closed my eyes, it would have been like looking up into a storm cloud as it unleashed an abundance of rain. But this wasn't rain. Rain was not sticky. Rain did not tack in my eyelashes. Rain did not taste like old copper coins.

I pinched my eyes closed, flinching with every drip that splashed against my skin.

Drip. Drip. Drip.

I couldn't look away. Mumma's eyes were wide and all-seeing above me. Her face was squashed into the floorboard that separated us. Dead eyes peered through the gap, bloodshot and discoloured.

Mumma had such pretty eyes, even when they sang of death.

Drip. Drip. Drip.

I clamped my hand over my mouth. My mind commanded me to scream, but I couldn't. The dead would hear me. Just as I could hear them sucking, slurping. Pappa would have slapped the back of my hand if I ate like that. Smacking one's lips whilst chewing loudly on a meal, it was not good manners. The dead didn't care what noises they made. They had no manners when draining their prey.

Drip. Drip. Drip.

As Mumma's blood dribbled through my little hands and spread across my lips, I couldn't help but ponder why the dead craved blood with such desperation. The copper tang was vile. My stomach cramped, and I felt as though I would be sick. I wished to spit it out and scream and scream. But I couldn't. No. No.

As I stared deep into Mumma's eyes, I remembered what she said as she hid me beneath the floor. *Keep quiet, Eamon, don't make a sound.*

Drip. Drip. Drip.

My skin itched where her blood spread. I wanted to scratch at my face and rub away the gore, but it was the only thing smothering my scent from the vampires. My hair was drenched by it; my eyes were blinded by it.

Drip. Drip. Drip.

Where were the Crimson Guard? They would come. They should come and save us.

Drip. Drip. Drip.

The blood ran dry by the time the vampires finished drinking from my parent's corpses. So much time passed that the blood no longer bothered me. I was frozen to the spot, looking up through the gap in the floorboards as they creaked with the monsters' movement.

Drip. Drip. Drip.

One of them boasted about the taste of Mumma's blood. Fresh peach, it said. The other thought Pappa tasted like vintage wine. I thought they would leave, but they didn't. They were in no rush. No one was coming for them. I recognised the familiar sound of a chair scratching against the floor as they took a seat. Whilst I was hidden beneath the floorboards, covered in Mumma's blood, the monsters sat at our family table and laughed with full bellies.

Drip. Drip. Drip.

They laughed.

Drip. Drip. Drip.

They sang.

Drip. Drip.

I had been hiding for so long, I felt as though my body would never break free of this position. Spiders welcomed me into their domain, crawling over my bare feet and blood-coated face. I used to hate spiders. Now they were my only comfort.

Drip. Drip.

The monsters leave, not because the Crimson Guard had come for them, but because dawn had arrived. With the light of day, it ushered them out of my home. Mumma watched me. Her skin looked blue. I used to think she had pretty eyes, but now the whites were grey, and the blue looked like it bled out from their circles.

Drip. Drip.

Light spilled in from above. I lifted my hands before my face. They were not red as expected. It looked as though I dipped my hands in rust. The blood had dried to a flaking brown stain. The Crimson Guard were still not here.

Drip. Drip.

Night came again. Sick covered my chest and face, mixing with Mumma's dried blood.

Drip.

Three times, the world above the floorboards had brightened with daylight. It was on the fourth day when my saviours came. They came when there was nothing left to save.

Drip.

I hated them.

Drip.

Vampires. The Crimson Guard.

Drip.

They were all monsters.

Drip.

I hated them.

Drip.

I...

I...

2

I DO LOVE YOU, Rhory Coleman.

It's strange how such words hurt far greater than the physical pain left in their wake.

Eamon always seemed shocked when he spoke them to me. His piercing sky-blue eyes would glisten with tears of regret. He would look from his hands to the part of my body he'd chosen to mark during his blackout of rage, and whimper as though he was the one with a body riddled with pain. For such a towering broad man, in those moments he was more akin to a child looking between their favourite broken toy and the hands that tore it in two. I recognised remorse; I thought. If only for a moment, which made the bitter taste of fault hard to swallow.

He never said sorry. No. It seemed Eamon could not allow such a dirty phrase to grace his lips.

All of Darkmourn would tell me how kind he was. Which made the understanding of *why* he acted with such ferocity towards me confusing. Kindness caused bruises, broke bones and drew blood.

I couldn't pick up bread from the bakery in town without being told how wonderful Eamon was. Even during my frequent visits to the local medic, they'd remind me about the many great things Eamon had done for them. It was those encounters I found most difficult to hear when I was forced to lie about how two of my fingers even became shattered in the first place.

That is one nasty bruise you've got, Jameson would say, pointing his finger towards my swollen eye.

I would smile and exhale the lie with such ease, one would have thought it was rehearsed. *The door picked a fight with me and won.*

Jameson would tut, smile and dismiss it. And no matter how many times I visited, or how many aliments I collected across my body, he never questioned me. No matter how ridiculous and fictitious the excuses became.

Of course, it was Eamon who left those marks, but I couldn't ever say that. Not out loud. And it wasn't because I was scared about what he would do to me. The days of fearing him were long gone. It was what others would say. And how I would be looked at, like a crazed fool, for even suggesting Eamon Coleman had such a capacity for evil.

No one would ever believe Darkmourn's leader of the Crimson Guard—the man tasked to protect every living creature from the monsters of the world—was that very thing to me.

My monster.

My devil.

My husband.

But he loves me, I reminded my reflection. Which made sense, because love had only ever caused me pain.

My fingers had only recently healed, making my movements awkward as I tied the velvet laces of my scarlet cloak around my neck. The splint and cloth bindings had been removed days ago, and I couldn't ignore how skeletal they looked. Thin from the lack of use, like the fictional description of a witch's finger. Fitting, I thought.

The thick band of iron and gold spun around my emaciated finger. I hardly spared it a thought before my heart dropped into the pit of my stomach. There was a time looking at the ring filled my chest with breath, and my mind with the wonders of a future with the man I loved.

Now, it simply reminded me of the harsh truth of my reality.

"You must be looking forward to getting some fresh air, Rhory."

I turned my back on the scratched glass mirror to regard Mildred, who stood in the foyer before me. Mildred had been in my life for as long as I could remember. The Coleman residence wouldn't have been the same without her stout, hunched body shuffling across the waxed oak floors. She was part of the furniture, as Father used to explain. Which I always disliked, because Mildred was far more than that. She was, to me, the soul of this house with its countless rooms all empty as the next.

I almost folded in on myself at seeing her again.

"Eamon called you back?" I asked, not meaning for my voice to sound as relieved as it did.

"He did indeed," she replied with a smile that tugged the wrinkled corners of her mouth upwards. One thing about Mildred, she had been old for the twenty-seven years of my life. She had the same nest of wiry, grey hair and a face that bore more resemblance to the surface of a melted candle.

"Poor soul!" She rushed towards me, waddling like a duck on two of the same feet. "Bed bound for all those days. I almost demanded to be let back in so I could care for you myself! But, of course, that would not have been necessary since your darling husband has kept you fed, bathed, and rested. Lovely man, that Eamon. You are very lucky to have him."

I allowed Mildred to fuss over me, not stopping her as she reached towards the poppy-red curl of my hair that fell before my eye. With a motherly brush of her finger, which smelled of pine oil and lemon, she moved it out of the way.

At least I knew what excuse Eamon had spread about my imprisonment whilst my fingers had healed. It had been a long while since he blamed my absence on an upset stomach. Mostly because when he hurt me, the damage was easily concealed. This last time was a lapse in his judgement, one he would likely not allow again.

Or would he?

"Never mind that," I said, lifting my fingers to her shoulders. They felt like dough in my hands. I wanted her to envelop me in her arms so I could melt into the safety of her motherly aura. "I'm glad you are back. How about I fetch you a tea before you start, and you can update me on all the books you have devoured during your time off?"

It was Mildred who had encouraged my love of reading. From when I was a child, she had smuggled books past my mother, and we had discussed the stories in great detail. Reading was an escape, one that we both thirsted for.

Mildred waved me off, pushing me with unseen strength towards the main doors at the end of the shadowed foyer. "Go, Rhory, get going with you. Your skin looks as pale as death itself; some sun might do you well. Bring some of that lovely glow back to those cheeks of yours. If you would wish to entertain an old woman, you can do so tomorrow. But today, I would be happier knowing you were out of this house."

"Are you sure?" I asked, almost expecting she would go back on her word.

"I'd rather you were not under my feet whilst I caught up on weeks' worth of neglected dust since I last stepped foot inside this house." She drew the feather duster from her belt, unsheathing it like a sword. With a great swing, she clobbered my arm with its soft end. If she noticed me flinch, she didn't mention it.

"Go, go, go."

My back thumped against the door. The chill of the autumn breeze slipped through the cracks, tickling across the back of my neck as though seducing me with the promise of the *outside*.

"Will you stay for supper?" I asked, hopeful. *Please say yes, please say yes.*

Mildred pulled a face, one that would've been best carved into the expression of a statue in mid-contemplation. "Dearest, I have a feeling I'll be cleaning from now until sunrise tomorrow. Although Eamon wouldn't allow that, would he? Darling man, the moment he walks in that door, he will relieve me of my duties. Such a caring soul."

I shook my head, the same pesky curl of red hair falling back into place over my eye. "Indeed."

A cloud passed behind Mildred's honey-coloured eyes. For a moment, her brows furrowed in wonder, searching for something that my face must have given away without me realising.

"Is something bothering you?" she enquired, eyes trailing me from head to foot. "If you are still feeling under the weather, I could see you back in bed, and then I'll rustle up some soup for you."

From the pits of my belly, I dredged up a mask to adorn. One that eradicated weakness. An expression which oozed—*I am fine*—in abundance. "And what, I leave the patrons of St. Myrinn without a visit from me? How could I possibly deprive them of my presence? After the past couple of weeks, I am surprised the infirmary has stayed afloat without me."

Mildred's face cracked into a smile. "Only if you're sure. If Eamon thought I sent you on your way whilst still unwell, he would have my guts for garters. He cares greatly for you, you know."

I took Mildred in my arms before she had another moment to contemplate the wince that shattered my mask of strength in two. There would've been a time, years ago, that I buried my face in her forest of silver hair and inhaled the scents that clung to her. I was far too tall for that now. So, I rested my chin atop her head and held on tight.

"It's just so good to have you back," I said.

"Oh, my darling." She expelled a breath, her concern melting away like butter on a hot spoon. "I've missed you too."

Over her shoulder, in the distance of my home's entrance, sat the tall-standing mirror. I caught my reflection in it. Wide, unblinking eyes stared back at me, with a mouth drawn tight, all exposed by the golden glow which encompassed my hands.

Light spilled beneath my splayed fingers as though I held onto a star. A shard of sunlight grasped in my very palm. The magic was cold, like dipping my hands into the bottom of a frozen lake. But there was nothing painful about the light. It was peace. An emotion that reminded me of the sensation of snow falling upon my upturned face.

The brushing of flakes as they tickled across my skin, before melting and leaving the icy kiss as a physical memory.

My power didn't always feel like this. Sometimes it pained me. Stung like the needle of a bee. Burned like the wick of a flame on skin. Shattered like finger bones beneath a hammer—

"Go on, get out of my sight, sappy fool," Mildred cried, pulling away suddenly, drawing me from the sudden, horrific memory.

The magic spluttered, winked and died out, all before she would've noticed anything was amiss.

"Don't tire yourself out too quickly. A woman of your age shouldn't be overdoing herself," I said, gripping the brass knob of the door with a firm hand. I forgot, for a moment, of my aching fingers. It shot a stab of pain up my arm. I drew blood as I bit down on my tongue to stop myself from yelping. It made hiding my pain easy when Mildred whacked me with her feather duster once again.

"Cheeky boy." I heard the mellow laugh in her tone. "If you were any younger, I would've made you eat soap for such a remark."

I yanked the door open, allowing autumn to spill into the foyer with its crisp wind. Leaves the colour off rust, wine and gold, shot towards and skated across the waxed flooring with ease. Mildred barked out a swear word that would've made the drunkest patron of our local tavern look like a saint.

"Who needs their mouth washing out now?" I retorted, skipping out of the threshold before a third smack of her weapon of choice reached me.

Mildred's deep rumbling chuckle followed me down the three steps from the door, along the overgrown pathway of shrubs and reaching rose bushes, and out onto Darkmourn's main street. The childish joy it filled me with lasted until the screeching garden gate slammed closed behind me.

I hated lying to Mildred. It pained me. But I knew I could never burden her with what truly happened behind the closed doors of my family's home. It would break her, and I needed her whole. Selfishly, if it meant lying kept her laughing and… safe, safe from his gaze, then I would keep it up.

It wasn't like lying was a new concept between Mildred and me. I had been doing it to her since as long as I first learned to do so much as crawl.

Mildred didn't know of my magic. My heritage, beyond being the only son of the founder of Darkmourn's Crimson Guard, was a secret. Which, Mother would tell me, was very different to lying. Keeping secrets came from a place of protection.

When in reality, I knew otherwise.

It was tradition, when I navigated Darkmourn, to glance towards

Castle Dread. I found myself drawn to the ominous place, like a moth to a flame. It sprouted in the distance. A dark scar across Darkmourn's landscape, and memory. A smudge of gloomy stone, stained-glass windows and the remnants of scaffolding from the recent renovations. Every year, it seemed the castle grew bigger. Swelling like the pregnant belly with more *halflings* imprisoned inside its walls.

It was a place my mother swore to keep me from.

Eyes down, trained on my scuffed boots, I pulled the red cloak over my head and moved with speed.

The sooner I reached St Myrinn's Infirmary, the better.

3

I REMEMBERED the day I was asked to identify the lumps of torn flesh and bone, as though it were yesterday. It wasn't the memory that haunted me, but the way death invaded my senses. How it clung on, refusing to give me any reprieve.

It had taken months for the smell of my mother's bloodied corpse to leave me. *What a mess.* That had been my first thought as Jameson, our family's personal physician and lead practitioner at St Myrinn's Infirmary, pulled back the blood-stained sheets and revealed the parts of the body beneath.

Then there weren't any other thoughts that followed. Only a mess of grief as the reality of what I looked upon crashed over me.

There was a slick, wet sound as the material tugged at ruined flesh, pulling loose bits back with it to expose the hollowed-out insides and the ribbon of guts that dribbled out onto the metal table. I'd vomited down my wedding suit. Over and over, my body expelled the day's joy and festivities. How could the happiest day of my life end in such a way? Ana Coleman, my mother, was laid out on a metal cot with skin of alabaster splattered with gore and grime. Only hours before my mother had raised a glass to me and my husband. Now she was scattered across a metal table with her legs beside her and her chest open and empty of what should have been inside.

As I stared down at her, vomit spread down my chin and tears sliced scars down my cheeks. I wanted Father to be with me, but his mind was already broken, and Jameson feared what would happen to him if he saw his wife like this. Eamon had kept him in the hallway beyond this room. I could still hear him. My father, whispering his pride and happiness to Eamon, whilst not knowing where we were and what had happened.

My father's mind had not been his own for years by this point. Mother had cared, night and day, for him. Now she was dead, I feared what would happen.

I'd vomited again. My throat burned with the bile conjured from heavy contractions gripping my stomach.

Eamon didn't waste time in convicting a rogue vampire for my mother's brutal murder. Days later, the nameless vampire was hung for all of Darkmourn to see as he screamed and pleaded his innocence. He hung from the noose, pale neck pinched by thick rope, as we all waited for the sunrise to come and claim him.

And, the worst part was, I had believed his innocence. I believed the vampire, who supposedly tore my dearest mother to shreds, because of the... blood.

There was so much of it. I couldn't understand why a vampire, whose requirement for blood was limited by law, would leave so much wasted. The foyer to my home was covered in it. Hours later, Mother still oozed blood across the metal table in the cellars of St Myrinn's Infirmary.

To me, it made little sense.

I had told Eamon my concerns, and it was the first time he showed me the monster that lurked beneath his perfectly crafted illusion. He had gone from the man who stole my heart to the one that held it in his hands and squeezed as he refused to listen to my disbelief. Eamon said I was blinded by grief. That I was a fool, stupid, pathetic—all because I refused to believe her killer was brought to justice.

The vampire was killed anyway.

He died, screaming for his innocence, and the case was closed.

"Keep going," the sleepy scrap of a girl mumbled from the bed before me. The crack of her tired voice drew me out of the painful memories. I gave into its siren pull, thankful to be reminded that it was all behind me.

"Where did I get to?" I said, tracing my finger across the page of the book resting across my lap. My mind had wandered to old memories, making it hard to locate where I had stopped. The girl, Sallie, giggled through a yawn as she watched me struggle.

"Is the story boring you to sleep, or are you just that tired?" I asked.

Sallie did a good job at widening her eyes as she pleaded. "It is the best story ever. It could never bore me!"

I closed the book as another yawn overcame her. Her milky teeth were stained a blush pink. Even the corners of her little mouth had the remnants of dried blood from her last coughing fit.

"Good," I replied. "That is the most precious thing about stories.

They wait for you. And this one will not run away. So, how about you get some sleep, and we can pick up again tomorrow when I am back?"

"Will you come back *this* time?"

Her question had the power to break me. I leaned forward, chair creaking beneath me. The book became an afterthought as I deposited it on the sheets crumpled beside her. Then I took her hand closest to me, the one that always seemed to reach out when I read to her.

"Sallie, I promise."

She blinked heavily, turning her head to the side until she faced the ceiling instead of me.

"You promised me before, and then you didn't come, and... and. And you forgot about me."

Phantom pain speared up my two fingers. It was only a hint of the agony I had felt when Eamon shattered the bones, but it was enough to have me hissing through my teeth. "I could never forget you, Sallie, never."

"It hurts, you know," Sallie said, a jewelled tear rolling down her swollen, colourless cheek. "No one could take the pain away but you. And you left me."

Sallie didn't know of my magic. Nor did any of the other patients that frequented St Myrinn's Infirmary. The ones whose discomfort I softened, and pain I blanketed, during my visits. If anyone knew, I would have been thrown into Castle Dread, never to help anyone else again.

Sometimes, that didn't sound like such a bad outcome. To be taken from this life and kept from returning. But that was a selfish wish, one I squandered quickly.

"Well," I drew the word out, offering Sallie a warm smile. "How about I don't promise you again since I'm the world's worst promise-maker. Instead, I would suggest a contract between me and you. One which legally binds me to return to your side come morning and finish that story you love so much."

Sallie scrunched her eyes closed. It was her way of pretending she couldn't hear me. "Con-ter-acts..." I almost chuckled at the way she echoed the word back to me, fumbling over its newness. "Mummy said they're for old people and vampires. Not for me."

She wasn't wrong, I had to give her that.

"A deal?"

Sallie peeked one eye open and shook her head defiantly, golden hair spilling around the feather-down pillow that propped her up in the bed.

"Okay then, I suppose there is nothing I can do—"

Sallie's eyes burst open as a gravelly cough clawed itself out of her throat. Her sudden jolt tore my hand forward. But she didn't let go.

Not as the whites of her eyes bulged a dark red, and blood splattered across the sheets before her.

"It's okay, Sallie. It's going to be okay." I opened myself up to Sallie's emotions. Taking a deep breath in, my magic roused deep in my core; like a butterfly cracking out from its cocoon, it awoke in a flurry of spreading wings.

I *felt* her turmoil and pain. It struck me like an arrow into my chest. Claws cut into my lungs, echoing the very agony Sallie was currently lost to.

This was what I visited St Myrinn's for. For this very moment, and the peace I could offer. It made me feel less useless. My being here gave me purpose. I recognised how selfish it was, but still, I returned. Because if someone couldn't take away my pain, how all-consuming and haunting it was, then I could at least do it for others.

I had been visiting St Myrinn's since Mother was killed and Father was moved here to be cared for daily. It took a year for his mind to kill him and return him to my mother's side in death. Even without him here to visit, I came anyway. It made me feel closer to him.

Sallie cried out, gasping for air as the coughing fit subsided for a moment. I sunk the fangs of my magic into her hurt and dragged it out of her like a dog to a bone. Sallie's coughing spluttered and calmed. Blood spread across her lips, dribbling down the sides of her mouth as though she was a vampire and had just completed a feed. But it stopped bursting from her ruined lungs the disease slowly ate away at her.

The small lines on her face melted away. I watched the hint of a smile return to her pink-stained mouth and even her eyes seemed to widen without effort. Slowly, as the storm of her pain continued to thrum within me, Sallie relaxed. Laying back into the pillow, her eyes drew heavy. I separated her exhaustion from her agony and fed it back to her.

I removed her terrible emotions, allowing more pleasant ones to replace them in their void. To give Sallie some form of peace, I harboured the pain and claimed it for my own.

∽

I didn't wish to leave Sallie's side, but the sky beyond the infirmary was growing dark. If I didn't return by nightfall, Eamon would come and find me himself. And that thought alone had me dropping Sallie's hand and leaving her in the grips of painless sleep.

Jameson must have sensed my presence as I reached the main atrium of the building because he raised his hand in farewell. At least, that was what I thought before he called out my name.

"Rhory, can I borrow a moment of your time?"

My rushed steps slowed as I glanced hesitantly between the deep maroon sky and Jameson, who watched me expectantly.

"I really should be getting home…"

"Just humour me, for a moment."

I swallowed a hard lump in my throat. "It's Eamon, he doesn't like me staying out past dusk."

Jameson's grin beamed at that. "I hardly imagine there is any human, vampire or witch, that would wish to see you harmed knowing the man that waits at home for you."

It was not those who lurked in the darkness of night that scared me, but the very man who waited in the warmth of my home. But I couldn't say that. And I hardly thought using Jameson as an excuse for why I was late would prevent the lashing of Eamon's belt.

That very excuse didn't work the last time.

"What is it I can do for you?" I asked, unable to keep the annoyance from my tone. If Jameson noticed it, he didn't react.

"I've been meaning to ask this of you, but of course, you have been… out of action for a while." He looked to my broken fingers, marvelling at how well they healed. I could almost hear his inner praise, gloating to himself about how his work alone had seen my fingers heal straight and with little scarring.

Unlike Mildred, Jameson didn't need to be told I had fallen ill with a stomach sickness. He was so blinded by infatuation for Eamon, he would never have questioned my disappearance being a result of my husband.

"I have something for you. Here." He plucked a torn, aged parchment from the pocket across his chest and held it out to me between two fingers.

"What is it?" I caught the hint of scrawled, untidy writing between the folds as my firm question spilled out of me.

"He said he needs aid with his grandmother. The note explains it. Pleasant chap, he was. He said he heard of the wonders and effects your visits have had on our patients at St Myrinn's and wishes for you to offer the same for his grandmother."

"Grandmother," I echoed.

"Auriol Grey. She lives in a cabin outside of Tithe's old wall. Directions can be found on the note, as well."

Tithe was an old village that was once surrounded by a wall that kept the monsters out and the humans in. Since the covenant between the humans and vampires had been signed in blood, there was no need for such separation of our kinds. Which was odd why Auriol Grey deemed Tithe a place to live when it had been abandoned many years ago.

"You said a man gave you this?"

Jameson nodded. "Indeed. Didn't catch his name, but he said you would know him."

I pulled a face which screamed how untrue that statement was. "And you are confident he asked for me?"

One of his plucked brows raised and his lips screwed into a pout. "You can't turn it down."

"Pardon?"

Jameson stepped in close, looking towards a gaggle of bed maids who rushed past us in a cloud of hoods and aprons. "Rhory, funding for St Myrinn's has dried up. Since Lord Marius has suggested the opening of healing facilities at Castle Dread, it seems the more mundane route of medicine is being forgotten."

I shook my head, unsure how the Lord of Vampires, the creature that ruled over the undead of Darkmourn, had anything to do with me and this note.

Reading the confusion across my face, Jameson continued. "Money, Rhory, I have been offered an abundance of it if you visit Tithe and provide care for this Auriol Grey. Your father had always been such a supportive sponsor for our infirmary, but I'm afraid the reserve he left us is running out. This." He jabbed at the note currently strangled within my fist. "May just save us."

There were so many things I wished to say. I felt the excuses tingle across the tip of my tongue, begging to be released. Except, I didn't have the courage to speak my mind the way I wished.

"I'll think about it," I replied finally.

"Rhory—"

"Tomorrow," I said. "Give me until tomorrow. Of course, I would need to pass this by Eamon. If I was to go elsewhere, it would make him... worried. He likes to know where I am."

Jameson bowed his head, the dull light from the brass chandelier above casting a ruddy halo across his balding scalp. "Certainly. Although Eamon is a man of pure heart, if you explained that an elderly woman requires your company to ease the suffering of age, then he would not refuse you the visit."

He would, if he so wished.

"Tomorrow," I repeated then turned on my heel with a gentle yet blatant air of dismissal around me.

"Or you could stick your hand into your pocket, Rhory Coleman, and show some of that generosity that has seemed to perish alongside your father?"

I stilled. A cold rush flooded up through my body, and back down again, until my legs were ice and my bones as dense as stone.

Behind me, I heard Jameson fuss over himself and the words that his lack of self-control spilled. Not that I hadn't contemplated this myself before Jameson had said it. It'd been three years since my parents had died and the money which was left to me had fallen into the hands of my husband. Even if I wished to dig my fingers into the piles of coin that came with my family name, I couldn't.

Eamon had it locked, with the key secure and far away from me.

Guilt coursed through my body and soul. It was thick as tar and as hot as boiling oil. Just as I had that fateful night when I stood in this very building looking at the brutalised body of my mother, I wished to scream.

"I've spoken out of line," Jameson mumbled beneath his breath.

"Forget about it." I couldn't bear the silence that would have followed if I didn't say something.

"No, I was wrong to say such a thing."

"I will do it," I said, speaking from the raw place of guilt that would make even the strongest of men do another's bidding. "Tomorrow, I will go to Tithe. For your sake, I hope it gives you what you desire."

"St Myrinn's thanks you," Jameson said, reaching out and squeezing my upper arm. My body cringed at the contact. "As it always has, and always will."

4

101 YEARS BEFORE

"AURIOL GREY, *do not deviate from the path.*"

Perhaps it was my anger that diluted Marius's warning, or was it the rush of sickness that spread across my stomach? Regardless, I didn't *fucking* listen. I would scorn the day that bastard wolf bit me. From the moment its fangs sank into my arm, tongue lapping at the oozing blood, I would never forgive myself for stepping one foot off the path.

My mind was elsewhere as I exited the grand doors of Castle Dread. I never looked back when I left Lord Marius's domain, not because I feared what I would find but more because I just hated the ambiance. It was all cobwebs and dust and was so fucking cold.

Night still dominated Darkmourn, but dawn would arrive soon. I had always found the early hours of day the most beautiful, but today I was far too angry to care for its splendour.

It had been ten years to the day when the covenant between living and death was signed, and my brother had let me down. Arlo had promised to return to Darkmourn with his husband, Faenir, to celebrate our success.

Darkmourn had never been the same since that fateful day when the treaty was signed.

But, not to my surprise, Arlo had not arrived. I had waited in the presence of vampires, peering meekly into my glass of red wine, trying to convince myself it was not blood whilst trying to conjure a good enough excuse not to drink it. I had hoped Arlo would distract my hosts from seeing me tip the wine into the nearest plant pot, but that didn't happen, because Arlo never arrived.

Arlo was older by a few years, but I couldn't help but feel as though he was younger. He had spent his youth protecting me, and then nothing. Of course, that was not my story to tell. My story was far more... mundane.

I kicked through the wisps of mist which clung to the castle's outer grounds. Ghostly shadows danced across the floor, obscuring the gravel path that crunched beneath my feet. I was far too focused on my disappointment from the evening's festivities to notice when the crunching of my footfalls ceased. I didn't notice when the ground had grown soft with dewy grass.

Not until the wolves were upon me.

As the first rumbling growl echoed though the dark, I protectively cupped the doughy swell of my lower stomach. The baby was only a handful of months old, but I already felt overwhelmingly protective of them, now more than ever.

The wolf parted from the darkness as though it was born from it. Shadows clung to the thick hide of dark fur. Silver droplets of saliva fell from its open jaw, every single pointed tooth flashed in my direction.

I had been aware of the shadow hounds that lurked the grounds of Castle Dread, wolves that were cursed alongside Marius all those centuries ago. Sometimes I could hear them sing all the way from my home on the outskirts of Tithe. Even now, as the wolf padded on large paws towards me, I couldn't help but admire its deadly beauty.

The mist had devoured the stone path I had stupidly stepped from. Even if I wanted to find it, I couldn't, not without taking my eyes off the creature which prowled towards me. There was only one I could see, but I heard the rest. They waited in the shadows, watching as a diligent crowd viewed a show. Yipping and snapping jaws were their applause as this brave beast picked on me.

I drew the stake from my hip, one I always kept close when breaking bread with the undead. Thrusting out the point towards the monster, I bent my legs and readied myself to run or fight.

"Now, now," I cooed, as though speaking to a child. "Steady yourself, pup."

The wolf snarled, splashing drops of saliva across its thick neck. It must have been the alpha of its pack. Even I recognised the command rolling out of its jaws; the sound kept the other wolves at bay. This would be the one to attack first, the rest of them would have the scraps.

I was fully prepared to drive the stake into the beast's neck and run. If that was what it took, I would do it. Gods knew I needed to get out some of my frustration from the evening. And it was not fear I felt. Instead, I buzzed with adrenaline that resulted in a strange sense of calm to settle over me.

I took a deep breath in and gripped my weapon tighter.

The wolf's eyes burned like molten gold. It stopped moving, gaze flickering from the stake, then back to my face.

"Yes," I sang. "That is a good boy."

It walked back and forth in a line, regarding me with narrowed eyes as I praised it.

"I am going to leave you in peace, just as you are going to leave me. I'm afraid you'll not be feasting tonight."

Damp grass flattened beneath each careful footfall backwards. Every time I put my boot down, I longed to hear the tap of stone beneath it.

One hand was still outstretched, pointing the stake towards the wolf whilst the other held the faint swell of my stomach.

I would have told Arlo tonight that I was expecting. All day I had pondered what his reaction would be to finding out he was to become an uncle. Part of me convinced myself that the news would make Arlo visit more often. And yet he did not show. Disappointment was an understatement. It was fury that I truly felt, even if I didn't want to recognise it. Which was why, if this creature lunged, I would be ready. In some sadistic way, I longed for it. At least something about the evening would be exciting.

"You wouldn't like the taste of me anyway," I said softly, refusing to take my eyes off the creature. "It has been days since I have kept down a meal, and longer since wine has passed my lips. I would be unseasoned and bland. Trust me."

The wolf tilted its large head. For a moment I caught some recognition in its expression.

"My mistake," I said. "I should have focused on where I was going. The nurse at St Myrinn's told me my brain may grow as foggy as a bog, the larger the baby grows."

What did I think to achieve, having a conversation with the unholy creature before me? Of course, it couldn't understand me. The only conversation it knew was hunger. Something I sympathised with since I found out I was with child.

The wolf followed at a distance. It never allowed too much space to grow between us. Just when I believed it would forget me and move on, it padded forward.

"You're such a handsome beast," I said, swapping my tactic to one of compliments. If the wolves were anything like Lord Marius, stroking their ego would work enough as a distraction.

I was wrong.

"Such big eyes you have—"

The wolf threw itself through the air, shadow and night blending as one. I stumbled back, falling over my feet as the monster's jaws split wide. Time slowed, and I refused to scream. All I thought of was my baby and the stories I prayed to tell it.

I bit down into my lower lip, blood bursting across my mouth as though I chewed down into a ripe fruit. The wolf latched onto my wrist. At first there was no pain, only the lapping of a rough tongue against my broken skin.

Then the agony came, like wildfire. It overcame me. Devoured me. Enough to set each of my bones ablaze.

I swung my spare arm wide. It took two powerful stabs for the stake to drive into the wolf's skull. Only then did it release my wrist. I had to pry it from me, then push the weight of the dead wolf from my lap where it rolled over into a heap at my side.

The pain was murderous, but I refused to scream. I wouldn't cry out for help.

I fell back across the ground as the beast's burning poison spread from my wrist, up my arm and across every muscle and through every vein. The rest of the shadow hound's pack still watched in the darkness. I felt them, stalking and waiting. In time they would come for me, picking the crumbs and leftovers from the beast I had just killed.

Soon enough, the sky was blessed with pink and oranges of a new day. I watched the sun rise, hand on my belly and arm covered in my blood, waiting for the wolves to come and claim me.

They never did.

I picked myself up. The ground swayed. I blinked, and I was in Darkmourn, walking the streets before the world truly woke up. I blinked again, and I was in the forest, walking the path to my home where my beloved waited for me.

Relief flooded through me as I caught a flash of the cottage through the trees. A home he had built for me, for us. The trance I was in broke as I lifted my knuckles to the door and knocked. Before they rapped against the door for the first time, I noticed something. The pain was subsiding. My wrist, although covered in blood, showed no marks or wounds.

My skin was pink with fresh skin.

Although my outer body was fine, my insides still ripped and tore. Even the baby, deep within me and no larger than a bean, stirred. The cramp followed swiftly, spreading across my torso and stomach. I almost excepted the spotting of blood between my thighs. I had been warned about what the pain could mean if it ever happened. But this was different. It was not the baby.

It was... hunger. And not for blood.

This hunger was primal. And my stomach longed for the soft chew of flesh.

5

Darkmourn was an entirely different world at night. When the sun set beyond the town, and the human residents of Darkmourn curled up in their beds behind locked doors, it was the dead who came out to play.

Vampires roamed the night as though it belonged to them.

I pulled the cloak tight around myself, fending off the evening autumn breeze. It ruffled through my hair, so cold that even my teeth chattered, no matter how I tried to grit them closed.

All around me, fellow humans clambered on chairs and short wooden ladders to prepare the town for its evening dwellers. One by one, the stained red glass lampposts were lit. The glow bathed the streets in an ominous haze of scarlet.

My pace quickened, and I buried the coiling discomfort Jameson's words left within me as I raced towards my home. I was late. And I dared to contemplate how Eamon would react when I returned, far past the time he allowed me out.

I thanked my lucky stars that Mildred would be waiting. At least she would hold off the wrath, perhaps even dilute it.

The red glow cast down from the many lampposts was not the only thing that changed when the sun departed and gave way for its silver counterpart. If I navigated the poorer, more clustered streets on the outskirts of the town, I would have found deep bowls of blood left upon doorsteps. Offerings to the undead, who left bags of coin as thanks.

Blood faired more than money. Its value was steep. But it was illegal to trade, not that it stopped those humans, in desperate need, from taking a knife to their skin and flaying it just enough to fill a mundane kitchen bowl.

Because of its illegal nature, there was no saying how much coin the vampires would leave as payment. It was a gamble. One I was thankful I would never have to partake in. Even if Eamon had cut my ties to my family's fortune, he would first kill me than let me bleed for the undead.

Up ahead I heard commotion coming from the White Horse. The tavern was named after the steed which Death was believed to ride upon. Humans stumbled out into the street, shouting thanks to the landlord inside with stomachs full of beer. Many still carried the glass tankards home with them, not wishing to waste the pricy drink just before the town's curfew was about to begin.

Inside the White Horse, the landlord would be busy swapping out barrels of ale for those containing blood farmed from livestock. Cows, pigs, chickens… it didn't matter what animals were slaughtered to provide the vampires something to drink, as long as it was not human.

Darkmourn's history suggested the vampires had spent years drinking blood from rats once the humans were kept safe within their walled dwellings, like Tithe. It was that fact which was part of the motivation for the Covenant to even be drafted.

They needed us. So, it was best to live in harmony than separated.

The Coleman's residence came into view as the drunk singing from the White Horse's patrons faded behind me. I picked up my pace into a slow jog, as if it would stop me being late. Perhaps, if Eamon saw me out of breath and hair plastered to my forehead with sweat, he might just be more understanding.

The wrought iron gate screamed on its hinges as I pushed it open. My skin crawled at the sound, alerting even the undead within the towering three-story houses that spread down my street, that I had arrived. If they could hear it, Eamon would have.

By the time my hand pushed against the black-painted door, my heart was in my throat threatening to strangle me. I hesitated. If only for a moment, nails digging into the already flaking paint.

Breathe.

If only someone had the power to take my emotions away. To remove my fear as I entered my home.

I was welcomed by the glorious scents of cooked food. One step inside the foyer and my mouth was watering profusely. The air's warmth suddenly made me feel overheated in my cloak.

"Eamon, I'm home," I called out, grappling with the lace ties at my neck. I hated how meek I sounded. My voice barely echoed in my home, as if it knew I was not worthy of it.

Silence reverberated around me. I stretched my mundane hearing out for signs of Mildred's heavy shuffling of her feet. By the smells that oozed within the dusty air of the foyer, dinner must already have been prepared.

"Mildred?" I called out, inhaling the pungent aroma of roasted chicken, potatoes baked in thyme and carrots bathed in spices. How I missed her cooking. For a moment, I forgot I was late, or the events at the infirmary had even happened. The smell alone conjured a smile and a hearty rumble of appreciation in my stomach.

"She isn't here." A voice purred from the darkness. "I dismissed her hours ago."

Dread traced its frozen finger down my spine as a shadow departed from a doorway to my left. There was once a time when seeing Eamon at the end of the day was something to look forward to. We had been in these exact positions before, except I would have run across the foyer and thrown myself into his arms.

Now, it filled me with dread. I'd much rather run away from him than towards him.

But you can't, I reminded myself.

I recognised his smile first. Wide and proud, displaying almost all of his perfectly lined white teeth. Shadows peeled from his face slowly, exposing his cobalt eyes followed by the high cheekbones and the subtle divot in his perfectly carved jaw.

Eamon's jet-black hair was slicked back away from his face. The flames from the chandelier above revealed that he had recently washed, which was not uncommon after a day's shift running the Crimson Guard. He would clamber into the scalding water of a bath, only to leave it once it had grown tepid.

He wore a loose white shirt, unbuttoned down to reveal the hard chest that lingered beneath. The sleeves were rolled up to his elbows, and in his hand he gripped the stem of one of my father's beloved wine glasses that had been blown for him as a gift during his marriage to my mother all those years ago.

We only ever drank from them when we had something to celebrate, which unnerved me beyond imagination.

"Mildred said she was staying for dinner—"

Eamon strolled towards me so suddenly I flinched backwards. The door pressed firmly into my spine.

"Are you disappointed, Rhory?"

I swallowed hard, not wishing to inhale too deeply. Eamon was so close I couldn't ignore the heavy aura of lavender that seeped off his skin and hair. It was sickly. The type of smell that burned your nose and throat on the way down.

There was a time I used to long for his scent. I would've found it on my hands and my clothes and smile at the thought of the man that left it on me.

Now it haunted me, alongside the sweeter memories.

I wished to say otherwise, but I retorted with a single word. "No."

Eamon's gaze stalked me from head to foot. I felt the question glossed across his thin, red lips. "Where have you been?"

"I—I..." My chin dropped to my chest. It was easier to look at my boots than into his bright, inquisitive eyes. "Jameson asked to speak with me. I told him you would've wanted me home, but he was adamant he needed a moment of my time."

I almost closed my eyes in preparation. Scrunched them closed to protect myself from the hand he would likely raise in punishment.

When nothing happened, I hesitantly glanced towards him. Eamon rocked back a step and lifted the lip of his glass to his mouth instead. "Well, I am sure *your* tardiness will not be a bother again. Come, let us eat. I have some good news I wish to share with my darling husband."

Eamon swept away, back towards the door he had slipped from. Our dining room waited on the other side, which led straight through to the kitchens at the back of the house. By the smells of food that weighed heavily on the lower ground of our home, I knew the table had likely been set.

Eamon must have sensed my hesitation to follow. It was not by choice that I didn't fall into step behind him. My body had betrayed me, refusing to move from my place against the door.

"Come." His command was short. Unignorable. I almost relaxed at the sudden anger behind it. I expected it with the first thing he had said to me, not the last. The presence of the nasty side of Eamon had finally shown itself, and I felt at ease. It was better facing the monster than waiting for it to strike.

"It would be nice to eat before the food grows cold," he said.

My bones creaked as I took that first step away from the front door. Still, I couldn't muster a word to say to him.

The dining table stretched the length of the room. It was so large it could have seated at least twenty dinner guests. Mother and Father used to host Darkmourn's nobility at the turn of every season. The feasts they put on, with the help of Mildred of course, would be all that was spoken about amongst their friends, and Father's colleagues at the Crimson Guard. Our wine cellar would be raided, only to be filled again by the time the next celebration begun.

All those chairs had been removed from the room, leaving only two left. One for me, and one for Eamon. He could have sat anywhere but chose his place directly beside me. Every time his knee brushed mine beneath the table I stiffened.

"Are you not going to ask me about my day?" Eamon raised Father's celebratory glass up as if he was hinting the question I should ask.

I always found that my movements were rigid around my husband. Whatever I did, whether it was cutting potatoes on my plate, or walking at his side... I did so carefully. Carefully was certainly the right word.

I lifted the napkin from my lap and dabbed at the gravy that stained the corner of my lip. I did so because Eamon grimaced as though disgusted by my table manners. For my husband, there was never a hair out of place or food on his face. He was above that.

"I trust it was good, considering we are drinking one of Father's oldest wines and from his special glasses," I replied, forcing a smile that never reached my eyes.

Eamon took a deep swig of his drink. He didn't stop for breath. Not until the flakes of red wine sediment was the only thing left at the bottom of the glass. "Seven of our most wanted killers were found today."

What little appetite I had faded immediately. "Seven?"

"Yes. Those vampires think they can hide from us," Eamon barked a laugh, "Pathetic."

"Will they go to trial?" I didn't know why I asked it when I knew the truth. Darkmourn had not seen a public trial since Eamon took over my father's role of Head of the Crimson Guard.

"There is nothing to discuss. They are murderers, Rhory. Monsters. One less vampire on Darkmourn's streets is one step closer to purifying it completely."

"One less killer, do you mean?"

Out of the corner of my eye, I caught Eamon shift his head around to look at me. I felt it, two eyes boring holes directly through my skull. "Oh, Rhory, of course that is what I meant."

"Good," I replied, mouth dry.

"Is that it?" Eamon slammed his glass down upon the table so hard, I was surprised when it didn't crack. "You know how restless my days make me, yet you do not share my celebration."

"I'm sorry," I said calmly.

"Do you even care for the effect this job has on my—"

"Temper?" I interjected, shocked that the word slipped past my walls of inner control.

Eamon's face flushed red. His chest rose and fell dramatically, and he didn't blink once as he regarded me.

But he didn't tell me I was wrong.

Before he could act out on the thoughts that clearly poisoned his mind, I raised my glass that had been left untouched until now and spoke with as clear of a voice as I could muster. "To my husband, Eamon Coleman, may he be successful in his *hunt*."

"Did you doubt otherwise? Rhory, I *shall* always be successful." He didn't join me in my cheers. Instead, he clutched his knife and fork as though they were weapons in his arsenal. "It would all be much easier if the Crimson Guard didn't have to pass authority through Lord Marius. The clean-up of the vermin of this town would be completed in one bloody night. Instead, I am forced to wait."

Eamon's hate for the vampires seemed to have begun after the brutal murder of my mother. But I believed it started long before that, although he would never have admitted it.

The Crimson Guard, under my father's lead, were a force that protected both the humans and vampires of Darkmourn. Since Eamon had sunk his nails into them, it seemed the scales of justice always tipped towards the living.

I would never have said this aloud, but I thanked the stars that Lord Marius had his say in those the Crimson Guard brought to justice. His sway would have saved many unnecessary slaughters at the hands of my husband.

If my father could see the obvious corruption of his Crimson Guard, he would roll in his grave.

"I can still see the bruising," Eamon said, after finishing the mouthful of roasted chicken in a matter of a few chews. I thrusted my hands beneath the table, not wishing for his eyes to linger on my fingers.

"They are fine," I blurted, feeling the heat rise in my cheeks. "No one noticed."

"But what if they did?" Eamon asked. "You should have stayed at home until it had completely faded. I shouldn't have let you out today."

The tension rose between us, sharp and electrifying as a summer storm. I panicked, knowing what was going to come. With Eamon, I always waited on the edge of a knife, unsure which side of his tolerance I would fall into.

My knuckles rapped underneath the table as I drew them back out again. The golden wedding band caught the amber glow of the burning sconces as I reached across and took Eamon's hand in mine.

His mouthed parted at the sudden touch. I gripped on, feeling the urge to let my power out to calm him. But I restrained myself, not wishing to know the truth of how he felt inside. Instead, I let my emotion bleed out of my wide eyes as I leaned towards him.

"Darling," I whispered, the word only for him. "I am fine. No one noticed, and if they did, they wouldn't question the bruises as it would seem everyone in Darkmourn knows I am cursed with a never-ending spell of clumsiness. I thank you for letting me out today. I needed it."

Eamon contemplated my words in taut silence. His teeth ground against one another, the muscles feathering in his jaw, as though he chewed what I had said, determining if he could taste sincerity or the lie that it actually was.

"I'm good to you." It wasn't a question, but a statement. One with no room to contest, not that I would dare.

"I know you are. You have my best interests at heart."

Slowly, Eamon's raised brows lowered and the tension around his mouth smoothed out.

I wondered if he saw how my other hand shook as I raised it to his face and placed it there. My fingers tickled against the short hair at the side of his head. Grey strands of hair mixed among the black, exposing the ten years of age Eamon had on top of me.

"What you do for me, for Darkmourn, is something undeniable. I know you will complete your work and we can celebrate together."

Eamon exhaled the remaining tension out of his nose. The corners of his lips turned upwards, giving me a glimpse of the man that I had met all those years ago. How his cerulean eyes had been so kind. He always looked at me as though I was the only person in the room, the world.

What I thought then was admiration and love revealed itself to be a nasty possessiveness. My skin crawled at the knowledge.

"You should get some rest," Eamon said, pulling away from me. I allowed my hands to drop awkwardly to the table as Eamon stood from it. He took the empty glass, and the burgundy bottle of wine in each hand. "Come morning, I'll be gone by the time you wake."

Relief swelled in my heart, but I bit down on the inside of my lip to stifle it from showing on my face.

"You work too hard," I said.

"Someone must. I have a town to protect." Eamon moved to the door. My eyes tracked him as though I was his prey, hiding in the shrubs as my predator passed.

"Will you be joining me tonight?" I asked, holding my breath for his answer. It was rare for Eamon to share a bed with me. I couldn't remember the last time his body had provided me warmth at night, not that I wished for him to do it.

The dread of where he would sleep was only another worry that cursed me during the day.

"Not tonight," Eamon replied.

I tipped my head in a bow.

"I *do* have your best interest at heart, Rhory," Eamon muttered, his gaze landing on my hand, to the fingers he had not long broken. "Everything I do is for you."

"I know," I replied. It was all I could say.

Eamon paused, as though he had something else he wished to say to me. Then he moved from the room, his knuckles white as he grasped the neck of the bottle.

I waited, steadying my breathing, and listened to his footsteps move through the foyer, up the curved stairway and across the landing far above the dining room. Only when the door closed to his personal room did I relax.

Even if this peace only lasted until I next saw him, I held onto and cherished it.

6

It seemed autumn had awoken today and chosen war.

As I walked towards my destination, the note Jameson gave me gripped in my fist, I battled through the season at every given turn. Frigid winds nipped at my ears. I drew up my red cloak and held the hood over my head for protection.

Leaves billowed from the bending trees lining the path towards Tithe. They were like the heads of spears, all varied shades of golds and jewels. I was attacked from all angles and couldn't do anything to stop it.

There was no denying the beauty of the season. It brushed the world in a shade of warmth and gave it a song of crunched leaves beneath feet and the whistle of winds.

I would've preferred to enjoy the drop in temperature if I was inside my home, curled by the fireplace with a book from Mother's personal library. Perhaps with a glass of mulled cider to warm my stomach and one of Mildred's muffins laced with maple syrup and topped with pumpkin seeds. Except that would mean staying home, and the guilt that woke me hours before had made me draw the note from yesterday's clothes before it forced me out the door towards the forgotten town of Tithe.

I remembered Father telling me stories of when the great wall that surrounded the commune of Tithe—keeping its occupants safe from a world ravaged by vampires—was finally torn down. He had only just been born and didn't remember the events first-hand. But, like much of Darkmourn's twisted past, the story of its destruction was added to the ever-growing storybook. Those tales were repeated to children with caution and warning. His parents had recited the tale to him, just as he'd recited it to me.

During my youth, me and my friends would run to Tithe, clamber over the rubble and used the deserted town's streets and buildings as our very own playground. We whispered about the elves that used to frequent Tithe, even daring one another to touch the tree in Tithe's centre, the very place those fey beings were told to have come through.

The elves had not been seen in years, but I imagined adults still used their memory as a warning to children who misbehaved.

Do not be naughty, or the fey will come and snatch you from your bed only to replace you with another.

Of course, my parents never used such a concept to threaten me into behaving. Not when my mother was the very product of such a thing. Not completely human, and not completely fey. They called them halflings, but history called us by another name: Witches.

But being called a *witch* was no different to being a devil. The stigma was one of the many reasons Jak Bishop, eternal mate to Lord Marius—collected halflings as though they were coins, and he was a magpie with a thirst for gold.

Witches belonged to Castle Dread. Unless you knew how to hide from its all-seeing eye. Father, being the Head of the Crimson Guard, had the power and authority to keep those prying eyes from me and my mother. But it was not his will that kept us from Castle Dread. When his health declined, it was Mother who kept her strong thumb down on me, ensuring I was safe.

If it was not for her, I would have been taken years ago.

The only other trusted with the knowledge was the man who stole my heart. Eamon. At first, we all believed he could be trusted. Oh, how wrong we were.

No one knew what happened to the witches. Only that they never came back. It was as if the castle devoured them whole, keeping them from ever returning to Darkmourn's civilisation. Eamon reminded me of that often. So much so that I no longer took his words as a threat, but silently begged him to make it a promise.

The life Castle Dread offered must be better than what currently faced me at home.

I found the supposed path towards the cabin on the outskirts of the woods, just shy of Tithe's shattered stone-wall. Never had I ventured in this direction during my adventures to Tithe as a child, and nor had anyone else by the look of it. The woodland had overgrown; the worn path buried by debris, roots and foliage.

I wrestled myself through the skeleton hands of trees. One particularly low-hanging branch dug its spindly fingers into my cloak and threatened to pull it clean off. It seemed nature didn't fear the Crimson

Guard. Anyone else would have seen my cloak and kept their distance, which was why Eamon ensured I wore it at all times. The colour marked me as his. His property. And I knew what he would do to me if he ever saw me without it.

I was thankful for the thin twig that snapped back and slapped across my lower face. It caught my chin quickly, drawing me out of those dark thoughts.

The deeper I drew into the woodland, the darker it became. By the time I found the cabin and the low light spilling beyond the windows, it was like dusk had fallen over the world whereas it must have only been midmorning.

Who would live this far from everything? The thought haunted me as I closed in on the front door. It was shrouded in climbing vines that had turned a russet brown.

Someone must have dwelled inside because the chimney pot billowed with a dark cloud of grey.

I knocked on the door, three times. The sound of my raps filled the woods. It was so loud that birds burst from their hidden perches in the surrounding trees. For a moment, far off in the distance, I was sure I even heard the howl of a wolf.

Silence responded. No one called out for me to enter, nor could I hear movement from inside.

After a moment, fear reared its ugly head. How stupid could I have been? One note, and the promise of funding for St Myrinn's. That was all it took to draw me here. Standing before the derelict building, I couldn't fathom how anyone inside could give so much more than a single coin to the infirmary.

The note crumpled in my shaking fist. I grew uncomfortably hot so suddenly. The warmth spread across my neck, my palms and even coiled across my chest until sweat blossomed across my forehead.

I almost missed my footing as I stepped back from the door. The sound of leaves screeched painfully loud as I stood on them. I winced, pinching my eyes closed as I continued putting distance between me and this place, my footsteps heavy with trepidation.

Father always said I was too trusting. He was right in so many ways, but it seemed even he was cursed with the same blindness as I.

Just as I was prepared to leave with haste, my eyes wrenched open at the sound of groaning hinges, and the door before me swung inward. A man stood in the threshold, an expectant glint in his eyes. Eyes the colour of molten gold.

"Rhory Coleman?" His deep voice seemed to silence the woodland entirely. I felt the power of his voice travel up from the ground beneath my feet. It took me a moment to discern that he had said my name, for it sounded so familiar on his strange tongue.

I swallowed hard, unable to draw myself out of the dark gilt pools of his eyes. Instead of forming a word in reply, I raised my arm out before me, the crumpled note suddenly exposed between my fingers.

It was all I could muster to explain my presence.

"So, Jameson *is* a man true to his word," the stranger said, one corner of his mouth drawing up into a smile. When he finally removed his gaze off me, I felt my marrow soften. My knees almost gave way from relief, or disappointment, I was not sure.

The man looked to the crumpled note, one thick dark brow raised. He didn't glance back to me when he said, "You better come inside."

"I am here to see Auriol Grey," I said, trying to force as much confidence into my voice but failing; it cracked as though I was merely a boy. He smiled at that. Smiled. Full lips, shadowed by an equally full beard, tugged upwards. It was the colour of warm sand, as was his hair which was drawn back into a bun at the back of his head.

"Yes, that is what I requested." Lines creased around his eyes as they naturally narrowed.

Heat rose in my cheeks at his reaction. "Is she here?"

"As I have said, come inside and I will take you to her."

Once again, as he spoke, the world grew silent. As if it, like me, hung off every word. There was a slight bit of annoyance radiating off him, proven by the subtle roll of his unnatural eyes.

"Excuse me," I said, chin lifted as my gaze widened whilst I regarded him. He currently blocked me from entering. Unless he wished for me to barrel through him, there was no way I could enter the cottage.

As though breaking out of a trancelike state, the man stood to the side of the doorway, giving view to the rickety hallway his broad figure had blocked. He waved a hand, mimicking the gesture a lord would have provided to the person they wished to dance with.

"After you," he murmured.

My limbs felt as though they waded through mud. Each step towards the cottage's threshold was stiff, but I managed it. I almost excepted the stranger to move out the way, but it seemed he wished to make me as uncomfortable as possible. His sly grin only proved my point, his gaze tracking the red glow which stained my cheeks.

He was tall. Very tall. The man had to bend his neck forward so the top of his head didn't bump across the doorframe. As I stepped in, shoulder almost brushing his abdomen covered in leathers, I had to bite back my gasp.

Instead of biting it back, I choked on it.

"Do you know my name?" he asked, expectantly.

"Unless you have told me and I ignored you, then no."

Disappointment winced across his expression, if only for a moment.

"Calix," he whispered beside me, body leaning in to ensure I could hear him. "Perhaps knowing my name will dampen your *fear* of me."

I could have sworn his nostrils flared. Was he… sniffing me? I stumbled forward, slightly out of his reach, only to feel more unnerved knowing I had my back to him.

"Should I fear you?" I asked, stumbling over my words enough to answer him.

"That would depend."

I didn't dare look at him, but I could certainly feel his gilded eyes boring holes into me.

"Calix, you gave Jameson the summons for me, did you not?" I said.

"Indeed, I did."

I forced a smile, feeling the skin on my face crack with the involuntary expression. "Then may I see Auriol? Or do you insist on keeping me from her?"

Calix exhaled slowly, sizing me up from head to foot. "Straight ahead. You'll find her on the last room to the left."

"Is she… troubled?" Troubled? My brain was so *scrambled* that was the word I had picked!

"Terrible," Calix replied, his smile slipping until his face looked as though it had never known a smile before. "Go on ahead. I will follow right behind you."

I suspected he thought that would make me feel more at ease, when it had the complete opposite effect.

Wishing to get this visit over with, so I could return to Darkmourn with enough time to scold Jameson and get home before Eamon ever knew I had been here, I paced away from him. All the while, I felt his stare on my back.

My skin erupted in gooseflesh, and the hairs across my arms stood on end. As if sensing my discomfort, Calix emitted a low chuckle from behind me.

Except, it sounded more like a growl than anything else.

7

NESTLED within the mounds of feather-stuffed pillows and ivory bedsheets, an ancient-looking woman waited. Her piercing eyes tracked my every movement. One was as bright as the summer sky, whereas the other was the richest of browns. Wire-framed spectacles balanced on the end of her neat nose; an old book laid out across her lap.

I could not place an age on her. She looked older than anyone else I had seen before. Her face was set with deep wrinkles, her hair the colour of freshly laid snow. Even her skin seemed translucent and lacklustre of colour. If it wasn't for the life that screamed out of her two mismatched eyes, I would have believed she was merely a corpse.

She leaned forward from the pillows. They had been stacked behind her hunched back to keep her upright. I could have sworn I heard every joint and bone creak in song.

"We have a visitor, Grandmother," Calix called out from behind me, making me jump.

The old woman, Auriol Grey, looked me from boot to head and exhaled a raspy breath. "What good is a visitor who doesn't bring me cake?"

My cheeks stained a deeper red, if that was even possible.

"Hello, Rhory," Auriol said, voice as clear as her gaze. "I should thank you for coming all this way to see me."

I stood in the doorway, hands clutched before me to give them something to do. My entire being buzzed, knowing that Calix lingered behind me. Like an unwanted shadow, he haunted me.

"Jameson passed me your summons but didn't specify how I could help."

Auriol narrowed her eyes, screwed her face up and patted the bed at her side. "Please, come closer. My hearing is not as famed as it once was."

As if sensing my hesitation, Calix leaned in and whispered, "Don't worry, her days of biting have long passed."

I couldn't dispel the feeling of deep-rooted discomfort. My soul was screaming at me to conjure some excuse and leave, never to see this place and the strangers it harboured again. But the note weighed heavy, back in the pocket where I had returned it, reminding me of why I had come here. Although, looking around this room alone, I couldn't understand how the Greys had the means to offer St Myrinn anything worthwhile, especially not money.

Calix hovered in the doorway as I paced towards the old woman, his prickling gaze never once left me.

Dust riddled the air. My nose tickled. The two bay windows at the west of the room were closed, and the curtains half-drawn. I almost had the mind to open them, if not for Auriol but for my sake.

No matter how I felt, the closer I got to the bedside and the smaller Auriol became in her perch, the more I felt unhappy that she was here.

"Forgive me if I come across rude, but this doesn't seem like the best place for someone of your... experience to live."

Auriol's laugh rumbled like a storm through a forest. The sound was more feral than pleasant. "Wise choice of words, dear boy. I could almost hear you say *age* beneath it."

I looked down, feeling as though I was scolded by a teacher.

"Is there a problem with my home? From where I sit, it is pleasant enough. Calix sees I am well cared for here."

I couldn't help but read the undertone of her comments and the mockery that seemed to thrum between Auriol and her grandson.

"Then may I ask why you called upon me?" I asked, unsure where the confidence came from. "I mean, the note was clear. You asked after me by name, it could have been any of the infirmary's healers or carers, I am simply a volunteer at St Myrinn's—"

"I am well aware of your charitable position, Rhory Coleman, and that is not why I asked after you. I hear you deal in pain, and I have an abundance of debt which I wish for you to collect."

Auriol looked down the length of her nose at me. Her bright eyes were alight with knowing. I couldn't hold them for long. Instead, I focused on the book in her lap, trying everything not to expose the panic that overcame me.

"I'm sorry, but I don't know what you are referring to."

"*Halflings* have a scent you know," Auriol said, nose twitching. "It is enough to fill a room, pungent and demanding."

I stumbled away from the bed. Instinct fired through me, scolding my urgency to get away from them. But there was nowhere to go. Calix stood in the doorframe, his broad body blocking it entirely. And there was the imprisonment that Auriol's gaze locked me in. It was heavy and all-encompassing.

"Do not worry yourself, Rhory. One's secrets are best kept by those familiar with secrets. Yours are safe here."

I shook my head, swallowed the lump in my throat and forced the fakest of smiles which cramped my cheeks. "You've got it all wrong. I think my coming here has been a mistake. I am sorry, Auriol, there is nothing I can do to help you."

"Calm yourself down, child," Auriol scolded. In a strange way, her clear annoyance silenced me. The feeling of displeasing her outweighed my worry. "Your panic is going to give me a migraine. Calix, make yourself useful and fetch some tea."

"Grandmother," Calix said, a hint of warning in his tone.

"*Leave* us to talk."

I glanced to the stoic mountain of a man. He ran a calloused hand through his length of honey coloured hair. A strand fell from the messy bun and draped across his face. "Would that be wise?"

"Your presence clearly unsettles the poor boy." Auriol waved a hand in dismissal, as though sending a dog away to its bed. "Shoo. Away with you."

Calix must have sensed the pure command in Auriol's ancient voice. He fell into the shadows of the corridor at his back. It seemed the cottage muffled his footsteps, swallowing any sound beyond this room entirely.

My blood thundered through me, echoing in my ears as though someone held a shell up to them. They knew. They knew what I was. But what caused my body to crash with anxiety was wondering what they would do with the information. I felt as though I had walked into a cobweb of iron with my eyes closed.

"If it is money you want from me…" I spluttered, ready to divulge that her attempts would be in vain because Eamon had my fortune locked in a chastity belt of his own design.

"Do I look like I need money? As I have told you, I have pain which I desire a reprieve from. Age is not kind. And you, from my knowledge, are the only one to offer me relief in the comfort of my home." Auriol gestured to a chair pushed into the corner of the room. "Fetch that and take a seat. I'm sure you would love to get this over with and return home before dusk."

I hardly took my eyes off the strange old woman as I followed her command and brought the chair close to the bed's side. The legs screeched as they were dragged across the worn wood-panelled floor.

"How did you know?" I asked, whispering as if the whole of Darkmourn could have heard.

Auriol reached out a hand across the bed. Her skin exposed rivers of blue and red veins hardly hidden beneath. Her arm was as thin as a twig, the skin melting from the bone as it sagged down with gravity. "I knew your mother, Ana, very well. In fact, there was a time when I knew you, Rhory Coleman. Although it would seem you *have* forgotten that all together. That is the curse of youth. Your minds are so busy that you can hardly remember what you ate for supper the night prior."

My mind had numbed to most of what Auriol had said. It was focused solely on the name she had spoken.

"You knew my mother?" I repeated. It wasn't a question for the old woman, but I felt the need to say it aloud myself to make it real.

"I did." Disgust tugged down at her face. For a moment, even the whites of her eyes dulled as her mood sobered. "It was terrible to hear of her..." Auriol hesitated. "Passing."

Grief always stalked me, lingering just over my shoulder. In moments like this, it struck hard and sudden. A sharp pain stabbed in my chest as Auriol continued speaking.

"I kept her secret. I promised to take it to the grave but did not expect it was her grave in which I spoke of."

There was no knowing if Auriol lied just to make me trust her. But the way her emotions clouded across her face, it was familiar. It seemed the old woman was whisked away, to another place and time, whilst the memories of my mother haunted her.

I couldn't find the words to reply. Instead, I took her hand in mine. It was frail and as fragile as glass. "Then I trust the same sentiment applies to me."

"Certainly, although I hope it is my grave this time. That is if Death ever deems me worthy enough for the peace it keeps from me."

Somewhere in the darkness of the forgotten cottage, a stove kettle whistled to life.

"Well," I said, lifting the lid on the power within me. Gold light emitted from my palms and the light seeped into Auriol's skin. There was something so freeing of showing my power so blatantly. I felt... seen. "Until Death lays their judgement on you, let me take some of this pain away. It would be a wasted journey if I left without helping."

Auriol's pain was physical. I closed my eyes and sensed her discomfort. It lingered between every joint. There had been others at St Myrinn's whose body suffered with age, who I had helped during my visits. But nothing compared to the agony I took on for this woman. Hers beat any others by tenfold. It was so sudden and sharp. I sucked in an inhale and dug my teeth into the soft skin of my lip.

We sat in silence. Auriol grinned as I clawed the pain out of her body, whereas I felt as though mine was being torn apart. In the darkness of my closed eyes, I felt my skin split open. My bones cracked and splintered. Whatever this pain was that ruined her small, hunched body, I could have sworn it was inhuman.

"That is more than enough." Auriol pulled her hand out of my stiffened fingers, breaking the link between us. I didn't know how much time had passed, only that a silver tray of bone mugs waited on the cabinet beside me, milky tea still steaming with heat.

Calix had been in the room, all without me knowing. My skin prickled at the thought.

"Thank you," Auriol purred. It seemed she sat up straighter. The apples of her cheeks had flushed with vitality. "I cannot remember the last time my body felt so... light."

I went to stand, but the room swayed.

"And I do not think I can recall a time that I felt so much pain," I said.

"One grows used to it," she replied.

I couldn't imagine how that was possible. "St Myrinn's can help you. Give you longer term relief. I really think it would be wise if you—"

"That won't be necessary," Auriol interrupted. She pulled a face, which deepened the lines across her forehead. "You know, I always found it strange why Darkmourn's infirmary was named after the woman who sold my brother out and nearly had him killed."

"Pardon?" I spluttered, head still pulsing with agony.

"Ignore me," she replied, ending the conversation before it had even begun. "My brother would be the first to tell you I was always the hardest to please. Tea?"

I passed her a cup and picked one for myself. The handle was warm to the touch. The liquid inside was almost clear, all besides the flakes of mint that had fallen to the bottom. I inhaled the smell, desperate to have the tea wash away the lingering pain Auriol had left inside of me.

"I see you are familiar with the ball and chain? Your husband, Eamon is it?"

Her mismatched eyes had settled on the golden ring on my finger. I had the urge to place my hand between my thighs so she could not look at it. One mention of Eamon, and I felt the atmosphere shift. I wondered if Auriol sensed it too.

I nodded, noticing a dull, diamond encrusted silver band on Auriol's finger. "It is. What would be the name of your spouse?"

"Unimportant," she replied, smiling over the lip of her cup.

"That is a strange name, and where is *Unimportant*?"

"I ate him."

Tea burst up my throat, choking me. By the time my breathing had steadied, my eyes streamed with tears and my lungs were raw.

I waited for her to tell me she was joking, but that never came. Instead, she continued sipping her tea with eyes never once leaving me.

Until now, I had wondered why I didn't remember Auriol. If she was a family friend, why had she not been around? Surely, I would have remembered such an eccentric soul. Or perhaps that was the very reason I didn't recognise her. Maybe my mother distanced herself because of the very nature of this old woman.

"Dusk arrives in the wood long before it graces Darkmourn's clear skies," Auriol said, filling the silence. "I think you should take leave. I wouldn't wish for Eamon to be forced from his duties at the Crimson Guard just to come searching for you."

"There is nothing more I can say to entice you to visit St Myrinn's?" I asked, placing my half-drunk tea back on the tray.

"Rhory, I am going to *pay* the infirmary just to keep me out of its grasp. I am fine, just as I am and have been."

I smiled, itching to leave. Her mention of providing donation to the infirmary was enough confirmation that my good deed was well and truly over. "I thank you for your generosity on St Myrinn's behalf."

My eyes kept falling back to the shadowed door, expecting Calix to be haunting it once again.

"You know where to find me," I said, offering her a smile as I edged away from the bed. I knew, deep down, if she reached out for me to visit again, I would soon burn the letter than do as it asked.

"Oh, I certainly do. But I will not require sending a summons for you again. You'll be back soon enough."

Her words unsettled me.

"Goodbye, Auriol," I said, finality plainly clear in my tone.

I could see the doorway now, right at the end of the corridor beyond the room. Calix was nowhere to be seen, but his presence lingered in every shadow.

"You have her eyes," Auriol called out, the sorrow I had seen earlier returned once again. "So bright, an emerald would be jealous."

I resisted the urge to lift a hand to my face.

"Your eyes are the windows to your heart. Not your soul. That is guarded, I can sense that."

I held Auriol's stare, not wishing to be the first one to drop it.

"There is much I must protect myself from." As soon as I said it, the pressure constricting around my chest loosened a little. Auriol would not know what I meant by that, but I did. And I had never given myself the chance to voice such a thing before.

"Stay safe, Rhory Coleman. There are monsters in Darkmourn, the likes that you could not even comprehend."

"I know," I replied as I took my leave.

I paced out of the cottage into a world of brass and golds and ran directly back towards the very monster Auriol warned me about. All the way back to Darkmourn, through the dense underbelly of the wood, I kept my pace up. Not because of my desperation to return home. It was the lurking presence at my back that kept one foot in front of the other.

Only when I exited the expanse of towering pine trees did I finally hear it.

A howl.

8

THE LAST I REMEMBERED—BEFORE sleep claimed me—was the muffled humming of Mildred from somewhere within my home's many rooms. To stop myself from thinking about Auriol and Calix, or the impending doom which had settled in my chest, I latched onto the sound and allowed it to lull me into a false sense a security.

Until I was woken, abruptly.

There was no discerning if a noise pulled me from my dreamless slumber, or it was the sudden silence that spiked fear from me. What I knew with all certainty was something was terribly wrong. Bolting upright in the bed, the sheets barely covering my modesty, I scanned the dark room. The only light was that of the ominous red glow of Darkmourn's nightly world, spilling through the thin crack between my heavy stone-grey curtains.

Disorientated, my panicked eyes waded through the shadow cloaked room. My heart dropped when I saw my bedroom door was wide open. Then the thudding organ split in two when my eyes fell to the man slumped on the reading chair, legs spread and elbows leaning on both armrests.

"After everything I have done for you," Eamon said. His voice was deep and slurred. I could practically taste the sting of spirits that muddled his speech.

I gripped the sheets and brought them up to my chin. It did little to still the wave of shivers that overcame me.

"Eamon," I rasped. "What is wrong?"

He leaned forward, the chair creaking in protest. The crimson glow bathed over his twisted, furious face. His eyes were wide, his mouth pursed and colourless. In his hand he gripped the neck of an almost empty bottle. It seemed more like a weapon in his hold than the means to quench a thirst.

The cold claw of dread sliced down my spine.

"I am going to ask you something, and you are going to make sure you tell me the truth. Do you understand?"

I couldn't form the words to reply, so I nodded meekly. Eamon caught the way my gaze flickered to the open door. He stood, swayed on his feet, then walked to it. It closed with a sickening click.

I knew what was coming. Even though my mind raced for what possibly had caused the lashings I would soon endure, I could foretell the future in those moon-wide eyes of his.

"Is Mildred still here?" I asked, not wishing for her to hear the screams Eamon would soon conjure. Part of me didn't fear it. In a strange way, I almost felt relief that it was finally here after weeks of tiptoeing around the *beast*. I'd soon rather face it, knowing it would be short-lived and a time of reprieve from the pain would follow.

"No," Eamon snapped.

I swallowed, cold relief creeping across my neck like the grasp of a hand.

"I saw Jameson this evening and imagine my confusion when he told me you had not visited St Myrinn's today. My Rhory would never deviate from my rules. I had the right to call that man a liar. But is he? A liar?"

Bile crept up the back of my throat. It took great will to keep it at bay whilst I contemplated my answer.

"I can explain…"

Eamon shot forward, bottle raised high. His shout rocked the very rafters of our home. "Then do so!"

I threw my hands up and shielded my face, squeezing my eyes shut. Only when no pain followed did I open my eyes and lower my shaking fingers. When I did, I saw the long-drawn smile sliced across Eamon's face.

"Jameson asked a favour of me," I replied, voice trembling as violently as my hands. "I tried to tell you last night—"

"Quiet." The mattress creaked as Eamon added his weight to it. No longer did he hold the bottle like a knight wielding a sword. Now he simply sat. "He said. But what I cannot understand is why you agreed. You owe that man nothing. I am your husband, not Jameson. How is it you seem to follow the commands of others who do not care for you, yet you choose to ignore me? Do you wish to hurt me, Rhory, is that what you are trying to do?"

"Not at all." I reached out for him. Eamon's shoulders had hunched forward, as though his misplaced sadness weighed heavily on them.

As my fingers brushed his sticky, sweat-damp shirt, Eamon struck forward. He had tricked me into his trap, leaving me helpless and uncovered. Eamon threw his arm towards my face. His entire weight must have been behind it, because the force blinded me. Pain burst across my skull. I didn't register how my teeth were jammed into my lower lip until the blood nearly suffocated me.

Suddenly, Eamon was atop of me. His powerful legs straddled either side of my waist, pinning me down. Not that I would fight him. It never ended well when I did that, so I kept still and compliant as my lip bled wildly into my mouth.

Eamon leaned down over me, teeth bared like a rabid dog. The bottle was still gripped in his large hand, the other had taken my wrists and pinned them above my head.

"Care to tell me where you went?" he growled.

I turned my head to the side as much as I could, wincing at every drop of spit that touched my skin.

"Tithe," I spluttered quickly, repeating the word in hopes it was clear. I didn't wish to give him any reason to prolong this punishment. "Tithe."

"You little fuck!" Eamon slammed the bottle into the bedding beside my head. I felt the power in the thud that vibrated through every feather-stuffed in the mattress. "I give you rules to protect you and you defy me. It is though you ask for this. You like it, don't you? Is that why you disobey me, because you beg for me to punish you?"

Tears sliced down my face as a sob wracked through my chest. All I could do was lay there, whilst my torn lip spread blood across my teeth, and the skin of my wrists bruised beneath Eamon's grip.

"No, no. Please," I begged. "I don't mean to upset you."

"Don't you?" He knocked his forehead into mine and held it there so all I could look into was his wide, feral sky-blue eyes. I inhaled deeply, drawing in the sickly scent of lavender mixed with whatever harsh spirits he had drunk. "What was so important that you picked Jameson over me? I should kill him for—"

"He told me of an old woman, someone who needed me to visit to help with their pain!" I shouted, arching my back to try to force him off of me. He held firm. Eamon knew what he was doing, holding my hands above my head. It stopped me from reaching for his skin and manipulating his emotions.

One touch and I could absorb all of his fury. I could take it away and fill that void with something kinder, more loving. So many chances I had before this night to do that, and only once had I ever tried.

I still bore the scars across my shoulder blade, left from his teeth.

"What woman?" His voice had calmed as he asked the question.

I felt the need to hold her name back. To protect it somehow. Names had power, that much was known. Revealing such a thing would turn Eamon's sights on them.

But maybe...

"She knew Mother and Father," I spat, almost laughing at the revelation. If Auriol had known my family, she must have known Eamon. He had been as much a part of it since I was barely eight and he the eighteen-year-old, fresh faced, Crimson Guard recruit who was more known for being my father's shadow.

Eamon completely released my wrists. He rocked back, still straddling me, but instead stared down at me with an inquisitive look across his face. "Who was it?"

"Auriol Grey," I started, watching the recognition deepen the lines across his furrowed brow. "Jameson gave me a note that said she requested my visit. He said she would fund St Myrinn's, and I was made to feel as though I could not turn it down."

"Auriol," Eamon seethed through gritted teeth. I cared little for the spit that flecked across my face. "Grey."

"Yes," I said, "Eamon, I'm sorry I didn't listen. I should have told you—"

The glass bottle smashed across the wall at the head of the bed. I barely had the time to close my eyes before shards rained down over me. Something wet dropped over my cheek and I hoped it was the spirit in the bottle, and not my blood.

Hands gripped down on my throat, thumbs pressing into my soft skin. I gasped like a fish out of water, but the air refused me. My lungs burned with fire.

"You'll never leave this house again," Eamon bellowed. I only hoped someone beyond the house would hear and come to help. I often thought that, but no one ever came. "I gave you freedom you never deserved, never!"

Stabbing jolts of pain exploded within my skull. I reached up and tried to claw his hands away, but he held on with a grip of iron. Eamon hissed when my nails drew blood, but it was no good. He seemed to thrive off pain. His hands tightened, his thumbs dug deeper into my throat and the world seemed to slip away.

The darkness behind my closed eyelids was both peaceful and welcoming. I didn't feel pain or panic as the starless night engulfed me, claiming me as its own.

"You made me do this!" Eamon screamed. "This is your doing. Not mine."

For a moment, I *felt* his fury. In my weakness, the door to my power could not be kept closed. It crept open enough, just a crack, that I was certain gold glowed from my fingers. If I had the strength to open my eyes, I would have seen it.

Instead, it stole my peace away and buried me in an emotion I would never be able to comprehend. Eamon's fury was as hot as a fire's heart, as sharp as a fork of lightning. Beneath it, I felt something else. *Panic.* I could not discern if it was my emotion reflecting at me, or his. But what I recognised was its power and strength. It careened into me, smashing me into the darkness and banishing me into a realm ruled by agony.

Just as the world slipped away, the pressure was torn from my body. Air flooded back into my lungs, threatening to burst them entirely. I grasped at my throat, no longer feeling hands upon me. My skin was raw. I coughed and gasped, my throat shredded to ribbons.

Eamon was still shouting, but I didn't care. It didn't matter. He likely melted into a puddle of guilt, pleading how much he loved me and how sorry he was.

None of it mattered. What was done was done, and it would happen again.

It was only when another voice registered that I dared open my eyes. I rolled my head over slowly, wincing at the bruises that likely spread hungrily across my skin.

Eamon had his back to me. He was still shouting, facing something unseen in the door's direction.

"By the creed of the Crimson Guard, you will be drawn and quartered for breaking into my home!"

Every beat of my heart rumbled like thunder across my chest. It was so fast, I thought it would explode free from its confinement of ribs and flesh.

"Didn't I warn you before—"

A low laugh vibrated through the darkness, interrupting Eamon's frantic shouts. It tickled across my skin as I pushed at the bed in my attempt to sit up. Every muscle and bone screamed in resistance, but I fought on, fuelled by the wish to see who Eamon threatened.

Mildred? No. Gods, no.

The thought alone dampened my discomfort, enough for me to shift myself and get a better look at the door, to the person standing in it.

"If you wish to see morning, Eamon," Calix Grey growled, his eyes glowing a bright gold that would have made the stars jealous of its vibrancy, "I suggest you move out of my way."

9

For the first time, I felt Eamon's fear. It was an emotion I didn't think possible for such a man, but here he was, riddled with it. And I didn't need to touch his skin to know it, not when the emotion cascaded from him in undulating waves.

"I was wondering when you would break and come for him." Eamon stood straight, his shoulders rolled back and chin high. Whereas Calix held my husband's gaze, I watched as Eamon slowly slipped a hand into the belt of his trousers, flashing the hilt of a short dagger.

Calix prowled forward with the confidence of a man adorned in countless weapons. Except, from what I could see, he was without a single one.

"So, *this* is what you do to him? All your effort has led to this. The Leader of the Crimson Guard delights in causing harm to those he loves… as well."

My heart thundered in my throat as Calix risked a glance at me. His rich amber eyes traced across my bare chest, to my hands clutching the sheets at my waist and then back to my face. Pity slowly drew down his thick brows.

"What I do with my belongings does not concern you," Eamon spat, edging his body in the line of Calix's sight.

"But what you do with *mine* concerns me."

Eamon snatched his hand back from his belt and produced the dagger in a swift gesture, the dull blade held out before him, the tip aimed directly towards Calix's chest.

"One more step…" Eamon warned.

I winced when Calix threw his head back and roared with laughter.

He clapped a large hand to his chest as though to catch his breath. "And what do you plan to achieve with that? I cut my meat with blades bigger, you fool."

Fear slipped back into Eamon's posture. This time I couldn't so much as feel it, but I could see it. His hand shook, knuckles paled white, as he gripped the blade's handle. Eamon stumbled back a few steps as Calix continued to move into the room, undeterred by the blade.

"He is mine…" Eamon spluttered; his voice was octaves higher than normal. It seemed Calix's presence had gripped him by the balls and squeezed.

"By all means," Calix spared me a look which sang with unseen pain, "You can have him."

Surprise leaked from Eamon at Calix's dismissal. "Then who brings you here this time?"

"You know who I want."

"What is to say he still lives?" Eamon said, goading Calix.

"Oh, *he* lives."

Who was it they spoke of? The thought was as sudden and lingering as the bruising Eamon had left around my neck.

"Get. Out," Eamon sneered, baring his teeth like some rabid animal.

Calix pointed towards me all without caring to look my way again. "Give me who I want, or I am taking him. It would be a fair trade after all."

It was Eamon's turn to laugh. My skin itched with discomfort as both men glanced towards me. I wished to draw the sheets above my head, pinch my eyes closed and pretend I was somewhere else.

"No, no, no," Eamon sang. "He is mine."

"Care to stop me?" Calix raised both hands out to his sides as though welcoming Eamon to try. And try, he did.

Eamon shot forward, his frantic growl giving him away. I screamed out, unsure if it was because I worried for him, or for Calix. *Or myself*.

Calix moved at the last moment. He side-stepped the blade, turned his broad body towards Eamon's outstretched arm and grabbed it. Eamon was torn from his feet as Calix heaved him forward.

I cried out as my husband's body slammed into the wall beside the open door. The dagger was still in hand, but soon slipped out of unconscious fingers. Eamon's body left a dent in the wall's plaster. Debris and dust, old paint and splinters of wood, rained down upon his unmoving body.

All the while, Calix showed no sign of effort. His breathing was steady as he looked down upon the body, a smile creasing his beard-shadowed face. "How I have wished to do that."

"Get out!" I screamed at Calix. It clawed out of my belly and filled the room. Even the volume surprised me. "Get out! Get out!"

Calix snapped his attention towards me, confused. "Unless you wish to alert every Crimson Guard in Darkmourn, I suggest you stop shouting!"

But I couldn't. My panic urged me to scream and shout, whereas it froze my body to stone in the bed.

"Eamon!" I cried out, wishing for him to wake. A small trickle of blood oozed from his hairline, staining the blond a harsh pink.

"Shh," Calix urged, suddenly beside the bed. He clapped a hand over my face, muffling Eamon's name from passing my lips again. "Stop it!"

Calix didn't remove his calloused hand, not when my tears danced across the dips and curves of his fingers and traced around his wrist.

I couldn't take my eyes off my husband. His chest rose and fell slightly, but it was not his welfare I cried for. It was the fury that would follow. The anger he would hold when he woke. I cried for myself. Knowing my skin would endure his embarrassment in the form of pain. He would take this out on me. *That* was why I called out his name.

"Listen to me," Calix whispered, trying to make me look at him. His face was so close to mine. It was impossible to look anywhere else but his moon-wide eyes. I inhaled deeply, smelling pine and earth on his fingers. If I closed my eyes, I would have believed to have been in the heart of a wood after a summer storm.

My breathing was ragged, and my shouts had died down. I sensed hesitation in Calix's soft touch. He didn't wish to hurt me, but also didn't want me to ruin whatever plans he had.

"Promise me you are going to stop shouting," Calix murmured. "Promise me that, and I will explain everything."

He searched my tear-blurred eyes for that promise, because gods knew I couldn't speak it aloud with his hand still muffling me. I nodded my head sharply, as much as his grip allowed.

Calix dropped his hand from me and stumbled back. He withdrew so suddenly it was as though I had burned him.

"He... he will kill you for this," I said, throat sore from my anxiety and Eamon's necklace of bruises.

"I know. There is much you do not know, and I am sorry it has come to this." Calix didn't look sorry. In fact, his expression had hardened into a mask that revealed no emotion. His gaze was distant. "Can you walk?"

The question caught me off guard.

"You either walk, or I will carry you out of here."

"No," I snapped my refusal, gripping onto the sheets across my lap as though they had the strength to keep me in this bed, "Don't you touch me."

"So be it." Calix shot forward again. His hands slid beneath me. Effortlessly, he hoisted me from the bed. I gasped as his rough hand brushed the soft skin under my thigh. The widening of his eyes, and the way his mouth parted open, suggested he had not expected me to be completely naked.

"Get your *fucking* hands off me!" I shouted out again. It only rushed Calix more. He drew me towards his chest, one hand digging fingers into my skin and the other wrapped around my shoulder, to stop me from fighting back. "Eamon!"

My husband didn't respond. He was left on the floor, breathing but unconscious. If he witnessed me in the hands of another man, his heart would have stopped beating entirely.

"I'll ask you again," Calix grumbled into my ear. His cool breath sent a shiver down my naked spine, and conjured gooseflesh to erupt all over me. "You are welcome to walk, or I will carry you."

"Tell me what you want from me," I said, baring my own teeth. "Then I have adequate knowledge to provide you with an answer."

"You," Calix said, not a single hint of a smile on his powerful face, "You are my hostage. However, unlike your caring husband, I do not wish to hurt you in the process of what must be done. So, walk or carry?"

My hostage? Why didn't the words sound as horrifying as it should? I looked to the four walls of this room and pondered what prison would await me when I left this one. I could have clawed my nails down Calix's thick neck or tangle them into his length of honey-coloured hair to pull it from the root.

But an odd calm rushed over me, and I replied, "I'll walk."

Calix put me on the ground, the bedsheet trailing around me like the dress of a bride. I sensed his control, and he fought against the urge to look me up and down. Instead, he kept his deep eyes on mine. "You can have a moment to gather any home comforts you wish to bring with you. And some... clothes perhaps."

"There are no such comforts here," I replied, jaw aching as I gritted my teeth.

"Clothes then, and quick. I'd like to leave before Eamon wakes, or his Crimson Guard come searching for the cause of your screams. Our carriage awaits."

I hurried to dress my naked body. Calix didn't turn away, which made me rush quicker. He stood guard at the door, beside Eamon's slumped body, his tapping foot like the ticking of the grandfather clock in the foyer downstairs.

My cheeks reddened as I clothed myself. I had turned my back to him, offering myself some reprieve from my embarrassment. By the time I was dressed in the slim leather breeches buttoned at my waist, and the red corset was slipped over my long-sleeved cream tunic, my hands didn't stop shaking.

If I could just get outside, then I could scream bloody murder. It was clear Calix would do anything to get me out of this house, but the second we left I would make sure the whole of Darkmourn heard me.

I hardly had my boots on when Calix shouted. "There is no more time, come!" He had moved to the window, peering out between the crack of two curtains to the red glow bathing the streets beyond.

Another voice joined his from the door he had not long stood guard at. I expected it to be Eamon, returned from his forced slumber to stop me from becoming an *unwilling* hostage.

A woman stood there. Sheets of long, straight black hair fell across each shoulder, parted down the middle of her head. Not a hair out of place. Her skin was as pale as snow, her lips colourless in contrast to the burning red of her eyes. My blood buzzed in my veins, panicked by the final detail of the woman I noticed. Two, pointed teeth were longer than the rest, and rested slightly over her lower lip.

"The Crimson Guard are minutes away from storming this building," she hissed, hardly sparing me a glance.

"Millicent, how many?" Calix asked as his deep voice rumbled like thunder.

"Enough that the dance would not be enjoyable for us both," Millicent replied. "Get him into the carriage. Now!"

In a blink, she was gone. Her speed... her eyes and teeth. The deathly glow of her ice-white skin.

"You heard the vampire," Calix said, putting a name to what my mind refused to believe she was. He too had moved quickly, and without sound. "It's time to go. And I think it best I reclaim the standing offer for you to walk. You'll come to learn I am not one to keep promises."

With one swift move, I was back in his arms. The ground fell away from me, and I threw my arms around his neck to steady myself from the suddenness of it all. His grip on me was not as hesitant as it had been when I was naked. He held me as though I was his most prized and coveted possession.

"He will kill you for this," I repeated to Calix, sparing a glance to my husband splayed across the floor.

"I'm counting on it," he replied.

Then Eamon was lost to the blurring of walls, floor and shadows. My stomach jolted violently at the speed. I scrunched my eyes closed against the sickening speed. Only when the world stilled, and the kiss of cold night graced my sticky skin, did I open them again.

A carriage waited at the end of the path from my house. Millicent was sat at the front, leather reins wrapped three times around both hands, connecting to the towering steeds of night before her.

I took in a breath, readying to shout out with all the air in my lungs.

"Inside," Millicent barked, red eyes silencing me. I saw hate in them. Danger. It made me cling to Calix against my better judgement whilst he forced me into the carriage, without any fight or resistance from me.

10

DARKMOURN PASSED in a blur beyond the window of the carriage. There was only the screaming of the wheels slicing across the cobble street and the whipping of leather against the hinds of horses to occupy the thundering of my heart.

Calix didn't speak, not even to utter a single word of comfort.

It seemed comfort was a strange concept to the man who burned holes into me with his eyes. Not once did he look away from me, sitting on the velvet cushion seat in front of him. I didn't have it in me to enter a competition of stares, so I stared aimlessly out the window.

It was easy to lose myself in fear. With everything that had happened, it was hard to truly grasp the reality of my situation. But now, as Castle Dread was no more than a speck in the dark distance, it overwhelmed me.

I drowned in it.

My breathing became ragged, my eyes filled with tears. The cushion beneath me groaned as I dug my nails into it. And all I could think about was Eamon. I could picture his wrath, when he woke, to find me gone. Missing. Already I prepared myself for the blame of this situation. My skin prickled with discomfort of the hand that would surely strike me. The booted foot that would drive the air from my lungs, and the hands around my throat that would keep the air from returning to them.

Beyond the window, the towering sentinels of trees revealed themselves. It was so sudden, I flinched away from the glass with a rasped gasp.

I pinched my eyes closed and lost myself to the storm inside of me. In that moment, I did not understand the world around me.

Hands found my thighs. The touch was reassuring in the dark, enough for me to open my eyes and regard the man kneeling before me.

"He cannot hurt you," Calix growled. There was something ancient and feral in his stare. "Not anymore."

I opened my mouth to explain to him how wrong he was, but all that came out of me was unkept breaths.

"Rhory, I need you to calm yourself down."

How was it this man's voice had the ability to sink deep into the frantic part of my soul? I felt him try to rein it, like a wild mare. The feeling was so strange that it caught me off guard... it was almost familiar.

All without removing his eyes from mine, Calix reached for my hand and pried my fingers from the cushion. A new thought seemed to demand my mind for a moment. He was so... warm. So... alive. My stiffened bones melted like butter over flame at his touch. I gave him no resistance as he guided my hand then took it in both of his.

Perhaps Calix sensed my thoughts, because his fingers tightened and he said, "Do it."

Those two words were as clear as his calm demeanour. It was that emotion I desired. I thirsted for it as a vampire thirsted for blood.

Blinking through the tears that continued to blind me, I opened myself up to him. There was no hesitation.

Golden light seeped from my fingers. It glowed like a star, captured in Calix's hands. The light blazed between the cracks of his fingers and bathed us each in the warmth of light. It banished the shadows that clung to the proud bones of Calix's face until every pore and strand of hair could be accounted for.

I did not borrow his calmness. I stole it. I clawed it from him, swapping my storm of anxiety for this blessed emotion.

His face creased with discomfort as I forced my anxiety into him, filling the space his calm had once claimed. Brows furrowed, and his full mouth thinned into a taut line of tension, but he didn't pull away. His hold on my hand tightened, refusing for me to pull away even if I desired.

My tears dried up. My breathing slowed and mind stilled. All the while, I watched as Calix struggled with the emotions I forced upon him. And he did it, all without complaint. He swallowed the acidic bite of the anxiety, warring with it internally.

"That is enough," I whispered, pulling my hand from him. All at once, the light dissipated until the carriage was coated in shadow once again.

Calix rocked away from me. The muscles in his arms bulged as he gripped the seat behind him. He used the leverage to seat himself. He slouched in on himself, his dark brows furrowed deeply until his entire forehead was cursed with worry lines.

"What a useful little trick," he said, tired eyes surveying me.

With my mind no longer clouded with fear and panic, I asked the only question I deemed important. "What do you want from me?"

"Straight to the point," Calix muttered. He lifted a lazy fist and rapped it on the wooden panel his head rested on. A hatch slid open almost immediately, revealing the burning red of Millicent's eyes.

I let Calix's calmness falter for a moment as the vampire looked directly across the carriage to me. Captured in the nightly winds, her sheets of obsidian hair whipped around her angular face.

"Have we lost them?" Calix asked.

"Of course," Millicent replied, rolling her eyes at the question as though it was the most ridiculous thing she had heard. "Is that a lack of confidence I hear in your voice?"

"Far from it," Calix replied. "Simply wondering why we haven't reached our destination yet."

Millicent bared her teeth, the two elongated points nipping at the skin of her lip. "Auriol's orders were clear. *Little Red* cannot be conscious upon arrival. It puts us all at risk."

Her use of the nickname shocked me. I had not heard it in years, not since my father had passed. It had died with him, yet here was this vampire speaking it without knowing the power it had over me.

"I know," Calix replied plainly.

If it wasn't for Calix's calm that still captured me, I would have reached for the handle of the door and thrown it wide.

"It's locked." Millicent glowered, drawing my attention from the door handle and back to her. Amusement burned in her eyes only to disappear when she slammed the hatch closed, leaving us alone once again.

"Don't mind her, Millicent has justified reasons for her lack of trust," Calix said. "But she is right, you cannot know where we are going."

"Why?"

"Because you are our hostage, and in the hostage rule book, being unaware of your whereabouts is pretty high on the list."

I swallowed hard.

"What do you want from me?" I repeated, this time my words as sharp as a blade.

"It is not what I want from you, but what I want from having you. Don't worry, *Little Red*, you'll get your answers soon enough. For now, we still have the issue about what I am to do with you if we ever want Millicent to stop taking us on this detour of Darkmourn's landscape.

Trust me, she is stubborn enough to ride until the sun rises and burns her to ash. I rather enjoy her company, so we better figure this out soon."

"I thought she made it clear," I replied, sensing the chill of uncertainty slice up my neck.

Calix narrowed his gilded eyes, making them darker in colour and emotion. "I am not in the mindset of knocking you out cold."

"Thank my lucky stars. I was beginning to believe I'd been handed from the hands of one abuser to another."

He winced, as though my words had slapped him. "I am nothing like *him*."

"Yet you've broken into my home and taken me from it?"

Calix leaned forward, elbows resting on his spread legs. "Would you have preferred I left you?"

It was my turn to wince. My facial reaction and silence were answer enough.

"Right," Calix added. "Now, may I?"

From his pocket he withdrew a square of material. He folded it neatly into a thin length and held it towards me.

"And what are you going to do with that?"

I couldn't discern if my silver tongue was a result of my situation, or if the confidence had slipped into me from Calix when I had invaded his soul and swapped our emotions. I certainly hadn't spoken like this to anyone before. Or, at least not for a long time.

There was once a time when Mother would say my tongue was sharp enough to cut stone. That sharpness had dulled the night she died. Until now, it seemed.

"Blindfold you," Calix said; his voice was barely a whisper.

"Pardon?" I looked to the cloth he held out as though it was a viper that could strike me.

His laugh was deep and rumbling. It came from far within him and caused the skin on my arms to prickle with bumps.

"Did I stumble over my words?" Calix leaned forward more. "You can decide, if you wish for me to do it or you can do it yourself."

Not wanting to feel his touch again, I shot forward and tore the material from his grasp. His hand was left hanging out before him, fingers curling slowly inward.

I kept my stare pinned to his as I lifted the material. His smile was the last thing I saw as I brought the blindfold to my eyes and tied the length in a knot behind my head.

"Good boy," Calix drawled from the darkness that now blinded me.

My mouth became parched at his praise. I almost choked on it, finding the two words harder to swallow than the reality that I had become his hostage for some unknown reason.

"Sit back and enjoy the ride," Calix continued; I sensed the smile in his words. "We will reach our destination soon. Then you will get your answers."

"Good." It was all I could manage as I leaned back in the seat and folded my arms over my chest.

"You're welcome, by the way." Calix sounded so close as he spoke. If I had torn the blindfold from my eyes, I was confident he would have been inches from me because of the smell of forest and rain infiltrating my nose, and the soft brush of his breath.

"For kidnapping me?" I asked as my cheeks filled with crimson heat.

"For saving you," he replied.

"Eamon is my husband," I snapped, not willing to hear the pity in Calix's tone. "You have not saved me from anything."

"This…" A coarse finger traced the tender skin of my throat. My breathing hitched. I didn't need to look in a mirror to know the skin had bruised, Eamon's fingers imprinted in blues and dark purples. "…suggests otherwise."

11

Calix guided me from the carriage. There was only the scratch of material across my eyes and his warm, firm hand pressed into my lower back. Now and then short bursts of light shone through the top of my blindfold, like a glow through the crack of a narrow door. Then it was gone, and I was lost in darkness.

It was easier to rely on my other senses to help give me some clue as to where Calix led me. At first, the crunch of autumn leaves screamed beneath each of our footfalls. But that soon gave way to a patter as we walked across the smooth edge of stone. We had found some sort of path, or road. Soon enough, the sound of our footfalls echoed all around us. I knew we had entered some sort of tunnel from both the sound and the way the air seemed to grow thicker and damper with each inhale. I expected a reprieve, that we would come out the other end and be greeted with the much-needed kiss of fresh air. But I was wrong. The ground beneath my feet sloped downwards and the echoing only intensified. Even my heavy breathing and Calix's low humming became unbearable in the strange place.

We walked for an age until my thighs ached and my feet seemed peppered with blisters. At some point I lost my bearings completely, feeling that I was alone on this odd journey into the darkness without light to guide me, only the desire to not stop. Then Calix's hand would shift on my back, fingers drumming in rhythm, as if to remind me he was there.

I almost forgot the vampire's presence until she spoke. It seemed she had the ability to glide across the earth, with little need for making sound. Her footfalls were as silent as her breathless body. "Auriol will desire to know about this, Calix."

"Oh, I know."

Shivers trailed down my spine at the closeness of Calix's whisper.

"Then would you wish to do the honours to wake her and tell her what you've done?" Annoyance graced Millicent's stoic tone. There was something scolding about the way she spoke to Calix, as if she was his mother, and he, her son.

"Does my grandmother scare you, Millie?" Calix retorted, using a nickname for the vampire that was poisoned with jest.

"Only a fool wouldn't fear Auriol," Millicent snapped.

"Exactly why I wish for you to be the one to inform her of this evening's events," Calix replied. "If she doesn't already know, that is."

It took a moment for Millicent to reply. Her silence unnerved me. Calix's deep chuckle suggested he sensed my emotions as if he had my abilities.

When the vampire replied, she was further away, her voice muffled by distance, but as clear as newly forged steel, "You owe me."

"Add it to the list," Calix retorted.

We continued walking, me blind to everything but the symphony our breathing made and the choking intensity of the damp earth-filled air, Calix humming his tune to entertain himself.

It was cold in this place. The chill was deeper than what winter gifts to the air. It was the type of cold that came hand in hand with the dark, so intense that it belonged in the furthest parts of the deepest lake, where sunlight could never reach.

I was thankful for the thick red cloak I had taken with me. The cloak that I had worn since the death of my father, with its gold trim around the hood, was a symbol to his position in the Crimson Guard. Many had wondered why Eamon, now taking the mantel my father once possessed, didn't insist to wear this very cloak himself. Whereas I once believed it was my husband's wish for me to have something of my father, I now knew it was simply a way of marking me. Possession of the Crimson Guard, it screamed. Possession of Eamon.

He would have thought this cloak and the meaning behind it would have made me untouchable.

I laughed suddenly, the sound echoing around the dark.

How very wrong you were, Father.

The direction we took changed suddenly. There were turns. Left and right, right and left. Sometimes it seemed we turned corners in circles, as if Calix had attempted to trick me. However, I didn't sense that would be the case.

Perhaps it was his borrowed calm, that still rallied within me, which tainted my vision of him.

"Rhory," Calix said as we slowed to a stop. "We can take this off now."

His fingers tugged at the knot of material at the back of my head. Although he had not stopped touching me since we left the carriage, the new place his fingers graced still made me quiver slightly.

I squinted against the flare of light before me. It took me a moment for my eyes to settle, enough for me to distinguish the glow was not the sun but a burning torch. Fire hissed and spat whilst it devoured the oil-soaked head as it hung on a sconce beside a large metal door.

Calix allowed me a moment to gather my surroundings. As I had thought, we were within some form of tunnel. Dark stacked bricks glistened with water, mould and moss. The glow from the sconces revealed the arched brick ceiling above my head. A droplet of stale water fell from the ceiling where it splashed across my cheekbone, startling me.

"If I asked where we are, I guess you wouldn't tell me," I said, drying my cheek with the back of my hand.

"Darkmourn," Calix answered through a grin, his deep voice echoing all around us.

I fought the urge to roll my eyes, finding it easier to look anywhere else but his intense gaze. "No, would have been an easier answer."

"I'm not one to lie, Rhory."

Gods, he really was leaning heavily into his sarcasm, using it as support to hold him in place.

"Are you planning on having me stand here or...?"

Calix leaned close towards me. I stiffened as his face neared mine. A surprised gasp broke out of me. The sound deepened his grin, only to make me feel foolish when his arm snaked out behind me and reached for the handle to the metal door. With a push, it opened. The hinges wailed, demanding oil.

"If I had a red carpet to roll out, I would've." Calix swept his muscular arm towards the shadows of the room beyond the door. "Welcome to your holding cell."

It should have filled me with dread, but as the glow of the sconces filled the room before me, I felt nothing of the sort. Firelight raced across the modest dwelling, revealing a large fourposter bed with mounds of pillows and rumpled sheets tangled atop the mattress. The dark wood furniture had been pushed up against the walls, cabinets and tall wardrobes that seemed more like doors leading to magical worlds within.

Carpets covered the slab stoned flooring, overlapping one another in contest. Even the walls were draped with rugs to conceal the evidence of leaking bricks and patches of moss.

The glow of fire shifted, stealing my attention back to Calix. He had lifted the burning torch from the sconce and drifted into the room without invitation. I waited at the threshold, awkwardly watching as he shared the flame with waiting candles throughout the room. By the time he was finished spreading his fire, the room held some inviting warmth.

"This should be comfortable enough for you to get some rest," Calix said, as if his simple suggestion could erase the fact I was now his hostage.

"Do you concern yourselves with the comfort of your prisoners?"

His eyes sparked with golden fire. "Should I not?"

I shrugged, feeling self-conscious beneath his devouring gaze. "What do you want from me, Calix Grey?"

He flinched. "My wants do not matter in this circumstance. Auriol can answer those questions come morning, but until then you need to rest. Regardless of what you think, I'm not a monster." He paced towards the door, needing to put as much distance between us as possible. "I'll return for you come morning with food."

The thought of being left alone caused fear to spike within me. It encouraged a desperate plea to burst out; it stopped Calix dead in his tracks, "Wait!"

He stilled, glancing over his shoulder enough to see me. "Is *my* room not up to the standards of a Coleman?"

I swallowed hard. "This is your room? Here?"

"Indeed," he replied.

I wished to ask him where he was to stay, but the question failed me. "Shouldn't you be chaining me to a wall? Isn't that what captors do to their victims?"

The torch cast shadows across Calix's face. It gave him a sinister glare as he slowly smiled at me from his place by the door. "Now, tell me why I would wish to give pleasure to my victim, if that is what you think you are?"

My mouth dried at his comment. I ground my teeth together, trying to keep the impression of strength when, in fact, my insides had turned to sludge and my knees threatened to give out at any moment.

Calix reached for the door, this time to close me in.

"I could escape, you know!" I snapped. "Nothing is stopping me."

There was no lock on the door on the outside, only two small sliding bolts on the inside. I could keep him out, but there was nothing stopping me from leaving.

"And pray tell, what would you do then?" Displeasure flashed across Calix's face. I had yet to place an age to him, but the threads of silver within his honey-coloured hair and beard suggested he had passed his thirtieth year. "Even if you could work out the maze of tunnels and find yourself in the fresh grace of Darkmourn's landscape, would you run home? Back to *him*?"

"My husband?" I asked, voice high and light. "Is that whom you refer to?"

"Yes," Calix replied, voice as cold as the brick walls surrounding me. "*Him.*"

I didn't need to answer his initial question. The answer, although not spoken aloud, was obvious. No, I wouldn't run back to Eamon. And Calix knew it.

"What you should understand, Rhory, is tonight should never have happened," Calix stared straight into my soul as he spoke, "Eventually, we would have been in this situation, your being here and what that means for us all. But that shouldn't have been tonight. I understand you have questions and deserve answers… but I ask that you wait for tomorrow. It is best to come from Auriol herself."

I should have refused. Should have slammed my foot into the ground and demanded every detail that Calix kept from me. The hows, and whys, burned through my mind like a wildfire in summer.

"One thing," I said as Calix closed the door. "Just tell me one thing. It is the least you can do."

He surprised me by nodding, when the grimace and tension in his jaw suggested he wished not to tell me anything. "Fine. Ask your question."

"Why did you come for me tonight if it was not supposed to happen?"

Fury pinched Calix's strong brows forward as his nose scrunched. His pale pink lips pulled back from his teeth, enough to mimic the expression a vampire gave before sinking teeth into human skin. Except, Calix was no vampire. I had felt his warmth, the heartbeat that thundered in the tips of his fingers.

"I heard what he was doing to you," he replied finally. I blinked and was back in my room at home, with Eamon above me and his hands wrapped around my throat. The bruises seemed to burn with agony as Calix's eyes brushed over my neckline. "Rhory, I am many things, but I couldn't just leave knowing what was happening to you."

I dropped my eyes to the floor, finding the memory and the truth of his words too harsh to bear.

Then he asked me a question: "How long has this been happening?"

I wanted to tell him that it didn't matter. To inform him that the happenings in my home, in my marriage, had nothing to do with him. Or anyone for that matter. But when I opened my mouth to tell him just that, I replied with the truth, "Since my mother…" Grief struck again, promising to strangle me. "Since their influence could no longer protect me."

I stood in the middle of the room, feeling as though the entire place was about to cave in on me. Calix gripped the metal door, using it to hold himself up, or hold himself back; I could not tell which, only that it practically groaned beneath the force of his hand.

"Don't tell them," I snapped. Calix didn't owe me anything. There was no reason he would care to harbour my dark secret, but I found him agreeing without question.

"It is not for me to tell," Calix said. I sensed there was more that he wished to share, but the metal door swung closed, and he was gone.

Calix left me alone. Except that wasn't entirely true. His scent was everywhere. It lingered in the air. It stained the sheets I slowly climbed into on shaking legs and arms.

I forced myself to close my eyes, with no idea if it was day or night or if my body was as violently lost as I was in this strange, tunnelled place.

12

I WOKE beneath the glare of burning red eyes. My mind took a moment to differentiate them from cauldrons of endless depths filled entirely with blood. I choked back a gasp, gripping the sheets of my bed with iron fingers. *Calix's bed*, I hastily reminded myself. Beneath the vampire's watchful gaze, the comfort of the feather-stuffed bedding suddenly dissipated, leaving only the sensation of being weighed down by someone's attention.

"Oh dear. Did I wake you?" Millicent asked, reclining into the downy cushions of the aged reading chair. The leather of her trousers squeaked as she crossed her legs with dramatic flair.

"Yes," I replied, throat dry, and unsure on what else to say.

Millicent smiled, flashing the two sharp points of her canines as her lips drew back. There was nothing friendly about the expression. The smile never reached her eyes, which still hadn't left me. "Well, I apologise."

I didn't need to touch her skin to sense the dishonesty that dripped from every syllable she spoke.

"Rhory, isn't it?" Millicent's gaze narrowed. I was completely trapped beneath it, like a mouse in the paws of a bloodthirsty cat. "I see Calix decided against the suggestion of chains. He has always been more… pragmatic with his choices, however I can't help but sense he has had a lapse in judgement. Door unbarred. You, in his bed no less. What next, will he be offering to spoon-feed all his prisoners?"

Hostility rolled off her in formidable waves. As Millicent off-loaded her spiel at me, her upper lip continually curled upwards until her face was screwed in a snarl.

"Does my presence offend you?" I asked.

Even I was surprised by my question. I no longer had the dregs of Calix's calmness I had drawn from him the last time I was awake, but still this confidence was new. No, not new, but simply buried for a long time. Lost.

"Offend me?" Millicent's laugh cracked the air like lightning. It was so sharp it whipped at my bare soul. "Come on, Rhory, don't play the idiot. You know who I am."

"Millicent, isn't it?" I sat forward, knuckles turning white as my hold on Calix's sheets tightened. I could tell from her pinched expression she didn't like me using her own tone back at her.

A darkness passed behind her eyes, turning them almost black. The air shifted, bringing with it a new scent of lilies. Then she was before me, inches from my face, with teeth so close my blood retreated into the far corners of my body.

Fury brought some semblance of scarlet to her cheeks. So brutal, it defied her dead flesh and gave her a sense of humanity.

"Look at me," she demanded. The vampire moved with fluid grace and unnatural speed. Her nails pinched the skin of my chest as she took a handful of my shirt and tugged me towards her. Naturally, I reached for her single hand and clasped it with both of mine. It was the extra leverage I required as she practically tore me from the bed and held me aloft.

She was cold to the touch. As I pinched my eyes closed in fear, I remembered the same chill in the skin of my mother as I held onto her hand the last time I had seen her in St Myrinn's morgue.

"Please," I begged, turning my face away from her. "Whatever I have done, I'm sorry!"

I opened up my magic to her and instantly regretted it. The hate that slammed into me was as powerful as a wall of stone. I felt my bones crack at the impact and immediately drew myself out.

It had been many years since I had last been so close to a vampire. During the days when my life wasn't poisoned by Eamon, my family would host Darkmourn's vampiric nobility in our home. Mother and Mildred would conjure feasts that even the dead couldn't turn their noses up to. Then came Eamon. After my mother's murder and father's shortly followed death, the last vampire I had been close enough to see was the man who hung for a crime I didn't believe he committed.

"Open your eyes," Millicent sneered. "I do not have your powers, *witch*, but I can sense a mistruth better than any hound. Let me see it."

I didn't feel like I could refuse her. Prying my eyes open, I couldn't do anything but look directly into the pits of blood-red orbs that were now inches from my own.

If Millicent needed to breathe, she would have taken a hulking one at that moment. "Do you know what you took from me?"

My skin grew sticky, my heart thundered with the agony of my impending doom. All I could do was answer her again.

"I don't know, but I see that I have caused you great pain. Millicent, I'm—"

"Don't you dare. Your apology is unwanted if you do not know what it is you must be apologising for."

"Then tell me," I said, recognising the pinch of my skin across my already bruised neck.

Millicent parted her dark rose painted lips to answer me. Before a sound came out, her head snapped towards the closed door of the room. Her ears pricked at a sound that was out of the mundane reach of a mortal. Then she released me. I fell back into the bed with a thump that jarred through my body. When I looked up again, Millicent was sitting in the chair with her legs crossed and gaze focused on her nails as if they were the most interesting thing in the world.

That was when I heard the footsteps. Only a few seconds later the door creaked open, and Calix stood beneath its frame.

"Good morning," he said, eyes boring into me.

"Evening," Millicent corrected, all without looking up from her nails.

Calix snapped his head towards her, a look of surprise betraying his face for only a moment. It melted into one of fear which had him looking back towards me. It was only when he saw me again did he relax.

"I told you not to come," Calix said with false calm; he stared at me as he spoke to the vampire.

"And *I* do not abide by your commands, Calix."

"I asked for company," I added quickly, steeling my face and holding back any hint that I was lying. "Millicent found me exploring. I was lost, and she kindly returned me back to the room. Since then, we have just been... catching up."

"Catching up?" Calix raised a single, thick brow.

I threw my legs over the side of *his* bed, planting my feet on the cold ground; it helped the room stop spinning so violently.

"Is that so?" Calix sighed, looking from both of us with an expression of distrust.

Millicent glanced to Calix, a hint of her snarl returning to her pristine face. "You could have at least guarded the door. Your judgement is clouded."

I felt the unspoken thrum around me like winds coiling around my legs and arms. There was something in the way they looked at one another, then to me, that revealed a secret they both wished not to speak aloud. Did it have anything to do with what Millicent accused me of?

"Auriol wishes to see us," Calix said, ignoring Millicent's comment about his judgement.

Millicent stood, clicked her head from side to side and faked a yawn that I hardly imagined the undead were privy to. "You can go without me. I have had enough of Auriol's fury to last me a lifetime and the next. Plus, I need to hunt. Our little *catch up* has built a rather burning appetite."

Millicent cut her gaze to me. I swallowed the lump in my throat, making the most audible gulping sound.

"It's been a pleasure... Rhory."

Calix sidestepped the door without a word. Millicent mocked a bow before she passed, disappearing into the shadows of the tunnel system beyond the room.

"Are you alright?"

I forced a smile at Calix but couldn't hold his gaze for long. There was something intense about it that had me preferring looking at the ground instead. "Should you be concerned about the welfare of your hostage?"

"Others would say I shouldn't, but I do."

His answer was plain. Simple. It spread a warmth across my chest, one that I wished would leave me.

"Regardless of my treatment, I *am* still your hostage. Your kind words and offerings mean little to me when you have stolen me from my home."

"You are not wrong. And if you would like some answers, then I suggest we make a move. By sunrise, I must leave you for the day."

I wished to ask why, but I couldn't show such interest.

"I want to go home," I said, almost stamping my foot like a spoiled child.

"That is not how this works."

Pacing across the room towards him, I made it a few feet from the door when Calix pointed to the ground beneath me. "Perhaps you should put something on your feet, unless you wish for me to carry you again?"

I turned my back on him, quick enough that Calix couldn't watch the scarlet spread up my neck and across my face.

"I'll wait for you outside," Calix said, his voice dripping with warmth.

Hunger cramped my stomach, causing it to roar.

"What was that?"

I faked a cough, rushing to grasp my boots that waited beneath Calix's bed. "Nothing."

Calix released a laugh that echoed through his room and the tunnels beyond. "If you are quick about it, you may find that some warm tea and cake waits at our destination. And before you ask, no. Not all our hostages are fed cake. Just you."

"Lucky me," I whispered to myself.

Calix heard me, replying loud enough for every dust mite to hear, "Indeed."

∽

The blindfold was removed when we stepped out of the dank air of the tunnels, into the blessed chill of the nightly breeze. We continued walking a short while before we reached our destination. Twigs and leaves crunched beneath my footfalls. Calix even found it necessary to turn me around in circles a few times before removing the blindfold. *Just to be sure*, he had said.

Auriol's cottage was before us, the dark forest cocooning us entirely. I turned around, trying to search for the direction we had come out of the tunnels from, but it was no good.

"I've slept for an entire day?" I asked, studying the dusk-bathed sky above the thick canopy of trees above.

"Just about," Calix replied, reaching for the brass knob of the door. "My grandmother comes alive when the moon is high. I would have woken you sooner if she was able to host a conversation, but her age exhausts her."

I nodded, glad that his focus shifted to the soft glow of candlelight in the corridor beyond.

It wasn't that I had slept for a day that worried me. It was that I had been kept from Eamon for a day that did. As I watched Calix's broad back ahead of me, I had the urge to turn and run. Surely Eamon's wrath would dilute if I ran back to him now? The longer I was kept, the more kindling would be added until his blaze would spill over.

Pain jolted through my chest.

"Care to join me?"

I looked up, breath ragged, as Calix watched me with obvious concern. Before I gave into my desire to run, I fought against myself. Each step into the cottage was hard. Only when the door swung closed behind me did I feel like I could breathe again.

The cottage's air was filled with the sweat aroma of tea. It wafted in clouds that clung to the corners of rooms. Mint, camomile, ginger. I could taste the scents on the back of my tongue with a single inhale.

I had never met my grandparents on either side of my family. They had died when I was too young to hold my own bottle. I had often wondered what it would have been like having them and could imagine that it would be like this. Hearth warmed houses, tea and the smell of cooking that seemed as part of the furniture as the floral décor I now passed.

Auriol was nestled within her bed, as she had when I had first seen her. It seemed she hadn't moved, but there was more energy to her mismatched eyes as she lifted her attention from the book held in her crone-like hands.

"I knew we would see each other again, but not so soon as this," Auriol said, taking the round spectacles from the bridge of her nose and placing them on the hardcover of the book on her lap. "First, let me apologise for my grandson's actions. Know that he did not act on my authority, but his own, no matter how misplaced it is."

Calix tipped his head, unable to hold Auriol's gaze. When she regarded him, she did it with anger and disappointment. Those expression's relaxed when she focused back on me. "Come, sit with me. You must be hungry, and I know the tea will help."

Not wishing to offend her, I stepped away from Calix's side towards her bed. As I passed him, he leaned in and whispered, "She doesn't know about Eamon."

A chill sliced down my spine. There was no keeping the discomfort from my expression.

"Your presence bothers the poor lad," Auriol barked. "Calix. Make yourself useful… elsewhere."

I heard him retreat without comment, leaving us alone once again.

Auriol's eyes fell on the bruises at my neck. "Which one did it?"

I lifted a finger and traced the sensitive skin. "It is my fault."

"Nonsense," she replied. "However, I know hesitation well. No need to tell me, I will see both Calix and Millicent punished as one party since they were both at fault for taking you."

"Please," I blurted. "Don't do that."

She narrowed her gaze on me. I sensed her reluctance to let it go, so I took hold of the conversation and changed it.

"Wasn't this always your plan?" I asked. "Taking me from Eamon. Having me as your hostage?"

There was no hesitation when Auriol replied, "It was, in time."

"Then why wish to punish Calix and Millicent, when you wanted this outcome?"

"Shouldn't you wish to see them both punished? They stole you from your home, your husband. We are keeping you against your will for our own gain. You, of all people, should wish to see them flogged for their actions."

She was testing me. I could see it, like a glint in her eyes.

"Why?" I asked, choosing to ignore her question. "Tell me what it is for, then I can answer."

"Eat something first. And drink. Once I see the bottom of your mug, I will tell all."

Her hand shook as she gestured towards the set-up of cake and tea at the bedside. I didn't waste time to slather the thick slab of pale sponge dusted with sugar and filled with smooth jam. I devoured it quickly. The tea washed it down. It was cool enough to knock the entire mug back. I cared little for the sprig of fresh mint that followed.

"Now tell me," I said, clearing my lips with the back of my hand.

"Yes," came a voice from the doorway. I didn't need to turn to know Calix had returned. "He deserves to know."

"Okay, okay," Auriol said, wincing as she shifted in the bed. Three pillows were propped behind her to help her old bent frame sit up. Calix rushed forward to help her, but she batted him off with a wave of her hand.

"Rhory, we need you to see that something is returned to us. I promise, beneath our hands, no harm will come to you, but you must know that your being here is a plan that has taken years to complete. Of course, it was not entirely prepared before my grandson decided to flood your home and snatch you like some common criminal. However, here you are. And thus, the plan must begin."

"You are a bargaining tool," Calix added, at the displeasure of Auriol, "A means of a trade."

"Trade? For what?"

"In a manner of speaking, yes. My grandson, Calix's younger brother, was taken from us. We are under the understanding that it was your husband, Eamon and his Crimson Guard, that are behind the abduction. We had believed he was killed, but recent information suggests that Silas is alive and if we ever wish to see him returned home, we must do so by using you."

"I don't understand," I admitted as a storm captured my mind and twisted it into a vortex of thoughts.

"I will put it plainly. Eamon will know you have been taken from him and he will know why. Until he returns Silas back to me, I am afraid you cannot go home to *him*. Our terms will be sent to Eamon and they shall be clear. One for the other." As Auriol spoke a heavy sorrow weighed down on her. It aged her before my eyes, deepened her wrinkles and dulled her eyes with a milky sheen.

"You are going to send me home?" I asked, already knowing the answer as I looked up at Calix. Not once did he take his gaze off of me. It was what I had asked for, but the thought unsettled me deeply.

"Yes," he replied, voice deep with regret.

"Eamon loves you," Auriol said. "We know your importance to him, likely the only thing with enough leverage to give me back my Silas. Someone who is equally important to me."

I found tears filled my eyes. There was no discerning which emotion pricked them into existence, but I couldn't find it in me to fight them.

"Eamon is not as controllable as you believe him to be," I said, looking back at Auriol. "I'm sorry, but you will fail. If he really has your grandson, I will not be the person who sees that he returns home to you."

Auriol's shoulders sagged. "I do hope you are wrong."

"When?" I asked. "When do you hope to begin this bargain of yours?"

Auriol and Calix shared a look, one that spoke volumes.

"After the turn of the full moon," Calix answered me. "We will both be…"

"Indisposed," Auriol answered for him. "Then we will send our terms to Eamon. Until then, Rhory, I promise to provide you as much comfort as possible. It is the least we can do."

"And if he doesn't do as you wish?"

Calix placed a hand on my shoulder. The touch surprised me, but I found I didn't flinch. There was something familiar about the weight of his hand. My body recognised it, but I couldn't place why.

"Then you stay until he does. No matter how long it takes," Calix said.

I stood, knocking the empty mug of tea from my lap where it smashed into pieces across the wooden floor.

"Take me back," I demanded. "Take me back to the room."

Calix looked to his grandmother, for the permission she granted with a nod of her head.

"I am sorry," Auriol said. "I wish I could tell you this was a hard decision to make, but I cannot lie to you. Not you."

I didn't wait to hear the rest. None of it mattered. I left the room, knowing that Calix followed close behind me. He didn't stop me as I burst out of the cottage, leaving the tendrils of comfort behind for the cold of night. Perhaps it was because he knew I couldn't go anywhere, or that he knew I wouldn't.

There was only one person who would suffer the consequences of this bargain. And that was me. All I could think about was Eamon and his reaction to when I was finally handed back to him. My skin prickled at the promise of pain that would soon welcome me home.

13

4 YEARS BEFORE

My tongue traced across the back of my teeth. It brushed over the dead flesh caught between them, coating it with the taste of spoiled skin and blood. No matter how much I swallowed, the sickly tang of copper would not ease. It stained my cheeks, my throat, and thrashed within my stomach with every slight movement.

Vaguely, through the roaring in my head and the settling of my human bones as they fused back together, I was aware of the cold gore spreading down my chin, my neck and coating my bare chest.

I should wash before anyone found me, but I didn't dare move. My eyes were entirely fixated on the two vampires I had killed. Through it all, just looking at the torn flesh and tooth-scarred bones, I felt a swell of pride. I did that. I killed them, and they deserved it. If I could have done it over and over, I would have.

My grief was so fresh, so new, that I had hardly recognised it for what it was. Hours had passed since Calix and I found our parent's slaughtered by their vampiric friends. Friends who now lay, body parts scattered throughout the forest bed, before me. And the grief was only starting to seep in.

My ears, still keen from the recent shift, picked up a snapping of wood far off in the darkened forest. I snapped my head towards it, nose flaring to catch a scent on the subtle wind which raced around the thick trunks around me.

Was it Calix? He knew what I planned to do and threatened to come after me. Or perhaps it was Grandmother. Auriol would have been able to stop me with a single command. I gathered, from her silence, she wanted me to avenge her daughter's murder as much as I longed for it.

That was the difference between Calix and me. My brother didn't have it in him. He couldn't kill anyone. He fought the beast inside of him, whereas I welcomed it.

There was another crack of wood, followed by the heavy step of a boot as it ground leaves into the dirt. I opened myself up, allowing my ears to pick up the rhythmic steady beat of a heart. One heart banged far greater than the others as it was closer.

I was all but naked, with nothing but the blood of my parent's murderers to warm me. Yet the vampire's blood was nothing but a frozen presence against my burning skin.

"I know you are there," I called out, throat slick with vampire blood.

Through the darkness, from behind a wall of thick oak trees, stepped a man adorning a cloak of dark ruby. His hair was as black as night itself, where his eyes were the colour of the clearest of summer skies. He was tall and carried himself with confidence. Shoulders rolled back and spine pin-straight, the man moved through the forest towards me as though he owned it.

This man was part of the Crimson Guard, obvious from the cloak tied around his neck, and the way his watchful gaze slid over the discarded corpses of the vampires and then back to me. He held a jewel of scrutiny in his blue eyes, which filled me with a claw of dread.

"What a mess you have made," he said, voice as smooth as silk. I felt as though I could drown in it.

I steeled my jaw and levelled my eyes with his. Something about it made him smile, viciously.

"Have you come to arrest me for my crimes?" My voice echoed through the dark, repeating back on myself until it faded to a silent whisper.

The man pulled at his red cloak as through righting it on his shoulders. He pouted his lips and drew his brows down into a deep frown. "And why would I do that?"

I lowered my eyes back to the corpses that separated us. "Because I have murdered someone."

"More than just someone I gather," he replied, not even a wince across his face as he looked to the mutilated body parts, then back to my blood-soaked and naked body. "Care to tell me how you have done it?"

My teeth forced themselves closed. I didn't dare open my mouth, because I could not tell him. I wouldn't. It was the very reason my parents had been murdered in the first place. They trusted their friends enough to reveal our secret, and that secret led to their death.

"Your name, at least."

The silence haunted me.

"Silas," I said finally, voice cracking, as I lost myself in the endless pits of his stare. There was something alluring about him. Perhaps it was his stillness, or the lack of care that I knelt in the leaves before him, naked and covered in blood. Or maybe I was drunk. Drunk on the adrenaline left in me from murder and revenge.

One thing I knew for certain was the man's heart skipped each time he allowed his gaze to leave mine and trail my body. His reaction to me was intoxicating.

"I admit, I am rather disappointed," he said. "I was hoping to be the one to kill these two this evening."

His words stole my breath away.

"Why?" I muttered. "Should you not be protecting them?"

"Who from? Monsters like you, or monsters like me?"

Slowly, as though proving he was not a threat, the man unclasped the red cloak from his shoulders and extend it to me.

"Take this," he said quietly. I felt his restraint as he kept his eyes on mine. "Cover yourself up before you catch your death."

I regarded the offering, deciding whether to accept or refuse. The stranger made my mind up for me as he stepped carefully over the gnawed arm of the vampire and brought the cloak to me himself. As he settled it over my shoulders, the air picked up his scent and washed it over me.

I inhaled the pungent waft of lavender. It was as though I stood in a field of it. The brush of his knuckles across my bare skin sent an alarming shiver through me. This man, whoever he was, screamed danger. Why was it I was so completely stuck by it?

"Did they deserve it?" he asked, standing at my side and looking down at my chaos.

I inhaled sharply, now smelling both him and the blood of my victims.

"Yes," I said, finding it the easiest word I had ever said. "They... they killed my parents."

The man hissed through gritted teeth. Then he draped a warm arm across my shoulder, until his hand gripped my bicep to steady me. "Then I have no questions. All crimes must be answered for. And between me and you, Silas..." he spoke my name, extending each syllable as though he hissed like a snake, "We are no different. I am sorry for your loss. Come, let us get you cleaned up, and this... dealt with."

He attempted to move, but my feet were rooted to the spot.

"Who are you?" I asked, eyeing him as distrust stormed within me.

"My name is Eamon," he said, whispering as though it was only me and him in the entire world. "And I too lost my parents to these vile monsters."

Eamon reached a hand to the side of my face where he brushed his fingers over the tacky blood that coated it. He hardly blinked as he drew it to his nose, sniffed and then brought it down to his trousers where he cleaned it off.

"When my parents died, I was the one who was covered in their blood. I am glad to see you covered in the enemies." Eamon gestured to the scattered remains at our feet. "Come on, let us get you somewhere safe. The woods are a dangerous place."

His comment was edged. From the glint in Eamon's eyes, he knew the forest caused me no danger, not when I was the beast which lurked in it. As Eamon said, I was the one covered in the blood of vampires. And Eamon had yet to question why I was alone, naked and caught red-handed, let alone how I killed them. But I felt the question lingering. It would come.

"What are you going to do to me?" I asked, unable to hide the shake in my voice.

Eamon pouted as the lined skin around his eyes softened. "I am going to see you are cleaned, and the bodies are burned. Then we can have a discussion about how it is you came out in the woods and murdered two vampires... all alone."

I exhaled, searching his bright eyes for a reason to run. "Why does it matter?"

"Because we need someone like you."

"Who is we?"

Eamon smiled, leaned his forehead into mine and spoke. "The tides are changing. Our enemies align. Silas Grey, come and let us talk in a more suitable place. I want to hear about it all. Believe me, you can trust me."

And he was right because I allowed myself to slip down the stream of his charm, all the while not realising I had never been the one to tell him my surname. In the days which followed, I was far too deep in revealing all my secrets before I realised Eamon's first slip up—the first of many.

14

I QUICKLY BECAME aware that I was walking with no real knowledge of my destination. And Calix knew it. Every time I looked behind me, he was there. A shadow, lurking at my back whilst always keeping a distance.

I picked my pace up. Twigs scratched at my face, lacing my skin with small kisses of pain but I didn't care. On I pushed, fighting my way through the dense woodland with only one desire. *Don't stop.*

The forest swallowed me whole. It bathed me in its darkness and welcomed me into its belly. Nothing scared me more than the thought of home, yet I found myself trying to find it. I searched my memory of the directions Calix's note had provided but couldn't grasp the image. My mind was a storm of revelations and accusations.

Eamon had someone hostage. Calix would use me to get him back. I was a pawn on a gameboard I never asked to play.

Cold air stabbed at the back of my throat with each inhale. My feet stumbled awkwardly over roots and mounds of Gods knows what. But on I pushed, defending myself from the branches, vines and earth that fought hard to keep me within its hold.

"Rhory, wait," Calix finally called out for me. His voice was void of warmth. In its place was a tempered command. I felt the urge to listen to him as though it was the natural thing to do. *No*, I reminded myself, *Keep going.*

He could have stopped me. We both knew it. Calix was far stronger. It was not impossible to imagine him catching up, throwing me over his shoulder and carrying me back to his underground dwellings.

What held him back?

I could have been walking for an age before I finally stopped. Frustration bubbled up my throat, exploding out of me in a cry that brought the forest alive.

By the time I turned to Calix, he too was standing still. There was distance between us, so much that I had to squint through the dark to even make sense of his features. Only his eyes were clear. They no longer held the soft honey glaze, but now blazed like two beacons of burning gold.

"Please take me back to him," I said, breathlessly.

"Are you certain that is what you want?"

I could hardly calm myself enough to ease the thudding of my heart. "As if you would even allow it."

"I would," Calix replied slowly. "If that is what you wanted, I would take you back myself."

My laugh surprised me. The narrowing of Calix's eyes revealed his discomfort the sound caused.

"I don't believe you. You heard what Auriol said. What *you* already know."

"Tell me," Calix said. "Say it."

"You need me. You need me so you can trade me to see your brother returned…"

"And I am sorry if I gave you the impression that I was your knight in shining armour, come to save you from your awful life."

I hadn't felt anger like this since the first time Eamon raised a hand to me. My bravery to even allow such an emotion had died long ago. The feeling was so fresh and familiar that it took me back to that day.

It was the morning of my mother's accused murderer's execution. Eamon didn't wish to hear my pleas of the vampire's innocence, to acknowledge that I didn't believe the vampire was at fault for her death caused him too much of a headache. I had barely got five words out before his fingers had slapped themselves across my mouth, and the other ran across my scalp where they knotted with my hair.

"*Enough*," he had hissed, splattering spit across my face. "*That's fucking enough.*"

Even if I wanted to scream back at him, his harsh palm prevented that. He must have seen my desire in my wide eyes because his grip on my hair tightened until I could hear strands breaking one by one. I was frozen in shock, surprised and worst of all… fearful, an emotion I never thought possible to be conjured by Eamon.

"Rhory." I drew out of the memory to find Calix inches before me. "I shouldn't have said that."

It took me a moment to pull myself from the nightmare. Where my body was and my mind had been were two entirely different places. I had no recollection of Calix reaching me, nor when he put both hands on each of my shaking arms.

"You couldn't save me from him," I replied finally, speaking through the sorrowful lump in my throat. "No one can. Don't flatter yourself for even a moment, Calix."

I was highly aware of his closeness now. His warm touch reminded me of just how cold I was. The long autumn nights were far more deadly than winters. They made you believe they didn't have the power to freeze one to the bone by distracting with jewelled toned leaves, when in reality it was lethal.

I waited for Calix to say something else. It was the way his eyes flinched that told me he had something lingering on the tip of his tongue. Just before his lips parted, he dropped his chin to his chest and sighed.

"How are you so certain Eamon has your brother?" The question had been at the back of my mind until now. In a blink, I traced through my memories for any sign or familiarity that suggested Eamon was truly responsible for Silas's abduction.

"Because I know. And I am sorry if that answer is not good enough, but that is all I can tell you."

My mind told me to pull away from him and continue my blind journey back to Darkmourn. To Eamon. But something stopped me. Was it the warmth his touch gave me, or the way it seemed to cut through my emotions and give me some sense of grounding that kept me from listening to my better judgement?

"What would Eamon want with your brother? Make me understand... I deserve as much."

I sagged forward when Calix was the one to break contact. My shivering intensified immediately at the lack of his touch.

"You are not the first to be blinded by his charm."

I was caught in the web of Calix's gaze. My power reared itself to the surface, conjuring a glow of gold that illuminated the minimal space between us. Usually, I would have to touch another to sense their true emotions, but Calix's was so powerful they rolled off him in undulating waves. His helplessness had the power to barrel me over. But it was the undertone of guilt that unnerved me the most. Touching him wouldn't answer the question as to what he felt guilty about, but I was prepared to find out.

"What has this got to do with Silas? With Eamon?"

"Silas and Eamon." He paused. "They—"

Discomfort coiled around my heart and squeezed. Jealousy burned at the back of my throat.

"Are you suggesting my Eamon and Silas..."

"I am."

I turned away from Calix, not wishing for him to see the storm of emotions pass, one by one, across my face. I silently questioned if I believed Eamon had such a capacity for loving another. The answer came quickly to me.

Eamon wasn't capable of love.

"You could have reported this to the Crimson Guard directly. If Eamon has kept your brother hostage, they would have the authority to help you!"

Calix shook his head, long strands of his unkept hair falling around his face. "They are as corrupted as the man who heads it."

"You are wrong about them," I replied. The accusation hurt more than the idea of Eamon in love with another. The Crimson Guard were good. They stood for everything right in the world. Their entire existence was a product of my father's devotion and heritage.

It broke my heart to think Eamon's poison had not only slipped into my life, but into the very legacy of my father's efforts.

"I can imagine this is a lot for you to take in." Calix placed a careful hand on my shoulder, reminding me he was there. When I faced him, my knees grew weak to the pity he looked down at me with. It conjured bile to creep up my throat and sting with every swallow.

Calix saw me as weak. As something which required gloves to hold. Something breakable... as if I wasn't anything entirely whole in the first place.

"Do not pity me," I said, refusing to blink for fear of what it would unleash.

"Touch me and you'll find that pity is not the emotion I hold for you, Rhory."

The offer was there, but I ignored it. Reading Calix's emotions wouldn't help untie the strange knot his closeness conjured deep in my chest.

I blinked and a single tear fell from the corner of my eye. Calix reached for it before I could. The rough pad of his thumb brushed across the soft skin of cheekbone. He spread his warmth, caught my tear and drew it from my face.

"No, no crying." I sensed the command hidden beneath the soft whisper of his voice. It was reminiscent of when he called out my name only minutes before this moment. "I want to propose a deal, something for you to ponder."

I swallowed hard, sniffling. Part of me was distracted by the phantom heat of his touch, whereas the other part of me couldn't loosen that demonic tightness in my chest.

"Surely I would need something of worth to enter a deal, and I am afraid I am worthless to you."

Calix ignored me. He continued to stare deep into my eyes. "If you wish to be returned to Eamon, then I will take you. But only if you agree to one thing."

"What about your brother?" I muttered, fear kindling at the thought of Eamon but recognising it as the only outcome.

"Forget the trade, forget Silas. In truth, I would sleep better knowing you would not be in the midst of a tension you have no need of... knowing." Calix paused and took a hulking deep breath before continuing. "If you wish to go home, then I will see it done. But only when these fade."

My breath hitched as Calix brushed his thumb across the tender skin of my bruised neck. I gasped at his touch. A shiver spread across my entire body, leaving not one inch of skin without prickles. I reached up and put my fingers atop his as Calix studied the marks Eamon had left on me during our last encounter.

"Regardless if I demand to return to him now, or if you see this trade through... Eamon will paint my body in deeper bruises than these, Calix. How well would you sleep knowing the type of hands you are placing me back into?"

Calix's eyes narrowed. The colour darkened as he lowered his hand from beneath mine and returned it to his side. "Who is to say he will have hands left? I said I would return you to him; I didn't say in which state he would be in when I did so." I had never worried for Eamon before, not until this very moment. "If Eamon is smart enough to heed my warning, then all would be well. He can decide his fate, just as I wish for you to decide yours."

I stood awkwardly as Calix's threat to my husband's life sunk in. Each word settled over my consciousness like spits of ash from a spilling hearth.

"Fine," I said, breaking the tension. I fought the strange urge to raise my hand and offer it to him. Weren't deals not solidified with a shake of a hand, or the sharing of blood upon pricked fingers?

"Fine," Calix echoed.

He glanced skyward and frowned. I followed his gaze to the flashing of the near full moon that crowned the dark skies beyond the canopy of the forest. When he returned his attention to me, all concern had faded once again. "Before Millicent comes looking, I suggest we return you to your room. Her mood is always more erratic after she hunts."

Calix started away from me, and it was I that chased to follow after him.

"Millicent," I began, fumbling over roots and fighting my way back from the outstretched foliage of the forest. "Millicent said something to me..."

"Before you continue, no I will not say anymore; that is Millicent's story to share, not mine."

The conversation was dead before it even took its first breath.

Soon enough we had made it out the thickest part of the wood. The trees were thinner, allowing the starlight and moon to cast some silver across the world. Enough to see the opening of a tunnel stretched out within a mound of earth that stood thrice the size of Calix's height.

It was the entrance to the tunnels hidden beneath trailing vines that clung to the arched wall of brick and mortar.

"Shouldn't you be tying the blindfold back over my eyes?" I asked as he waved me into the dark shadows of the tunnel's gaping mouth.

"With such a proposed question, I am beginning to think you enjoy it."

Scarlet blush crest over my cheeks like a breaking wave. Calix sensed it and chuckled deeply to himself, except the sound came alive as it echoed throughout the darkness before me.

"Never mind," I grumbled as I passed him, sensing the way my stomach flipped as my shoulder brushed his firm chest.

"Trust. It is imperative when embarking into a deal," Calix said, following steps behind me. "I trust that you are not going to run away before we see it through, and I want you to trust what I have to say in return. The lack of blindfold is the first step. Again, unless you would prefer it and I would happily put it on—"

"Lead. The. Way." Each word was forced out of me with urgency.

"Pretty please," Calix replied, pouting.

I rolled my eyes. He laughed again. And Calix led me without further jibe or comment until we returned to the door to my room.

His room, I reminded myself once again. *His.*

15

IT HAD BEEN an entire turn of a day since I had been standing in the belly of the forest with Calix, and still I felt his touch across my neck as though it had been only minutes before. My skin was tender beneath my fingers as I inspected the bruises in the scratched mirror. The bruises had muted to pale blues and greens but were still there. I felt relief at seeing them. Even if I knew my decision to return to Eamon had not changed, part of me wished for these marks to never fade.

Although I had not long woken, I beheld a deep tiredness that told me night was upon us. Nothing was stopping me from walking out this bedroom door, through the winding tunnels and back towards the promise of fresh air in the world above. Calix wouldn't stop me. Not because he wished to keep me here against my will, but because he had kept his distance from me. I hadn't seen or heard from him since he deposited me back into this rather comfortable prison. Because that was what it was, deal or not.

Calix had provided me with the key to my own metaphoric shackles.

I stared deep into my reflection. The green of my eyes looked more vibrant compared to the dark circles beneath them. I hadn't washed in days, so much so that my poppy red hair had grown wiry and stuck up in strange angles across the back of my head; no manner of wet hands could smooth the hair and keep it down.

At least I looked the part. When Eamon would see me, I prayed he would see the state I was in and find some relief that I had returned home to him. Perhaps this forced space between us would soften his touch and remind him of a time when his language of love was not hard fists and pinching fingers.

Ever since the day he first raised a hand to me until now... I was simply waiting for the chance to save him from his darkness. Darkness I had long blamed on myself for causing. I had changed him; it was the only reason I could find for his shift in personality. Which meant this was not only my fault, but my sole responsibility to fix him.

Pushing thoughts of my husband to the far reaches of my skull, I chose to distract myself until Calix came for me. Or Millicent, except I hoped the vampire kept her distance.

I finished the plate of food that had been waiting for me when I woke. The jug of fresh mint water was now half empty. Most of the cuttings of mint were between my teeth, which I chewed all the flavour and relief from them.

Then the screaming started.

It came out of nowhere. The wall of silence that sang in the tunnels shattered as a deep, rumbling howl erupted from beyond the room.

My power burst to life and cast my hands in their golden glow. I raised them up before me, fingers shaking as another howling roar joined the echoes of the last. This one was louder. Stronger. Deeper. And it sang with pain. Agony. Hurt.

I ran towards the door which opened before I could reach for it. Millicent was waiting, her narrow yet powerful body blocking the doorway. There was no sign of panic or even a lick of concern across her stoic, red-gazed face.

"Going somewhere?" she asked just as another gargled shout sounded from down the tunnel behind her.

I looked beyond her shoulder, eyes narrowing as I tried to make sense of the location among the shadows. Millicent hadn't confirmed it, nor did I need to hear another shout to know who it came from; somewhere, deep within me, the truth lingered.

"Calix, that is Calix, isn't it?"

Millicent looked over her shoulder, an expression of boredom smoothing the creases that settled across her pale forehead. Her whip of dark hair had been collected into a single braid that hung down her spine like a snake. When she returned her attention back to me, I noticed her eyes flicker to the glow of my hands, if only for a moment.

"It is," she answered.

My blood turned to ice in every vein. "He needs help."

"Calix needs more than help."

I tried to step past her, but she moved her body in the way.

"Why aren't you going to help him!?" I gestured behind her just as another skin peeling cry sang through the dark. His pain was so raw it filled the air with a sour tang. Each inhale I took, I could taste it in the back of my throat like bile after a bout of sickness.

"Calix has asked me to keep you in your room. It's not safe for you outside it tonight."

I stepped in close to her. With the burning concern and desire to help Calix, I hardly registered the fear I once had towards the vampire. "From my impression, I didn't think you cared for my well-being."

Millicent smiled slowly. "I don't."

"Then move out of my way."

"Please?" Millicent cocked her head to the side. "Or is that word above you?"

I lifted my hands and Millicent flinched as the gold light spilled out of my skin. She reacted to my power as if I held the sun between my hands, ready to turn her dead skin to ash with one ray.

"Please," I said slowly, heart thudding in my chest. "I can feel his pain. Let me help him."

"Calix does not need your help, witch." Millicent moved out of the doorway now, almost gesturing like gentry for me to move past her. "But you do not look like the person who is willing to take no for an answer. Go. Be the fool you are destined to be. Do not say I didn't warn you."

I should have asked her what I was to be warned against. What danger waited for me and why Calix had her stationed beyond my door like some hired guard. But when the next scream stretched out for an unnatural length of time, I found myself running. Running towards it. Running from the safety of my room.

Running towards Calix.

∼

The golden cast of light from my hands guided me through the tunnels. I hadn't ventured in this direction before, but I felt the sense that I was losing myself. On and on, I ran. The screams echoed across the brick walls and curved ceiling. My feet splashed through puddles of stagnant water, splattering my lower legs in old dirty muck. From the corner of my eye, I saw marks etched into the walls beside me, circles and strange shapes. Some markings looked like words from a language no one old enough in this world could read.

It was clear these tunnels had been here a long time. Even the musky air smelled ancient as it burned down my throat while I continued running towards Calix.

My lungs burned. My muscles ached. Each bone rattled with the force of my footfalls. But my discomfort was nothing compared to Calix's. Whatever was happening to him, it sounded as though someone sliced every inch of skin from his body and snapped every one of his bones one by one.

I wished to claw for the red laces of my corset and free myself from the squeeze of material across my chest. There was no time to stop, let alone offer myself some comfort, not when Calix's screams of terrifying pain grew louder and louder the deeper I lost myself to the tunnels.

My light soon revealed a heavy iron door. It waited at the end of one tunnel and was locked from the outside. I came to a stop before it as Calix raged beyond. Whoever had put him inside had ensured he couldn't leave. He was locked in.

I fumbled awkwardly with the large slab of iron that rested across the width of the door. A growl of determination burst out of me as I lifted it from its confinements. The sound of the metal slamming into the stone floor joined in symphony with another of Calix's cries.

With a great tug, I pulled the door open and revealed the most horrific scene before me.

Calix was knelt in the middle of a room flooded in the glow of burning torches. Infinite chains kept him in place; he was trapped amidst the web of iron. The chains were bolted to the walls and floor. They were wrapped around his bulging arms, legs, chest, waist, neck. I could hear the very hinges scream as Calix fought against them.

He snapped his head up to me. Strands of his shaggy brown hair were plastered to his face with sweat. Spit dribbled down his chin, mixed with blood from his pierced lips where his blunt teeth had bit into.

"Go," he roared, honey eyes burning with fire from within, "Away!"

I stepped towards him, helplessly looking from the chains to his bare skin. He only wore leather trousers that hung across his powerful hips. His chest was naked, muscles rippling like water with every howl and breath he expelled.

"Who did this…?" I mumbled. The closer I got to him, the more Calix fought the bindings of chains.

If only I could touch him, I could take his pain away. My hands still glowed, ready to do just that.

Calix tried to say something again, but he lost himself to his pain. His head threw back and his mouth split in a deafening cry. His face crumpled into itself as the contraction of agony overcame him.

Then I saw the marks. Four harsh puckered lines sliced down the right side of his proud chest. Old scars. Marks similar to that I had seen before.

On the torn, mutilated body of my mother.

It stopped me in my tracks.

Calix stopped howling and looked back to me. His wide eyes roared with panic. Silently, he begged me to help him. I pushed my dread down and went to him.

"Let me get you out of this. Then I can help with your pain."

Calix didn't fight back. He didn't refuse me. He watched as I looped chains off from his limbs. He hissed, spitting and flinching.

"Rhory, run." He forced the words out as though it was the hardest thing for him to do. "Leave me."

"No!" I refused sharply. My knuckles grazed his scarred chest as I lifted the loop of chain from his waist and over his head. It was a puzzle to free him, but I worked quickly. Focus and determination had me solving it. His skin boiled. I had never felt such a fever in a person before.

Whatever was happening to him required more than the relief I could offer with my power. He needed St Myrinn's. Perhaps Jameson had concoctions or medicines that would ease Calix's affliction.

Once I freed him and dampened his agony, I would take Calix there myself. Millicent would have to help; I would *make* her.

I was so focused on freeing him from the web of chains that I didn't notice when his harsh breathing mutated to something entirely different.

He growled.

I stilled my hands and slowly lifted my gaze to his. At some point Calix had stopped shouting, stopped fighting.

Fear sang within me. It spiked when my eyes found his. Except it wasn't his, not the honey-tones I had grown familiar with. Now they burned a bright, molten gold with swirls of dark red dancing around his irises.

I stumbled back as the skin across his face shattered like broken china. Flecks of skin fell away, turning to ash in the air. Beneath it, I saw fur.

Calix opened wide to reveal a mouth full of teeth which seemed to grow before my eyes.

"Go," he growled. "Nooooow." His last word drew out into the sound that didn't belong to a human. It was the song of a wolf, crying to the moon.

I scrambled away from him as his bones bent, cracked, snapped and shattered. Calix's skin fell away from him like snow captured in the wind. His face elongated and spread with dark fur.

Calix grew before my eyes. The transformation happened with fluid grace. His arms lengthened and pulled against the remaining chains. His leather trousers ripped as his legs bulged through.

I was frozen to the spot. Even my power had faded from me. All I could do was watch as the monster lifted his dripping maw and settled its unnatural eyes at me.

It was not pain I sensed without the need of touch.

This was hunger.

16

IT SEEMED, when faced with a monster, one's senses betrayed them.

My ears muffled until the world sounded as though it was beneath a body of water. All I could discern was the faint *thud, thud, thud,* of my heart somewhere from deep within me. I blinked, slowly, and watched Calix stretch and mutate into a creature that was both human and wolf.

In place of skin was now washes of dark thick fur. Calix stood on two bent legs with paws the size of boulders with perfectly pointed, yellowed claws which carved grooves into the stone beneath him.

The stomach of the creature had shorter hair which outlined the sculptured mounds of humanoid muscles. His chest, thick neck, and the unnatural head of the ferocious wolf was maned like a lion and splattered with the creature's saliva.

I stared, helplessly, into the coal-red eyes of the monster and screamed. A part of me told myself to close my eyes, so I didn't watch as my end greeted me. But I couldn't. It was as though wooden picks held each eyelid up in its place whilst I couldn't help but study every pearly white tooth that snapped in the maw of the creature.

"Please…" I begged, tears wetting my cheeks. "Please, Calix."

The creature reacted to the name. As the final chains slipped free from him like loose trousers without a belt, the wolven beast flinched. Two pointed ears flattened back and its eyes narrowed in recognition.

Perhaps it was my desire to live that made my mind catch the subtle reaction. But I grasped onto it and shouted his name over and over, each time growing more feral and desperate. "Calix, Calix… CALIX!"

The monster bent forward until it rested on all fours. I caught the ridges of its spine ripple like water over stone as it pawed towards me.

A thick tail flicked left to right out the corner of my vision. At some point I had fallen to the floor. My palms were hot where the skin had ripped against the old floor. The pain meant little as the creature came close and I scrambled backwards until I couldn't anymore. A wall trapped me at my back. I didn't dare look away from the creature, but I felt the draft of air from the open door at my side.

If I could just get out, close the door and return the iron bar back to its hold… it would give me a moment to run. To do just as Calix had commanded before the monster replaced him.

Hot, sickly breath washed over me and destroyed all hope for escape. Warm globs of spit dripped across my thighs as Calix leaned in close.

I turned my head to the side as the wet kiss of the wolf's nose brushed into my neck. Every muscle in my body tensed. I blinked and saw, in my mind's eyes, a maw full of pointed teeth pressing into my soft flesh.

A low rumbling growl emitted from deep within the creature's throat. It vibrated through every shadow in the room as though they were the audience for some monstrous song.

Then, to my disbelief, the creature pulled back.

There was space between us so suddenly I cried out in relief. Even if I wished to call upon my power, as though such a passive magic even had the capability to help against this beast, it had utterly left me. I couldn't sense its presence even if I wished to.

Calix uncurled to standing once again. Powerful arms ending in blackened talons flexed. Monstrous, hungry eyes widened. Strings of spittle linked every tooth as his mouth split open. When he roared, I threw my hands up before my face as though they would do something to keep the attack from coming.

The noise I made was not a word but a guttural and ancient cry of panic that filled every tunnel, cave and place within this underground world. I continued expelling the sound until my lungs burned with wildfire.

Calix roar broke into a whimper. He threw his maw from side to side, snapping teeth. Even his tail, which whipped with a mind of its own, forced itself between his elongated legs.

Then the unthinkable happened.

The creature did not feast on my flesh as I sensed it wished.

It ran. Gouging scars into the stone floor as it bolted towards the open door and ran off into the dark beyond it.

~

It was Millicent who found me. Her cold touch shocked me out from the ball I had curled into on the floor. I hadn't moved since Calix had shifted into the wolven monster and fled the room. Not a muscle had dared relax ever since the last faint howl reached my ears as the creature disappeared deep into the tunnels of Darkmourn's underground.

"Get up," Millicent commanded. Her voice was careless, but her touch was gentle and guiding. Such a contrast that even in my panicked state I couldn't help but recognise it. "I need to get you back to your room before our dear Calix changes his mind and returns."

My bones ached as she drew me to standing. I was thin and average of height, but Millicent was shorter and smaller, yet could still lift me with a single hand and not break a sweat.

"He is a monster..." The words scratched at my throat as I spoke them.

"We all are monsters in someone's eyes, Rhory. Even you."

She was right. Because, for some unknown reason, that was exactly what Millicent thought I was. A monster. Her eyes flickered with hate every time she looked at me.

"What is he?"

The question hung between us. Millicent put my arm across her narrow shoulders and glanced into the shadows of the tunnel with a faint wariness.

"Quiet. He is stalking the tunnels. The further he loses himself to the wolf the more the chance that he comes searching. I've sealed him in so he can't leave out of the tunnel system, which is good news for life above ground but not for us."

Millicent started for the open door, pulling me in tow.

Her keen ears picked up in my intake of breath before I spoke. She slapped her icy fingers across my mouth and hissed, "No more speaking."

Just as Calix's eyes burned with feral warning, so did Millicent's. I swallowed my question and focused on keeping even my breathing quiet.

She moved me through the dark tunnels without need of torchlight. I found it easy to pinch my eyes closed because the natural dark threatened to drive me mad.

Millicent swore beneath her breath, picking up speed as she navigated forward. And I could hear what sped her up. The scuffling of claws against stone. The growling that sang through the shadows. And the pound of heavy paws as the monster ran throughout the underground maze in search for... a feast.

By the time we reached Calix's bedchamber, Millicent pushed me through the doorway and pulled the door closed with a careless bang. Gone was her desire to keep silent. The tremendous slam would alert even the smallest of cave spiders and the hulking monster Calix had become.

Millicent backed away from the door without turning away from it.

"I can't believe he let you live," she said, hands clenched to fists at her side. "Never has he turned down meat, whatever the kind, when he has shifted. Never."

Unlike the room Calix had locked himself... no, been locked within, this one did not have chains or iron bars to keep him out, only the single bolt which Millicent had not even bothered to draw closed.

"Will he come here?" I asked, my voice small and broken.

"Even lost to the monster he is now, Calix has enough instinct to stay away," Millicent confirmed, finally facing me. If it was possible, her pale skin had grown even more ashen. Even her lips had silvered with dread. "The wood of the door is soaked in wolfsbane. Silver has been threaded through the frame and hinges. In human form Calix could enter, but in this one... Calix would keep clear for fear of what the flora and silver could do to him."

I buried my face in my shaking hands. "If you knew what he was... why did you let me go?"

"Because I can't kill you, but I thought maybe he could."

Millicent knew all along and sent me to Calix as a judge sends a criminal to the gallows for hanging.

"What's stopping you from doing it now?" I asked, dropping my empty hands to my side in defeat. "It is clear you hate me, and now it doesn't even matter as to why. You could take whatever hate you have for whatever I have done and end it. So, why don't you?"

Millicent smiled, even her eyes glowed with it. "I see in the face of death you have found your bravery. And here I was beginning to think you didn't have any."

"Answer the question," I forced out. There was no room for fear in me now, not with the wolfish beast stalking the tunnels, or the vampire who smiled at me, eyes flickering from my gaze to my neck.

"I asked you if you recognised me, and you said no. Perhaps I should get closer." Millicent did as she said, stepping into me. I didn't flinch or move away. "What if I cut my hair and tied a rope around my neck... would you recognise me then?"

Her strange comment strangled me. "I—"

"My brother died because of you," Millicent revealed, a single tear of pure blood rolling down her pale cheek. "He died because it was easier pinning the blame of your mother's murder on a creature which humans already see as evil. He..." Millicent lifted a sharp nail and pointed it directly above my heart. "He died pleading his innocence. And you watched it happen."

I did see it then. Blinking, Millicent's face morphed into that of the man who was put to death by Eamon with the crimes of killing my parents. A vampire who I knew did not kill my mother.

Years of guilt poured out of me. I gripped Millicent by her shoulders, not caring for the way she pulled her lips back from her pointed teeth and hissed in surprise.

"I pleaded with him," I spat, words rushing out of me without thought. "Eamon didn't listen. I couldn't stop him even if I wished and begged. You don't understand…"

"No," Millicent said, stiffening beneath my touch. "I do *not* understand. I watched it happen, you know. How they strung him up with a noose around his neck, knowing that would not destroy him. Your husband displayed him for all to see as the dawn's sun crept over Darkmourn and set my brother's skin ablaze. I hear his screams even now. I can taste his flesh as though his ashes coat my tongue. And whilst they all clapped and jeered at his execution, you stood and watched silently. Complicit."

I couldn't hold her hateful stare, but nor could I look away. My apology died on my lips, knowing it would not bring comfort to Millicent, or me. The words were meaningless, the same words used by Eamon after his fist struck my head, or his nails dug into my thigh beneath a table. I didn't dare speak them.

"I deserve whatever punishment you wish to hand out."

Millicent pulled out of my hands and stepped back. "Which is exactly why you will not leave this place until the trade is done. I heard you in the forest striking a deal with Calix in a moment of his weakness. A deal to take you home. I know what waits for you there, and I want you to go back to him." She almost said it, but I knew *him* had the same meaning.

"Does Calix know?"

Millicent nodded once. "It is the reason I turned my back on my past and pledged to help Calix and Auriol in their cause. Calix knows why and how my brother was murdered, as a means to cover up the truth, to use an easy, blameable target whom no one would think twice to question for a crime. He knows everything."

"I did try to stop Eamon from killing your brother," I said again, eyes burning with hot tears which I did not deserve to shed. "He struck me hard before I could even finish my plea."

Millicent straightened and shed all emotion from her face. "You didn't try hard enough."

She was right. I didn't. Perhaps it was because a part of me wished that my mother's murderer had been found so I could have peace knowing justice was served. It was selfish of me. Regardless of Eamon and the temper he had kept hidden until the day I tried to plead the vampire's innocence, I should have fought harder. I knew he was not to blame, but I watched silently as the noose was lowered around his neck and how the rays of morning sun peeled the skin from his bones.

"His name," Millicent whispered, "was Loren."

All this time I had never known it. Never asked. I felt the weight of Loren's death push down on my shoulders and force me to my knees before his sister. She glared down at me with disgust and pity.

"When the trade is done, and you are turned back into your husband's uncaring hands... I want you to ask him why. Why he picked Loren. What it was that drove his decision. Then, and only then... will you understand it all."

Millicent turned her back to me, paced across to the chair and sat within it. There was no room for further conversation. She didn't look up at me again where I stayed, knelt in the middle of the floor.

Hours passed and the bones in my knees screamed and pleaded for me to move. But I refused. Comfort was not something I deserved.

The revelation of Calix and the beast he had become was no more than an afterthought as Loren and Millicent—and everything about what she said—occupied my mind.

Only when a firm knock sounded on the bedroom door before it opened to reveal Calix, human and dressed, did I stand.

Millicent left the room without a word.

The tension remained and only intensified as Calix finally spoke. His words pierced my chest and drove directly into my heart, aided by the heavy sorrow in his gilded but human eyes.

"You shouldn't be alive."

17

"Rhory, I *am* so sorry."

We stood at opposite ends of the room, glaring at one another as his apology stormed between us. I toyed with the concept of accepting it, but in truth I didn't know the extent of what part of our story he wished to apologise for. Was it the fact he wanted to use me? Stole me from my home, my husband? Or did he wish to apologise for turning into some monstrous creature and almost killing me? It was hard to imagine what I had witnessed as reality, let alone that a monster even lurked beneath Calix's freshly repaired skin.

"What are you?" I asked, breaking the tormenting silence.

Calix took a step forward only to stop when he noticed me flinch backwards.

"There isn't exactly a name for it," he replied, studying me carefully with his gilded eyes. "Not one that would encompass what I am, and what I become."

"A wolf," I answered for him. But that wasn't entirely the truth. No wolf had the shaping of a human, with the ability to walk on its hind legs and move with mundane grace. But he wasn't human either.

"That is a part of it."

"Are you the only one?" I knew the answer before asking it.

Calix shook his head, causing chestnut hair to fall over his eyes. "Our kind is rare. Auriol, my grandmother was the first. Then her husband, but he didn't last long…"

Something Auriol had said during my first visit chose that moment to occupy my mind. "Auriol ate him. She told me that herself… I thought it was a joke."

"My grandmother is many things, but a trickster is not one of them. Yes, she killed my grandfather when it became clear his change to the *beast* gave him some power over her. So, she devoured his heart and reclaimed her rightful mantle as alpha of our pack."

"Pack?" The word fell out of my lips without restraint. "Alpha?"

"There is not a handbook on what we are. What we know comes from instinct and more so, trial and error." He gestured down at himself with two proud hands. "But what we do know is the instinctual part that sings through our blood. Auriol is the alpha."

"And what about you?"

"Would you walk with me?" Calix replied with a question of his own. "I promise to tell you everything, but I would rather do it beneath the open sky. Last night was... torturous."

I didn't know what to say. There was a part of me that wished to refuse him, but another that thirsted for knowledge. "Is it safe?"

"With me, you mean?" I watched the lump in Calix's throat bob. "If you are wondering if I am going to turn again and hurt you, the answer is no. I am in control until the next full moon. And I promise, Rhory, I will not hurt you. I *can't* hurt you."

Before my very eyes, Calix struggled with the guilt of what had happened. I saw it in the cower of his gaze and the way he couldn't look at me for longer than a few seconds, before focusing on something unimportant like his hands or the cuff of his dark shirt.

"I know you won't," I replied. Shock creased across his face. I even caught the way his shoulders straightened, as if some weight on them had lifted.

Calix nodded. He ran his fingers through his hair and scraped it back completely from his face. The muscles in his jaw feathered as though he chewed on my words before swallowing. "Come then, I have something I wish to show you."

"Only if you promise to tell me all of it," I retorted, stepping in close to him. His scent invaded me. One deep breath and my ease had returned.

"Auriol was the first of our kind," Calix continued as we left the dark tunnels. "Her story is where this began, and it will be where it finishes as well."

It was early dawn in the world above the tunnels. Mist clung to the ground, twisting and curling around our feet as we padded through the forest. It was windy enough that the branches bent in the gusts, allowing leaves to be torn and scattered around us. I was thankful I brought my red cloak with me. It kept some warmth in and the chill of autumn out. I hugged it around myself, grateful for the comfort and the way it kept my dishevelled and dirtied appearance from view.

I had not been outside with Calix during the daytime since the first time I visited Auriol. Dawn light did little but accentuate my unwashed and messy state. Beneath Calix's attention, I felt more self-conscious than I thought possible.

"Is this some type of curse?" I asked, keeping pace at Calix's side. "Like the one the last witch put upon Lord Marius, the one that made him a vampire?"

Calix stared forward to some unseen destination he had yet to reveal. "Yes, I suppose you could say my grandmother's aliment was a result of the same witch, but not in such a direct connection. Auriol, although mortal, has been around far longer than you could comprehend. Back from times before humans returned from their walled communes. In fact, Auriol was born in Tithe, as was her brother, Arlo."

"That would make her over a hundred years of age," I said, breath fogging beyond my lips.

"One hundred and thirty-one to be exact. Although I recommend you don't mention her age. It would be unbecoming." Calix offered me a sideways smile that lasted a flicker of a second. It faded when he saw I did not hold one.

"How did it happen?"

"In the early days, after the covenant between life and death was created, my grandmother was visiting Castle Dread. Have you heard of the beasts that lurk within the castle's boundaries? Shadow wolfs, blood hounds. They have many names, all fuelled by speculation and uncertainty. But what is certain is they bite."

I had heard stories of the shadow beasts that dwelled outside of Castle Dread. They were used for stories that adults told their misbehaving children. A way to warn them from Castle Dread. And it worked. Sometimes, in the dead of night, I was certain I heard them howl.

"Auriol was attacked by... a shadow hound?"

"Attacked perhaps is not the right word," Calix replied. "Although my grandmother has not shared the details completely, and nor have I ever felt the desire to push her on the matter, but what we know is she was bitten and changed. She was the first."

Of how many? The question died on my lips as Calix added, "Ah, we are here."

Just beyond the border of the forest we cleared through was a lake that spanned out before us. Its surface was as still as glass and as blue as the sky. If it wasn't for the clouds above, I would have believed it connected seamlessly.

"I thought you might care to bathe," Calix said softly. "The waters are cold, but it should help with your bruising. If not, the cold will decrease the swelling."

Considering the natural chill of autumn was as cold as an iron blade, my cheeks blossomed with heat. Noticing my embarrassment, Calix quickly added, "I won't look, and I am not suggesting you require it. Consider it an apologetic gesture; I prefer mine to be more than words. I find actions speak far louder."

"Sorry for nearly eating me?" I suggested, offering him a smile.

Calix gave me his full, undivided attention. The ring on my finger seemed to burn as I allowed his gaze to jolt my stomach. "You should be dead, Rhory. When the full moon rises, I am lost to it. I know nothing but primal instinct and hunger. I should have killed you…"

Mood ruined. My stomach dropped like a stone so quickly I felt sick.

He stepped in close, the toes of his boots pressing into mine. Calix had to look down at me with his added height. The sun rose across the lake behind him, his shoulders cast me in shadow.

"What stopped you?" I asked. I blinked and saw the beast that had only hours before regarded me with starving hunger.

Calix raised a hand. Slowly, he drew his fingers to a strand of my red hair and brushed it back from my brow. His finger was soft against my skin. My sharp intake of breath was not because I was scared of the claws that lurked beneath his human hand, but from the tentative care his touch held.

How could such a monster be so gentle, when the hands I was used to left bruises, not goosebumps?

"You did," Calix replied. "It was you who stopped me. In that state I know nothing but what my instincts tell me. There are no thoughts, no negotiation, no will of my own, only that of the wolf. But here you are, standing before me unscathed. Breathing."

I felt myself leaning into him when Calix withdrew his hand and returned it to his side.

I raised my hand and pressed it into his chest. Calix breathed rapidly, chest rising and falling beneath my touch. It moved my fingers up and down, causing the light of dawn to catch against the faded metal of my wedding band. For a moment I lost myself. The ring reminded me with horrifying clarity.

"Promise me you will not watch," I said, drawing the conversation down a different path.

Calix noticed my sudden change. I had to look back to the lake to stop myself from reading the disappointment that glowed in his eyes. "I would do anything you ask of me. That is the problem."

My stomach jolted again. The feeling was so divine it made me want to cry. I bit down into the insides of my lips until I could taste blood. Only when I felt I had control of myself did I speak. "About our deal… I have changed my mind."

Calix took a deep inhale, readying himself for what he believed was further disappointment. "Until your bruises fade, that was the deal."

"That was if I wished to be taken back to Eamon."

"And do you?" Calix's deep voice rose to a peak with the last word.

"I do," I said, speaking the two words just as I had when I said them to Eamon on our wedding day. "But not before you get your brother back. I think it is clear now as to why Eamon took an interest in him. Your… affliction could give him the power he clearly craves."

Calix held my stare, eyes flickering across my face, making me feel as though he drank every detail of me in. "Are you confident you wish to be in the middle of this?"

"You ask that like I have been given a choice in the first place. May I remind you, Calix, you're the one that snatched me from my bedchambers and took me for this very reason."

"Was it me? What happened last night?" he asked. "Am I the reason you changed your mind?"

I could have revealed to Calix what Millicent had not long told me, but I couldn't bear to recognise the guilt which had only just been buried down deep enough to ignore. So, I picked my answer carefully, knowing it would drive a wedge between us. A wedge that would keep my ring finger from burning my skin, even if I wished to tear it free and place my hand back upon this man's chest.

There was something so familiar about the urge.

"Yes." I turned my back on him and began fiddling with the laces of my crimson cloak. "Now, turn away. I will not be long."

Calix spoke to the back of my head. "Very few know about us, Rhory. We are going to want to keep it that way. Our… existence puts those with power in positions of weakness. If you, or Eamon, or anyone decided to reveal our truth, then it would lead to so much death."

A violent shiver brushed over my neck as Calix took the cloak and lifted it from me. When I looked back at him, all signs of his previous gentle nature had vanished. A wall had been thrown up, and he barely looked at me. When he did, it was as though I was a stranger.

Which, I reminded myself, I was.

"I don't believe for a second that Eamon, or his Crimson Guard, would have the ability to harm you. Not after what I have witnessed."

"You are not wrong. But Lord Marius would have something to say if he discovered us. I hardly imagine he would allow such abominations to roam Darkmourn freely."

Calix read my unspoken question which glistened across my parted lips. "Why?"

"Bathe quickly," Calix said, diverting the conversation. "I should return you to the tunnels before Auriol catches wind of this. She would eat my heart next if she knew what you have learned."

He did as I asked, turned his back and walked back to the shadows of the forest's border. "Won't Millicent inform her?"

Calix's laugh rumbled through the shadows. For a moment, I caught the undertone of a growl from the beast I had met last night. "Millicent needs Auriol. She won't risk the promise of freedom for the chance to one up me. Believe it or not, her desires for a future outweigh her desire to see you pay for the death of her brother."

He knows. Panic surged through me. *He knows.*

"Enjoy the waters," Calix added, his voice cold as the chill that seeped from the lake's edge. "I can't promise such an offering again."

18

Calix stalked ahead, not once turning back to see if I followed. My hair was still drenched by the time he finally slowed, signalling our return to the tunnel's hidden entrance. My wet skin had spread stains of water across my shirt and trousers. Nothing could help against the kiss of ice the fresh lake left upon me, and the autumn breeze that seemed to want to torture me. At least I was clean. No longer did the autumn breeze remind me of how unwashed I was.

What I desired was a warm hearth and something equally warm to drink. But at least I was clean.

"Wait," Calix barked at me, breaking the competition of silence between us. His outstretched hand stopped me from passing him.

I glanced up to his profile and saw it was pinched into a deep scowl.

Something was wrong. The sense of dread nearly knocked me to the ground.

"What's the matter?" I asked. Every bone in my face ached with the cold the lake had set into it. I even had to sniff to stop my nose from running down my newly cleaned face.

Calix's nostrils flared. He tilted his head upwards and inhaled deeply. "Blood. I smell blood."

The one word set my world tilting. Suddenly, the forest seemed to cave in around us. I threw my stare around the thick wall of trees but couldn't see anything amiss.

"Stay by my side," Calix said, emanating a low growl from the pit of his chest. "Understand?"

Fear kept me rooted to the spot. My legs refused me; my arms stayed pinned to my side. I found that my mind went straight to Millicent. But daylight crowned the skies, meaning the vampire would be lurking deep in the darkness of the tunnels.

Before I could utter a word, Calix threaded his large hand into mine and captured each of my fingers between his own. His grip fought against the shaking that had set in.

Without him touching me, I didn't think I would have ever moved. It wasn't the thought of blood that scared me. Gods, I had seen enough of my own for such a thing not to bother me. It was the look on Calix's face. The way his frown aged him into something ancient and... feral.

I caught the tang of blood in the air soon enough. My sense of smell was nothing compared to Calix's, which meant I smelt it only just before I saw it.

My knees buckled and the ground raced up to great me.

Calix didn't have a chance to let go of my hand before I dropped to the forest's bed. Agony screamed through my shoulder and wrist from the great tug Calix's resistance caused.

The physical pain I felt was nothing compared to the shattering of my heart as I looked upon the body hanging from a branch before the tunnel's darkened entrance. The thick rope around the stout neck of a woman was all that kept her aloft. Her skin was burned raw from the friction as she swung like a pendulum in the breeze.

Mildred hung before me like meat in a butcher's display. It seemed her dead glassy eyes looked directly at me where I knelt. I felt the desire to scream, but I couldn't gather enough breath. The only sound that came out of me was broken and rasped.

She spun slowly, like a dancer on string. Legs and arms hanging limp. Her skin was already as grey as stone.

At some point, Calix had knelt before me. He tried to take my hands, but I swatted him away. His lips were moving but all I could hear was the creak of the giant branch that had become Mildred's gallows.

The back of her dress was split wide. Great flaps of blood-stained material gave the impression she had wings. Slow, so terribly slow, she turned until all I could see was the mutilated skin of her exposed back and the message carved upon it.

HE IS MINE.

Harsh, messy letters had been cut into the hunch of her back. A blade had been used. Not a pen or paper, but I recognised the handwriting immediately. The penmanship was horrifically familiar.

Sick burst out of me. Calix only just jolted back before the contents of my stomach spilled across the ground and my splayed hands. Over and over, I expelled everything possible until my stomach cramped, and my back arched in burning discomfort.

I blinked, and the world grew dark. I blinked again and the shadows refused to recede.

The third time I closed my eyes was the last. They didn't open, but the image of Mildred hanging was seared into the back of my eyelids, haunting me even in the dark.

※

Many things had become clear since we discovered Mildred's body, yet I still felt like I had more questions, and little access to answers. Eamon knew where I was being held. His placement of Mildred was more than the message that was carved into her flesh. It was to tell me—us—that he knew. Which posed the question as to why he had not come himself to claim me? He had the entire army of Crimson Guards at his disposal. Even a small number could outnumber Calix and Millicent. Auriol was bedbound and powerless. So, what was stopping him?

All these thoughts, and more, cascaded through my mind. It was a wildfire, and no one had the power to quench such flames. I was left to burn amongst it whilst grief gripped my ankles and held me firm.

I had not long woken and my hand still ached slightly from being held by Calix. It was the first thing I felt when sleep released me. When I opened my eyes, Calix was holding my hand to his chest. His forehead was pressed atop them as well.

He must have felt me shift because he looked up and released me with urgency. It was as though he had been caught doing something he shouldn't have been doing.

I pressed my aching warm hand to my forehead to find another ache. This one was heavy and dull, located somewhere deep within my skull.

"Here." Calix shuffled in the stool perched at the bedside. "I had some tea made. It might be cold now, but the camomile should aid with the head pains."

I took the mug from him because I felt like it was the right thing to do. In truth, the thought of putting anything into my mouth conjured the urge to vomit again.

My eyes stung, signalling the arrival of my tears. Calix watched as I brought the rim of the cup to my lips as my tears cut down my cheeks. I took a small, pathetic sip and brought the mug back to my lap.

"He killed her," I uttered, voice hoarse. There was the faint taste of sick across my tongue, but the sip of tea helped bury it. "Eamon knows how important Mildred is… was to me."

I couldn't finish speaking what I wished to say aloud.

Mildred died because of me. Because I cared. If I had pushed her away, just as Eamon had urged for years now, then she would never have been used against me.

I felt guilt; it plagued me. Guilt for holding her close, for keeping her as our staff because I was not strong enough to be alone with Eamon. And now she was dead.

Calix placed a hand atop the sheets resting over my thigh. I looked down, bewildered. I didn't dare look at his eyes because I could have drowned in the sorrow within them.

"Eamon is a monster." Calix spoke slowly and carefully. There was a sense of control as each word came out after a pause, whereas I sensed his fury lurking somewhere deep. It sang to my own. "What he has done is unforgiveable. But it will happen again. As long as we have you, he will harm another."

Should I have told him that there was no one left? No one Eamon could use against me. No one I cared for, or whom cared for me.

"What has been done with her body?" I asked. The thought of her hanging... left alone for Gods knows what creature to find her. A starved vampire looking to drink the dregs of her blood, or the wildlife that sheltered within the forest.

"I have tasked Millicent to deal with the body." Calix raised a hand towards me as I jolted forward, sloshing the tea across the sheets. "Nothing will happen to Mildred's body, Rhory. I trust Millicent to do as I have asked."

"Drink her dry?" I spluttered, gagging on the thought.

"No. I have asked that she is buried immediately. If you do not trust me, then I will take you to her."

"Yes, I do... trust you. But..." I swallowed hard, staring deep into his calming gaze.

Calix took my hand in his again, gripped it firmly and said with brows raised, "Use your power and take from me what you need. Just as we did when I brought you here."

"Would that not make me a coward?" I asked, wishing to pull away from his warm, gentle touch but finding I was incapable of moving. "I should face the pain. I deserve it because I caused it. Hiding beneath someone else's stolen emotions—"

"It is not stolen when offered," Calix said, squeezing slightly. "Please, I can't bear to see you like this."

I didn't refuse him. Not again. Gold light glowed from my hand. It reflected across Calix's face, highlighting each strand of his manicured beard, to his smooth skin and masculine features. As I drank in his calm, I drank him in. From the arrow point of his straight nose to the squared lines of his jaw.

He did the same in return.

Each breath became easier as I took in his clarity. Instead of pushing my emotions into him, I buried them. At some point I would need to face it, and I couldn't expose Calix to it. I wished to keep him sheltered from my anguish.

"Is that better?" he asked.

"Much," I breathed in response, finding the weight upon my soul lessen, if only slightly.

The light dimmed to a faint shimmer. It didn't completely retreat as my power picked up a new emotion. One that I had not felt in a long time. So long that it was foreign and strange. There was no naming the feeling that Calix exuded, only the way it warmed my insides like summer sun on naked skin. It was sweet as fresh spring apples picked from an orchard. It thawed my stomach like hot soup on a winter's day. Everything about it was pleasant. Wonderful. Beautiful.

"Calix?" I whispered, his name falling out of my parted lips. My chest blossomed with this new emotion. It sang through me, filling my veins until blood no longer pumped through them but liquid bliss.

He leaned in. I didn't stop him, *couldn't* stop him. "Yes, Rhory?"

"I feel something in you," I said, finding that I leaned into him as well.

"Tell me what it is," Calix replied. "I want to hear you say it."

I pinched my eyes closed and inhaled deeply, drinking this weightless feeling in. When I opened my eyes, Calix was inches from my face. His cool breath washed over me. My eyes darted between his half-lidded eyes to the subtle part of his blush lips.

If I had the words to answer him, I would have. But there was not a word I could find to express this emotion. There was only action.

I closed the small gap between us until our lips were pressed together. The kiss was gentle. There was no movement from either of us. Only my lips, pressed carefully into his. At first, I felt reluctance, but I was drunk on this feeling he gave me, so I didn't care.

With his spare hand, Calix lifted his fingers and danced the tips from the bottom of my neck up to my cheek. He rested it there, holding me in place. Then he pressed in deeper, forcing our lips further into one another.

I returned his urgency with my own. My spare hand gripped his shirt and crumpled the material up into my fist. He couldn't pull away even if he wanted to. And he didn't. I sensed his hunger for me dancing among other unnameable emotions. It thrummed like lightning through clouds, like wind through reeds.

The kiss changed like the seasons. It was soft at first, with slightly parted lips, and tongues entered the fray. Then the kiss was deep and wet. Vicious but tender.

It was everything.

I didn't know who broke away first, but I was breathless, and my mouth bruised raw. My jaw tickled with the memory of his coarse beard rubbing against me. No longer was he awash from the gold light of my power; our hands were not connected at all.

We stared at one another without uttering a word. Calix stood, the stool clattering to the ground. He backed away from the bedside, one hand on his hip, the other holding the lower half of his face.

"I took it too far," Calix growled. He could barely look at me. When he did, I saw disgust.

"No." The single word broke out of me. "Don't say that."

"Rhory, I'm sorry." He moved for the door. I wanted to cry out for him, but my words were caught by the sudden lump in my throat. "I'll send Millicent for you. She will take you to Mildred's body. I—I."

He looked at me a final time, brows pinched and face screwed. Then he turned and left, leaving the door wide open in his wake.

I watched the shadows of the tunnel beyond, half expecting for Calix to return. Still drunk off his borrowed emotions, it was as though the sense of what had happened had yet to hit me. I placed my fingers on my swollen lips. They were tender to the touch.

A flash of gold flickered in the corner of my eyesight. The lightness inside of me faltered as my eyes dropped to the glint of metal, to the wedding band strangling the freckled skin of my finger.

Reality returned, smashing into me all at once, allowing shame to assassinate me.

19

Auriol Grey stared at me from her chair, both brown and blue eyes full of judgement. I tugged the cloak around my shoulders as her gaze narrowed on my face then drifted to Calix, who sulked in the dark corner of the room. Could she sense something was wrong between us?

I fought the urge to lift a finger to my tender lips. Even hours after the incident with Calix they still felt sensitive to the touch.

"Are you certain our message has been received?" Auriol asked the moment Millicent had finished debriefing us on her quick trip to Darkmourn. She had not long returned when she had summoned me from Calix's room.

"Is that doubt I hear?" the vampire replied.

Auriol regarded Millicent with intensity. She may have been old, but even Auriol sensed the ancient presence the vampire held. Millicent's age was unknown to me, but there was something about the way she carried herself that suggested experience. Experience that came with being immortal. Most vampires I had encountered oozed the same aura, but not all of them sang with it like Millicent.

"It is no good to assume Eamon will receive it, let alone accept our terms," Auriol said.

"What did you want me to do?" Millicent retorted, arms crossed over her chest. "I hardly imagine knocking on the door and hand delivering the outline of our terms to him would help. My welcome wouldn't be warm."

I hadn't uttered a word since Millicent had brought me to this room within the underground tunnels. Keeping quiet was an easier option. I had nothing to add. Calix kept quiet too and hardly looked at me. If his gaze, framed by pinched brows, was not on Auriol or Millicent, he chose to look to an unimportant place on the wall opposite him.

Anywhere but me.

"In that case, I suppose we throw all caution to the wind. We are on the back foot. Eamon knows more than we ever wished he could. If our only chance is to go in blind, then we must," Auriol said, obviously displeased with the sudden rush to their original plan. Since Mildred had been murdered and left on their front doorstep, it was clear time no longer favoured them.

"He knows Rhory is here," Calix said finally. His voice was low and riddled with tension. "Our desire to set terms is a waste of time when Eamon could be rallying an army of his Crimson Guard to retrieve *his* —" Calix paused, swallowing back his words for a moment. "To retrieve Rhory himself."

"Except he has had all the chance to do so and has chosen to lurk in the shadows." Auriol looked so small in the chair. She was swaddled by blankets as if the cold tunnels were deadly to her. Regardless, there was something refreshed about her compared to the last time I had seen her. Auriol's voice had shed the slight gravelly tone. Her cheeks were flushed and her eyes brighter.

I couldn't imagine such a frail body breaking and splitting to make way for the monster which lurked beneath. Except when her gaze landed on me, I saw a hint of it. Something feral and old lurked within her, something that held enough power to frighten me.

"You know him better than the rest of us." Auriol glared at me once again, fixating her entire focus on me. Beneath her stare, I felt smaller than she looked. "What is stopping him from saving you, since we all know he has the power and influence to do so?"

I shrugged, unable to answer the very question I had been asking myself since we found Mildred. "Eamon is determined. His focus is sharp. If he wanted me back, he could have got me." I blinked and saw the message he had carved into Mildred's back. HE IS MINE. "Maybe I am just not as important to him as you first believed."

Auriol scoffed. Calix stiffened before my very eyes and Millicent exhaled a slow, long breath. They each shared a look that suggested they knew more than I did on the matter.

"You are very important to him, Rhory Coleman. I would wager that you are, perhaps, the single most important asset to him."

I opened my mouth to tell Auriol how wrong she was. There was not enough time in a day for me to go through the list of reasons to prove my theory. The bruises, the scars, the marks both visible and invisible. They spoke the truth. Alone they debunked Auriol's beliefs.

"Am I in a position to ask about this plan?" I asked, choosing to alter the conversation.

"No," Calix answered quickly. "The less you know, the safer you will be."

We stared at each other for the first time. I couldn't look away, and nor could he. The pressure of his attention snatched my breath, and burned at the skin beneath my wedding band.

"*Safe*," I repeated, tasting just how sour and wrong the word was in this situation. "We both know that is not right."

I sensed Auriol looking between us both again. The taut string of tension between Calix and I had pulled so tight I feared it would have snapped in two if it wasn't for Millicent.

"We are to meet Eamon during the witching hours tomorrow. Of course, we all know this is not a man to be trusted so I shall go ahead. It is less likely he will sense me. Us undead have a way of slipping through shadows. I will then confirm if he has answered our request and followed our clear set of instructions."

Calix continued staring at me. Even when I tore myself from him and forced myself to look at Millicent, I felt his gaze like twin daggers forged of fire, burning through my skin and into my soul.

"I want my grandson back," Auriol said. "The request we have put forward to your husband is simple. Eamon will either give Silas with the promise that you are returned to him. Or—"

"That is enough," Calix barked.

Auriol snapped her head to face her grandson. In the blur I noticed the shift in her eyes. They lost all colour, turning almost completely black besides the spark of gold glowing directly into their centres. "Do you need reminding who you give orders to, child?"

I felt the power weep from Auriol. It filled the air. Her words were so commanding I felt my own will desire to give into it. Millicent slunk back into the shadows, disappearing all but the glow of her blood-red eyes.

"D...Don't." Calix's body shook as he regarded the old woman. He winced, face twisting into a scowl. It seemed he fought against himself to speak the single word; he strained with every ounce of his being to complete it entirely.

Auriol didn't reply with words, but with a sound that rumbled from the pits of her being. Her lips pulled back from her tea-stained teeth and she snapped them together with a harsh clack.

Calix sagged backwards and... whimpered. The sound was bizarre, to be coming out the mouth of a full-grown man; it was more akin to a puppy after being scorned by its mother.

By the time Auriol focused her attention back on me, her eyes had returned to their normal state; only the deepest wrinkles across her brow took a moment longer to smooth.

"Rhory. I wish this was different. I do. If your parents knew of the choices I have been forced to make, they would hunt me down and skin me themselves. Know that I struggle with the truth of what must be done. It is not easy for me, but this is my family. My Silas has been taken and all I want is him returned. You must understand that."

The woman speaking was no longer a wrathful crone with the beast lurking deep within her. She was broken. Tormented. And I felt the truth of her plea in my heart.

"You must do what you must," I replied, straightening myself and forcing as much confidence into my stance as I could. "If I was given the chance to return my family to me, I would do anything."

Auriol relaxed in her wheeled chair, blinking back a wave of exhaustion that drained the colour from her cheeks. All vibrance she had moments ago had faded.

"If I could ask, I wish to be taken to Mildred's resting place." I choked through a sudden sob as I said her name.

"Of course," Auriol replied. "Millicent will take you."

A cold shudder raced down my spine. I glanced into the shadows of the room where the burning sconces didn't quite reach. That was where the vampire lingered. I sensed Millicent's hesitation. She didn't voice it, because there was no need.

Calix refused on her behalf. "*I* will be the one to take him," he said, deep voice strained.

Once again, Auriol looked between us, displeased. I half expected her to force her command back to Calix, but it seemed she was lacking such energy. Instead, she waved a defeated hand. "So be it. Millicent, return me to my cottage. I wish to sleep. And, Calix, be wary."

There was no further explanation as to what, or who, Calix had to be wary of. Eamon knew we were here.

"I don't need your warning; I understand the risks. Rhory is safe with me," Calix replied, stoic and face void of emotion.

"Oh, I remember," Auriol paused briefly before looking to me, "But does he?"

20

MILDRED'S grave was no more than a mound of overturned dirt. There was no marker of stone to confirm her presence. No offering of flowers or gifts laid atop her resting place. If Calix hadn't gestured towards the ground, I would have passed it without ever knowing.

It was raining. Not heavily, but the type of rain that felt more like a mist when walked through. I was already soaked to the bone by the time we reached her burial place. My boots were covered in mud that had splattered up the shin of my trousers.

I stood there, neck aching as I looked down at the ground trying to imagine how we even got here.

"Tell me about her," Calix said, standing vigil at my side. His brown hair looked almost black now it was wet. Rivers of water ran down the side of his face, falling over the hard edges of his cheekbone and jaw. "She may be gone but speaking of the dead keeps their memory alive."

I ground my teeth together as his request burned through me. It would have been easier to refuse him. But I owed it to Mildred to spread her story.

"She was my family. We didn't share blood, but we spent so much time together. Since I was born, she worked for my parents, and then for me when they passed. She had no one else. I used to think we were unfair to her, overused her and ruined all chances of having her own life, her own family. But I once asked her about it..." I choked on my words.

"Take your time," Calix said calmly.

I swallowed hard, feeling the memory swell as a lump in my throat.

"She said... how could she desire a family of her own when she has everything she ever wished for right before her."

Calix placed a firm hand on my shoulder just as the tears began. I had wondered why I had not cried since we reached her grave. There was something about speaking of Mildred aloud which made it real for me.

He didn't urge me to continue, but his touch and presence encouraged me to lighten the weight of guilt that clouded my chest.

"When my mother died, and Eamon... changed, I truly believed he would have laid Mildred off. He did move her out of our family home, but she was still allowed to return daily. I don't think I would have survived this long if it wasn't for knowing Mildred would be walking through the doors of our home. I had to be strong for her."

"Did she know?" Calix asked, voice thrumming through the smattering of rain.

He didn't need to express what he meant. I heard the true question beneath the first. *Did Mildred know how Eamon treats you?*

"No, and I never told her." I turned my body to face Calix completely. Watching rivulets of mud form across the grave was a painful reminder that once I left this place no one would ever know where to look for her. "Does that make me a coward, Calix? All these years I could have shared my burden, but instead I kept it all to myself."

Calix hesitated. I saw it in the wince of his stare and the way his hand formed a fist at his side. "You are not a coward, Rhory. I would never think such a thing, not when it comes to you."

"Then you tell me what I am." I narrowed my eyes and fixated them on his swirl of honey brown. Even if Calix didn't speak what was on his mind, I would fish the truth out of the windows to his soul. "Am I pathetic? Am I weak?"

Calix didn't so much as blink as he replied, "No. None of those."

"Adulterer?"

His brow furrowed. "Last night, that was my doing. I lured you into that. Do not add such a burden on your shoulders which you have already weighed down with the weight of the world."

I stepped in closer to him. A strand of wet hair had fallen beyond his ear. I reached up and tucked it back. Calix's breathing hitched as my finger brushed across the side of his face.

"Do you regret it?" I asked him. "Last night I mean. The kiss."

"Never," Calix said quickly. His rushed reply caught me by surprise as his face seemed to come alive with emotion. "I want to ask you the same question, but I don't think I am strong enough to face the answer."

"The only thing I regret," I said, lips coated with rain and tears, "Is that I never had the chance to meet you when this hand was free of my binding."

Calix winced as though I had slapped him. All his composure slipped, and I was certain the monster within would break free at any moment. His reaction was so powerful, I wished I could have clawed back what I had said.

"I shouldn't have... Calix, I am sorry."

He regarded my left hand and the dull light which glinted in the dawn light.

"Take it off," Calix urged.

"What?" I dropped my hand back before me and clasped it with my other.

"Take the ring off, Rhory," Calix repeated, slower. "Tonight, you will be sent back to Eamon, but until then let me show you what freedom feels like."

"I can't..." I turned my back on him and began to walk. There was not enough time to spare Mildred's grave a final look. All I knew was I had to get away from his suggestion. It was not because I didn't wish to do as he said. I longed to free my finger from the shackle Eamon had put on it. But memories of what happened the last time and the weeks of pain and broken bones that followed was still fresh in my memory.

Calix was before me. He moved with vampiric speed, but I now knew his true curse even if I didn't truly understand it. His leathers glistened with rain. His tunic was so wet it had darkened in colour and clung to every mound and curve of his torso beneath.

"Please, don't run away from me," Calix said.

"You are asking that of me, when you did the exact thing last night. You left me."

Calix held my gaze, both hands reaching out for my arms. He held them gently, and I let him. "I left you last night because I didn't wish to give you more regret to burden yourself with. If I had stayed, I need you to understand, you would have broken more vows to Eamon than you even knew existed."

The insides of my cheeks pinched as though Calix's words were an unripe fruit, and I had just taken a hard bite into its sour flesh.

"That makes you a coward," I said.

"It does. I'm not as brave as you, *Little Red*."

I buckled at the nickname. That nickname, Calix shouldn't have known it. It was a name my father had whispered into my ear as he walked me down the aisle and handed me over to Eamon. Without Calix ever being able to know their power, those two words enraptured me.

Glancing back down to my ringed finger, I didn't notice that Calix now held it in his hands. His thumb brushed across the metal over and over, spinning it around my finger.

"The last time I took my ring off, I was punished for it." I allowed the story to come out of me; it was no good to face such a nightmare on my own when I had someone to hold the light for me. "I had sent Mildred home early because it was her birthday and I couldn't stand the idea of her standing before the sink, washing our dirtied and spoiled pots. She left, and I finished the job for her. All I had done was remove the ring and left it on the side. It was so innocent, harmless. But to Eamon, it was the end of his world…"

I took a breath, realising I had hardly allowed myself one since I started talking.

"Go on," Calix urged, holding my hand and offering his warmth. There was no need to use my power and borrow his emotions; his touch alone calmed me. "I wish to know. I want to know it all."

"Eamon put the ring back on. He was drunk and sloppy. It was like something entirely demonic had overcome him. He took the meat mallet near him and brought it down on my hand. He wanted, I believe, to smash the ring into my flesh so I could never remove it again. Just my luck, his aim was shit, and he brought it down on my hand instead. He shattered most of my bones. He hurt me all because I wanted to clean the dishes."

Calix's breathing had grown ragged. His eyes had taken on its golden sheen. "Cunt," he growled. One word and it was cursed with so much fury even the surrounding forest seemed to bow away from Calix. "Eamon doesn't deserve you."

I didn't resist when Calix lifted my hand to his paled mouth. Wide eyed and with bated breath, I watched him. And he watched me. His rain-slicked lips pressed into my finger, covering my skin and the wedding band. Calix held my finger there for a prolonged moment. When his lips pulled back, his fingers worked with ease to remove the wedding band.

"He broke the sacred vows of your union," Calix said. He reached towards me, the ring pinched beneath his finger and thumb. A shiver spread across my skin as his knuckles brushed over my chest. I looked down the length of my nose and watched him discard the ring in the breast pocket of my shirt. It dropped like a stone, heavy and full of burdens.

Out of sight, out of mind.

"Eamon would never see it like that. I am his to do whatever he pleases."

Calix shook his head, eyes closed as he attempted to regain the composure that was quickly slipping away from him. "He defiles such a blessing. To have you, to be with you, should be the most coveted part of his life. He broke his promises. So, now you should shatter your promise to him."

It was unspoken, but I knew how this was going to end. I sensed it like a flame in my stomach, or fresh air in my lungs. Reading Calix's emotions was not required when his eyes glowed with his desire, his wishes.

"And how do you think I should do that?"

Calix stepped in closer. He trailed his fingers from my hands, up both arms. I shivered as he ran them over my shoulders, up my neck and to my face, where they rested on either side of it. "First, I will show you what you desire. Every place that monster has hurt you. Every scar, every bruise, every fucking mark. I wish to wash the memory of your hurt away and replace it with something else. If you would allow it of me. Tell me to release you and take you back to your room and I will do it. I would do anything for you…"

There was only one option for me. Only one thing I could say to him because, for the first time in a long time, I recognised my desire and selfishly claimed it.

"Stop talking," I said. "And show me."

Calix smiled. We were so close I could see the beautiful curve of the rain droplet that grew on the tip of his nose until it fell down into the limited space between us.

"We made a deal. I promised I would take you home when your bruises fade." Calix dove into my neck as he spoke. His scratchy beard tickled across my dampened skin. I pinched my eyes closed, lips parting in a moan as his lips greeted my tender skin. "I will kiss every one of them just to remind you of what you deserve. What *I* can offer you."

My head lolled back as Calix replaced his words with action. His lips branded my neck. His kiss was subtle to begin with. I faced the skies, rain pattering across my closed-eyed face, as Calix ran his lips, then his tongue, across my neck. He left a necklace of his saliva across it.

He guided me to the ground, all without removing his mouth from my neck. I knelt in the muddied moss-covered bed of the forest. Calix did the same before me. I found my fingers were now tangled in the wet length of his hair. My nails ran across his scalp, urging a moaning groan from deep within him.

I was disappointed when he suddenly pulled back from my neck. That feeling only lasted a moment until I found myself lost to the raging desire in his eyes.

"Rhory, I would like to take you. It would be my honour to offer you a memory to return home with. One that you can… remember this time."

I leaned into him, pressing my mouth to his as I answered, "No more talking. Take me."

Our kiss was soft and careful, whilst being desperate and rushed. We didn't require to use our eyes to know what we were doing. It had been a long time since I had laid with Eamon, but even that faded memory was easily incomparable to this feeling. Excitement bubbled in my chest, echoing the thunder in my groin.

Calix's fingers worked quickly to untie the red cloak. It slipped from my shoulders with ease. He broke away from my mouth long enough to lay the cloak out across the muddied and wet ground. "It may not be the comfort I wish to give you, but I promise you will not notice."

"For once," I said, breathless and lips raw, "I do not want you to be gentle."

"No," Calix replied, eyes narrowed. "Perhaps there would be a time for that, but this... This is something else. You mean more to me than a fuck, Rhory. Allow me to show you, if you trust me."

"But you do not know me," I said, unsure where the words came from, "Not for long."

Calix's lip curled into a snarl. "Do you trust me?" he asked, ignoring my statement as though it didn't matter. And perhaps it didn't.

"Yes, I trust you," I replied. "I am a fool, and you are a stranger, but I trust you, nonetheless."

"Good," he breathed, gilded eyes alight in the darkening storm covered sky. "Then I shall begin."

Calix took his time undressing me. It took a long time until the chill of autumn wind and rain graced my naked skin because he took breaks to kiss every part of me. His lips explored more of my body than Eamon had ever had the chance to hurt. They graced my bare shoulders, my chest, my stomach, my arms and my thighs.

I knelt on the red cloak and watched as Calix removed his own clothes. He refused my help. "I want to watch you. I want to see every thought in your eyes. I want to remember your face when you see me."

And watch him I did.

He was a god carved in flesh. Broad shoulders and a powerful, sculpted chest that gradually narrowed to his firm hips. If I had the time, I would have counted every muscle. Instead, I was hypnotised by the rivers of rain that ran over his body. I was jealous of them, wishing to touch him in the places they graced.

As Calix worked the belt of his leather trousers and plucked the buttons at his waist away one by one, I crawled across the cloak towards him. I stopped only when I knelt directly beneath him. My head was at the height of his waist. Calix didn't refuse my help now, not as my hands reached up the wet material of his trousers, over his powerful thighs to the lump of flesh that grew with every passing moment.

My palm glided over his cock. It was a monster, hidden behind material I would rip away with teeth and nails.

Calix removed his hands and placed them on the back of my head, all the while he stared down the length of his nose at me. I gazed up at him, not taking my eyes from his as I tugged down his trousers, undergarments, and freed the thick length of hard cock.

But curiosity forced my eyes further down.

My breath caught at the sheer size of him. I tried to hide my surprise, but no matter how hard I fought to steel my expression, I failed.

Calix chuckled softly at my reaction as he guided my head towards it. I offered no resistance. His hands pushed at the back of my head until my lips were inches from the glistening tip of his cock. It was as thick as my wrist was. Blessed with length, that even hard, it couldn't stand completely to attention for its weight was too great. It was crowned with dark hair that spread up to his lower stomach in a trail. My hands explored his waist, nails tickling among the coarse hair.

"Look up at me," Calix said, drawing my attention from his perfectly formed being, back to his face. "I want to see your eyes as you take me in."

He freed a hand from the back of my head. Calix took his cock in his palm, lifted it up and pressed the bell curved tip to my parted lips.

My tongue broke free. It slithered from the confines of my mouth. The moment it caressed the end of his length, I tasted his sweetness. It seeped out the eye of his cock and dribbled willingly into my mouth. The insides of my cheeks prickled with ferocious hunger that drove me forward.

I took him in, and Calix roared into the skies. I parted my lips wider as I forced as much of him into me as I could; my jaw ached and throat cramped but that didn't stop me.

I allowed him in until I couldn't physically take any more. His low chuckle encouraged me as I gagged on his cock. His fingers tensed in my hair and held me in place. I slapped both hands on his thighs for aid whilst tears gathered in my wide eyes.

"Good boy," Calix groaned, unsheathing his cock from my mouth with his hand still wrapped around its base. "Just like that. I want it all in that pretty little mouth."

I smiled with my own pride. Seeing Calix's reaction was encouraging and exciting. I stuck my tongue out, not caring for my dribble that fell onto my naked lap. Calix bared his teeth and hissed as he slapped his thick cock onto the pad of my tongue.

One. Two. Three. Four times, he smacked it as he bit down into his lip and groaned.

"More," Calix said. "Take me again, give me your mouth."

My cock was hard too. I didn't need to touch it to know it throbbed with desire between knelt legs. I feared if I did reach for it, a single touch would race me to my end. I was not ready for this to finish. There was so much I wanted from this moment. In Calix's half-lidded eyes alone, they held promises of more to come.

I wanted it all. I wanted him.

I sucked on Calix's length until it was him who stopped me. His hand was replaced with mine as it worked up and down, following the grace of my lips. I would have gone on forever if it was not for Calix who withdrew himself suddenly. He was close to finishing for I could taste his cum within my mouth. It was different to my saliva. Thick and salty. It was a pleasure to let it coat my lips and spread its taste all throughout my mouth.

"Careful," Calix said, joining me on my knees and taking my face in his hands. "I am a selfish man. Selfish enough to know that I am not ready for this to finish. Not yet."

"Your cock tells otherwise," I replied.

Calix crashed his lips into mine. His tongue entered my mouth and twisted with my own. I wondered if he could taste himself on me.

"That pretty little mouth," Calix groaned. His fingers were in my hair. My hands groped his rock-hard chest. "I wish to bury myself in it again. Over and over until I fill you."

"Do it," I urged, not blinking as I bored through him with my gaze.

Calix's sly smile was enough to melt me into a puddle. "I have nothing to aid it, Rhory. It is not my ego speaking when I tell you my cock is far too large to take without... lubrication."

I felt a mixture of excitement and disappointment. Calix was right. His length was considerable, and its girth even more so. My ass flinched at the thought of it entering me. It was not an unpleasant thought, but I sensed there would be discomfort and Calix didn't wish to hurt me.

"But I want you," I whined, nails tracing slight red marks across the hair-covered skin of his chest. What I wished to tell him was this was our only chance. Lust was fading, giving room for reality and I sensed the wedding band in the pile of clothes to our side. It called to me. I couldn't keep my conscience buried for long.

"There are other ways I can pleasure you," Calix said, his words like a promise. "Rhory, I am going to tell you what to do, and *you* are going to do it without question."

I gasped, stomach flipping as though I had reached the peak of a steep hill and was ready to be thrown off the top of it.

"Do I make myself clear?"

Calix's brows twitched as he heard me gulp.

"Yes, crystal."

"Stand up," Calix ordered.

I had never moved so fast before. In seconds I was standing before him. Calix shuffled on his hands until his body was stretched out across my cloak. He laid on his back, gazing up at me as the rain fell over him.

"Come to me," Calix beckoned me with his hands, "Here, come and stand over my face."

My breathing was rushed and heavy. It was as if I had run from Darkmourn and back and my body suffered the consequences. Calix watched me with his soft-gold eyes as I straddled his large frame and waddled all the way up, until my feet were on either side of his shoulders.

"Turn and face the other way," Calix continued.

I listened, wishing to discover what he wanted from me.

His hands reached up for my lower legs; the hairs prickled, and my knees grew weak.

"Sit back and let me take your weight."

I looked over my shoulder and down to Calix. His entire focus was on the curve of my naked ass. He licked his lips as though he faced a delicious meal. Then I realised quickly what he wanted, and my legs almost gave out.

"Slowly," Calix drawled as I gave into his hands and the resistance of his strong arms. "Slowly."

Soon enough I was squatting over his face. I felt his breath brush across the sensitive point of my ass, between the two cheeks he now spread.

"I want you to stroke your cock," Calix said, lips and beard tickling the skin on my ass. "If you want to cum, do it. But tell me. I want to hear you reach your bliss."

I found myself stuttering. "What... what about you?"

"Oh, my darling," Calix replied. "I've already found my bliss."

Surprised, I glanced down to his hard muscular stomach and noticed the cloudy milk-like liquid that dripped into the hair that crowned his softening cock.

Had he come as he pulled me from his mouth? How had I not noticed?

Pride swelled in my stomach. I had done that. I had caused that without even knowing and it made me feel powerful.

"Sit on my face," Calix demanded, tearing me from my thoughts, "I wish to devour you."

Calix's hands were firm as he held me in place. My knees hardly ached from the position I took. There was no room for discomfort when his tongue wreaked havoc on me. It lapped against the centre of me, twisting, licking, sucking. His teeth would come into play every now and then. When he nipped my ass, I was certain he left a mark.

I didn't care.

I wished for him to mark me. To cover me in his kisses, his bites, his sucks.

Only when Calix reminded me to stroke myself did I do so. I was entirely hypnotised by the way he ate at me. I had never felt anything like it in my life, yet my body seemed to convince me otherwise. It was all wetness and tongue. He lapped against the centre of my ass, even going so far as to force his tongue inside of me occasionally.

When my bliss raced towards me, I couldn't form words to warn Calix as he demanded. All I could do was let out a long, breathy moan that caused birds to flock from nearby trees.

"That's it," Calix sang, voice muffled as he pulled back from my ass. His fingers dug into my cheeks and squeezed as I lost myself.

My cum joined Calix's. It splattered across his stomach. Only when the convulsions of pleasure ceased did I recognise the burn in my legs and lower back from being kept in the unique position. He could have been eating me for hours, or minutes; it was impossible to know.

I felt the need to apologise for causing such a mess as I lied down on the cloak next to him. Exhaustion overcame me. I turned my head and glanced at him to find Calix was already looking at me.

"How do you feel?" he asked, weaving his hand into mine.

"Exposed," I said, smiling.

"Then I have let you down," he replied. "You should feel powerful. Strong. Unstoppable. Those are all the things I wish for you."

I rolled onto my side. Leaning forward, I rested my head on his chest, half expecting for him to roll away and stand. He didn't move. Instead, he encouraged me onto him. His heart thundered, thumping against the side of my head.

"I feel like I could sleep for a week...." I faltered, silencing myself quickly. We both knew we didn't have a week to waste together. Merely hours.

"Do you think, if we stay here, the world will forget about us?" I asked, not wanting to welcome the pain deep in my chest. But I was powerless to stop it from affecting me.

"Not here," Calix replied, staring up into the skies above. "But we could leave it all behind."

"You don't mean that," I said. I didn't dare focus on his words for the hope they provided could destroy me. In a strange way, as I closed my eyes and replayed his suggestion over, the words felt familiar, as though I had heard them before.

Calix faced me and his expression broke me in two. "Say the word, and I would do it. I would snatch you away and steal you for myself.

There would be no Eamon. No Auriol. No brother or Crimson Guard. I know our time together has been.... sparse, but I know deep down that I could provide more for you."

"And where would we go?" I couldn't keep back the anger from my question. I hated this. I hated the way he looked at me with pleading and longing, knowing full well that what we desired, and what had to happen, were two entirely impossible things.

"To a place where we would be nameless. We would be without a past. All we would have is what we take with us. A fresh start, a promise for a life without hurt."

"Then tell me why everything you are saying is the most painful thing I have ever felt?"

Calix sat up, his face twisting into a harsh frown. "Hope should not hurt."

"It does," I replied, sitting up beside him. I curled in on myself, hiding my naked body from the world. "To me, hope is a bait to lure me away from reality, lower my guard and destroy me."

"Then I should take you back to the tunnels," Calix said quietly. "We will have only hours until we must leave."

"Okay." It was all I could muster.

"Okay," Calix replied.

He offered me a hand, helped me stand and passed me the pile of my clothes. They were drenched and muddied, but better than being naked.

"Do you want me to turn away this time?" he asked.

"No," I replied softly.

"Good," he replied.

I turned my back on him before he could read my secret reply as it fell silently from my lips.

Never.

21

3 YEARS BEFORE

DEEP in the undead core of my body, I knew something was wrong. Loren hadn't returned home, and sunrise was almost upon Darkmourn. He never stayed out past the long evenings; in fact, he was always the first one home. My brother was, and had always been, introverted. When I changed him—offered him an eternal life of bloodlust and adventure—he almost did not accept it; not because he was scared of becoming one of the undead, or the idea of drinking blood unnerved him... He had said it was longer than a lifetime of speaking to people, and the thought of that displeased him.

Of course, Loren came round in the end. To my relief.

I was younger than Loren by five mortal years, but I felt maternal over him. Perhaps it was because our mother had died when we were nothing but small children, or maybe it was because our father left us when I was old enough to hold my own bottle.

Since then, we had been alone. Just me and him. We had survived together when the world first changed. Sometimes I allowed myself to think back to when Lord Marius first broke free from Castle Dread with his eternal mate, Jak Bishop. In fact, I remembered Jak from my childhood. He was like Loren, in a way. Shy and quiet, but with a dark streak lingering beneath the surface of that facade.

The difference between my brother and Jak was that Loren didn't lead to the destruction of Darkmourn. We were merely products of its obliteration. Victims.

I had been changed first. Not by choice. When the wave of the vampiric disease was freed from Castle Dread, it spread like fire to a dried wood. I remembered the hot burn of the bite to my neck, followed by the soft honey-dew liquid of blood the vampire had dribbled into my mouth.

He had wanted me as his eternal bride, admiring Lord Marius and Jak's story; he had wanted to create one of his own. Except, I had killed him before he had a chance to do any of the vile things he had whispered to me as I drank from his wrist.

Sometimes I still felt the cold slab of flesh that was his beatless heart gripped in my hand before it melted beneath my fingers and fell to the ground as ash.

When I changed Loren, it was nothing like my brutal re-birth. It was kind and soft. I would never have forced him—at least that was what I told myself. Gods only knows what I would have done if time went on and I watched my brother age, knowing he would soon die naturally and leave me in a world I did not wish to be in. Without Loren, I was nothing.

I stared out of the window of our dwelling in Old Town. Legally, it did not belong to us, but we had claimed it anyway. Our real home was down the street from this one, and I had remembered staring through the shutters of our window to this very building when I was a child. The Bishop's had lived here. I had often spied Jak as a boy looking out his own window with a look of distant pondering. Although I could not see what had caught his attention, from the direction his window faced I knew it could only have been Castle Dread he had focused on.

We had not known the Bishops were witches then, although many had speculated. It never bothered me though, I rather liked the boy even if we had never shared more than a word. Which was how I made myself feel better for taking the empty Bishop dwelling for my own and moving in with Loren as the centuries passed.

From Old Town, I had a good view into the main centre of Darkmourn. A blanket of night still fell over the world, but with the passing of time the stars winked out, readying to welcome the bastard sun.

Irritation swelled in my stomach, dampening the hunger which had returned. I should have hunted tonight, but Loren's disappearance had thrown me off. I didn't dare leave in case he returned, because I wanted to welcome him and shout until my throat was raw. He never left without telling me first. He should have warned me.

The Crimson Guard were out in full force tonight. Even Old Town—which was usually more silent than a graveyard these days—had its streets invaded with the roaches. That fact didn't help calm my nerves with Loren's lack of appearance. It only worried me more, knowing how unbalanced the town's protection force had become in the passing years. It was best for monsters like us to stay under the radar. It didn't take much for us to be snatched from the street and punished publicly for something ridiculous.

Tensions had been high since the murder of Lady Coleman, and the Crimson Guard looked for someone to blame.

Dawn was at most an hour away and Loren was still not home. I was moments from smashing our home up in frustration, which was what drove me to wear my woollen cloak and join the bustle of Darkmourn's streets.

I tucked back sheets of black hair into my hood, which I pulled down further over my eyes to hide the glow of red. It was common for vampires to frequent Darkmourn whilst the moon still ruled, but that didn't mean I wanted to catch the attention of the Crimson Guard.

Excitement thundered between the humans as I passed them. My ears picked up parts of the conversations as I slipped through the shadow of buildings around them.

Execution. Coleman. Criminal.

Beneath the ruby glow of the gas lamps lining the streets, I caught the movement of the living. There was never this many out at night. I could smell the sweet scent that oozed from their skin, and the promise of life nectar that lingered beneath it. As I moved further from Old Town into the residential streets, I spied empty bowls of blood left on doorsteps, and bags of coin left in thanks. The hunger within me was growing like a newborn child; if there was a bowl left, I would have taken it. Although I would not have left coin. I was old enough to remember a time where blood was free, and the demonic side of me missed it.

But I had promised Loren years ago that I would never drink from a human again—unless offered. That was a caveat in our deal I had been sure to add. Loren had never drunk blood from a human, not once. He boasted about the divine flavours of rabbit and deer. I never believed he preferred it, but his nature was far too kind to even sink teeth into the flesh of a mortal. I loved that about him. He drove me to be a better version of myself. Without him, I was nothing.

If I had a heartbeat, it would have been racing by now. I looked out across the outstretched crowd swelling in the town's centre. The Crimson Guard and humans I had passed all congregated here, joining the back of the crowd with equal excitement.

Dread cut through me. I didn't need to see what drew their attention to know something was terribly wrong. I felt it in my bones, in every muscle and vein. The discomforting emotion thrummed through me, and it was not fucking welcome.

There was no way I could have fought through the crowd, but I longed to get a better look. I had to see for myself.

Loren's name glistened across my lips. The overwhelming desire to cry out for him took over me. He was in this crowd, he had to be.

Whatever had drawn everyone here had captured his attention too. At least, that was what I attempted to convince myself.

"You," I snapped, gripping the arms of a young man to my side. His eyes threw open in surprise at my sudden presence, before his expression melted into disgust. "What is going on?"

I was far stronger than him, but that didn't mean I prevented the man from pulling out of my hold.

"I'm surprised you haven't heard," he grumbled, looking me up and down with tired hate-filled eyes. "They found the Coleman killer. They're going to hang him up so we can all watch him be brought to justice."

I looked away from the man, throwing my gaze across the sea of people as my mind put the pieces together.

"Who did it?" I asked, not wanting to know the answer.

"His name doesn't matter," the human man spat. "What matters is another one of you… monsters are slain."

I was running before I could even contemplate a reply.

Instead of moving towards the heart of the crowd, I ran around it. Darkmourn was more familiar than the lines on my palms. I knew every building, and who owned it. I had seen people come and go, die and change. Using my knowledge to my advantage, I slipped down a narrow side street as the noise of the crowd swelled behind me.

My nails tore and the skin of my palms ripped as I climbed up the side of the building. I used the old bricks as leverage beneath my feet, and my unnatural force to propel myself upwards as quick as possible. There was pain, but it didn't matter. By the time I reached my destination, I would have healed.

Towards the top of the building was an older apartment that had not been used by the humans in years. It was a hideout for vampires, a place those who needed the shadows in a time of need could use. When I threw myself over the wrought iron bannister and landed on the balcony, I caught the glint of many red eyes glaring through the darkened building within.

I was not the only vampire here today, and I would not be the last.

"Loren?" I called his name, waiting for my brother to step out of the shadows. He had to be here. With the swell of humans and Crimson Guard, he knew to use this place if he didn't feel comfortable coming home. The amount of people out this night would have sent him into the open arms of his anxiety. He knew this was a place of quiet for him.

"Brother, are you here?"

It was not my brother who replied. "He is not here." One of the vampires from the shadows spoke, voice husky and rich. They did not step forward, but that didn't prevent me from seeing as they raised their hand and pointed to somewhere behind my shoulders. "You are too late."

I refused to turn around and face what I had already known. Maybe it was our tie as siblings, or because I had been the one to sire him into this curse—my dread was justified. It was not just a misplaced feeling because he was missing, it was a feeling born from the instinctual bond between us.

"He killed the Coleman woman," the vampire from shadows spoke again.

"No," I sputtered. My knees faltered and I wobbled wildly. "He didn't—"

"We are not the ones to convince. They are..."

Tears of blood already slipped from my eyes as I turned and surveyed my living nightmare. From this height, I could see everything. Every horrific fucking detail.

The podium. The crowd. The hangman, noose and the man that stood still beneath it as the rope was lowered around his pale ivory neck.

"Loren!" I screamed, but my voice was muffled as a cold hand slapped over my mouth.

"Crying for him will not save him," the soft voice said. "Don't look, you don't need to see this."

Whoever held me tried to turn me away from the scene, but I was older and thus far stronger. I tugged free with ease, my entire body swelling with premature grief.

Standing beside my brother was a towering man with obsidian black hair. He spoke to the crowd, but I could not hear his words. The billowing cloak of red that flapped in the breeze confirmed who I already knew him to be.

Eamon Coleman, the acting Head of the Crimson Guard. And just beyond him was his husband, Rhory Coleman. The red-haired man had his arms wrapped around his thin frame, his eyes never leaving Loren. Not once. They never left my brother, not as Eamon lifted his hand and gestured downwards with a clean strike.

The sound of breaking wood broke around the entire world. My eyes flew from Rhory to Loren. The podium beneath his feet had fallen away, and my brother was left to drop. The rope stopped him from falling entirely, snapping his neck with the force and keeping him hanging.

It didn't kill him. It didn't give him the peace he deserved.

My brother was left to hang before the crowd. He gargled on his innocence, but no one listened. My dead heart broke, my soul shattered. Each one of his screams pierced me. And there was nothing I could do but watch because behind him the light of dawn crested over the world.

I was pulled back into the shadows of the building. This time I did not fight.

As the rays of light cast over Darkmourn, I watched from the safety of the room, as my brother erupted into an explosion of ash and flesh. As the crowd roared with applause, and my brother became nothing but bone—I didn't look away. I would not award myself the peace of looking elsewhere.

Unlike Rhory Coleman who didn't watch. He didn't watch as my brother died for the death of his mother, a death I did not believe my brother capable of doing. Rhory kept his gaze pinned to the ground before him whilst Loren answered for crimes he did not commit.

The crowd cheered and rumbled for hours after. I was stuck in the apartment, surrounded by vampires I did not know—as Darkmourn celebrated the death.

The death of my brother.

The death of my soul.

22

MILLICENT WAS LOWERING the blindfold to cover my eyes when Calix burst into the room. The slip of material fell to the floor, forgotten. It was no more than an afterthought when we both regarded the horror set into his face.

"Eamon," Calix practically roared, shaking dust from the corners of the room. "He's come."

Every ounce of warmth our last interaction gifted me vanished as though it never existed.

Millicent moved with such speed and had unsheathed two blades from her hips and gripped them in both hands within a single blink. "Fuck. Where's Auriol?"

Something darkened Calix's wide eyes. "He has her."

I moved, propelled forward by the thought of Eamon having his hands on Auriol.

"No!" Calix extended an arm to stop me. His hand caught my shoulder, preventing me from barging into the tunnel way behind him.

"He wants me," I said, heart thundering in my chest. "Not Auriol. Me. If you let me go to him, I can stop this."

Calix glared down at me as I stared up at him. "You know I cannot let you run to him."

"Oh, just let the boy leave," Millicent snapped, gesturing towards me with one of her sharpened blades. "The human is right. Eamon wants him, not Auriol."

"This is not how this was supposed to go," Calix warned, hissing through his teeth at the vampire.

"Millicent is right." I put a hand over his chest. Beneath my touch his heart hammered, like the stampede of wild horses. It matched my own. "Eamon knows little of sense. He will not entertain your wants and desires. But he will listen to me. Let me go to him before he comes looking."

Calix didn't need to use words to answer me, because I read them clearly in his eyes. *I can't do that.*

"He *will* kill her," I added, ensuring Calix not only heard, but felt what I had to say. "You have seen what he did to Mildred, you know what he is capable of. Please, Calix. Let me go to him. Let me try."

"Then what?" Calix rushed, pressing his hand atop mine to keep it in place.

"We fail," Millicent answers. "Auriol, or Silas. That is the decision we are faced with."

"Or Rhory." Calix glowered.

"You cannot be serious." Millicent's voice pitched. "Calix, you are thinking with your cock, not your head."

Heat rose in my cheeks. Calix seemed to falter over Millicent's brazen accusation, his entire body shook beneath my palm.

"Auriol told me to keep you from him, but I disobeyed her," Millicent snapped. "I should have listened."

"You do not know what you speak of." Calix was practically vibrating with built up tension.

"I can smell it on you, fool! On both of you. Old habits die hard." Disgust twisted her face into a scowl that sharpened her features. Her eyes burned a ruby red which emanated her power. "It was a mistake ever letting you fool around with our bargaining tool. Your past blinds you. And you..." She turned her gaze at me and pinned me with it. "What do you think your dear husband will do when he finds out? Oh, perhaps abduct Auriol and punish her for the both of you? Or worse. This is on you, Calix. What comes out of this will rest on your shoulders."

Blood thundered in my ears like the rush of a tidal wave. There was nothing but Millicent's words and the knowledge of what I had to do.

"Calix, let me pass."

His hand pressed down on mine, trapping it where it rested over his chest. "Millicent, you might be right. I am selfish. I am a fool. But I am also not letting Rhory go back to him. There are other ways out of these tunnels, ways that lead away."

I caught Millicent snap her pointed teeth at Calix out the corner of my eye. She dropped her knees, readying to pounce. "Then I will take him to Eamon myself."

"There will be no need for that," I said. Gold light emitted from beneath Calix's large hand. It spilled out as though he held a star between his fingers. The glow cast shadows across the bottom of his face, highlighting the realisation that struck him. "I can take myself."

I pulled the exhaustion from deep within my bones and forced it into Calix. The rush of sharing the emotion was violent. It came out of me willingly, without resistance or care. The more I pushed into Calix I felt revigorated. Alert.

His golden eyes grew heavy. His mouth slackened and the colour drained from his face.

I pulled my power back only when Calix's body had fallen to the ground. His breathing was even, his eyes closed.

"What did you do?" Millicent asked, wariness etched in her voice.

"I put him to sleep," I said, staring down at his large frame.

The vampire stepped to my side and peered down at Calix. "You made the right choice, for everyone."

"This is the only choice."

When Millicent looked at me, it was not with her usual disdain. The lines around her red eyes had softened. Even the scowl she wore with pride had faded, allowing room for a slight smile. "Then we should go before the *beast* awakens. Or, before you change your mind."

∼

The further we ventured out of the tunnels, the thicker my panic became. It was as dense as a cloud. I waded through it as if it was smoke stinging at my eyes and clogging my throat.

Millicent was unbothered, forging ahead only to stop when we neared the exit. Daylight spilled into the tunnels. Millicent regarded it with horror, hissing like a cat drenched in cold water.

"This is all you from here," Millicent said. "He will kill me for this."

She couldn't leave the tunnels with me, but I felt lighter knowing she had planned to.

I was numb, the only thought passing through my mind was of Auriol and her safety.

"It is fine," I said, finding myself reaching out for Millicent. Her strong arm was made of pure muscle. She did not flinch as I took it in my hand. "Go back to Calix. If Eamon comes for him, keep Calix safe. For me."

Millicent swore under her breath for a final time. "Calix will never forgive me for this. Good luck, Rhory."

I offered her a smile, one that pulled awkwardly at my face. "Millicent, for what it is worth, I never believed your brother was the one who killed my mother. His death has never left me, nor did it satisfy me to know he was cast the blame. I did try to stop him... Eamon made sure I never did again."

Millicent stared daggers through me. I felt her gaze burn at the far back of my skull. Part of me wished for her to say something, but she chose the path of silence. I let go of her arm. She turned, without a word, and ran back into the dark tunnel. Perhaps I should have told her that I was sorry, but I imagined those words were as meaningless to Millicent as they were to me.

Eamon waited for me beyond the tunnel's exit.

My eyes fell on him where he stood, unable to focus on anything else. His crimson cloak draped perfectly over his shoulders, tugged gently by the breeze flirting through the forest. Eamon held both hands before him, clasped with only his thumb drumming with impatience. At first glance it seemed he was alone. Then my eyes adjusted. For every tree in the clearing, there was a further two of the Crimson Guard waiting. And not a single one was without a weapon. All but Eamon, who was empty handed.

"I trust you received my message," Eamon said, unclasping his hands and letting them drop to his sides.

Each step towards him was difficult. I felt the resistance my mind placed on my body. It was like walking through knee-high mud.

"The one you had carved into Mildred's back?" I asked, surprised by my fury that overwhelmed me. Eamon didn't so much as flinch at my accusation. It was clear he had nothing to hide from his Crimson Guard. "How could you have that done... to her?"

"Oh, my darling, you know me better than to think I had someone else do that for me."

"You disgust me." My heart thundered in my chest, filling my ears with the rush of blood. "Only you have such capacity for evil."

Eamon pouted, stretched up on his tiptoes and made a spectacle of looking behind me. "Where is the mutt? From the strongly worded letter he had posted through our front door, I would have thought I was to be greeted by the big bad wolf himself."

"Where is Auriol?" I countered his question.

"Auriol Grey." Eamon raised his hands up as though to show he didn't have her hiding in his palms. "She is on her way to the reunion she has petitioned so tirelessly for."

"Silas," I echoed Calix's brother's name.

"See, I am not a monster." Eamon narrowed his eyes on me. In four large strides, he closed the gap between us. His closeness caused a shiver of disgust to roll over my skin. "And I don't like the way you are looking at me, dear husband. You should feel relief that I have come to save you. So why do you snarl like a feral creature? It would seem your captors have rubbed off on you."

He leaned in close as he whispered. I could smell last night's overindulgence of wine. It was sharp, lacing his mouth with a scent that revolted me yet still the sickly smell of lavender lingered beneath it all.

I opened my mouth to say something. To spill all the hateful thoughts I had harboured for him. The audience of his Crimson Guard would at least prolong the physical pain which waited for me, so speaking my mind would make no difference. But Eamon silenced me with what he said next.

"I saw you both," Eamon hissed into my ear. Flecks of spit hit the side of my face. I didn't dare move to wipe it clear. "Last night. You have betrayed me. Dishonoured me. Til death do us part, do you remember chanting those words? Because I certainly do."

"How could I ever forget?" I replied, filling each word with burning fire.

"You make me *sick*."

Eamon trembled with rage. I glanced out the corner of my eye to see the whites of his almost entirely red. He looked exhausted this close up. Dark shadows hung beneath his eyes, giving his face the gaunt expression of a skinless skull.

"I *will* kill him. Your mutt. I'll be the one to put him down."

"Calix was not the one to speak the vows. It was me. I am the one who deserves punishment," I hissed, jaw aching from clamping my teeth shut. Heat flooded my cheeks as some of the Crimson Guard began to quietly laugh among themselves. Eamon showed no sign of sharing their humour.

"You had him in your mouth." Eamon lost his control for a moment. It was long enough that he snapped his hand back and sent the back of it into my cheek. I blinked and saw stars. I tasted blood. It filled my cheeks as I unsheathed my teeth from the soft flesh of my tongue.

"That mouth is mine. You will do well to remember that." He pulled away slowly, righting himself and smoothing the fury from his expression. "We are leaving."

I flinched back a step. Eamon struck out like a viper and wrapped his fingers around my forearm. His nails pinched my skin through the layering of my shirt, uncaring and familiar.

"*If,*" he sneered, "You wish for Auriol to stay alive long enough to be reunited with her grandson, then I suggest you do as I say."

Tears filled my eyes. I didn't dare blink for fear they would show Eamon just how much power he had over me.

"Come," Eamon commanded, pulling at my arm. "It seems we have much catching up to do."

I couldn't refuse him as he tugged me from the tunnel's exit. As we moved away, the Crimson Guard filed in towards it, silver blades raised at the waiting dark.

"What..." I foresaw what was going to happen. "No, stop!"

I dug my heels into the ground, forcing my weight against Eamon. His grasp on me tightened, but it was useless as I was blinded by the desire to act. In the dark of my mind, I saw Calix slumped out across the ground, forced into his lured sleep. Millicent was alone. Although I had no doubt she was powerful, I hardly imagined the sea of countless and unending Crimson Guards would struggle to cut her down. Cut them both down.

"That beast deserves to die," Eamon shouted. My shoulder blade screamed louder with agony. "He has defiled my husband. He stole you from our home and ruined you. I am owed his head for what ghastly deeds he has made you do. And you should be thanking me!"

It was no good fighting against Eamon. He was too strong, his body accustomed to years of training and endurance, whereas mine was more used to bruises and scars.

I changed tactics, fuelled by my urge to stop the bloodshed that would soon spill within the tunnels.

Spinning on my husband, I tried to reach for any skin I could find. He had once warned me what he would do to me if I ever used my power against him. But there was no promise of pain that was as severe as murderous agony which would ensue if Calix was harmed.

The sudden lack of resistance set Eamon off-kilter. He lurched backwards as I threw my weight towards him. Eamon's eyes widened as my free hand reached for his face. My nails were inches from the skin of his cheek as he used my momentum, spun me around and held my back to his chest, arm pinned between us.

"Watch them do it," Eamon spoke into my ear. His lips brushed my skin, turning my stomach inside out. "Watch as my guards hunt for the wolf. Did you know that silver burns the monster's flesh? I didn't, not until I found out."

I was certain my shoulder had dislocated. The pain blinded me, but I wouldn't close my eyes. I couldn't.

"I'm sorry, I'm sorry! It wasn't him... please, Eamon. If you love me then leave him."

Eamon pressed a dry-lipped kiss to the side of my face. I recoiled as much as I could, but he had me trapped before him. My skin burned in the place where his lips had touched. "I love you enough to protect you from harm. Which is why I must hunt the wolf and see that its skin hangs from our walls. Perhaps I could make you a rug, or a blanket? Hush now..." He stroked my hair with his free hand. "If you listen you might just hear his howls. It's a magical noise, one you will never forget."

"Bastard," I spat.

Eamon tugged at my arm, sending a terrible pain across my

shoulder and back. If he wasn't holding me up, I would have fallen to my knees. "Am I? For killing the creature that pillaged you? I have seen men hung at the gallows for less."

"Calix didn't... it wasn't—"

"Enough," Eamon snapped a final time. "That is quite enough."

I could do little but watch and wait as the Crimson Guard flooded into the waiting dark. They filed in, one by one, in search of their prey. For Calix. And Eamon was right. It didn't take long before the screams started. Except they were not the screams he desired to listen for. The loosening of his hold on me confirmed that. As did the wave of men and women who ran out of the tunnels they had just entered.

"What...?" Eamon breathed but was quickly silenced by the screams of his guards.

A growl echoed from the shadows of the tunnel, following every human that left them. It rumbled through the earth until I felt the power behind it vibrate through my bones.

The howl of a wolf sounded from deep within the tunnels. It was a song. A song of hunger, anger, and most of all...

Hate.

23

Calix prowled from the shadows, thick paws padding heavily across the ground. I felt each one echo through the dewy bed of the forest and up my stiffened legs. In his mouth he held a torn and bloodied arm. As he moved, the fingers wiggled as though they waved. Which was impossible, because the arm was not attached to anything. Severed.

"Take him down!" Eamon screamed so loudly my ears felt as though they would bleed. "Stop running, you *fucking* cowards, and take that bastard down."

The Crimson Guard had mostly scattered, but it seemed they feared Eamon more than the monster moving towards them. Silver blades raised, the Crimson Guard did not so much as move towards Calix, but they didn't run away from him either. Instead, they held their ground, each one quaking like a leaf in wind.

"Calix," I breathed his name. His dark, pointed ears twitched. Slowly, he lifted his eyes towards me. The whites were completely black, all beside the star of gold in their centre. Power emanated from him, thundering and as demanding as the growl deep in his throat.

As before, Calix was part wolf and part man. His body had grown in size and width. Muscles had grown in places impossible to the mundane.

He had left the dark tunnels on all fours but uncurled himself when he saw me. Calix towered far taller than anyone else as he stood on his bowed, back legs. He snatched the severed limb from between his jaws and discarded it on the ground before him with a wet smack.

"Master Grey," Eamon said, demanding the creature's attention.

Calix snapped his monstrous stare from me, to the man who held me pinned before him. His maw pulled back into a snarl, exposing teeth coated in human blood and flesh. The growl Calix emitted sent a handful of Crimson Guards from their station as they fled into the forest.

A noise rumbled from deep in Calix's thick fur-coated neck and sounded like a word. *Eamon.*

My husband laughed, recognising his name as I had. "If you care for the safety of your grandmother, your brother, then I suggest you turn back into your tunnels and leave with your tail between your legs."

Calix took a giant step forward. It was clear Eamon's threat was unimportant to him.

I yelped in pain as Eamon tugged on my dislocated arm. One slight pull and it felt like my skin had been set ablaze.

Calix faltered. Eamon laughed again. "Oh, I see. Has family become an afterthought for you now? Perhaps I must alter my warning if my intentions are not clear. Another move and Rhory here will suffer the consequences." Eamon leaned into my ear. He traced a finger down the side of my face. Although his touch was soft, I felt the bite of his nail leave a red mark across my skin. "Tell him, dear husband of mine, warn the creature what will happen to you if he doesn't listen."

A wave of defiance crested over me like a wave. As it crashed down, my will was torn from me and hurtled violently from my control. Perhaps it was the knowledge that if Calix heeded Eamon's warning, I would suffer regardless. Pain would wait for me at home as it always did. Punishment for my actions, no matter how just it may have been, would greet me.

I pushed against Eamon's hand until my head was straight. My eyes settled on the monster named Calix. I levelled my chin and my eyes focused on the monster. When I spoke, it was clear and without panic, "Do it. Kill them all."

Eamon didn't have the chance to release me before Calix threw his head back to the skies and howled. Then the monster was running. On all fours, Calix tore at the ground. As he came to the line of cowering guards, he threw himself into the air. Powerful limbs forced him into the sky as he leapt over the wall of flesh and silver which kept us separated.

The force of his landing caused the ground to shake. But Calix didn't stop. Didn't falter. He ran fast, scratching marks deep into the dirt with his blade-like claws.

Only when the flash of silver reflected across the creature's face did he stop.

Eamon held a knife to my throat. The sharp bite of metal sliced into my skin, enough to sting. It was cold at first, until the warmth of blood began to trickle from the nick the blade had gifted me.

"Down!" Eamon snarled, "Dog."

Calix snapped his teeth at Eamon but didn't dare move another inch towards us. Already the Crimson Guard was gathering at Calix's back, creating a circle around the three of us with the points of blades held inward.

"Rhory is mine," Eamon growled, pressing the blade into my skin. I swallowed and felt my skin split even more. "Do you understand? He is mine."

The heckles across Calix's large back lifted.

"Leash the beast," Eamon shouted for his guards. "Remember, the silver will protect you."

Tension was thick in the air within the forest's clearing. It clogged in my throat and threatened to choke me to death. Behind Calix a band of guards were holding a thick chain which ended in a belt-like collar. It gleamed, entirely laced with silver. It was the type of collar the elite of Darkmourn tied around their pedigree dogs, as though to prove even the pets they owned benefit from more wealth than most of the city's population.

Except this was made for one creature alone: Calix.

"When we peel the pelt from your back, Calix, remember we gave you the choice. I gave you the choice all those years ago." Eamon spat as he spoke, his teeth equally bared as the jaws of the wolf before him. "I would have let you scuttle back into the dark place you have called home. Even after what you have done to my husband. I deserve your head, your hands, for what you did. I may even slice that devil tongue from your maw and hang it on my wall as a reminder to Rhory what happens to those who break the eternal vows of our union. Yes," Eamon barked a deranged laugh. "Yes! That is exactly what I'll—"

Calix pounced towards us, silencing my husband. Eamon shouted out like a child grasped in fear. The blade swiped from my neck and lifted towards Calix. I dropped just as the pointed jaw of the wolf lifted towards me.

I cowered on the ground as hot blood rain down across my head. It drenched me, mixing with the ruby red of my hair until it was entirely soaked.

Eamon's scream lit the forest. It was drawn out and breathless. A part of me wished to clap my good hand over my ear, but intrigue won. I glanced up to see Eamon clutching his handless arm. He had fallen back to the ground, holding his wound to his chest as blood spluttered like a fountain. My husband's skin had turned an ivory white as the colour bled from him and over me.

Calix pawed towards him. The wolf was chewing on something as he moved. A gag crawled up my throat as I saw the glint of a wedding band around a finger which was still attached to a hand. A hand that was more pulp, flesh and snapped bone as Calix devoured it.

The wolf prowled forward, ready to feast on more of Eamon's flesh. Until something stopped him. Calix yelped in pain, jerking his massive paw from the ground. I looked down and saw the silver knife Eamon had held to my throat not that long ago. It had pricked Calix's paw.

It was so small, so pathetic in comparison to the wolf, but the pain it caused him was overwhelming. Agony sang in the wolf's howl as he thrashed and cried. Eamon screamed too, with incoherent words. His Crimson Guard watched in horror and confusion as to what to do. Without an order, they were useless.

Whereas the forest seemed bathed in chaos, I felt oddly calm. I reached for the silver knife, covered in both mine and Eamon's blood. I snatched it from the ground. Calix flinched away from me, whimpering.

I turned towards Eamon. He was ashen and his eyelids heavy. He could hardly look at me as I towered over him, the knife held in my good arm.

"Look at me," I said, hand shaking as I pointed the blade at him. Eamon didn't listen. He was focused on the blood and exposed bone that once was a hand. "I said look at me!" I screamed over his caws.

He did. Eamon lifted his paling eyes from his wound up to me. They had glazed with pain and delusion, and he looked through me rather than at me. Slowly, he regarded the knife and then me, and smiled.

"What... what are you going... to do with that, darling?" he asked, struggling to speak as the agony of his severed hand clogged his throat.

I could kill him. Finish this. All I could think about was burying the blade in Eamon's skull so I could watch the light drain from his eyes.

And I would have done it. I would have killed him then and there if it wasn't for Calix.

The wolf swept me from my feet and held me to his powerful chest. He was all warmth and strength. It was as though a statue held me, one coated in fur and flesh. I resisted at first, but quickly gave in to my desires. Burying my head into the coarse fur which enveloped me, I blocked out my fear.

A rumbling echoed across the side of my face. It came from deep within Calix, and although it was wordless, it was not meaningless.

No.

Then, we were moving. I was vaguely aware of our direction, but I pinched my eyes closed as the blurring of the world made me feel sick. All that mattered was Calix had me, and I had him.

Wind ripped past my ears and slapped at my face. Even with my eyes closed I was aware that the light had vanished, and we were bathed in darkness. Calix never stopped running. He moved awkwardly on his hind legs, shifting us from side to side violently. It was painfully clear that he moved better on all fours, but that didn't matter. He was still faster than any human in this form.

He ran and ran until the air became thick with dust and age. All I heard was the scratch of his claws against stone and the thunderous roar of his breathing as it echoed around us.

Calix slowed to a stop. The world was spinning even after he placed me carefully on the floor and released me. The lack of his touch drove a shard of panic into my heart. I threw open my eyes, but it was pointless. There was no light here. Not natural, or fire blessed. It was pure darkness. Complete and unending shadow. I closed my eyes again, fearing that the dark would make me mad.

"Calix?" I asked the darkness, and it replied with my own echo. *Calix, Calix, Calix.*

The pain caught up with me as I waited for a reply. My shoulder burned with fire. The skin on my neck prickled from the slight cut Eamon and his knife had left on me. Even my fist ached. I relaxed my hand and the silver-bladed knife clattered to the dark ground. I hadn't even realised I still held it until it was no longer in my hand. The lack of its presence was not comforting.

In this dark place, there was no good trying to find it again.

"Ca-lix?" I asked the dark again. My voice broke this time. In the echo I could hear how pathetic and scared I sounded.

Had the wolf discarded me and left me here? I knew we had entered back into the tunnels, but it was clear we had ventured further into them than I had before.

"Calix!" I shouted this time, cringing at the loud screech of my plea. "Don't leave me."

Something soft shuffled across the floor before me. I searched the dark, but it was pointless. Still there was only gloom.

"I am here," the dark said. No, Calix. It was Calix.

Arms reached out from the shadows and folded around me. I felt the naked press of skin. Human skin. It was warm and welcoming so I scrambled into it and sobbed, not caring for anything but knowing I was not alone.

"Rhory," Calix said, his voice thick and rasped. A shiver burned up my spine as I felt the press of his chin rest upon the crown of my head. There was the familiar tickle of a beard, and the long exhale of relief which sang to my very soul. Although I could not see what I touched, I knew with complete certainty it was Calix. His skin was moist beneath the palms of my reaching hands which grasped his powerful naked back and held on firm.

"Don't leave me," I cried. "Don't go."

"I've got you," he said, brushing the back of my head with his hand. "I'm here."

24

MILLICENT FOUND us before the Crimson Guard had much of a chance. It could have been hours or minutes, I didn't know. In the dark, time didn't seem to exist. Neither Calix nor I heard her coming. She was a wraith, moving on soundless feet with the grace of air. It was the fire she held in the glass lantern which gave her away.

"Both of you," she snapped as firelight flickered over her stern face, "Get up."

How long had we been sat on the ground in the dark, grasping one another as though our lives depended on it? Long enough that my muscles stiffened, and my skin seemed to stitch with his.

"Eamon is alive." Her voice melted across me, finally pulling me out of the trance of Calix's embrace and the dread which had overcome me. Millicent's pale skin glowed as though a dying star was captured beneath it, reflecting the light of the lantern she held out towards us.

"I should have finished him—" I began, until Millicent shot her hand towards me, gripped my forearm, and pulled.

"You left the bastard without a hand. Do you know how serious this is?"

My bones creaked as Millicent pulled me away from Calix. I was aware he was without clothes, but beneath the exposing glow of fire, we both could see how entirely naked he was. And he didn't care, showing no effort to cover his modesty as he peered up at Millicent. What I also didn't account for was Calix still had the smudging of blood across his mouth and jaw. Eamon's blood was more a stain of black across the lower half of his face.

"It would not be wise to waste time worrying about the past," Calix replied coolly.

"What were you thinking?" she hissed, teeth flashing. "Auriol has been taken by the man you have mutilated. If you thought her treatment would have been kind before, it will be hell for her now! If she is even still alive."

Calix didn't utter a word. Nor did I.

Even though we had not said anything to one another, I knew we both shared the guilt. And even before Millicent confirmed Eamon survived Calix's attack, I knew he was not dead. I still felt the leash like tether binding us together, even if Calix had torn his hand clean off, taking the wedding band Eamon wore with it.

"Get up, Calix," Millicent snapped, glaring with ruby red eyes at him. "We don't have the luxury of sitting and doing nothing."

"And go where?" Calix's voice rumbled through the dark, blending with the inky blackness.

"There is only one direction we can go. If the path back is not possible, we must therefore venture forward. Calix, get your sorry ass off the ground and get moving."

Millicent had not once let go of me. Her skin was ice cold to the touch that it stung slightly. She was careful not to pull at my dislocated arm, which I clutched to my chest.

"Try not to scream," Millicent said to me, distracting me from Calix as he stood.

"Wait—" I couldn't finish my question before Millicent reached for my arm. I gulped just as her nails caught my skin. With a great jolt, she twisted it at an awkward angle. The sharp snap of pain lasted but a second, then relief settled in. The pop of my bone fixing into its socket echoed throughout the dark.

"Fuck me," I gasped out as a rush passed through my head.

"Better?" Millicent's smile elongated above the flickering lamp.

Slowly, I moved my arm around, testing for pain or lack of use. It was uncomfortable at most, but manageable.

"Thank you," I replied, rolling my shoulder backwards.

"I can do little for the cut on your neck," Millicent muttered to me, tongue tracing her lip as she surveyed the blood which had dried beneath the wound. "Your arm will feel sore for a day at most."

Millicent steadied her gaze to Calix. I watched her red eyes trail him from bare foot to blood-coated chin.

Calix turned his head away in silent refusal. "Take Rhory and get him somewhere safe. I need to—"

"Need to *what*, you sorry fool!" Millicent withdrew her hand from me kicked his foot with a firm boot. "Auriol has been captured, Silas has not been returned, and not only have you shaken the hornets' nest, but you also kicked, pissed, and set the bastard on fire. Now, if you wish for the chance to save them, I suggest you get moving. We have a way to walk. Then you can sit all you want and mope about your actions and their consequences."

Calix unfurled even taller than before, stretching his long naked limbs until he towered over us both. Millicent kept her eyes upwards with ease, whereas I felt as though I struggled to hold Calix's stare. I pulled the torn, bloodied red cloak from my shoulders and handed it to Calix.

His fingers brushed my hand as he took it with a smile that sang with thanks, although it never reached his eyes. Those golden orbs seemed lost to the moment, dazed almost.

"Wouldn't want to scare the shadows," I said, forcing a fake smile.

Calix wrapped the material around his waist. The red matched the dried blood that was smeared around his chest, his neck, the lower part of his face. He caught my stare. I found that I looked away, embarrassed he had caught me regarding the evidence of the death he had recently caused.

Should it have repulsed me? Because it didn't.

He didn't.

"It is not the shadows that you should fear," Millicent warned, her voice edged with unwavering seriousness. "Quick, follow me before the real demons reveal themselves."

I would have thought Millicent was playing some joke on us, but the stoic expression on Calix's face, and the way he placed a reassuring hand on the small of my back to urge me forward, proved otherwise.

As we navigated the dark tunnels, Millicent leading the way with her lantern held high, I kept looking behind me as though someone—or something—unseen followed.

～

I didn't know where our destination was, but as we climbed in single file up the iron-handled ladder and through the wooden latch far above us, I would never have expected this.

"What is this place?" I asked, rubbing at the ache of my shoulder. The climb up and into this room had reminded me it had been hanging out of its socket not so long ago.

Calix followed in last, closing the hatch that gave way to the sheer drop into the dark tunnels below. "Somewhere familiar, no doubt. Millicent, your scent is everywhere."

"What did you expect of me?" Millicent said, smiling as she looked around. There was a softness to her expression. "That I would rest in the dark corners of the tunnels whilst you stayed in your warm bed? Or that my life began only when I came to you? Because both concepts are ridiculous."

"This... is your home?" I stepped forward just as Millicent blew out the flame that danced within the lantern. Without it, we were covered in darkness. Shapes of furniture draped in dust-ridden sheets looked more like hunched crones spectating from the corners of the room. Where I trod, my footsteps left marks in the dust settled across the floor.

"Careful, *witch*. I am merely a squatter demanding my rights. This place does not and will not belong to me. However, its original tenant has found more... opulent dwellings. We will not be disturbed here."

Calix began talking to Millicent in hushed tones. Whatever they were discussing, it was not for me to hear. Perhaps I should have demanded to know what they spoke of, but I was transfixed by the beam of silver light which cut through the pitch-black room.

I paced across the space, aware of the old creaking floorboards. Each step caused the ground to scream. Before me was a window, or it should have been a window if it was not for the thick planks which had been nailed across it from the outside. There was only enough of a gap for me to see outside. As soon as my eyes settled on the darkened street, and the wall of buildings which leaned on one another for support, I knew without question where the tunnels had led us.

"We are in Old Town." I turned my back on the window, interrupting Calix and Millicent's somewhat secret conversation.

"Directly in its heart," Millicent confirmed.

"Which is exactly why we are returning to the tunnels and looking for somewhere else to stay. Somewhere far from Darkmourn." Calix stormed towards me, the muscles across his exposed chest and stomach etched into his body like stone. "Come, Rhory. We must leave."

"No," Millicent added, following behind me. "That is exactly why we are staying. Eamon will never know to look for us here. No one will. Even if they searched the tunnels, they would come out from many other exits before this one."

"I... I think Millicent is right." I felt the desire to look back out the window.

"Rhory," Calix breathed, reaching for my hand. I let him take it, glad for the comforting steadiness his touch provided me. His eyes were wide, pleading. "Old Town is a stone's throw from your home. From Castle Dread. We are directly in the line of sight of all who would wish to see us dead. I have put you in this position, which means I have taken on the responsibility to keep you safe. Please... let me do that. Let me keep you out of harm's way."

The silver beam of moonlight that sliced into the room from the window at my back illuminated Calix's state. He was covered in blood, naked and barely concealed beneath my cloak, with the weight of so much on his shoulders. He needed to wash, and rest. We all did.

I tore my eyes from Calix and looked to Millicent who hovered over his shoulder. "What is important is righting the wrongs of Eamon. I know my husband." The word soured in my mouth like spoiled milk. "He is as resilient as he is crazed. Something is driving him to act in such a manner, and he will not stop until he gets what he wants. I suppose it has been for a very long time. If we are to see Auriol and Silas returned in one piece, then we must find out what he wants from them."

"What good will that do?" Calix asked, his low voice causing shivers across my skin.

"It is how we are going to stop him. By finding out what he desires and tearing it from beneath him until all he can do is fall."

Millicent's laugh was as light and shrill as a bird. "Who is this man who has crawled out of the dark? I barely recognise him."

I gritted my teeth, tensing my jaw as Millicent pinned me beneath her ruby eyes. "He is someone who has been buried away, against his will, for a long time. Someone who is ready to shed the bindings put upon them and do the right thing."

"Survived," Calix said, squeezing my hand. "He is someone who has survived."

I nodded, swallowing hard as the lump persisted in my throat. "And I am someone who wishes to thrive. His control over me must end."

"Then I should give you some house rules," Millicent said, gesturing around her. "No one must know we are here. When it is dark, we keep it that way. During the day, we stay quiet. We cannot draw any attention to ourselves. Well, you both can't. I am still an unseen player on the board, and I wish to keep it that way. You'll find a bedroom upstairs. The one at the end of the corridor is mine, keep out. I trust you both will not complain if you are forced to share the other. It is that or one of you can flip a coin to decide who has the floor."

Even after everything that had conspired, I found my chest warmed and stomach flipped at the thought of sharing a bed with Calix. It was better than a dirt covered ground in the middle of a forest. Even Calix reacted silently to the suggestion. His was subtle, but clear from the way the lines across his forehead smoothed and the tension around his mouth eased.

"The bed," Calix said, unable to take his eyes off me. "Will be sufficient."

I found myself nodding like an overenthusiastic child. "More than fine."

"Good, because the rooms can be cursed with a nasty draft. The views are not the only breathtaking thing in this building."

"Seems like you read my mind," Calix added softly.

"Calix, you stink." Millicent's nose flared as she passed us. "And for someone who rather enjoys the delicacy of blood, you are spoiling it for me. You need to wash. The roof has an issue with leaks, as well as other things. This house is ancient, so the water supply is sparse. Use the gathered rainwater in the jugs and vases I have laid out to clean yourself. Come morning, I will see you both have something to eat and drink. Then, we discuss how three unlikely creatures are going to stop a raging mortal from tearing more families apart."

25

The old wooden box seat beneath the window in our bedroom creaked with aggravation as I sat upon it. Once the material atop it would have been a vibrant red, but time had sapped the colour from it. And the comfort. Moths and other unwanted guests had devoured the cushion's stuffing until it was left flat and lacklustre.

This window, like the rest in the house, had been boarded up; enough to stop prying eyes looking in, but not looking out. Through a narrow slit, I was transfixed by the breath-taking view of Castle Dread. It seemed this place was built for the very purpose of this view.

The waning moon hung far above its tallest peak, washing the castle's dark stone walls in silver light. The castle was alive from within. Golden warm firelight spilled out of the multitude of stained-glass windows. A shiver of comfort purred across my skin at the thought of luxury. There was nothing of the sort in this house.

"See something you like?" Calix asked as he entered the room, two cracked jugs full of water in either hand.

For once, I didn't feel the urge to look at him. Instead, I trailed my eyes down the castle's grandeur, imagining rooms teeming with halflings Jak Bishop collected, as someone would with shells on the seafront. I looked from the narrow street just outside this house, which opened up to the bridge separating the castle from town. It was as quiet as the dead, which was befitting for the vampire lord and his lover who silently ruled from the castle.

"I wonder why they called it Castle Dread," I said, finding that I whispered because I didn't wish to shatter the stillness of this place.

"That is the name given to a place people fear, or harbour discomfort towards. I can't help but see it in a different light."

"Auriol told me of a time when Marius, The Lord of Eternal Night, was trapped as punishment inside the castle's walls..."

"And the last witch, Jak, was sent to kill him but failed, and unleashed an age of death across Darkmourn. We all know the story. I'm surprised it hasn't been etched into our bones or carved beneath our skin, from the number of times it has been told to us. What I want to know is: why? Why the name? It would seem that Darkmourn and its people find it easy to remember the bad side of our history, but no one talks about the time before it. Strange that."

There was the clink of china against wood. I tore my eyes from the view to a new one. Calix covered in dried blood that now looked as brown as dirt or smeared mud. He had exchanged my red cloak with a spare pair of trousers Millicent provided; they must have belonged to her brother. The rest of him was unclothed. Until he was cleaned, he didn't want to spoil the only spare clothing accessible to him, and the jugs and bowls of water he had carried down from the house's attic was going to fix that.

"You are the only one of us who would ever have the chance to find the answers you seek," Calix said. He snatched a cloth that hung from the belt of his leather trousers. I watched as he wrung it in his hands, giving himself something to do as I drank him in. "If you wanted to walk up to the castle's doors and ask for entry, it would be given to you."

"Because of what I am," I answered for him.

"A witch, you can say it."

I pushed myself from the box seat, cringing at the loud cry of relief the wood gave. "I promised my mother that I would never go."

Calix's smooth face changed at the mention of my mother. It was a reaction I had seen before, as though he was disgusted by it. "With all due respect, Rhory, Ana is no longer alive. It is hard to keep the promises of the dead. Trust me. You could walk up to the castle now and put this all behind you. Eamon. Your pain. *Me*. We wouldn't matter when you are kept safely behind those walls."

I felt both pained and comforted by Calix's brash words. He was right, my mother was dead, but he was also wrong. Promises were immortal.

"What good would that do for my parent's legacy if I was to give Eamon what he wanted all along? My home, the Crimson Guard. Haven't I given him enough? My life, my happiness, my love. See what he has done with that and you will get a glimpse of what would become of Eamon if I walked into the den of vipers, never to look back."

Calix's face pinched in confusion. "The Crimson Guard is already his, no?"

I laughed. Of course, he would think that. But I knew the truth. It had been read out to me the night of my father's death. I have long believed it was the reason Eamon raised his hand to me the first time. Out of frustration and anger. Defeat.

"As long as I am alive, the Crimson Guard falls into Eamon's control. I die, and he loses it. It was my father's dying wish, literally; a change made to his will only days before my marriage to Eamon."

I practically witnessed the pieces of a puzzle fall into place within Calix's mind. His stare fell to the ground, his eyes flickering and mouth parted as he worked it all out.

The sorrow he regarded me with almost brought me to my knees. "All this time, you stayed with him because you had a death wish."

I nodded, not feeling anything but a deep, echoing numbness inside of me. "I am a coward. I couldn't end myself, but I knew Eamon might. His fits of rage grew the more he became used to hurting me. I knew it would only be a matter of time when his fist hit me too hard, or he strangled me long enough to kill me. Part of the reason I stayed with him is because I couldn't bring myself to do it. The other part of me—the sadistic and hateful side he created—stayed because I longed for him to do it, only for him to suffer the realisation that his actions are the reason he lost everything he ever wanted."

Calix discarded the cloth without thought, and took me in his hands. I felt so incredibly small when I stood before him. It was the way his neck craned down when he looked at me, or how his hands were so large that it made my arms feel as brittle and narrow as a twig.

"I'm sorry to disappoint you, but I am never going to let that happen."

I folded against Calix's chest, uncaring if my cheek pressed into the dried blood of the Crimson Guard. Calix ran his hand across my head over and over, soothing me with his touch and the beat of his heart that slammed within his ribcage. I felt every beat. Every single powerful pump as though it kicked against the side of my head.

My hands trembled as I traced my fingers up his hard stomach to the four, puckered red scars across his chest. I hadn't dared ask him about them for fear of what he would say. All this time I had allowed myself the bliss of not knowing. I couldn't hide from it anymore.

"These marks..." I began but stopped myself as my fingers brushed over the puckered lumps. It was the familiarity of the touch that silenced me. If I closed my eyes, it was as though I had been in this very position before with the question lingering across my tongue.

"What is the matter?" Calix asked softly, holding me close.

"I just... how is it I hardly know you, yet my body tells me otherwise?"

Calix's breathing hitched. His reaction stopped me and drew my hand away from the scars on his chest. His lips paled, and parted, but nothing but a choked gasp came out.

"Is it pathetic to admit?" I said, pulling free of Calix. My legs felt like they might have given way at any moment, so I took the chance to sit on the edge of the bed. Calix stayed standing, unmoving, as though something I had said rooted him to the spot.

"Your mind and your body are two separate entities, both carrying different memories."

"And why would my body hold a memory for you?" I asked, feeling my mouth become dry as I spoke. There was something in his gaze, an ominous shadow passing over the glow of the sun and blocking it out completely.

"Because it should. It remembers what you do not."

A nervous laugh burst out of me. It was the heavy weight of Calix's stare that unnerved me, because I sensed there was something hiding behind it. I recognised the emotion for what it was. Even without my power, his feelings sang in the air, thick and suffocating. *Sadness. Regret.* But there was something else. I had sensed guilt on Calix once before, but this was stronger. More prevalent.

"Auriol told me to leave it, but I.... I don't think I can, Rhory. I am selfish, I told you this. But all I want is for you to remember."

"Remember what?" I asked, unable to move as I glanced up at him.

"No, I shouldn't have said anything." Calix turned his back on me. I watched the rise and fall of his broad back as he struggled to calm himself.

Before he could take a single step away, I snapped, "Don't you dare, Calix."

He regarded me over his shoulder with thick brows pinched over his sorrowful gaze. The weight behind his stare was so powerful it almost knocked me backwards. "It has been a long day," Calix said softly. "I would feel better talking about this tomorrow."

"What should I remember?" I pushed on, refusing to give this up.

The question hung between us, a storm cloud of wonder which thundered in the silence as I waited for my answer.

Calix came and took a seat next to me. The old mattress lifted with the balance of our weight.

"Look at me," Calix commanded. "Look at me in my eyes and tell me you do not remember. I know the truth, but I need to hear it from you... One last time."

I did as he asked, frustration shimmering through me. The pressure was so strong; I was moments from bursting. It had not been the first time I had heard such a comment to my memory, or me remembering. My mind worked through the remarks Auriol and Calix had made, even something Eamon had said to Calix when he first came and took me from my home.

"What, Calix? Please, don't talk to me in riddles."

He raised his stare to me. There was something mesmerising about how his golden eyes glowed, even in such a dark place. But now, they were rimmed with sudden tears that snatched my breath away and conjured a harsh cramping in my chest. That one look, and the emotion behind it, made it hard for me to think.

"Me," Calix said, refusing to look away. "You should remember me."

26

"Rhory, you should remember me," Calix repeated. He stared at me, hopeful, his gilded eyes rimmed with sadness. The honesty in his gaze was so boiling, it scalded me.

Calix sagged forward and rested his blood-coated chin on his muscular chest. Whereas I couldn't take my eyes off of him, he refused to look at me.

A high-pitched whirling bounded through my skull. For a moment, the room and the world around beyond it faded out of view. There was only Calix, and his words which stabbed deep into me sharper than any knife could.

"Why should I?" I asked, and as I spoke, it was as though I was buried beneath a body of water, unable to hear anything clearly. Even though deep down I knew the answer, my mind still searched for Calix, but I couldn't find him in my memories.

"Yes, you should. But there has been a block placed upon your mind, a barrier keeping you from the truth. Trust me, I would never have told you if I didn't think—"

"I don't know what you are talking about!" Frustration riled out of me. I felt like a dog chasing a bone I could never reach. "Just shut up, please! This is unfair."

"Rhory, we have met one another before." Calix looked at me. "Many times, in fact. Auriol and me, when we requested for you to come to the cottage, it was a test. I opened the door and saw you standing there, staring blankly at me, and I knew. I knew, from the look in those beautiful eyes, you didn't remember."

My tongue felt swollen in my dry mouth. "Remember... what?"

Calix paused before replying. His eyes narrowed, flickering between my wide eyes and parted lips. He dropped his attention to his hands which were fist-sized boulders on his lap.

"In the forest," Calix said. "That was not the first time Eamon found us together. The night before your engagement, I was there with you. And that was the last time I saw you."

"I don't understand what you are saying, Calix!" I shouted now, uncaring for the vow of silence we promised Millicent. Her rules didn't matter when my brain felt like it would implode with what Calix was telling me.

"Our families had been friends for a long time. Auriol and your father's parents were alive during a time when the world was rebuilding and the living and the dead were learning to live together in harmony. My grandmother was there at the creation of the Crimson Guard. She hoped to protect the mortals in a world where the immortals thrived. She put your ancestors in charge because she knew they held the same morals and beliefs. Me and you. We..." Calix spluttered on the words. He looked down at his hands, as did I; his knuckles were white with tension.

I placed a hand over his and gold light spilled forth, and I eased his emotions enough for him to continue. With my power, I also searched for truth. And he had it in abundance. Everything Calix was saying was real, but why could my mind not believe it?

He looked at me as the lines of tension melted from his face.

"Continue," I breathed. "Please, I need to know."

Calix nodded, the muscles in his jaw flexing. "Eamon wormed his way into your family like an infection. He worked beneath your father, idolised him, we all thought. Then he turned his sights on you, and he was not prepared to stop at getting you, or what you could give him. My family tried to warn yours, and they were shunned for it. At the time Auriol didn't know about me and you. No one did. But Eamon... He knew because he found us, in your home, in your bed."

My head ached as I tried to make sense of what Calix revealed. No matter how much honesty I felt from within Calix, I couldn't find the memory of what he was saying. It was blank. My past was clear and colourful, and there was not one scene of him in it.

"These scars." Calix lifted my hand to his chest and pressed my cold fingers to his skin. He was warm as a hearth in winter. "Just as I told you the first time you asked, were given to me by my brother. He did it, the night he killed my parent's murderers. I tried to stop him from chasing revenge but failed. I failed him, just as I failed you. And I can see that telling you was a mistake. It was indulgent and has caused you pain."

"Why?" The word was more a command than a question. "Why do I not remember?"

"Eamon knew of a witch." Calix refused to look me in the eye as he spoke. "Someone with the power to tamper with your mind and make you remember what he wanted you to remember, whilst removing what he didn't wish for you to know."

As Calix spoke, I raised my spare hand and pushed my fingers into the soft skin of my temple.

"We heard of your engagement to Eamon the following day. I came back to see you. I didn't know what I expected to find, but you were happy. Smiling and celebrating an engagement you would never have even entertained the night prior. For a long time, I thought it had all been a game to you. Until you turned up at the cottage and looked at me as though I was a stranger. I knew then. What we had, what we shared… only a curse of a mind could bury that."

"Why didn't you tell me before…?" I asked, feeling tears cutting down my cheeks. Deep inside, I felt empty. Half made. Something was lost to me, and even knowing it gave me little comfort.

"Because I, like you, made a promise. Auriol commanded me to keep my silence. I tried to do as she wished, but I knew I was to break that promise the moment I laid eyes on you. I am a weak man for it, I know."

I retrieved my hand from him and called back my power. The room was bathed in darkness once again, except this time everything felt different. Nervous energy buzzed beneath my skin. It itched and ached, needing an escape that I couldn't give it.

"After everything you have said, I feel like I am drowning in questions more so than before."

Calix exhaled a laboured breath. "I wish I could make you remember."

I cringed at the thought of a witch tampering with my mind. Never had Eamon suggested he knew of someone with power. In fact, he always promoted the concept of those with magic being herded into Castle Dread like cattle.

"I need a moment," I said, standing from the bed and leaving Calix behind me as I paced towards the door. There was nowhere for me to go, but I couldn't sit down and let the knowledge of a past I could not remember scolded me. I had to move, I had to get away.

"Rhory," Calix called out for me. All this time he had spoken so calmly, but when he spoke my name, it froze me to the spot. "I'm sorry if I have hurt you with what I've explained. Know it has never been my intention."

"That's just it," I replied, looking back at him over my shoulder,

"There is nothing more debilitating than the truth. Even a truth I cannot remember."

"No," Calix replied, eyes cutting into me. "You are wrong. The truth is freeing if you let it be."

I held his stare, searching a feeling that told me it was familiar. I clawed through my mind, searching for a flash of a memory of him. Of Calix. And there was nothing. Just Eamon and my life, and the happiness before there was gloom.

"I don't remember you," I said with finality.

Calix flinched slightly before straightening and replacing the armour he usually wore across his face. "I know, but, Rhory, I remember you. My heart has known pain. Pain I wouldn't even wish upon Eamon. And I have ached for you. Longed for you. But I know, I know it will never be the same. You will never know the feelings I harbour for you, feelings that we once shared. And I am sorry about that. But if it is any consolation, I have held the same flame for you I did all those years ago. A flame not even Eamon could extinguish. I missed you with such terrible, boiling agony. Just the thought of you could undo me. Your mind might not remember, but your body does. You said as such..."

Fury crawled up my throat and came out as a vicious scream. It was not fury at him, but at the frustration that my mind was not my own. My memory, although belonging to me, had been taken from me. Eamon had infected my body, my will and now my mind and I felt wrath at that truth.

"But I don't remember you! Fuck my body. It matters little! I don't remember... I don't... remember."

Calix was there, kneeling on the ground before me. He moved with such speed that the still surface of the water in the jugs and bowls rippled as though a stone had been thrown within them. "I can't give you back the memories that have been taken from you, Rhory. But if you let me, I will replace them."

My entire body trembled with so many conflicting emotions, I felt as though I would burst if handled with uncaring hands. But there was nothing uncaring about Calix, not the way he held me now or looked at me. But it was the last thing I desired in this moment.

As I stared down at him, I finally understood the guilt and hurt which cursed him when I was near. It seemed my presence caused him pain, but his presence for me did the opposite.

"I want to remember you," I said, tears falling between us. Even Calix's eyes glistened, but he had enough control to keep them back. "I want nothing more than to look at you the way you look at me."

Calix's shoulders sagged inward. He exhaled a long, tempered breath before he replied, "And you will. Eamon is the only one with the knowledge of how to undo this."

"He won't do it freely," I said.

A shadow passed over Calix's face. His eyes narrowed, and the gold seemed to glow from within. Then he whispered words that had as much power in them as if he would have screamed it at the top of his lungs, "Oh, he will. If that is what you desire, I will ensure it happens."

27
3 YEARS BEFORE

RHORY COLEMAN WAS the most beautiful creature I had ever seen. I couldn't take my eyes off him. Although, if I closed my eyes or looked away, the image of him would have been engraved in the dark of my mind.

His hair was as red as poppies. No, it was deeper. Richer. A colour that would have made the flower jealous. I was transfixed by the deep gleam of his green eyes. I lost myself in them, just as I did with the forest. They were never-ending pools, welcoming me in and refusing to let me go.

Rhory Coleman had thirteen freckles which spanned across the bridge of his nose and fell over his cheeks. Each one was as perfect as the next. If there was not a table between us, I would likely have reached out and placed my finger upon each one in turn.

Conversation rang around the room, but I cared little for it. Even Ana Coleman—Rhory's mother—attempted to spark chatter with me, but it was useless. My focus was on her son. It was solely on him.

This was not the first time I had seen him. But before, it was always from afar. Even then, he captured my attention and held it hostage until he was out of sight. Then it was my mind he occupied.

Tonight would be different. It was the first time the Grey's had been invited for supper. It was the end of autumn feast. Across the table before me was plates piled high with pumpkin seeded bread, meats, bowls of spiced soup, an array of different flavoured cheese, seasoned and roasted potatoes with streams of steam which danced in the air above them. Glasses of wine never went empty, always refilled by one of the many housemaids the Coleman's hired.

All but my glass. I had not touched it since I had sat down. Nor did I reach out to spoon food onto my plate. I couldn't do anything but look at him. And he knew it. Rhory sensed my attention and glowed beneath it, his cheeks blossoming with a scarlet blush

Rhory's father was seated at the head of the table. To Michal's side was my grandmother, Auriol, and on the other was his shadow, Eamon, a young man who had climbed the ranks of the Crimson Guard in the past few years. It amazed me how bored he looked. Perhaps Eamon's mood was affected by my brother who practically chewed his ear off with one-sided conversation. Silas always was one to talk. Since we were children my younger brother was always better in crowds. Where he thrived, I wanted to slip into the shadows where I could prowl and watch.

Until now. Now, I wanted to be in the light so Rhory could see me.

And see me he did.

"Would you like some?"

I snapped out of my trance when I realised it was Rhory who held a plate of thinly sliced beef over the table towards me. My eyes fell from his, to the spreading of red across his cheeks and then down to his hand. He held the plate firmly and the way he did so gave me view to the dusting of freckles across his knuckles. I wondered just how far they went as I followed their constellation into the shadows of his sleeve.

"Thank you," I replied, realising quickly that Rhory was still holding the plate and some awkward seconds had passed.

"You're welcome," he replied quietly.

I took the plate. As I did, it was Rhory's opportunity for his gaze to wander. A warmth spread across my chest as I felt his eyes trail over me. Then they fell to his knife and fork, severing his attention.

It was disappointment that urged me to speak again. I wanted his eyes on me, not anything or anyone else. "All these years, and I am surprised this is the first time we have met."

Rhory looked back up, smiling. "Is it really?"

I nodded, feeling suddenly embarrassed I had not put more effort into my appearance before I came. My beard was unkept and my hair fell loosely around my face. It felt silly to keep having to tuck the unruly strands behind my ear, but it seemed to make Rhory smile at least.

"I believe so," I replied, taking the glass in my hand just to give it something to do. "I would have remembered if we had."

"And why is that?" Rhory asked, looking at me through his lashes.

Something uncoiled in the pit of my stomach. The suggestive gleam in his eyes was enough to undo me. How could a stranger have such an ability to disable me?

"Because you are rather memorable," I said, my voice edged with confidence.

The apples of his cheeks blossomed a deeper scarlet. Matching that of the cloaks Michal Coleman, Eamon, and the handful of other Crimson Guard's wore around the table. Rhory's eyes fell, once again, to his plate. Guilt twisted through me.

"I didn't mean to embarrass you." I couldn't stop myself from blurting out. Thank the Gods I held the glass of wine, otherwise I might have smacked my palm against my forehead.

"You haven't at all," Rhory said.

We didn't say anything again after that. I wanted to add something else in, but I feared my mouth would get me into further bother.

Ana Coleman had turned to Auriol and was speaking on how well Michal's health had seemed to steady. All of Darkmourn had known of Michal Coleman's mental decline over the past years, and even I had been shocked to have seen such a strong man being wheeled into the dining room. I was glad her attention was diverted, but I couldn't help but sense the way her eyes fell back over to me and her son. As well as Eamon. He watched, even as Silas leaned in and whispered something into his ear.

If Rhory had not filled my mind, I may have wondered further as to my brother's comfort with the Crimson Guard. He acted familiarly around him, which shouldn't have surprised me as Silas was always the more social of the two of us.

Since our parents' murder, he had come more out of his shell whereas I sulked further into mine. I almost refused to come tonight, but with Rhory so close before me, I didn't regret joining one slight bit.

I decided to join in and eat something. If anything, it gave me something else to focus on. No matter if I wanted to, I couldn't sit here and just watch Rhory. It was odd and would likely scare him off. And that was the opposite of how I desired to make him feel.

The evening moved on quickly. The savoury food was swapped out for a display of desserts. Not even the sweet smells of cinnamon, nutmeg and clove could distract me from Rhory. His attention had soured as the evening progressed, which caused an uncomfortable pang to fill my chest. Rhory watched his father every now and then. His smile had faded completely when his mother had to go and help Michal with his food. He had only so much energy to feed himself so Ana had to swap places with Auriol just so she could sit beside him and help him with each mouthful.

I couldn't bear to see Rhory in such a way. The sorrow didn't suit his face. He had the type of expression that deserved to smile. His face was made for it, not sadness.

Rhory was more focused on his parents than his dessert. He, like me, hardly touched his plate.

I had to distract him. I had to do something to make his smile return. In hindsight, it was a childish act but that was how he made me feel. He made me feel small and juvenile. So, I stretched my leg out beneath the table and knocked my foot into his.

Rhory looked back to me, surprise passing across his handsome face.

"I was hoping," I said, now I had his attention again, "Would you care to give me a tour?"

"A tour?" Rhory replied. "Of what?"

"Anything," I breathed, not caring. I just wanted to get him out of the room, alone.

Rhory held my gaze. I was prepared for him to refuse me, because of course my request was ridiculous. Then, my heart jolted as Rhory's chair screeched back and he stood.

The entire room fell silent.

"What is it darling?" Ana called out, lowering the spoon from her husband's mouth. He had food down the side of his lips. If it was not for the napkin she had tucked into his collar, his shirt would have been covered in caramel sauce.

"I am going to show Calix Grey our library, if you do not mind."

How did he know my name? Had I told him? I racked my brain, trying to remember when I had said it. But I knew, deep down, I had never revealed it.

Which meant he knew it before. And I longed for him to say it again.

Ana Coleman looked to me, her gaze narrowing slightly. "But we are having dessert. Mildred made your favourite—"

"And I am sure there will be some spare," Rhory interrupted. I got the impression he often got what he wanted.

"Let them go," Auriol said from beside me. My grandmother was half a bowl into the trifle. For such an old woman, she could certainly put away her food, especially if it was of the sugary variety.

I stood too, before anyone else could object. But nothing came. Ana agreed, allowing us to leave. Which was strange, because never in my thirty-two years of life had I needed to ask permission to leave a table. It only added to how young I felt around Rhory. I almost had the urge to giggle as he gestured for me to follow him.

We left the dining room quickly, moving into the warmth of the fire-lit foyer beyond. Sweeping stairs stretched out before us, disappearing up into the floor above.

"So," Rhory said, turning around to face me, "You've got me away from them all."

I opened my mouth to reply, but he promptly added, "And don't play coy, I rather enjoy honesty."

I exhaled through a smile, feeling my cheeks ache with the expression. Rhory was far shorter than me, but beneath his gaze he made me feel small. "And here I thought you were desperate to show me the library."

Rhory leaned his weight on one leg, popping his hip out and crossing his arms. "Are you much of a reader?"

I couldn't lie to him. "Not really."

"So, you wouldn't be bothered to see it."

"Is it empty?" I asked.

Rhory narrowed his jade green eyes. "All this just to get me alone. Is that it?"

I straightened my back, refusing to back down. "I must practice on my ability to be subtle."

Rhory pouted his pink-blush lips. "Yes, you should. It needs improving"

I prepared myself for him to tell me to go back to the dining room, but that was not the command that came out of his mouth. Instead, he turned his back on me and faced the stairs.

"But I must admit that I admire your effort," Rhory said, walking away from me. I was left, standing like a fool, in the middle of his foyer when he called back over his shoulder, "Come then. You've got me alone until dessert is over. If I was you, I wouldn't waste another moment."

∼

There was not much talking between us when we reached Michal's office. Before I could even admire the wall of bookshelves and the grand oak carved desk placed in the middle of the room, Rhory was on me.

His mouth crashed into mine before the door clicked shut completely at our backs. The suddenness of it took my breath away, but I didn't shy away from it. My back was shoved into the door, spine pressed into it with the weight of Rhory before me.

His hands were on my face, his fingers running through my beard and up my cheeks. His skin was warm, but I held back the urge to hold him in return. I feared it would shatter this illusion, if I dared move a muscle it would ruin this moment.

Noticing my lack of response, Rhory pulled back. He practically leaned on me, on his tiptoes, until he pulled away, wiping his mouth with the back of his sleeve.

"Perhaps I got the wrong end of the stick," he said. Even in the dull glow of the silver moon beyond the room, I could still make out the embarrassment creeping over his face. My eyesight was far better than most, but it was my ability to hear the beating of his heart which transfixed me. It thundered wildly, skipping every time he caught my gaze.

"No, you certainly are not wrong." I pushed from the door and closed the space between us in two strides. Rhory's chin was smooth to the touch as I slipped my two fingers beneath it and lifted upwards until he was looking at me again. "I just thought we might have had a conversation first, although I am not going to pretend I'm disappointed we haven't."

"Who are you?" Rhory asked, the question knocking me off guard. "And how dare they keep you from me. The feasts Mother and Father put on would have been more bearable if you had joined them."

"So, you are telling me you don't bring random men into dark rooms and kiss them?" I replied, still holding Rhory's chin in my grasp. Excitement bubbled in my chest, making it harder for me to take in a decent breath. "Because I warn you, if you say you do, I will be painfully disappointed."

"No," Rhory whispered, blinking his doe-wide eyes. "Never."

"Then I consider myself lucky," I murmured. "And if it helps curve the embarrassment you feel... I want to know you."

"Is that why you have always looked at me?" Rhory asked. "I've seen you do it for years."

"Does my attention make you feel uncomfortable?" I replied.

Rhory shook his head. A curl of poppy-red hair fell over his eye. I took my fingers from his chin and brought them up to the pesky strand. As I brushed it back in place, I felt Rhory's skin shiver beneath my touch. His heart pounded proudly in his chest, singing to me and my soul.

Knowing I had such a power over him almost brought me to my knees.

"You interest me," I said, feeling the words rush out of me. "Rhory Coleman."

"Is that a compliment?" he asked, gaze flickering over me as though he drank me in.

"It is if you wish it to be. I want to see you again," I said, tilting my head. "If you would care to."

"At the next gathering, or before?"

"No." I swallowed hard. "I want to see you tomorrow, and the day after and the day after."

"Is that obsession, or healthy infatuation?" Rhory narrowed his eyes as his smile cut wider across his beautiful face.

I couldn't hold myself back anymore. There was something about the gleam in his eyes which was as irresistible as a siren's call. I lowered my mouth to his, stopping only when our lips were a hairsbreadth away from each other. "Maybe a helping of both. I *want* to know you. Everything. Your mind, your soul. I want to know what makes you tick. What gets you out of bed in the morning. I want to know that smile, how it looks and feels. I want it all."

Rhory closed his eyes slowly. "Mother would not like it. She doesn't really like your family, you know."

"Ah, now it makes sense. The refusing son, are you using me to upset her?"

"Yes," Rhory said, matter-of-factly. "But it doesn't mean I don't wish you to use me in return."

"Tell me then, if I am going to willingly let you use me... What is it you want?"

"A comfortable life," Rhory said, still keeping his eyes closed. "One of my choosing." As he replied, his lips brushed mine. The touch clawed a ragged moan from deep within me.

"I could give you that, and more."

Rhory leaned into me, just as I pulled away. His eyes snapped open wide as I allowed myself to create distance between us. Each step was hard to complete, but I did it because I had to.

"Prove it to me," I said, wanting nothing more than to snatch him back in my arms.

"How would I do that?" Rhory asked breathlessly.

I glanced outside, regarding the slither of the moon. It had been two days since I had turned last and I still felt the violent night beneath the tunnels and the chains Auriol and Silas had wrapped around my body. Rhory was safe with me until the moon was full again. I was in control, and I wanted him.

"Tomorrow morning," I said finally. "I will come for you then."

"Mother will not like it," Rhory repeated.

"I get the impression you do not care what she approves of or not."

The corners of Rhory's mouth lifted. The smile was becoming and overcame his entire face until his eyes glowed with it.

"Tomorrow it is then," Rhory said. "But I don't know if I have the patience to wait that long."

A laugh bubbled out of me, echoing the lightness that filled my chest. "Believe me, Rhory, I have waited a long time for this. I think you can wait until tomorrow morning. I'm not the type of man to steal you away in the night."

"That is a shame." Rhory pouted, flexing his fingers at his sides as though he didn't know what to do with himself. "And what type of man are you, Calix Grey?"

"Meet me tomorrow, and you will find out."

"I," Rhory swept towards me, snatching control of the moment with the press of his chest into the firmness of my stomach, "Very much look forward to it."

I knew, with complete certainty, Rhory spoke with honesty as my ears focused on the steady hum of his heart. He didn't refuse me as I lifted my stable hand and pressed it over his chest. It beat beneath my soft touch, and I knew then that it was the most precious thing to me in this world and the next. And I would do anything to protect it. *Anything.*

28

I WOKE to the muffled murmurings of Calix and Millicent, far beneath the bedroom. The gaps in the floorboards did little to silence their conversation. At first, the sound was comforting and kind, for my mind was still gripped in the bliss of rest. But that bliss quickly vanished. Straining my ears, I could pick out words here and there through the groggy tiredness that lingered in my mind. But then the events of the night prior came flooding back in full destructive force.

My first mistake was to stretch my arms out of the cocoon of warmth the quilt provided me. I was instantly scolded by the cold chill that seeped in through the broken glass windows and thin old walls. My second mistake came quickly after as I chose to face the memories from last night and the new understanding that my mind was not, in fact, mine at all.

Calix and I had hardly spoken after he revealed our shared history. History I could not remember, no matter how hard I tried. It would have been easier to believe he had lied about it all. But that didn't feel right, not when one touch of his skin revealed to me the truth. He was not lying.

The headache I had fallen asleep to was back in full force.

Throwing my legs out of the bed, I stood beside the mound of a pillows and tangled sheets where Calix had slept on the floor beside me. I should have offered for him to stay in the bed with me. Gods know there was enough room. But selfishly, I needed space. Not that it helped. My mind told me that was what I required, but my heart longed for his touch, his closeness. Instead, I afforded myself escape only when his breathing slowed, signalling he had found sleep. I followed soon after, lulled into rest by the symphony of his inhales and exhales.

By the time I made it down the rickety stairs, Calix and Millicent came to an abrupt halt in whatever they discussed. Although I had heard enough. My name was mixed in with the low murmurings about Eamon.

"Good afternoon," Millicent said from her seat. She was placed far in the shadowy corners of the room, far from the little light of late day which infected the shadowed space. Although there were wooden boards across the windows which kept the majority of the daylight out, Millicent was taking no chances.

Calix smiled weakly at me but didn't speak a word. He could hardly hold my stare before dropping it back to his hands which toyed with one another on his lap.

I took my seat between them. The legs of the chair were uneven, causing it to rock as I put my full weight down on it.

"Have I interrupted?" I asked, voice light with caution.

"Not at all," Millicent said, muffling Calix's quiet answer. She extended a rolled parchment across to me. I plucked it from between her fingers, already recognising the wax seal and the emblem it bore. "We were discussing this. Here. Feast your eyes on your husband's new attempt to get you back."

Dread filled my stomach and coiled itself down my legs. "Where did you get it?"

"They are practically blowing with the breeze through the streets," Millicent added. "The devil works hard, but Eamon works harder. He has put the notice up across town. But this one, this I found back at Auriol's cottage last night. It was nailed to the door like an eviction notice."

I spared Calix a glance before unrolling the parchment; he never met my gaze. His knee was bobbing with nervous energy, and the skin around his thumb had been picked raw. I resisted the urge to reach out for him and take his hand, knowing how natural that would have been but also knowing I didn't have it in me to hold him.

"At least, this time, the message has not been carved into someone's skin," Calix said as my eyes trailed the wording across the parchment. "Although, give him time and Eamon will grow desperate when this attempt fails and he is forced to find another."

My name had been scrawled in untidy and thick penmanship beneath the word **Missing**. It was a short notice which detailed the incorrect account that I had been missing for days and whoever found me would be awarded a trunk of coins.

"...to be paid in abundance by the Crimson Guard for the return of Rhory Coleman," I read it aloud, twice.

"So much money that, if I needed such a thing, it would have me turning on you," Millicent added, grinning over the lip of a mug. Her lips were stained a deeper red than usual. Even her teeth looked darker, until her tongue cleared the liquid away. It quickly dawned on me that she was drinking blood, although it took a moment for the scent to reach me and invade my nose. As though noticing my shock, Millicent smiled. The harsh tang of copper flooded the air, as though she sucked on the very coins Eamon had promised Darkmourn as payment for my return.

"Smart, I will give it to Eamon," she continued. "He has placed more of the notices in the poorer areas of Darkmourn. Because he knows they will give tooth and nail to get that money. And atop that, he has practically tripled his force of Crimson Guards overnight with the promise of reward."

"But it also tells us something else," Calix added as he took the parchment from my hands and rolled it up in his. I hadn't realised I had started to shake until my fingers were without something to hold. "He knows we are in Darkmourn and it will only be a matter of time before he gains entry into every home, establishment, and dwelling to find you."

"Are we are going to sit and wait until he does?" I asked, because it was the only question I could fathom.

"That is one option, one of many," Millicent said. "I have a few other suggestions—"

Calix stood abruptly, the notice no more than a crumpled ball of paper in his fist. His breathing was ragged. Even his eyes were wide and unblinking, the whites almost entirely bloodshot.

"Steady boy," Millicent said, but there was no humour in her voice. She feared him or feared what he'd be as he was moments from losing control and shifting. "It will do none of us well if you let out the wolf now."

"Calix." I was beside him, my hand around his wrist. "It is going to be okay. Look at me."

He did, just as my power slipped from my skin and snatched his uncontrolled rage and replaced it with something easier to breathe through.

The force of his emotions slammed into me. It was boiling, so hot my skin prickled raw, as though I had been an inch away from a roaring inferno. When I couldn't take any more of his fury, I released him and slumped back into my chair.

"Thank gods for that," Millicent cooed from her chair. "I rather like this house; I wouldn't want it destroyed."

"Sorry," Calix fussed, running a hand through the length of his brown hair. "I can't bear the feeling of being forced into a corner.

Eamon took something very dear from me, and I will not let it happen again."

Millicent leaned forward. "We will save Silas. And Auriol."

Calix didn't tell Millicent that they were not who he spoke of, but one subtle glance my way proved my suspicions. He spoke of me.

"Eamon is painting a picture for the public." The words came out of me without thought. "To combat it, we should paint one of our own."

"What do you mean to do?" Calix asked.

"I never was one for art," Millicent mumbled.

"Millicent, I know you said you were not one for money either," I said, the idea coming to me quickly. "But if you give me to Eamon and claim the prize, he will never expect the truth behind it."

"No, absolutely not." Calix slapped his palm on the table. The glasses and china mugs clattered against one another violently.

Millicent leaned forward, smiling with a glint in her ruby eyes. "Keep going."

"Eamon needs me alive if he wishes to keep control of the Crimson Guard. He may hurt me, but he cannot kill me. Take me back to him. He knows not of Millicent's involvement, and will never blink twice at a vampire trading in a human for their own benefit."

"Did you not just hear what I said?" Calix whispered. "Rhory, you can't possibly think we will let you do this."

"We?" Millicent echoed. I was never more thankful for her thinly veiled and blatant untethered disloyalty to me. "Unless you can come up with another idea that doesn't involve eating the limbs of the man who is literally tying the noose around your family's neck, then I suggest we listen to Rhory. The boy is finally speaking sense."

"Let me do this," I said, ready to fall to my knees before Calix and beg. "He is my husband and the Crimson Guard is my father's legacy. Allow me to right his wrongs, return your family back to you and prevent this from happening again. Calix, I am no longer scared of him. I can only stop him if I am close enough, and if Darkmourn knows that I have been returned home, all eyes will be on me and my welfare. It will be harder for Eamon to hide with so many eyes on us."

It took a moment for Calix to answer me. It was not another refusal, because he likely saw it was pointless to try. Defiance and determination danced within the blood in my veins, and if I felt it, he surely could see it.

"What has changed?" he asked, gold eyes softening at their edges.

"I finally have something to fight for."

"Rhory has a point," Millicent said over the rim of her cup. This time she didn't add any sarcastic comments. "He can get into the nest and get the information needed about Auriol and Silas's whereabouts."

"Best to strike the monster whilst he is down," I said, eyeing them both. "Eamon has been wounded. He is weak. Darkmourn's attention is on him. One wrong move and he fucks everything up."

"If you go to him, Rhory, I cannot protect you." Calix's words settled over me.

"It is time I protect myself," I replied, feeling a swell within my chest at the notion. My hand uncurled before me, fingers peeling away like the petals of a flower until my power glowed between them. "It is time this ends."

29

IT QUICKLY BECAME apparent that this house once belonged to witches. Strange marks had been carved into doorframes, dust coated candles had been piled within old cabinets full of curiosities. But the most obvious evidence was the worn-leather book I found beneath the bed I had slept in.

I had not exactly gone looking for it, but the distraction came at a perfect time. Millicent had faded back into the tunnels, and I had left Calix pacing in the room downstairs. He had hardly looked at me since our conversation earlier that afternoon, and I had to distract myself from his silence.

As much as I desired his company, it only reminded me of what I was missing: my memories.

A part of me felt wrong for even touching the book, but the moment it was in my hands, I felt some desire to lose myself to it. Growing up with my mother and her wishes to keep our powers hidden, I never had the chance to contemplate what it meant to be a witch. There was nothing in our home that could reveal our truth. No books or objects that would incriminate us. If it did, we would have both been shipped to Castle Dread, never to be seen again. And Mother would have done anything to stop that from ever happening.

Finding this book, and the untold secrets within, made me feel as though I was doing something entirely wrong yet entirely right.

A star had been worn into the leather-bound cover, the grooves painted with gold leaf which had survived the ages. As I opened it carefully, pages cracked. They were stained brown with age and worn at the corners from the many fingers which had touched it. The spine was delicate, I had to lay it out across my lap carefully just to ensure I didn't crack it.

There was a name scrawled onto the first page, nothing else.

"Bishop," I read it aloud. Dread uncurled deep within me as I repeated the name aloud. If there was one witch family that was infamous among Darkmourn, it was the Bishops. The book confirmed that this house belonged to Jak Bishop, Lord Marius's eternal mate.

I flicked through the pages, in awe that I held something that once had been touched by a Bishop witch. Some pages held no writing at all, but drawings and marks much like the ones around the doorframes and carved into the stone slabs at every entrance point. I even recognised some symbols and shapes identical to those I had seen etched onto the walls within tunnels beneath Darkmourn.

Other pages were crammed full of writings. Words and poems, which I knew in my heart of hearts to be spells. I had the urge to read a few aloud, but bit down on my tongue for fear of what would happen.

"Found anything of interest?" a voice asked from the room's entrance.

I looked up, surprised at Calix's sudden appearance. He leaned against the doorframe, studying me just as I studied the book. A cloud of dust exploded as I slammed it shut, feeling embarrassed I had been caught, although unsure why.

"It was under the bed," I said quickly, as though I had to come up with some excuse. "I couldn't bear the idea of sitting still and doing nothing. At least a book is good company."

Calix pushed himself from the doorframe and paced towards me. "Care to tell me what it is about?"

I placed it behind me, childishly hiding it from view. "Some erotic love story. You wouldn't like it."

"Wouldn't I?" Calix asked, one thick brow raising in jest. "And suddenly you know everything about my likes and dislikes?"

"Well," I snapped, "You seem to know all of mine. Doesn't seem fair to me."

His sarcastic gleam faded as my words slapped into him. He knew what I referred to. The untouched conversation we had left from the night prior was still taut between us, the tension so thick it was like wading through a frozen lake.

Calix took a seat next to me and sighed. "I shouldn't have told you. It was not fair to play with your mind like that."

"What isn't fair is my mind is not my own. My memories should be mine, but they are not. I do not know what has been tampered with and what hasn't."

"I wish I could answer that for you, Rhory, I really do."

I wished to recite all the warm memories I held onto. The ones of me and Eamon in love. My mind was full of scenes, replaying over and over as though I tried to search for missing details and reasons to prove to myself that they were not real. There was the one of Eamon and me leaving a feast and scampering up into Father's library where Eamon had kissed me for the first time. No, I had kissed him. There were others. So many vivid visions of us together, courting and moving from Darkmourn as though we were the only two in the entire world. How could all those memories, colourful and real that I could almost taste, almost smell them now, be fake? If it wasn't for the truth that scorched from Calix as I read his emotions with my power, I would have dismissed what he said as a lie. It would have been easier.

"I could tell you everything. Gods knows I wish to share the burden of these memories I have with someone. Perhaps then it would make everything feel real, and not some made-up scenarios which I have been made to feel they are. Since it happened, since you were taken from me, I have driven myself mad. What good is the truth if you are the only one who bears it?"

My answer came out quick. "No. Calix, I don't want to hear it. I can't—"

I buried my face in my hands, sensing the pang of a headache beginning.

Calix couldn't hide the hurt in his reaction; when he replied, his voice was low and tired. "Understood. I may want many things, but to burden you with something unwanted is not one of them. I should leave you to your—"

Before he could leave, I gripped his wrist and held on desperately.

"Show me," I pleaded, addressing my innermost desires. "I don't want you to tell me about the past. I want you to show it to me. Show me what it was like. My mind cannot remember, but my body... I think it remembers. It remembers you, where I cannot."

His lips parted slowly. I thought he would say something; instead, he exhaled a long breath whilst lifting a finger towards my face. A shiver spread down my spine as his fingertip trailed from my temple, across the rise of my cheekbone and down to my jaw. He was an artist. His hand was his tool as he painted my face in a scarlet blush.

"Are you sure this is what you want from me?" he asked, voice dropping to a low whisper.

I nodded, unable to remove my eyes from his. "I am certain."

Calix guided me without words. He took my hand, urged me slowly from my seat and pulled me on to his lap. The bed creaked loudly beneath us. It made his expression break into a smile. I smiled back, not because of the sound, but the knowledge of how badly I wanted this. Neither of us spoke of what was to happen. We both knew it. We both *wanted* it with equal measure.

A distraction. From memories and illusions. Something to take our minds off a world I could not understand, at no fault of my own.

In a blink, I was straddling him. My knees were on either side of his hips, pressing into the warmth of his legs. His hands gripped on my thighs desperately. I felt the pinch of his nails through the cotton of my trousers.

There was something about the way Calix touched me that made thinking of anything but the now impossible. Our past didn't matter, and nor did the events that would come in the future. All I could focus on was him, whilst he was solely focused on me.

Calix wove his hand up my arched back and spread his fingers through my hair. He tugged on the roots, ensuring his grip was firm before he brought my face to his.

I kissed his smile. It was feather soft and lingering. He held me to him, exhaling through his nose and tickling the blushed skin of my face as his lips melded with mine. Both my hands found either side of his face. The hairs of his short beard scratched my soft palms, sending a new shiver up my arms, across my shoulders and down to my ass.

"Does your body remember?" he asked, breaking away momentarily from our kiss. "Only you can answer that."

I rocked on him, our kiss intensifying from gentle to hungry. By the time our tongues danced together, Calix was as hard as stone beneath me.

There was a thrill coming from the knowledge that I had such power over him. I didn't need to pay attention to his cock to make it stand to its desperate attention. He groaned into my mouth as I swayed my hips back and forth. I enjoyed the ache his hardness gave me as it pressed into my ass cheeks.

Pulling back slightly, I marvelled at Calix's lips; how pink and swollen they were.

"From the moment I saw you, my body craved your touch. I believed it to be sinful thoughts, but now I know otherwise. There is nothing sinful about you," I whispered.

He dropped his hands from my face and let them linger on my shoulders. Calix's fingers moved, easing the tension from my taut muscles, as I stared directly into his golden-glazed eyes.

"I like the idea of being someone's sin," Calix replied, speaking softly.

"Then be mine,' I said as warmth unfurled in my chest. 'Entirely."

Calix's lips twitched upwards, but it was his eyes which shone with his glee. "It would be my pleasure. This—what is to happen—will not be like it was in the woods."

"By that," I said, biting my lip, "Do you mean you are not going to finish so... prematurely?"

His brows furrowed, giving his expression one of danger and desire. "That wasn't exactly what I was suggesting, but yes. If you care to know, I am going to hold back until I am buried inside of you. Only when I ride your tight hole until you beg for me to finish will I plant my seed."

My stomach flipped; my mouth burst with saliva. "And what if Millicent returns?"

"She won't." His answer was clear and final.

A new spreading of warmth cursed my cheeks. "Does she know?"

"That we are going to fuck in her house? Perhaps not."

"Fuck?" I barked a laugh. "Were you always so vulgar?"

Calix lowered his forehead and pressed it to mine. I pinched my eyes closed, gasping as his cool breath washed over me. "Believe it or not, but you were rarely in the mood for making love. Although when we did so, from the moment I entered you, you would *beg* for me to fuck you."

"Did I?" My mind reeled at the thought. This time, it was not painful to hear of something I could not remember.

"Indeed," Calix growled through an exhale, "You did."

I opened my eyes slowly, holding back a childish giggle as I found his intense stare boring straight through me into the back of my skull. Beneath it, I felt naked. Exposed. Even with my clothes still clinging to my body.

"Would you like to play a game?"

Calix tilted his head in amusement, his golden eyes glinting with intrigue. "Well, that depends on the game."

I pushed off him, feeling his fingers lingering on me as long as they could, until I was standing out of reach. "I am going to ask you a question about the *before*."

"Before?"

I nodded. "For every answer you give me, I will remove a piece of clothing. Care to play?"

Calix reached for the hard mound of flesh pressing through the cloth of his trousers. His hand gripped it and held on, thumb moving slowly as he watched me. His touch alone had the power to fix me, undo me and fix me again. "Ask away, *Little Red*."

"That name," I started, exchanging what would have been my first question for this. "You used it before, but I couldn't understand why you would know my parents' nickname for me."

Calix pouted. "Well, that is not a question. If you are asking why I used it, it was because I secretly hoped it would spark some memory back to life in you. It didn't work. And it was not a nickname your parents gave you. It was mine. Perhaps, when your memory was tampered with, it took those memories and morphed them into something new. Little Red, it belongs to me. Like you did."

"Belong to you? Is that so?"

"It is, and I belonged to you."

My cheeks warmed with a blush beneath his intense gaze and equally intense words.

"Next question. That one was just a warmup." I began unbuttoning the shirt whilst Calix massaged his cock through his trousers. He hardly blinked as he watched me. Slowly, I lifted the material over my head and dumped it on the floor beside me. The movement had ruffled my hair; it took effort not to lift a hand and smooth it back down.

"Hurry, before I grow tired of waiting and decide to rip your clothing off you myself."

I breathed out a laugh, one that smoothed the serious lines of Calix's face. His beauty was heartbreaking and breathtaking.

"Did I know what you were before?"

Calix's hand movements faltered. "No. I was going to tell you, but Auriol forbade it. It is dangerous to tell others, even those you trust most. It was what led to my parents…"

Calix faltered as a look of pure sadness spread across his expression. I couldn't bear to see such a look spoil his eyes, so I lifted my hand and brushed it down the side of his face. As though Calix was hypnotised by me, his unexpected turn in emotions faded like smoke and his hungry desire returned as I popped the single thread button at the top of my trousers; a simple wiggle made them fall to my ankles.

"Only one more question," Calix said, gesturing to my undershorts, entirely distracted by my nakedness.

"I didn't say it was going to be a long game." I thumbed the elastic band of my undershorts, nail brushing slowly across the skin coated with fine ginger hair. Calix moved from the bed, got on his knees before me and took the position of a man in prayer.

I looked down at him. "What are you doing, you fool?"

"Ask me the last question," Calix said, staring up at me from the floor. "And when I answer it, I want to be the one to remove… these." He flicked his hand towards the remaining piece of clothing.

My final question took a moment to locate. When it came down to it, I was uncertain if it was out of jealousy or perhaps hope. "Since…"

"Spit it out," Calix said, smiling mischievously at me. "Or swallow it, your choice."

Every hair on my arms and legs stood to attention. "Have you been with anyone else since… our before?"

Calix smiled proudly, lifted his chin and released a low hum before answering. He raised his large, powerful hands and hooked his fingers into the band of my undershorts. I lifted my hands out of the way, cheeks pinching with excitement.

"Not a soul," Calix answered. "Perhaps it is the curse that floods my blood, but like the wolf... when I have found a *mate*, no one else compares. Ever."

Calix removed my undershorts, his eyes fixated on my cock which slipped free and stood proud and hard between my parted legs. "Hello again," he moaned, eyeing it with an intensity that made my mouth prick with saliva.

I parted my lips to reply, but soon gasped as Calix opened his mouth, extended his wet tongue, and brought it to my tip. Bliss exploded through me as Calix took me into his mouth. My knees threatened to give way as the pleasure of his warm soft suck overcame me. I closed my eyes and gave into the feeling. Part of it was from fear that if I watched him take me, I would be the one to reach a premature finish this time.

From the tip to the base of my shaft, where curls of short ginger hair covered me, Calix devoured me. He didn't use his hands, but moved his tongue in beautiful circles, ensuring every inch of me was glistening with his spit.

My eyes shot open when the feeling stopped suddenly. I hardly cared for the dribble of his saliva that slithered down the base of my cock, onto my balls, where it elongated into a drip and splashed on the floor between my separated feet. Disappointment wracked through me. Calix rocked back on his knees, staring up at me. His cock was free of his trousers and in his hand. He worked it slowly, allowing a bud of spit to fall from his lips onto the curve of his cock.

"You taste just how I remembered," Calix said. "Sweet as summer berries."

As he spoke, I felt a seeping of cum slip from the head of my cock, followed by a knee-buckling shiver which spread from my length across my entire body and soul.

"Fuck me," I said quickly. Desperately. Without thinking, simply speaking my deepest desire into existence. It was the way he looked at me, drank me in, and the way his large hand rubbed his cock, which conjured such sudden starvation from me.

"There it is," Calix said, standing from his knelt place on the floor. For a moment, I forgot how tall he was. When he uncurled to full height, it was he who now looked down at me. "I am not even inside of you yet, and you already want me to fuck you."

"Perhaps my body does remember then," I said, voice barely a whisper.

"Hmm. We will see."

I walked around Calix. He was rooted to the spot, whilst his rich eyes tracked me until he was forced to turn around to continue watching me.

"Where do you think you are going?" he asked, voice rumbling like far off thunder.

I sat on the bed, pushed myself into its middle and laid down on my back. "To bed. Care to join me?"

"I want nothing more," Calix groaned, stepping in until the wooden frame of the bed pressed into his shins. His trousers, like mine, fell with ease to his ankles, which he had stepped out of on his way to the bed. "You always did enjoy this position; however, you were partial to riding me as though I was a throne, and you the king who ruled from it."

I lifted my knees up, cocked my legs, and spread them. There was something thrilling about being so exposed before him. How his eyes flickered to the centre of my ass, then back to my face.

"I want you so bad," I beckoned him, "Let me watch your face when you enter inside of me."

Calix joined me on the bed, crawling over me. His long cock flopped down, heavy; I felt it crash into the inside of my thigh as he brought himself atop me.

"I will be careful with you," he said, reading the moment of fear that washed over me. His thick length was far greater than Eamon's cock. It'd be a miracle if it would enter me without hurting. Eamon was not as blessed as Calix, but still caused me discomfort. It was something else he never apologised for.

Before my mind could move away from this moment to darker thoughts, Calix lowered himself down and kissed me. I was vaguely aware of his bulging arms flexing as they held up his weight. Soon enough, there was no room for thoughts of Eamon. Only Calix, his cock, and the way he was about to fuck me... just how I wanted it. Just how he *knew* to give it to me.

"Spit for me," Calix said. He brought his hand to my mouth.

I did as he asked. My neck strained as I pressed my lips to his fingers, gathered the spit in my mouth and forced it out. Once I was done, and he had lathered his cock with it, he brought his hand back to my mouth, slipping a finger to my lips and parting them.

"More," he demanded.

I was pleased to give him what he wanted.

Calix did the same. Three times he took the saliva from his mouth and stroked it across his cock. Every time, his moan of pleasure grew. He bit down into his lower lip by the last time, straining against his urge to continue working his wet cock with his hand.

Nerves bubbled in my chest. Calix must have heard the skip of my heart as he turned his attention back to me. "Are you nervous?"

I looked to his spit-glittered fingers. "Is that enough... to, you know?"

A sly grin etched across his handsome face. He playfully glowered at me through his thick brows and spoke, "Reach into my jacket pocket."

I did as he asked. His jacket was on floor beside the bed. The cold brush of wind toyed with my bare hole as I bent over, plucked the jacket up and wove my hand into the inner pocket. The tips of my fingers met the kiss of glass.

I pulled free a small vial, no bigger than the palm of my hand. Clear liquid sloshed inside, stopped only from spilling by the cork stuffed in the top. I held it out to Calix, as though displaying evidence. "You've come prepared."

A blush crept over his face. "It wasn't that I expected this but..."

I stifled Calix's excuse by popping the cork and tipping the contents atop his already wet cock. It dribbled out of the vial, thick as honey but as clear as spring water. My hand soon became lathered with the lubrication, which I promptly brought to my hole and spread it around.

Calix didn't say a word as he watched me. The vial smashed on the floor beside the bed, signalling its uselessness now that it was empty.

"Then I suppose you should stock up," I said, lowering my legs back over his waist until I straddled his cock.

"Oh, I will. Tell me when it is too much," Calix said, guiding his length and pressing the hard, curved tip of it to my ass.

"Okay," I breathed, bracing myself for the pain.

But it didn't happen. The burn was not scalding, but warm and welcoming. Calix used a hand and lifted my lower back up, creating a natural arch. His touch relaxed me, which eased his entrance. He completely focused on ensuring I was not harmed. All the while, I sensed his desire to bury his cock in me.

I didn't know I was moaning until I felt the press of his hips. He was in. Completely, with not a single inch spared. The knowledge had me gripping my cock whilst I rolled my hips, familiarising myself with the swell of his length inside of me.

"You..." Calix breathed as his eyes became glassy with desire. "You are so tight. So... good."

He pulled himself out of me, unsheathing his length from my ass. He did so slowly, ensuring my hole grew used to his presence before he ruined me. Calix had been so careful and gentle, but it was not what I desired now. Urgency had me thrusting myself back and forth, enjoying the slide of his cock in me. His thick and demanding presence stretched and pleased me.

"Fuck me, Calix. I want you to take me, fuck me, devour me."

Calix lowered himself back down over me. I kept my knees raised skyward. He folded my legs between us, placing my shin to his chest and keeping me trapped. "Oh, I am going to do all that and more. Again, and again. This... this is something no magic can ever make you forget. I will make sure of that."

Calix, of course, was correct. I could never have ever forgotten this. He fucked me just as I begged him to. In fact, over and over I said those words.

Fuck me. Fuck me. Fuck me.

He always delivered.

Each time I spoke the words, whether aloud or screamed in my mind, his thrusts got harder, faster, to where each slam of his hips caused the words to jolt out of me.

Gone was the warning of keeping quiet in this house. It was a miracle if all of Old Town didn't hear my screams of pleasure.

"Open your mouth," Calix commanded. As I did, he took his middle finger and slipped it between my lips. "Suck it."

I kept my gaze fixated on his as I sucked his finger, just as he'd sucked my cock. He thrusted into me, grunting each time he was buried completely in my tight warmth. My tongue wrapped around his finger and my lips pinched down on it.

"Good boy," Calix groaned. "You are such a good boy."

Thank the Gods I had something in my mouth to stop me from crying out, because Calix reached for my cock and began stroking it in rhythm with his thrusts.

Sweat beaded on his temples, running down the line of his face like rain on a glass window. His length of hair was wild and untamed. Everything about him was a *beast*. Which was why when Calix howled, it didn't scare or shock me. It was natural, although the sound was anything but.

His howl rocked the very walls of the house. It sang of his pleasure and I knew he was racing towards the edge of it, ready to throw himself off the precipice. My ass tightened as I knew he reached his climax, just as his hand worked me to the edge of mine. Breathless, I sucked harder on his finger whilst moaning in tune with his howl.

Calix came inside of me. His cock throbbed as it expelled its milky seed deep within. I raced to my climax as Calix jerked my cock with his fist. The world became sensitive and soft. The rub of his hand became too much to bear. He let go, as though he read my body's reaction. Everything he did, *everything*, was thought-out and familiar, as if he knew my likes and dislikes like the lines on his palms.

Which, in fact, he did.

Calix flopped on the bed beside me after he eased himself free of my hold. There was no care for clean-up. Nor did I mind, as I felt a little of his seed seep out from my ass and spread across the sweat-damp sheets of the bed. All there was room for was the enjoyment of his lingering feeling of pleasure that stormed through me.

He rolled his head to the side and faced me. I did the same. Calix smiled at me with heavy eyes. "If Millicent didn't know about us before, I am sure she does now."

"It doesn't matter," I replied breathlessly, even though I had done little of the hard work. It seemed I was rather inept at lying on my back. "Hell, even if Lord Marius himself heard your howl, it was worth it."

Calix brought his hand to my finger and brushed his thumb over my lip. A kiss followed. It was brief before he flopped back down on the bed, exhausted but smiling with closed eyes.

I stared up at the ceiling, still reeling from the joy his sex had given me. "It was worth it. All of it."

"And it will not be the last time."

I smiled to myself. "How are you so confident in that?"

"Because it is in my nature. Threaded through my very being. You are part of my pack. You always have been. And I will be damned if I ever let you stray far again. No matter the consequence."

"Does that make you my alpha?" I asked into the dark.

"If that is what you wish to submit yourself to."

"How does it work?"

Calix sighed as he gazed up into the darkening ceiling. "In a pack of wolves, there is always an alpha. It is instinctual. However, any leader can be contested."

"Auriol," I said softly, finding it odd to speak of her when her grandson had just been buried within me. "She's your alpha?"

"She is. Until I contest her title."

"It is that easy for you to take it?"

Calix rolled over to face me. The bed creaked with the weight of his movement. "I would need to kill her and devour her heart if I wished to become the true alpha. Just as she did with my grandfather after she turned him with her bite, and he *turned* on her."

Part of me was repulsed, where another part of me felt excited intrigue.

"You wouldn't do that though," I said.

"No, not unless the moment called for it."

His words settled over me, draining the warmth from my body at the thought of such a vile act. I felt the atmosphere we had created in this room slip away like ice in the first thaw of spring.

"Then you better keep your heart safe from me," I said, stretching my hand over his chest and resting it over the solid beat of his heart. "Otherwise, I might be forced to contest my alpha and eat it."

"You can have it," Calix said. "It is yours. It has always been yours;

it always will be. No matter what happened or what happens... It belongs to you."

His words took my breath away. They solely returned the warmth to my body, sparking heat in the kindling of my soul until every limb, finger, and vein hummed with *him*.

"Get some rest," I said. "I am going to need you back to full strength come morning. Before I have to—"

"No, no, no." Calix grabbed me, brought me into his side, and nestled me into the crook of his arm and chest. "No talk of tomorrow. One night, just one more night, and I want to pretend we have nothing to face outside this room."

I pressed a kiss into the damp, sweat-slicked skin of his hard chest before granting him a reply. He knew what was to come when the sun set tomorrow. Our plan would start its first stages, and Calix would be forced to leave my side.

"One more night," I repeated his sentiment. "Until we can claim another, my alpha."

30

IN THE HOURS WHICH PASSED, Calix and I didn't remove ourselves from one another. If our fingers were not entwined, or my hands draped carefully on his scarred chest, we were kissing and dancing with naked limbs and a burning thirst for one another. We slept too, a little. Only brief breaks between the exhausting yet thrilling entanglement we had entered. The night passed into day and day into night. Time slipped away from us, replacing our enjoyment for one another with the feeling of impending doom.

Our bliss was short-lived when Millicent came knocking on our closed door.

Her red eyes surveyed the state of the room the moment she pushed it open. Millicent didn't wait for us to answer her knock, nor did she require to. This was her home; we were merely visitors. Calix hardly stirred at her presence. Instead, he pulled me in closer to his chest with a muscled arm scooped under my neck, and rested it on my upper arm.

"If you are done defiling my brother's room, we should make haste and get this over with," she said, nose flaring as she smelled the air and the tang of sex the hours had poisoned it with. "May I suggest you wash before I return you back to your husband. I wouldn't want him smelling another man's scent all over you."

I slipped from Calix's hold, pulling the crumpled sheets with me. "There is no need. Eamon saw me and Calix in the forest, he would likely expect nothing less."

"And let him," Calix growled.

Millicent grinned like a cat seeing milk. "Very well. Both of you, meet me downstairs to discuss the next steps. If I am to walk Rhory to his front door and deposit him, it should be with a believable story. A solid one, which explains how and why I found him."

The vampire turned on her heel and departed into the shadows of the hallway beyond the room. Her quick visit had shattered the aura of peace we had conjured, allowing room for the impending anxiety to overcome me.

I sat on the edge of the bed, gaze stuck to a spot on the wall. A warm hand trailed up my back and slipped over my neck. Where Calix placed his fingers, he finished with a brief kiss.

"Tell me how you feel?" His question was as dark as the skies beyond the house. "Voice it aloud, it may help."

"Frightened," I replied. It was the easiest answer to give. "But determined. There is nothing Eamon can do to me which he hasn't done before. He may hurt me, punish me. This time, I know what it is for."

"I will remind you, you don't need to do this," Calix said, lips purring into the skin of my neck. "If you told me you had changed your mind, I would not care. You mean more to me than I could put into words."

"You also care for your family, and I will see that they are returned to you. I know what it is like to lose everything you ever loved; I cannot see you go through that."

"And what will you do when it is over? When it is you that I desire the most?"

"Find a way." Tears filled my eyes, but I refused to let them fall. I was in control of my emotions, just as I could be with others. And now, I was the master of them all. "Calix, listen to me. I *will* find a way to remember you. Eamon has the key to many things, and if he refuses to give it to me willingly, I will break the damn lock myself."

"There he is," Calix exhaled, as though some weight had been lifted from his shoulders. "The man I love. He is returning. Seeing you as the broken shell I found standing outside my door was never who I had been forced to leave. Knowing you leave me with a slither of your past self gives me the confidence that you'll see this through. I'm rooting for you. We all are."

∽

Our plan was simple. Millicent would say she found me roaming the streets of Old Town after fleeing Calix. Eamon was not to know that I was aware of our past, and I would lean into that. It would be easy to perform the unknowing fool, since it had been the part I had been playing for years. Of course, Millicent would have to make it look unsuspecting.

"Is this really necessary?" Calix asked, soul brimming with distress.

The thin leather cord he used to tie his hair back from his face did wonders to show every line and crease of concern as he looked between his hand and my face.

"If we want Eamon to believe Rhory fled you, it would be more credible if he was returned...marked," Millicent replied, "By you."

"It's fine," I said, lifting Calix's chin with my finger so he would focus on me, and not the dark claws that had replaced his fingers. The shift from human to the wolf had only reached up to the crook of his arm. Not a single scrap of skin was left; in its place was dark fur and yellow talons. "I will be okay."

"If you can't see it through..." Millicent began, but Calix stopped her with one look.

"No one else is to lay a hand on Rhory. No one."

I marvelled at the warmth that spilled from Calix's fur-coated arm as I took it by the elbow and lifted it to my exposed chest. There was slight resistance, but Calix allowed me to guide his claws up until they pressed firmly into my skin. "You can't hurt me."

His gold eyes brimmed, and thick brows quivered. "I can."

I knew Calix could not draw his claws across my chest without encouragement, so I did it for him. We held one another's stare as I pierced my skin with his claws. I pushed only enough to draw beads of blood. Then, with great effort, I guided his powerful touch downwards.

Pain lashed through my chest, cramping every muscle in my body. I offered Calix a smile, whilst concealing the discomfort I was in. If it wasn't for the insides of my cheeks which I bit down on, I would have hissed out in agony.

"That is enough." Calix drew back.

"Yes, that is more than convincing. Rhory, take this." Millicent thrust her hand towards me, whilst keeping her gaze the other way. Pinched between her painted nails was a square of cloth with embroidered frills sown around its outside. "Clean yourself up before I forget myself."

As I dabbed away the dribbles of blood that oozed from my new cuts, I watched as Calix's fur melted from his arm like ash caught in the wind, revealing pink flesh beneath. By the time I had wiped away most of the gore, his arm was mundane once again.

"I hate myself for hurting you." Calix leaned forward, taking the blood-stained cloth and dabbing it across the bloodied marks.

"You could never hurt me," I whispered, not wishing for him to know how the stinging of the wound felt more like fire blossoming across my skin. "Never."

Calix studied my lips as though he attempted to understand my words.

"It is highly imperative to our plan. So, let us leave whilst the blood still weeps." Millicent stood quickly, still averting her eyes from me. As she referred to the blood, it seemed she strained at the word. "Rhory, say your farewells and meet me by the door for the next part of our ridiculous plan."

Calix took me into his arms before Millicent's footsteps faded into the darkness of the Bishop's house. I pressed my face into his chest, closing my eyes and inhaling the moment so I would never forget it. No longer did I care for the stinging of my fresh wound, not when he held me.

"This is not a goodbye," Calix whispered, his lips tracing the words on the top of my head.

"Then why does it feel like it is?" I asked, not daring to move. All I cared for was the smoothing circles his hands made on my back, and the way his earthy scent filled my nose with each breath in.

"I will not be far," Calix said. "If you need me, I will come for you."

He had given me the option to call this all off if I required it. Part of me wished he had never told me. It made giving up easy, knowing something so simple was the only thing from preventing him from coming to save me. All it would take was setting a lit candle by my window, and Calix would come bursting through the door to my home to claim me, as he had before. The thought was tempting. I feared I was not strong enough to ignore it when the time came.

"Let's hope it does not get to that." I pulled back, feeling Calix's reluctance to let me go. His touch fell down the length of my arms and took my hands in his. He squeezed them, and I squeezed back.

We stared at one another in silence. His eyes flickered across my entire face, drinking me in. Every second I stayed with him was another closer to me giving up before I had even stepped out of the door.

"I will remember you," I said, watching Calix's proud face break with every word of my promise.

"That doesn't matter to me," Calix pleaded, pulling me to him a final time. "What matters is that you come back to me safe and sound."

"But it matters to me. Eamon has taken from me, and it is time I claim it back."

Calix took my face in his hands and lifted it until we were looking at one another again. We were inches apart. No longer did he bother to control his tears, which he let fall freely from each corner of his pinched eyes.

"Just come back to me," Calix whispered through quivering lips. "That is all I wish for you to promise."

I reached up and brushed a single tear from his cheek. He leaned into my hand, closed his eyes and exhaled a long and taut breath.

"Calix, look at me."

As he did, gold light spilled gently from my hands. My use of power was not to take his emotions from him nor provide him with replacements. It was different this time. I simply wished for him to feel my burning honesty as I answered him.

"I cannot explain it yet, but I do not think we could ever be separated. Not forever. It seems we will always find a way back to one another."

The lines around his eyes lessened. The tension around his mouth relaxed. In the glow of his handsome, honey-pure eyes, I knew he felt the truth I spoke. It eased his tension, smothering it like a flame within the eye of a storm.

"Two days," Calix said calmly. "We will give you two days. Eamon has had you long enough. No matter your success, or failure, I will come for you. That is my promise to you."

I guided his face down to mine. He followed willingly.

"What are you going to do this time?" I asked, stopping him only when his lips were a hairbreadth away from mine. "Break into my house, throw me over your shoulder and take me away into the night?"

"Well, it would not be the first time. Why would it matter if I did it again?"

My stomach flipped. "Something to look forward to then."

"Indeed, it is," Calix purred. Slowly, he brought his lips down to mine and kissed me as though it were our first and last time. The gentle caress of his mouth against mine, and the memory it left on my lips, carried me from the house in Old Town, all the way back to Eamon.

To my husband. To my monster.

This time, it would be different. I would no longer allow Eamon to hold any power over me. It would be my turn to force power on him until he was completely suffocated beneath it.

31

My throat burned as I expelled my feral screams. The noise shattered the night. My lungs constricted as I shouted over and over until I felt the strain of breathlessness force me to my knees. Millicent had told us to keep quiet. But that rule no longer mattered. Not as I shouted into the night with all the frustration and determination of my promise to Calix.

This was the first part of our plan. A fine pencil sketch on a canvas, which would soon become the picture we would paint to combat Eamon's story of a missing man.

Millicent reached me before the patrons of the Darkmourn, dead or alive, had much of a chance. She claimed me publicly, as windows were thrown open and people came rushing out to see what caused the ruckus. Of course, it was planned. For me to run through Darkmourn screaming bloody murder with a torn crimson cloak, claw marks down my chest. It was all to paint the very public picture that I was a victim of something horrific. Something unseen and terrible.

I was a survivor, and all of Darkmourn would find out before Eamon. Just that alone made me scream harder, shout louder.

Our plan was well thought out. *Manipulative*, Millicent had said. I gave props to the vampire where it was due because she played her part well. She had her arm draped over my shoulder, tugging me in close to her side as we navigated the dark streets of the town whilst they filled with an audience.

"Keep it up," Millicent had whispered as we moved closer towards my home. She had to flash her teeth at others who attempted to step in our way. I could see their starved desire to take me from Millicent and return me to Eamon so they could be the one to claim the prize. But when they saw the points of her teeth, and the deep flashing of blood-red eyes, they all backed away.

No one crossed Millicent. Not even the Crimson Guards, who came rushing over to see what the fuss was about. One of them looked at me. That was all it took. They all recognised me instantly.

I half expected them to take me from Millicent, but they didn't dare. The posters they had spread around Darkmourn made it clear, and if they went against the promise of money, it would not have done well for their imperfectly laid illusion.

Instead of taking me from Millicent, they formed a wall around us as we moved through the streets, bathed in the red glow of streetlamps. With the sketch of my face plastered upon buildings we passed, there was no denying I was Rhory Coleman, and I had been found.

Eamon was waiting for me. I saw him through the crowd of heads the moment we turned onto our street. He stood within the doorframe of our home, highlighted by the warmth of fire and light behind him. My heart quickened its pace as I regarded him. Millicent sensed it and held on tighter. She didn't offer me words of comfort, nor did she need to.

With the Crimson Guards around us, and the street full of nosey townsfolk following at our back, this was exactly the show we wished to put on. I was not surprised when I had to fight the urge to smile.

"Rhory?" Eamon called out. There was a slight rasp to his voice, a congested tone that suggested he was not well. The exasperation in his voice did well to show him as the broken man who'd had his love taken from him. I hated how genuine his sorrow looked, and the way he leaned against the doorframe, as if one look at me would bring him to his knees.

As we grew closer and Eamon's outline became more defined, I could see exactly the cause of his weakness. Eamon's arm was bandaged. He had his arm lifted in a sling across his chest. Where his hand should have been was now a stump of wrapped bandages. The urge to smile at the memory of his pain was almost too powerful to ignore.

I was stopped before the pathway that led to our front door. Bathed in the glow of firelight from the many windows before me, I was illuminated for everyone to see.

"Tell me this is not some cruel trick." Eamon mumbled, clutching his chest with his remaining hand. "Or have you truly come back to me?"

The surrounding crowd was silent. All I could hear was the thundering of their following footsteps, and the symphony my heartbeat played in pace with them. My dearest husband was playing his doting part well, but I would play it better.

"My love," I cried out, pulling free of Millicent and stumbling up the stone path to our front door. As I reached him, I fell to my knees. I sensed Eamon's shock within his reluctance to catch me. Not that he could help with a missing hand and a body riddled in pain.

The clapping began as Eamon lowered himself to me with a hiss of pain. Once again, I fought the urge to smile. Knowing he was suffering at the hands of Calix was thrilling. Regardless, he had to believe my reaction, just as the crowd did. If we were to be successful, Eamon had to believe Calix had harmed me, and I escaped. It all mattered to my manipulation of him, and the crowd who watched.

"I'm home," I cried out loud enough for all to hear. "I found my way back to you."

I cringed into Eamon's cold chest as he pulled me into him. Choosing not to shy away, I threw my hands over his shoulders and placed a hard and rushed kiss onto his unsuspecting mouth. Our faces clashed into one another, and I felt the nip of my lip against his teeth.

His entire demeanour was tense and uncomfortable. Knowing that only urged me to kiss him deeper. The crowd ate it up just as Millicent said they would. The cry they gave out was like the strike of lightning in a storm. It was Eamon who pulled back first. I would have continued kissing him until his mouth was bruised and bloodied.

"What has *he* done to you?" Eamon asked through gritted teeth as he took in the torn cloak and my dishevelled nature. His blue eyes studied the wounds on my chest, but his gaze showed no care or compassion. It was as though he was surveying something new, something he was unfamiliar with.

I couldn't answer truthfully, although the urge to lean into Eamon's ear and whisper to him how Calix had fucked me so hard that I still felt the echo of his cock even as he held me now. Instead, I forced my face into a fearful frown as I took Eamon's hand in mine and brought his fingers to the clawed marks on my chest. His touch was cold and as soft as silk. My skin itched and stung, but I made certain to press his hand into the wound, until it was smeared with blood.

"He did this," I forced out, blinking out the fake tears I had conjured. "Please, I just want to be home…"

"You're ruined," Eamon hissed into my ear as he guided me to standing. I inhaled sharply, feeling my lungs swell with dread as my husband faced the doting crowd. He righted his tone and spoke more to the crowd than to me. "Rhory, you are safe. I won't let anything happen to you again."

I couldn't focus on the lack of his emotions as he spoke, not when he steered me towards the door and ushered me inside our home. The

Crimson Guard followed swiftly; I caught their movement out of the corner of my eye. In their midst was Millicent, who couldn't break away from them even if she desired to. By the time the door closed, shutting off the chaos of the streets, Eamon called an end to the grand show we had all put on. The second we were out of sight, he released me, almost pushing me away with a shove that hurt him more than it did me.

We stood in the foyer's centre, with Millicent and a handful of Crimson Guards lingering on the opposite side.

I continued my act, forcing tears out of my burning eyes as I tried to press myself back into Eamon's hold. He refused me again.

"Do not touch me," Eamon snarled, teeth clashing like a rabid dog. He looked me up and down, then spat at the ground before my feet. "You are unclean. Spoiled."

"But, husband—"

"I'll take my prize and be on my way," Millicent called out, interrupting the tension between us. "I wouldn't want to ruin such a precious moment with my presence."

Eamon ignored Millicent, showing no sign he even recognised her presence. My skin burned beneath his scrutinizing gaze. There was a darkness behind his eyes. A silent promise of hateful thoughts. It was as though he searched for proof; proof Calix had, in fact, ruined me.

Eamon's nose flared slightly as disgust rolled over his face.

"One of you, see that the bath is filled," Eamon said whilst beholding me, but his words were directed to his Crimson Guard. What he said next was for me, and only me. "You are covered in his stink. Before we discuss anything, I want to see him scrubbed from you."

Hate swelled within me. I felt protective of the knowledge that Calix lingered on me. It took great effort not to refuse Eamon.

"Yes," I forced out. "Just don't leave me." I cringed at my own pleading. More so when it didn't conjure the reaction I'd hoped from him. Eamon's lack of physical touch was not proving well for my act.

"About that prize—"

"Silence yourself," Eamon barked, finally turning his attention to Millicent. "*Vampire.*"

The Crimson Guard swelled around her, closing in on her from all sides.

"My apologies, but did I misunderstand the notice?" Millicent held her ground as rough hands reached towards her from all sides. "You promised coin for his return."

Eamon spat at Millicent's feet, just as he had mine. The splash of phlegm crashed into the wooden panelled flooring at her feet, some droplets hitting into her boots. Loathing deepened his face into a mask that mirrored something of a beast. "Oh, you shall get your thanks."

Eamon looked back at me, ushering with his remaining hand for me to step towards the stairs. "Come, *husband*. Let us clean you up."

I couldn't refuse him. But I didn't want to leave Millicent. Something felt terribly wrong, and from the panic that set into her face, Millicent sensed it too. I could hardly see her through the swell of red cloaks, who closed in on her from all sides.

"She saved me," I pleaded. Eamon kept his gaze on the stairs, urging me forward with a push to my lower back.

"*She* is a vampire," he answered coolly. "Money matters little to her kind."

Millicent was struggling, hissing curses at those who grabbed her.

"Stop it." I pulled back enough from Eamon to step back towards Millicent. But Eamon's strength surprised me. His hand gripped the back of my neck and squeezed, yanking me backwards with a harsh tug.

"Oh, my darling," he said; although his words sounded as though they should have been filled with compassion, his expression was distant. "Vampires do not deserve to be rewarded. Don't you see? They are the problem with this world. They always have been."

"But you—"

"Do not concern yourself with it," he snapped. "It was her misfortune she found you, and my fortune she did. Now, are you going to continue to struggle, or would you prefer I ask a few of my guards to help you up the stairs?"

I struggled beneath his grip. How could someone pale and sickly from his wound hold such strength in one hand? I knew his touch well. But this... this was different.

"Darkmourn knows she is here," I said, urgently reminding Eamon that many people had witnessed Millicent come into the home. If they didn't see her leave, there would be questions. And Eamon hated questions.

His hand squeezed harder until the skin beneath his pinch felt as though it was on fire. "Then it will be a lesson to Darkmourn. I no longer care for their approval; it matters little to me now. Now I have what I want most."

Millicent's vulgar shouts and struggles followed me all the way from the ground floor of our home up to my bathroom. I didn't dare say another word for fear of what would become of her. Eamon didn't know Millicent had anything to do with Calix, but his reaction to her had been birthed from something entirely different.

I trusted the Crimson Guard would not act out of turn. Their entire purpose was to see the protection of all kinds, both the living and the undead. That was what they were created for: balance and peace.

Eamon was muttering something beneath his breath, but I couldn't make it out, not as the hallway we passed suddenly filled with bodies.

Men and women spilled from the many closed doors, exiting rooms which had not been used in years. Faces I didn't recognise surrounded us, all human, and all watching.

Our home had gone from a place for only the both of us to the opposite; even before they revealed themselves behind the closed doors there was a sense of fullness to our home.

"I was lonely without you," Eamon said, pulling me the final stretch towards the door that spilled with steam from beneath the small opening; the air grew heavy with it.

We walked into the cloud of warm air and into the bathroom. There was heat everywhere. It choked me.

"Who are those people in our house?"

"My people," Eamon said before correcting himself, "My warriors."

It didn't make sense, nor could I work it out as I struggled to navigate the steam filled room.

Eamon finally let go of my neck, allowing me to crash to the floor. I could see the outline of his dark frame move through the steam. He closed the door with a slam. The click conjured a jolt of childish fear to slip around my soul.

"Remove your clothes," Eamon commanded, watching me from a distance. He was no more than a dark shape through the thick cloud of steam and moisture.

"No..." I said, pulling the strength to resist from deep within me.

Eamon flinched, then expelled a breathy laugh. "Don't make me ask again, Rhory. You will not like it."

He was right. There was no point in fighting him. At least not yet. I focused on the reason for my being here and used it to lift my fingers to the buttons of my shirt. Eamon watched me undress. He didn't offer to help, although I felt his gaze follow every subtle move as I removed each piece of blood-coated clothing. It had been a long time since I was last naked before him. Being so now felt demoralising and wrong. Discomfort flooded through me, thickening in my veins.

"Do you know how I feel?" Eamon asked, brow creased with deep lines. He stepped in close, the mist peeled away from his features until he was fully corporeal again. "You belong to me, but you gave yourself away to another. Every inch of your skin should be mine, but it doesn't feel like it is. Looking at you *sickens* me."

His words conjured a shiver to spread across every inch of skin his eyes surveyed. I felt completely and utterly exposed. My hands shook as I clutched at my length, hiding it from the scrutiny of his tormented stare.

"I... I came back for you." I forced the words out. "Everything that I have done... everything that has happened, it has been a mistake."

"Do not lie to me!" Eamon shouted, body trembling with fury. "Do not dare utter another fucking lie out of that mouth or I swear…"

He raised his hand up suddenly. I flinched backwards, almost tripping over the pile of clothes I felt on the floor, as I raised my arms protectively before me. But there was no pain which followed. No slap of a palm, or smack of a fist. When I peered back through my shield of my arms, I saw Eamon smiling.

"Get in the bath."

I couldn't move, even if I wanted to.

"Get *in*," Eamon commanded again, voice steady. His words echoed throughout the room. It disrupted the steam that oozed from the water's surface.

"I'm sorry—"

"In!"

I skipped forward, no longer caring for my nakedness. My mind screamed for me to obey. Doing so would protect me from him.

My toes burned as they slipped beneath the tub of water. It was hot, but not scalding. The temperature was warm enough that my skin prickled with discomfort. I fought the urge to itch. Giving myself over to the pain gave me a sense of clarity. It reminded me of what I was here to do. Giving in, I slipped beneath the water until only my head was above it. Eamon stepped to the tub's side, parting the thick steam. With his remaining hand, he pulled up a three-legged stool and perched himself upon it. From somewhere unseen, he produced a dried sponge.

"Lean forward," he said, flicking his hand in dismissal. I did as he asked, not wishing to show any resistance. "As it seems your back is your preferred place to lay, I will start by cleaning it."

His insult stung, but that didn't prevent the sly smile that spoiled my lips as I leaned forward and curved my back for him. Where the water was so warm, it made the air of the bathroom have a terrible chill. I couldn't help but shiver, which Eamon soon noticed as he began pressing the sponge to my back and moving it methodically.

"No, no. This will not do," he said. I felt him withdraw the sponge. The skin he had rubbed stung from fresh scratches. "I cannot have my husband cold."

There was the shuffling of feet, soon followed by the splash of water against water.

"Fuck!" I screamed out, lurching forward. I gripped the side of the tub, trying to pull myself away from the splattering of boiling water Eamon poured into the tub.

"I must purge *him* from your skin," Eamon said over the cascading water. "Do you think I want to do this? Do you truly believe I enjoy hurting you? If you would just do as you must and behave, you would not force my hand."

I cowered in a ball at the furthest point of the tub I could move towards. My back hissed with agony from the splashes of boiled water which splattered upon my skin. There was no denying I would be greeted with punishment upon my return. Perhaps I deserved it for breaking our vows. But as I leaned back into the scalding water I reminded myself just how little the vows of our marriage meant. They were spoken from lies. Whatever Eamon had done to my mind, whatever tinkering and altering he had seen done to my memory, had led me blindly into our union.

It means nothing, I reminded myself, *it all means nothing.*

I repeated the statements over and over as my body acclimatised to the hotter water. As I eased back into it, thankful as the boiling water diluted to a bearable point, I didn't stop internally screaming the sentiments on repeat.

"No one is making you do this..." I hissed as he returned to scrubbing my back with the sponge. He pressed harder now. The coarse edges of it scratched the hot water into my skin. I didn't need to see my back to know it was covered in cuts.

"I love you," Eamon said, as though that was a justified answer. "Everything I do is because I love you."

I hated hearing those words from him. He spoiled them. Tore all meaning from them and ruined them. Between the pain he caused me physically, and the mental disgust his declaration of love cursed me with, I couldn't help but forget myself.

My lips grew slick. Words came out of me without so much as a thought to them, or what reaction they would conjure. "It is not me you love. It never has been. You love me because I am the leash connecting you to the Crimson Guard. That is what you love—"

Eamon cracked his fist into the back of my head. I blinked and saw stars. Blood burst across my tongue as my tooth cut into the inside of my lip.

"Never think as though you can speak on my behalf, Rhory. I fear you forget yourself. And it would seem that it is not only your body that requires cleaning, but your mind." Before I could react, Eamon had discarded the sponge and reached down for another jug of boiling water.

Except, this time, when he poured the scalding water into the tub, he aimed it at my lap.

I felt red. I saw red. I tasted red. The world was bathed in it, but the pain was delayed.

I took a deep inhale, and then it came so sudden and sharp, I almost lost control and gave into the darkness of peace. My cheeks filled with spit and blood as I did everything in my power not to scream.

His remaining hand gripped my neck. Nails bit into the tender flesh and squeezed. Eamon was leaning over the tub, holding me in his vice-grip so I could not squirm away from him. He brought his lips to my ear and hissed, "Another word and I will—"

He didn't finish. He *couldn't* finish. I slapped my hand around his wrist and streams of gold billowed out with such force the entire world exploded in light. With every ounce of my desperation and rage, I thrust the pain from my body and poisoned Eamon with it.

One moment, it stormed through me. The next, it had vanished.

Eamon's blue eyes bulged. His face cracked into a mask of terror. Then he erupted in a scream of pure agonising pain. I grinned at him, my teeth stained with my blood.

"It would do you well to remember," I said, each word coming out with ease, "You, my kind husband, need me more than I need you."

I released his wrist, and the power blinked out. Eamon fell backwards, howling viciously into the darkened room. The sound of his suffering was the most beautiful thing I had ever heard. He whimpered and cried as he scuttled away from me. He had landed awkwardly on the bathroom's flagstone floor and pulled his body with one hand as far from the tub as he could manage, all whilst I never took my eyes off of him.

Slowly, the pain returned, but it was not as bad as it had been. It was worth it, in a way. As though I bathed in warmed milk, I eased myself back in whilst Eamon whimpered like a scorned dog. I ensured I left the majority of my agony inside of him, as both a reminder and a warning.

"I wish to bathe alone," I called out, languishing in the sickly calm which soothed my burned back. I knew, in time, it would stop me from moving. But for now, I relished in knowing that Eamon would suffer from the pain he had caused me. "Leave me."

Eamon couldn't form words as the agony sunk its talons into him and refused to let go. I lolled my head to the side and watched as he picked himself up from the floor and dragged his body towards the door. He didn't spare me a glance as he left. He wouldn't. I would make sure that every time he laid his eyes on me it would hurt.

That was my promise to him.

32
3 Years Before

"Can I ask you something?" As Rhory spoke, his voice vibrated through my body. He had laid his head upon the hardening muscles of my chest, whilst tracing his finger over the mounds across my abdomen. I felt the press of his ear as he enjoyed the song that was the beat of my heart. And gods how it thundered when he touched me.

The cold breeze of early winter filtered in through the open window of his bedroom. Not only did it provide fresh air to the room, but it was an attempt to remove the scent of sex we had left. If Ana or Michal were to find us, it would have shattered the illusion we had crafted in the months that'd passed. A world where there was only us. Together. An illusion which would only last as long as we allowed it.

"Anything," I said to him, tracing my fingertips across his back. As much as I enjoyed our silence, when there was only his breathing and the song of hearts beating proudly in my skull, hearing Rhory's voice was one of the wonders of the world.

He shifted himself so he could peer up at me. I adored the swell of his lips after we kissed. How I painted his face in a smile with my touch. It made me feel powerful.

"Why don't you ever speak about your parents?" he asked.

The question caught me off guard.

Rhory must have noticed my reaction, because he quickly pushed himself off me as he fumbled over his apology. "I shouldn't have asked, forget it—"

"No," I said, urging him back down onto me. I hated how quickly the cold affected me when his warmth was removed. "It is okay, Rhory. I have nothing to hide from you." As I spoke my lie, it sent a shockwave of pain through my chest. Even if I dared to contemplate it, I always lied to Rhory. I lied to him about what I was, what my history consisted of. There was always a mistruth as I exposed my past to him, knowing I could never tell him about what I was—even if it was all my soul told me to do.

Auriol would never allow it.

"My parents were murdered," I said aloud. I found that every time I spoke the words, it hurt less and less each time. "It is not that I do not honour their memory by refusing to speak about them. You see, my brother and grandmother took their passing badly. I have grown used to tiptoeing around the conversation of my parents because I do not wish to hurt my family."

"My father said it was a vampire who killed them." A heavy sadness filled Rhory's eyes. I hated seeing such an emotion on him.

"It was, but it was also their friend. Michal is right, it was."

I felt the question lingering on Rhory's lips, but it seemed he didn't dare speak it aloud.

Why?

Part of me waited for him to ask it, knowing I could never reveal the entire truth. When he didn't speak the word out loud, I was relieved. It was one less lie I had to tell him.

What was known about my parent's murderer was it was done by a rogue vampire, which was not uncommon in Darkmourn. What Darkmourn didn't know was the vampire killed my parents because of the threat they posed to him.

Auriol warned us not to tell others about our affliction. Our curse. My parents didn't listen. They believed they could trust someone, and it only ended in their demise.

"It must hurt," Rhory said, drawing me out of the terrible memories. He always had a way of clawing me out of the dark.

"Terribly," I said. "It seems those who pose the most danger to you are the ones closest."

"That is not true, Calix. I wouldn't hurt you," Rhory said quickly. There was an urgency to his words which I felt deep within me. "Not ever."

In the pause that followed, I wished I could promise Rhory the same. But I couldn't. It was not a lie I was willing to offer him.

"You underestimate the power you have over me," I said.

A dark cloud passed behind Rhory's eyes, darkening them. He glanced away from me, proving I had said something wrong.

"It's getting late," Rhory said, filling the silence. "Father will be back from his check up at St Myrinn's soon and…"

"And I should leave, before they find me in bed with their darling son." I brought my mouth down and pressed a kiss into his forehead.

As I did, I inhaled deeply, drawing in his scent so it would last me until we next stole a moment together. My body and soul warmed by the way his heart skipped a beat when I touched him. If only he could hear mine. He would know it did the same.

"I hate this," Rhory said as I pulled back. "It does not feel right hiding... what we have."

It had been almost three months since that first night we had spoken. And a glorious month it had been. Stolen moments. Hours lost to one another.

"One day," I said, offering him a promise I was unsure I could keep.

"When?" Rhory asked, frowning deeply up at me.

"If I am to court you, I want to do it properly. With your father's permission."

Rhory took his hand and ran it across my stomach. Beneath where his touch trailed, my muscles hardened in anticipation, as did the proud muscle which waited beneath the sheets.

"It is not my father's permission you should be worrying about. It is Mother's. And if you do not speak with her soon, then she might end up forcing me with someone of her own choosing. Someone she thinks would be best for me. The more Father's health declines, the more her urgency to see me cared for intensifies."

The thought of Rhory being with anyone else woke the monster within me. The feeling was swift and overwhelming.

"There is no one else," I said, pressing down the force within me.

"No?" Rhory teased, not knowing the command he had over me—over the wolf. "What about one of the Crimson Guard? I am sure Mother would love to see me with—"

"No. One. Else."

Rhory exhaled through a sly grin. He narrowed his eyes at me whilst continuing to draw his hand down the mounds of my stomach, towards the thin slip of bedsheet that covered my cock. The wolf within me was not the only thing to awaken. The growing lump just shy of Rhory's hand was a physical result of his touch.

"Then be quick about it," Rhory said, fingers disappearing beneath the sheets. "Because you are right. There is no one else. There is you and only you. I want you and if all of Darkmourn doesn't know, then it is pointless."

"What did I say, Little Red?" A shiver passed across Rhory's skin as I used the nickname I had given him all those nights ago. "Those closest to you are the most dangerous. Get too close to me and you might regret it."

"What are you going to do?" Rhory sang. "Bite me?"

My stomach jolted as Rhory's hand found my cock. His fingers wrapped around it, urging it to harden like stone. "If you so desire."

"Well," Rhory said, slipping down the length of his bed. He never once took his eyes off of me, not as he gripped my cock firmly, pulled the sheet back to reveal it, and placed himself beneath it so he looked up my length towards me. "Stay with me tonight."

"I—I can't."

Rhory lifted my cock and pressed the tip to his parted mouth. I gasped at the tickle of his soft lips, knowing full well what was to follow.

"Then I will make you."

"And how do you propose you are going to do that?"

Rhory finally diverted his stare from my eyes and settled on the curved head of my cock. It looked larger in his small nimble hands. With the length lifted to his face, it swelled me with pride.

"I have my ways," Rhory said.

"Auriol would not be pleased if I do not return home."

Rhory's fingers tightened, drawing a moan from deep within me. "Are you really going to make me get on my knees and beg?"

"As much as that would be a pretty sight, no. You do not need to beg."

Rhory's eyes lit up as he read the suggestive look I painted across my face.

"Does that mean you will stay?" Rhory murmured, looking up at me with doe-wide eyes. "Tonight?"

I nodded and reached down, running my fingers through his poppy-red hair. "How could I refuse you, Rhory Coleman?"

"You will not regret it," Rhory said, allowing my hand to guide his face closer to my cock. "I promise."

His heartbeat quickened in sync with mine. My gaze looked towards the closed door just as Rhory wrapped his little wet mouth around my cock. Then there was only darkness and pleasure. As much as I wished to watch him take me in, I had to tilt my head to the side and bite my teeth down on the pillow. If I didn't, the howl which brewed deep within me would have burst free.

Rhory's tongue had magic all of its own. It twisted and caressed my cock, whilst his fist moved gently up and down. He was my undoing. My destruction. He was bliss in physical form. My everything. Our time together had been short, but it had been equally full.

Even with the wedge of my mistruths between us, I had never felt closer to anyone. He took my mind off my world and created a new one where we existed solely in it, together. There was no wolf. There was no Crimson Guard. No death and responsibility. If only we could keep the door to this room shut forever, never to leave again. But one glance across the room to the dark night beyond the window was enough of a reminder that our time was limited. The moon hung heavy and almost full. In a matter of days, my control over the lurking wolf within would be torn from me. Instead of Rhory being draped across my body, it would be silver chains and bolts.

It was a reminder of what I was, and the danger I posed to Rhory.

And as he sucked my length, taking it all in until I felt the soft warmth of the back of his throat, I knew this would never last. Not like this, not in Darkmourn. Our responsibilities would forever keep us apart. Until the day I was brave enough to tell him. Brave enough to leave Darkmourn, together.

One day, I told myself as Rhory fought a spit-riddled gag, *One day soon.*

Our perfectly crafted illusion would become our reality. Even if we both had sacrifices to make before that could happen.

My chest warmed as I looked down and studied Rhory taking me into his mouth. He too glanced up at me, through long lashes, with eyes that screamed with desire. I couldn't continue watching him without the threat of exploding entirely in his soft throat.

I gripped Rhory's jaw and withdrew him from me.

"Something wrong?" he asked, lips glistening with his spit and my pre-cum.

"Sit on me," I said, unable to hold the command from my tone. Rhory's eyes widened and glistened with excitement. "Now."

Rhory didn't hesitate. As he slithered up my body and positioned his legs over my hips, I reached for the vial of natural oils which would aid my cock into him. There was never a vial far from me; one always knocked about in the inner breast pocket of my jacket, in easy reach. With Rhory's insatiable appetite, I had to be prepared.

"I'll do it," Rhory said, snatching the vial and tipping the clear oil into his waiting palm. Without taking his eyes off me, he rubbed his hands together and reached behind his ass. I couldn't see his hands grip my cock, but by the gods I felt it. A shiver burst across my length and spread like wildfire across every inch of skin.

His soft hands were a pleasure in their own right. I melted beneath them and he ensured every inch was coated in the oil. Although, if he was not careful, I would spread my seed before I could grace his tight, glorious hole.

I had to put my hands behind my head or they would wander across Rhory's bare torso. It was selfish, I recognised, but all I longed to do was touch him. So, when I closed my eyes, I could recount Rhory's body without the need to see it. I desired to learn every brush of soft skin and hard corner of bone and muscle. I wanted it all.

Rhory eased himself onto my cock, expelling the longest and loudest moan I could imagine. I joined in, unable to contain my enjoyment as his tight hole strangled the length of my cock.

It was a miracle the entirety of Darkmourn could not hear.

Rhory gripped my tensed chest, his thumb and forefinger spreading the oil across my nipples which he twisted between his touch.

The bedsheets crumpled around us as he took me in and bounced himself up and down. He continued fucking my cock until his knees ached. Then I took over. I retrieved my hands from behind my head, happy to give them something to do. I gripped Rhory's legs, where his small ass met his thighs. I held him up and thrust myself skyward, knowing from the roll of his eyes that my tip pressed firmly into his prostate; the shivers which coated his freckled arms revealed as much.

We were both lost to one another that neither knew the door to his room had opened. My ears betrayed me, focused solely on the thumping of Rhory's intoxicating heart, that when the second joined in it was too late.

I pulled Rhory down on top of me as though it would shield his modesty from view. Rhory gasped out, the sound accompanied by the wet pop of my cock escaping him.

Eamon stood in the doorway, his wide blue eyes surveying the room.

If Rhory didn't have his hand on me, I would have broken free from the bed and devoured the intruder. My instincts burned for me to do it, to explode from the sheets and destroy Eamon before he could leave and reveal what he had seen.

Silence bathed the room. There was only room for our heavy breathing and the slow, steady beat of Eamon's heart.

"Pardon me," Eamon said finally, bowing his head but not before his smile cut across his face. "I should have knocked."

It was Rhory that replied, for words failed me. It was the wolf who lingered within me, and I knew if I opened my mouth, it would only be to howl in threat.

"Get out," Rhory said, quietly at first.

Eamon didn't move.

"I said get out!"

When Eamon lifted his stare back towards us, his smile was nothing more than a memory. Although his paled lips were straight, I still recognised the glint of it in his bright eyes.

"Ana sent me back earlier," Eamon said. "She wished for me to check on you. But I can see you are being... well cared for—"

"OUT!"

Eamon didn't dare speak again. Instead, he walked backwards out of the room and closed the door with a soft click.

How could such a quiet sound be so wholly world-shattering?

33

My body felt as though it had been ridden over by a stampede of wild horses. Every small move and my skin ached. It was tight from the burns, and raw as sun-bleached hide. No matter if it was clothing or bedsheets which rubbed, the discomfort was agony. Whereas my mind was exhausted, the pain encapsulated in my body refused sleep and rest. What little time I got was soon interrupted by the brush of silk across my burns. Just a simple touch, and it restarted the wildfire of torture across my back.

I had stared at the burns in the mirror of my bedroom. Although it felt like my entire back was on fire, it was only a lashing diagonally across my shoulder blades which caused my pain. I knew from my time at St Myrinn's that the burns were not the worst, but enough to blister and scab in the coming days.

Between my body's discomfort, and my mind's reeling, it was the noise of a full house that kept me awake into the early hours, until the dark of night eased into the lighter tones of dawn.

I had found it easier to sleep on the cushioned ledge beneath my grand window, where the cold breeze beyond flirted with my back. I had watched the night pass, searching the street for Calix or Millicent, in the hooded faces that passed below me. The game of seeking was the catalyst to my eyes growing heavy and sleep finally claiming me.

By the time the obnoxious knock on my bedroom's door came, I felt as though I had only found rest for a broken hour or two, at most.

"Eamon wishes to have your company during breakfast," a light voiced woman said from my door. She had not waited for me to allow her to enter. When she stepped into the room, it was with a smirk plastered across her freckled face.

"And if I say no?" I asked, shifting to a sitting position, my back screaming from the movement.

"Eamon doesn't like that word," she sneered, grinning through thin, freckled lips. "It would best you come with me before he comes to retrieve you, don't you think?"

This stranger was right, of course. And the glint in her gaze told me she knew what Eamon did to me behind closed doors. But her smile confirmed she was unbothered by it—in fact, she seemed rather pleased by the fact.

I gathered myself, steeled my expression, and walked past her. This was my home. It belonged to me. And I would not let anyone make me feel otherwise.

∼

Our dining room had not been so full in years. Since my parent's respective deaths, there had only ever been two seats occupied. Today, there was not a single space free. In fact, chairs and stools from other rooms within my home had been brought to the table, creating more places for the men and women of the Crimson Guard to take a seat.

They had disrobed from their red cloaks. If it was not for their conversations, I would have not known they were Crimson Guards at all. Instead of the heavy red material that confirmed their station, they were each dressed in leathers that hugged their athletic builds. Most had blades at their hips, whereas others had placed them heavily on the table. One stout man with a proud beard and a face marked in scars used his short blade to cut into his eggs.

Conversation bloomed throughout the room. Yet I was not the only one who didn't speak. Eamon sat at the head of the table, opposite to me, and watched me the entire time. His food was left untouched, as was mine. Although the eggs looked fluffy and white, with a yolk which popped and spread beautifully over charred bread, I couldn't face a mouthful.

Eamon was my enemy, and I was not about to break bread with him.

I allowed my mind to slip to that of Calix. It felt good to let him occupy my mind whilst in Eamon's company. The betrayal of it gave me a sense of confidence I would need to get me through this. I had just over a day to get the answers I required before Calix came for me. It was my fuel. I refused to leave Eamon again without knowing where Auriol and Silas were being kept.

Perhaps a part of Eamon's vindictive nature had slipped into me as a tithe for the pain I had given him in the bathroom last night. Whatever had dampened my fear of him was welcomed.

The chair screamed across the floor as I stood abruptly from the table. All around me, the conversation faded into silence. Every head turned to look at me, each expression one of dislike. I picked up my glass of freshly pressed apple juice and lifted it. "If I may, I would like for us to each raise our glasses in a toast."

My smile faltered when not a single one of the Crimson Guard followed my request. Instead, they glared at me as though I was the stranger in their home.

Swallowing hard, I continued, "It has been many years since I have seen so many faces in this room. My father would smile down on us now if he knew the Crimson Guard shared our—"

The laughing began before I could even finish my sentence. Not a single person around the table kept their composure. Even Eamon roared with a bark that shook the chandelier above us.

Slowly, my husband stood. "Sit down, Rhory, before you make yourself look even more a fool."

My knees wobbled, but I locked them in place. I refused to be shunned in my own home, before the very people that belonged to me. Not him, me. Although my cheeks burned, and my face likely turned a red richer than the cloaks these men and women wore, I stood firm.

"I have not finished," I snapped, grasping onto the confidence which burned through me, not wishing to let it go.

The pale liquid in my glass shook with my hand, but I refused to lower it.

Then Eamon lifted his glass.

"Then allow me to offer a toast of my own," Eamon responded, staring directly through me. His lip curled into a faint snarl as his eyes sang with the memory of the night before. The pain I had forced into him had faded. In fact, he looked more rejuvenated than he had when I saw him waiting for me on the front step of this house.

"I am confident Rhory needs no introduction." Eamon leaned down to the woman close at his side and shared a smile that screamed of secrets. She was the same person who collected me from my room. Her hair was as red as mine, her face as equally freckled. It seemed Eamon had a type, which made me wonder if Calix's suggestion that something had occurred between Silas and Eamon was true. "What do you think? Should I include Rhory in on our little secret?"

My blood turned cold as he looked back at me.

"Can he be trusted, sire?" The woman tilted her head, brown eyes glowing with an emotion that stung at my chest.

"Does it matter if he cannot?" Eamon replied. "He isn't going anywhere, and if he does it will be over far before then."

The room laughed again, each nodding in agreement with Eamon's comment.

I lifted my chin, trying to force some confidence into my expression. Eamon acknowledged the silent thoughts that passed through my mind.

"Rhory, there are no Crimson Guards in this house."

I looked across the table, gesturing to the crowd who watched with faces of glee and humour. "Then who sits at my father's table, if not his people?" I asked, voice faltering enough for Eamon to notice.

It was as if the entire room faded away, and it was only Eamon and I left.

"My people," Eamon corrected. "These are mine."

"What are you saying, *husband*?" I spat the title, using it as a weapon, much like he had used it against me.

Eamon tutted, smacking his tongue to the roof of his mouth. He moved from around the table with steady grace and walked the length of the room towards me. "Something you said to me last night... it stuck with me. I need you. It was true, at first. I needed you, but that is no longer true. Not in the sense which I imagine you believe, or have been *told* to believe."

I sat down as his proximity overwhelmed me. Eamon stopped prowling as he reached the back of my chair. His hand gripped the wood and squeezed, causing it to creak beneath his strong hold.

"The Crimson Guard belong to you because *I* belong to you," I hissed through gritted teeth. "Without me, you have nothing. Am I wrong?"

"Oh, no. You are not wrong." He swept his hands to his sides as though he were an actor, and the room was his stage. The men and women audibly reacted, playing their part as his doting crowd. "The Crimson Guard are mine as long as you are alive. But I no longer have a need for the Crimson Guard. I have something better, something stronger. Which means you, darling husband, have lost your importance to me."

Horror cut through me. Eamon brought his head down to my ear and sniffed. The sound shocked me into a trancelike state.

As though reading my mind, he whispered something into my ear, "Do not worry, I won't kill you. You are safe from that at least..."

There was something unfinished about his comment.

I stood again, forcing Eamon back with my sudden movement. The raw skin of my back screamed with agony as I stepped from my chair and tried to move towards the room's door. But I was stopped when two bodies pressed in behind me. I'd turned too late; two men blocked me from reaching the door.

"If I am safe, then you will let me leave this room."

Eamon pouted, his sharp brows pulling down over his vivid eyes. "Do you not want me to introduce you to our new family?"

I wished to wrap my fingers around Eamon and pour all my dark emotions into him. "What I wish is to return to my room."

"You were not always so spoiled, brat."

"I would say the same for you, but I cannot remember what you were—"

"Ah, so you know." Eamon smiled broadly. "But how much did he tell you?"

I tried to step in close to Eamon but was stopped by rough hands on my shoulders.

"What you are looking at, Rhory, are the saviours the Crimson Guard had hoped to be," Eamon said. "I couldn't have them, not completely, so I've made a new legion of my own. One that will do as I bid, one who shares my vision of a world we deserve. And together," Eamon raised his glass higher, enjoying himself as he watched his followers cause me pain before him, "We will purify the world and return it to the way it should have always been." He believed every word he said aloud. His eyes were alive as he preached his sermon to the room and his followers reacted by slamming their fists down on the table whilst stomping feet beneath it.

"And how do you believe you'll accomplish that?"

His expression hardened. Eamon's smile dropped until his lips were pinched into a thin, taut line. "What I care about is the lives of mortals. The living has suffered beneath the rule of the dead for long enough. It is time we take back what was ours to begin with."

"Then release Auriol and Silas. If you care for the living, you will not hold them hostage."

"Hostage?" Eamon repeated, eyes wide in shock. The room murmured in quiet words and giggles. "What other poisonous lies has he fed you?"

"Calix," I said his name aloud. It was clear the act I had returned home with was useless. If Eamon had bought it at first, that was long gone. There was no need to keep up pretences now.

"He told me the truth." I leaned in as close to Eamon as the rough hands allowed and whispered the final words into his ear. "He told me everything."

"Is that so?" he replied. "Then, if you know everything as you say, you know the truth of what became of your mother?"

"What truth is this?"

"How Calix slaughtered Ana in his madness and jealousy?"

"You lying cunt…" I breathed, laughing at the absurdity of his words. "Are you so desperate to keep me beneath your thumb that you would allude to such…"

Eamon's expression did not crack or waver. "Oh, so he didn't tell you everything."

The ground fell away from me. A haze passed over the room, shrouding my vision and deafening my ears. It was as though a sea had washed over me. Violent hands dragged me down into the dark depths of Eamon's words.

"Here," Eamon said, offering his remaining hand to me. "If you care to find the truth, let me repeat it to you again so you can feel it."

I glanced at his hand as though it were a strange thing. Blinking back tears, I couldn't move my arm even if I wished to. I knew Eamon offered for me to use my powers on him, but I didn't dare. He lowered his hand to his side and sighed, as though it pained him to tell me. Although his voice was heavy with sadness, his eyes glowed with enjoyment.

He loved every moment of this.

"If you do not believe the truth from me, then perhaps you will believe it from someone else." Eamon shot a look at the room and every single person in it stood. Soon enough, the walls echoed with heavy footfalls as it emptied, all but the nameless woman Eamon had shared his prolonged look with.

"If you do not wish to believe the words from my mouth, then perhaps you would like to hear it from Auriol?" Eamon asked, gesturing for the open door. "I am sure she will gladly share the truth with you."

"Auriol," I mouthed her name. "She is here?"

Eamon's brows pinched downwards in the centre. His frown was the most genuine thing about him. "Where else would she be?"

I couldn't answer him.

Eamon offered me a final, pitiful smile and then turned his back on me. He left the room, and the two men holding me made sure I followed. Without them, I wouldn't have moved an inch.

There was nothing I could think about as I was led out of the dining room and up the stairs towards the left side of our home, an area Eamon had banned me from entering, the part of the house which had once belonged to my father. Suddenly, we stood before a door I had not seen open since Eamon had Father moved to St Myrinn's Infirmary.

"Protecting you from the truth has been a great struggle," Eamon said as he retrieved a brass key out of his breast pocket. "I should have given up long ago."

"I don't believe you," I murmured. A numb wave rolled through my body, leaving no inch spared. "I won't. All you have done, all you do, is lie."

"Don't, or can't?" Eamon asked as he slipped the key into the ancient brass lock and turned. The dull click reverberated through me as the door was pushed open.

"I will let you discover the truth yourself," Eamon said, leaning in and pressing a cold kiss to my cheek. I didn't have the energy to cringe away, not as I faced the room I had not seen for a long time. My eyes fell first on the ancient woman slumped in a wheeled chair in the centre, her frail body draped in woollen blankets and thick silver chains. "When you are finished, I will wait here to welcome you back."

I couldn't move a muscle, not because I was weak, but because I feared what I would discover once I stepped into the room before me.

"He wouldn't do it to me..." I murmured, mind fixed solely on Calix. Even the thought of him murdering my mother was a ridiculous concept. It was laughable to even suggest it as the truth.

"Sometimes," Eamon said, "The truth is not always the freedom you believe it will be. Go claim it. See that you will not find the solace you expect. Rhory, I know you see me as a monster, but I am merely a product of what the world has made me. We—even those you loved most—are monsters. We all are."

34

THE DOOR CLICKED SHUT at my back. It was not a loud sound, but I flinched regardless. Anxiety stabbed its talons into the top of my spine and dragged itself downwards as I took in the situation before me.

It was the stale smell that slammed into me first. The musk was so thick in the air that I fought the urge to gag as it wormed its way down my throat. It was the scent that came with a room being refused fresh air for years. Dust had claimed Father's study. Unable to remove my eyes from the slumped form of Auriol, I waited for the turn of a key and the click of a lock. It didn't come. I held my breath as I listened out for Eamon's muffled voice. He was whispering to the woman, and I couldn't make out a word. Soon enough, they had both faded away into the house, leaving me in the almost quiet.

Auriol showed no signs that she recognised my arrival. Her head had lolled to the side, resting upon her shoulder at an ungodly angle. The sour tang of her breath came out of her parted mouth, and her lips were crusted with dried spit.

She was illuminated by a single bright strip of daylight that cut through the gap within the heavy curtains. It fell perfectly upon her, ensuring her terrible state was proudly put on display; without it, I would have believed her dead. Only as I stepped towards her, tiptoeing cautiously across creaking floorboards, could I see the slight rise and fall of her chest. Relief flooded through me, regardless of the horrible rattling sound that spluttered from within her chest.

"Auriol," I mumbled. My hands shook with the desire to tug the chains from her until I saw they had been bolted into the wooden planked floor beneath her chair. It reminded me of when I found Calix, locked within a room in a web of chains. This was no different, except her chains were layered with blankets across her ancient and frail body.

Her mouth moved. She said a single word through a rasped exhale. At first, I didn't make it out, until she said it again. "Arlo..."

I knelt before her and reached out for her hand which waited upon her lap. Her skin was sickly warm.

"It's Rhory," I corrected. "I'm here."

It was a natural response for my power to rear its presence in moments like this. I couldn't count how many times I had spent with the old and suffering. Even during father's last days, I took away his discomfort and replaced it with something softer. Lighter.

As the golden glow of my gift shone across her wrinkled face, I caught the flutter of her eyes. Auriol was not in pain. Not exactly. The feeling I took from her was one of deep exhaustion, the type that worked its way into one's bones like woodlice to walls. Except there was nothing natural about this feeling. It was forced. As I took it in, easing the feeling from the old woman, I couldn't help but feel poisoned by it. Drugged or drunk. My mind felt as soft as cotton.

"Let go of me," Auriol demanded. Thin fingers gripped my wrist and pushed me away. As we broke contact there was a faint ringing in my ears.

Auriol was alert now. Her mismatched eyes were wide with the wisps of silver brows furrowed over them. I fell back from her chair and landed hard on my ass. A dull ache thrummed around my head. I lifted my fingers to my temple and exhaled a long groan.

"Wolfsbane," Auriol confirmed, her voice rough as though something filled her throat. "No matter the food they present me, or the drink they force down my throat, it's laced with the herb."

It took a few deep breaths for the heavy sensation to fade; all the while I held her stare, as she held mine.

"Rhory, I am disappointed to see you before me," Auriol said, her voice no longer sounding as if two people spoke at slight intervals from each other. Her words were clear as they were honest.

"As am I," I replied, sensing the drunk sensation fading slowly from my body. As it did, I was reminded with the single burning question I had to ask her. But, no matter how my mind replayed what Eamon had said, I couldn't find the words to speak it aloud.

"Auriol," I said quietly, "Tell me it is not true."

Her mismatched eyes darkened. If it was not for the chains across her lap, she might have leaned forward and grasped my face in a motherly way.

"Dearest," she murmured, her voice strained and tired. "I am going to need a more specific question if you are hoping for me to answer you."

"Did..." I gathered myself with a breath. "Is my mother dead because Calix killed her?"

Auriol hardly flinched, let alone blinked. Instead, her eyes widened, and the corners of her thin lips pulled downwards. My heart dropped too as she lowered her gaze from mine, unable to hold it any longer.

"No," I breathed, my skin itching with disbelief as I read the answer in her widening eyes.

"I do not know," Auriol said quickly. "Eamon has a sure way of getting into someone's head. Do you know, even when your father's mind was being gripped by his debilitating sickness, he had his suspicions about Eamon?"

My body ached as I pushed myself to standing. Skin still raw from the night prior, I was glad for the discomfort; it helped me focus. "What do you mean? Please, Auriol. You must tell me the truth. I need to know, hell I deserve to know!"

"I cannot." When Auriol looked at me, it was not with her usual frown. Sadness aged her face. It caused her eyes to droop and her wrinkles to deepen. "I wish I could be the one to vouch for my grandson's innocence, or guilt, but I cannot."

"Why!?" I said, practically begging. "Eamon told me Calix killed her. The marks... the damage her body endured." As I inhaled sharply, my mind was full of the memories. Torn limbs. Deep marks etched into flesh. Shattered bones. I didn't dare close my eyes again for fear of being lost to the horror forever. "I saw her. There were marks left on her body, the same as what Calix has on his chest. We both know no human would have the strength to cause such damage, and no vampire would leave so much blood..."

Auriol tempted to reach for me, but the chains restrained her from only being able to lift her hand an inch from her lap. Frustration whipped across her face with a snarl. "There are only two people who know the truth of that night," she said. "In the years since your mother's murder, I questioned Calix. He has never given me an answer."

"And who is the other?"

Auriol winced as she said the name, "Silas."

The world went oddly still.

"Could he have done it?" A strange, warped sense of hope filled me. Was it someone else who broke my world apart?

She shook her head, not in refusal, but because she didn't have the answers I sought.

I dropped my chin to my chest, feeling a wave of exhaustion rush over me.

"It happened the night of your wedding to Eamon," Auriol said suddenly, telling me something I already knew. "We had each been invited. Some twisted joke Eamon played on Calix, knowing your history. The Grey's and the Coleman's have been allies for many years, so it was not strange for us to be invited, but Calix understood the message behind it. It was that night when Silas was taken from us. I refused the invite, not wishing to see a union between you and Eamon, knowing your father's lack of confidence in it. Perhaps if I had, I would have been able to prevent whatever had happened that night."

I buried my face in my hands, head thumping as though thunder ruled within it. Everyone knew my past but me. Understanding that fact caused me such vicious pain.

"Who did this to me!?" I cried out, slapping my hand against the side of my head as though it would loosen the buried memories and return them to me.

"Rhory," Auriol sang, her tone motherly and soft. "Rhory. Tell me why you are here and not leagues away."

"I came back to find you, and Silas."

"You should have left us," Auriol said, matter-of-factly. "What of Calix? Does Eamon have him?"

"No," I replied, head raw from my own self destruction.

Auriol exhaled, sagging forward in her chair with relief. "Good. That is good. And it is important he does not come."

"He will..." I hissed. "Calix will come for me by tomorrow evening, that's if I don't summon him with a candle in my window before then."

Auriol's face opened up in fury, eyes widening and mouth gasping. If the chains were not binding her, she would have thrown her body out of the chair just to stifle me. "That cannot happen. Do you hear me, Rhory? Calix must stay far away. There is nothing good waiting for him here."

Even without touching her, Auriol's panic almost floored me. "It is not safe. For you. For him."

"Eamon is going to kill me," I said, breathless. "He said as much, in his way. He no longer needs me."

Lightning coursed over my body, raising every hair across my arms.

"I hope not." It was all she said. Even I could recognise that there was no comfort in her words. "Do you know it was in this very room your father altered his will? I was here as witness as he wrote in the covenant, tying your life to Eamon's command of the Crimson Guard. It happened days before your wedding to Eamon. An engagement most did not expect, but to your father, you seemed joyful and in your right mind. Which, of course, you were. But by then, your mind was an altered version, one to benefit your sudden union with Eamon. Your father had his concerns over Eamon's intentions, but you were the happiest he had seen you. He didn't wish to think the worst, but he was always a careful and well thought out man... even when his own mind had deteriorated over the years. He may not have known himself, but he knew you."

My eyes pricked with tears, and the dull thud in my skull worsened. As Auriol spoke, I pressed the heels of my hands into my eyes and focused on steadying my breathing. In the dark, I could almost make out the scenes she described, played out in colour and sound.

"You knew," I said. "You knew about Calix and I."

"I did," Auriol replied. Hearing her say it aloud was strange. It confirmed what I was trying to convince myself was the truth. But in turn, it frustrated me more.

"Did you not think to tell my father what had happened to me? That my mind had been tampered with, poisoned with witchcraft, so my reality was actually not mine at all?" When I dropped my palms from my eyes, they came back slick with tears, silent droplets that were without sobs. They poured from my eyes as though the heavens had opened and unleashed a storm.

"At that point, it was not clear as to what had been done to you."

"And when did it become clear? When did you work out what Eamon had done to me, just to get close enough to marry me and take the Crimson Guard as his own?" I couldn't hide the fury from my voice. Likely, the entire building and its occupants could hear me shout. Not that I cared. Let them hear. Let Eamon hear me, for it was only a matter of moments before I found him and demanded to be fixed, no matter the cost.

"I understand you are in pain, but the answers you think you seek will only hurt further. What matters now is that Eamon no longer requires the Crimson Guard. Which means he no longer requires you. It is only by the grace of his humanity that he's kept you alive long enough for you to talk to me."

"And what grace would that be?" I asked, gazing at the old woman through a blur of tears.

"I am afraid I cannot answer that either." The chains across Auriol's lap shuffled as she tried to right herself. "Rhory, I need to ask this of you. Forget about this, all of it. Get out of this house, find Calix, and convince him to do the same. Leave Darkmourn."

I blinked, confusion riling through me. "Do you truly believe we can forget about this? How can I possibly move on, knowing the hurt and danger Eamon poses to you, to Silas? To everyone?"

"But you could," she said, wincing slightly at the weight pressed across her. "Do not be ashamed to admit it."

"If you have given up, what about Silas? All of this is because you wanted him back. Surely we cannot just turn our back on—"

It was not Auriol's words which interrupted me but the look on her face. Her mask of age deepened before me; even her eyes seemed to glaze with a feral sadness that aged her by years.

"I was wrong," Auriol muttered, voice broken. "So very wrong."

I reached forward for her. "About what?"

Slowly, she found my eyes again. The whites of hers had stained a scarlet red and she seemed to shake as though a cold chill flooded the room. "He is..."

A knock sounded at the door behind us. Three loud raps of knuckles to wood, each with prolonged gaps of time between one another.

Silence followed. My eyes locked on the brass knob of the door, waiting for it to turn and open. It didn't. When the knock came again, it was more a ferocious bang. It made me jump to my feet and call out in reply, "Yes?"

There was nothing, no reply but the string of tense silence.

"I'm tired," Auriol groaned from behind me, "Let him in so I can be put to rest."

There was no ignoring her exhaustion as she spoke. Unable to follow my body's urge to keep still, I paced across the room and reached for the door just as another knock came again. It was louder and faster. Impatient. Urged by it, I pulled the door open.

Shock blazed across my mind. It kept me immobile as I regarded the man before me.

"Have you finished with my grandmother?" the man said with a forced smile.

I blinked hard, unable to make sense of what I had witnessed. It was as if Calix stood before me. Bright honey eyes full of life, a proud square jaw with bones chiselled from stone. His hair was shaved close to the scalp, not swept and lustrous as I last saw it. He wore a burnt brown cloak pinned across his neck, the colour of spoiled blood and rust.

But this couldn't be Calix...

He was thinner and taller. This person's skin did not have a glow but looked as pale and colourless as a corpse. Drained. The dark circles beneath his gaunt eyes looked more like old bruises than tiredness.

"Excuse me," he hissed through gritted yellowed teeth.

My body moved without thinking. I stepped aside as the man strode past me, focused solely on the old woman trapped in her chair. He had a slight limp in his gait. It caused the china pot and cup on the tray to clink together as he crossed the room.

I shifted my attention from the man to Auriol. Her face had morphed into a snarl. She bared her teeth, wide eyes not daring to blink as she studied the man setting the tray down and pulling up a stool beside her.

It was as though he just remembered I still watched from the doorway because he snapped his attention to me and barked, "Get out."

No matter the fear his command gave me, I still could not move. It was not until Auriol spoke, her voice as soft as it had been the first time I had met her, "Rhory, would you be so kind to leave me with my grandson? Silas and I have much to catch up on."

Silas. His name repeated in my mind, as though it was both familiar and unfamiliar. How could he possibly be here, before me? It made little sense. Eamon's supposed captive, walking freely in my home. But, Silas *was* here, in this room, dressed and somewhat well. And very much alive.

He glared at me like a starved feral hound would while it guarded a bowl of rich cooked meat. Unable to hold his attention, I scampered from the room, wishing to put distance between us and the hateful gaze he regarded me with.

35

I HAD TO FIND EAMON. It was all I could think of as I left Auriol and Silas, closing the door on the impossible scene. Never had I felt the desire to run towards my husband, until now. Now I needed him with a burning need which only he could quench.

My mind still reeled on having seen Silas. So much so, I didn't fully contemplate why the house was so... empty. Whereas the rooms and hallways had been filled with men and women, I couldn't find a single soul.

It was not until I made it down into the foyer, through the dining hall, and into the kitchen that I heard the horrifying sounds. I stopped, shocked at first, as I surveyed the empty rooms whilst my hearing stretched out for the sound. It took a moment to register what I heard, were muffled by layers of stone and mortar, but loud enough for me to hear. Screams. Blood-curdling screams which set my soul aflame. So powerful that the ground beneath my feet vibrated with them.

I followed the shrieks into the pantry and down the curving steps towards the dank room beneath. Mildred used to refer to the cellar as her castle of curiosities. Once filled with hanging meats, vegetables in towering crates and a wall of bottled wine and liquor, it was now full of a sea of humans.

Silas was not the only one to wear a cloak of russet brown. They all did. I looked across the room stuffed full of humans and found they were all adorned with an identical cloak. It had a similar design to the red cloaks I had grown used to the Crimson Guard wearing, except the noticeable difference was its colour. These were the shade of dried, old blood.

I pushed my way through the wall of bodies. Grunts and displeased mumbles followed me, but I didn't care. Nothing mattered beside the skull-piercing screams which lit the room in a blaze far greater than any burning sconces could reach.

My mind revealed to me who it was that cried out. I refused to believe it, but there was something so familiar which sickened me.

Eamon was in the centre of the crowd. I caught a flash of his bright, sky-blue eyes staring down at someone on the floor before him. They were wide. Feral. It wasn't until I forced myself to the front of the mob, and the large open space in the heart of it opened up, that my worst fear was confirmed as truth.

"Millicent!" I shouted so loud my throat burned with her name. Desperation to reach her fuelled me. It dampened the pain in my back and the confusion rioting in my mind.

The vampire was sprawled out on the ground. Her shirt had been torn, exposing the raw skin of her back. It was smeared with blood, but I couldn't see any marks. Her wounds had healed, but the evidence was there. And the sharp tipped whip Eamon had curled in his fist explained the blood. There was an abundance of it.

No one stopped me as I threw myself towards her. She didn't seem to notice my arrival either, not at first.

"I've got you," I cried out, covering her body with mine. She felt so small beneath me. If it was not for the violent shivering that overcame her, I would have believed she was already dead.

"Get away from it," Eamon growled, towering above me. His face screwed in a scowl. Sweat dripped down the side of his jaw and plastered the dark-black hair across his forehead. As I regarded him, I was repulsed by the splash of blood on his cheek. It was the same dark gore that smudged my chest; it covered the silver-tipped end of the whip and coated Eamon's knuckles.

"You're a monster!" I screamed, spitting and hissing like a cat. "She doesn't deserve this."

Eamon didn't look surprised at my reaction. Instead, he pulled a face, one a displeased parent gave a child who bothered them. I too was vaguely aware of his crowd watching, equally pissed off that I had ruined their show.

Eamon simply replied, "She is a vampire." As though that was a good enough reason for such a crime.

"No, Eamon. This is not what you stand for! You have sworn yourself to protect all. That was your pledge to the Crimson Guard and your promise to the people of Darkmourn. What crimes are you punishing her for… Eamon, tell me!"

He inhaled deeply, lips quivering as they parted, and he answered, "Existing."

Millicent groaned beneath me. I felt her weight shift, but I refused to move off of her. If I did, I couldn't bear the thought of him bringing down the whip on her. I would rather have taken it.

"I won't let you do this," I said, tears of fury and sorrow cutting down my face.

I flinched as Eamon lifted the whip. He smiled, releasing a sharp tutting sound from his tongue. "How noble. You truly do take after your father. Shame, I always preferred your mother's company."

The sharp lash of the whip never came. I refused to look away. Holding Eamon's gaze in contest was my form of defiance. To my surprise, he handed over the weapon to someone in the crowd.

Once his only hand was free, Eamon brushed it down over his dark trousers, smudging Millicent's blood from his fingers.

"Perhaps we shall take this conversation elsewhere?" he asked as he knelt before me, pity tugging down his face.

My jaw ached from the tension. It was a surprise my teeth did not completely shatter beneath the force as I gritted them together.

"I am not leaving her," I spat.

"No?" Eamon muttered, looking over my head to his throng of watching humans. "Then we will have this conversation with an audience."

"There is nothing I have to say," I said, ready to reach out and grab him. If I could just grasp a slither of his skin, I could immobilise him with some haunting emotions. Gods knows I harboured enough of them. Millicent had warned me never to take her emotions, but I felt her pain, even without the use of my power. I could transfer it into Eamon, and ruin him with it. But what of the crowd? There was thirty, perhaps close to forty, of Eamon's brown-cloaked followers watching. I could never fight my way out, but I would be damned to try.

"Eamon, you do not want to do this."

He sighed. "Believe me, it is all I have ever wanted to do. There is not an ounce of compassion I have for such monsters. Rhory, I don't have the energy to convince you as to why this is the right thing to do…"

"Torturing her is not the right thing to do," I growled as my body boiled over with hate for this man.

Eamon leaned in close until the waft of lavender with the undertones of blood washed over me. "You have no idea what these monsters took from me. No idea what I was forced to watch, all because the monsters require blood to survive."

A tension thrummed through the crowd. It was a ripple of muted voices, each in agreement with Eamon.

"Is that why you kept Silas alive all this time? Does your hate only extend to vampires?"

"Kept Silas alive?" Eamon repeated. "What did you expect to find? His supposed abduction is just another lie Calix fed you. You see, Rhory, being with me will reveal all sorts of truths."

Millicent whimpered beneath me. She sounded like a child, calling out for a mother who was long dead.

"If you wish to be in the deal of truths, then do so," I said. "Tell me, all of it."

Eamon reached out his blood-stained fingers and drew them towards my face. I pulled away before he could touch me. His hand hovered in the air for a moment before he lowered it, defeated. It was the first time he had done that before. If he had wanted to touch me, he would have. Something had changed.

"Rhory, I am going to save the world." His words shocked me to the very core.

"You are delusional."

"Perhaps I am, but that doesn't take away from what I am going to do."

"Save it from what?" I asked, spitting. "Because the only monster I see is you. Eamon, the hate that feeds you will be your demise."

Eamon's eyes flickered to the hunched form I separated him from. As he looked at me, his scowl twisted into something feral. "Those creatures have taken enough from us."

"Yet you are sworn to protect them," I snapped before the crowd erupted in laughter that drowned me out.

"I have sworn many things, partaken in many vows, except there is only one that matters to me. The vow I made myself as I was forced to hide beneath the floorboards of my childhood home while my parent's blood splashed across my face, drenching me from head to foot. Days, that is how long your precious Crimson Guard took to save me. Days. And those monsters were given the time to luxuriate in my parent's blood, feast and escape without punishment. Every vampire I slay is another vampire closer to those who destroyed my life. It is worth it."

I had never seen Eamon cry before. Never did I believe he even had such a capability of that emotion. Until now. Now, his eyes filled with defiant tears as he spoke. I watched his restraint as he refused to blink and release them.

"You told me your parents died from a sickness," I said, unpacking yet another mistruth from him.

"And they did." Eamon jabbed a finger towards Millicent. I lowered myself over her further, feeling the press of her cold, still body as a constant beneath me. "They are a sickness. A disease that started and spread. It ruined our world for years, broke families apart and sent the humans to live behind walls. Suddenly, we were expected to live beside them. To break bread and share wine, never knowing if they will turn on us just for the need to feed."

I saw hate in his eyes, it oozed from him. And the sentiment behind each word... the crowd who watched agreed wholeheartedly.

"Why did you join the Crimson Guard?" I asked. "Why go through all those lengths to join a force that is supposed to protect all kinds? Living and dead, when you only ever favoured one?"

"Because they failed me. Do you know what the Crimson Guard, what your father did, when they found me covered in my parent's blood, hiding beneath floorboards, days after vampires broke into my home and destroyed my life?" Eamon's entire body trembled as he spoke. "Tell me!"

I flinched back at his sudden display of anger.

"Nothing," he answered for me. "The Crimson Guard did nothing. Your father did nothing. They let my parent's murderers roam free and closed the investigation when the perpetrators were not found. So, I knew I had to save myself if no one else would. No matter what it would take, I would get penance for what *they* took from me. Tell me, dear husband, does that make me a terrible person? To hunt the *monsters* of this world, to right their wrongs?"

I took my time to answer, mostly because I couldn't find the right words. The man before me was broken and twisted. He was a monster created by his experiences. "What makes a monster? Is it their actions that justify such a title? Because, if so, you would see one every time you look in a mirror, *husband*."

Eamon regarded me with honest disappointment. He exhaled a breath, rocked back on his heels and stood. Still, I refused to move from Millicent who had gone so terribly still beneath me.

"I *am* going to save this world," Eamon repeated his earlier statement, as though saying it again would convince me.

"And how do you suppose you are going to do that?" I asked.

"I am going to destroy them," Eamon said. "All of them. It is about time Darkmourn returns to its former glory. Where the living rule, and the dead are no more than forgotten bodies buried beneath the ground."

It was my turn to laugh. It came out of me, echoing across the crowd.

Eamon winced, as though my reaction stabbed him in the chest. He soon righted himself, steeling his expression and glaring down at me. "Do not underestimate a desperate man. He would do anything to get what he wants. *Anything*."

We both knew what he referred to.

"Does that include having a witch alter my mind to forget my past just so you could marry into my family and steal the Crimson Guard from beneath me?"

Eamon's frown broke into a smile. He flashed teeth as he grinned, looking down at me with the flickering of fire casting monstrous shadows across his face. "Ah, I suppose it does."

"Give. It. Back." The three words broke out of me.

Eamon leaned forward, washing his breath over me. "I'm afraid I do not have the capabilities for that."

I jolted towards him, fuelled by my own desperation and hate. My nails missed his face by inches. Someone from the crowd broke forward and grabbed me with harsh hands, yanking me back. I was torn from Millicent and shoved into a wall of waiting hands who pinched and squeezed until I was completely entrapped in a web of them.

"Return him to his room," Eamon commanded. He flicked his wrist, gesturing for me to be swept away.

"Millicent," I growled. "Millicent, get up!"

The vampire pressed two hands on the ground either side of her and raised herself up enough for me to see her face. Her eyes were burning ruby, her fangs overlapping paled lips. Spittle burst from her mouth as she snarled towards Eamon, who hardly flinched in response.

"Fight," I cried, putting everything I had in my resistance to Eamon's followers. "Fight them, Millicent!"

"Get out of here," she managed, tears of blood tracing down her eyes. "Foolish boy."

Millicent's fight lasted only a moment. Eamon brought down his boot onto her back, knocking her to the ground. The crack of her skull reverberated across the room, followed by her broken cry.

"I would have allowed you to stay and watch," Eamon called out to me as the hands of his followers dragged me back towards the stairs. "To see what becomes of a vampire when bitten by a wolf. But you ruined it, as you always do."

It took a moment for what Eamon had said to register in my mind.

"All these years, and it took Calix to give me what I desired, when Silas refused me. Imagine how deeply Silas hates his brother—especially after the one thing he kept from me was handed to me by Calix, the same man who never wished to save his brother."

Eamon was just about to slip from view when his words finally made sense. My eyes shot from Millicent's unconscious body to Eamon, then around the crowd of his followers who seemed to flood towards her.

"I'm sure I will have the chance to thank Calix myself," Eamon said as the outline of his body shivered. "It was a fair price to pay, my hand for power."

Before my very eyes, Eamon's skin shattered, bursting apart like ash. Shadows coiled outward, dark as a winter's night. My blood ran cold, my mind reeling from the impossibility of what I witnessed. Then, from among the cloud of shadow which engulfed him, came a howl. Then another. And another. Just before the cellar disappeared from view, I watched as the remaining men and women in the room burst into plumes of shadow, replacing their human form for another.

Wolves.

They were all wolves.

36

I LISTENED TO THEIR HOWLS, each one clear as day all the way up in my bedroom. The sound rocked the walls, seemingly never-ending. Every soul in Darkmourn, living and dead, would have heard them. But why would they come looking? Why send for the Crimson Guard, when they were standing sentry before my home stopping anyone from interfering? I was left alone, with nothing but the truth to keep me company. All I could do was sit on my bed and listen to Eamon's wolves as the reality of what it meant settled over me like burning ash.

Eamon had changed. He had become a wolf. When Calix had bitten him, it had mutated him, just as the shadow-hound had with Auriol. I could only make assumptions about how the change occurred, but it certainly explained Millicent's reaction. What I knew as a solid fact was Eamon had truly become the beast he was supposed to hunt.

I picked through the facts, trying to make sense of what was happening. Eamon's wolf form did not look the same as Calix's. Whereas Calix presented like a monster, with long limbs and the remnants of a human shape, Eamon was more similar to a large wolf, one I would have found lurking in the woods beyond Darkmourn.

It was the same with the rest of his followers. *His pack.*

The streets of Darkmourn heard it all. I could see them from my window, looking towards the house with confusion or fear, scuttling off as though the house itself was cursed, and they had to flee it. Beyond my home, the Crimson Guard loitered, but they never came to investigate. Instead, those red cloaked protectors stopped inquisitive beings from coming up to our door.

They were complicit. And whatever Eamon was doing, he no longer cared to hide.

Millicent had stopped screaming, but I couldn't tell if it was hours or mere seconds when the cries of anguish silenced. Her cries of pain and terror echoed in my ears. Although I felt her suffering in every cry, at least I knew she was still alive. Now, I was not so sure. Her silence spoke volumes. I couldn't bear it. I longed to hear her cry out, just to know if she still lived.

My knuckles were bloody, as were my torn palms and bruised fingers. The wooden door to my room was scarred from where I smashed into it, trying to break myself free. Shattered remains of a chair were scattered across the floor before it. Everything I could use to break myself free didn't work. All it did was conjure muffled laughter from those Eamon had stationed on the other side.

I was left staring at the candle in my hands. My last option. Night had fallen upon Darkmourn and all it would take was for me to light it and place it in my window, and Calix would come. For me. He would save me, save Millicent. But then there was the problem of Silas, Eamon, and the wolves. Calix wouldn't stand a chance. Calling for him would only put him in grave danger. No matter how I longed for him, I didn't dare put him in that situation.

There had to be a way out of this. Something I could do to work myself free. It only took one look back to the door and the smashed furniture before it to dwindle my hopes.

I soon heard the familiar rattling of wheels and the stamping of hooves upon the street beyond. Picking myself up, I discarded the candle on the bed and moved for a better look. Beyond the house, lining the streets, were carriages; a row of them stretched for as far as I could see. Crimson Guards moved among the coaches, opening the doors and lowering the steps to allow for someone to exit, or enter them, with ease.

The wall beneath my palm shook as our front door burst open. I jolted back, pulling the velvet curtain over me, enough to obscure me from view, but not completely so I could still watch what was happening.

I recognised Eamon first. The top of his head caught the red glow of the streetlamps. From this viewpoint I could see his black hair had thinned, revealing bald skin beneath. Behind him followed the same red-haired woman that seemed to always be close to his side. I felt nothing as I watched Eamon stop and offer her a hand as he hoisted her into the carriage with him.

Then the rest of his followers joined them. No longer were they in their wolf forms but dressed in finery befitting royalty. Except, unlike the Crimson Guards, who welcomed them and helped them into the carriages, they wore cloaks of russet brown.

My breath caught in my throat as I watched Auriol exit my home. She was being helped down the path by two of Eamon's followers. Her head was bowed, and her legs hardly moved. She was practically dragged into a carriage. I longed to call out for her, but I stopped myself when I caught the flash of silver beneath the blanket across her shoulders. She still wore chains of silver as though it was armour. It was clear Auriol's limping body was riddled with wolfsbane.

Movement from Eamon's carriage snatched my attention. He climbed out and paused. His gaze shifted from the front door as it closed with a bang—the tremor vibrating in the wall beside me—and lifted his chin to my window. His sky-blue eyes pierced through me. I gasped, breath fogging on the glass between us. The red glow of the streetlamps bathed his face in the colour of blood. Eamon smiled up at me, his lips parting in a word which I could make out even without sound.

Goodbye.

"Are you enjoying the view?"

My blood ran cold at the voice behind me. I had not heard the door open, but the visitor was not discreet when it was slammed shut again.

Silas stood in my room, his hands clasped over his waist with his head bent slightly at an angle. As I had the first time I'd seen him, it took me a moment to discern him from Calix. They looked so similar, except Calix glowed with health and vitality. Silas looked sickly and pained, as though standing was enough to hurt him. His skin was a strange colour, as though he had not been blessed with sunlight for years. Even the whites of his eyes had a yellow tinge, which matched perfectly with the stains across his teeth. He wore a cloak matching that of Eamon and his followers. It made Silas look smaller as it fell over his narrow shoulders. His shirt and trousers hung around him like a tent, clasped together by a scruffy belt decorated with a bone-carved wolf in the hilt of a blade. Beside it, looped around his belt, was a twine of rope.

"Did... did Eamon deem you unimportant enough to leave you behind tonight?" I asked, hearing the clatter of hooves and the screech of wheels against stone. If I looked over my shoulder, I would have seen the carriages move away.

Silas noted the shift of my eyes to the door he stood before. He clicked his tongue, shaking his head like a displeased parent. "Eamon has asked that I see you to bed. Then I will join him for the evening's celebration."

I swallowed my discomfort and stared directly into his eyes. Calix's eyes glowed like molten gold. Silas's eyes seemed more comparative to the colour of piss. "And do you enjoy obeying the commands of someone who has kept you captive for years?"

"No," Silas replied calmly. "No, I don't." Hope burst in my chest like a breath of fresh air. It was soon suffocated when Silas's smile widened, and he continued, "However, we both know just how... forceful he can be. So, for both our sakes, would you get into bed?"

I couldn't move even if I wanted to. "Why are you helping him?"

Silas pondered the question for a moment, wringing his hands together. "It is not that I am helping him, Rhory, but merely helping myself." He put a finger to his lips as though he didn't want anyone to hear.

"So, this has nothing to do with the fact you are in love with him."

My words hit their mark. Silas rocked back a step, widening his unblinking eyes until every red vein was visible. "Love is fickle. It means little."

"I don't mean to offend you," I said. "Eamon has a way of infecting a person's mind and blinding them. What he has done to you, he did to me. You don't need to do this."

"Yes," Silas snapped. He jolted forward, nostrils flaring. "In fact, I do."

"Calix could save us—" Before I could finish, Silas's entire demeanour cracked. He sprung forward, gripping my upper arm with his hand. I tried to pull back, but he was quicker than me. With a fast tug, I crashed hard into his chest.

"Bed," he hissed, nails breaking into the skin of my arms. "Now."

With a push, I was sent sprawling to the ground. Pain shot up my back from the fall, jarring every bone in my spine.

"Do not think for a moment that Calix would ever wish to save me."

I scrambled back from Silas as he prowled towards me. He never seemed to blink. His eyes were always wide and watching. *Let him watch*; the thought was as hot as it was sharp. Just as Silas leaned down over me, I raised my hands, ready for him. The only bare skin was his hands, neck, and face. It didn't matter what I reached for as long as I touched him.

Light spluttered to life at the tips of my fingers. Silas regarded them with a frown before stepping back.

"Touch me again," I sneered, spit flying out of my lips, "See what happens."

"I am not your enemy, Rhory."

My power brightened. "Then what are you?"

"Someone who would like to see you in bed so he can enjoy his evening. Please, do as I ask." Although his words were calm, I saw a flash of the monster pass behind his eyes. It was brief, but enough to take my breath away.

We regarded one another for a moment. Silas with his hands held before him, and me on the floor with the glow of gold bursting from my palms.

"Stubborn as ever," Silas said, eyes tracing over every inch of me.

"You have no idea," I replied.

"Oh, I do. In fact, I know there is no way you are going to do as I ask. So, if you are willing to get into bed all on your own, I will offer you something you cannot resist."

"There is nothing—*nothing*—you could give me."

"No?" Silas said, narrowing his eyes. "Not even the name of the witch, the very one who fucked around with your mind?"

"You're lying."

"Am I? Get into bed and see."

My body moved with little thought. Silas smiled, knowing he had bested me.

Without completely withdrawing my power, it faded to a faint shimmer. Still, Silas kept back as I stood from the floor. I stepped towards the bed until its frame pressed into the back of my legs. He watched me with such interest as I took a seat on the sheets and shuffled back.

"I don't remember me, but I remember you," Silas said.

I shook my head. "Good for you."

"It is." Disappointment curved his thin pale lips. "The curse is as strong as the witch who cast it. I was rather hoping you would be freed from it when she died, but I gather such power has a life of its own, beyond its caster."

His words immobilised me, enough that I hardly cared as he unlooped the rope from his belt and walked to the foot of the bed.

"She is dead? The one who did this?"

Silas smiled, but it didn't quiet reach his eyes. They looked almost… sad. "Of course, she is. And I am surprised you haven't figured it out yet."

"Name," I said. "I'm on the bed, so tell me her name."

Silas's hands were already on my ankle before I could pull away. He traced his fingertips over my foot so gently it almost tickled. Then, in one swift motion, he looped the rope around my feet, binding them together and tethering them to the frame of the bed.

I pulled hard against it, but the rope pulled tighter. The rub of it over my skin burned. "No… stop!"

"Quiet. You know what happens when we don't listen, and I do not want the evening's festivities to be spoiled by Eamon's wrath if he knows I didn't do as he asked."

I sat up and reached down for the rope to free myself. In a blink,

Silas had moved to the head of the bed. His hands gripped my shoulders. With one harsh push, he slammed me back down on the bed, the force so harsh my skull shook with the impact. The mattress was soft, but the slam of my body into it still drove the wind out of me.

There was no chance to fight against Silas as he withdrew another length of rope and tied it around both of my wrists. Before I could have had so much as a chance to scream out, he stretched my arms back and knotted the rope to the bedframe.

"That's better," Silas said, his lips brushing close to my ear. "So much better. And how the tables turn. It was your darling husband who last tied me to a bed, but I expected a much... happier ending. Instead, he left me tied up for three years, begging me to change him. I refused, because it was the right thing to do, but as always Calix came in and gave him exactly what he wanted. I can't say you'll last as long as I did, but you will appreciate how I felt, even if it is for a brief time."

I pinched my eyes closed, turning my head as far away from him as I could. Struggling only pinched the ropes further into my skin, but I couldn't calm myself. The guttural urge to fight for my life overtook me. When Silas brought his face over mine, all wide eyes and glistening lips grinning, I thrust my skull upwards and into his nose. Bone cracked. I felt the splash of warm blood fall across my face before Silas jolted back with a howl of agony.

"You little cunt!" Silas roared. He had his hand clutched to his face. Blood spilled between his fingers and down his chin, splashing across his brown cloak.

"Go on," I screamed over his cries of pain. "Run back to your master like the good little pup you are!"

I could taste his blood in my mouth. It didn't disgust me as I thought it would. Not even the dull ache across my skull from the impact bothered me. I revelled in watching him suffer.

Silas paced the room, thrashing himself around as though he was in the grips of a tantrum. I felt the feral urge to laugh at him. But my adrenaline quickly faded from a roar to a dull whisper.

"Do you know?" Silas said, his teeth stained red with blood. "I was going to defy Eamon tonight. For the first time, I was going to refuse him something. Now, I am not so sure."

Silas jolted forward. His hand shot towards me, but no impact came. Where I thought he was going to strike me, he didn't. Instead, he picked up the candle I had forgotten I'd left on the bed.

"I heard you," Silas said, returning to his pacing. "I heard what you said to my grandmother."

He moved towards a wall lamp and lifted the candle to the flame. The wick caught instantly. Silas didn't bother looking at me again. His gaze was focused back on the windows.

"How quick do you think my brother will be?" Silas asked, still refusing to look at me while all I could do was look at him.

I continued my struggle until my wrists and ankles rubbed raw against the rope. The pain mattered little. All I focused on was getting free, whilst I watched Silas with unwavering intent.

"Do not trust his word, Rhory. Anything that comes out of Calix's mouth is fabricated. He lies with ease. Calix has known, all these years, where Eamon had kept me. Yet all this time, he has played into Auriol's wishes to save me. Except he lied to her. He pretended like he had no clue where I was when he did."

Silas moved across the room, his broken nose already drying.

"Lies," I spat. "Calix has only ever wanted to see you returned home. He would do anything to—"

"For the sake of your life," Silas growled, snapping his head towards me. He stood before the window, burning candle in hand. I knew in that moment what he had heard me reveal to Auriol. That if I placed a candle in the window, Calix would come for me. "I suggest you stop. Stop preaching lies for I have no patience to listen to them."

Silas lowered the candle and placed it on the floor. It was just out of view from the window. At first, I felt relief, then disappointment. Calix would never see the light from the candle's position on the floor.

"You know my power," I said. "If anyone can know the difference between a lie and truth, it is me. I have felt Calix, and I know what he has wanted, and it has always been to save you."

Silas exhaled a long breath from his nose. The lacklustre yellow of his eyes stood out against the rust brown of his drying blood. "Okay, then do something for me. When he comes for you, and he will, I want you to ask him a question." Silas drew the curtain closed, covering the window completely. Straining my neck up as far as the bindings allowed, I saw the bottom of the material flirt with the open flame of the candle. There was hardly any space between both.

Silas moved for the door, not taking his eyes off me as he spoke. "Touch him, look into his eyes, feel his truth when you ask him what the reason was behind him leaving me with Eamon. Was it because he didn't know where I was being held? Or…"

I could hardly breathe as Silas opened the door.

"Or was it because I am the only one who knew that he had your mother murdered? That he killed her."

The world seemed to fall away from me. "No… I don't believe you."

"Did you hope I did it? Not that it would matter if you did. It is clear you would only care to hear the answer from Calix himself. So, do it… when he comes, ask him yourself. Ask him why he murdered your mother in cold blood. He never wanted to save me; he simply hoped his dark secret would die with me."

"Fuck you!" I screamed. The volume of my cry was muffled beneath the noise in my head.

"What a mouth you have," Silas said, amusement brightening his face. He glanced a final time towards the candle beneath the curtains and smiled. "You know, Eamon wanted your death to look natural. An accident. A candle misplaced. No questions asked. Except Eamon does not account for fighters, he never has. And I think you are a fighter, Rhory. We will just need to see if Calix comes and saves you, or if you are ready to save yourself for once."

37

The fire caught quickly. I watched, the muscles in my neck screaming, as the flame sparked on the hem of the curtains and licked upwards until the window was ablaze in flame. I was transfixed by the hunger of the fire, so much so that the ceiling of the room was thick with dark clouds of smoke before I even attempted to break free.

My wrists burned as I yanked hard against the rope. Circlets of bloody skin wrapped around my ankles, making my foot slick and wet. But no matter how hard I fought the bindings only seemed to tighten.

"Help!" I screamed, my frustration as hot as the fire that scorched the room.

The glass of the windows cracked against the heat. Wood spat and hissed as the flames soon spread across the wall, charring everything black in its wake.

I kicked out at the wooden frame of the bed, hoping the force would break it so I could work myself free. My attempts were useless. Pointless. My eyes streamed with tears, stinging from the smoke that desired to choke me. Its opaque fingers infiltrated my nose and mouth until I felt the smoke with every inhale.

If the fire didn't kill me, the smoke would.

I fought until my wrists and ankles were bloody, and pain no longer mattered. Something Silas had said about me saving myself was all that I could focus on. If I didn't swear as I screamed, I would have called for Calix. But I didn't know him anymore. Perhaps I never did. I feared he would come, and I would be forced to face what Silas had suggested. That Calix had killed my mother. He was the monster that tore her into pieces and left her for dead.

Quickly, the fire ate away towards me. Snakes of it slithered across the floor, spreading up reading chairs and melting the portraits on my walls.

"Rhory!"

My name was so clear that it dwarfed the noise of the fire's roar of starvation.

"Rhory!"

It was closer now.

I turned my head towards the door just as it burst open. It was not knocked in but ripped from the hinges on the other side and thrown into the hallway beyond.

Calix stood in the doorway, the crook of his arm held over his nose. It was hard to see him as my eyes blurred with tears, nor could I focus as the coughing begun. The hacks rocked my chest, each as powerful as the one before. My lungs bellowed in agony. I couldn't help but take in the breaths my lungs cried out for, but each time only encouraged more of the smoke to enter. I welcomed it in, to drown me from the inside out.

"I've got you," Calix said, his voice closer now. "Little Red, I have you."

I hadn't realised I had closed my eyes until the closeness of his voice surprised me. Part of me believed the darkness was because the smoke had finally overcome me, but when I opened my eyes, it was to watch Calix reaching up to my hands. I didn't feel his touch; I tried to, but felt nothing.

Calix quickly moved from my hands to the bottom of the bed. Still, I could not feel what he was doing, but I could see. His hands took the bedframe. I blinked, noticing his arms bulge as he pulled it towards him. With a violent snap, the wood came away in pieces.

My ankles were still bound with rope, but that was no longer connected to anything. Before I could so much as wiggle a toe, I was out of the bed. Calix carried me, pressing my face into his shirt and holding it there. When I breathed in, it was not smoke and heat I smelled, it was forest and open skies—it was Calix.

I was vaguely aware as the cold kiss of fresh air graced the back of my sticky neck. A shiver spread across my skin, passing across my arms and shoulders as though I had wings of my own. I parted my lips and breathed in a mouthful of air. Fresh air.

Each inhale was both painful and beautiful. I must have been crying because Calix's hand was running across the back of my head as he whispered words of encouragement into my ear.

"It is okay, Rhory. You are going to be okay. I should never have left you."

When I was brave enough to open my eyes, it was to see the wash of red across a busy street. I pushed back from Calix, still held in his arms, and surveyed the world around me. The street was full of people. Their faces were on me or looking up at the blaze that had overcome my room above them. The fire cast a vicious glow across the street, making people wince and pull away in shouts of fear.

At some point my windows had burst outward, shattering the glass across the street beneath it. Black smoke billowed out into the night, blending seamlessly with the darkened sky.

"He must go to St. Myrinn's," a voice said from beside me. I couldn't see the speaker but could hear the honest concern in it. It was as thick as the smoke that spread above us. Smoke that still clung to my lungs, no matter how hard I fought to clear them.

"He will be fine," Calix said, dismissing the person.

"Where is the Crimson Guard?" another voice cried out. "This is Eamon Coleman's husband; someone must alert Eamon to this!"

"There is no need…" Calix began. Hearing his voice awoke me from the hypnotic trance the fire had lulled me into. I slammed my hands into Calix's chest as hard as I could. As I did so, I thought I heard one onlooker call out *rope* as they saw my bindings.

His hands have been tied.

Can you see his ankles?

On and on, I fought. I had to break free. I had to get away from him.

"Rhory, stop," Calix said, forced to put me on the ground by my erratic movements. I thrashed and kicked, remembering everything that had been revealed to me.

"Let him go!" someone called as cold hands tried to help me away from Calix. I glanced towards the woman who assisted me. For a moment I thought it was Mildred, with her nest of silver hair and eyes magnified by round spectacles. The trick of my mind almost broke me, because of course she was not Mildred. Mildred was dead, just as I should have been.

As the woman coddled me and tried to lead me from the path beyond my house, I didn't once take my eyes off of Calix. "We must get you to see a healer, dear boy. Then we will find your husband—"

"No," I broke free from her with ease, "No, I don't want him. He did this!"

The crowd murmured into silence. For the first time, I saw just how many people watched on. Vampires with eyes glowing red and humans dressed in their nightclothes. Not a single person looked elsewhere, all eyes were on me.

"Eamon did this!" I raised my arms until the frayed rope dangled for everyone to see. Blood and rope-burned skin were illuminated. There was no hiding from it anymore. No excuses and lies to keep up Eamon's illusion of the kind and loving man everyone believed him to be. It was time they knew him for his truth. "And this... this is only a glimpse of what he is capable of."

No one spoke. No one but Calix, who was suddenly at my back, hand resting on my shoulder. "It is over. No more lying for him."

My arms shook as I kept them aloft. I scanned my eyes over the crowd, which seemed to grow with each passing second. I heard their whispers, felt their judging stares. It didn't matter if they believed me or not. I knew it was the truth, and for once, I would not conceal it.

"Lying," I laughed, mouth slick with smoke and ash. My stomach cramped, threatening to overcome me and make me sick. "It seems everyone is adequate at such a skill, even you."

Calix fell back a step as I turned on him. My mind told me to look at him with hate, but my heart sang another tune. The conflict within me was overwhelming that I didn't know whether to run from him or run to him.

I glanced back at the open door to my home. It looked more like the gaping mouth of a burning devil. Then my heart dropped like a stone in my chest.

"Millicent," I breathed, forgetting about Calix. About all of it. "She is still in there!"

Calix snapped his head back to the house. "I thought she..."

There was no time to tell Calix about what had happened. How Millicent had returned me home, expecting a prize but getting pain and torture in the cellar instead. It was the fire which spread across the upper floor of the house that screamed, but if I closed my eyes, I was certain I heard Millicent above it all.

I moved passed Calix, only to be stopped by his hand. He held my arm, urging me to stop. "I will go."

It was easy to pull out of his hand. "No."

That single word looked as though it broke Calix into pieces. He let go of me, his hand falling back to his side, fingers flexing as though they didn't know what to do with themselves. His wide gaze spoke a thousand silent words; it seemed he was choosing which to say.

"I do not need you to save me, nor anyone else," I whispered.

Calix's jaw hardened, then he nodded. "I will be right behind you."

~

We found Millicent in the cellar. The fire had not yet reached down here, but one look up the stairs from the foyer and it was clear the fire was enjoying its feast. There was no coming back from this. As I ran through the dining room, to the kitchen and down the cellar's stairs, I couldn't help but think the same thing over and over.

Let it burn. Let it all burn.

Millicent's clothes were torn and bloody. Her skin was covered in bite marks, huge puckered scars which had refused to heal completely. Whatever they had done to her, she should have healed by now. But she hadn't. Her body was a storybook of the horror she had faced down here. One look and I could read it all.

"We need to get you out!" I yelled in a panic.

She was lying on her back, staring up at the dark ceiling with wide, unblinking eyes. I fell to my knees beside her, hearing Calix swear beneath his breath behind us. Vampires were cold to the touch, but when I grasped her hand, her skin was like ice. She shook as though a fever had overcome her. Dark circles haunted beneath her reddened eyes. Her lips were moving as she mumbled to herself in the dark.

"*She* needs blood to heal," Calix said, rushing to her other side. He stared at me over her body, sorrow drawing his face into a mask of distress. "If she doesn't drink, she will die slowly and painfully. Our bite is deadly to a vampire."

"I..." Millicent croaked, a tear of blood rolling down the side of her face and falling into her greasy hairline. "I am already dead, you fool."

"Millie," Calix said, brushing a hand across her head. He winced, as though the touch burned him. "I thought you left. You didn't come back... and I thought you finally decided it was easier to turn your back on all of this."

Millicent laughed, but soon broke into sobs of pain. "And I should have. It would have saved me a lot of discomfort."

"You need to drink," Calix said again, frantically glaring across her.

Millicent turned her head away from him, pinching her face as though the thought alone was disgusting. "Tell him... Rhory, tell Calix to leave me in peace. Let me go, both of you."

I looked between them both. "Not today. You need to heal. We don't have long until the fire reaches down here."

"Fire?" Millicent asked as her eyes pinched closed. She spoke slowly, as though it was painful to do so. "Oh, I always wondered what it would feel like to... to burn. It would be better than having those beasts bite and chew at my body. I am certain... certain of that."

"Eamon is a wolf," I said, looking back at Calix. He looked across Millicent's marked body as though he couldn't understand what he was seeing. "Him and all of his followers. They are all..."

"Mutts," Millicent spat. "Fucking mutts."

"I did it." It was the only word Calix could manage. "Didn't I? This is my doing."

If I told Calix about his brother, it would open up the other conversations we needed to have. But it didn't feel right accusing him of the murder of my mother when Millicent was suffering on the ground between us. That time would come.

"Don't say I didn't warn you," Millicent moaned.

She opened her eyes again and looked directly at me. If it was not for the red and the flash of sharp teeth, she looked almost human. A human who suffered with pain they wouldn't survive.

"I begged him to kill me," she said, laughing and crying at the same time. "But he refused. Every time he bit into my body, or his wolves tore into my skin, I begged, pleaded for him to finish me. When he was done, and I was left to die, do you know what he told me? Why he never finished the job he so desperately wanted to do?"

I pressed my hand to her face. With burning desperation, I wished to provide Millicent comfort but didn't know how. She had made me promise not to use my power on her, and I couldn't break it.

"He cannot hurt you anymore," I said.

"Oh, Rhory," Millicent pinched her eyes closed, and another tear of blood dribbled down the side of her face, "He means to kill all vampires… Tonight."

"What do you mean?" I asked.

"No more talking. We need to get you both out of here!" Calix said, voice breaking as he pleaded. "Before the fire reaches us."

Millicent pursed her lips and hushed Calix. "Eamon has gone to the place it all started. In his words, he wishes to rip the head of the viper who rules the nest. Do you know what happens when you kill a vampire, Rhory?"

I blinked and saw the execution of Millicent's brother in the dark of my mind. The scene of him hanging would haunt me, but the way the sunlight peeled his flesh clean from his bones as he bellowed in agony felt so real; I could almost hear him now.

"Millicent, we need to—" I started, but she snapped at me with pointed teeth.

"Listen to me!" Millicent said, wheezing. "I have endured this because of you, so you listen to me." Her words pierced through me, cutting deep into my soul; they stung far greater than anything I had faced. "When a vampire sires another, it binds them. By killing one, you kill them all. Eamon knows this. And he means to enter the nest this evening, with his newfound power, and use it to purify Darkmourn. To destroy Lord Marius is to destroy us all."

I held Calix's stare across Millicent's ruined body as she broke into a fit of laughter. Blood bubbled out of her mouth, staining the pale skin around it.

"Then we must stop him," I said, voice shaking. Whether we saved Millicent now, she would soon perish if what she revealed was true. If Eamon succeeded in his plans, all vampires would perish. This was not what the Crimson Guard stood for. It was not what *I* stood for.

Eamon had torn too many people apart with his thirst for revenge. And I felt responsible for stopping him.

"Is... is the offer of blood still on the table?" Millicent broke the tension between us.

I raised my arm above Millicent. Rolling back the sleeve, I exposed my skin and the blue veins that webbed beneath it. Millicent was hesitant as she regarded my offering.

"Well, well," she sang, tongue lapping up at her paling lips. "I would be lying if I said I hadn't fantasised about what you tasted like, Rhory."

I brought my arm down and guided it until the skin tickled across her mouth. "Drink your fill. Then we will stop my fucking husband."

"Do it gently," Calix warned quickly. "Millie, I don't want him to feel any pain."

Millicent's reply was muffled as she pressed her lips to my arm and inhaled through her nose. "Oh, he will enjoy it. They always do."

Millicent's teeth sank into my skin with ease. I didn't feel any discomfort, only the lap of her tongue against my skin and the pressure of her suck as she drew the blood out. All the while, I gritted my teeth and stared at Calix.

I looked through his eyes, deep into his skull, searching for the truth.

There had been a time when I had felt guilt lurking within Calix. The emotion was sour and left an aftertaste in me the last time I had used my power on him. It had never crossed my mind that it would be because he killed my mother. But, as I looked at him now, regarding his furrowed brows and sorrow-filled eyes, I felt as though I knew my answer without asking it.

What I didn't know was why. Why he had done it? What happened that night, when I was celebrating my union with Eamon, believing the day to be the happiest of my life?

"Tell me," I said to Calix as Millicent drew blood from my arm and my home burned above. "Why did you do it? Why did you kill my mother?"

Calix bowed his head, glaring to his hands as though they were deadly weapons resting on his thighs. Then he opened his mouth and told me the truth—all of it, no matter how dark and deadly it was. There was no detail spared as Millicent drank from me, and Calix offloaded the burden he had hidden from me...

He told me *everything*.

38
3 YEARS BEFORE

THIS IS A MISTAKE. *I should not have come.*

The thought overwhelmed me as I stood, dumfounded, before the door to Rhory's home. A place I had vowed to myself never to return to. Yet here I stood because I was pathetic. Weak.

A flurry of snow fell around me, casting Darkmourn in a blanket of pure endless white. It was late afternoon, but the fresh layer of winter kept the world brighter than it should have been at such an hour. Flakes soaked through my heavy jacket, making the leather smell damp. I was certainly not dressed for a wedding, one I had never intended to attend... until the invite arrived.

And yet here I was, waiting before the door like a fool.

The invite was no more than a crumpled ball of parchment within my fist. I should have thrown it out the moment Silas brought it to me. And I would have. Except my brother was adamant he was going to attend. And Auriol commanded me to retrieve him. I couldn't refuse her. Her control over me was powerful enough to move my limbs even against my better judgement.

I convinced myself I had only come here for Silas, not because I longed to see Rhory again. Which was a lie, but perhaps if I kept repeating it to myself, I would wish it into existence. If I saw Rhory, it would destroy those last surviving parts of me.

Rhory and Eamon's ceremony shouldn't have finished by now, but the house was dark. Quiet. I would have taken the emptiness as a sign to turn away and forget this. Silas could find his own way home, likely drunk and merry from the enjoyment of my sorrow and pain. He always thrived in my pity, but what little brothers didn't enjoy the downfall of their elders?

Except the house wasn't silent. Not completely. I could hear the heartbeats; the regular thumps thundered in my head as though they demanded my attention.

Auriol's command just raged within me. The siren song of her request had me raising my fist to the door. I knocked, two loud raps that disturbed the peace inside. The sound of my knuckles against wood interrupted the beating hearts, causing one of them to skip. In all my years, I had memorised Silas's heart-song. And he was here. I heard him above the rest. And I needed to get him out. Once I did, I would never return here again.

Never.

The door was thrown open, and Ana Coleman stood before me. Her sudden presence surprised me—enough to take a step back from the doorstep—as did the vicious smile that spread across her beautiful face.

"I was beginning to think you had ignored my invitation, Calix Grey. Please, come inside before you catch your death. This weather is... wicked."

"My apologies," I replied, bowing my head from her intense gaze. "But I have only come to retrieve my brother."

I could hear Silas from inside the foyer, talking loudly to another with a deep voice. Ana soon stepped aside, revealing who my brother spoke with, although I would have recognised the deep tones of the man's voice even in the darkest of rooms.

Eamon. Now, Eamon Coleman.

Fury sparked deep in my chest as I regarded him, until Ana blocked him from view. The deep maroon dress Ana wore slid across the polished floor of her home, giving the impression she floated more than walked. Her waves of dark brown hair had been pinned up and off her face, all except a single strand that fell perfectly before her azure eyes.

"We are not strangers, Calix. Please, come in and enjoy one drink with us. It is a momentous day," Ana said.

"Momentous indeed. It is not every day I get to marry the love of your life." Eamon stood, dressed in a fine suit of obsidian material, with the clasp of a crimson cloak draped from his shoulders. He held a glass in his hand and raised it to my brother, who held its twin.

"Eamon, I believe you have misspoken," I said, glaring as both men turned and looked at me. Neither one smiled.

"No, not at all," Eamon replied with a cruel smile.

A rage swept over me as I watched my brother toasting to the man who stole my heart and kept it for himself. It took great effort to stay standing on the step. What I desired was to run through the foyer and tear Eamon to shreds. To make him feel every scrap of agony he caused me when he took Rhory from me.

I might have, if Ana hadn't had leaned forward. "Calix, dear, one drink."

"Silas, come." The command snapped out of me.

Disgust crawled over Silas's face as he swept his gaze across me. "I don't bow to your requests, brother."

I swept past Ana and into the warmth of her home. Silas rocked back a step, whilst Eamon held firm. Ana closed the door. The slam of it almost made me lose my composure. I stiffened when she slipped up behind me, her nails tickling up my back and over my shoulder like a spider.

"Allow me to fetch you something to drink. A toast is without merit if you do not have something strong to raise."

Eamon nodded his head to Ana, smiling his thanks as she slipped from the foyer into the darkened dining hall beyond. The same place I had first shared a conversation with Rhory. It was hard not to forget myself in the forest of memories we had shared in this home. Our history together was stained across every room. I felt the intoxicating call of them wishing to drag me away in its current.

"Master Grey." Eamon offered me a handsome smile, the very same he had when he opened the door to Rhory's bedroom and found us, entangled, together in it. I didn't see how Rhory could have fallen in love with him. He was everything Rhory despised. He was perfect, from the brush of his midnight hair across his head to the bright sky-blue eyes. Even the way he carried himself, straight-backed and always displaying his charming smile. This was the type of man that would make Rhory shiver. At least that was what I believed. I was wrong, of course, because my eyes caught the glint of a wedding band around Eamon's finger, confirming my greatest fear.

Eamon caught the shift of my attention and lifted his finger up before him, showing off the polished metal for all to see. "Silver. Pretty metal, isn't it?"

"Silas," I snapped. "I will not ask you again. It's time to go home."

My brother stepped forward, half positioning himself between Eamon and me. "And I will not remind you again, brother. I am not some dog you can bark orders at."

He was right. I was not the alpha. Not yet. Auriol could have given him a single command to leave, and he would have raced out of this house before dropping the glass from his hand. That power was not mine to claim.

"You're drunk," I said, disgust creeping across my face. I couldn't hide my emotions, nor did I desire to.

"Oh, come on, Calix. Do not spoil the mood of the day." Ana danced back into the foyer, glass in hand. I kept my arms folded across my chest, refusing her offer. I was not here to toast to my heartbreak.

"Shouldn't you be with your guests?" I asked, no longer caring for anyone but Eamon. "What would Rhory say if he discovered his newly wed was raising glasses with his previous lover?"

Ana smacked my shoulder. "Oh, Calix, please do not say such vile accusations. I can't bear to hear them."

Eamon smiled at that and raised his glass again. Silas followed suit, quietly amused by the tension that thrummed between us all. I snatched the glass from Ana, praying that something strong was promised. A rush of spirits would help me walk out of this place without blood on my hands.

Eamon placed his arm over my brother's shoulders and pulled him close to his side. Their proximity disgusted me. It was not an emotion Silas shared, as he seemed completely entranced by Eamon's touch.

"Now," Eamon said, pulling a face of forced confusion. "Whatever should we toast to?"

Silas looked directly at me as he replied, "To love, perhaps."

"Very good," Eamon purred, sharing a quick look at Ana. I couldn't make out what it spoke of. By the time I glanced at Rhory's mother, she was hiding a snicker behind her painted nails.

"To love then," Eamon said, raising his glass higher to the sky. "And to remembering it."

I was the first to drink, draining the glass of the wine and thrusting it back towards Ana, who carefully took it from me. Silas was next. He laughed as a dribble of the red liquid spread down his chin. It was Eamon who plucked the pocket square and brought it to my brother's face, tentatively clearing him of the spillage.

"If we are done here," I said, enjoying the ease of the wine as it slipped down my throat and numbed my chest. Sweeping my hand towards the door, I focused on my brother. "Silas."

Silas frowned, took a reluctant step towards me, and stumbled. Confusion pinched his dark brows down, creasing his face. It was a moment of embarrassment, as though he didn't understand how he had lost his footing.

"Careful," Eamon sang, but refused to step forward and help.

Silas opened his mouth to say something. Perhaps to make some childish joke about the wine and his head, but the words that came out of him made little sense. The glass slipped from his fingers and shattered at his feet, coating the floor in shards of glass.

Instinct took over. I shifted my weight to step towards him, but I didn't move. I fell over myself as the world tilted on its axis. The ground raced up to greet me. I couldn't even raise my arms to soften the fall. My face crashed into the cold panels of the floor, bone and wood clashing together in a jarring crack. Pain split my skull. Claws pierced my brain and pinched down hard, attempting to tear it into multiple parts.

I blinked as the dull light of the room grew too harsh. When I opened my eyes again, it was to watch feet moving towards me. Then a voice spoke through the haze.

"Wolfsbane," Eamon said, tutting down at me.

I tried to shift my face around so I could see him, but everything was blurry. I was only vaguely aware that Silas too was on the floor, hands gripping his stomach as he moaned and wailed.

"Such a pesky weed to locate. Did you know it grows in abundance beyond Castle Dread? I didn't, not until Silas revealed it all to me. The weed grows from the blood of a dead wolf. Hence the name, a wolf's bane, tragic but almost poetic. I wouldn't hold it against him, of course. His youth and, well... how do I say this without sounding as though I am gloating? Silas's obsession with me has led him to have rather loose lips."

Eamon squatted over me. A smile broke out across his face, twisting it into a mask of horror. "Do you find it strange to know that I have not only fucked Rhory, but I have also fucked your brother?"

Ana clicked her tongue from somewhere out of sight. "Eamon, how crude."

My mouth seemed to have been sewn together. I couldn't speak even if I wished to. The wolfsbane was spreading through me like wildfire. It turned my muscles to stone, and my marrow to honey. It was a feeling I was familiar with, from years of Auriol testing our resistance to the plant, but the dosage Eamon had provided was far greater than anything I had devoured before.

I must have been crying, because Eamon lifted a hand to the side of my face and brushed something cool away from my cheek.

"Now, now," he sang. "I will not kill you. You, Calix Grey, are not my enemy. In fact, you are the means for me to see my enemies destroyed. Once and for all. What I am going to do is offer you peace, as thanks for everything you are going to give me."

Peace? I scoffed at such a ridiculous concept while my wolf stirred with hungry vengeance. *You are my enemy. And one day I will destroy you.*

"Let this be a warning," Eamon said, pointing his finger in my face. "If you come back for Rhory, if you so much as go near him, it will be his pretty little skin I mark."

"Oh, Eamon, do not speak in such ways. Or do I need to remind you of our deal?" Ana moved into view above me, the tap of her heels teetering across the floor. Her outline rippled as the drug took hold. Her features were blurred and warped, but her grin was as clear as the sun breaking through the clouds of a storm.

A name formed on my lips. It may not have made sense as I spoke it aloud, but to me, it rang true.

Rhory.

"You are going to forget all about him, just as he forgot about you."

The pain dulled, lightening if only a little.

"Ana," Eamon said, standing and making room for Rhory's mother. "I trust I can leave you to work your magic whilst I deal with Silas?"

Ana lifted her dress up, enough for her to have room to kneel before me. With each blink, the wolfsbane was fading. My gaze sharpened first, followed swiftly by my other senses.

"You," I managed as Ana leaned over me, hands outstretched.

"I have only ever wanted what was best for my son. My first and only child. And you, Master Grey, are not worthy."

Her power burned to life like fire blossoming across her hands. The glow was a cold white. It filled the protruding veins in her fingers, lighting her skin up from the inside.

"What... what have you done to him?" Each word was hard to force out, but I did so with every ounce of effort I could muster.

She scowled down at me, face ageing before my eyes. "I made him forget you. Every part of his mind you occupied, I changed, altered. I filled it with Eamon, placing him in all the slots you once invaded. He is a far greater match. Where you would have only been dangerous for him... Eamon would be his saviour."

"W—Why?" I fumbled over the words.

Ana glanced over her shoulder. I followed her attention, seeing that Silas and Eamon were no longer with us. I could hear the creak of boards above us, and the drag of a heavy body against the floor.

Satisfied no one else could hear, Ana leaned over me and whispered her answer into my ear. "Because Eamon gave me a choice. What Rhory is, what I am. Eamon knows. I did it to keep Rhory from being dragged to Castle Dread and being disposed of like the other halflings and witches discovered in this godforsaken town. Your proximity to my son puts him in danger, which I cannot allow. Be thankful Eamon simply wishes for me to alter your mind and not kill you, because I certainly argued that ending you would be the easier of options."

She pulled back, hands swirling with white light.

"Michal... would not—"

"Michal doesn't even know his own name, let alone what is best for Rhory. His mind is mine, just as Rhory's and yours will be. Now, careful... otherwise, the outcome may leave you... ruined, as my dear husband is now. He is the perfect example of what happens when you resist me."

"You are a monster," I hissed through clenched teeth. My jaw ached as I fought the wolfsbane and the beast within me. It longed to be freed.

"No," Ana said, face lit from beneath by the glow of her magic. "I am a mother. And I will do everything to see my family thrive."

"Rhory... will... remember."

"This will hurt," she said, lifting her hands towards my face. "As all good things do. And I would sooner die than break the curse. Rhory will never remember you..."

Perhaps it was the fury at what had been revealed, or the desire to never allow myself to forget Rhory, but my desperation blew through the cobwebs the wolfsbane settled over me. The change happened before she could lower her fingers to my head.

My skin split in two. My bones shattered like glass.

Without hesitation, the wolf within me burst beyond its cage of flesh, past my better judgement. There was no more thinking. No more Calix. Silas. Eamon. There was only flesh and blood as the wolf tore into Rhory's mother, snuffing out her power. Her life. As the monster's jaws bit down into her neck and severed it from her shoulders with the ease of melted butter, Ana hardly had the chance to scream. When she did, it was a song of gargled blood and death.

39

CALIX HAD KILLED MY MOTHER. He was the murderer, the monster. That fact alone was hard to bear, as was the knowledge that Ana Coleman was the name I had longed to uncover, the witch who altered my mind. My *own mother* was the one responsible for tearing into my memories. She ripped them apart and, in turn, stole everything away from me. Because of her, I was married to a monster. Since her death, I have faced pain both physically and mentally. Because of her desire to see me safe, she handed me over to the man who stripped the last remaining scraps of my life away with his bare hands. And what I couldn't fathom atop it all was that was not her only devilish sin. Not only did she play with my memories as though they were hers to own, but she also tampered with Father's mind, destroying him slowly from the inside.

She killed him.

She did this to me.

Her power tore our family apart. Her actions led to this very moment as I walked out of our house, bathed in smoke and ash from the fire, towards the battle which waited for me within Castle Dread.

It should have pained me hearing what Calix had kept from me. The events which happened the hours before I found my mother's body torn to shreds. Instead, I drowned in fury; not because Calix had done it, but furious I would never have the chance to confront her. By killing my mother, Calix had taken any chance from me of ever asking her the only question that seemed to poison my mind.

Mother, was it worth it?

I couldn't form words as we travelled to Castle Dread. No one spoke to me. Not Millicent, who slowly, but surely, healed from her wounds. Or Calix. Even though he was not in my viewpoint, I felt him look at me. There was an expectant shimmer in his eyes. He trod carefully around me, as though he walked on glass. I couldn't fathom the chance of catching his gaze for fear it would be the final straw that broke me. All I could do was face forward as we moved through Darkmourn towards our final destination.

Millicent led the way. Although the scarred teeth marks had not completely faded, my blood had given her enough vitality to walk herself out of my burning home without aid. Each step seemed to provide her with more strength. Soon enough, her gait evened, and her shoulders rolled back until she was once again a picture of health.

I did what I did best and buried everything. All my thoughts and feelings, I forced them deep inside of me until I felt only the physical echo of pain. Now was not the time to focus on self-pity, not with the real threat which still hung over Darkmourn, like the axe held aloft by an executioner.

If Eamon succeeded in killing Lord Marius, it would lead to Millicent's demise, as well as every other vampire sired from him. I kept my focus on the back of her straight black hair, waiting with bated breath for her to stop and crumble to ash before my eyes. As long as she was moving, we had time.

The walk was torture, as was the silence that occupied it. All I could think about was what Calix had revealed. No matter how hard I tried to fill my mind with other concerns, it always led back to my mother. How Eamon seemed to have enamoured Silas, leading to his eventual imprisonment. What Mother had done to me, and her warped reasonings. And mostly, what would have happened if she had made Calix forget about me? Above it all, knowing that was almost a possibility drove daggers into my heart.

Even after everything he had done, and everything I could not remember, Calix was my tether, whether or not I wished to admit it.

I found myself stifling the urge to laugh. The feeling came over me so suddenly as Castle Dread loomed ahead. After everything Mother had done to ensure I never set foot near this place, here I was walking across the bridge directly into the harsh shadows the monstrous building cast across Old Town.

The presence of the castle had our party of three slowing. I was so used to the silence and the patter of our boots against cobbled stone that when Millicent spoke it jolted surprise through my soul.

"I'm all for going in knifes out and poised for blood, but this may be one moment when a plan would be a good idea." Millicent glanced between the glowing windows of Castle Dread, to Calix and then to me.

Before us stretched the ancient stone bridge that connected the castle to Old Town. It was weathered from years, and the stones stained a dusty black. There was no light here, beside that of the fire-lit windows and the waning moon far above. Even the stars seemed to disappear. Perhaps they too sensed the darkness in this place.

From our vantage point, the face of the castle looked more like a grinning face with hungry eyes, promising damnation inside it.

"Just keep to the path," Calix said, striding past us. "You both know what waits in the shadows if you leave it."

Wolves.

"And I have had just about enough company with wolves for a lifetime," Millicent muttered, unsheathing the twin daggers Calix had returned to her. "No offence."

Calix continued walking, ready for the shadows to swallow him whole.

"Wait," I called out, "Calix."

He stopped in his tracks as my voice echoed. Nerves overcame me as I waited for him to turn back to look at me. Calix hesitated, likely caused by the fact my calling his name was the first thing I had said to him since he revealed his crime.

My breath hitched when he finally looked my way. His gold eyes glowed through the darkness between us, casting me in a warmth and chill of equal measure.

"We don't have the time, Little Red."

His use of the nickname weakened my knees. It would have been easier to fall to them and sob, to unleash the storm of emotions which riled throughout me.

"You do not have to do this," he said, as though that was what immobilised me.

I shook my head. "It is not myself I am worried about. Not this time."

How could I tell him what I truly feared? Speaking it into existence would only make it seem more of a possibility. Because when Marius discovered the danger Calix's kind was to him, what was stopping the vampire lord from destroying every single one of them?

I walked towards Calix, carefully stepping from one stone slab to the next. He stiffened as I closed in on him, but soon melted when I reached up with my hands and graced my cold-tipped fingers against the warmth of his face.

My lover. My heart. My mother's killer.

"I'm so sorry, Rhory." Calix broke the moment my touch graced him. He dropped his chin to his chest and loosed a weighted breath, one I imagined he held in for a long time.

"Not now," I said, jaw clenched. "You do not get to say that to me now. Not yet."

"I never wanted for any of this," he replied as the grim expression furrowed his brows and rimmed his bright eyes with a devious glint.

"Nor did I. But here we are and eventually we have the truth to face. Together."

I glanced behind me, but Millicent was nowhere to be seen. Calix didn't seem alarmed, nor surprised.

"What I deserve for the pain I have caused you... I deserve to—"

"Together, did you hear me? Calix, look at me."

Calix took my face in his hands, holding me in place with gentled ease. "I should have told you sooner."

"And why didn't you?" I said, breathless. "Tell me that, at least."

Calix paused. He took a moment to gather himself whilst his eyes roamed across my face, my body, leaving no inch unattended. "Because I have taken so much from you. And what I didn't wish to be responsible for was ruining the image you held for your mother."

"Knowing the truth would have freed me."

Calix shook his head. "No. You are the only one who can free yourself. I thought, by upholding the lies, I would shield you from more agony. If I told you the truth of what she did, I feared it would break you."

"You are right," I replied, mesmerised by the glow of his eyes in the dark, and the way his breath blew out in clouds of silver beyond his lips. "It *has* broken me, but you are the only one who can see that I am put back together. Which is why I do not want you to do this."

"Do what?"

"Expose yourself," I snapped. "Doing so will reveal what you are. And I need you, Calix; I need you to survive this night so you can help me put together the mess in my mind. You owe me that, at least. And if something happens to you, our *before* dies with you."

"Oh, Little Red. But that is exactly why I must," Calix said. "Rhory, let me fight for you."

"There will be nothing left to fight for if you are dead, Calix. Lord Marius will not allow you to live if he knows what you are... the threat your life is to his and to his kin. If you die, you take the truth with you. I cannot remember what happened between us and my mother is not alive to fix it, which means you are the only one with the knowledge of our truth. If you die, you take it with you, and I can never be whole. I will never be fixed."

"When will you learn?" Calix whispered, using his leverage and guiding my face to his. The winds whipped at his hair, casting it across his face. "You need no one but yourself. There will come a time when you'll understand that others do not have the power to fix you. We can help you hold the parts together, but only you can truly patch them together. You do not need me for that."

"I do," I forced out. My throat seemed to squeeze in on itself. "I need you, and I want you."

"Then I am the luckiest man alive," he said, brushing the tear from my face. "And that is why I am going to see this through. My brother must be reasoned with, and Eamon dealt with. I can only pray to whoever listens that Lord Marius finds it in his cold still heart to pardon me if we save him."

"Promise me," I said.

"I promise. Which means little unless I seal it with a kiss."

I closed my eyes, providing no resistance as Calix lowered his lips to mine.

"I have killed six of them... no, maybe five. It is easy to lose count when the sound of breaking necks is all so similar."

Reluctantly, we pulled away from each other to see Millicent standing in a cloak of shadows. Her hands were covered in blood, as were the sharp blades which she cleaned methodically on her trousers. Only when the blood had been cleared from each side did she force them back into the sheathes at her hips.

"Crimson Guards?" I asked, noting the deep red of blood.

Millicent pulled a face, with one brow raised far above the other. "Rhory, I am not sure that is the name they are using anymore."

"Eamon's pack," Calix corrected, his voice thick with darkness.

"Yes, and it was definitely six of them I killed. Enjoyed every single moment." After what they did to her in the cellar, I couldn't fault Millicent for the wide smile she displayed as she spoke.

"Eamon has the outskirts of the castle surrounded or did. I know, from experience, there are far more than only six of the fuckers. He'll have the rest of them inside with him, no doubt."

Adrenaline buzzed through me. It started at the ground, working its way upwards until I was filled with a fresh sense of confidence. "Let's get on with it. I have something I wish to say to my husband."

Millicent giggled maniacally and unsheathed one of her blades, extending it to me handle first. "Here, this might help with that conversation."

I felt the weight of the blade the moment it was passed to me. Holding such a weapon gave me a new sense of power, which both frightened and thrilled me.

"You know how to use that, don't you?" Calix slipped in behind me, put his arms around my waist and brought his lips so close to my ear it sent shivers across my back.

"Stab him with the sharp end," I replied, feeling my heart swell in my chest at the thought.

"Precisely," Calix replied. "Just like that."

A howl sliced through the night. It demanded our attention, forcing us to look towards the source of the noise. Toward Castle Dread, and the sound which came from within its old stone walls.

"Auriol," Calix said, releasing me and moving towards the sound. "It is her. She calls to her pack."

By the time the next long pained howl reached us, we were running towards it. I could only focus on following Millicent and Calix as they moved with unnatural speed and urgency.

I caught something out of the corner of my eye as we moved, unusual enough for me to look properly. What I saw was something no story could have warned me about. Shadows in the shape of hounds ran amongst the darkness within the castle's grounds beside us. They too heard Auriol's cry. A pack of cursed wolves listened as their creation cried out for help.

We all prepared to heed it.

40

THERE WAS NOT a single one of Eamon's pack to greet us within the main entrance of Castle Dread. Where we expected his followers to fill the space, there were only ghosts and the echoes of far-off voices. The only evidence of life where the scattered remains of those Millicent had left in the castle grounds for the shadow hounds to feast upon.

Calix stormed ahead, his speed increasing every time Auriol howled. His hands were balled into fists, which he used to propel himself through the foyer, up the grand stairs that stretched out directly before us then around the balcony atop it. Millicent stuck by my side, her hand on my arm in some protective manner.

My lungs burned, as did my legs. My body was a patchwork of pain, from Millicent's bite mark on my arm, to the burns across my back and the raw skin at my wrists and ankles. I used every ounce of agony to keep me going. It fuelled me, and reminded me it was nothing compared to what I felt inside.

Every muscle felt strained as we followed in pursuit of Calix. Even my fingers ached as they grew used to holding onto the dagger Millicent had gifted me. In an ideal world, I would have had the time to grow used to its weight and balance. Instead, I could only grip on harder and hope it would provide me some comfort with whatever we were about to face.

It wasn't until we had taken another flight of stairs upwards, and rounded multiple corridors lined with closed black doors and walls decorated with hanging paintings in gilded frames, that I recognised something was missing. *Witches*. This place should have been teeming with them. For years, Lord Marius and his beloved Jak had collected those with powers like rare items to be studied. Except the castle felt empty. It was the quiet that made me question if Mother had been right all along. If the witches were not here, then what became of them?

Before I could allow a new dread to enter me, Calix stopped beyond a door which looked no different to the many others we had passed.

"How many are there?" Millicent asked.

"Enough to cause us a problem," Calix whispered, the side of his face pressing into the wood of the door as he listened to something beyond it.

I strained my ears but couldn't pick anything up but the thundering beat of my heart; Calix must have heard it too, because he turned his full attention on me and winced.

"I should not have brought you here," Calix said, lips drawing back into a tight line as he inhaled. "It's not safe. There are too many of them."

"Which is exactly why I am here." I stepped from Millicent, who finally released my arm. The tingle of her grip didn't leave me, as though her fingers had left an imprint on my skin.

Calix's eyes searched my face for something, then glanced down at the dagger in my hands. Did he see the way I shook?

"You have another weapon in your arsenal," Calix muttered. "Do not be afraid to use it when the time comes."

I wanted to share my concern about the missing witches, but there was no time. Auriol howled again, making Calix recoil backwards.

"Go," Millicent hissed, her eyes glowing red and teeth bared, "Now."

Calix offered me a final look before opening the door and slipping inside. I took a step to follow him, but the door closed, and Millicent had returned her fingers back to my arm.

"He can't go alone!" I choked out, unable to pull free.

"Give Calix a chance," Millicent replied. 'Do this for him, as he is doing this for you.'

I stopped resisting at her comment for it had the power to immobilise me.

Do this for him, as he is doing this for you.

With a swift tug, we were moving away from the door, back in the direction we had come. My chest panged with a bitter shock that sang similarly to betrayal or jealousy.

"Millicent, we need to go back to him," I spat as we raced down the corridor, my feet slapping the ground as I tried to keep up.

"And we will," Millicent replied. "But first we must create a distraction, something to allow time for Calix to have even the slightest chance against Eamon and his pack."

I almost tripped as Millicent pulled me down one set of stairs after another. Soon enough, we were back at the main entrance. It was not the front door we moved for. Hidden in the shadows beyond the grand staircase was another corridor. It was narrow, and likely used as a place for servants or maids to slip through unseen.

"Millicent," I snarled, trying once again to pull away. "Tell me what we need to do!"

"I'm sorry," she said quietly, her voice buried beneath my heavy footfalls. "Know that I will let nothing happen to you."

Panic clawed up my throat. I opened my mouth to scream out for Calix, but the terror did well to silence and strangle me.

Auriol howled once again, and this time the noise was so close it rocked through the dark space and echoed across the stone walls beside us. I felt like being back in the tunnels beneath Darkmourn, the way the sound grew the more it shattered the dark.

"I have always wanted to make a grand entrance," Millicent said, unbothered by the fast pace of our running, or my struggling. "Books suggest it would have been better received if I was dressed in a ball gown that looked more like the decoration on top of a cake. I never understood the appeal. I prefer my entrance to be more... memorable than that." After she finished speaking, she added as an afterthought, "Hide your dagger."

There was no arguing with the look in her eyes. I slipped it into the belt of my trousers and folded my tunic over the hilt. The cold press of the blade against my back was a welcome relief.

"Am I a fool to trust you?"

Millicent giggled lightly. Even in the dark, I conjured an image of her deadly smile. "We are all fools, Rhory. Some more deadly than others."

The hallway stopped at a smaller door than the others we had seen. The paint on this was worn and scratched. It almost shattered completely when Millicent raised a boot and kicked into it.

Light flooded the narrow corridor, spilling out from the room beyond. For a moment I was blinded by it, enough that I couldn't make anything out as Millicent pulled me into the light.

"Eamon Coleman," Millicent cried out. The name alone turned my body to stone, as well as the realisation of exactly what distraction Millicent had alluded to. "I believe I have something that belongs to you."

I blinked, and the world steadied.

We had entered a monstrous room overspilling with grandeur. Golden sconces burned across the walls, each one glowing with roses of ruby flame. The light reflected off the stone walls, bathing shadows across the ceiling far above, making it seem endless.

To one side of the room stood a man who glowed as bright as a star.

His skin was pale as death, and his hair so white even winter's first snow would be jealous of its colour. Blood-red eyes picked up the glow of fire and seemed to swallow the light and reflect it from within—and they looked directly at me.

Marius, Lord of the Eternal Night. Father of the Dead. Sire of the vampires.

He stood alone atop a raised dais, his entire body trembling with fury.

It was the whimper that drew my attention from the vampire lord to the middle of the room. Covered almost entirely in a blanket of webbed silver chains was a wolf. Auriol. She was splayed beneath the net like a creature captured in the woods by hunters. She was both human and wolf, like Calix had been. Her limbs were long and drawn out, covered in patches of grey fur that showed a leathered skin beneath.

Seeing her blew away the trancelike state which gripped me. Her name formed on the tip of my tongue. As if sensing it, she opened eyes of swirling honey and looked at me. It was brief. Then she closed them and whimpered softly like an animal welcoming death.

"Rhory?" My name broke out in question. All I had to do was look to the opposite side of the room to see its speaker.

Eamon stood within a halo of his followers. Once the Crimson Guard, they were each dressed in cloaks of russet brown that looked like aged, dried blood instead of the new lifeblood they were sworn to protect. Just beyond Eamon's shoulder was Silas, sulking behind him with his head down, but eyes raised up and looking through his long lashes.

"What is the meaning of this?" Boomed the voice of Lord Marius. It was demanding and powerful but did little to sway me from the confusion that crossed my husband's face.

As the corners of Eamon's lips tugged downward, mine seemed to rise.

"My apologies, sire," Millicent sang loud for all to hear. The grip of her fingers released me. She leaned into my ear and whispered, "Go to him, Little Red. Run to him."

The use of my nickname was a gift, one which overspilled with newfound confidence.

With a shove, I was moving. Running, just as Millicent said, towards Eamon. As I had when Millicent last returned me to my husband, I put on the show of my lifetime. Throwing myself down the final steps, I crashed into his chest and wrapped my arms around his waist. He didn't lower his arm over me, which was rather lucky because if he did, he would have found the dagger hiding in the waistband of my trousers.

"Are you surprised?" I whispered, feeling Eamon stiffen beneath my arms. Part of me wondered if he could smell the remnants of our burning home on me, whilst the other part was focused on how we were to save Auriol and Lord Marius.

"Enough of this," Eamon growled, shrugging me away into another set of arms. It was Silas who withdrew me into the throng of the crowd, placing me behind Eamon who regarded Lord Marius once again.

Millicent paced into the room, her short blade drawn. "Lord Marius," Millicent called out, "Would you do me the honour of following me out of this room before those men and women attempt to kill you?"

The bark of the vampire lord's laugh was sharp, whipping the room and everyone in it. "You have broken into my home and interrupted a meeting with my Crimson Guard. Whatever spectacle you believe to achieve here, I would stop whilst you are ahead."

I was surprised when Eamon called for his followers to restrain Millicent at Lord Marius's order. Silas slapped a hand over my mouth as I cried out, ready to break my act and admit that Millicent was right.

"Not. Yet," Silas whispered through gritted teeth. Then he said, "So, you are a fighter."

My body stilled as Silas ensured I watched the wave of Eamon's followers overcome Millicent. I expected her to put up a fight, but she didn't. She took a pathetic swing towards the first woman that reached her, but it was poorly timed. The blade was knocked from Millicent's grasp and she was taken by multiple hands.

She could have fought them off if she wanted, but Millicent behaved. It was the knowing glint in her eyes that calmed me. This was all part of the plan she had not revealed to me, a plan that had seemed to change as the minutes went on.

"Pardon my suggestion, Lord Marius, but this would be a better time than any to prove to you the danger these creatures pose to you." Eamon gestured towards Auriol, and then Millicent, who stood as still as a statue in the grasp of the five strangers who held her.

Lord Marius's face was expressive. No matter the emotion he held, he showed it across his handsome face in dramatic flairs. And Eamon's suggestion had displeased him.

"You forget yourself," Lord Marius said, taking a step down from his dais. Both his hands were clasped behind his back, putting a strain on the decorative jacket he wore. It seemed to have been crafted from the richest of velvets that rippled like the surface of a lake as it reflected the firelight. "I am not in the sport of watching my chosen protectors of Darkmourn suggest a display of murder, all to prove a point." He nodded his head slightly towards Auriol, looking almost pained to see her suffering beneath the weight of the silver. "This is not a creature I am familiar with, but I hear her heartbeat and recognise she is a living being. Which begs me to ask you why you cause her to suffer. Is this what the Crimson Guard have become? A group inclined for the dramatics? Now, I will not ask you again. Remove these chains so I can discuss directly with Ms Grey the details of this..." Marius tilted his head. "...Issue."

"I'm afraid I cannot do that." As Eamon spoke, his remaining followers fanned out across the room, russet cloaks brushing the floor. Marius watched, eyes following each one of them. It was then he brought his hands before him, flashing the sharp points of polished nails.

"May I remind you, you stand in my home," Marius spoke carefully. "I have extended my invitation to you, and now I revoke it. Do not make me remove you myself, and that cloak you are wearing."

"Do you mean this cloak?" Eamon was the only one wearing the original red cloak that confirmed his station. He reached for the clasp with his free hand and unclipped it. He drew the material from his shoulders, extended his arm, then dropped it. "Oh, you can have the fucking cloak."

Darkness swelled beyond Marius as though wings of pure night burst from his back. His eyes burned as he split his mouth and bared a jaw full of teeth sharper than any forged blade. "Get out of my home. All of you."

"No," Eamon replied, speaking the word as though it brewed in the fires of his chest. "Marius, there was once a time your monsters invaded my home without invitation. They left only when they desired. And I wish to do the same here, tonight."

"I sense my brother is close," Silas whispered into my ear beneath Eamon's speech. "Waiting for the right moment to come and save the day."

My lips and teeth brushed Silas's palm as I tried to bite him. He emitted a low chuckle at my attempts and held down firmer. I clawed my hands into it as much as he allowed. No matter how I tried to pull his hand away, it didn't budge.

Marius was surrounded within seconds.

"Eamon Coleman," Marius growled. "What have you done?"

"I remembered what it means to value life over death," Eamon replied.

For a moment, I saw fear pinch across Marius's deep stare. He looked to his side, almost expectant that someone was there with him, except the space was empty.

"Take this man and remove him," Marius called out his command to

Eamon's pack. No one listened. Marius repeated himself, this time his words laced with viperous danger. "Remove Eamon Coleman from this room now, or you will all face the same punishment."

"They do not take orders from you," Eamon sang, pacing freely up and down the space where Auriol lay. "These fearless humans are loyal to me, not the Crimson Guard. Not you. They are mine."

Silas's chest rattled as he chuckled to himself. "Hmm. Are they?"

Marius bowed his knees and lowered himself. His fingers curved into claw-like points and he hissed to the men and women who slowly closed in on him. Ancient determination boiled in his blood-red eyes as he prepared to defend himself.

I looked at Millicent, waiting for some sort of signal. Her eyes were focused upwards, towards the shadows above. I followed her attention as much as Silas's hold allowed, looking up to see a narrow walkway that hid in the shadows. Millicent saw something out of my line of sight. When she looked back at me, I caught the subtle shake of her head.

Not yet, her actions said. *Not yet.*

My power lurked far beneath my skin. I felt its presence rear its head and prepare. Calix was right. I had a weapon. Something not forged by steel, yet still as deadly. And I would use it when the time was right.

"Your rule must end," Eamon shouted, almost hysteric as his voice cracked. "It is time I right the world you destroyed. To balance the scales back in favour of the living."

"Do you think you are the first to try?" Marius spat, more beast than man. "Fool, to think you have a chance against me. I have slaughtered more numbers than those you have brought with you. This is no threat, simply an annoyance."

"Oh?" Eamon said, scanning his eyes across his followers. They seemed to glisten with tears of pride. "I can see what made you think such a thing. But, Marius, I tried to warn you. What Auriol has become poses a great threat to the vampire kind. *We* are the threat. I think it may sink in just how deadly if I show you."

"Strange what trauma can do to one's mind," Silas said, mouth so close to the side of my face I could smell the harsh rotting of his teeth. "It either empowers you or blinds you. Which one will it be for Eamon?"

"Now!" Millicent was released suddenly as those holding her melted into clouds of shadow. From within, the rumbling growls of wolves called out.

As I unleashed my power on Silas with lightning precision, I could not tell if he underestimated me, or knew this would happen and simply waited patiently for the inevitable. Gold light erupted across his hand as though my fingers cast flame upon his skin.

His hold on me relaxed as I pushed an avalanche of feelings into his body. I fed him fear and panic, exhaustion and pain. Every negative emotion I harboured released out of me and into him. The force was sudden and vigorous.

Breaking free of him, I reached my hand into the back of my trousers and pulled the blade out. My legs pumped hard, and I seemed to forget to breathe. All I could focus on was Eamon's back as I closed in on him, dagger poised and ready to strike.

Somewhere I heard Marius expel a battle cry as wolves leaped out of the clouds of shadow. Millicent was calling my name. Eamon was too focused on his grand revelation. He was lost to watching Marius's reaction that he didn't see me coming.

I lifted the blade above my head and thrust it downward with the full momentum of my body. Then the ground fell away from me with such force the blade went flying from my hand. Commotion lit the room as it was suddenly filled with wolves far larger than normal, although not humanoid like Calix and Auriol.

"Did you truly believe such emotions would work to destroy me?" Silas hissed into my ear. He tore me backwards. I couldn't do anything to stop him from dragging me away from Eamon—who, all the while, still had not noticed how close he came to death.

"I have lived with those emotions for years." Silas gripped the back of my neck, his nails breaking skin as he pulled me away. "They are meaningless. I am numb to them."

I searched the room to find Millicent now standing at Lord Marius's side, dagger raised and teeth flashing. She held my gaze for only a moment before tracking the large brown wolf that pawed the stone floor before her, as though it sized up its prey.

"I want you to understand," Eamon called out, "Your death is for all those families your creations have destroyed. For the children who lost parents, and the parents who lost children, all because you had no control over the undead. When my pack tears into you, limb from limb, I wish for you to recognise that you caused this. This is your doing, let that be your last thought. Just as your monsters ripped into my family and killed them as I watched, my monsters will do the same to you."

The wolves throughout the room buzzed with a feral energy. Each one yipped and whined, hardly able to contain themselves.

"Take my word for it," Lord Marius shouted out a final time. "Revenge does not fill the void. It simply whets its appetite and fuels its hunger. It never satisfies."

"Thank you for your wise words, but I think I will decide that for myself." Eamon dismissed him, lifted a finger and pointed directly at Lord Marius. Then he called out his command which echoed across the room's sudden silence before it exploded into chaos.

"Feast. Kill Lord Marius. End it. *Now*."

41

EAMON'S PACK of wolves broke the line and pounced towards Marius, unsuspecting of any danger which awaited them. Their jaws were split wide, flashing teeth far larger and sharper than the vampire lord had.

Marius hissed, readied himself, and the shadows at his back flared as though they came alive when a new howl lit the room. My head shot skyward—up towards the shadowed ceiling—as a shape emerged from the walkway above me. Blinking, I hardly could watch as it moved with unnatural speed. From the balcony, it threw itself over and fell towards the ground. It was nothing but a blur of fleshy mass, dark limbs, claws and bared teeth. The first of Eamon's wolves who leaped towards Marius never would have had the chance to survive.

It was Calix who fell from above, faint wisps of shadow still spreading from his newly changed form. He landed atop the leaping wolf, using its body to soften his fall. I felt the crack of bones reverberate in my body as the wolf was thrust to the ground beneath Calix's large paws. It exploded beneath the force; limbs and gore splattered outward in a circlet of destruction.

Blood misted the air, filling it with a sickening copper coating that seemed to lather the back of my throat. It was everywhere. Leaking around the ground, spreading like rivers through the grout between the slabs.

Eamon's wolves closest to the impact zone broke apart from their formation, some completely covered in chunks of their kin. Droplets had sprayed across Marius's face too. Compared to the glow of his ice-pale skin, the wolf's gore looked black.

Calix uncurled his monstrous form, taloned feet digging into the mess of flesh, blood and shattered bone beneath him. He towered before Marius and Millicent; his large form blocked them both from view.

Calix flicked his golden eyes away from the wolves and settled his attention on Eamon for a brief moment before looking at me. Silas's grip on me tightened. Calix's maw creased into a mask of pure fury, and he threw his head skyward, bellowing a howl that shook the foundations of the castle itself.

"I was hoping you would show yourself," Eamon said, silencing Calix's roar as he spoke. His voice oozed confidence, as did his posture, which he kept straight with shoulders rolled back. "I have been meaning to thank you."

Calix fell forward, landing on all fours. The thick tail at his back swished side to side, just beyond the mountainous curve of his strong back.

"You took my hand, but you gave me something far more useful. Power. Which is why I am going to give you a chance. You've earned it." Eamon didn't flinch as Calix prowled towards him. The wolves around Calix scattered, whimpering and yipping, but Eamon held firm. "Step aside, and I will allow you to take Rhory from this room, unharmed. He will be yours." Eamon looked back at me briefly, flashing me a smile. "It is what you have always wanted, isn't it? And you can have it. If, that is, you turn away and allow me to finish this."

Calix bowed his head, peeled his lips away from his teeth, and erupted in a growl of refusal. Although the sound was far from human, the meaning behind it was clear to all.

Eamon shrugged. "Then my *pack* will rip through you and everything in this room to see the vampires destroyed."

At his words, the wolves throughout the room continued to fuss. Eamon was far too focused on his wish to destroy Lord Marius that he didn't seem to notice his pack lacked confidence as they faced down a true monster before them.

I had stopped fighting against Silas whilst I watched the man I love contest the man who attempted to see me destroyed. All I could think about was how I burned with longing to see Eamon murdered. If I was not the one burying a dagger in his back, it hardly mattered; as long as his blood spread across this floor, that was all I wished for.

"Would you care to see what you made me?" Eamon asked, raising arms to his sides. One hand flexed with fingers, the other was simply a mound of bandages from where Calix had torn it off.

Drool leaked from between Calix's serrated teeth as he studied Eamon. I wanted to shout out and demand he finished this, but a part of me kept as silent as Marius, who watched on with blood drying on his face.

"Dear me!" Eamon laughed out. "It is a wonder what Rhory ever saw in you. You are a terrible conversationalist."

Calix snapped his jaws. Eamon thumped backwards as his skin burst into shadowed ash. As the cloud of it took over him, he disappeared for a moment and re-emerged as a wolf. His fur was as white as snow, and his eyes were so blue it made the sky look dull in comparison. He was larger than the rest of his pack, but still did not compare against a monstrous form like Calix.

The pack of wolves reformed as Eamon padded into their line. His presence re-fuelled them. Eamon howled and barked, throwing his head around frantically. It was a wonder his mouth did not froth.

Millicent raised her short blade and pointed it directly at Eamon. Her straight black hair was caught in the unseen wind of Marius's shadows. Her dark eyes peered down the sharp length of her blade as she spoke.

"When you fail, and you will, know that I will proudly wear your pelt in memory of what you took from me," Millicent vowed.

Eamon snapped his teeth. He likely did not know what Millicent spoke of, but I did. And I knew the dark promise of death that lingered in her vow.

I only hoped she was right.

The line of wolves fussed, snapping teeth at one another as they burned with an uncontrolled energy. *Hunger.*

"Everything Eamon has done to get to this very moment," Silas whispered from behind me, "And what was it for?"

I tried again to pull back, but his nails dug deeper into me and my mouth was covered firmly by his hand.

"Eamon is a bad man," Silas murmured, suddenly withdrawing his hold.

"Then stop him," I pleaded, unable to stifle the shaking of my voice. Without Silas's hand, I longed to call out for Calix but feared my distraction would be his demise.

When Silas replied in a loud shout, my entire body stilled; I tried to inhale but choked on air as his command strangled me, invaded my conscience and undid me from the inside out. "*Attack.*"

The tension in the room changed. It cracked like lightning, splitting the wolves apart until every single one of them shifted and faced a new threat.

They each faced Eamon.

My husband's eyes burst wide, and his pointed ears flattened to his head. He couldn't do so much as whimper before the pack of wolves flooded over him in a wave of exposed teeth and claws.

42

I DIDN'T SO MUCH as cry out as I watched Eamon being ripped apart.

My stomach cramped with pain, and the burn of bile crept up the back of my throat. No matter how sick it made me, I couldn't turn away.

Eamon's snow-white fur stained black with his blood. I listened to every tear of skin as the pack ripped apart his limbs with their teeth and claws. The cracks of bone breaking beneath powerful jaws revolted me, as did the bellowing laughs that came out of Silas who watched on, his eyes glowing as bright as a dying star. Limb from limb, I felt the wet tear of skin and snapping breaks of bone deep from within me. Growls of hungry torment devoured the room. Blood sprayed until the majority of it was coated across the wolves who feasted upon Eamon.

When the pack pulled away, jaws smeared with blood and skin, the corpse they left behind was unrecognisable.

"Brother." Silas turned his attention on Calix as the pack gathered around him. "It has been such a long time since I last saw you. I would ask if you missed me, but I regret to admit I already know the answer."

My entire body trembled. I looked to the mess that could no longer be described with any other word, and searched deep within me for the relief I expected to find. There was nothing. Eamon's death was unexpected, but it should have made me feel lighter. Free, perhaps. But the shackles did not lift. Grief sunk its talons into my stomach and squeezed.

"You... killed him." The words broke out of me. As I finally looked away from the pile of blood-coated flesh and fur, Silas became my focus.

"Is that not what you wanted? What you asked of me?" Silas asked, peering over his shoulder whilst Calix still prowled in his monstrous form before the vampire lord and Millicent. "You asked me to stop him, and I did."

"Why would you..." I failed to finish, gaze flicking to the dagger that waited a stretch away on the floor. The tension had not evaporated with Eamon's death, but grew heavier and more potent. Millicent hissed at the wolves closest to her, sensing the same strange emotion in the air as I did.

"You were not the only victim of Eamon's narrowed focus on revenge. He used me for what I was, and when I didn't give him what he desired, he broke me down bit by bit until my choice was taken from me. And then you... brother, you had to bite him, didn't you?" Silas focused solely on Calix again. As though reading some silent cue, three wolves separated from the pack around him and faced me. Teeth bared and covered in Eamon's blood, they narrowed their ferocious gaze upon me.

"You *turned* Eamon," Silas spat. "You revealed to him it was possible. I hid it from him for years, and you ruined it. Do you know what he did to me when he discovered what your bite did to him? What it made him?"

Calix's wolven face seemed to soften as his brother spoke, ears flicked backwards, and a light whimper broke at the back of his throat.

"I thought I knew pain, but that night when Eamon first turned..." Silas looked downward, choking on his words. "He tore into me over and over until I broke and gave him what he desired. A pack. A group of loyal men and women he could use to take down Lord Marius and complete his lifelong search for vengeance. A source powerful enough to resist the undead. To end them."

Millicent slipped from Lord Marius's side, dagger still in hand and fangs on display. Carefully she paced down from the dais like a cat on silent paws. Each step was well timed and precise, and not once did she remove her ruby stare from Silas.

"It is over," Millicent said. "Eamon is dead. Lord Marius is safe. Why don't we take this family matter elsewhere?"

Lord Marius straightened, his voice booming out across the room. "No one is to leave."

"The vampire is right," Silas sang. "You see, what first drew me to Eamon was his desires and aspirations. Eamon was not the only one who lost parents because of a vampire. I'm surprised Calix can even bear your company... bitch."

Millicent stopped only when Silas spat at her feet. Disgust wrinkled across her face as she regarded it.

"You don't want to do this," I called out, stepping towards Silas. "I know better than anyone what hurt follows Eamon in his wake. Whatever has happened, we can get through this."

"Together?" Silas spun wildly on me, a look of feral humour creasing his face. "Get your head out of the clouds, Rhory."

"And how will it end? With more bloodshed? More families torn in two?" I snapped, unable to catch a breath as the presence of my anxiety swelled in my chest.

Silas trailed me with his sickly gaze, all the while the room was filled with the growls of wolves. Beneath it all, a small whimper sounded. Auriol.

"There is nothing you can say to sympathise with me. If it is humanity you are looking for, then my dearest brother should have saved me all those years ago before Eamon tore it from me."

Auriol gasped out again. The silver chains holding her down hissed into flesh and clattered against stone.

"What about her?" I said, gesturing to Auriol. "Auriol loves you. She played no part in this."

Silas glanced to his grandmother, and for a moment his face pinched in a painful sadness.

"Her suffering will end," Silas said, his voice detached as his gaze was lost to us all. "Soon."

Millicent edged slowly towards Auriol. Her movements were slight and soundless that Silas didn't notice as his focus was fixed on me.

"Silas, please. End this. I know there is a part of you left. A part Eamon could never reach. Grasp it—"

"Enough!" Silas screamed, his voice catching in his throat. "I don't wish to hear this anymore."

Calix shot forward, ready to leave Marius's side to help me.

I raised a hand and looked the monster dead in his gilded eyes. "Stay."

He couldn't refuse me, even if he wanted to. Calix's tail folded between his legs. He stopped his pursuit, falling back into line with the vampire lord who hissed like a feral cat at the wolves who prowled around him.

"Well." Silas clapped, the sound echoing around us like thunder. "Would you look at that. My brother, the man Auriol believes worthy enough to snatch the mantle as alpha, yet here he is... whimpering under the command of some worthless weak man. I pity you, brother, truly I do."

Calix flashed teeth, spittle dripping down his thick maw. Millicent was only a stretch away from Auriol now. Silas was focused on his brother and the humour of watching him follow my command that he didn't notice as she reached her.

If she could free Auriol, only she would have the power to command Silas to stand down. She could end this.

"They killed our parents, Calix. Eamon was many things, but he was right in his want to purify the world. And we, we have the power to do it. We are the key. You can either stand in my way and be torn down or stand beside me whilst we fix this world. No more hiding in the shadows, brother. No more tunnels. We can be free."

I couldn't swallow without feeling the swell of my heart in my throat. How could Eamon have died, yet his words still lived on so vividly?

"Killing me will not solve your torment," Marius called out.

"It may not," Silas said. "But I will still enjoy every moment."

The clink of chains falling upon stone silenced the room. All heads turned towards it, to see Millicent helping Auriol from the ground, the tatters of her clothes around her human frame barely covering her modesty. Her skin was a patchwork of burns and marks. Without Millicent holding her up, the old woman would never have had a chance to stand.

"No," Silas breathed, understanding what was to come.

Auriol's shadowed eyes flickered open. Her eyelids were heavy, her skin almost tinged with purple from the poisoning of wolfsbane. Limp silver hair fell over her shoulders, obscuring the sagging of skin which clung to her old bones like wax to a candle.

Millicent's lips tipped upwards in a sneer as Silas began moving towards them. In one arm she held the only person powerful enough to control the pack, Calix and Silas. In the other, she held the twin blade to the one she had given me.

I held my breath, waiting for Auriol to do something. Her mouth parted, exposing a paled tongue between clenched teeth. My mind screamed with the desperation for Auriol to end this, to call out and finish this war of blood and family.

Calix howled with fury, unmoving from his place beside Marius just as I commanded him. I was not his alpha, but he followed my words without hesitation. Silas shouted out, hoping to smother his grandmother's pending command.

"Come on," Millicent mouthed, her grin fading the closer Silas got. "*Do* something."

The whites of Auriol's eyes where bloodshot with violent veins of red and purple. She could barely keep them open. I began to move. Power swirled around my hands, coating my skin in curling flames of gold light, as I chased after Silas.

Silas changed too. Shadow burst from his skin, peeling it away in ash and dust, to reveal the arm of a monster beneath. Yellow curved claws dragged beside him as he reached his grandmother.

Millicent released Auriol, forcing the woman behind her, just as Silas met them. She clattered to the floor with a thud, no more a flesh filled bag of brittle bones.

Silas couldn't stop himself. He thrust his clawed arm forward as the rest of his body broke apart to reveal the wolf beneath. Millicent met him, shielding Auriol with her body.

I would never forget the sound of Silas's claws ripping deep into Millicent's stomach. It seemed every other sound faded into the room, allowing the slow wet tear to sing through the silence. Millicent's red eyes bulged wide as her face broke into a snarl. Silas hoisted her from the ground, holding her up with only the claws he'd embedded deep into her. Gravity tugged her downward, encouraging the claws to continue their pursuit through her stomach and up to her chest.

A noise tore out of me. It was feral and pained and boiled with my emotions. Millicent's name rushed out of the incoherent sounds, leaving its own scarred mark in the flesh of my throat. I couldn't take my eyes off her. Not once did Millicent scream out in pain. Beside her paled taut lips and wide red eyes, her face was not a mask of agony... but a mask of determination.

She raised the dagger aloft before the monster and brought it down with a warrior's cry.

Silas couldn't pull away completely, not when his claws had trapped him close to her. The dagger missed the intended mark of his forehead. Instead, it sliced down the side of his face, clean through his eye.

The blade fell from Millicent's hand as Silas threw his large, wolven head from side to side. Blood sprayed across Millicent, casting her in droplets of gore as dark as her obsidian hair. She smiled through it all, catching Silas's blood in her mouth and across her teeth.

Every being in the room watched as Millicent's smile faded. It was cleared from existence as Silas gathered himself enough to wrap his large powerful jaw around her neck. With a sickening wet snap, Silas tore Millicent from his claws with the force of his mouth and threw her, as though she was nothing but a discarded bone.

I didn't dare blink. There was nothing I could do but watch, vaguely aware of the muffled sounds of chaos as the room exploded in it. All I could do was study the strange scene as Millicent's body crashed against the floor, smearing blood in its wake, until she came to a perfect stop directly before me.

43

MILLICENT BLED out in my arms, her blood staining my clothes and skin. To the touch, she was as cold as fresh winter snow, so cold it almost burned as my fingers graced her skin, brushing hair from her face until they came back completely slick and wet.

"Please," I begged her, tears rolling down my nose and falling upon her upturned face like rain. She could hardly keep her eyes open. They fluttered shut, and each time it took longer for her to find the strength to open them again.

"Did I hurt him?" she gasped, flashing pointed teeth covered in her blood. Millicent coughed, forcing blood to pump out of the jagged tears across the skin of her neck.

I could hear Silas's thunderous roars above the howls of his pack. Calix was fighting them back from Marius, throwing his powerful limbs wide to knock those who attempted to attack out of the way. Bodies of wolves skittered across the floor like skipping stones on a lake, but they didn't sink. They got back up and raced towards him with more desperation and fury.

"You did," I replied, swallowing the bile that burned at the back of my throat.

Silas could hardly calm himself. He clutched at his gouged eye, pressing the pad of his monstrous claws to the now empty socket as he roared in agony and fury.

Millicent smiled weakly before breaking into another fit of coughs. I placed my hand atop the wounds on her neck. Flaps of flesh moved beneath my palm. Silas's teeth had cut so deep it prevented her from healing.

"But I didn't kill him, did I?"

I shook my head, more tears falling. "No, you didn't."

Although his eye was shattered beneath the force of her dagger, and he was momentarily blinded, Silas could still fight. He would fight, as soon as he gathered himself.

"The fucker... he really hurt me," Millicent hissed, skin turning ashen before me. Cracks formed across her blood-soaked skin. Time was finally catching up with her. I blinked and her youthful face sank in on itself. Even the lustrous obsidian of her hair faded, leaving grey and silver in its place.

"Tell me what to do," I pleaded, not willing to let her go.

Whilst I cried over her ageing body, Millicent smiled up at me, looking skyward at something she only seemed to see. "I am going to see my brother again. Don't cry for me, Rhory... I have lived more lives than you could imagine. And I'm ready... I'm ready for this curse to end."

Her eyes fluttered as she looked back at me. Her skin peeled away in clouds of ash beneath my fingers, making it hard to hold on to her.

"And just as I was beginning to rather like you, Rhory Coleman."

I traced my hand over her face, feeling her skin come away beneath it.

"I'm sorry," I sobbed, heart breaking in my chest. "I'm sorry for everything I have caused you and the loss you have endured because of me."

Millicent raised her hand up to my face. Her arm shook and trembled like a leaf stuck in a storm. Her hand was aged and bent with crooked bones that belonged on a corpse. I didn't pull away from her. Selfishly wishing to prolong this moment, I closed my eyes and leaned into her freezing touch, wishing to memorise it for a lifetime.

"Be quiet, you sappy fool. I do not wish to hear it."

I placed my hand on hers and held it there. Now was not the time to honour past promises or heed old threats. Millicent was dying, and she could do little to stop me from using my power to sooth her. It was the easiest choice I had ever made.

Gold light slipped outward from my hand. It blossomed to life, enveloping her crooked fingers in a halo of pure, painless emotion. As I had many times before, I drew in all her discomfort and buried it deep inside of me. In her final moments, I would ensure she felt nothing but the kiss of peace and serenity. That was the very least I could do for her.

Millicent's mouth parted. She exhaled a long gasp as her eyes rolled back into her head. A single, blood-red tear ran down the side of her face. All the while, her smile never faded. When she reached her end, it was with her smile proudly cut across her face.

"Goodbye, Rhory," she whispered, her lips coming apart and melting in ash. "Thank you for…"

Beneath my hand, hers crumbled to nothing. Where her body had been was now a pile of ash and dust buried among blood-stained clothes.

Grief stabbed its talons into my heart and refused to let go. I levelled my stare from her remains to Silas who threw his wolven head back and forth. All I could think about was his death. I focused on the boiling fury that sparked deep within me. It burned hot, but regardless, I reached down and grasped it.

I got up, allowing Millicent's ash to fall from my legs in a cloud of death around me. My power raged around my hands, gold and brilliant. One hand was fisted, the other held tight onto the dagger Millicent had used to tear out Silas's eye. The leather-bound handle still held Millicent's frozen touch, and that also fuelled me.

Emotions swarmed around me. Pain, anger, hunger, desperation, hate. Each step from Millicent's remains felt as though I waded through mud. My legs fought against the resistance of emotions, kicking through it as I navigated towards Silas.

Silas calmed suddenly. He must have sensed me coming because he snapped his large head towards me and bored through me with his one remaining eye. Where the other golden orb had been was now an empty socket of dripping blood that oozed down his black fur and smeared freely into his parted jaw.

Then I felt another presence behind me. Strong talon-tipped claws sliced at the stone floor as Calix loomed over me at my side. I risked a glance and stared deep into his glowing eyes. He had left Lord Marius to fight for himself against the onslaught of Silas's pack. I longed to tell Calix to leave, but his presence stilled the frantic clash of my heart. Lord Marius cried out in anguish as he fought tooth and sharp nail against the beasts that were commanded to kill him.

"Your first mistake was not killing me when you had the chance," I spat, pointing the silver-bladed dagger at Silas. He dropped on all fours, claws scratching against stone and jaws snapping vigorously. "It ends. Now."

I stepped back, allowing Calix to prowl forward. As much as I longed to draw the silver across Silas's body, I would be dead within moments. Winning a fight was knowing one's strength. And this was not my fight, no matter how I wished it damned was.

Silas regarded his brother, tilted his head knowingly, and I was certain his elongated jaw peaked upwards into a smile. Calix exploded in a howl, matched by the rumbling growl his brother made. Silas leaped skyward first, and Calix joined in. As both bodies crashed, I felt the boom rattle my bones.

Lord Marius cried out as I watched, slightly dazed by the vicious grace the monstrous wolves attacked each other. It was the second cry from the vampire that had me turning to face him. A wolf was on him, jaw clamped around his outstretched arm.

I blinked and saw Millicent in the waiting dark, screaming out in pain as Eamon and his pack tore into her in the cellar of my home. It was enough to steel my mind. Energy buzzed through me, brightening my power and forcing my body forward. Silver blade slicing out before me, I ran for the vampire lord. Lord Marius wailed on the floor, clutching his blood-soaked arm. The pain of the wolf's bite was like liquid fire, I felt it sing as my power picked it up. It was so powerful, I didn't need to touch him to sense it.

I swung the blade fast and hard, bringing it into the neck of the wolf. It yelped, releasing Marius and skirting back from me. The silver was enough to disable the creature. It gave me the spare moment to raise up a glowing hand before it could completely escape.

As my fingers graced its fur-coated skin, I forced my exhaustion into it whilst stealing its strength as payment. My mind sparked, rejuvenated with the wolf's energy, whilst the creature slumped in a heap before us. I kicked hard, forcing the limp body down the steps of the dais when it knocked down the wolf who attacked next.

On I fought, muscles burning and mind alive. Time mattered little. Nothing mattered but surviving. If we failed, Millicent's death would be pointless. I couldn't allow that.

I snarled back at the wolves that were brave enough to come for me. I cut through so many that the silver of the blade was buried beneath dark blood.

With each death, I drew on my past self. The part of me who had been stolen. The part Calix had gifted back to me with his return to my life.

I was blindsided as a wolf pounced on me out of nowhere. Its jaw snapped inches before my face, but I knew from the agony I felt pouring off its skin that my blade had buried itself deep into its soft underbelly. I drew it upwards with everything I had. Its skin separated with ease until the ropes of its innards spilled over my chest and legs.

Pushing the wolf off, I ensured he felt the pain tenfold as I used my power to intensify what it experienced.

Three wolves were left, howling in chorus with Marius's cries and the roars of the brothers caught in their battle. I sensed the remaining creature's trepidation as they regarded me. One of them raced forward but lost its confidence as I swung the blade towards its face. He tumbled down the dais steps, reeling onto its side with a sharp whimper.

"Come on then!" I screamed, waving the blade around as though it was a sword of great myth. I saw the golden glow of my power reflected in the wolf's eyes as they looked from the death I had caused, and the promise of more death leaking with light from my hands.

The wolf who had fallen did not stay down for long. When it got up from the floor, it whimpered, barked its jaws at me, and ran towards the door at the far end of the room. The final two who remained followed it, nipping and yipping at its heels.

"Witch," Marius hissed, fingers coated in his own blood as he held his arm close to his chest. The sound snapped my attention back to him. The dais was awash with blood. It coated the stone floor, pooling it in the vision of a dark lake. As was Marius, whose skin glistened with the obsidian gore of his lifeforce.

"Help," he gasped, blood gargling in his throat, "Me."

There was no room to think. I almost tripped over the intestines of the wolf I had sliced open as I threw myself towards the screeching vampire lord. He reached out towards me with blood-slick nails, and gripped on with the last bit of strength he had.

"I can take your pain away," I said, breathless as I brought myself to Marius's side.

He glanced up at me, broken and weak. With my power glowing around my hands like fire, I felt the whispers of his agony. It was enough to make someone beg for death.

"But I cannot save you." That was beyond my capabilities. I was the puppeteer of emotions, not life.

"Jak!" Marius cried out for his love, spit flying out from his mouth. There was a glassy haze to his dark red eyes. It passed over like a cloud, sending the man into a maze of deliria. "Jak. Jak! I do not want to die."

I clasped Marius's hand and forced my will into him. He was in no mind to accept or refuse, so I acted as I knew I must. The vampire lord's eyes burst open as though breaking free from the trance his pain had trapped him in. I felt his fear. The fear of death. Fear of being forced to leave someone behind without saying goodbye. And I took it. Snatched it alongside any other feral or vile emotion I could find.

Lord Marius blinked up at me with his moon-wide eyes, as though seeing me for the first time. I sensed he tried to pull himself away, but I held on firm. I would not let go until every ounce of his pain was mine to claim.

"You need to help Calix," I cried out, grasping the burning fire of the wolf's bite until it became so real to me that my arm burned as though I had been bitten. I felt the skin rip and blood leak out, although there was no wound to see on me. Regardless, the agony was real.

The dull light of the room had become too much. My head throbbed, and I felt death lingering, but it wasn't my death. This was

Marius's impending doom. And, if he didn't heal, the poison of the bite would claim him.

"I cannot—"

I released his hand, withdrawing my power. His pain dulled almost instantly, flooding back into the vampire in a tidal wave. He was knocked backwards by its return, so much so that the vampire lord could not fight me as I brought my wrist to his mouth, sliced it across his exposed fangs, and let my blood spill freely into his throat.

My head spun from the release. It was the second time I had given blood today, and my body knew it. Weakness crept in at the sides of my vision, but I refused to pull away. At first, Marius did not flinch. He gargled on my life's essence as it dribbled down his throat. Then his lips closed down on my wrist and I felt his tongue lap at my cut skin like a dog to water.

Pleasure rolled down my spine. It was all consuming, I forgot about the world as it crest over me in a wave of pure force. Cocking my head back, I groaned skyward, with my eyes drawing closed.

Marius attempted to pull back after a while, but he had not drunk enough. I held the back of his head and forced his mouth to my wrist harder.

As the vampire lord drank my blood from me, sucking my veins dry and making the room feel distant and strange, I watched the wolves fight as though I observed them through a muted lens.

Calix and Silas threw themselves around the great room in a bundle of claws and teeth. Walls cracked as they crashed into them. The ground thundered with their force. Even the air seemed to hum with their howls and cries. Both were covered in blood. There was so much. My eyes couldn't track their movements long enough to discern whose blood it was, not as they both moved with such speed and strength. It didn't matter. All that mattered was the sucking and nipping of Marius's mouth on my wrist and the feeling of warmth that spread across my chest.

I gasped out in disappointment when Marius finally withdrew his teeth from my skin. This time, it was me who was far too weak to refuse him.

Marius was no longer lying on the floor. He knelt before me, lowering me to the wet ground until it was I lying down. His lips were painted red, some blood stained his chin and neck.

A sorrowful pain creased his forehead and passed behind his bright, alert eyes.

"Thank you," Marius said softly as he released me. My head pressed against the floor, making the world look as though it was on an axis. Marius brushed the red curls from my head, his cold hand welcome against the burning temperature which gripped my body.

"Calix." The name broke out of me, taking the final dregs of my strength. If I could have raised my hand and pointed, I would have. But my body was numb, and my mind detached.

Marius nodded. The grimace caught across his face, twisting it into a mask of something deadly. Then, in a blink, he moved. His body was a blur as he joined the fight between brothers.

Calix was on the ground whilst Silas towered over him. Darkness swelled in at the corners of my eyes, making it harder to keep them open. I could do nothing but watch as Silas brought down his split jaws towards Calix's exposed neck.

I didn't wish to look away, but my heavy eyes betrayed me. I fought hard to open them. When I managed only a slither of a parting it was to find that Silas no longer pinned my love down. Marius had his arm wrapped around the Silas's neck, distracting him long enough for Calix to get off the floor. The vampire clung to the beast's back like a child whilst he brought his teeth down into Silas's thick neck. Over and over, Marius bit. Flesh tore away and gore burst from the fresh wound. Silas roared, claws reaching up for Marius to tear him free.

Calix was there. He grasped his brother's jaw with one large talon-tipped paw. Marius continued to feast on Silas, who could no longer howl in pain, not with Calix grasping the lower part of his jaw as though it belonged to him. Silas's single eye remained wide and knowing as he sensed what was to come. He kept it open the entire time, refusing to look away as Calix growled inches from his face.

Then Calix's growl exploded in a howl.

He jolted his muscular arm and ripped Silas's face into two parts. Silas's jaw came away with little resistance. Marius leapt from his back before the limp body fell to the ground with a shuddering thump.

Calix discarded the dripping mass of bone and flesh. I winced as the wet slap of the jaw was thrown to the ground where it slid to a stop at the bottom of the dais before me. Teeth and bone flashed through slick meaty flesh as it dribbled blood, wetting the stone beneath it.

Sickness stormed deep in my stomach, but I couldn't move, couldn't look away. If I closed my eyes, I understood the shadows would be waiting. But it was growing harder to fight them. My body was no longer my own. Nor was my mind.

Soon enough, the darkness closed in, shielding me from the horror of the lump of Silas's useless meat. It finally claimed me. Somewhere beyond it, I heard my name, but I couldn't be sure. I would have opened my eyes to see if someone spoke it, but I was married to the darkness. And, like Eamon, it refused to let me go.

The only thing I was certain of was the pain across my wrist. The echo of Marius's kiss lingered as a reminder of why I was fading.

"It is over, my love." A voice from the darkness sang. It was familiar and warm. It was home.

Again, I fought with every last scrap of strength I had, but I couldn't open my eyes. Not even a little.

When the voice spoke again, it was intimate as it was distant—far off, as though it spoke through miles of darkened tunnels. Three words, that was the last I heard; I focused on them as they echoed, growing quieter with each recurrence until there was only silence.

"I've got you."

44

I WOKE to the caress of lips against my mouth. The touch was gentle yet commanding, enough to discard the shadows and draw me back out into the light. My eyes fluttered open, adjusting to the warm amber glow that coaxed me out of sleep. As my body came alive, I was vaguely aware of the pressure of bedsheets strewn across my lower half. Pinpricks of needles tickled across my legs and feet, causing them to dance beneath the silken sheets.

Disappointment purred through my confused mind as the lips finally drew back and left me. I longed to call out, to demand they return, but my body did not yet feel like my own. Not entirely.

The familiar brush of a finger pressed to my forehead. Beneath its sudden presence a cascade of shivers spread over my skin. The single touch was the stone that was thrown into the still lake, creating gargantuan waves of disturbance. I opened my eyes enough to make out the shape of a man hovering above me. He was haloed in golden light.

The owner of the tender touch drew a finger across my forehead, down past my temple and along the curve of my jaw. "For a moment there… you had me thinking I lost you, Little Red."

My heart burst in my chest as the blurred figure came into focus. Calix leaned down close, blocking out the light so all I could focus on was him. He wore a smile that had the power to break my heart and remake it. His light brown hair had been gathered in a bun held together by a tie of leather string. A single strand fell over his face as he leaned in once again and brought his lips to mine.

"Calix," I exhaled his name, the word muffled by the press of our mouths.

My body arched upwards, desperate to eradicate every inch between us. I lifted both arms and linked them around the back of his neck. This time, Calix would not pull away from my kiss until I desired.

"Careful," he moaned as my tongue met his.

"Don't let me go," I managed, voice rough as stone.

"I will never let you go," Calix replied before diving back into my kiss. "Never."

Slowly, my mind woke alongside my body. Flashes of the bloodied room and the death that haunted it flooded my mind, replacing the warmth Calix gifted me with a terrifying chill. Questions overwhelmed me, distracting me from the man in my arms. I found my eyes drawn to the wrapping of white bandages across my wrist and the faint pink stain of blood that seeped from beneath it.

Calix felt my body stiffen beneath his hold. It was his signal to draw away.

"Where am I?" I asked, trying to get a better look around me but my neck ached and the light was suddenly too bright to bear. Calix lowered me slowly back to the cloud of pillows that supported my neck. As he stepped back, I could make out grand stone walls, elaborate sconces burning with pillar candles that reflected light off gilded frames with time-worn paintings. The room was somewhat moderate but adorned with rich coloured rugs and dark-wood furniture.

"Lord Marius insisted you stayed here until you healed," Calix said, his face creasing with obvious concern. A shadow passed behind his eyes as he spoke. I wondered if the same shadow mirrored in my gaze—we both could no longer hide from what had happened.

"And where is here?" I repeated, knowing I was certainly not being seen in St Myrinn's. Beside the narrow bed I lay in and the dark wood cabinet at the bed's side, there was little other furniture in the room. It was the perfect blend of plain, whilst also feeling as though I had stepped back in time. Even the air was thick with age. With each rasped inhale I felt the history of this stone room seep within me.

"Castle Dread," Calix confirmed.

Alarm clawed my body. My sore muscles spasmed at my physical recoiling and I gasped out, "I need to get out of here..."

"You are safe," Calix said quickly. "You are safe, Rhory. I will let nothing happen to you."

I looked to the closed door at the end of the room, half expecting someone to barge in and take me for being a witch.

"You need to drink something," Calix offered, fussing with a chalice on the bedside cabinet. "It has been three nights and you have hardly had anything to eat or drink besides what little water I have encouraged you to take. Finish a glass, and then we can talk. About it all."

Three days. I could hardly comprehend the time I had missed, so much so that I didn't refuse Calix as he brought the cold metal to my mouth, held the back of my neck with his hand and tipped the chalice. The cold rush of water was divine and I groaned as it soothed my dry throat. I had not realised just how thirsty I was until my eyes stared at the empty bottom of the chalice.

"More," I gasped as water dribbled down my chin and the burning in my throat soothed.

Calix poured another. The sound of water filling the chalice was the most beautiful song. I finished the second offering quicker than the first, gulping each mouthful down as though it was my last.

Dribbles of water slipped beyond my lips and fell into my hairline. Calix took his thumb and gathered the stray droplets with it. "I cannot express the relief I have for seeing you with your eyes open. Rhory..." Calix's voice faltered. It faded into a long sigh.

I had not yet noticed the exhaustion that painted Calix's face. His eyes were ringed with dark shadows, his skin pale as though the castle had drained the colour from him. Across his neck, I could see the faint red marks from newly healed wounds. I longed to reach up and touch them, to kiss them just as he did with the marks Eamon had left on my body.

My eyes drank him in with the same thirst my body had for the water. I trailed him from head to foot, recognising the shirt he wore was far too tight on his torso. It was clear he had not washed, nor was he dressed in his own attire.

His fist was pressed into the side of my bed. I crept my fingers across the sheets and wove them around his balled-up hand until it unravelled like a flower to sunlight.

"Take me home," I asked, staring deep into his eyes.

Calix held my gaze for a moment, then dropped his stare to the floor.

"What is wrong?"

Calix exhaled. It was long and slow. His sigh alone told tales of the tension he harboured inside of him. "My invitation to stay here has expired. Lord Marius has given me instructions to leave."

"Then we will go," I said, trying to push myself up, but fire burned at my wrist as I leaned on it. I hissed out through clenched teeth as my mind spun from the sudden rush of discomfort.

"Careful," Calix fussed, a deep growl emanating from deep in his throat. "The bite marks will take time to heal. If you tear open the fresh skin, the wounds will persist."

I could still feel the haunting pleasure of Lord Marius's bite. How his tongue lapped at my skin and sucked hard. But I also remembered how it was Calix's face in the dark of my mind. It was him I had imagined when the world faded.

"I'm fine, Calix. I am. Come on, help me up and we will leave..."

Calix's eyes screamed with refusal. "Rhory, I cannot take you with me."

"Yes!" I snapped with urgency. "Yes, you can."

Calix shook his head, returning his hand to the side of my face. He held it tenderly. I leaned into him, never wishing for him to pull away.

"Lord Marius has bid me a pardon. He allows me to keep my life, but I must leave Darkmourn as part of our arrangement."

I couldn't bear the broken gleam in his eyes. "Arrangement?" I echoed, the word tasting strange in my mouth.

Calix winced but didn't look away; I could see the pain that statement gifted him. "They know the danger I pose. Marius will not take any further risks."

"You killed Silas. You killed your own brother to save Marius! What more do you need to sacrifice to prove you would be no threat?" I didn't dare to blink, fearing of seeing the bloodshed. In my mind's eye, I could still see the torn half-formed jaw of Silas on the floor before me. Discarded. Useless. No one could survive that. Then another death flooded over me. Millicent. And all at once, I felt debilitated by the memory. If I wasn't in this bed, I would have been knocked down by the force of my grief.

"I may have helped save him, but that does not change what I am."

"This is wrong," I said, almost shouting.

"It is done."

"Then I will talk to him!" I said, fumbling over my words. "I saved his fucking life. If I didn't give him my blood, he would have died by the wolf's bite. Just like..."

I couldn't speak her name. It lodged in my throat like a thorn.

Calix smiled down at me, although the upturn of his mouth did little to conceal the sadness in his eyes. "Millicent got what she always wanted," Calix said. "It was what she asked Auriol for when she first found us."

Suddenly, the light of the burning sconces grew too harsh. I pinched my eyes closed, trying to unscramble Calix's words.

"She always wanted to be released from her..."

"Curse," I answered for him, echoing what Millicent had said when she perished in the cradle of my arms.

I opened my eyes to find Calix staring through me with his. The gold sheen of his irises glowed as tears pooled within them. There was something so heartbreaking and beautiful to see such a man cry.

"How could you leave me?" I complained as the sharp stabbing pain exploded behind my eyes. "After everything."

"I told you, I could never leave you."

"That makes no sense!" I shouted now, wanting to grasp Calix's shirt so I could prevent him from ever moving away.

Calix didn't answer. Instead, he brushed the hair away from my forehead and brought a kiss to my sticky skin. "I am so proud of you, Rhory."

"As am I," another voice sang from the doorway. Neither of us had noticed it had opened, nor that someone had entered.

Lord Marius stood before us, skin glowing bright as a star. His posture was pin-straight, with shoulders rolled back and hands held behind him. I felt Calix tense; he moved and stood at the end of the bed, blocking the vampire lord from view.

"Am I not permitted to say my farewells?" Calix asked, voice laced with something feral.

I could not see Marius's expression as Calix shielded me, but I could certainly hear the slight edge of fear in his voice as he chose his next words carefully. "Of course. I simply wanted to check on our patient, to ensure he is improving."

"Rhory is fine."

I shouldn't have enjoyed another man speaking for me, but when Calix did, my entire body buzzed with adrenaline. It was an emotion which seemed entirely misplaced in such a situation.

"Then my offer of blood would not be required?" Marius asked.

"As it hasn't been required for the past three nights," Calix replied, stone cold.

"Even if my blood could have healed Rhory sooner?"

The thought of ingesting the blood of a vampire displeased me. It was strange to hear it so blatantly offered, when Lord Marius himself was the one to outlaw such a thing.

"I am sure it would," Calix said, glancing back at me. "But Rhory is strong. He does not require your aid. He needs no one."

That was a lie. I wished to shout at Calix, to remind him just how wrong he was. I needed someone. He was the one who I needed the most.

"Indeed, he is strong." Marius stepped aside so I could see him. I caught the flash as his tongue traced his lower lip. A contemplative glint passed over his ruby eyes as he regarded me. "As he had just so beautifully put it, he *fucking* saved my life. I am in debt to him."

I cringed with embarrassment for being overheard but refused to lower my stare from the vampire.

"And because of your bravery, I am forever in your debt," Marius said. "I also have someone who is *dying* to meet you and thank you himself."

I wanted to spit at him, to show just how little I cared for his gift of thanks. The only gift I wanted stood before me and was moments from being banished from Darkmourn entirely.

"There is only one thing I want," I spat.

Marius regarded me for a moment before turning his eyes back to Calix. My proud protector, who had hardly moved an inch since the vampire lord stepped into the room.

"Master Grey," Marius said. "Your grandmother has awoken too if you would like to visit her. Then, I am afraid, it will be time for you to take your leave."

"Auriol, is she alive?" My question broke out of me, demanding both of their attention. I had almost convinced myself that she had died. In fact, it pained me to admit, but I hardly paid her any mind after Silas murdered Millicent.

"Of course, she is," Marius said, dark brows pinching over his brow. "If there is one thing about my friend Auriol... she is stubborn in the face of death. She is an example of the defiance of the mortals she so cares to protect. And she is a long-standing friend, and I treasure friends. The years we have known one another have made us family, although she wouldn't care to admit it. Auriol's wellbeing is of my utmost importance."

Calix scoffed to himself, granting him a sideways glance from the vampire lord.

"Will you be banishing her then? Is that how you treat friends, or just those who kill their own family to save you?" I asked.

"Auriol," Marius said carefully, her name rolling over his silver tongue, "Will stay here with me until her brother, Arlo, returns to care for her. I am sure he would be highly interested in what she has become during his absence—as am I."

"A weapon who can destroy you, that is what you mean. That is why you are sending Calix away, even after he proved he is no threat to you," I spat, anger boiling at his decision to care for Auriol, but to discard Calix as though he was nothing.

"Yes, exactly, however I think your annoyance should not be aimed at me entirely," Marius confirmed, bringing a sharp nailed finger to his jaw and scratching at it. "Calix, have you informed your dearest that the decision for you to leave Darkmourn was, in fact, your own suggestion?"

My heart stilled, quivered, then felt as though it would shatter entirely.

Calix turned his head sideways so I could witness his profile draw down into a frown. "I had not."

Marius tutted, pulling a face with wide eyes and raised brows. "Oh, well. Perhaps I will wait beyond the door as you say your final goodbyes."

I couldn't utter a word as Marius swept from the room, leaving the destruction his revelation had left in it.

"Tell me he is lying," I said.

"Rhory, I am sorry."

"What was the other option?" My voice was stoic, and as empty of emotion as I felt.

Calix tensed, his eyes flashing a molten gold as he looked away from me. "It doesn't matter—"

"What was the fucking option, Calix!?" I screamed, not caring for the cramping of pain that seized across my chest.

Calix slowly looked up at me. Even without my power, I could read the guilt that oozed from him. "I am a monster. The big bad wolf that killed your mother, my brother, Millicent, and almost you. I am dangerous. If a rabid dog attacked someone, it would be put down."

"Death?" I said, hating how the word sounded when it came out of my mouth. "That is no option."

"No," Calix corrected. "Marius is a fair man. He would not have killed me."

"Spit it out then," I said, anger and love coiling inside of me in an inferno. "For once, take your chance and be honest with me."

My words struck Calix and he stumbled back. It took a moment for him to right himself. When he did, he paced towards the side of the bed, his hand racing across the sheets tentatively. He knelt beside it, forcing me to turn my head on the pillow to see him. Wide-eyed and face sheet white, he leaned in and pressed a lingering kiss to my forehead.

"Sometimes we make sacrifices for the better," Calix said softly. "Just know I am proud of my decision, as I am proud of you."

Exhaustion kept me from fighting him. I felt the finality in his words and didn't wish to spend our last moments arguing over something that would not change. If he desired to leave me, I would not give into my pity and wallow in it.

"Tell me where to go... where to find you?" I asked, unable to hide the quiver in my voice.

"The world is a large place." Calix brought his lips from my forehead to my mouth and kissed me again. His lips lingered far longer than the one on my head. I refused to kiss him back. Refused to show him I cared, when internally I felt as though I was being torn into pieces. "Someone dear to me once told me that Darkmourn is merely a small part of a large world. Who knows what else is out there."

"The world is not a big enough place to stop me from finding you," I said, determination burning in my eyes. "Calix, I will find you."

He leaned in, eyes racing over my face as though he drank me in for a final time. "I am counting on it."

"I am serious," I said, tears cutting down my face. "No one can stop me. Not Marius. Not Darkmourn. Not anything. I lost you once and found you. Do you hear what I am saying to you, Calix? I *will* find you again."

Calix steeled his expression but couldn't hide the tears that lingered in his eyes. "You are free, Rhory. Free from Eamon, from me. You can decide the path you take. I do not deserve your promises."

"The only path I wish to take is the one with you standing beside me," I said, choking on the truth of the words. "Because I love you."

"I know," Calix replied, smiling through the palpable sadness.

"Is that it? Is that all you can say?"

"The last time I told you I loved you, you never came back to me. I pondered if I had never said it in the first place, you would have come to me that night we were to run away. The night before your mother cursed your mind to forget me. If I don't say it now, then you really will be forced to find me."

"You are cruel," I said as I urged his mouth back to mine. My fingers knotted in his hair, keeping him in place.

"Well," Calix said. "I am the big bad wolf. Being cruel seems like a fitting title for me."

"Okay, if that is what you wish to be… Then I will hunt you down. Hunt you down and slaughter you myself for leaving."

A shiver ran across my entire body as Calix's lips moved to my ear and whispered, "Is that a promise?"

I grasped his hand and let my power spill out of me. It lit the room with a glow of gold light that mirrored the stunning tones of Calix's eyes. When I replied, I wanted Calix to feel my honesty. To recognise the burning truth in my words deep in his soul. I let my emotions pour into his being as I replied.

"I promise."

45

JAK BISHOP WAITED for me in the library, just as Marius had said he would have. The vampire lord patted a hand on my shoulder as he left me beyond the door, bidding me farewell with a final thanks for saving his life. I couldn't respond to him. Words failed me, as all I felt was numb. *Empty*. Empty without Calix, who had been forced to leave hours before this. Knowing it was Calix's choice to go not only drove the knife of pain into my chest but twisted it thoroughly.

He had left me.

There was certainly nothing beastly about Marius. All the stories my mother had told me, all her warnings to keep my power hidden, seemed almost misplaced as I stood before the door to Jak Bishop's haven.

I raised my hand, ready to bring my knuckles down to knock, when a silken voice rang out from within.

"No need for formalities," Jak said, his voice barely muffled by the thick wooden door. "You can enter, Rhory Coleman. My home is open to the likes of you."

The brass handle of the door was freezing to the touch as I grasped, turned, and pushed it open. Warmth welcomed me, as did light. The glow of freshly lit fires bathed the library in gold and amber. I had not noticed just how cold the rest of Castle Dread seemed until I was engulfed in the room's embrace.

The door shut with a final click at my back. There was no going back now. Now I faced the very thing I had hidden from. The very being my mother had betrayed me and my father to keep me from.

Jak sat on a large red cushioned chair with his legs drawn up and a big leather-bound book open across his lap. From my vantage point at the door I could see only the side of his face. Dark curls fell over his forehead, gently brushing just shy of his perfectly shaped brows. He was a beauty, just as the stories told. With large all-seeing eyes and smooth skin stretched across the proud bone structure of his face. The fire lit him from a certain angle that made the hollows of his cheek deep, and the red vampiric glow of his eyes like the freshest of blood.

He closed the book with a thud and hugged it to his chest. As he beckoned me over to him, I caught the silver foiling of lettering across the spine. For a moment, I thought the swirling calligraphy spelled out his name.

"So, you are the witch who saved my husband," Jak said calmly, eyeing me up and down as I sat in the thick-cushioned chair before him. "In doing so, saving me and all those we have sired since Darkmourn first fell."

"I did what I had to do," I replied.

"Then it is only just that I personally thank you."

"It was the right thing to do," I said, voice void of emotion; Jak furrowed his perfectly sleek brows downward as he noticed. "But it was Calix who saved your husband. Not me. Perhaps your thanks would be better off given to him, for it would be wasted on the likes of me."

"Keeping him alive is our thanks. We have yet to understand what he is, but it is clear how deadly he can be." Jak lowered his eyes, fingers picking at the leather bindings of the book.

"So, the tales are true. You *are* unkind."

Jak smiled, welcoming my backhanded comment. "Oh, is that what they say about me? Seems rather tame, considering..."

My body trembled. I gripped the edges of the chair and picked at the thinning velvet with my nails. The cool kiss of Jak's red vampiric eyes fell to my wrists, and the freshly tied bandages which had not long been replaced.

"I know your story, Rhory. I know what you have lost to be sitting in that very seat." The caring nature of his voice surprised me, as did the softening of his eyes as he glanced back at my face.

"We all have made sacrifices," I replied. "Some more than others."

"Millicent." A sorrowful glint darkened the ruby of his eyes. I pondered what colour they had been before Marius changed him. "That is a name I will not forget. She fought beside Marius, and for that he will ensure her story is written to last an age and the next."

Pain stabbed through my chest. I felt it pierce slowly into my heart, inch by inch, until the thud of the hilt was all that was left. It seemed I was rather accustomed to the pain and I pondered if I would never be without it now.

"I'll never forget her either," I said, turning my attention to the licking flames in the fire at my side. The warmth tickled the skin of my face but did little to prevent the tears from pricking in my eyes at the thought of her.

"Tell me, because I admit I am curious. How is it I have not known of you before?" Jak asked. It was a question I knew was on Marius's lips when he saw me use my power against Silas. Before Calix ripped his jaw in two. "You are a witch, and yet you have been kept from me all this time."

There was no hiding anymore. Not that I cared to. Jak could take me, lock me away and it wouldn't matter. I had nothing left, nothing to fight for.

"My mother warned me about you," I said, levelling my eyes with Jak once again. "She told me you collect witches. And they are never seen again. She didn't wish for me to become another name on the list, so she became the very devil to ensure that never happened."

"Well." Jak smiled. "She should have tried harder."

There was nothing for me to say.

"Humour me. What is it you have been taught to believe happens to the witches I take?" Jak asked, tilting his head and narrowing his eyes at me. The fire beside me flared unnaturally, the flames turning a cold, cobalt blue in my peripheral.

"The answers are endless," I said before answering his question with one of my own, "What I know is Castle Dread is empty of them. Beside you, and Marius, there is not another living soul here. So, you humour me, Jak. Where are they?"

Jak's pink blush lips turned up into a grin. "Safe."

"My mother didn't trust you," I said.

Jak's smile faltered as honest hurt pinched across his brow. "Is this from the same woman who used her hidden power to alter your mind, poison it, and marry you off to a man who hurt you?"

My mouth parted, but no sound came out.

"Auriol told us everything," Jak confirmed. My first reaction was to ask if she was well. I had not seen her since she was carried out from the room in Marius's arms. But Jak continued before I could even draw a breath.

"It is why I wished to speak to you. Alone. Rhory, you and I are not as different as you may think. We are both products of the poison of our mothers. The Darkmourn we all know today is built on the backs of parents who use their children to settle old scores. Look at those parents now, they are all dead. Six feet under, so to say. Mine. Yours. You survived her, whereas I helped destroy the world to seek revenge on mine. It is all in here." Jak tapped the plain cover of the book. The leather looked almost wet as the unnaturally blue flames reflected across it. "If you stay with me, you will learn it all."

"No," I said. "For all I know you kill the witches."

"Of course, I don't. I train them. Ready them."

"For what?" I asked, chest filling with a strange, unwanted worry at Jak's dark expression.

Jak uncurled his legs, placed them on the ground, and stood. He was no taller than me in height, but as he towered before my chair, bathed in his cobalt firelight, he looked like a giant from old tales.

"The world requires balance. Who knows what new threats will come—just as Calix and Auriol have proved… they can be lurking anywhere."

It didn't exactly answer my question, but I sensed from Jak's demeanour that he didn't want to elaborate.

"Do you know I was once foretold to return magic to the world? I may not have done it as my mother wished, but I am now doing it in my own way. I never take the witches against their will. They are invited to join me. To train and learn about their powers in a world who would prefer to scrub all mention of witches from existence. It was my fault the hate and discrimination against the witches started, and it will be my legacy to fix it."

"Did you ask me to see you to thank me, or extend that same invitation?"

Jak didn't reply at first. He lifted the heavy tome, slotted it into a gap on the shelf and pushed it in. The sound of the book sliding against the wooden shelf sent a comfortable shiver across my skin. *Who knew such a noise was so pleasant?*

"It would not feel right to offer such an invitation because I know you would answer from a mind that is still not your own."

When Jak looked back at me, the force of his attention nearly knocked me out of the chair. I raised a hand and tapped my fingers to my temple, knowing exactly what Jak alluded to.

"My answer would be the same, no matter the state of my mind."

"Let us test that theory, shall we? Rhory, I would like to offer you a gift. A thanks for what you have done for my family."

"I want nothing," I said, voice breaking as I scrambled for an excuse to give him. "There is nothing you could give me, nothing I desire."

"Strange," Jak said, screwing up his face as he regarded me with a mischievous smile. "When I last spoke with Master Grey, he warned me you would say that. So, he made me a deal."

The world seemed to quiet at Jak's words, as though his voice had the power to still everything around us.

"Oh, I know all about his deal," I replied, feeling the numb agony that had settled on me since Calix left, intensify.

"Then I trust Calix told you what he asked of us? What he wanted in return for him leaving Darkmourn?"

The question hung between us. My silence was enough confirmation that I didn't know what was offered as part of the deal. Calix had a way of keeping secrets from me, it seemed.

"Calix left Darkmourn under one condition. In fact, I seem to remember him being rather passionate about what he wished for."

"What did he ask for?"

"I was simply going to give you wealth and an abundance of comfort as thanks for saving Marius's life, but Calix had a better idea. He promised to stay out of Darkmourn as long as I was the one to break the curse put upon your mind. Calix made a deal to stay away, as long as your mind is freed. He wanted you to remember... he said he wished for you to remember your *before*."

I choked on my breath as my words flew out of me. "Is it possible?"

Jak laughed, the light sound like the fluttering of bird's wings. "Anything is possible in Darkmourn."

A smile of disbelief creased across my face.

Jak grinned in return. It was breathtaking and wonderful, captured on a youthful face which his immortality had frozen upon him. Jak Bishop was older than I could imagine, but he looked slightly younger than me. It was the tone he spoke in and the way he carried himself which truly revealed the many years he had on me.

"With the power us witches hold anything is possible. If you wished to learn it all, I would teach you. If you decided that was not the path you wish to take, then I would not question it."

I leaned forward in my chair, my body moving closer towards Jak. All I could think about was the possibility that Jak could fix me. I longed for my mother's influence to release me, so I could not torment myself with knowing what I remembered was real or conjured.

I longed to remember with every ounce of my being and it was possible because of Calix.

"Do it," I begged, tears streaming down my face and slipping over my smile. "Please."

Jak bent down towards the lit hearth, scooping his hand into the blue flames. He brought out a bud of fire which twisted an inch above the skin of his palm. It hovered silently, not burning or maiming him. He turned his attention to me and closed the space until he stood carefully between my separated legs. A wash of his scent brushed over me. It was as light as spring air, with the underbite of spiced cinnamon.

"Be free, Rhory Coleman. Reclaim your mind. Your life. For it starts, anew, today."

I pinched my eyes closed as Jak Bishop brought the flame towards my temple and pressed it against my cool skin. At his touch, a rigid breath of power rushed through my skull. In the dark of my mind, I felt his magic penetrate through barriers; the force knocked them down, crumbling the mental walls one after the other.

There was pain, but I didn't shy away from it. I welcomed it, embraced it. And in the dark, slowly emerging through the heavy fog which had been forced over my mind, was a face. A face I knew from now, but slowly remembered from before.

Calix Grey stepped free, and with the phantom of him came the monstrous wave of our story careening towards me. I surrendered willingly to it with nothing but the swell of bliss within me.

46

3 YEARS BEFORE

We will run away, Little Red. Together. Come to me, come to the cottage. I will wait for you, and then we will both be free from secrets. We will be free, together. I love you.

Calix's promise repeated over in my mind as I clambered around my bedroom, stuffing clothes into a bag until its seams stretched. I was fuelled with desperation and urgency. My mind was so lost to it I hardly paid attention to what I packed. I was completely focused on the darkening sky beyond my room, and the knowledge that Calix would be waiting for me. In my mind's eye, I could see him waiting at Auriol's cottage, prepared to flee Darkmourn and all its shackles the moment I arrived.

I wondered if he felt the same swell of excitement as I did. Had the same feeling clogged his throat and quickened the pace of his heart until his ribs ached? As I stuffed another shirt into my pack, I smiled. I hadn't stopped smiling since this morning when I had seen him last and he presented this idea of us leaving Darkmourn, together.

Since then, it was all I could ponder, which was not a new concept because Calix always filled my mind.

Snatching up the pack, I didn't bother to glance back at the room as I left it. Knowing it was the last time I would pass through its door filled me with renewed excitement. Yes, I had memories made within its walls which I would always think back to with a full heart, but those memories involved Calix. And we were about to step out of our boundaries and create far more than I could ever imagine possible.

The house was silent as I passed through it. It was not uncommon for me to be alone here, and this time I almost felt sad knowing I was to leave it. Mother and Father were still at St Myrinn's for Father's weekly health check. Mildred had likely left for the day, after ensuring the rooms were full of the smells of cooking and freshly washed bedding.

I would miss Mildred. If I thought about her long enough, I might have stopped in my tracks. Of course, I would miss my parents as well; there was no denying that. But watching Father's health deteriorate was painful, and Mother had locked me up in my cage long enough. Father had always longed for me to see the world, but Mother kept the key to my cage on her at all times. She had grown complacent that I would never leave. Perhaps she believed the years of drumming in the horrors of the world would prevent me from even opening the door to my cage a fraction. Now, I would kick it down.

I had to leave before Eamon revealed to Mother what he had seen the night prior. Fear clawed up my throat as I thought back to him. All it had taken was the Crimson Guard to slip his head around the door to my room, to find me sat above Calix, bare for all to see. That one moment had ruined everything, or had it freed me?

Eamon was loyal to my father, and I had no doubt he would expose our secret in time. Which was why I had to leave tonight before Mother found some way to keep me from Calix, just as she always had.

It had been her fear of our truth ever being exposed which had kept me smothered. Until Calix, I had not cared to mind. Now, knowing what freedom and the fresh air felt like, I longed for it.

My feet smacked against the freshly oiled wood floors. As I took the last step down into the foyer, I nearly slipped. Catching myself on the banister, I took a moment to calm down—whereas my mind willed for me to leave and I would, my body reacted to the guilt I should be feeling.

"Careful."

A gasp broke out of me as I glanced up to see Eamon standing sentry at my front door. My breath lodged in my throat, blocking the string of curses that wished to spill from my mouth.

"Good evening, Eamon," I said, grasping my pack of clothes tight to my side. His bright azure eyes glanced towards it for a brief moment before returning to me.

"Rhory," Eamon replied, bluntly. "Are you planning on going somewhere?"

I lifted my chin, steeling my gaze as I regarded him. "What does it matter to you?"

"Your wellbeing matters to me," he replied quickly, watching me as though I was his prey. I refused to allow it to deter me. I continued moving towards the door, towards him. Only when the tips of my boots were close to him did I stop.

"Excuse me," I said, gesturing with a flick of my eyes for him to move out of my way.

Eamon hardly moved, only so much as to lift his arms and cross them over his broad chest. I hated the way he looked at me, how his eyes traced across my body, his sly grin lengthening at its corners.

I fought the urge to shiver, knowing exactly what thoughts plagued his mind.

"It is good to see you dressed more... appropriately," Eamon said. "Or, just dressed—"

"Didn't you hear me?" I snapped as my skin crawled in response to his comment. I squared my shoulders, but my small frame was unimportant compared to Eamon's. "I said, excuse me."

"Oh, I heard. But I am afraid I am under strict instructions to keep you from leaving tonight."

For the first time, I was unable to keep the panic from infecting me. I felt its chill spread across my chest, travelling with numbing speed down my arms and legs, until I was entirely numb. There was something sinister about the glint in Eamon's bright eyes. How he found this entire interaction... amusing.

"By whose orders?" I asked.

"*Mine.*"

Eamon didn't shift his gaze to the new voice, but I did. Before I even turned and looked, I knew it was Mother who had slipped into the room behind me. She always had a way of moving with silent grace—some people admired that about her, whereas it made me uneasy.

Ana Coleman danced across the foyer towards me. I couldn't see her heels beneath the long skirt of her maroon dress, but I could certainly hear the click of them. The swish of material around her ankles gave my mother the impression of floating.

"Allow me to take this from you," Mother said, reaching out for the pack I held.

My knuckles tensed on the strap, turning white beneath my grip. Mother kept her hand extended, but soon realised I was not going to give it to her. Her nails curled inward, likely pinching the skin of her palm as she fisted her hand and returned it to her side. There was no concealing the flash of displeasure that creased across her beautiful face.

"I thought you were out for the evening," I said, finally locating the courage to speak.

Mother pouted and drew her eyebrows down until her forehead pinched in wrinkled lines. "Jameson thought it best for your father to stay over at St. Myrinn's for observation this evening."

"And you left him?" I said, accusation lacing my tongue. Mother never left Father's side. Never. Where he was, she was there, hovering beyond his shoulder like a second shadow.

"Well, I would have stayed with him, dear, but how could I knowing my only son was home attempting to betray us behind our backs?"

I stumbled back a step beneath the force of her blatant, unapologetic accusation.

Unluckily, Eamon was there to stop me with a firm hand to my shoulder. His touch shocked me, as did the way his fingers curled over my shoulder bone and held firm. I tried to pull away, but his grip was iron.

"Rhory, how could you do this to me?" Mother breathed through her obvious hurt.

I couldn't fight Eamon off whilst holding the pack to my side. Mother took her moment and snatched it from beneath my arm. I called out to stop her, but one look scolded me into forced silence.

"Leaving me, leaving your father, all when you know just how dangerous the world can be for people like us."

My blood chilled, knowing Eamon was behind me and Mother had alluded to the very secret she fought to keep hidden. *Did Eamon know?*

"I am going, Mother."

She paused, eyes widening more than I believed natural.

"Pardon me—"

Eamon couldn't stop me from jolting forward, not as I threw my elbow back into his ribs and then slammed my hip into his groin. I marvelled at the way the wind was driven from him, enough to loosen his hold for me to break out of it.

My skin burned beneath his fingers as I pulled free of him. Mother was far too shocked at my refusal of her that she put up no fight when I reached for the pack and yanked it from her.

"Please," I snapped, breathless as adrenaline flooded through me. "Don't try and stop me."

Mother glanced over my shoulder to Eamon, snarling at his moans of discomfort. When she looked back to me, the lines of her face only deepened. "Calix Grey isn't suitable for you," she said, finally broaching the very topic I wondered if she knew about. "He is dangerous."

I almost laughed. How could Mother accuse another of being dangerous when she was the one who kept me under lock and key?

"You don't know him," I said. "Mother, I know you love me, but your need to smother me has driven us to this very moment. Please, you need to let me go."

She took a step forward, her arms raised out before her as though she didn't know what to do with them. "But, Rhory... everything I do is to keep you safe. There are sacrifices I have made, ones you could not even comprehend. I cannot just let you go when my only task in life is to keep you safe."

"Calix has my best interests at heart," I said, calmly. If Mother cared for me, and truly understood I was safe with him, then she would let me go. If she loved me enough, she would do it. She would do it, for me.

She took another tentative step towards me, continuing to hold out her arms as though I would run into them. Except, I wasn't a child anymore. I hadn't been a child for a long time. And it was high time Mother recognised that.

"Why didn't you tell me about him?" she asked. "Do you know how painful it was to find out from…" Her eyes flickered to Eamon once again, who kept silent and sentry before the door. I still felt his phantom touch on my shoulder; my skin ached from both disgust and tension from where his fingers had gripped me.

"Would it have mattered if I had?" I retorted. "If you knew, you would still not have approved. Even if I am the happiest around him. Even when he makes me feel loved and safe and…"

"He is a monster," she snapped, reaching forward and grasping me by the upper arms. Her face was twisted into a mask of desperation, with wide eyes and lips which paled with tension.

"Anyone else, Rhory. Anyone. But not Calix. Not any of the Grey's."

"Let go of me, Mother," I demanded, refusing to fight her off. It was not only this moment I longed release from her. I wanted her to let me go entirely. I wished nothing more than her to allow me to walk out this house without a fight. But if it was a fight she desired, I would do it. "If you love me, you will step aside and allow me to finally claim my life. My way."

She recoiled, my words striking true. Through the material of my shirt, I felt her nails scratch lightly over skin before she did the unthinkable. She withdrew her hands and returned them to her side.

"Is this truly what you want?" Sadness crept across her face, ageing her before my eyes.

"Yes," I said. It was the easiest word I could muster. "*Calix* is who I want."

Mother paused, taking my words in. My heart broke seeing her so sad. So defeated. I knew, deep down, she cared for my best interests. But she would learn that I was in safe hands. We would prove it to her.

"Okay," she said finally. "If this is what you want from me."

Mother looked to Eamon and nodded, dismissing him with the faint flick of her head.

"Thank you," I said, gripping the pack of clothes again as tears pricked in my eyes.

We stared at one another, mother and son. I felt guilty for leaving her to care for Father alone, but I knew he would want this for me. Before his mind was claimed by his sickness, Father had always encouraged me to follow my heart, and now I was finally able to heed his desire for me. I would make him proud.

"Rhory, before you go," she said, eyes brimming with tears. "At least permit me to hold my son for one last time?"

I nodded, selfishly allowing myself to fall into her open arms. She pulled me to her, grasping the back of my head with her hands and keeping me to her. We were of equal height, but there was something about being in her arms that made me feel small again.

I pinched my eyes closed and held her close.

"I love you, Rhory," she whispered into my ear. "Which is why I am not sorry."

A talon of panic sliced down my spine. I tried to withdraw, but Mother dug her nails into my hair and held on tight. I couldn't begin to fight, not as Eamon's hands were suddenly on me. Both of them applied pressure to keep me locked in place.

"You are hurting me," I gasped out, feeling the skin of my scalp sting from the scrape of her nails. My power reared its head, but even it refused me in the presence of Mother.

"I promise it will not last. I must do what is necessary," Mother said. "I vowed to keep you safe, but you continue to defy me."

"Get off of me," I pleaded, unsure if I spoke to Mother or Eamon, for both of them treated me with equally unkind hands. "Fucking let me go!"

"Quiet now," Mother sang. Somewhere in our struggle, she had passed me into Eamon's arms. He held me strong, with my arms bent behind my back and his body forced up against mine. I felt his mouth near my ear, but I didn't dare move for fear of getting closer to him. His proximity made me sick.

All I could do was look at my mother as cold light brewed from the tips of her fingers and covered her hands in the flame of her power. Our magic was forbidden to be used, especially in front of someone. Eamon didn't flinch as Mother revealed her magic, nor did she care. Her gaze was entirely focused on me.

My own magic awoke in response, but the way Eamon held me prevented me from touching his skin. Which could only mean he had been warned. In that moment, I knew one thing for certain. *This had been planned.*

Mother stepped towards me, her sharp face cast in the light from beneath her. It elongated her features, making her frown look more like a menacing smile. Seeing her open display of magic stifled me. In all my years, I had never seen her use her power. She had kept it hidden from me, never daring to speak about it.

As she brought her glowing hands towards me, I longed to call out for Calix. His name filled my mouth, but I couldn't muster the breath to speak it.

"If it is freedom you search for," Mother said, eyes glowing unnaturally with the reflection of her power, her determination, "Then I, as your mother, will be the one to give it to you."

I turned my face as much as Eamon allowed. Mother continued raising the glow of her hands towards me until I felt the frozen bite of her magic grace the skin of my cheeks.

"It is time I rid your mind of the poison that is Calix Grey."

"You can't," I breathed, stilling completely in their grasp.

"Yes," Ana said, tracing her nails up the sides of my face until the tips rested over my temples. She laid pressure on them and pierced her nails into the soft skin. "Yes, I can. Do not worry, my darling boy. This will only hurt a little, and then you will be free..."

"No!" I squirmed.

"Eamon, hold him," Ana snapped.

"Mother, please don't!"

"You left me no choice, Rhory. You forced my hand. You made me do this. But I promise, when it is over, you will be happy. I know what is best for you. Mothers know best. And I refuse to let you squander your life away with a monster when there are others who would better suit you. Others who would do as I please to keep you safe."

"Calix!" I screamed his name with every fibre of strength in my being. "Calix *is* what is best for me!"

"Shh," Eamon murmured into my ear, lips caressing the skin as he tightened his hold. "I've got you now."

There wasn't a moment to fathom Eamon's words as Mother pressed her hands to my skull and pierced it with her power.

I gasped out, a single tear tracking a cool river down my cheek as her cold fingers of magic rooted through my mind. Then, the room fell away from me. The world faded from view. There, in the darkness of my mind, stood Calix. Waiting, just as he promised. He was before me, smile illuminated by the light of Mother's power as it raced towards him in a tidal wave. I cried out for him as the power swept over the vision of Calix and engulfed him entirely.

I blinked, and he was gone. Swallowed whole by her magic. Then, when the light finally settled, there was no one left standing before me. In fact, I didn't know who it was. Who did I see only moments before? I focused on the shadows, willing them to reveal themselves, to calm the confusion and panic that gripped me from feeling so lost and out of sorts.

Out of the darkness, the figure stepped forward.

Eamon materialised, smiling and corporeal. My deep inhale lifted the weight of panic from me. *He had come back.* No darkness could ever hide him from me. No light could wash him away from my mind.

He was there.

My love.

My Eamon.

47

I KNEW, without a doubt, where to find Calix—now more so than ever before. Because it was one of the first memories that had come back to me. Perhaps it was because I was searching for it, but I knew with complete certainty Calix would be waiting, just as he had promised all those years ago.

The red cloak of the Crimson Guard whipped behind me as I ran from Castle Dread, my feet pounding against the pavement with the same fury as my heart in my chest. Marius and Jak had gifted the cloak to me, Jak even going so far as to tie it around my neck.

Darkmourn passed in a blur, as did the forest that separated Darkmourn from Tithe. My journey didn't matter, it was the destination I was focused on.

Jak's gift to me felt like reading a book backwards. The flooding of memories as they returned was strange. One after the other, I was in the eye of a storm as the winds of the past battered into me. I could have let them knock me down, but I didn't. I held firm and drank them all in.

I remembered the *before*. It was both painful and beautiful, like breathing in fresh air after being stuck in a room infested of smoke.

Auriol's cottage revealed itself before me. I had reached it without truly thinking. I slowed, panting viciously. But at no point did I stop. If I was not running with purpose, I was walking with desperation to reach him. To reach Calix.

The cottage was as I remembered it. Crumbling white-weathered walls, and vines that left scars across its surface. There was the flickering of orange light from the window at the side of the house. He was here, just as Calix promised before my mother had altered my mind to suit her own purpose.

Warmth crashed into me as I pushed open the front door. It squealed on its hinges, signalling my arrival. Maybe I should have called out that it was me. But I knew Calix was here, and he knew who entered his grandmother's home. I couldn't explain it, but we knew. We always would.

It was only when I walked up the hallway and turned into the room awash in candlelight did I truly feel like I exhaled for the first time.

Calix was lying across Auriol's bed. His long body stretched out, with a pillow propping up his head. His lips parted as he regarded me, blinking a few times as though the vision of me would quickly fade.

"Rhory?" My name was a question, encompassing every thought that passed behind his bright, gleaming eyes. He shuffled up, regarding me with suspicion.

I inhaled deeply through my nose. There was so much I longed to say to him. So many words and promises which I felt as though I could drown willingly in. Instead, I picked three words which held the most power.

"I remember you," I murmured.

Calix sat up, powerful arms straining as he righted himself. "Tell me, Rhory. Tell me it all."

I blinked and the tears I fought hard to hold back spilled without restraint. They ran down my face, leaking between my upturned lips until all I could taste was salt.

"You," I whispered.

Questions passed across Calix's golden stare. He pressed his hand across his chest, long fingers splaying directly over his heart. "Please, don't play tricks with me."

I stepped to the end of the bed. "You... you asked me to run away with you. The last time I saw you, you asked me to meet you here and we would run from it all." I kicked off my shoes and climbed onto the bed between his legs. "I was coming to see you when Mother stopped me. That is when... when she stole you from my mind. But I was coming to you, Calix. I was."

Calix broke. He reached over for me, taking my face in his hands and kissing me with years of passion he was forced to keep to himself. I melted into him, letting his strength pull me further onto the bed and into his lap.

"Shh," he hushed, lips pressed to mine. "It doesn't matter anymore. You are here. You came back for me, just as you promised you would."

My greedy hands touched him with years of my buried passion for him. I traced them across his torso and chest, his shoulders and upper arms. I longed to feel him, just as I remembered from before. This differed from sleeping with him in Jak's house, or on the grounds of the forest. This was familiar. Because now, I knew him. Truly knew him, and I couldn't imagine a curse powerful enough to ever remove him from my mind again.

"I waited for you," Calix said, pressing his forehead to mine. He brushed red curls from my forehead, ensuring not a single strand fell over my eyes. Calix wanted me to see him just as he saw me. Entirely.

"That night, I waited for you. Every noise I heard outside, I thought it was you finally coming. But you never did. Then, when I came to find you that following day, it was to see you in the arms of Eamon. It..." Calix took a shuddering breath in. For such a large, powerful man, he wore his emotions across him with pride. It was one of the many most wonderous things about him. "It destroyed me, but I loved you enough to give you what I thought you wanted. And, Rhory, I would do it again and again. Over and over, no matter the agony. If it meant you lived the life you choose."

"But I never chose that life," I said, grasping his face and holding it so he could look only in my eyes. "The one I wanted was with you. I would have escaped that night and found you. We would have been leagues away now, years deep into the life we wanted. That was what I desired. I choose you, always."

Calix smiled through his sorrow. He brushed a tear from my cheek with the pad of his thumb. The feeling was so gentle; I leaned into it and closed my eyes.

"There is so much time we must make up for missing," I murmured, "Starting now."

"Tell me, Little Red. Where do you wish to start?" Calix asked, his voice a soft purr.

I took Calix's hands and pried them from my face. Gently, I placed them down on his lap. Then I moved myself down to the end of the bed where I stood freely.

"Such large eyes you have." I lifted my fingers to the clasp of my cloak and untied it. It fell to the ground, like a puddle of blood beneath my feet.

Calix inhaled deeply through his nose. His eyes widened at my words, words only he would know. "You *do* remember."

"Answer me," I demanded, my stomach jolting with excitement.

Calix raised a single brow. "All the better for seeing you with, every inch and all."

Slowly, I unbuttoned my shirt, stopping only when I felt Calix would look away. He knew, as before, that I deserved his entire focus. And he gave it to me, licking his lips and rubbing his hands up and down his thighs with unspent excitement.

"Such big hands you have," I sang out, mouth watering as Calix moved his hands from his thigh onto the growing mound protruding between his thighs.

"All the better to touch you with," he replied, gaze narrowing with desire and hunger.

I wiggled free of my trousers, undershorts and all the remaining clothes until I was completely naked.

Calix trailed his eyes up and down my entire body three times. By the fourth, he lifted his finger and curled it inward. "Come to me."

The bed creaked as I climbed back on it. I crawled over to him on all fours, watching him as he drank me in. His mouth parted, pink tongue spreading out over his lower lip.

"Such a big tongue you have," I said, forcing Calix to flatten beneath me. I stopped only when my face was above his. A shiver passed over my skin as he lifted a hand to my thigh and slowly crawled his fingers up towards my ass.

"All the better to taste you with," he replied. "Now, are you going to let me do that?"

"All in due course," I replied.

"Do you remember how much you loved when I would fuck you with my tongue?"

Calix stuck it out. I brought my lips around it. He groaned into my mouth as I sucked his tongue up and down. When I pulled away, he grinned like a cat who found the cream.

"I want those lips around my cock," Calix said.

"Why wait?" I asked, tilting my head and raising my brows. "Tell me if I remembered this wrong, but I recall a time when we pleasured one another at the same time."

"You do?"

"Hmm, maybe I am wrong," I said with a sly grin, knowing I was, in fact, not wrong at all.

Calix brought both hands to my hips and brought me down hard on his cock. With his guidance, I rocked across the lump of muscle, enjoying the press of it against my ass.

"Now you mention it," Calix said, lifting his hips beneath me so every single inch of his cock had the pleasure of rubbing against me. "I think you are right."

"Oh, I am. Aren't I?"

"Turn around," Calix commanded.

I did as he asked. Calix released me enough to shift my position on him. I stopped when I faced his cock, and my bare ass was pressed directly before his mouth. We laughed as his long limbs knocked into me awkwardly while he frantically took off his clothes. When his teeth nipped at my skin, followed by the wet lap of his tongue, excitement rushed him, throwing every item of clothing into a forgotten pile on the floor beside his grandmother's bed.

I gripped the base of Calix's cock. My fingers couldn't touch around its width. I opened my mouth to make a comment but failed spectacularly as Calix brought his tongue to my ass and drew it upwards, slowly and tenderly. All I could do was release a long, breathy moan.

It would have been easier to give into the pleasure and forget the world. But I wanted Calix to experience it alongside me. So, I brought him into my mouth and wrapped my lips around the curved tip of his cock. My cheeks were entirely soaked with spit, making it easier to take him in, deeper and deeper. My jaw ached slightly, but that only encouraged me more.

Calix had each of my ass cheeks in his hands, separating them so he could bury himself deeper into me. He fucked me with his tongue. It slipped in, spreading warmth across my lower half. If he didn't hold me up in place, I would have fallen on top of him.

Calix made my knees weak with his devouring.

We competed with one another. I longed to make him groan as I moved up and down his length, sucking the tip and caressing as many of his inches as I could with my tongue. He breathed into my ass, exhaling his pleasure, which also spilled from the tip of his cock and sweetened the insides of my cheeks.

I loved how his taste filled me. And I wondered what I tasted like to him. Whatever it was, he must have craved it, because he was prepared to devour me all the way to my core. Whatever it was, he must have craved it because he ate, nipped and devoured me without breath.

"Careful," Calix said suddenly, shifting his hips and pulling his cock away from my mouth. "If you carry on like that, I will have another unfortunate accident."

"Unfortunate?" I asked, breathless.

Calix released my ass and allowed me to crawl into a different position. This time I turned to face him, sitting upon his hips and rocking across his hard cock with my spit-glistened ass.

"For whom?" I murmured. "I want to taste your cum. I want it all."

"And I *want* many things," Calix replied, his face pinched in a thrilling scowl.

"Like?" I teased.

"Like burying my cock in that tight hole. Your little mouth can't take all of me, but your ass can. And I want to submerge myself in you."

"*I want. I want,*" I repeated, mockingly. "That is all I hear from you."

"Oh, don't play coy. You will beg for it the second you feel the head of my cock so much as flirt with your hole."

"Is that so?" I countered.

"Care to test my theory?"

Calix reached beside him and produced a vial of lubrication from the beside dresser.

"Tell me that is not Auriol's own stash?"

A deep laugh rumbled out of Calix. "This is mine. Call it a precaution for if Jak unlocked your memories and you came back to me. Which he did, and one cannot be caught unprepared."

I smiled, licking my lips as they turned up. "Care to do the honours?"

Calix quickly uncorked the vial with his teeth, spat it out and emptied the contents until his hand, crotch and cock glistened with lube.

I reached beneath me, taking his length in my hand and positioned it before my entrance. Calix was right, of course. The second I felt the curved tip of his cock brush against the heart of me, I felt myself open and the muscles relax.

I lowered myself upon Calix, welcoming every inch of him as I did so. The further I sat on him, consciously tightening the muscles around my hole to provide him as much enjoyment as possible, Calix's eyes glazed over. His mouth parted, tongue swelling as he exhaled a groan of pure pleasure.

At some point, he pressed both hands on either side of my ass, spread my cheeks with his grip and slammed the final inch inside of me. The force of it took my breath away.

"Rock for me, Little Red." Calix urged me to do as he asked, moving my hips as I familiarised myself with the swell of him inside of me. "Ease into it. I don't want to hurt you."

I leaned down over him, pressing my forehead to his. Breathless, I replied softly under my breath, "Fuck me."

"What was that you said?" Calix asked; I could hear the grin buried in his tone.

Our faces were so close that my eyes crossed when I looked into his pits of gold. "Fuck me, I said fuck me."

A growl rumbled out of Calix's throat, conjuring a new wave of shivers to race across my skin. He released his hands from my ass and raised them behind his head. When he replied, it was with all the cocky arrogance I had first fallen in love with all those years ago. "From my vantage point, you are the one sitting on me. Ride it, if you want it. Fuck me yourself."

And I did just that.

Lifting myself up on my knees, I moved carefully to ensure his hard cock couldn't retreat from me. I contorted myself into a squatting positioning. For leverage, I grasped onto my thighs, which already burned from the position. It was a pleasant feeling, one that sang in harmony with the pleasure of his length inside me.

"Try not to finish too quickly," I warned, winking as I pinched my nails into the skin of my thigh.

"That," Calix said, narrowing his gaze at me, which mirrored the smirk plastered on his handsome face, "Was a onetime thing. And believe me, if I cum inside of you, that will not stop me from continuing. We have years of catching up to do."

"Thank my lucky stars," I breathed.

There was no more talking as I bounced myself upon Calix's length. He threw his head back, thumping into the pillow as I moved myself up and down. Soon enough, the discomfort in my thighs vanished as the swell of indulgence enraptured me. Deep inside, I felt the tip of his cock play with the soft spot of my centre. Each time they joined as one, it sent a jolt across every bone, muscle and vein, threatening to undo me.

Sweat spread across my forehead, running down the sides of my face and dampening my hairline. At some point, I fell backwards onto the bed. I was afforded only a moment's break from his cock until Calix took over. With my legs still bent between us and my arms holding up the rest of my weight, Calix thrust skyward. The faint muscles across my stomach rippled as I lost myself to my heavy breathing.

Somewhere in the back of my mind, I was thankful that we hid in the belly of a forest with no one around. Because I screamed and Calix howled. The symphony of our pleasure would have frightened birds from nests and sent burrowing creatures back into the holes in the ground they called home.

A rush of blood flooded my head as Calix shot forward and spun me around. It happened so quickly, I almost didn't hear the sloppy pop sound his cock made as it fell out of me.

"Rhory..." Calix whispered. "Look in my eyes."

I hadn't even realised I had closed my eyes. My mind was far too lost to the euphoria that the world seemed somewhat detached. Only when I opened my eyes and saw him did it all rush back into focus.

Calix had laid me on my back. My knees were brought up to my stomach and held in place by his hand. He had not yet entered me again. Instead, he watched me from his perch above as he leaned over. His hair fell over each side of his face, shadowing his expression but never dimming the glow of gold that was in his eyes.

"Are you okay?" I asked.

"I have never been better."

I craned my neck upwards and looked down the length of our bodies. In the shadows he created his muscles looked huge across his torso and stomach. His cock hung between his legs, only an inch from brushing the sticky sheets of the bed.

"Then why have we stopped?" I asked him, unable to hide the disappointment in my voice.

Calix shifted his entire body weight onto one hand and balanced on it whilst he took the other and brushed the side of my face. He was warm and slick with sweat. I didn't care. I wanted it all.

"I want to see you," he said. My heart stung at the sadness in his voice. "And I want to look into your eyes and see you seeing me. It's all I have wanted for years. Not your body, not your sex. You."

I leaned up as much as his body's imprisonment allowed. My hands were free, so I spread them across his head, digging my fingers into his scalp. I used his hair as leverage, making sure he couldn't look away from me even if he desired to.

Which, we both knew, he didn't.

"I am here," I replied finally, feeling my chest swell with his shared sorrow. "And I see you."

"Rhory," Calix breathed my name out as though it were the heaviest of burdens.

"Calix," I replied.

"From now, until you decide you no longer desire it... I wish to give you my love."

"How can you give me your love?" I asked, pulling his face down towards mine. Warm light spilled from my hands and cast the surrounding room in a halo of my power. Calix's eyes widened as I opened him up to my emotions. I took nothing from him this time. Instead, I showed him just how I felt through our connection, so he not only heard everything I had to say but believed it, with no room for disbelief.

"I stole it for myself years ago. I love you, Calix. I love what you are, who you are and everything in-between. I have loved you when my mind belonged to you, and loved you even when it was taken and given to someone else. There is no curse in the world strong enough to ever make me forget that."

Calix crashed his mouth into mine. The kiss was powerful with passion, but soft in equal measure. It was all lips and tongue, and the silence allowed me to read his response through my touch as he drove his emotions into me.

Love. Warmth. Happiness. Joy.

There was not enough time in the world for me to name everything I felt coming from him.

"You love me?" he asked once he pulled away. I smiled at the bruising of his mouth and the swelling of my own. "Even though I am the big bad wolf of Darkmourn?"

"I love you," I replied, aware that Calix took his cock in his hand and brought it back to my ass. "Big bad and all."

"Say it again," Calix groaned, slowly easing his cock back inside my hole. "I want to hear you scream it."

"I love you," I moaned as I felt every inch of him sheath within me.

"Then I'm the luckiest man in Darkmourn and beyond." Calix lowered himself atop me, pressing his chest to my chest and his lips to my lips. His pace was softer. He moved his hips in circles, the motion like the shore of a lake during the calmest of winds. He didn't fuck me now. He made love to me and I lost myself to it entirely.

'Then say it, tell me you love me.'

"I *do* love you, Rhory Coleman," Calix whispered. "Completely, entirely and with every fibre of my being. I love you."

As he spoke those final words, I truly understood their meaning. They no longer hurt. Those words were once my undoing, but now made me whole again.

ALSO BY BEN ALDERSON

The Darkmourn Universe - Adult
Lord of Eternal Night
King of Immortal Tithe
Alpha of Mortal Flesh
Prince of Endless Tides - January 2024

The *Dragori* Trilogy - Young Adult
Cloaked in Shadow
Found in Night
Poisoned in Light

A Court of Broken Bonds - Adult
Heir to Thorn and Flame
Heir to Frost and Storm
Book Three - 2024

A Realm of Fey Series - Adult
A Betrayal of Storms
A Kingdom of Lies
A Deception of Courts
A War of Monsters - 2024

Printed in Poland
by Amazon Fulfillment
Poland Sp. z o.o., Wrocław